w y t c h e s

story
scott snyder

art
jock

colors
matt hollingsworth

letters
clem robins

editor
david brothers

IMAGE COMICS, INC.
Robert Kirkman – Chief Operating Officer
Erik Larsen – Chief Financial Officer
Todd McFarlane – President
Marc Silvestri – Chief Executive Officer
Jim Valentino – Vice-President

Eric Stephenson – Publisher
Corey Murphy – Director of Sales
Jeremy Sullivan – Director of Digital Sales
Kat Salazar – Director of PR & Marketing
Emily Miller – Director of Operations
Branwyn Bigglestone – Senior Accounts Manager
Sarah Mello – Accounts Manager
Drew Gill – Art Director
Jonathan Chan – Production Manager
Meredith Wallace – Print Manager
Randy Okamura – Marketing Production Designer
David Brothers – Content Manager
Addison Duke – Production Artist
Vincent Kukua – Production Artist
Sasha Head – Production Artist
Tricia Ramos – Production Artist
Emilio Bautista – Sales Assistant
Jessica Ambriz – Administrative Assistant
IMAGECOMICS.COM

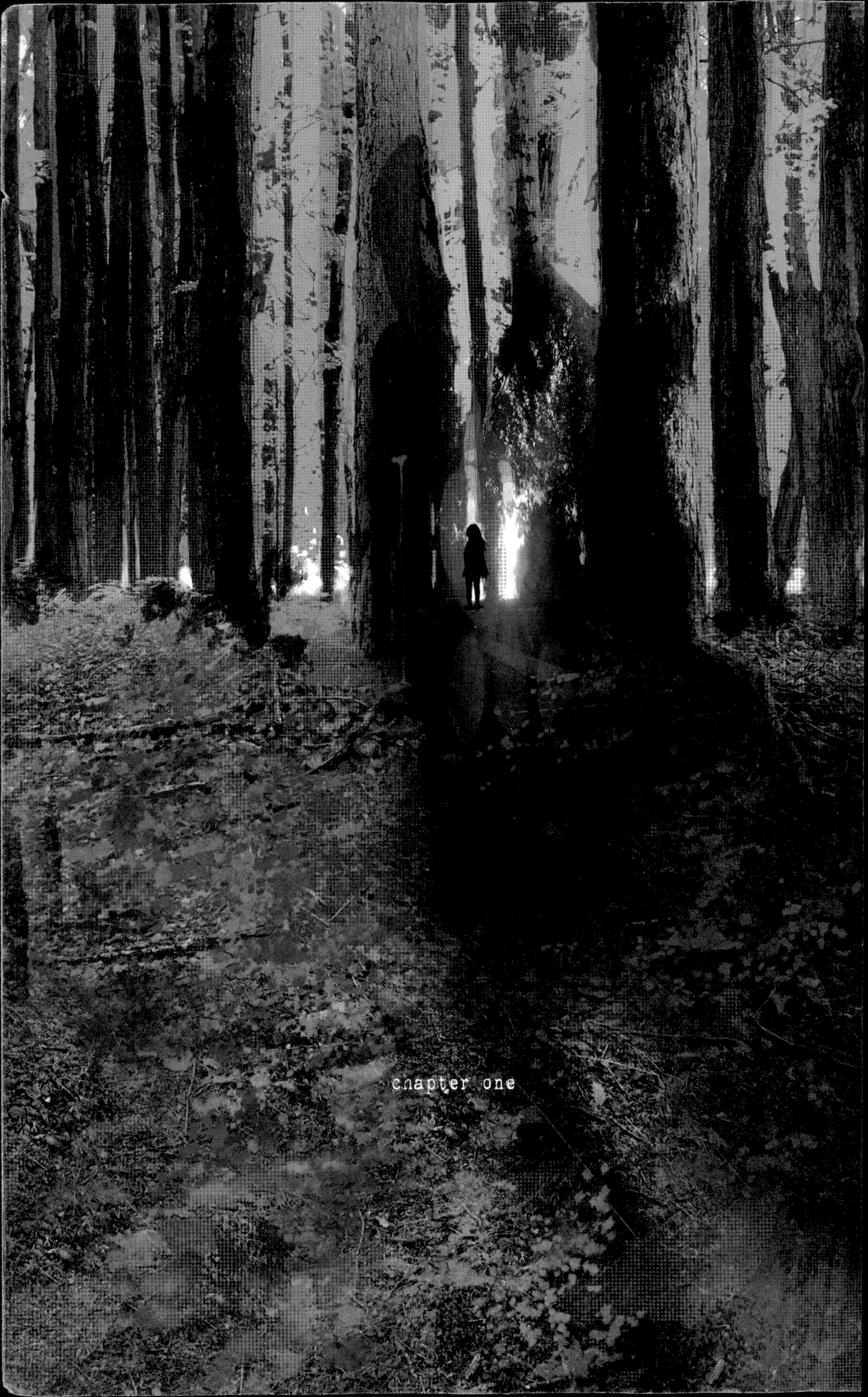

chapter one

witch (wich) *n.* [ME *wicche* < OE *wicce*, fem. of *wicca*, sorcerer, akin to MDu *wicken*, to use magic < IE base "*weik*", to separate (hence set aside for religious worship) > Goth *weihs*, holy, OB *wig*, idol] 1 a person, esp. a woman, having supernatural power as by a compact with the devil or evil spirits; sorceress 2 an ugly and ill tempered old woman; hag; crone 3 a practitioner or follower of white magic or of WICCA 4 [Informal] a bewitching or fascinating woman or girl 5 *short for* WATER WITCH (sense 1) —*vt.* 1 to put a magic spell on; bewitch 2 [Archaic] to charm; fascinate —*vi.* DOWSE —witch'like' *adj.* —witch'y *adj.* witch'·i·er, witch'·i·est

witch (wich) *n.* [ME *wicch* < OE *wicce*, fem. of *wicca*, sorcerer, akin to MDu *wicken*, to use witchcraft < IE base *weik-*, to separate (hence set aside for religious purposes) > Goth *weihs*, holy, OB *vig, idol*] 1 a person ... man having supernatural power as by a compact with the devil or evil spirits; sorceress 2 an ugly and ill tempered old woman; hag 3 a practicer of or follower of white magic or of WICCA 4 Unformal a bewitching or fascinating woman or girl 5 short for WATER WITCH (sense 1) —*vt.* 1 to put a magic spell on; bewitch 2 [Archaic] to charm; fascinate —*vi.* DOWSE —*witch'like' adj.* —*witch'y adj.* witch'-er, witch'-i-est

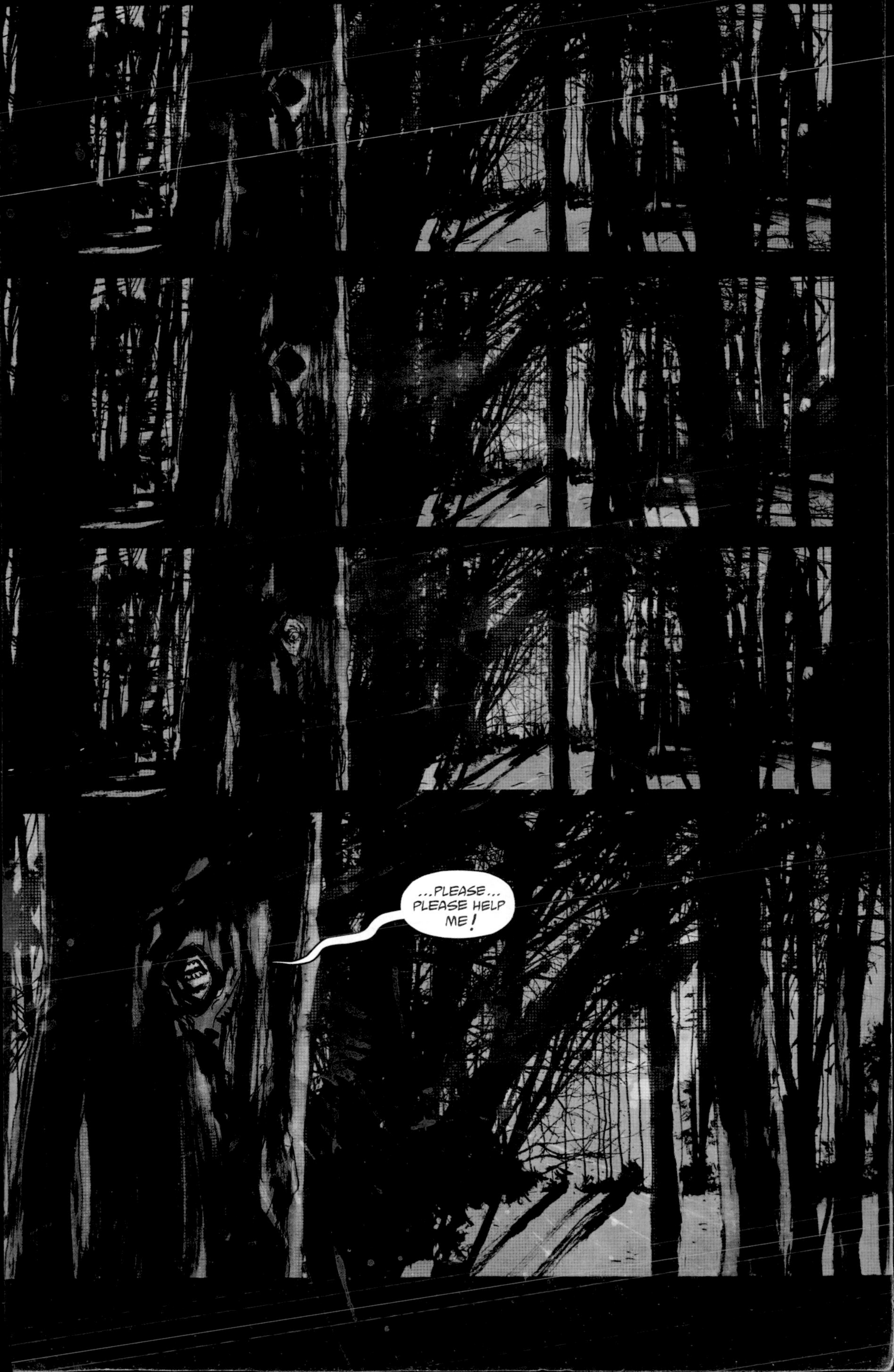
...PLEASE... PLEASE HELP ME!

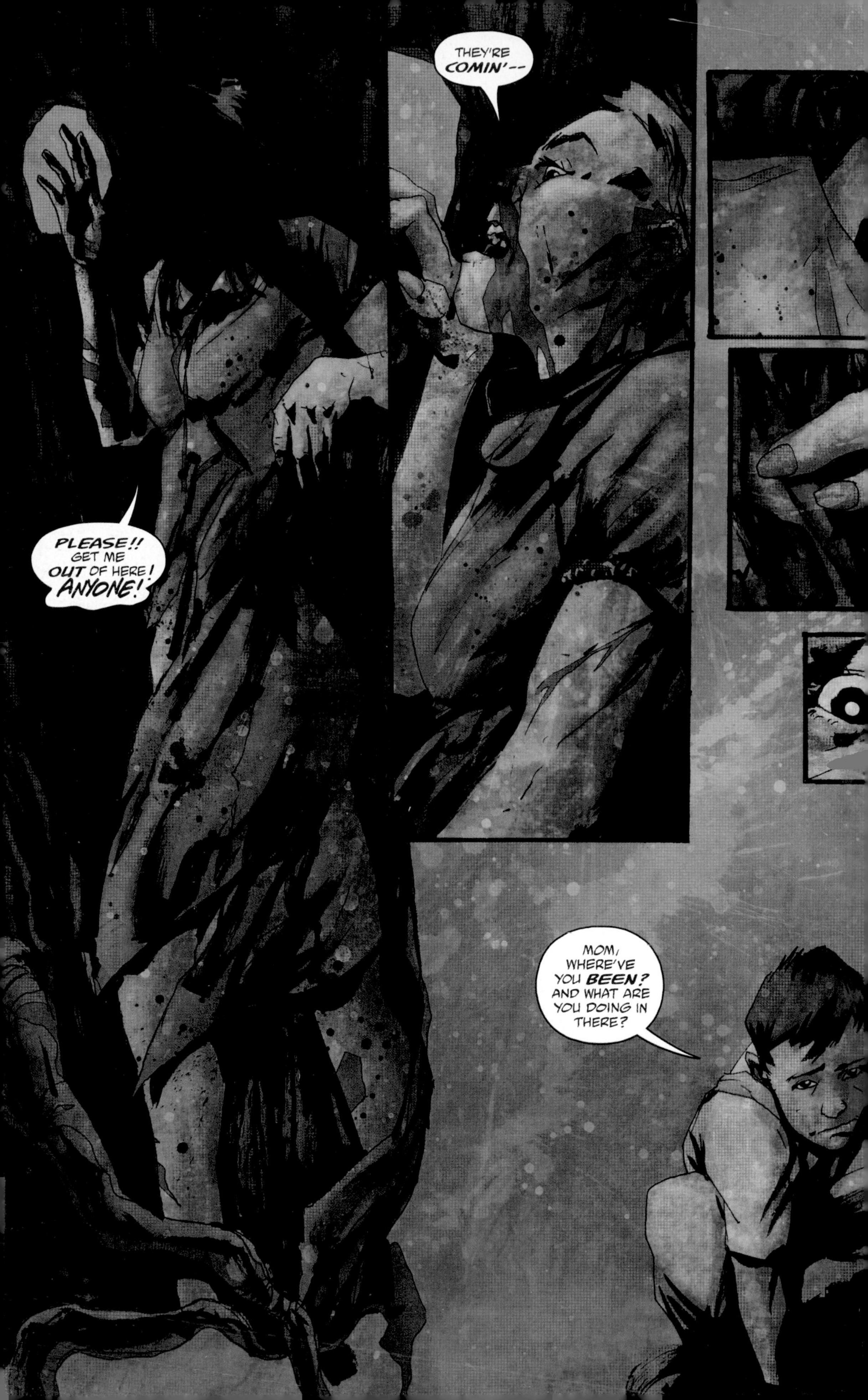
THEY'RE COMIN'--
PLEASE!! GET ME OUT OF HERE! ANYONE!
MOM, WHERE'VE YOU BEEN? AND WHAT ARE YOU DOING IN THERE?

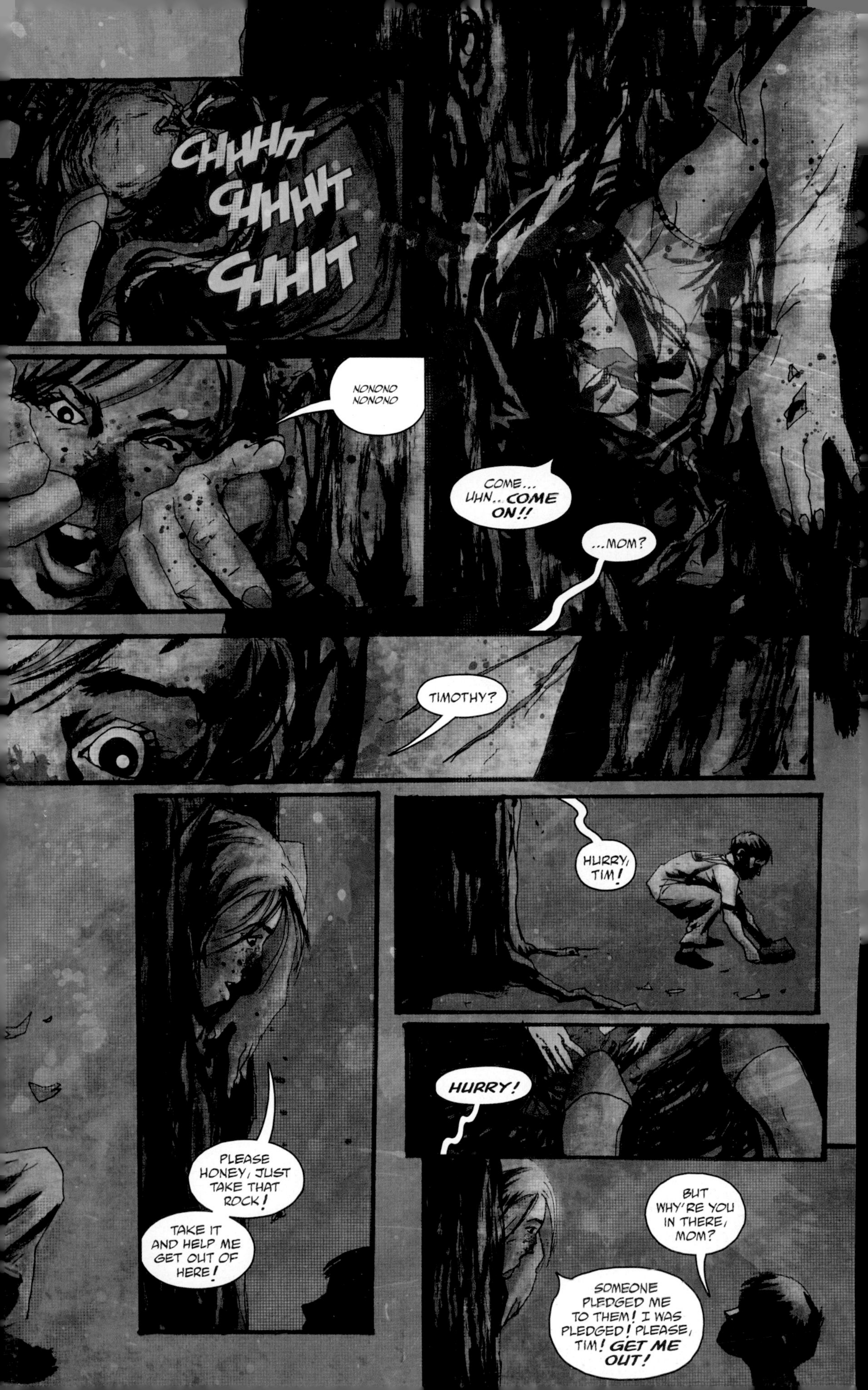
CHHHIT
CHHHIT
CHHIT
NONONO NONONO
COME... UHN... COME ON!!
...MOM?
TIMOTHY?
HURRY, TIM!
HURRY!
PLEASE HONEY, JUST TAKE THAT ROCK!
TAKE IT AND HELP ME GET OUT OF HERE!
BUT WHY'RE YOU IN THERE, MOM?
SOMEONE PLEDGED ME TO THEM! I WAS PLEDGED! PLEASE, TIM! GET ME OUT!

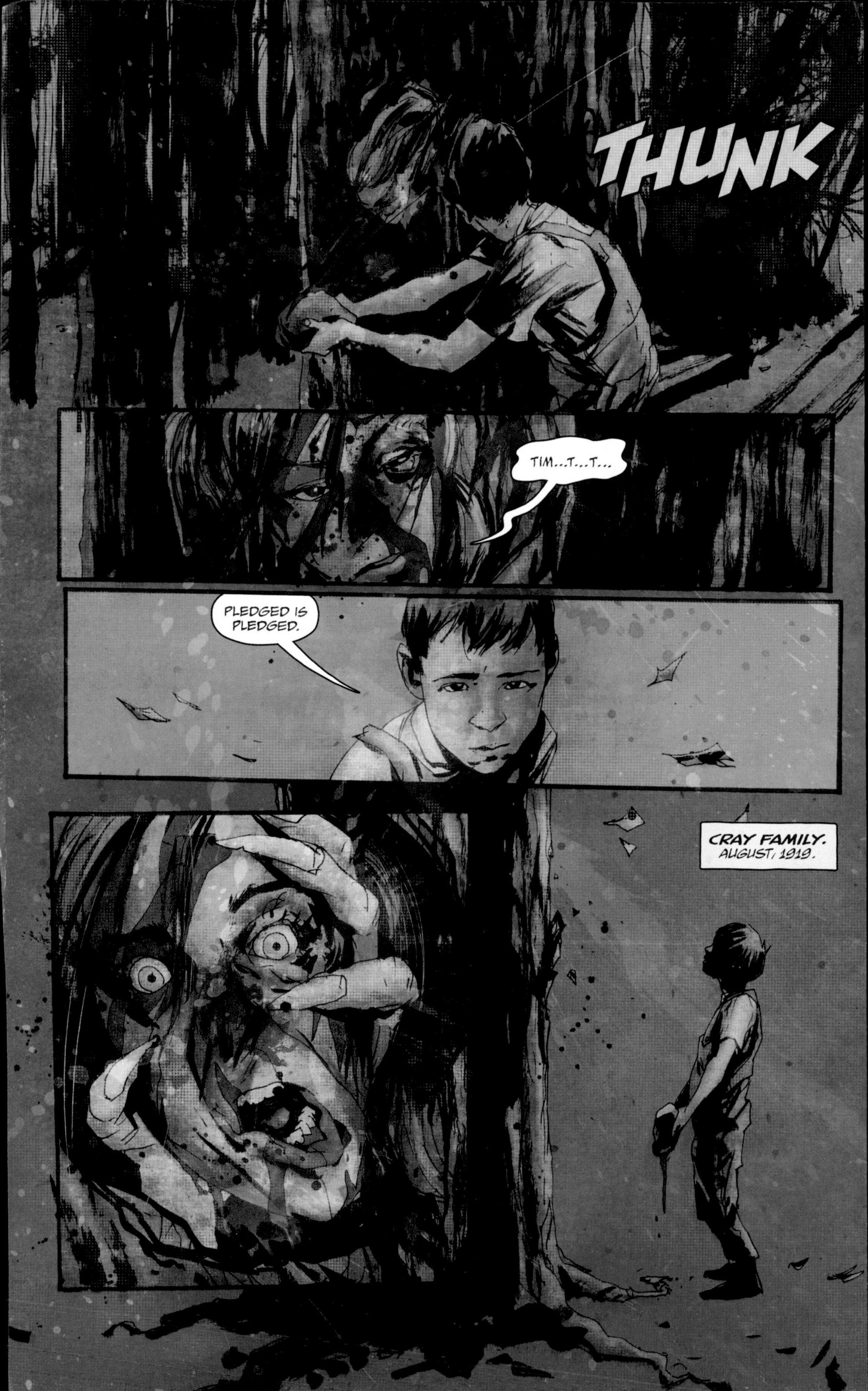
THUNK
TIM...T...T...
PLEDGED IS PLEDGED.
CRAY FAMILY.
AUGUST, 1919.

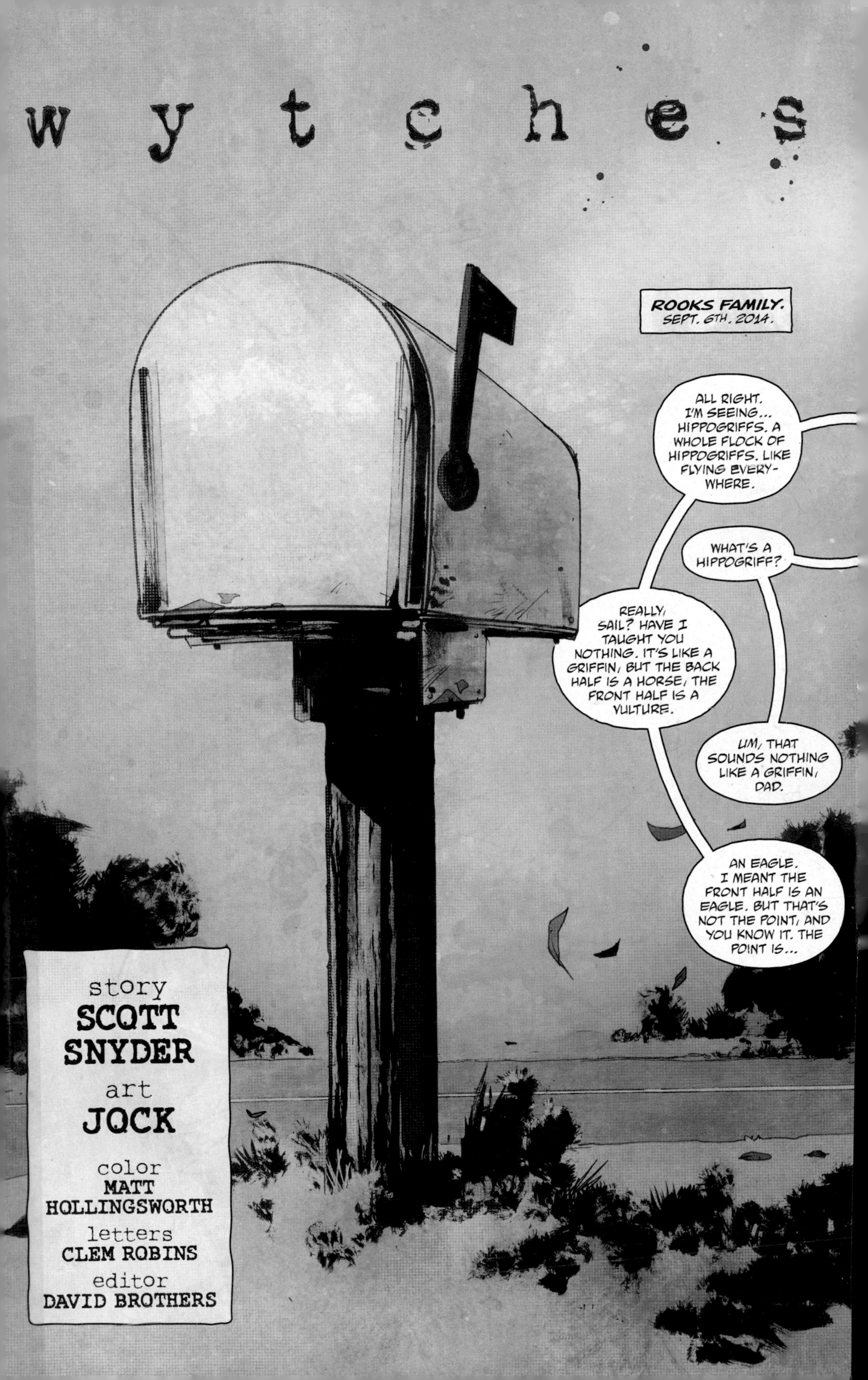
wytches
ROOKS FAMILY. SEPT. 6TH, 2014.
ALL RIGHT. I'M SEEING... HIPPOGRIFFS. A WHOLE FLOCK OF HIPPOGRIFFS. LIKE FLYING EVERY-WHERE.
WHAT'S A HIPPOGRIFF?
REALLY, SAIL? HAVE I TAUGHT YOU NOTHING. IT'S LIKE A GRIFFIN, BUT THE BACK HALF IS A HORSE, THE FRONT HALF IS A VULTURE.
UM, THAT SOUNDS NOTHING LIKE A GRIFFIN, DAD.
AN EAGLE. I MEANT THE FRONT HALF IS AN EAGLE. BUT THAT'S NOT THE POINT, AND YOU KNOW IT. THE POINT IS...
story SCOTT SNYDER
art JOCK
color MATT HOLLINGSWORTH
letters CLEM ROBINS
editor DAVID BROTHERS

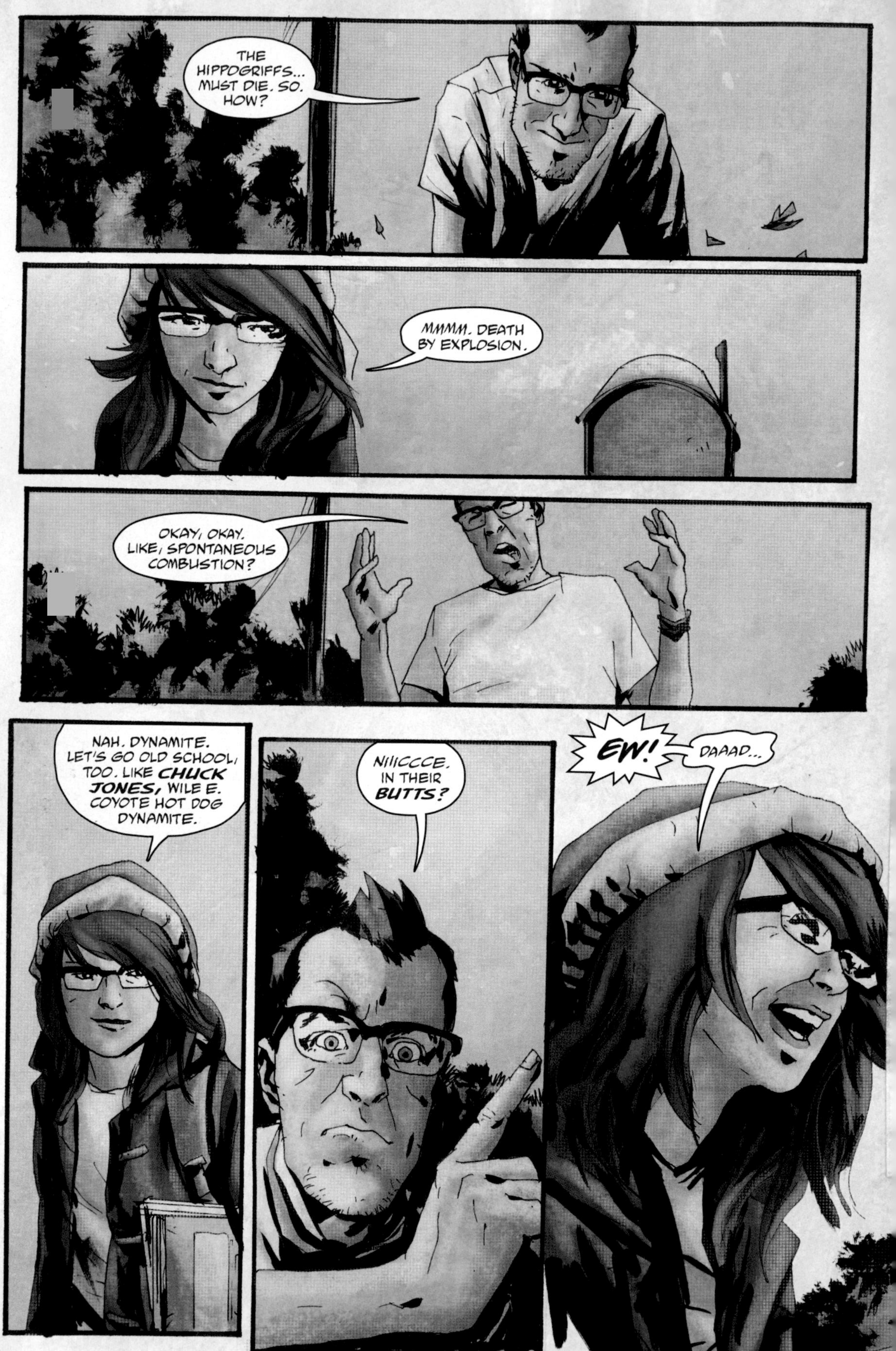
THE HIPPOGRIFFS... MUST DIE. SO. HOW?
MMMM. DEATH BY EXPLOSION.
OKAY, OKAY. LIKE, SPONTANEOUS COMBUSTION?
NAH. DYNAMITE. LET'S GO OLD SCHOOL, TOO. LIKE **CHUCK JONES,** WILE E. COYOTE HOT DOG DYNAMITE.
NIIICCCE. IN THEIR **BUTTS?**
EW!
DAAAD...

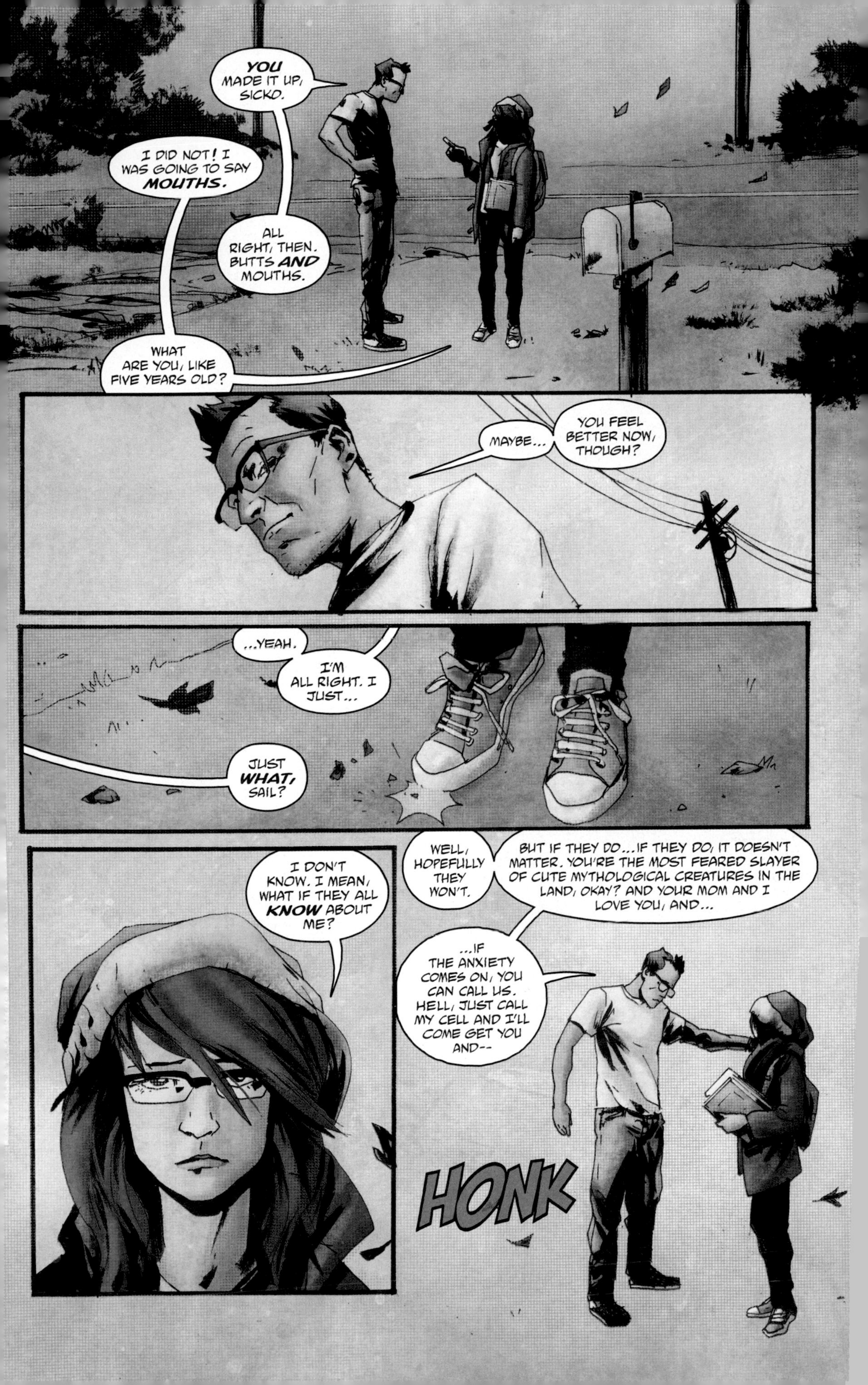

YOU MADE IT UP, SICKO.
I DID NOT! I WAS GOING TO SAY MOUTHS.
ALL RIGHT, THEN. BUTTS AND MOUTHS.
WHAT ARE YOU, LIKE FIVE YEARS OLD?
MAYBE...
YOU FEEL BETTER NOW, THOUGH?
...YEAH.
I'M ALL RIGHT. I JUST...
JUST WHAT, SAIL?
I DON'T KNOW. I MEAN, WHAT IF THEY ALL KNOW ABOUT ME?
WELL, HOPEFULLY THEY WON'T.
BUT IF THEY DO...IF THEY DO, IT DOESN'T MATTER. YOU'RE THE MOST FEARED SLAYER OF CUTE MYTHOLOGICAL CREATURES IN THE LAND, OKAY? AND YOUR MOM AND I LOVE YOU, AND...
...IF THE ANXIETY COMES ON, YOU CAN CALL US. HELL, JUST CALL MY CELL AND I'LL COME GET YOU AND--
HONK

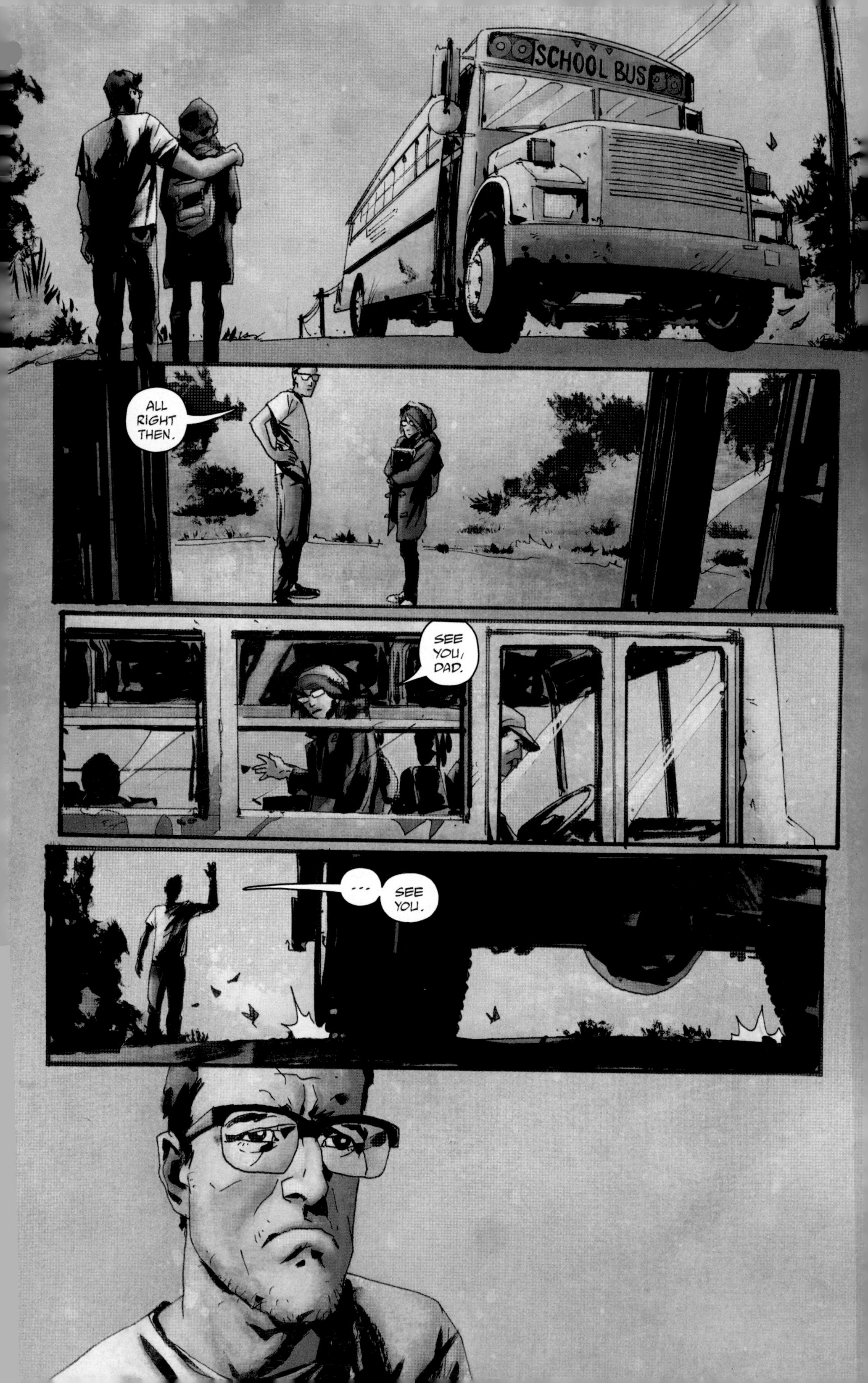
SCHOOL BUS
ALL RIGHT THEN.
SEE YOU, DAD.
...
SEE YOU.

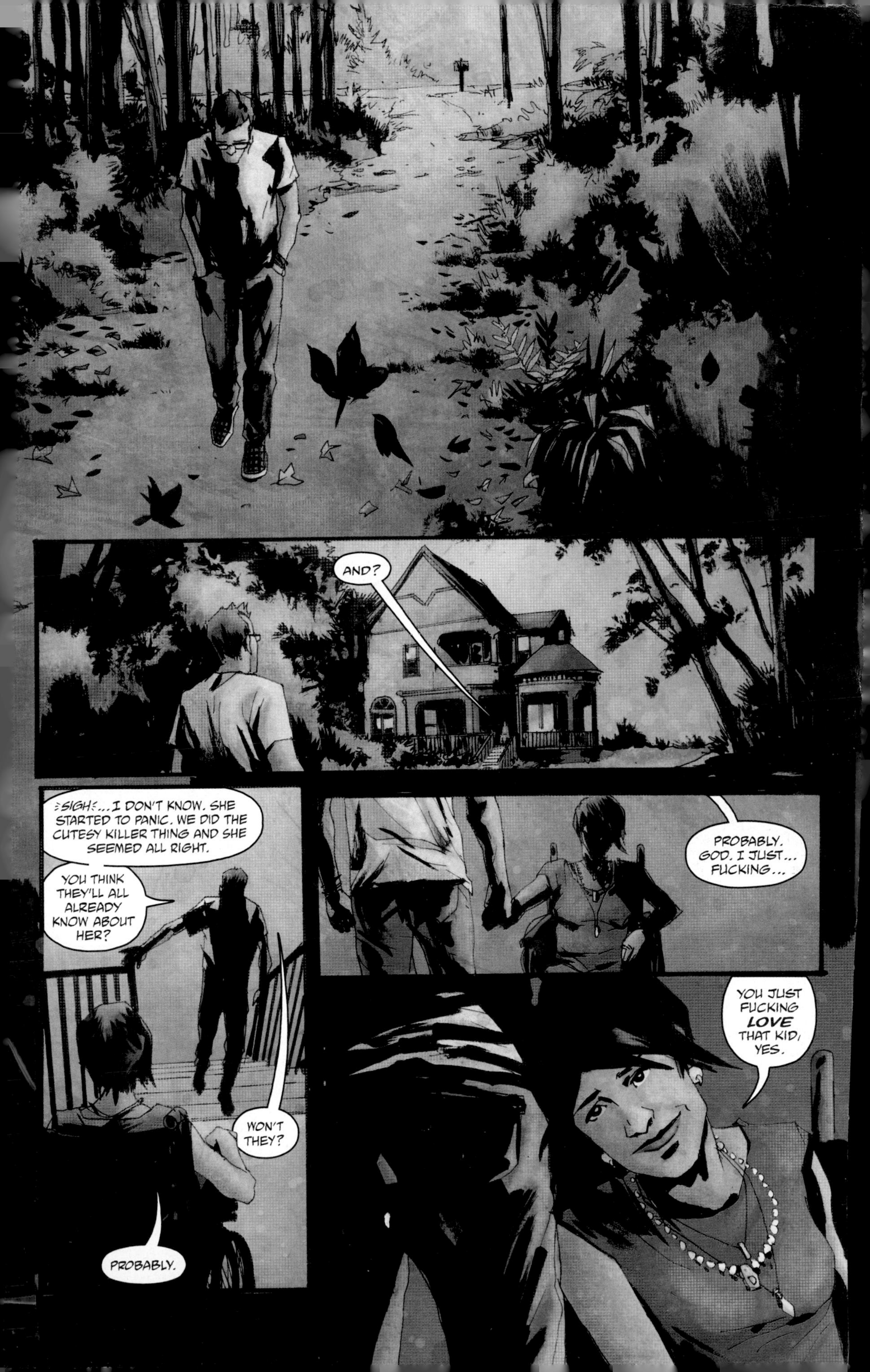
AND?
:SIGH:... I DON'T KNOW. SHE STARTED TO PANIC. WE DID THE CUTESY KILLER THING AND SHE SEEMED ALL RIGHT.
YOU THINK THEY'LL ALL ALREADY KNOW ABOUT HER?
WON'T THEY?
PROBABLY.
PROBABLY. GOD. I JUST... FUCKING...
YOU JUST FUCKING **LOVE** THAT KID, YES.

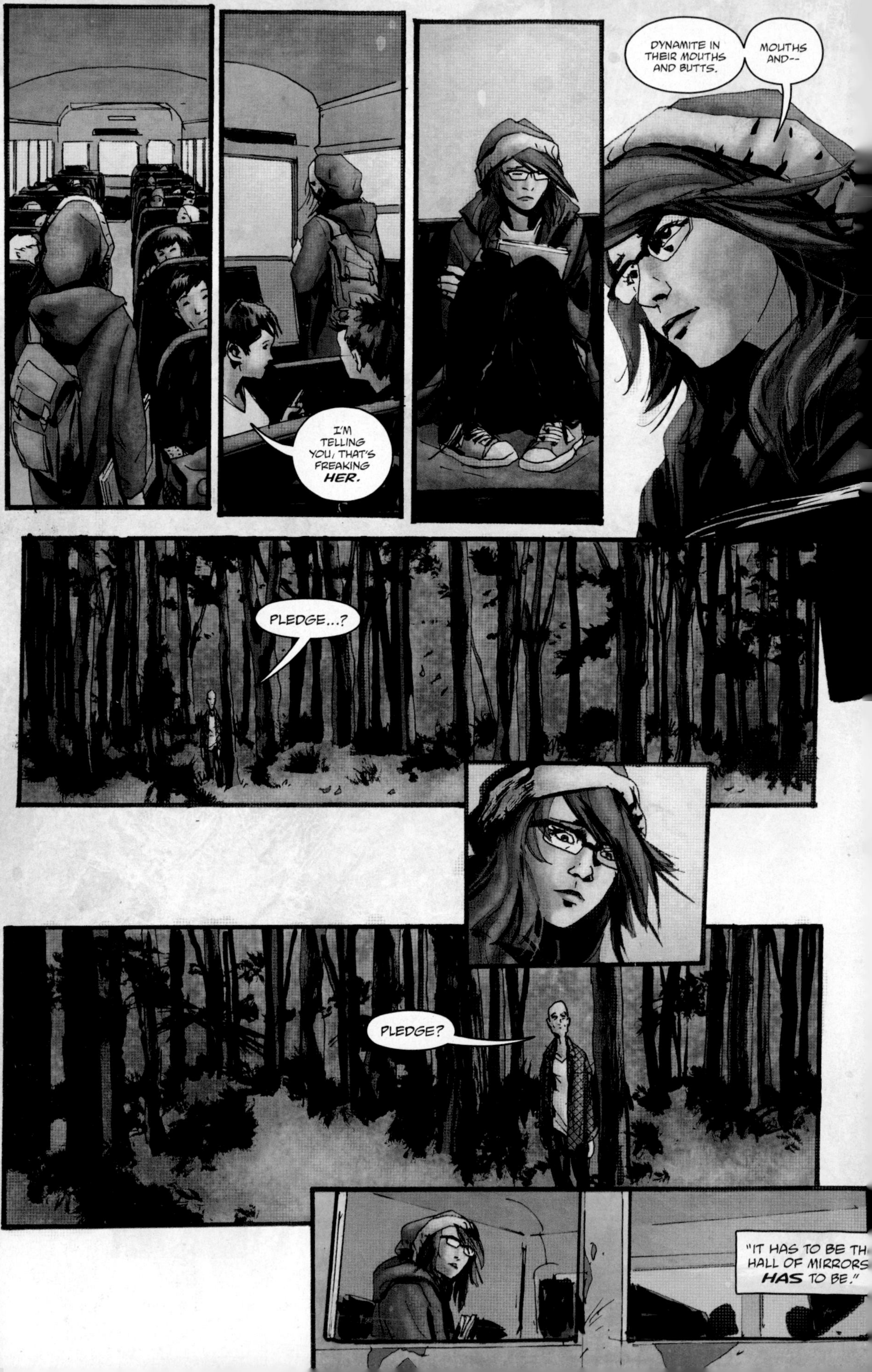

I'M TELLING YOU; THAT'S FREAKING HER.
DYNAMITE IN THEIR MOUTHS AND BUTTS.
MOUTHS AND--
PLEDGE...?
PLEDGE?
"IT HAS TO BE TH
HALL OF MIRRORS
HAS TO BE."

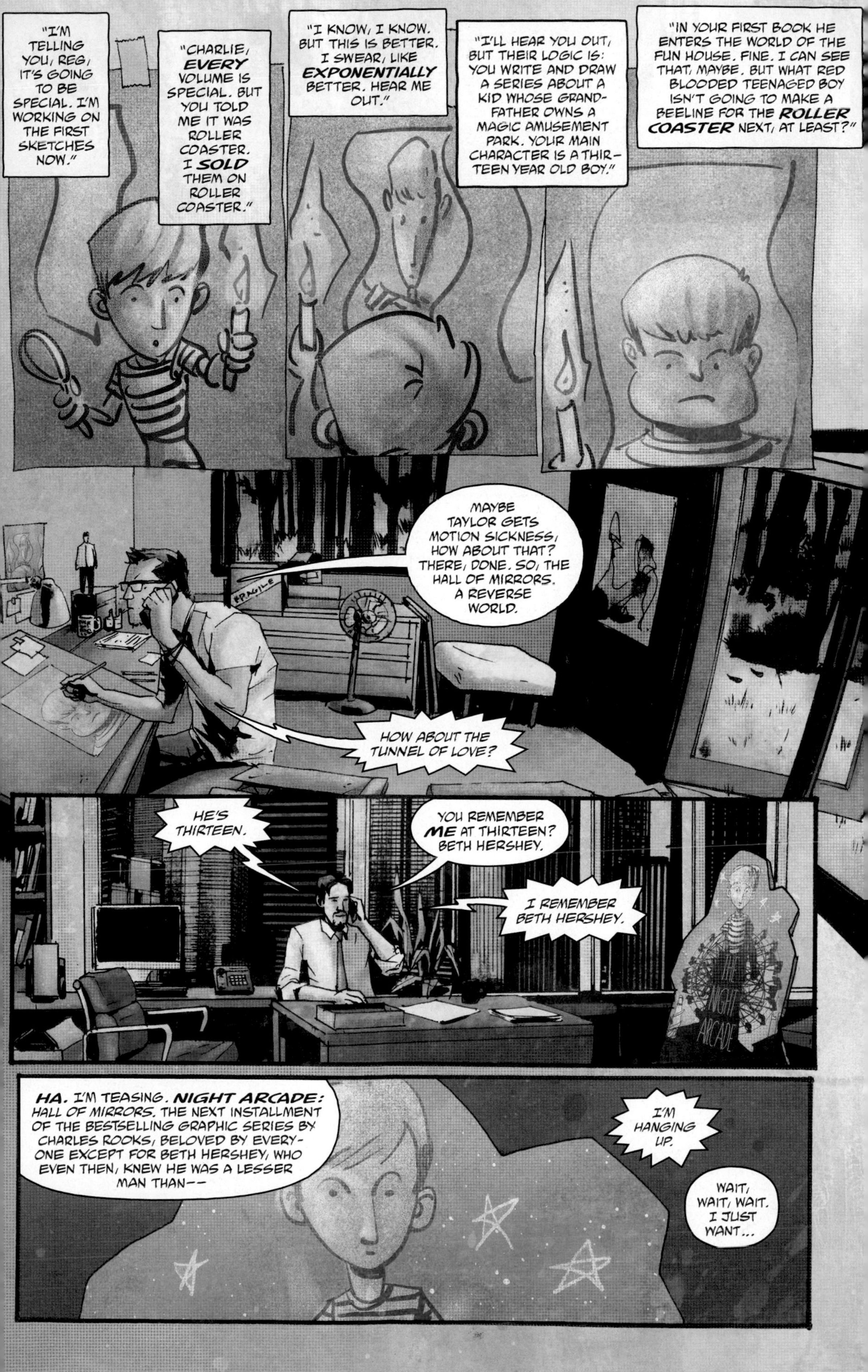
"I'M TELLING YOU, REG, IT'S GOING TO BE SPECIAL. I'M WORKING ON THE FIRST SKETCHES NOW."
"CHARLIE, EVERY VOLUME IS SPECIAL. BUT YOU TOLD ME IT WAS ROLLER COASTER. I SOLD THEM ON ROLLER COASTER."
"I KNOW, I KNOW. BUT THIS IS BETTER. I SWEAR, LIKE EXPONENTIALLY BETTER. HEAR ME OUT."
"I'LL HEAR YOU OUT, BUT THEIR LOGIC IS: YOU WRITE AND DRAW A SERIES ABOUT A KID WHOSE GRANDFATHER OWNS A MAGIC AMUSEMENT PARK. YOUR MAIN CHARACTER IS A THIRTEEN YEAR OLD BOY."
"IN YOUR FIRST BOOK HE ENTERS THE WORLD OF THE FUN HOUSE. FINE. I CAN SEE THAT, MAYBE. BUT WHAT RED BLOODED TEENAGED BOY ISN'T GOING TO MAKE A BEELINE FOR THE ROLLER COASTER NEXT, AT LEAST?"
MAYBE TAYLOR GETS MOTION SICKNESS, HOW ABOUT THAT? THERE, DONE. SO, THE HALL OF MIRRORS. A REVERSE WORLD.
FRAGILE
HOW ABOUT THE TUNNEL OF LOVE?
HE'S THIRTEEN.
YOU REMEMBER ME AT THIRTEEN? BETH HERSHEY.
I REMEMBER BETH HERSHEY.
THE NIGHT ARCADE
HA. I'M TEASING. NIGHT ARCADE: HALL OF MIRRORS. THE NEXT INSTALLMENT OF THE BESTSELLING GRAPHIC SERIES BY CHARLES ROOKS, BELOVED BY EVERYONE EXCEPT FOR BETH HERSHEY, WHO EVEN THEN, KNEW HE WAS A LESSER MAN THAN--
I'M HANGING UP.
WAIT, WAIT, WAIT. I JUST WANT...

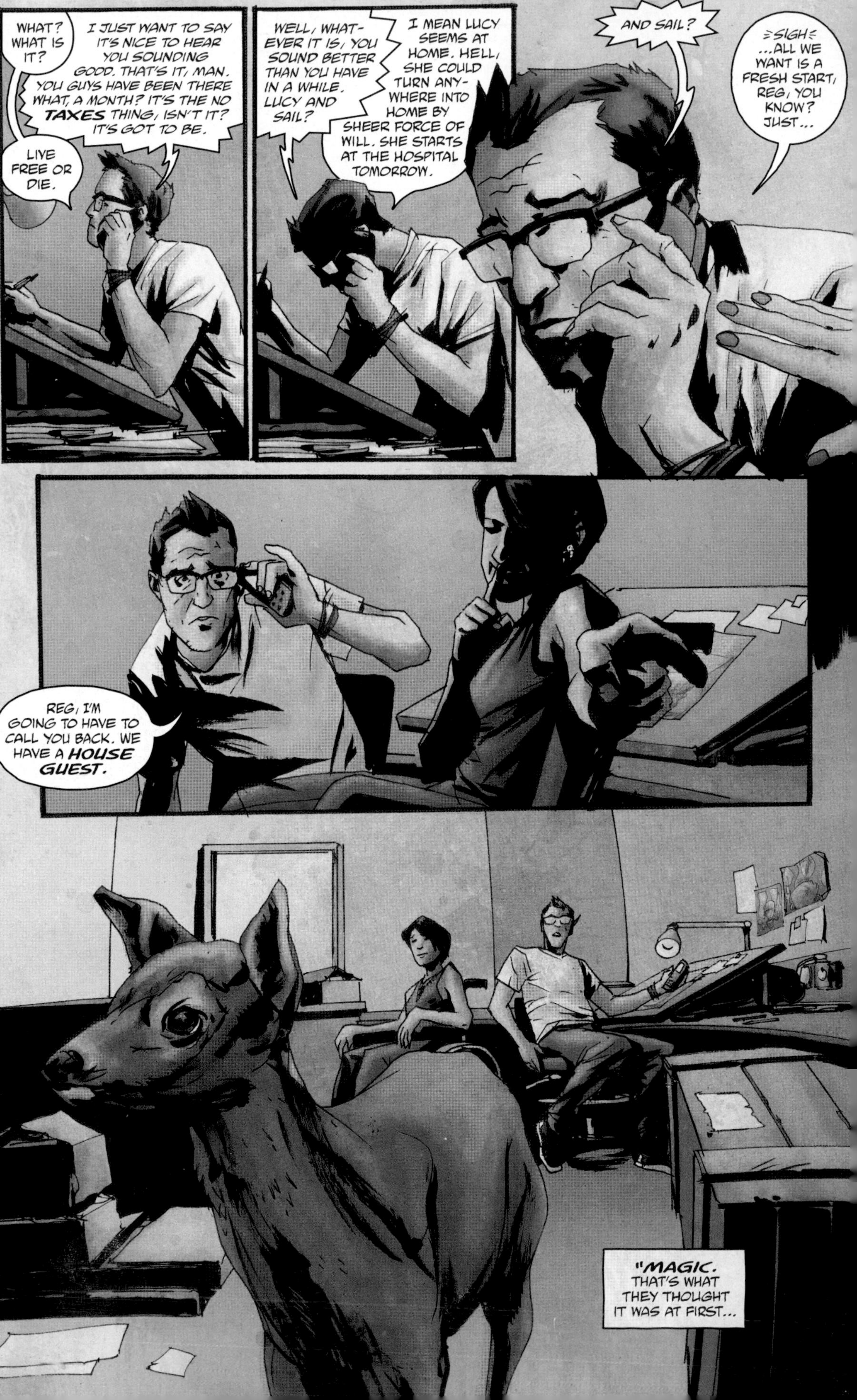
WHAT? WHAT IS IT?
I JUST WANT TO SAY IT'S NICE TO HEAR YOU SOUNDING GOOD. THAT'S IT, MAN. YOU GUYS HAVE BEEN THERE WHAT, A MONTH? IT'S THE NO TAXES THING, ISN'T IT? IT'S GOT TO BE.
LIVE FREE OR DIE.
WELL, WHATEVER IT IS, YOU SOUND BETTER THAN YOU HAVE IN A WHILE. LUCY AND SAIL?
I MEAN LUCY SEEMS AT HOME. HELL, SHE COULD TURN ANYWHERE INTO HOME BY SHEER FORCE OF WILL. SHE STARTS AT THE HOSPITAL TOMORROW.
AND SAIL?
SIGH ...ALL WE WANT IS A FRESH START, REG, YOU KNOW? JUST...
REG, I'M GOING TO HAVE TO CALL YOU BACK. WE HAVE A HOUSE GUEST.
"MAGIC. THAT'S WHAT THEY THOUGHT IT WAS AT FIRST...

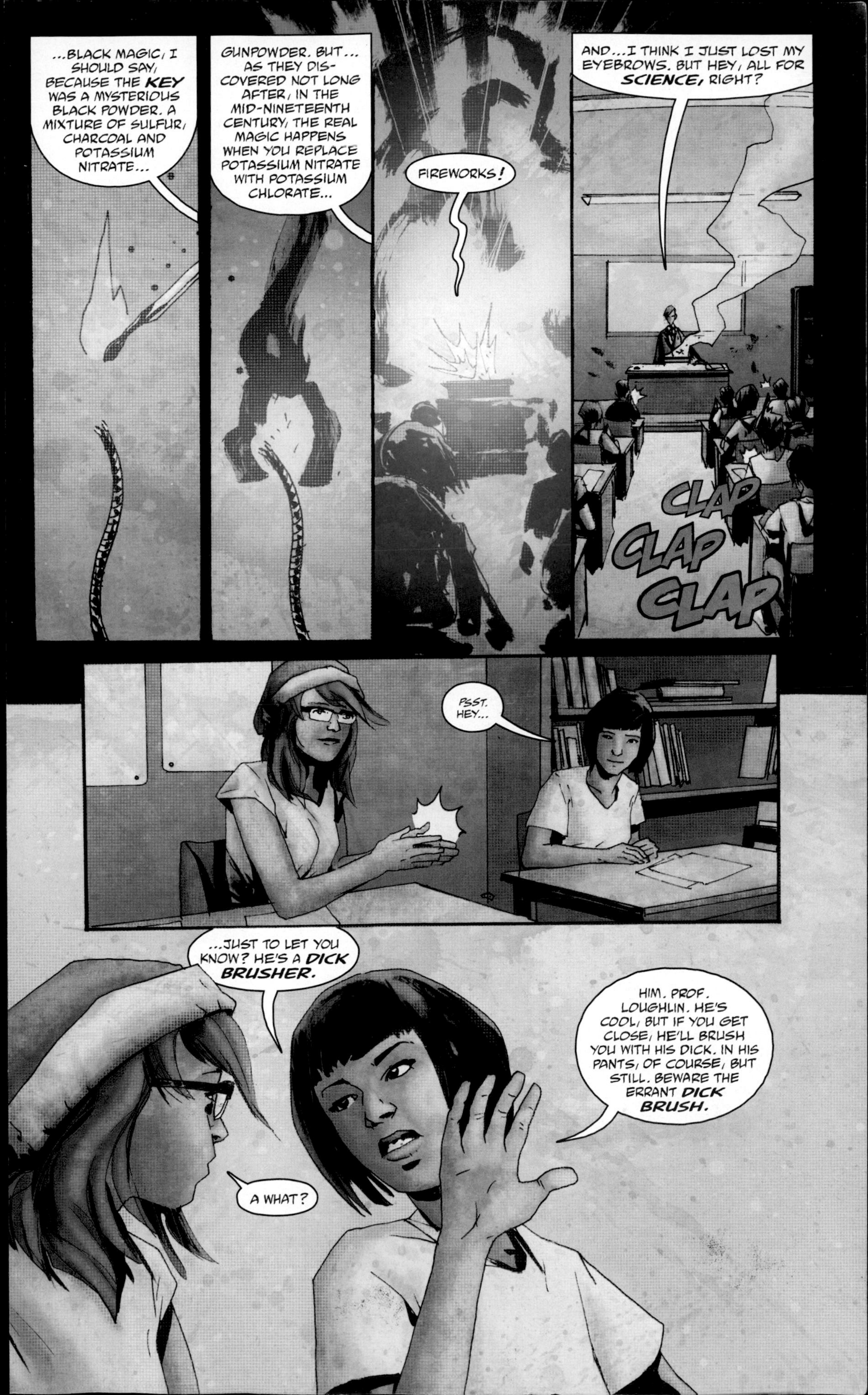
...BLACK MAGIC, I SHOULD SAY, BECAUSE THE KEY WAS A MYSTERIOUS BLACK POWDER. A MIXTURE OF SULFUR, CHARCOAL AND POTASSIUM NITRATE...
GUNPOWDER. BUT... AS THEY DIS-COVERED NOT LONG AFTER, IN THE MID-NINETEENTH CENTURY, THE REAL MAGIC HAPPENS WHEN YOU REPLACE POTASSIUM NITRATE WITH POTASSIUM CHLORATE...
FIREWORKS!
AND...I THINK I JUST LOST MY EYEBROWS. BUT HEY, ALL FOR SCIENCE, RIGHT?
CLAP
CLAP
CLAP
PSST. HEY...
...JUST TO LET YOU KNOW? HE'S A DICK BRUSHER.
A WHAT?
HIM. PROF. LOUGHLIN. HE'S COOL, BUT IF YOU GET CLOSE, HE'LL BRUSH YOU WITH HIS DICK. IN HIS PANTS, OF COURSE, BUT STILL. BEWARE THE ERRANT DICK BRUSH.

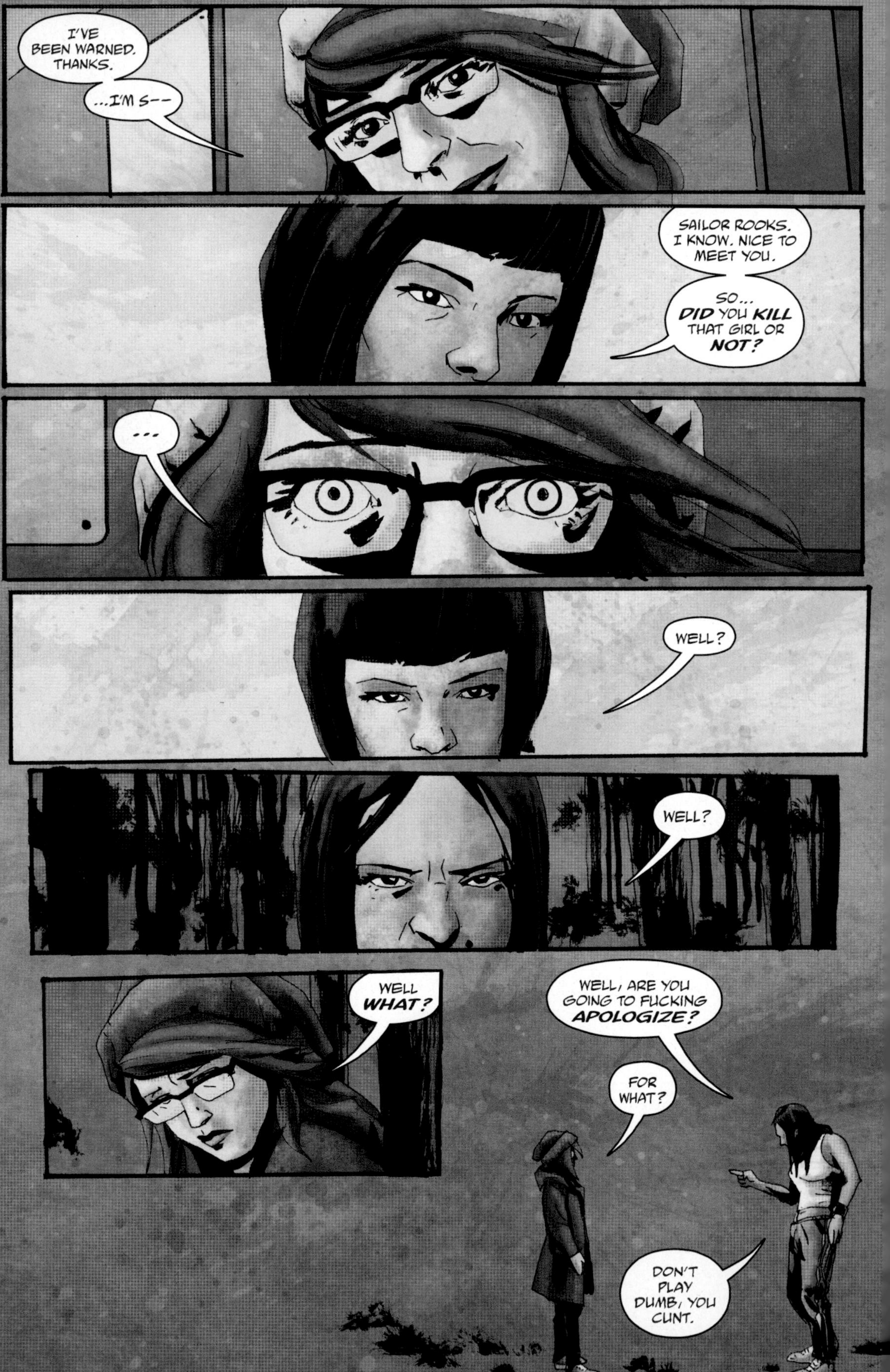
I'VE BEEN WARNED. THANKS.
...I'M S--
SAILOR ROOKS. I KNOW. NICE TO MEET YOU.
SO... DID YOU KILL THAT GIRL OR NOT?
...
WELL?
WELL?
WELL WHAT?
WELL, ARE YOU GOING TO FUCKING APOLOGIZE?
FOR WHAT?
DON'T PLAY DUMB, YOU CUNT.

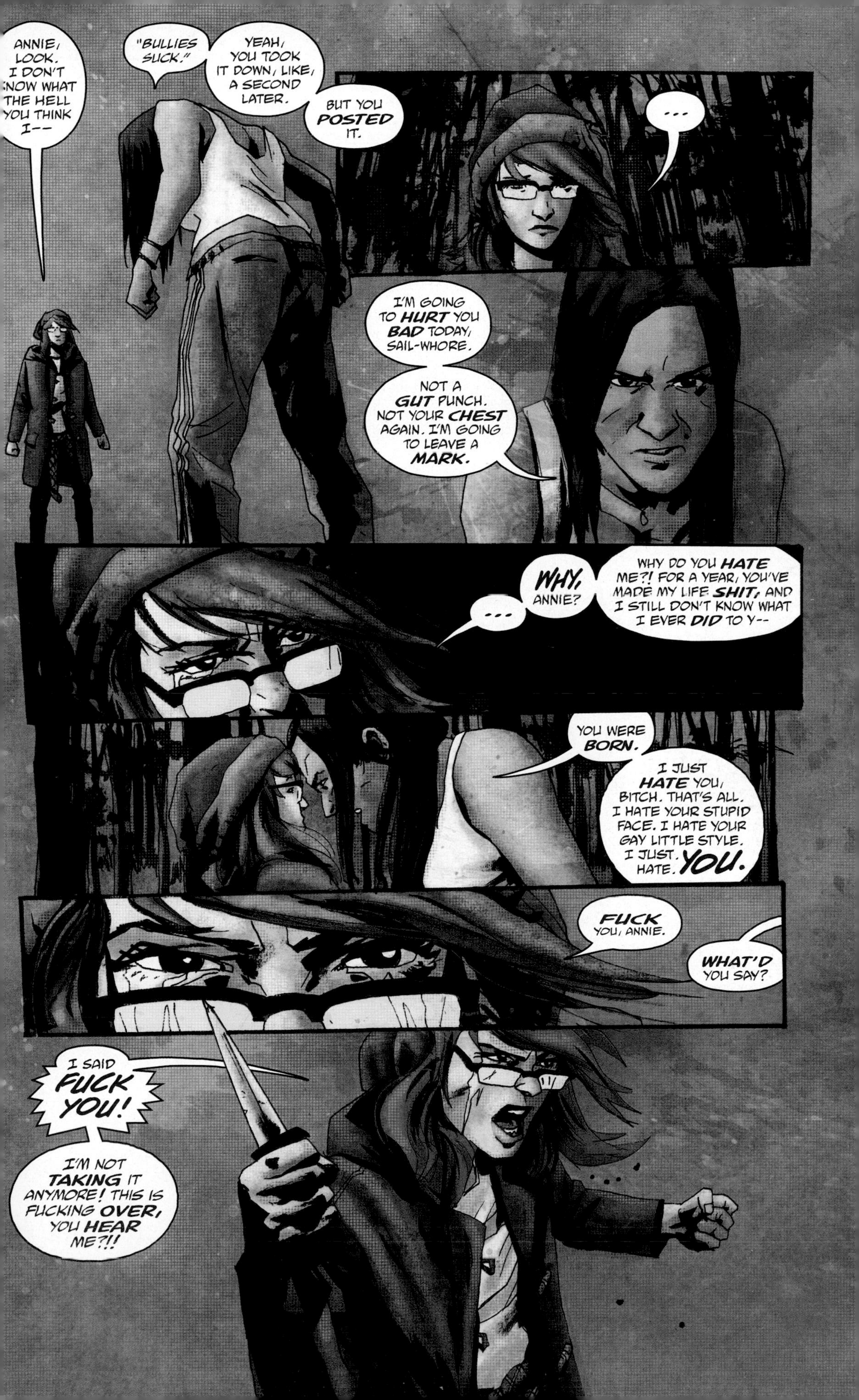
ANNIE, LOOK. I DON'T KNOW WHAT THE HELL YOU THINK I--
"BULLIES SUCK."
YEAH, YOU TOOK IT DOWN, LIKE, A SECOND LATER.
BUT YOU POSTED IT.
...
I'M GOING TO HURT YOU BAD TODAY, SAIL-WHORE.
NOT A GUT PUNCH. NOT YOUR CHEST AGAIN. I'M GOING TO LEAVE A MARK.
...
WHY, ANNIE?
WHY DO YOU HATE ME?! FOR A YEAR, YOU'VE MADE MY LIFE SHIT, AND I STILL DON'T KNOW WHAT I EVER DID TO Y--
YOU WERE BORN.
I JUST HATE YOU, BITCH. THAT'S ALL. I HATE YOUR STUPID FACE. I HATE YOUR GAY LITTLE STYLE. I JUST. HATE. YOU.
FUCK YOU, ANNIE.
WHAT'D YOU SAY?
I SAID FUCK YOU!
I'M NOT TAKING IT ANYMORE! THIS IS FUCKING OVER, YOU HEAR ME?!!

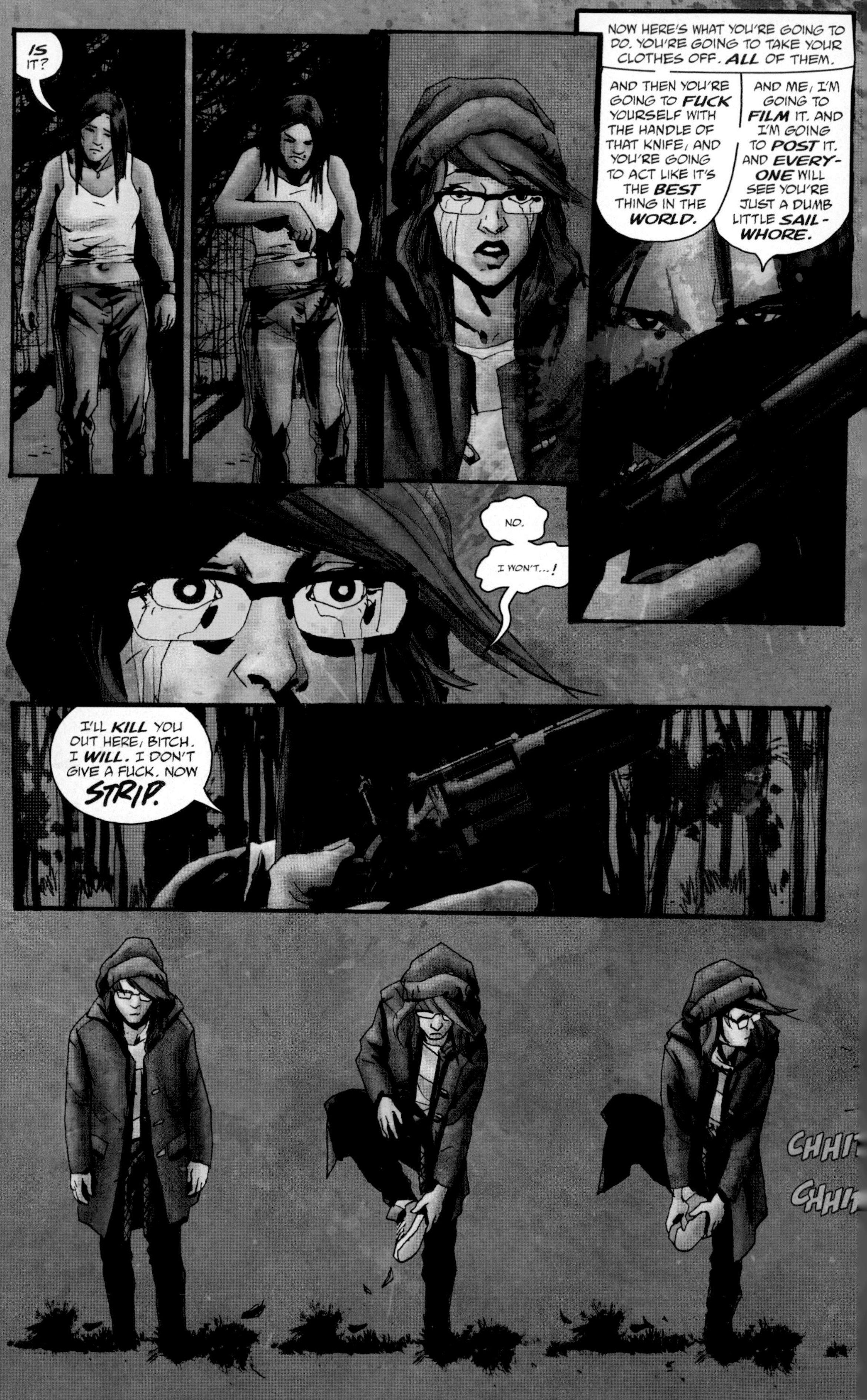
IS IT?
NOW HERE'S WHAT YOU'RE GOING TO DO. YOU'RE GOING TO TAKE YOUR CLOTHES OFF. ALL OF THEM.
AND THEN YOU'RE GOING TO FUCK YOURSELF WITH THE HANDLE OF THAT KNIFE, AND YOU'RE GOING TO ACT LIKE IT'S THE BEST THING IN THE WORLD.
AND ME, I'M GOING TO FILM IT. AND I'M GOING TO POST IT. AND EVERY-ONE WILL SEE YOU'RE JUST A DUMB LITTLE SAIL-WHORE.
NO.
I WON'T...!
I'LL KILL YOU OUT HERE, BITCH. I WILL. I DON'T GIVE A FUCK. NOW STRIP.

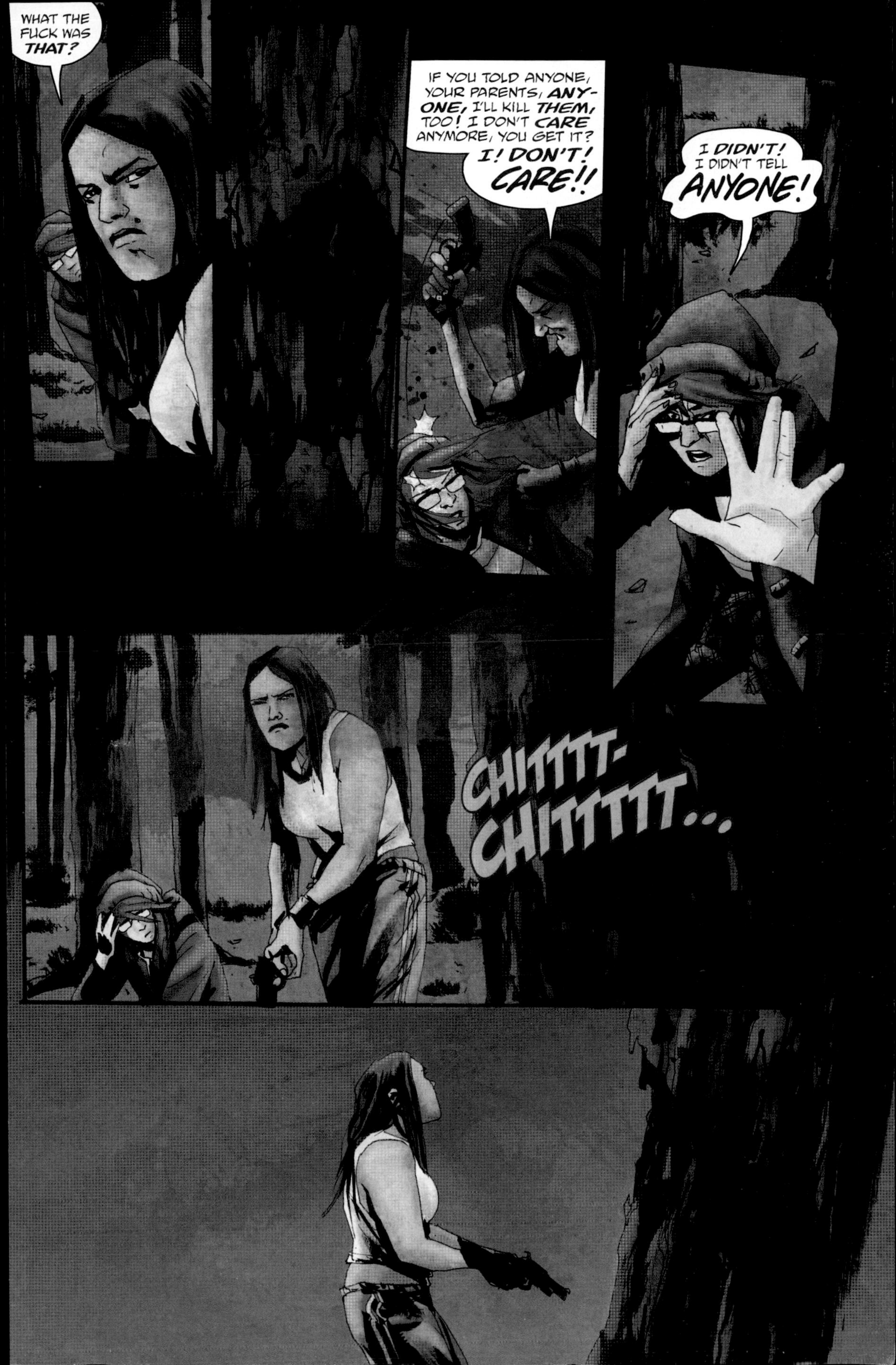
WHAT THE FUCK WAS THAT?
IF YOU TOLD ANYONE, YOUR PARENTS, ANY-ONE, I'LL KILL THEM, TOO! I DON'T CARE ANYMORE, YOU GET IT? I! DON'T! CARE!!
I DIDN'T! I DIDN'T TELL ANYONE!
CHITTTT-CHITTTTT...

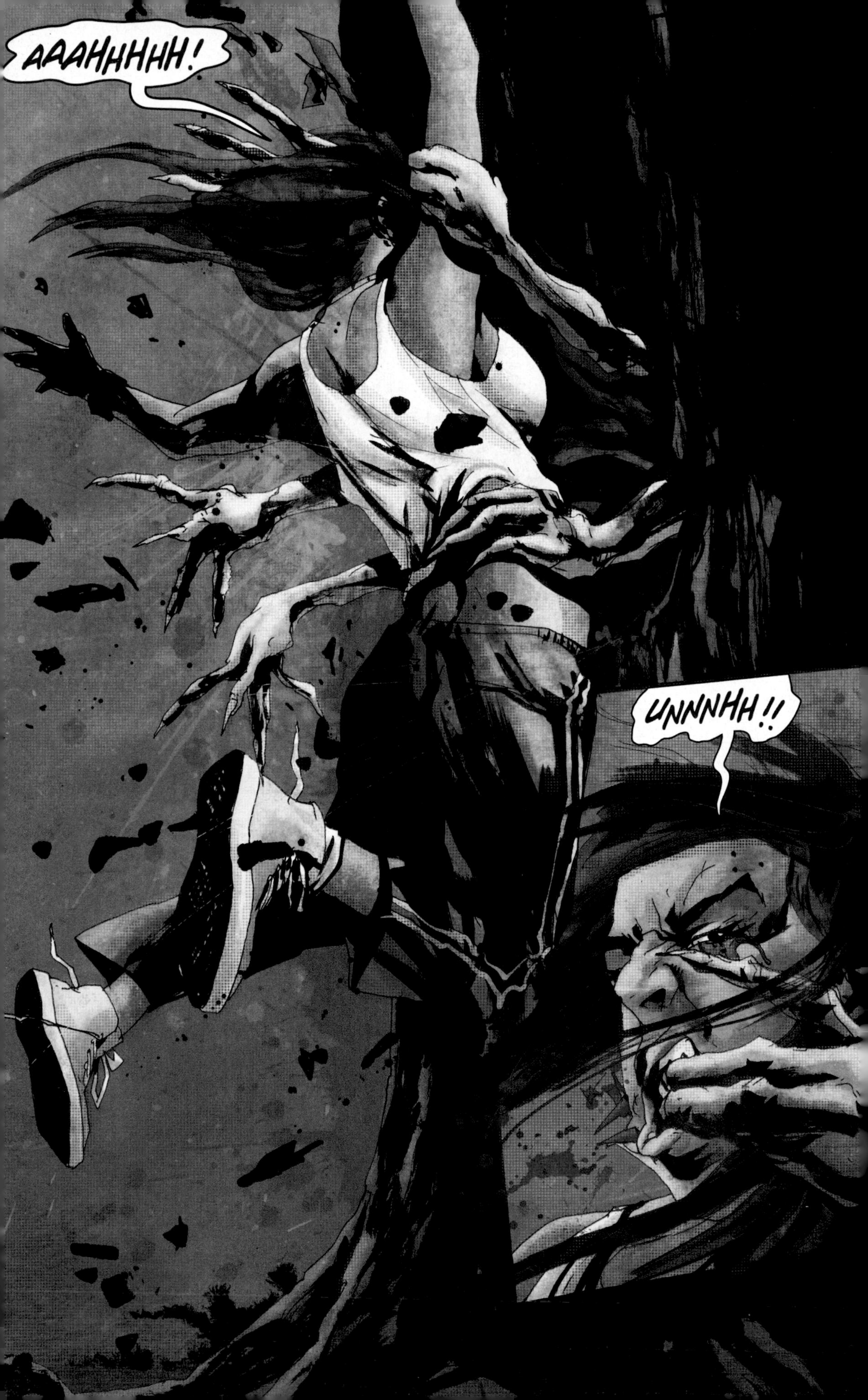
AAAHHHHH!
UNNNHH!!

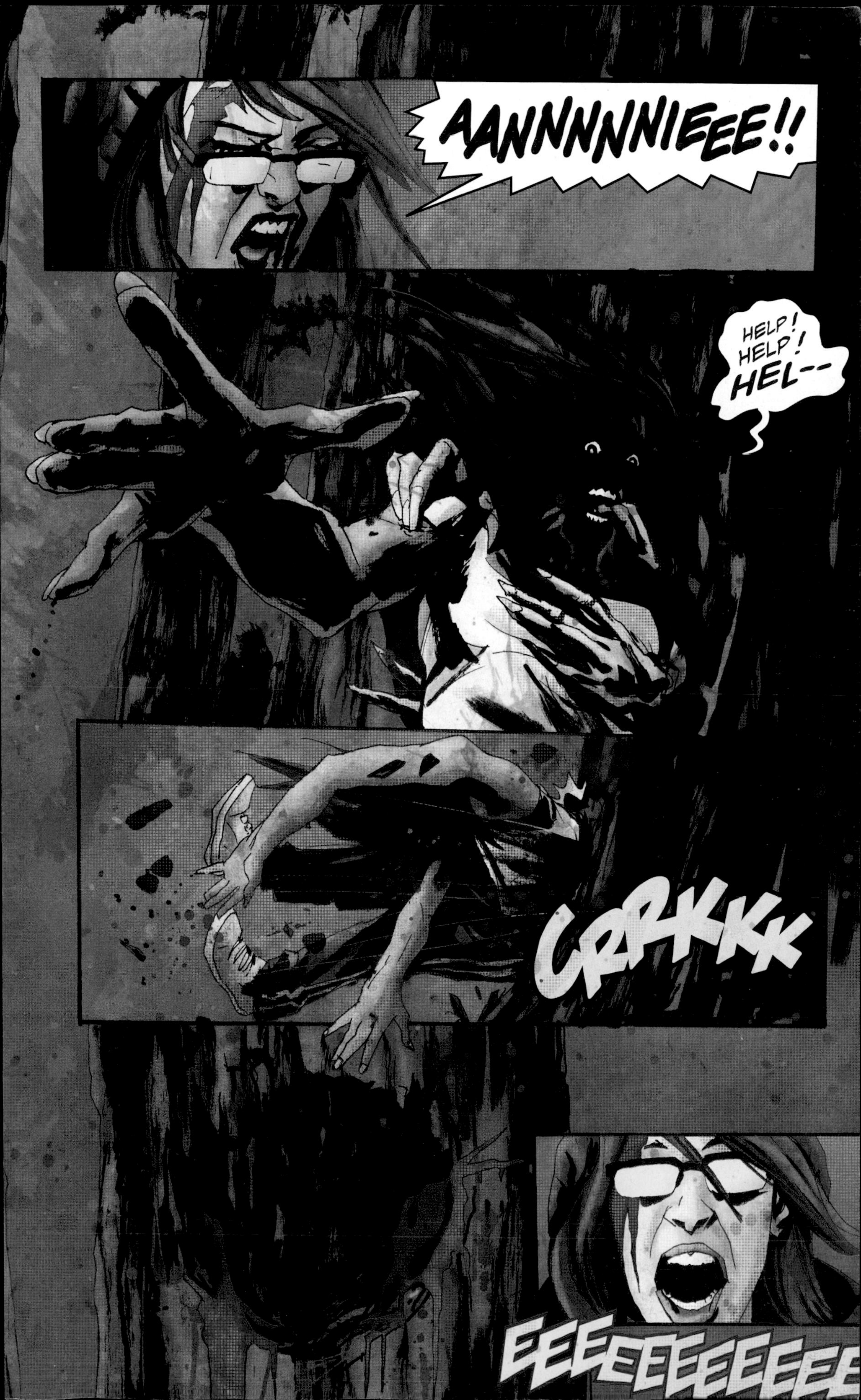
AANNNNNIEEEE!!
HELP! HELP! HEL--
CRRKKK
EEEEEEEEEEEEE

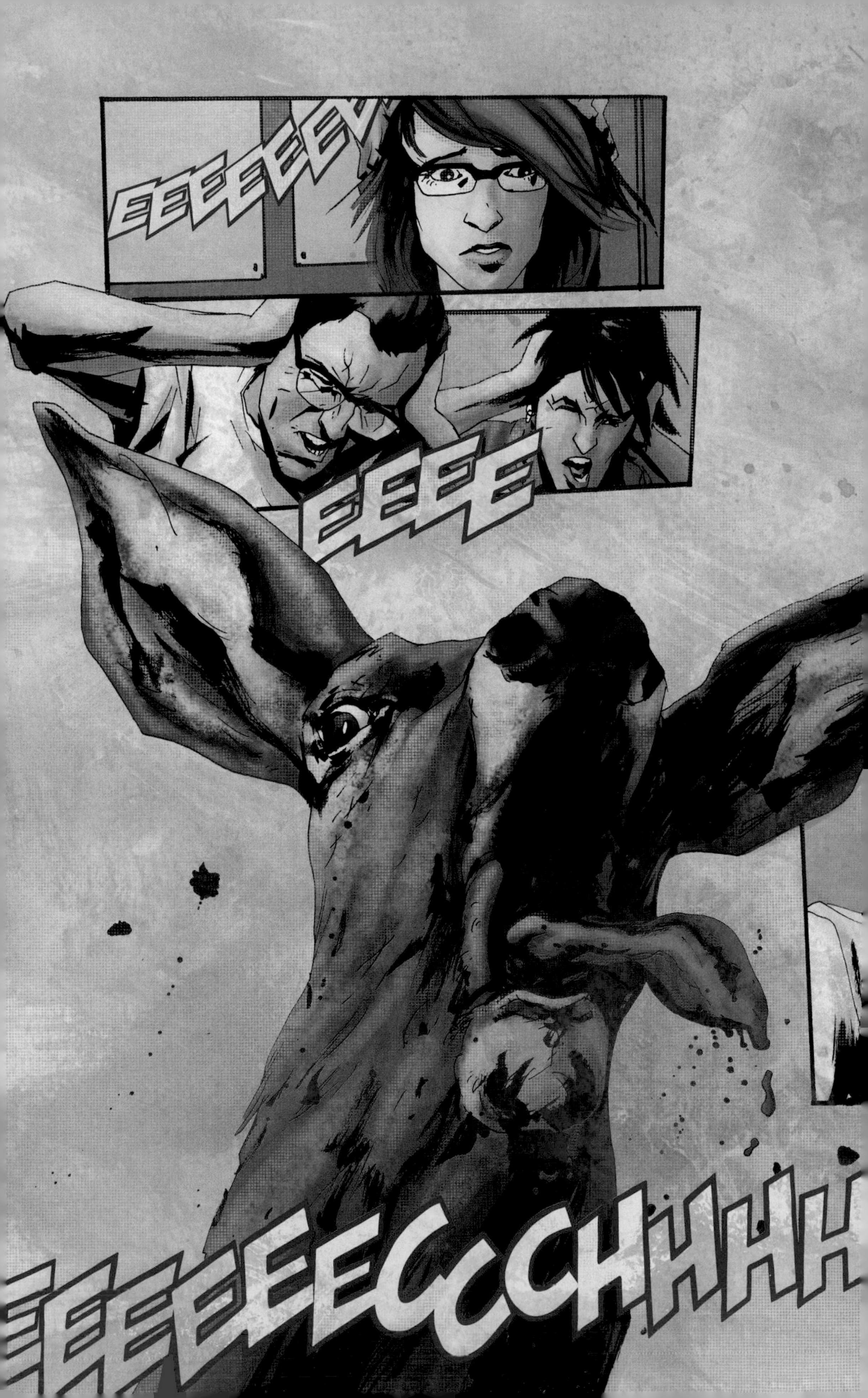
EEEEEEE
EEEE
EEEEEECCHHHH

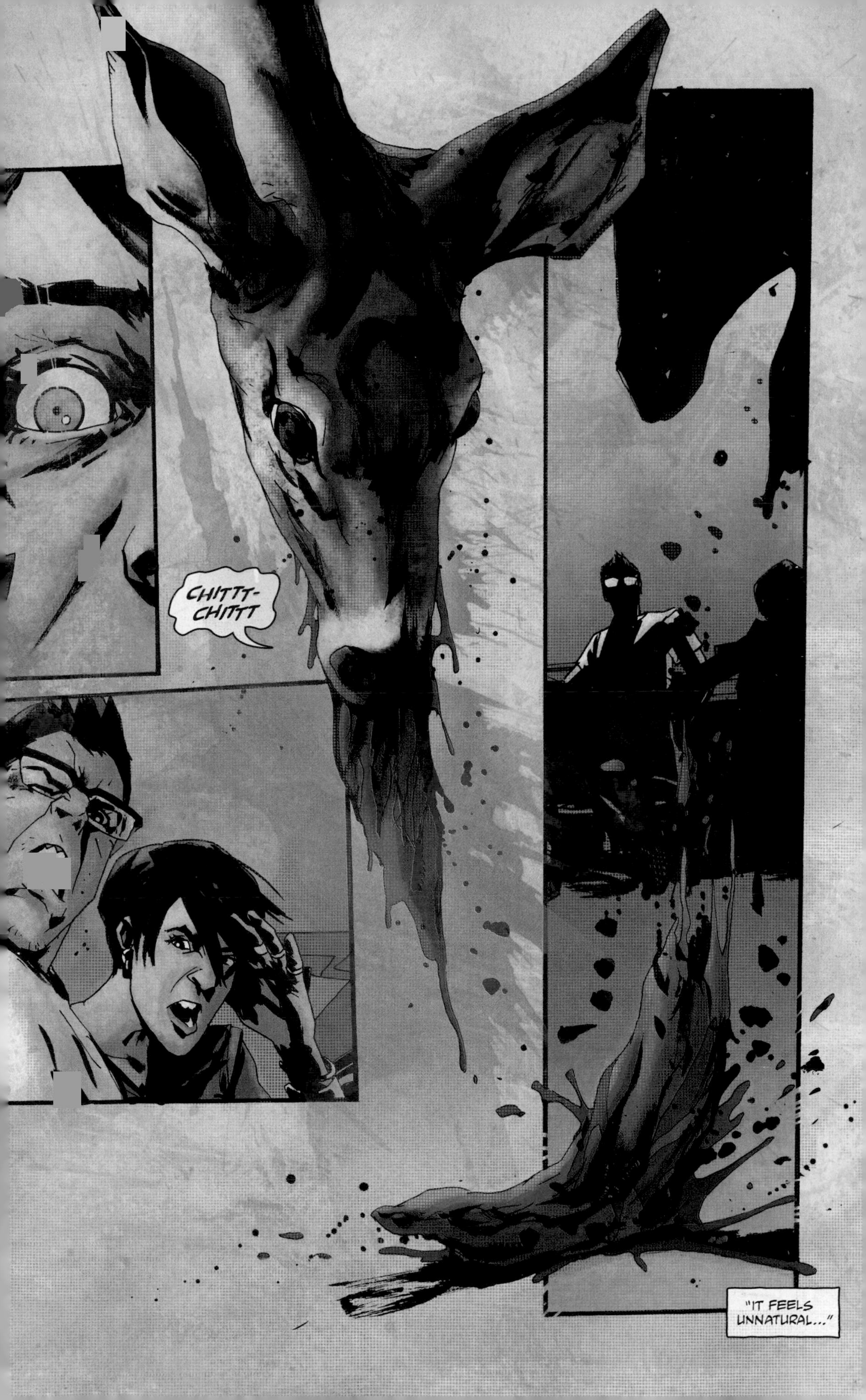
CHITTT-CHITTT
"IT FEELS UNNATURAL..."

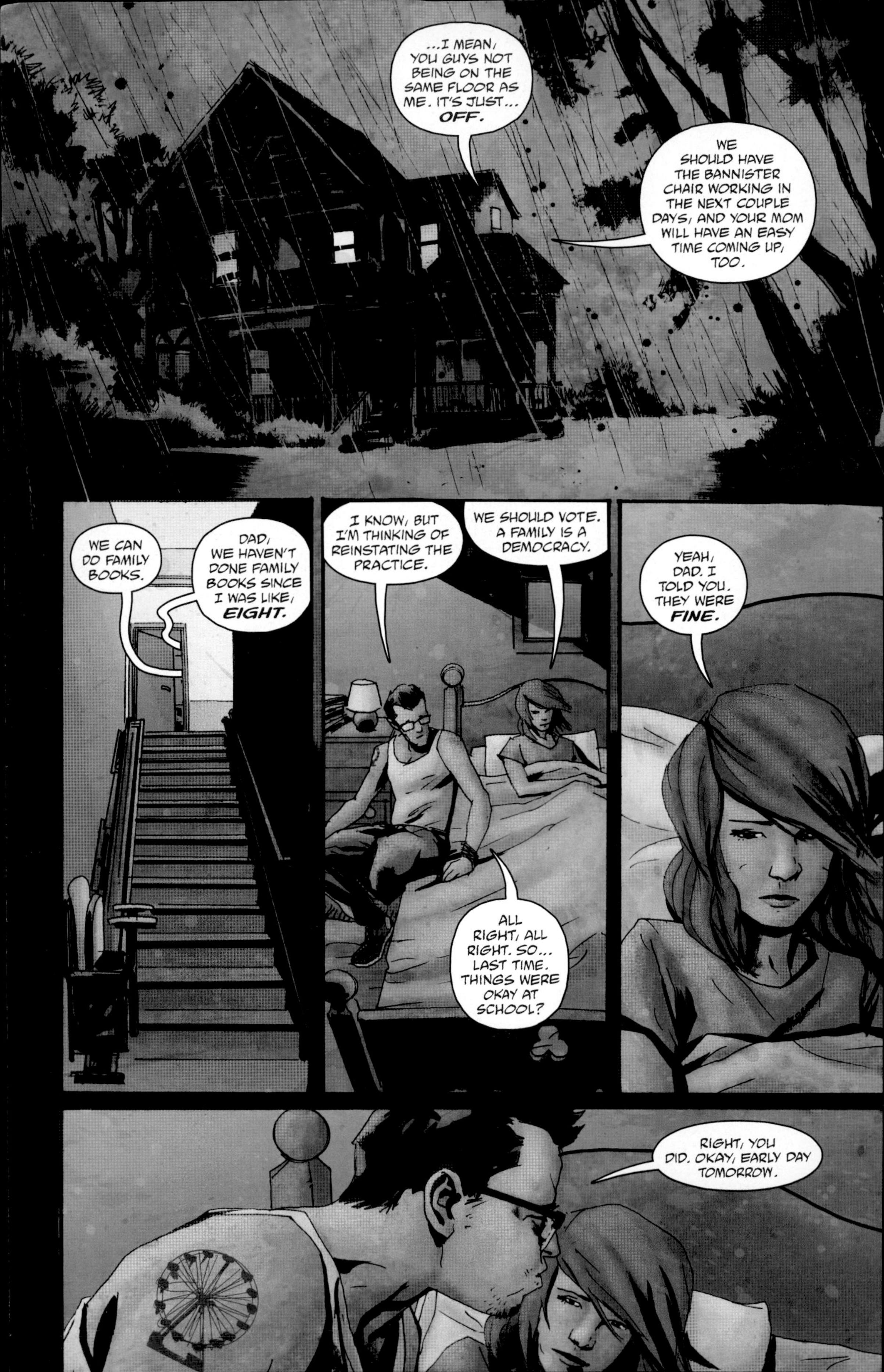
...I MEAN, YOU GUYS NOT BEING ON THE SAME FLOOR AS ME. IT'S JUST... **OFF.**
WE SHOULD HAVE THE BANNISTER CHAIR WORKING IN THE NEXT COUPLE DAYS, AND YOUR MOM WILL HAVE AN EASY TIME COMING UP, TOO.
WE CAN DO FAMILY BOOKS.
DAD, WE HAVEN'T DONE FAMILY BOOKS SINCE I WAS LIKE, **EIGHT.**
I KNOW, BUT I'M THINKING OF REINSTATING THE PRACTICE.
WE SHOULD VOTE. A FAMILY IS A DEMOCRACY.
ALL RIGHT, ALL RIGHT. SO... LAST TIME. THINGS WERE OKAY AT SCHOOL?
YEAH, DAD. I TOLD YOU. THEY WERE **FINE.**
RIGHT, YOU DID. OKAY, EARLY DAY TOMORROW.

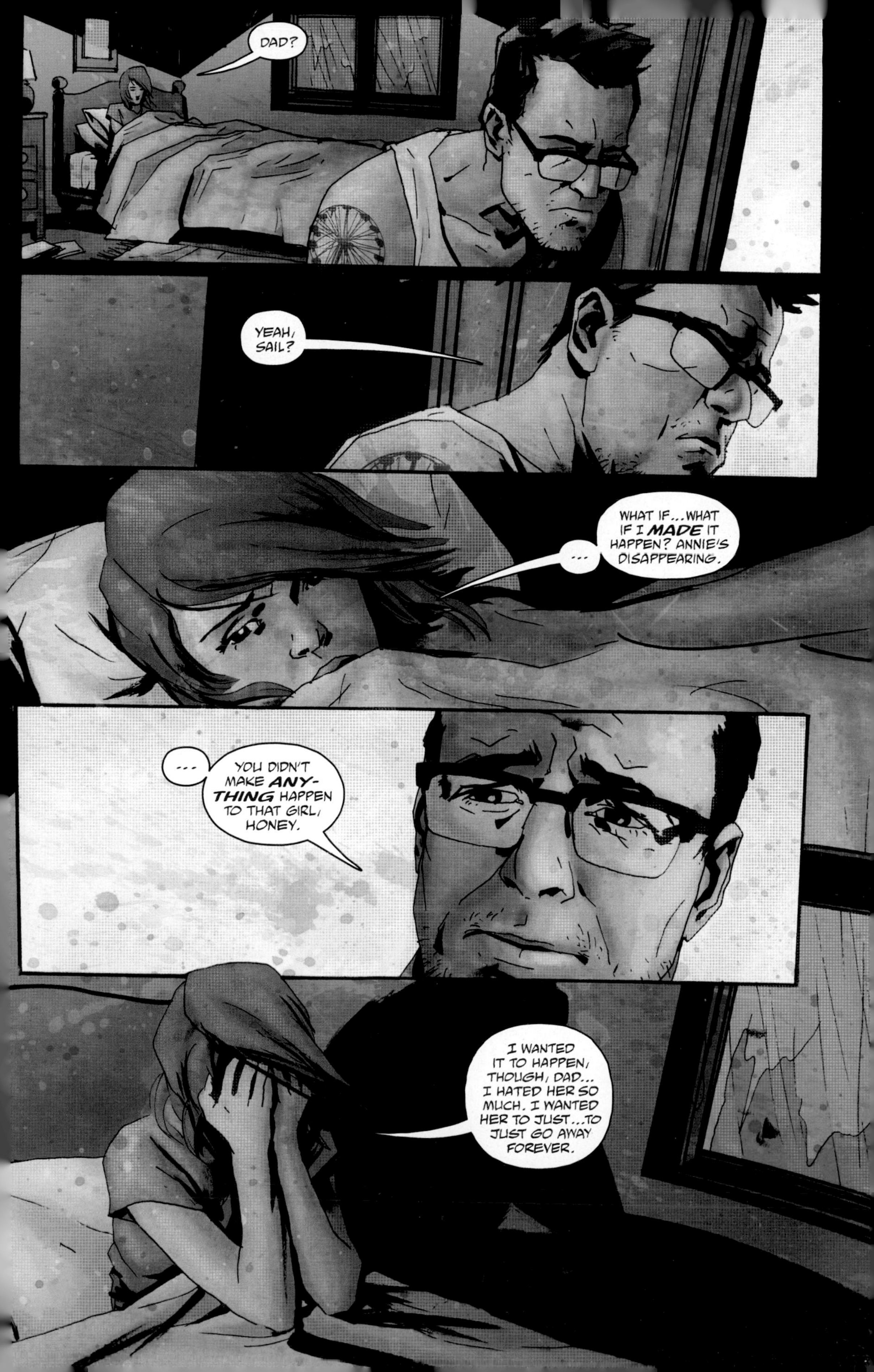
DAD?
YEAH, SAIL?
...
WHAT IF... WHAT IF I **MADE** IT HAPPEN? ANNIE'S DISAPPEARING.
...
YOU DIDN'T MAKE **ANY-THING** HAPPEN TO THAT GIRL, HONEY.
I WANTED IT TO HAPPEN, THOUGH, DAD... I HATED HER SO MUCH. I WANTED HER TO JUST... TO JUST GO AWAY FOREVER.

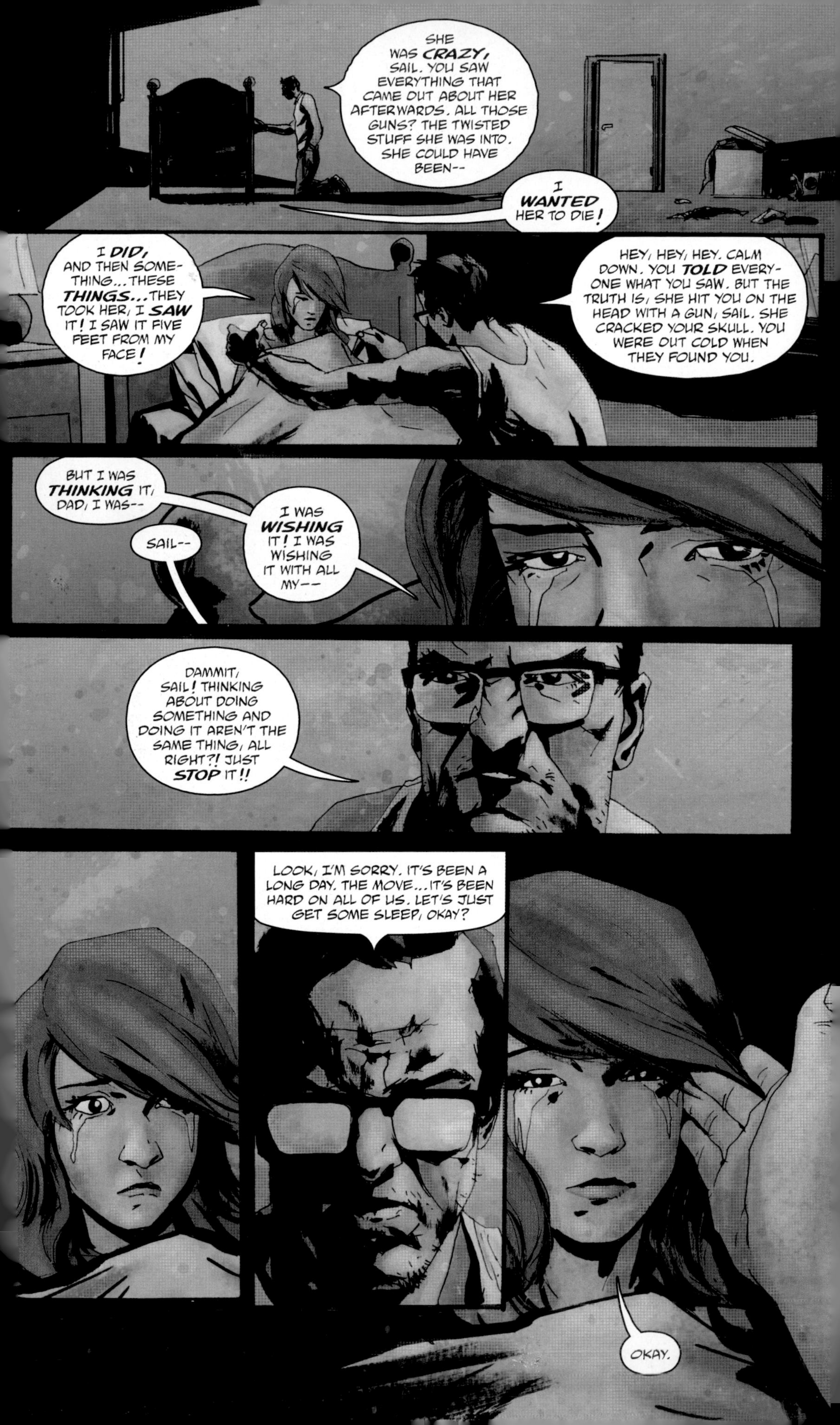
SHE WAS CRAZY, SAIL. YOU SAW EVERYTHING THAT CAME OUT ABOUT HER AFTERWARDS. ALL THOSE GUNS? THE TWISTED STUFF SHE WAS INTO. SHE COULD HAVE BEEN--
I WANTED HER TO DIE!
I DID, AND THEN SOME-THING... THESE THINGS... THEY TOOK HER, I SAW IT! I SAW IT FIVE FEET FROM MY FACE!
HEY, HEY, HEY. CALM DOWN. YOU TOLD EVERY-ONE WHAT YOU SAW. BUT THE TRUTH IS, SHE HIT YOU ON THE HEAD WITH A GUN, SAIL. SHE CRACKED YOUR SKULL. YOU WERE OUT COLD WHEN THEY FOUND YOU.
BUT I WAS THINKING IT, DAD, I WAS--
SAIL--
I WAS WISHING IT! I WAS WISHING IT WITH ALL MY--
DAMMIT, SAIL! THINKING ABOUT DOING SOMETHING AND DOING IT AREN'T THE SAME THING, ALL RIGHT?! JUST STOP IT!!
LOOK, I'M SORRY. IT'S BEEN A LONG DAY. THE MOVE... IT'S BEEN HARD ON ALL OF US. LET'S JUST GET SOME SLEEP, OKAY?
OKAY.

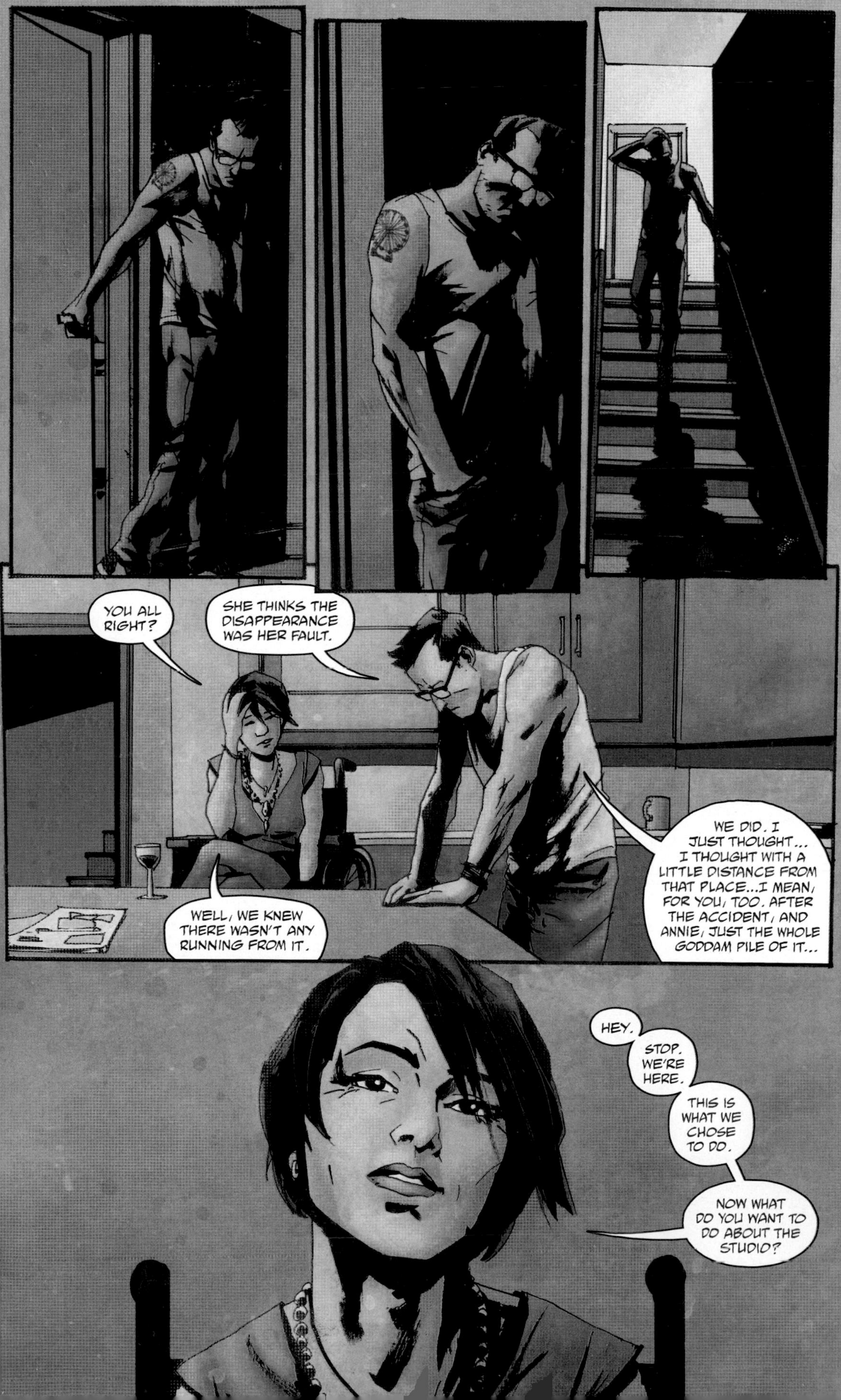
YOU ALL RIGHT?
SHE THINKS THE DISAPPEARANCE WAS HER FAULT.
WELL, WE KNEW THERE WASN'T ANY RUNNING FROM IT.
WE DID. I JUST THOUGHT... I THOUGHT WITH A LITTLE DISTANCE FROM THAT PLACE...I MEAN, FOR YOU, TOO. AFTER THE ACCIDENT, AND ANNIE, JUST THE WHOLE GODDAM PILE OF IT...
HEY.
STOP. WE'RE HERE.
THIS IS WHAT WE CHOSE TO DO.
NOW WHAT DO YOU WANT TO DO ABOUT THE STUDIO?

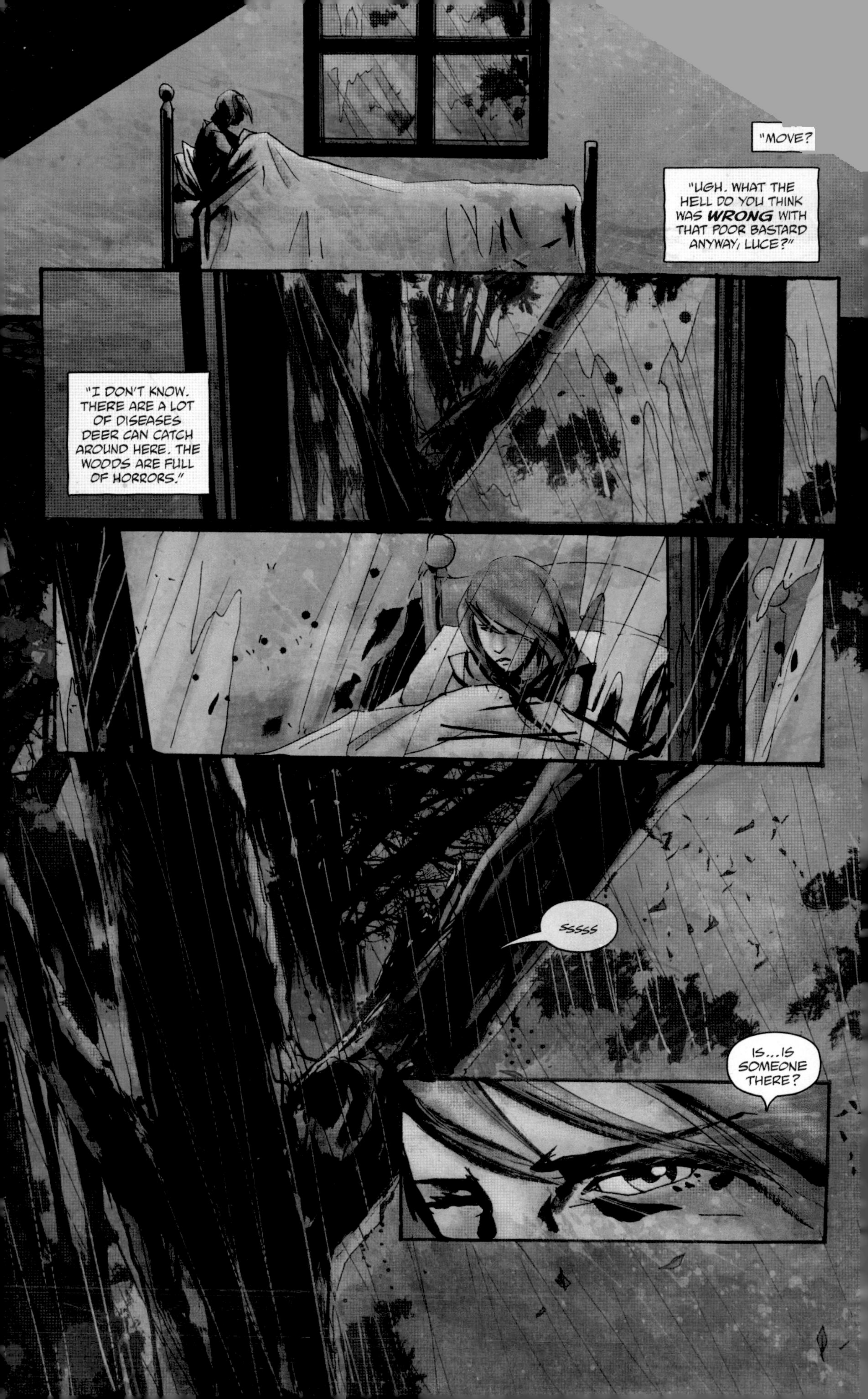
"MOVE?
"UGH. WHAT THE HELL DO YOU THINK WAS WRONG WITH THAT POOR BASTARD ANYWAY, LUCE?"
"I DON'T KNOW. THERE ARE A LOT OF DISEASES DEER CAN CATCH AROUND HERE. THE WOODS ARE FULL OF HORRORS."
SSSSS
IS...IS SOMEONE THERE?

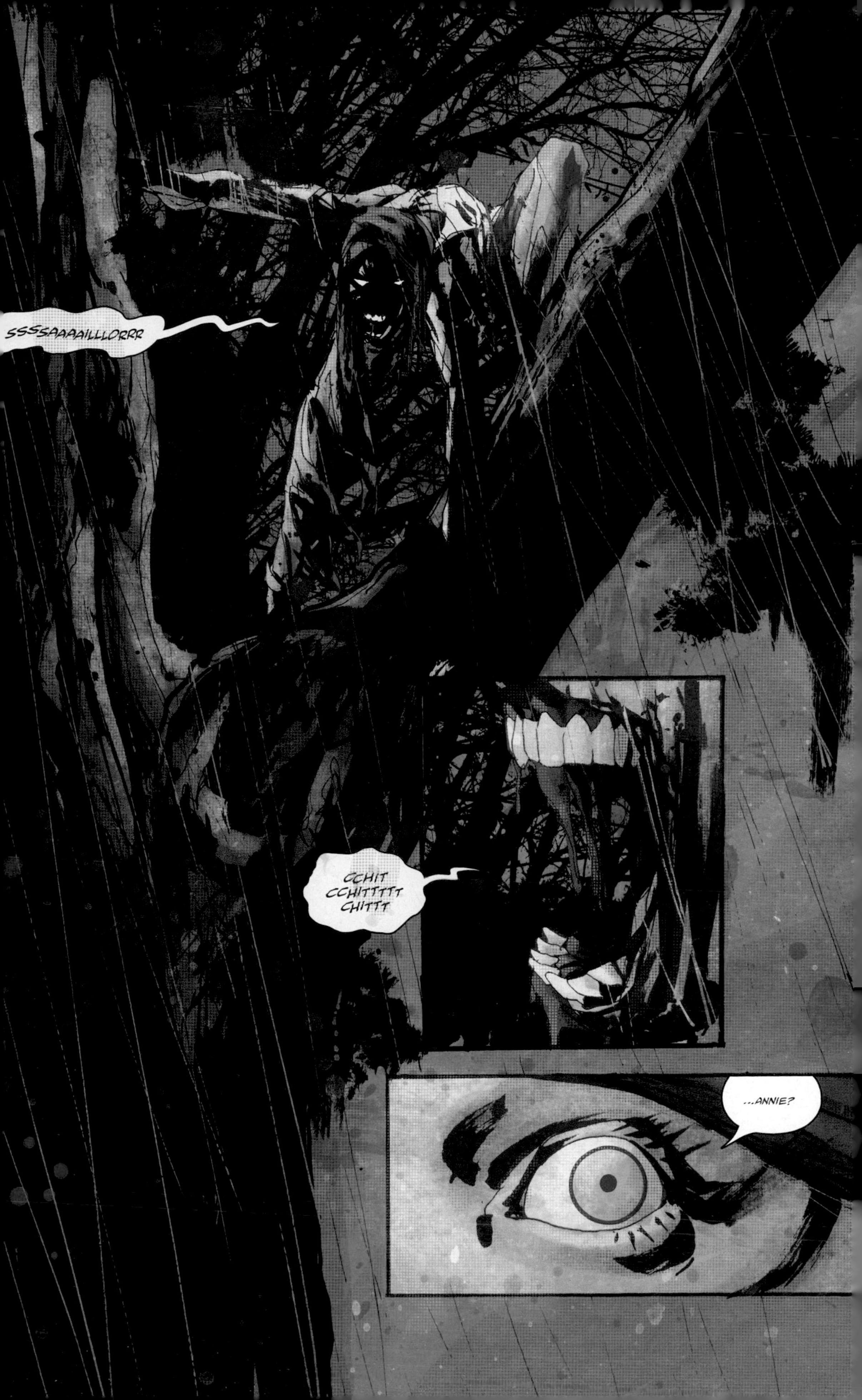
SSSSAAAAILLLORRR
CCHIT CCHITTTTTT CHITTT
...ANNIE?

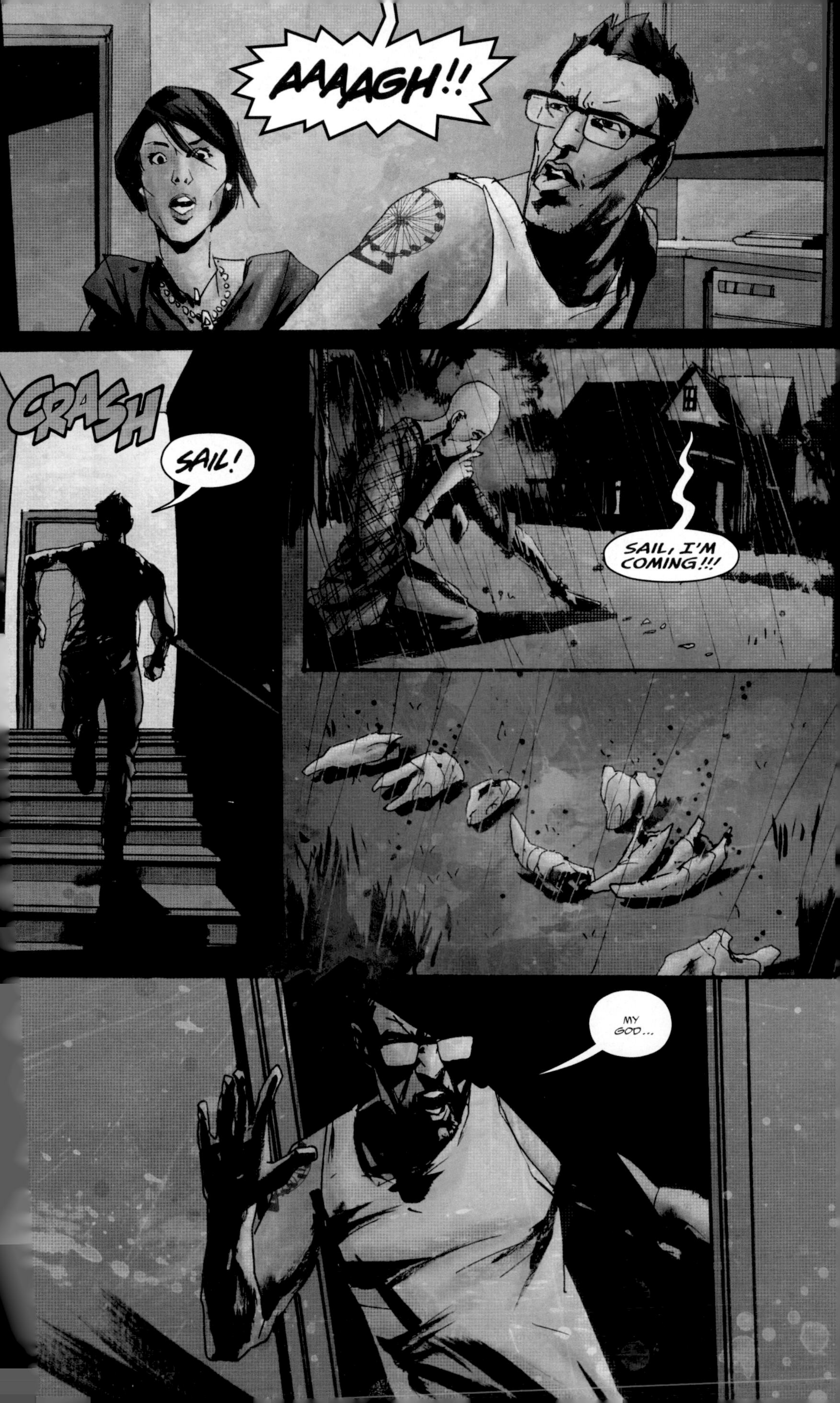
AAAAGH!!
CRASH
SAIL!
SAIL, I'M COMING!!!
MY GOD...

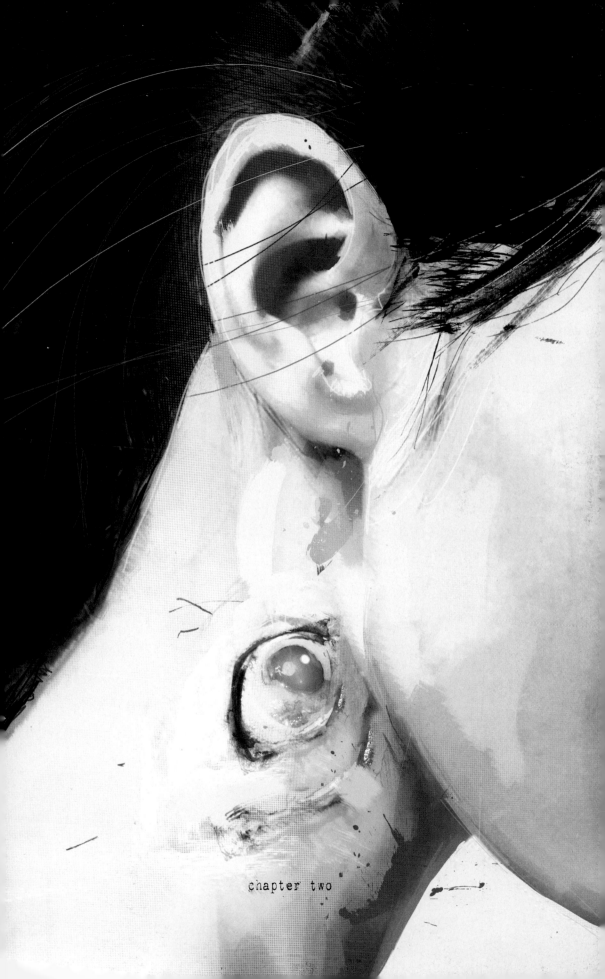

chapter two

CHAPTER 2.

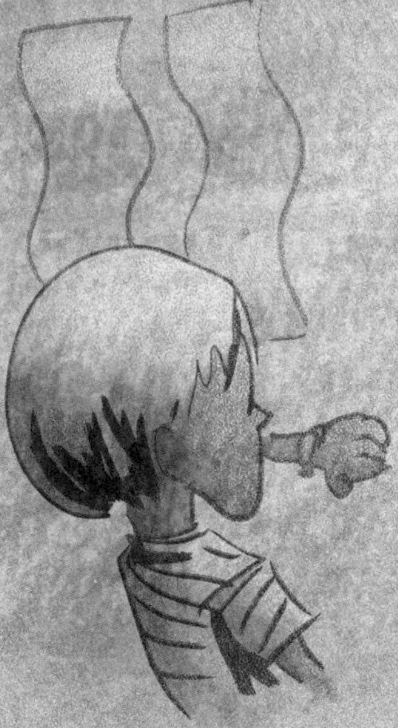

But by now the night was ending.

The sun was up and the glow began to fade from the old hall. Taylor blinked and rubbed his eyes and when he opened them, the mirrors had lost their luster. Instead of looking through portals, Taylor was simply staring at his own face again, twisted in the cracked and dusty slabs of glass. There he was. Small and blond and rumpled and...(he checked his watch) late for school. Ugh.

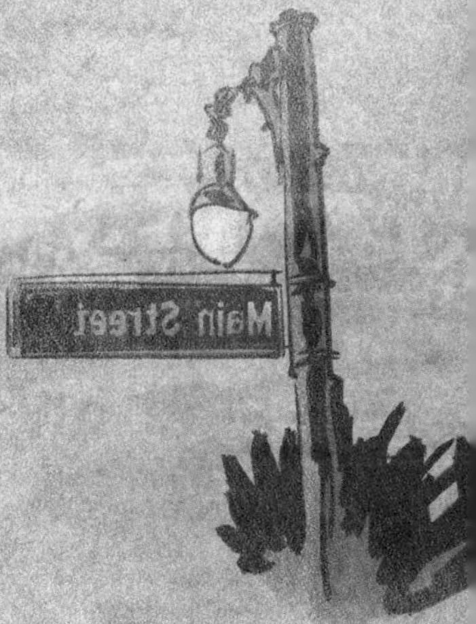
Main Street

He ran from the hall of mirrors and crossed the main fairway of the night arcade. Fast as he could, he hopped the rusty fence and set out for town. One by one he passed the streets, but the blocks seemed to stretch forever. He passed Orchard Street, Poplar Street, and then he was on Main. He was running so fast he barely noticed the slight change to the street signs. In fact, he barely noticed anything until he saw Lula coming up the street on her skateboard, practicing tricks.

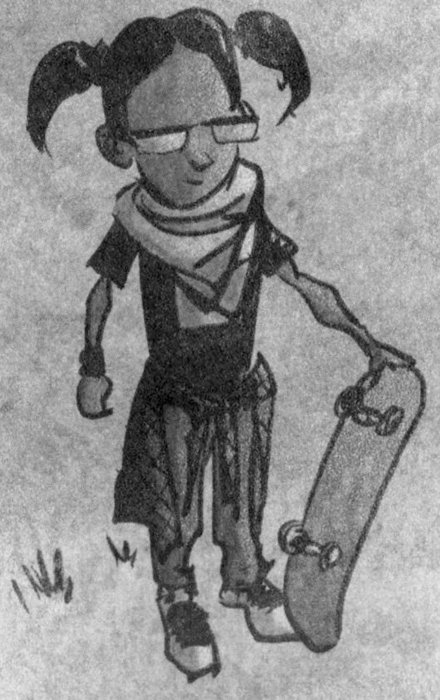

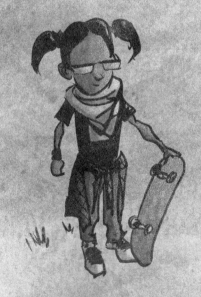

"Lu," he said, panting. "What are you doing? We'll be late for school. Come on!"

But Lula just stared at him.

"?loohcs s'tahW" she said.

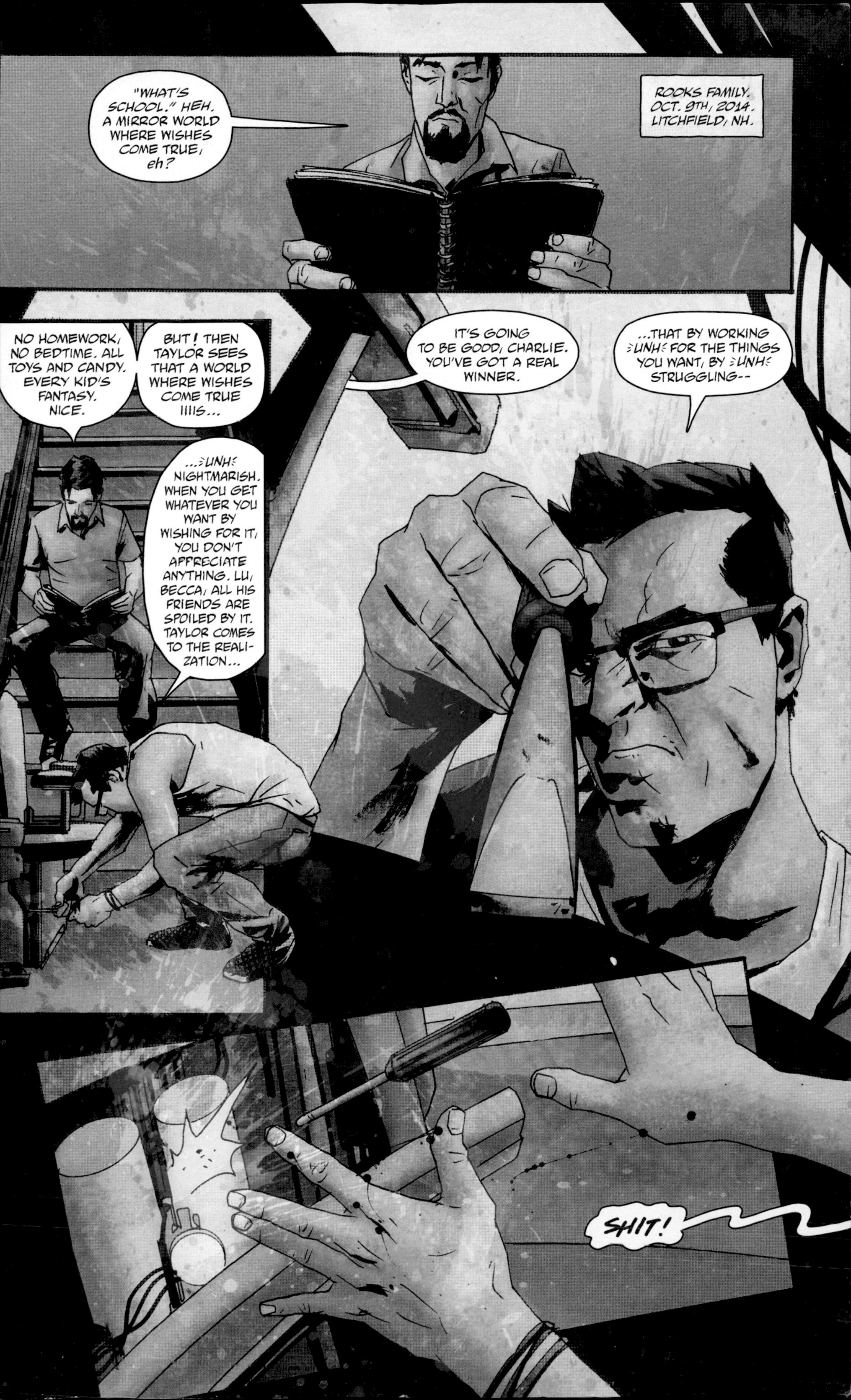
"WHAT'S SCHOOL." HEH. A MIRROR WORLD WHERE WISHES COME TRUE, eh?
ROOKS FAMILY. OCT. 9TH, 2014. LITCHFIELD, NH.
NO HOMEWORK, NO BEDTIME. ALL TOYS AND CANDY. EVERY KID'S FANTASY. NICE.
BUT! THEN TAYLOR SEES THAT A WORLD WHERE WISHES COME TRUE IIIIS...
IT'S GOING TO BE GOOD, CHARLIE. YOU'VE GOT A REAL WINNER.
...THAT BY WORKING UNH FOR THE THINGS YOU WANT, BY UNH STRUGGLING--
...UNH NIGHTMARISH. WHEN YOU GET WHATEVER YOU WANT BY WISHING FOR IT, YOU DON'T APPRECIATE ANYTHING. LU, BECCA, ALL HIS FRIENDS ARE SPOILED BY IT. TAYLOR COMES TO THE REALIZATION...
SHIT!

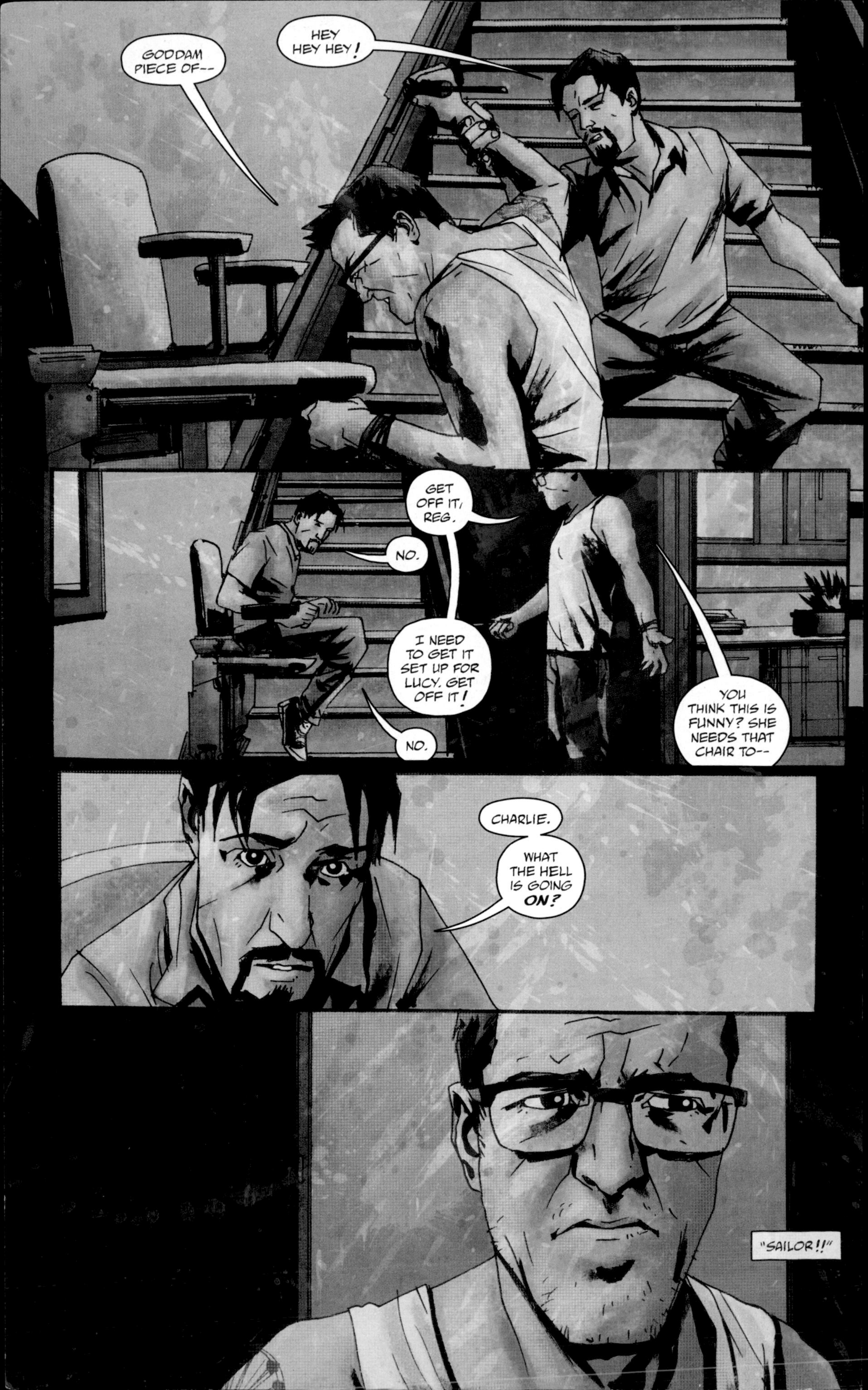
GODDAM PIECE OF--
HEY HEY HEY!
GET OFF IT, REG.
NO.
I NEED TO GET IT SET UP FOR LUCY. GET OFF IT!
NO.
YOU THINK THIS IS FUNNY? SHE NEEDS THAT CHAIR TO--
CHARLIE.
WHAT THE HELL IS GOING ON?
"SAILOR!!"

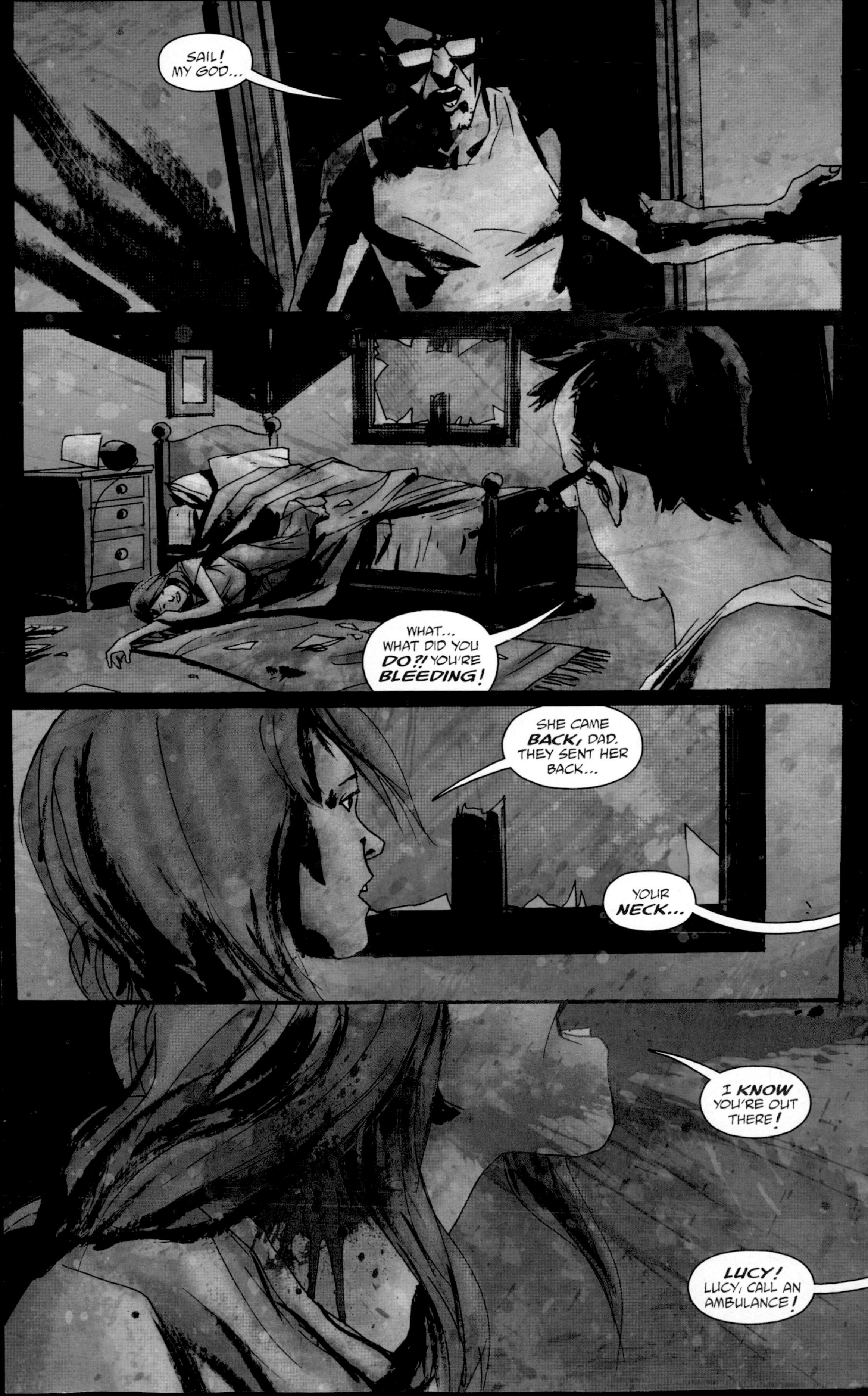
SAIL! MY GOD...
WHAT... WHAT DID YOU DO?! YOU'RE BLEEDING!
SHE CAME BACK, DAD. THEY SENT HER BACK...
YOUR NECK...
I KNOW YOU'RE OUT THERE!
LUCY! LUCY, CALL AN AMBULANCE!

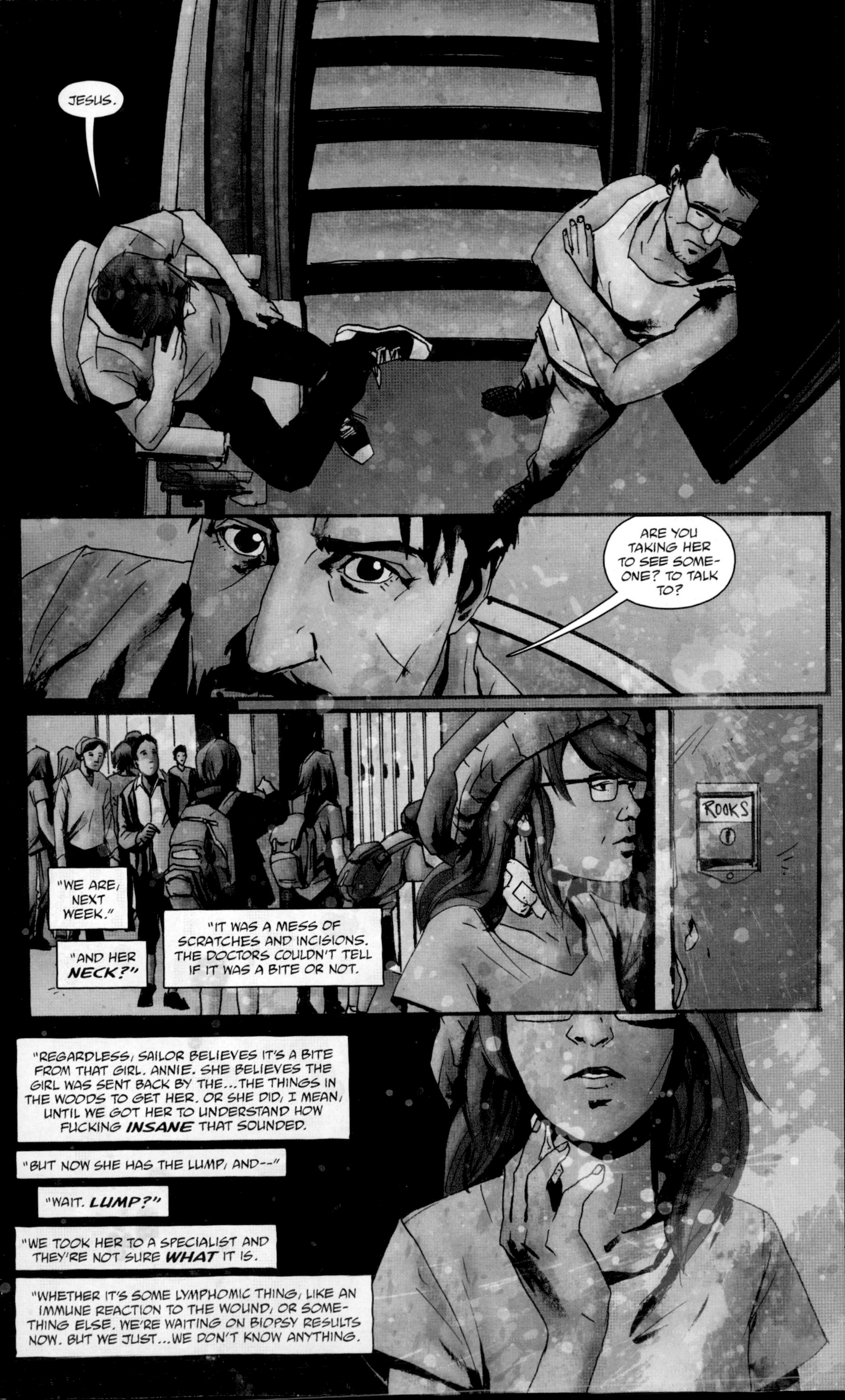

JESUS.
ARE YOU TAKING HER TO SEE SOME-ONE? TO TALK TO?
"WE ARE, NEXT WEEK."
"AND HER NECK?"
"IT WAS A MESS OF SCRATCHES AND INCISIONS. THE DOCTORS COULDN'T TELL IF IT WAS A BITE OR NOT.
ROOKS
"REGARDLESS, SAILOR BELIEVES IT'S A BITE FROM THAT GIRL. ANNIE. SHE BELIEVES THE GIRL WAS SENT BACK BY THE...THE THINGS IN THE WOODS TO GET HER. OR SHE DID, I MEAN, UNTIL WE GOT HER TO UNDERSTAND HOW FUCKING INSANE THAT SOUNDED.
"BUT NOW SHE HAS THE LUMP, AND--"
"WAIT. LUMP?"
"WE TOOK HER TO A SPECIALIST AND THEY'RE NOT SURE WHAT IT IS.
"WHETHER IT'S SOME LYMPHOMIC THING, LIKE AN IMMUNE REACTION TO THE WOUND, OR SOME-THING ELSE. WE'RE WAITING ON BIOPSY RESULTS NOW. BUT WE JUST...WE DON'T KNOW ANYTHING.

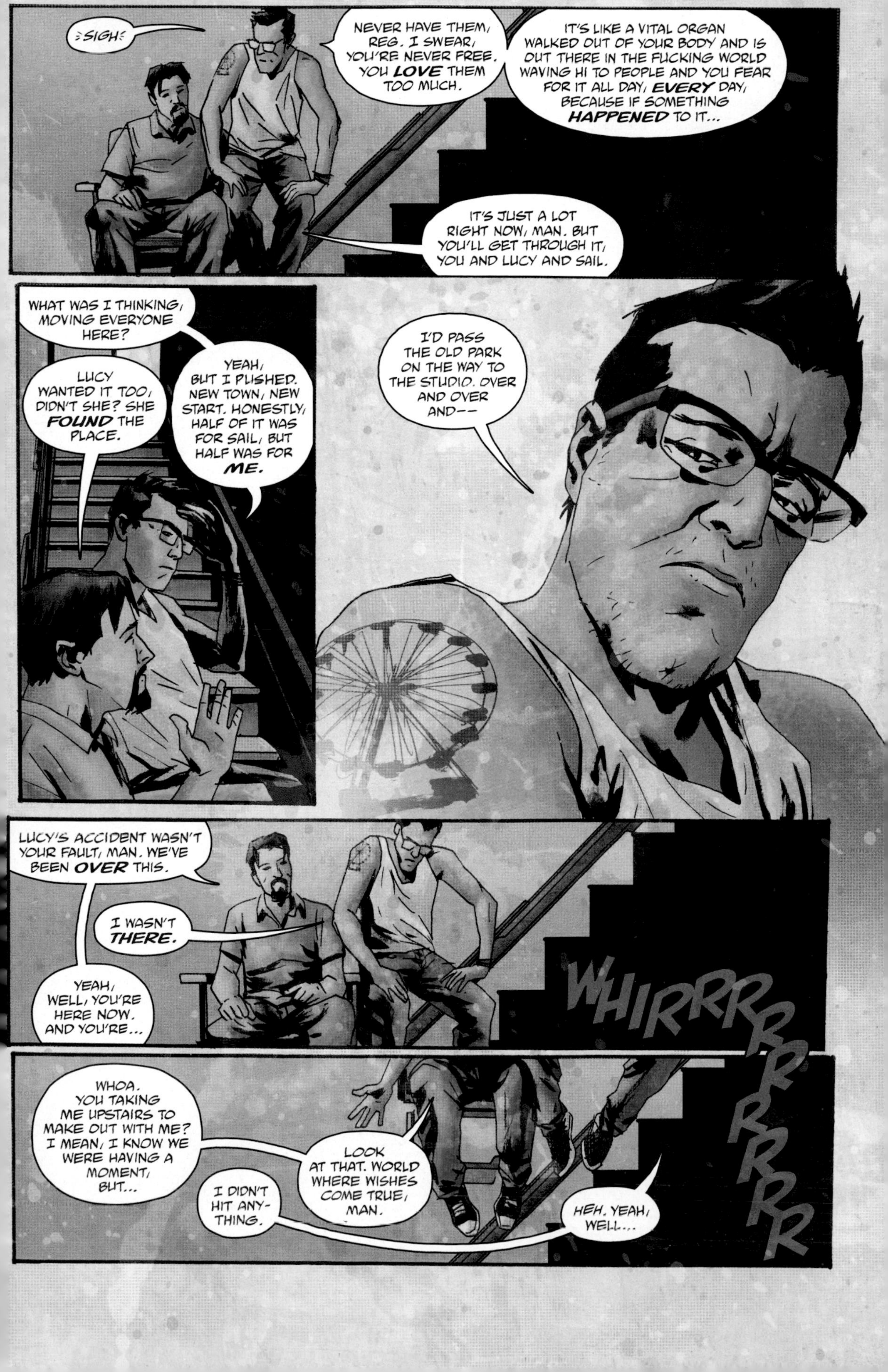
SIGH
NEVER HAVE THEM, REG. I SWEAR, YOU'RE NEVER FREE. YOU LOVE THEM TOO MUCH.
IT'S LIKE A VITAL ORGAN WALKED OUT OF YOUR BODY AND IS OUT THERE IN THE FUCKING WORLD WAVING HI TO PEOPLE AND YOU FEAR FOR IT ALL DAY, EVERY DAY, BECAUSE IF SOMETHING HAPPENED TO IT...
IT'S JUST A LOT RIGHT NOW, MAN. BUT YOU'LL GET THROUGH IT, YOU AND LUCY AND SAIL.
WHAT WAS I THINKING, MOVING EVERYONE HERE?
LUCY WANTED IT TOO, DIDN'T SHE? SHE FOUND THE PLACE.
YEAH, BUT I PUSHED. NEW TOWN, NEW START. HONESTLY, HALF OF IT WAS FOR SAIL, BUT HALF WAS FOR ME.
I'D PASS THE OLD PARK ON THE WAY TO THE STUDIO. OVER AND OVER AND--
LUCY'S ACCIDENT WASN'T YOUR FAULT, MAN. WE'VE BEEN OVER THIS.
I WASN'T THERE.
YEAH, WELL, YOU'RE HERE NOW. AND YOU'RE...
WHIRRRRRRRRRR
WHOA. YOU TAKING ME UPSTAIRS TO MAKE OUT WITH ME? I MEAN, I KNOW WE WERE HAVING A MOMENT, BUT...
LOOK AT THAT. WORLD WHERE WISHES COME TRUE, MAN.
I DIDN'T HIT ANY-THING.
HEH. YEAH, WELL...

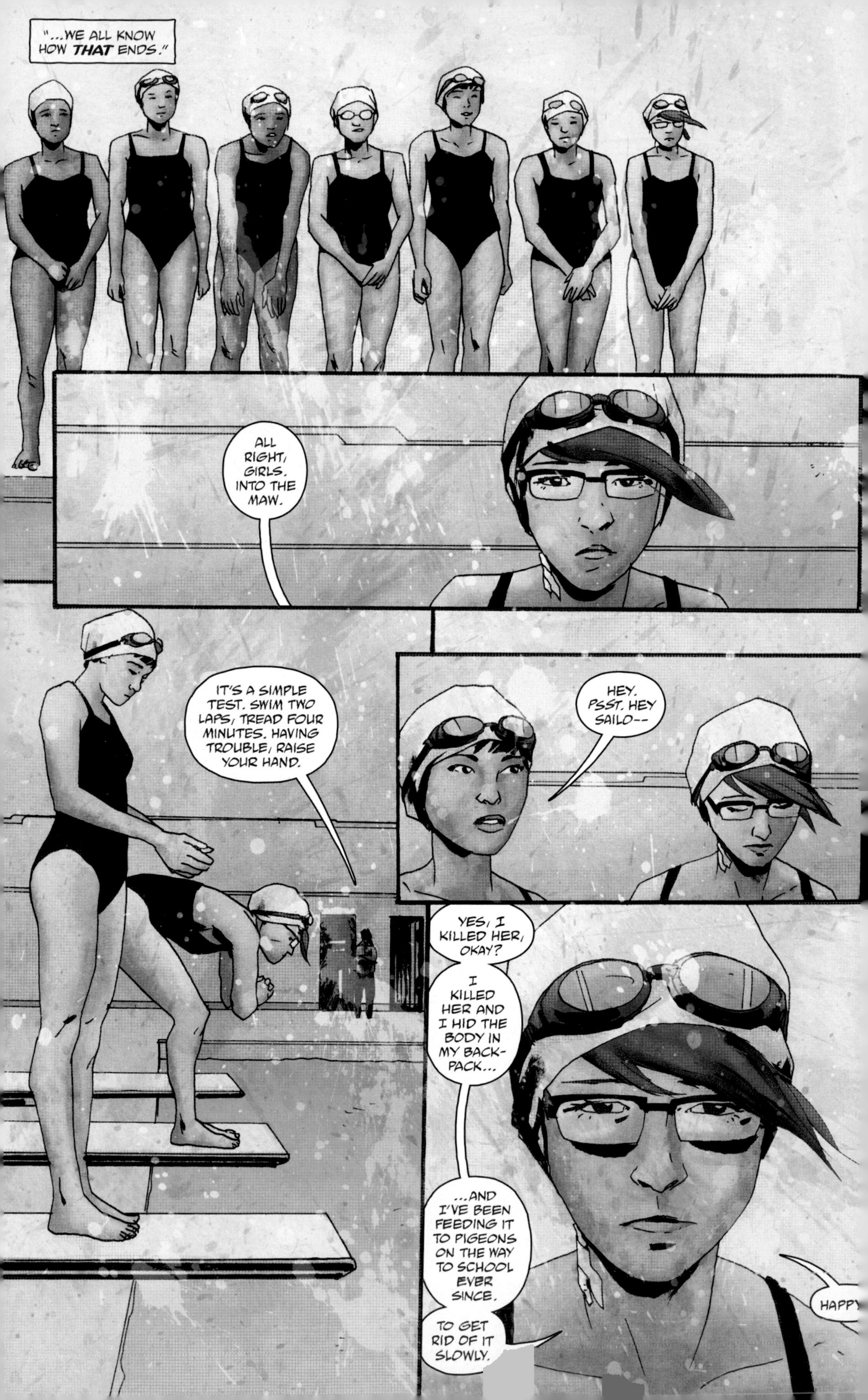
"...WE ALL KNOW HOW THAT ENDS."
ALL RIGHT, GIRLS. INTO THE MAW.
IT'S A SIMPLE TEST. SWIM TWO LAPS, TREAD FOUR MINUTES. HAVING TROUBLE, RAISE YOUR HAND.
HEY. PSST. HEY SAILO--
YES, I KILLED HER, OKAY?
I KILLED HER AND I HID THE BODY IN MY BACK-PACK...
...AND I'VE BEEN FEEDING IT TO PIGEONS ON THE WAY TO SCHOOL EVER SINCE.
TO GET RID OF IT SLOWLY.
HAPPY

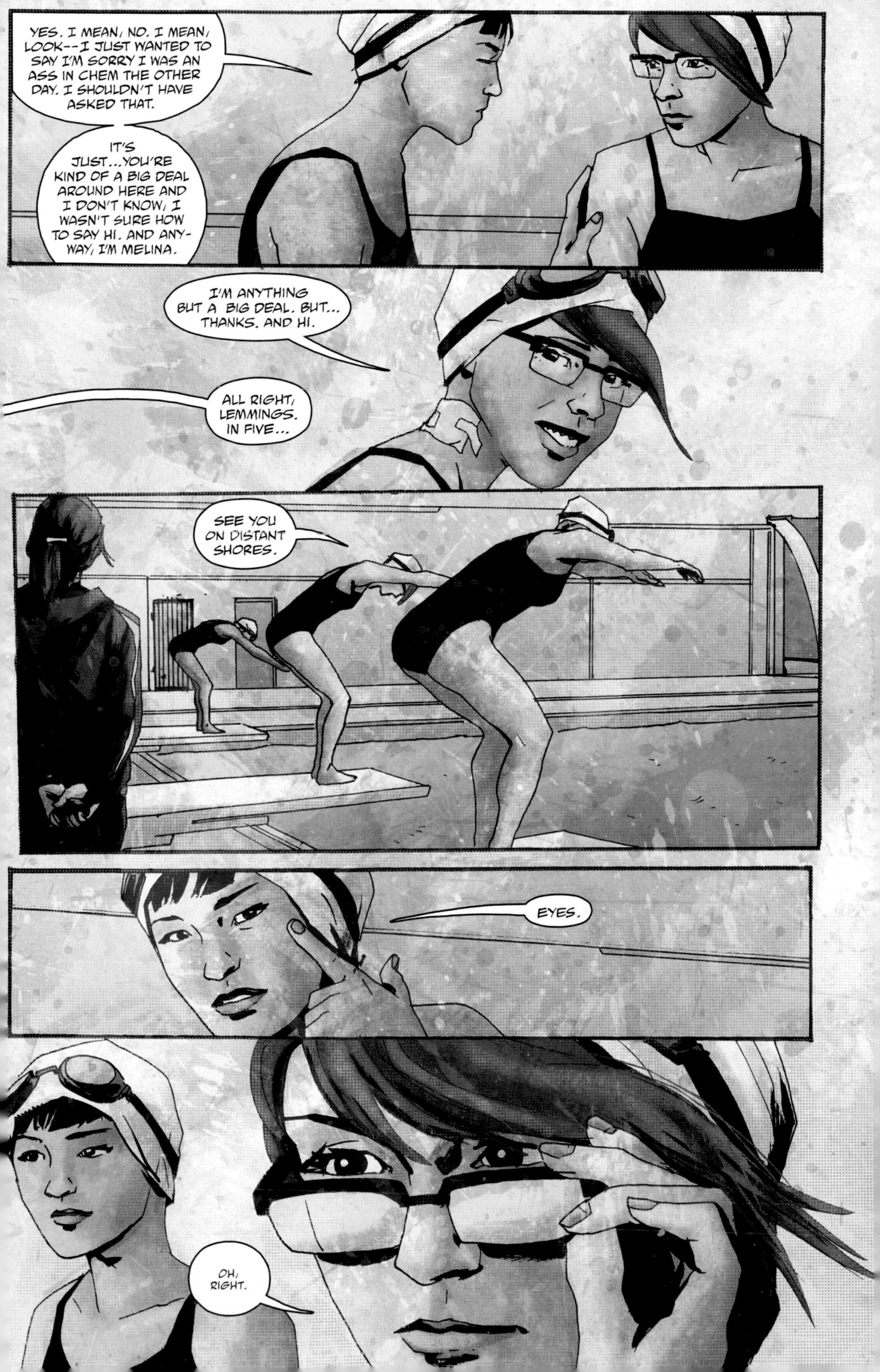
YES. I MEAN, NO. I MEAN, LOOK--I JUST WANTED TO SAY I'M SORRY I WAS AN ASS IN CHEM THE OTHER DAY. I SHOULDN'T HAVE ASKED THAT.
IT'S JUST...YOU'RE KIND OF A BIG DEAL AROUND HERE AND I DON'T KNOW, I WASN'T SURE HOW TO SAY HI. AND ANYWAY, I'M MELINA.
I'M ANYTHING BUT A BIG DEAL. BUT... THANKS. AND HI.
ALL RIGHT, LEMMINGS. IN FIVE...
SEE YOU ON DISTANT SHORES.
EYES.
OH, RIGHT.

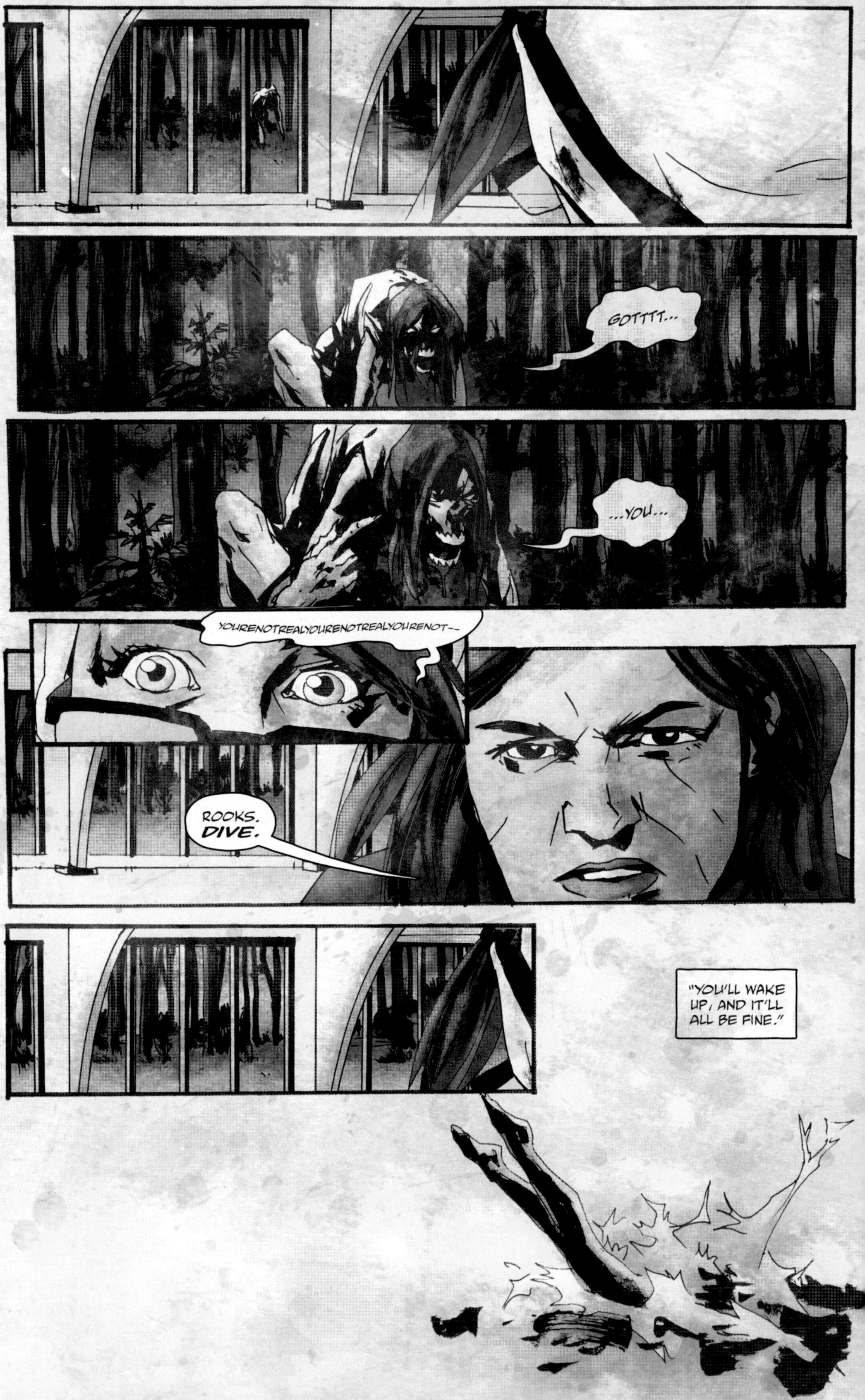
GOTTTT...
...YOU...
YOURENOTREALYOURENOTREALYOURENOT--
ROOKS. DIVE.
"YOU'LL WAKE UP, AND IT'LL ALL BE FINE."

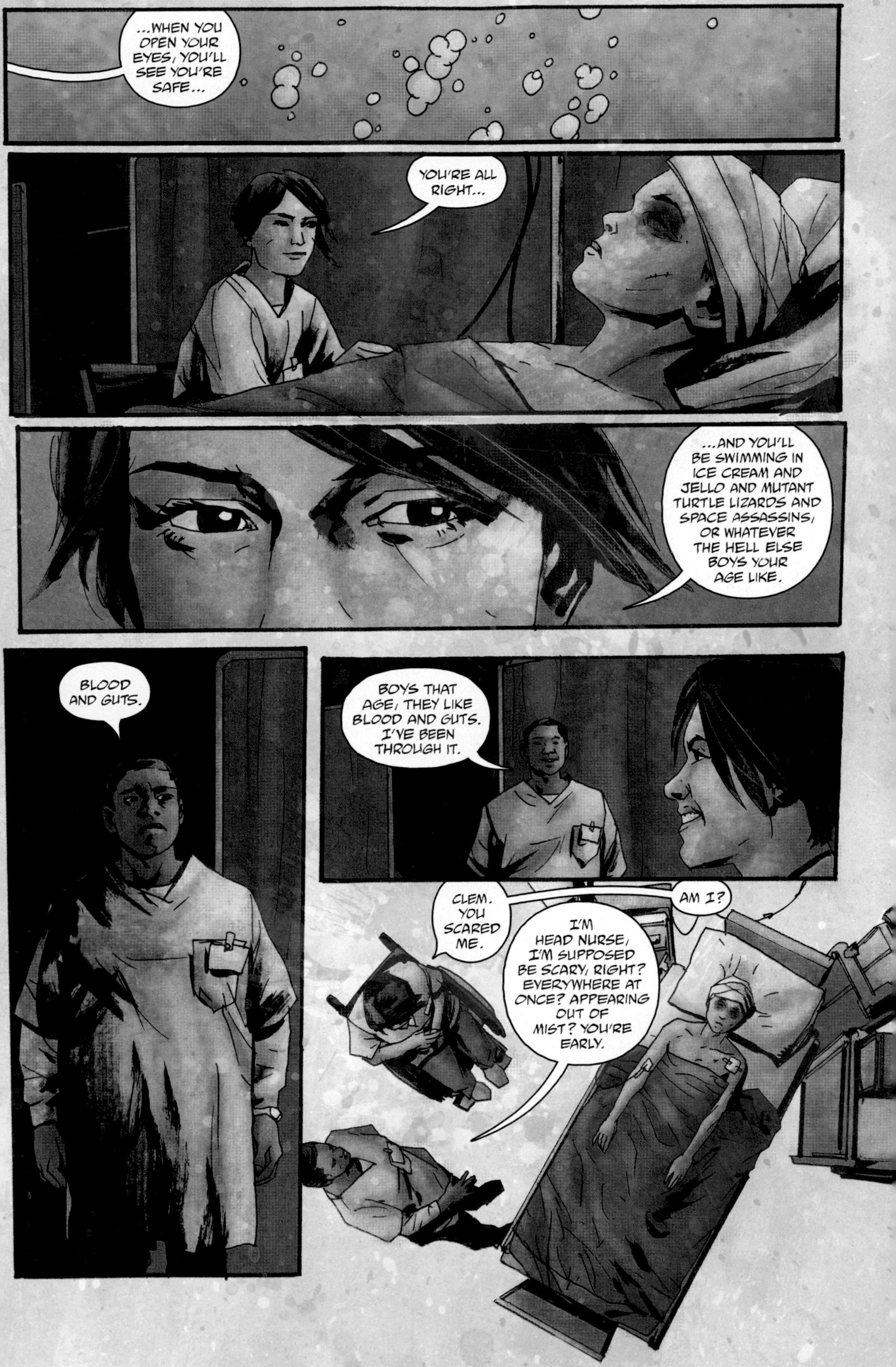
...WHEN YOU OPEN YOUR EYES, YOU'LL SEE YOU'RE SAFE...
YOU'RE ALL RIGHT...
...AND YOU'LL BE SWIMMING IN ICE CREAM AND JELLO AND MUTANT TURTLE LIZARDS AND SPACE ASSASSINS, OR WHATEVER THE HELL ELSE BOYS YOUR AGE LIKE.
BLOOD AND GUTS.
BOYS THAT AGE, THEY LIKE BLOOD AND GUTS. I'VE BEEN THROUGH IT.
CLEM. YOU SCARED ME.
AM I?
I'M HEAD NURSE, I'M SUPPOSED BE SCARY, RIGHT? EVERYWHERE AT ONCE? APPEARING OUT OF MIST? YOU'RE EARLY.

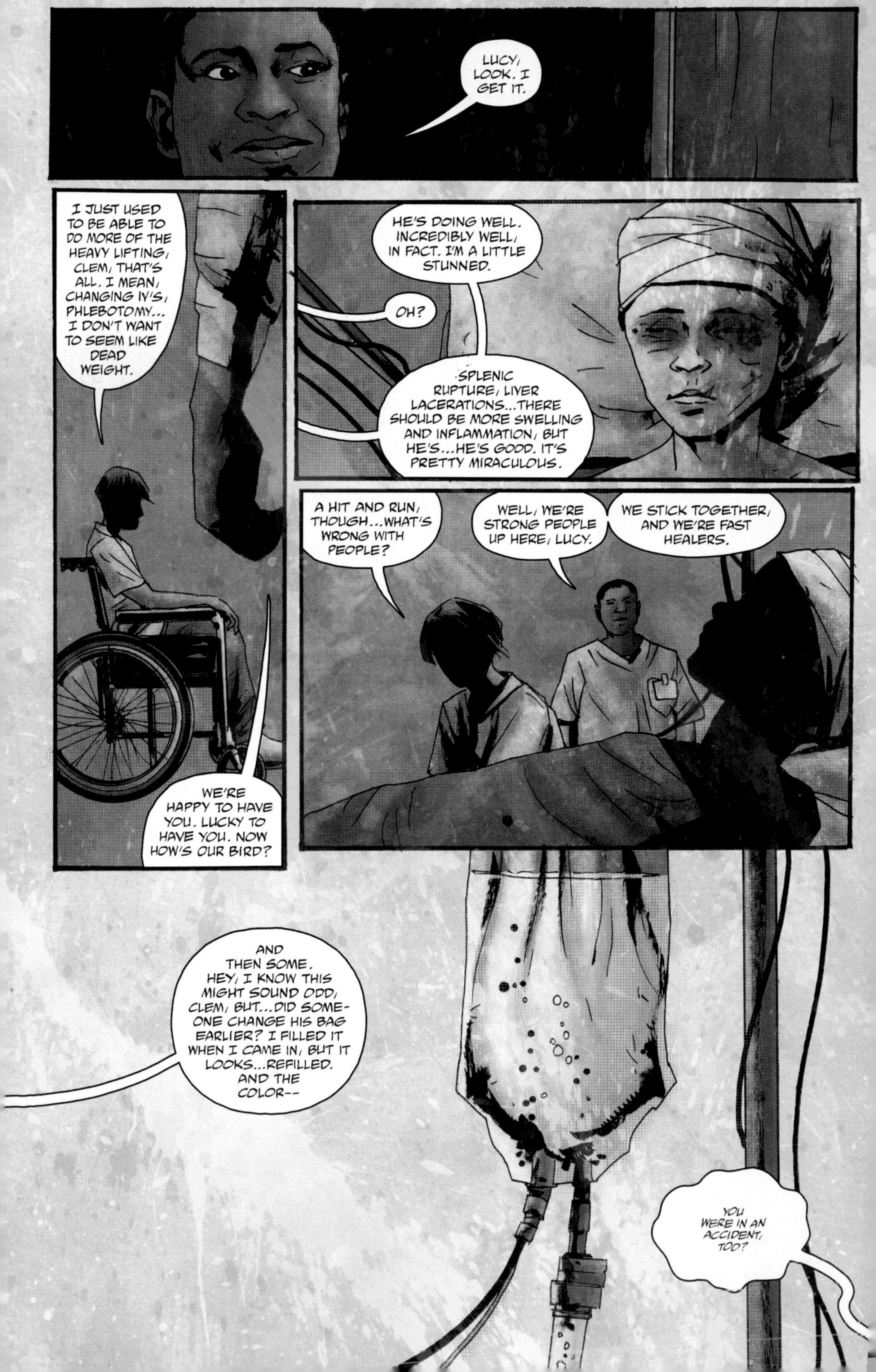
LUCY, LOOK. I GET IT.
I JUST USED TO BE ABLE TO DO MORE OF THE HEAVY LIFTING, CLEM, THAT'S ALL. I MEAN, CHANGING IV'S, PHLEBOTOMY... I DON'T WANT TO SEEM LIKE DEAD WEIGHT.
WE'RE HAPPY TO HAVE YOU. LUCKY TO HAVE YOU. NOW HOW'S OUR BIRD?
HE'S DOING WELL. INCREDIBLY WELL, IN FACT. I'M A LITTLE STUNNED.
OH?
SPLENIC RUPTURE, LIVER LACERATIONS...THERE SHOULD BE MORE SWELLING AND INFLAMMATION, BUT HE'S...HE'S GOOD. IT'S PRETTY MIRACULOUS.
A HIT AND RUN, THOUGH...WHAT'S WRONG WITH PEOPLE?
WELL, WE'RE STRONG PEOPLE UP HERE, LUCY.
WE STICK TOGETHER, AND WE'RE FAST HEALERS.
AND THEN SOME. HEY, I KNOW THIS MIGHT SOUND ODD, CLEM, BUT...DID SOME-ONE CHANGE HIS BAG EARLIER? I FILLED IT WHEN I CAME IN, BUT IT LOOKS...REFILLED. AND THE COLOR--
YOU WERE IN AN ACCIDENT, TOO?

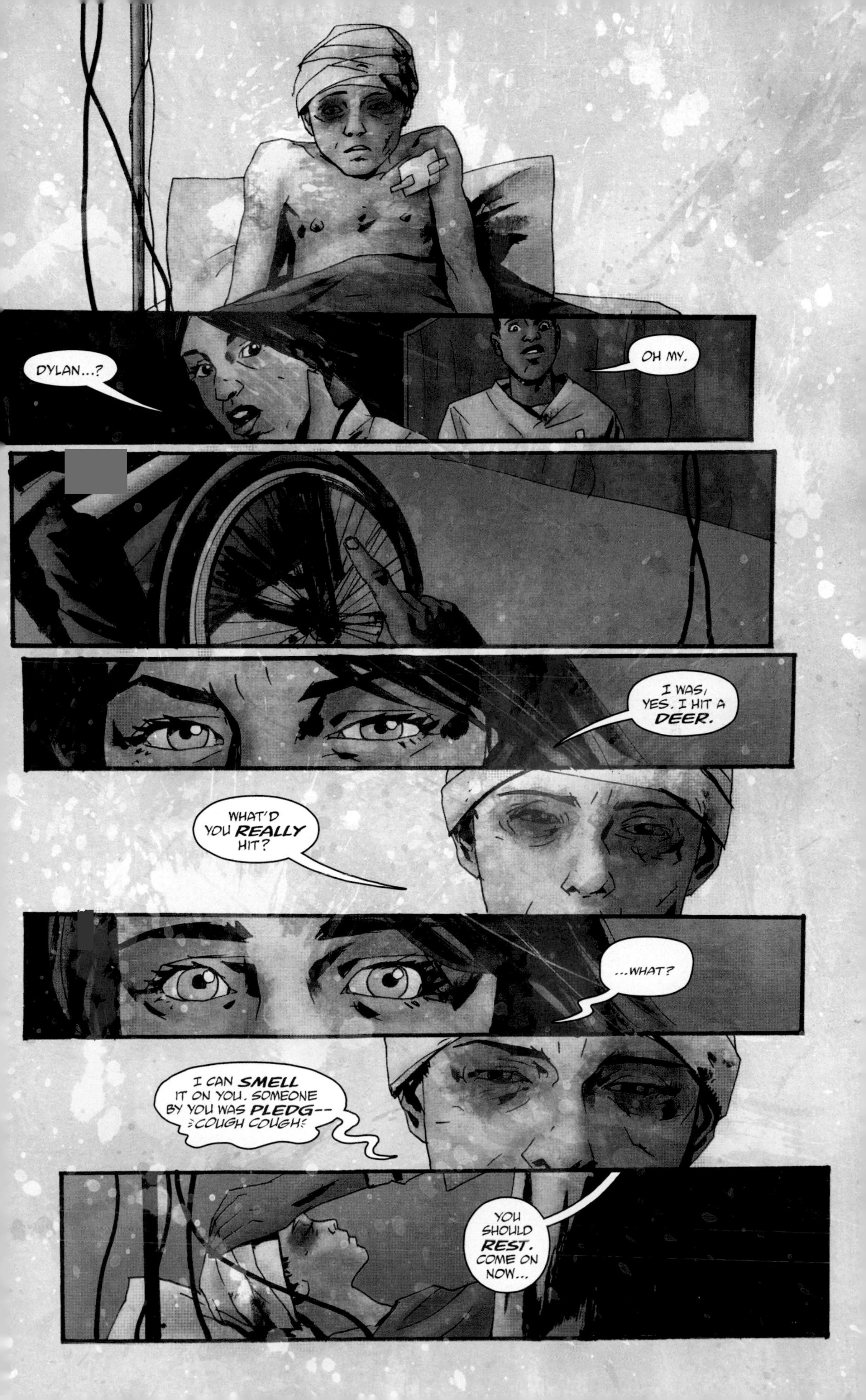
DYLAN...?
OH MY.
I WAS, YES. I HIT A **DEER.**
WHAT'D YOU **REALLY** HIT?
...WHAT?
I CAN **SMELL** IT ON YOU. SOMEONE BY YOU WAS **PLEDG--**
COUGH COUGH
YOU SHOULD **REST.** COME ON NOW...

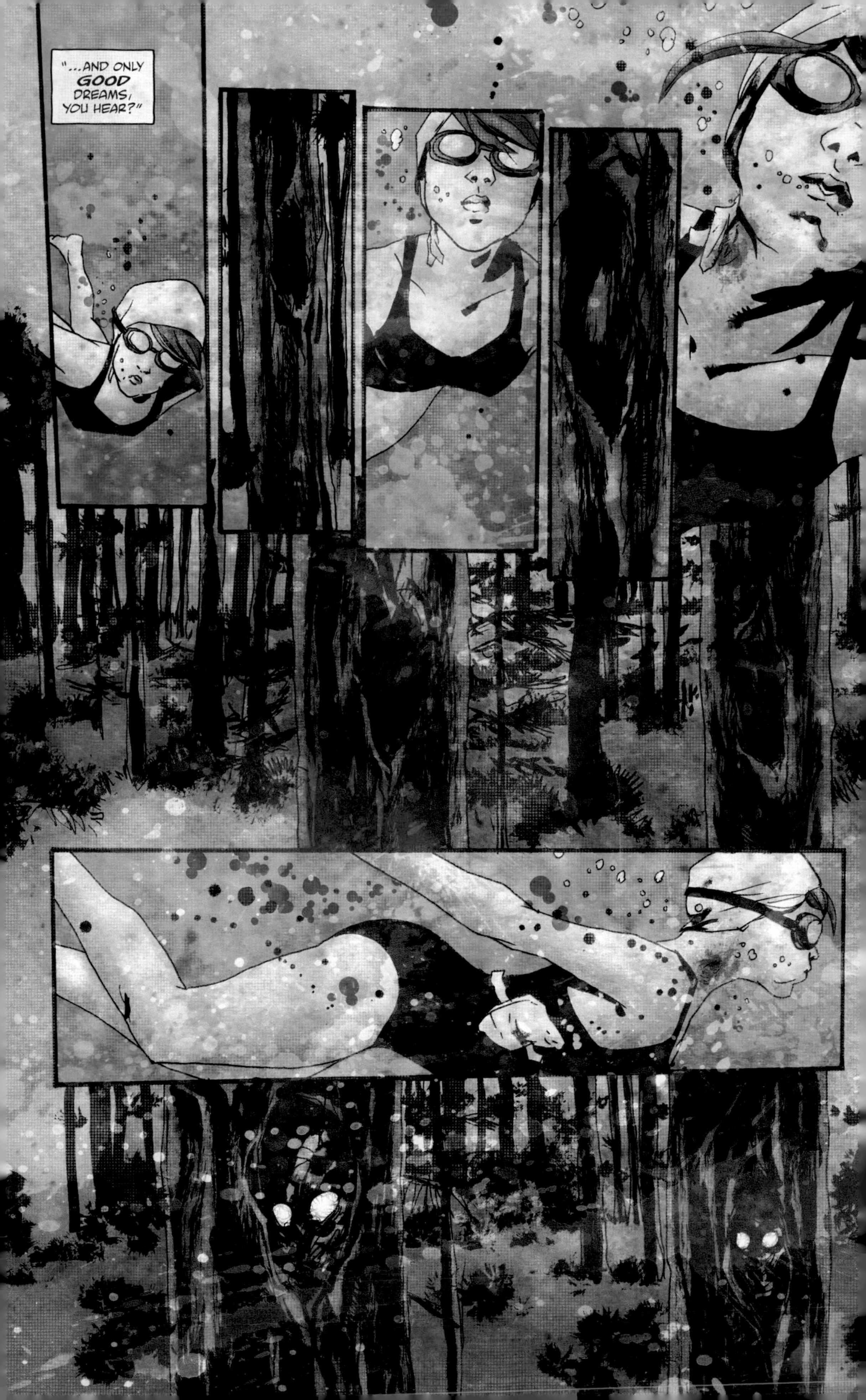
"...AND ONLY GOOD DREAMS, YOU HEAR?"

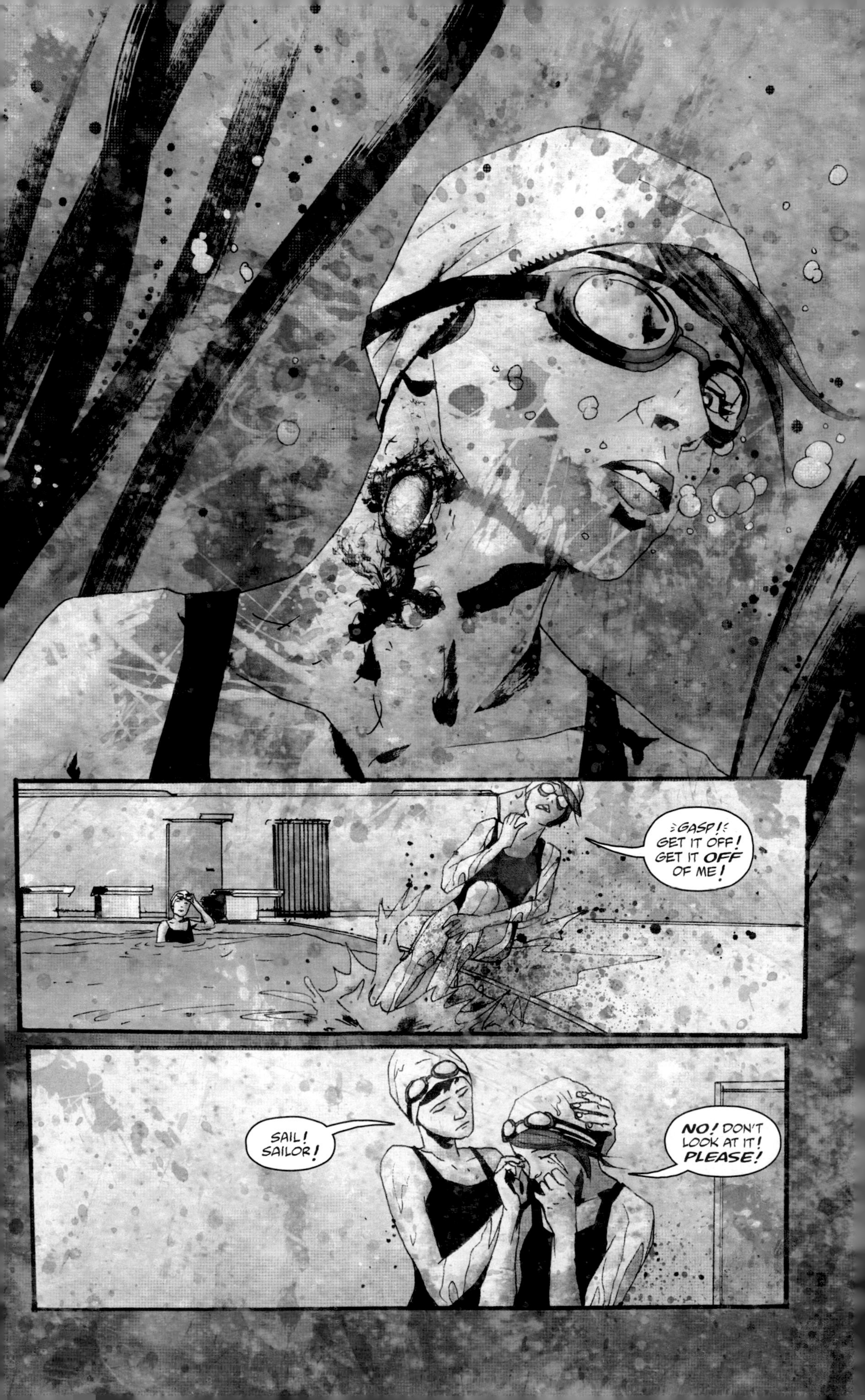
GASP! GET IT OFF! GET IT OFF OF ME!
SAIL! SAILOR!
NO! DON'T LOOK AT IT! PLEASE!

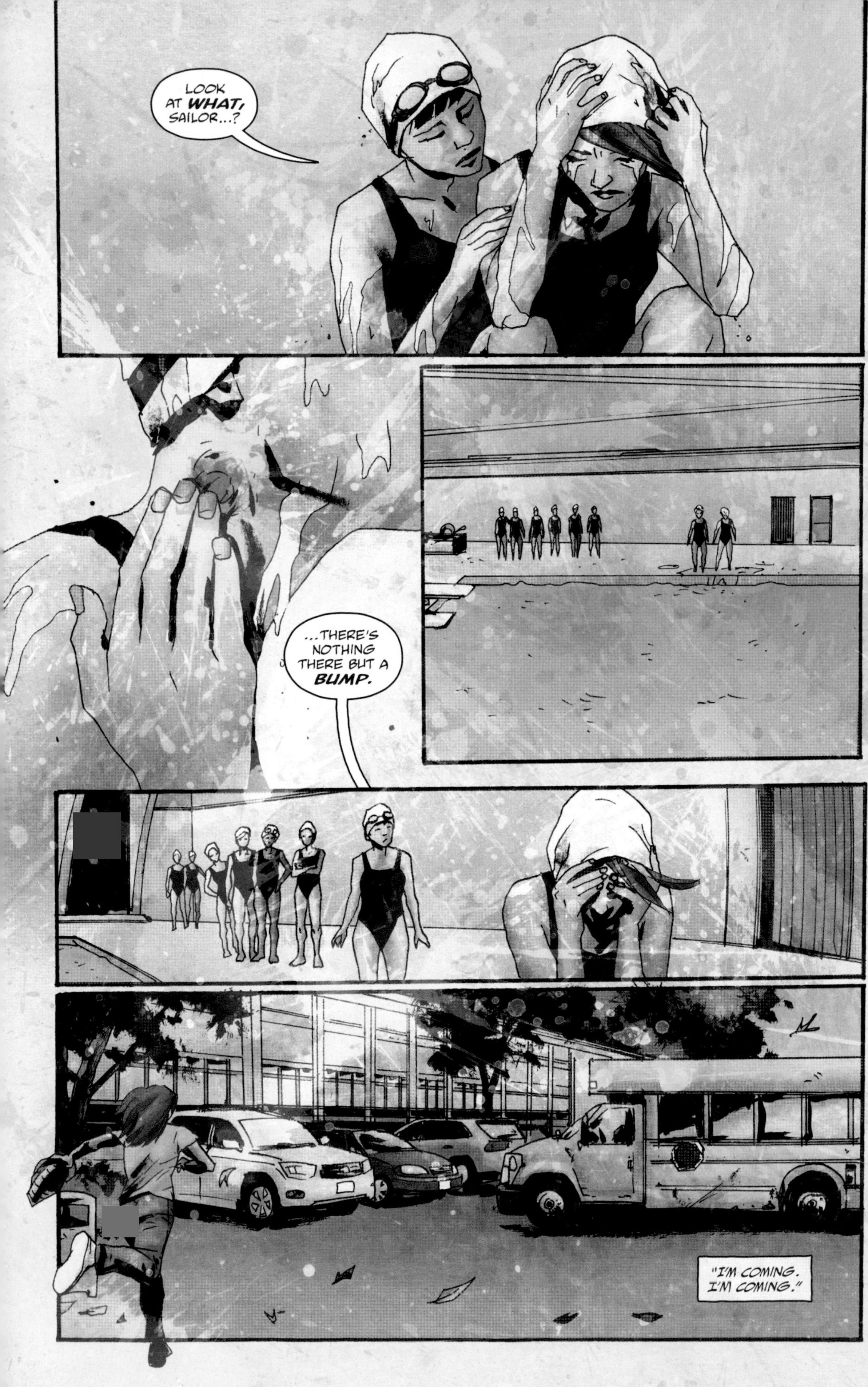
LOOK AT **WHAT,** SAILOR...?
...THERE'S NOTHING THERE BUT A **BUMP.**
"I'M COMING. I'M COMING."

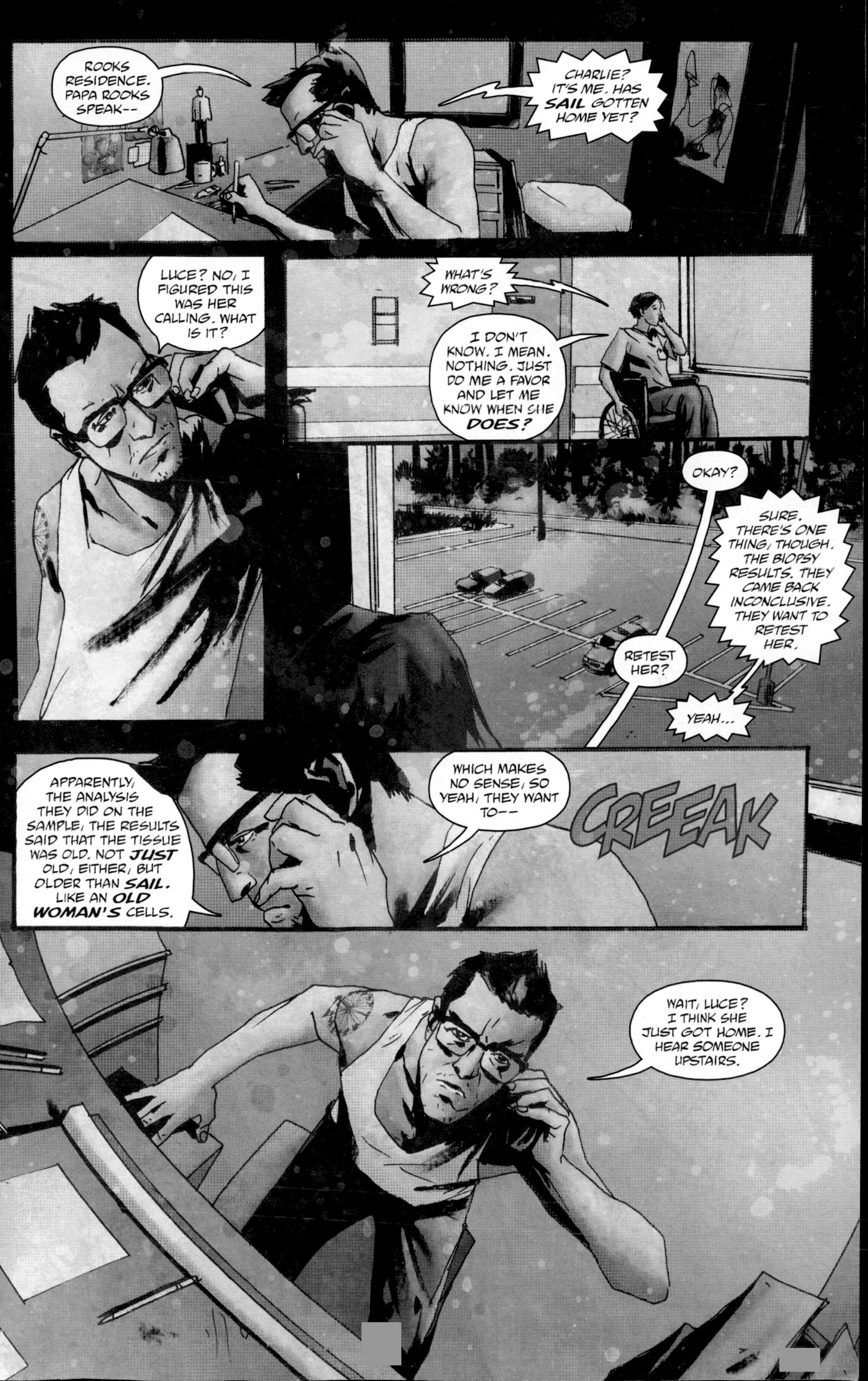
ROOKS RESIDENCE. PAPA ROOKS SPEAK--
CHARLIE? IT'S ME. HAS SAIL GOTTEN HOME YET?
LUCE? NO, I FIGURED THIS WAS HER CALLING. WHAT IS IT?
WHAT'S WRONG?
I DON'T KNOW. I MEAN. NOTHING. JUST DO ME A FAVOR AND LET ME KNOW WHEN SHE DOES?
OKAY?
SURE. THERE'S ONE THING, THOUGH. THE BIOPSY RESULTS. THEY CAME BACK INCONCLUSIVE. THEY WANT TO RETEST HER.
RETEST HER?
YEAH...
APPARENTLY, THE ANALYSIS THEY DID ON THE SAMPLE, THE RESULTS SAID THAT THE TISSUE WAS OLD. NOT JUST OLD, EITHER, BUT OLDER THAN SAIL. LIKE AN OLD WOMAN'S CELLS.
WHICH MAKES NO SENSE, SO YEAH, THEY WANT TO--
CREEAK
WAIT, LUCE? I THINK SHE JUST GOT HOME. I HEAR SOMEONE UPSTAIRS.

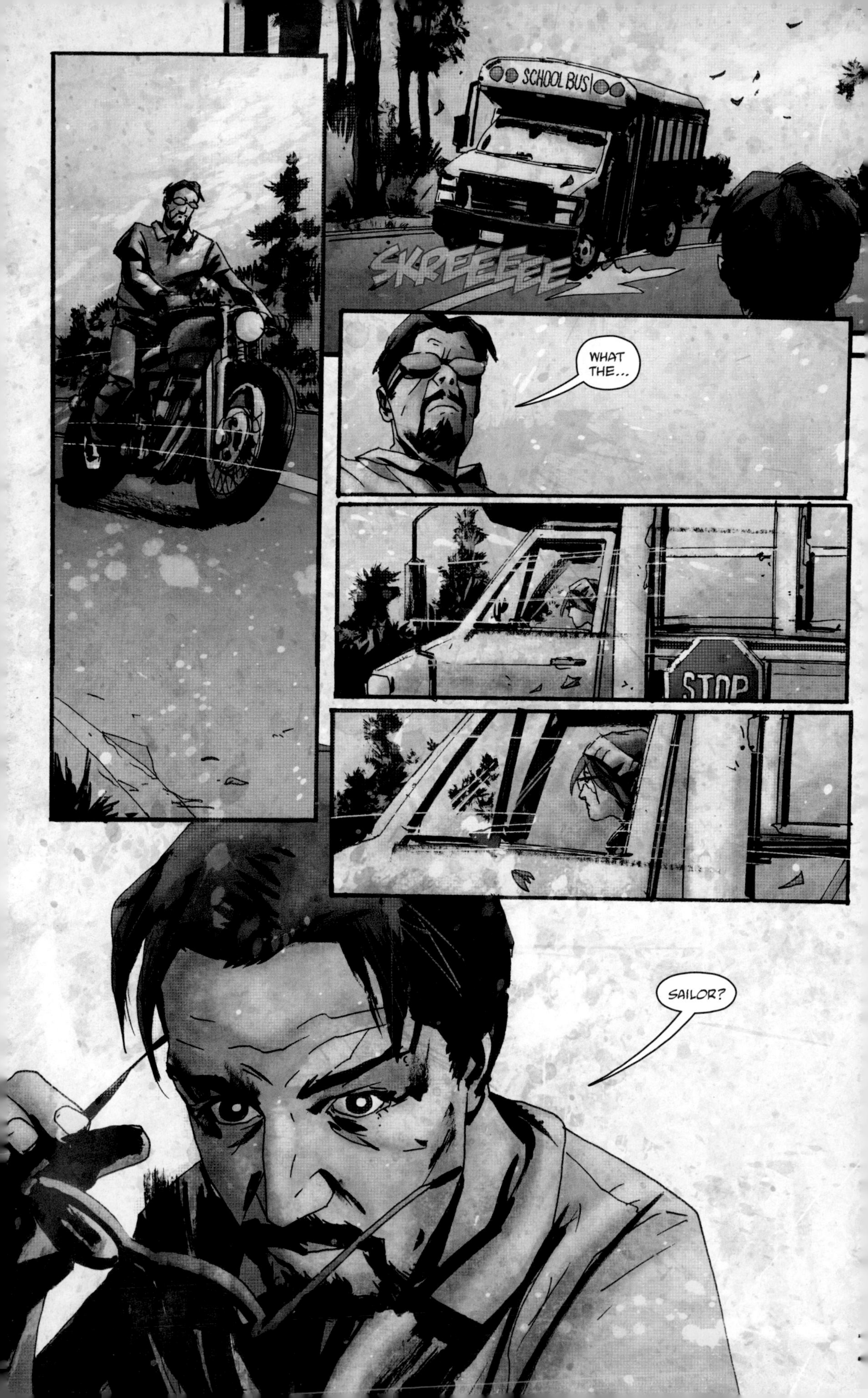
SCHOOL BUS
SKREEEEEE
WHAT THE...
STOP
SAILOR?

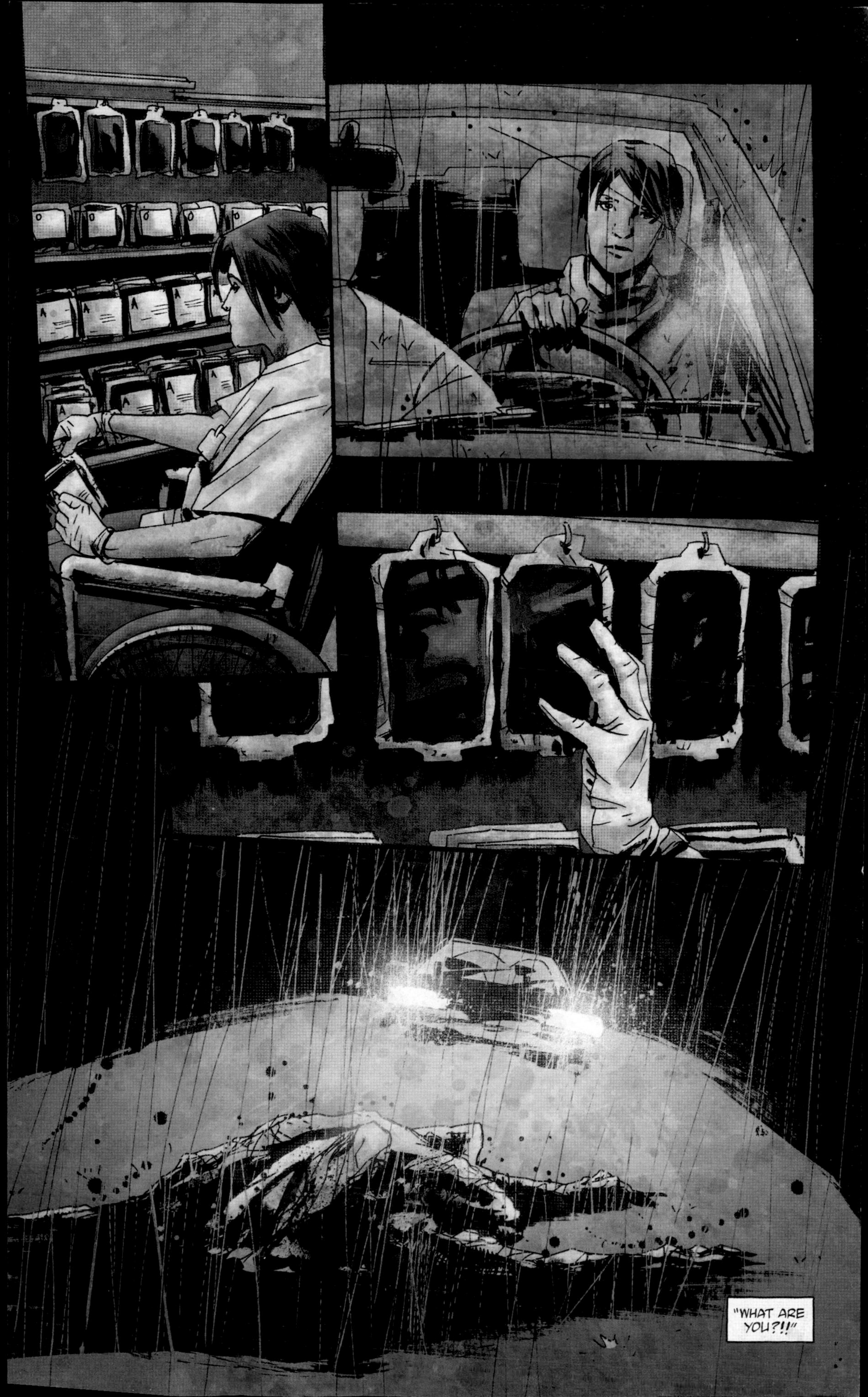
"WHAT ARE YOU?!!"

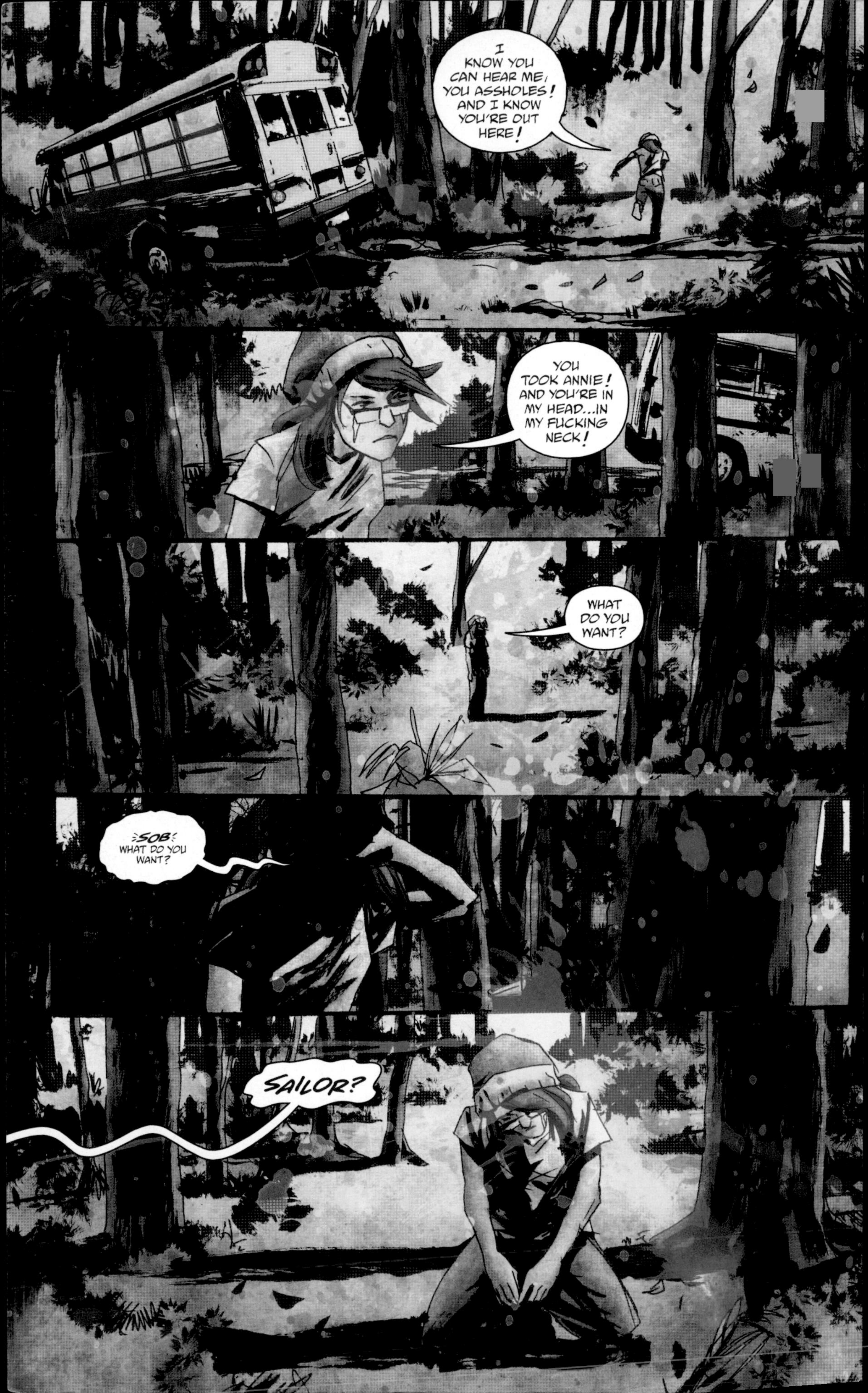
I KNOW YOU CAN HEAR ME, YOU ASSHOLES! AND I KNOW YOU'RE OUT HERE!
YOU TOOK ANNIE! AND YOU'RE IN MY HEAD...IN MY FUCKING NECK!
WHAT DO YOU WANT?
SOB
WHAT DO YOU WANT?
SAILOR?

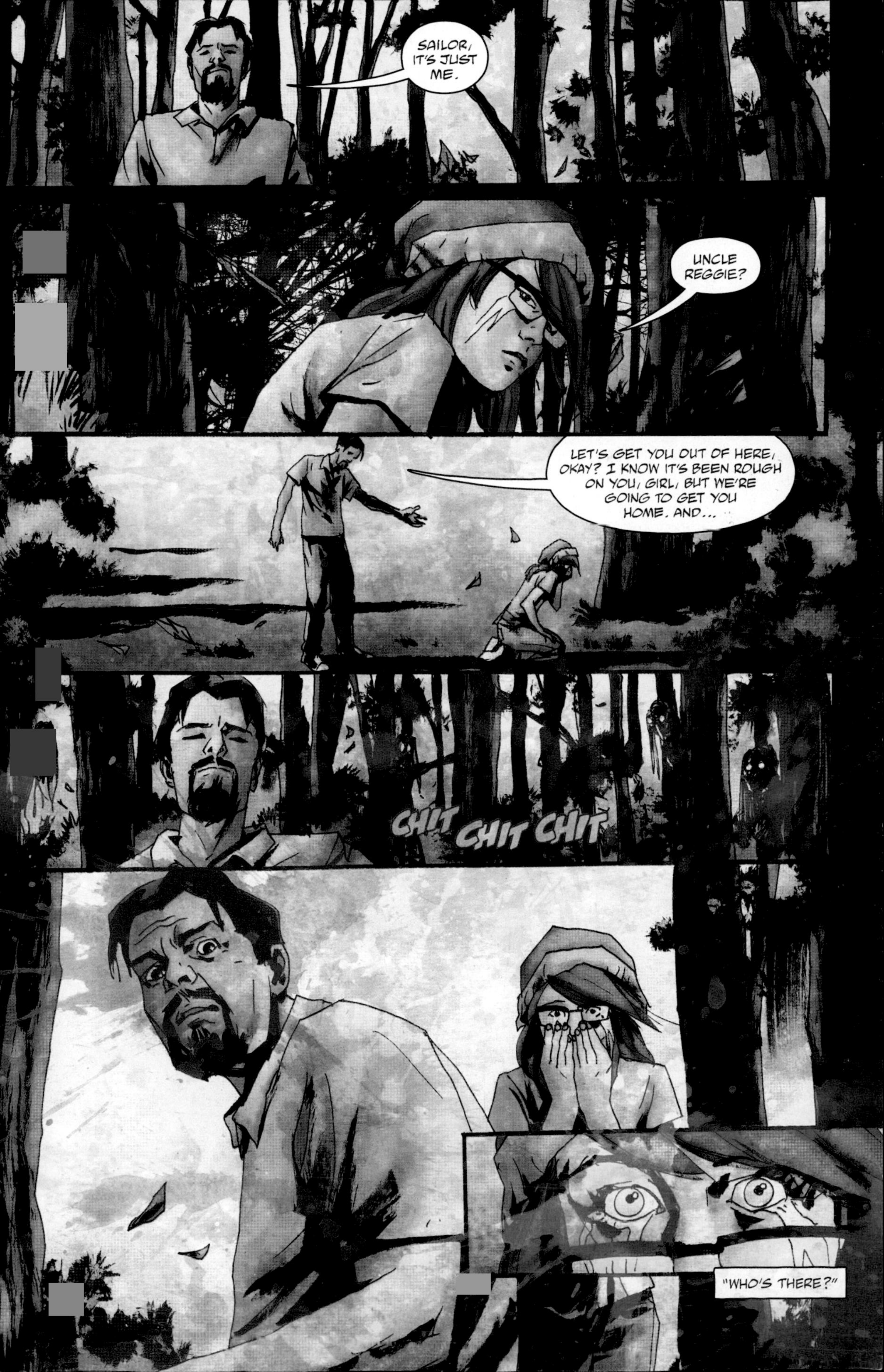
SAILOR, IT'S JUST ME.
UNCLE REGGIE?
LET'S GET YOU OUT OF HERE, OKAY? I KNOW IT'S BEEN ROUGH ON YOU, GIRL, BUT WE'RE GOING TO GET YOU HOME. AND...
CHIT CHIT CHIT
"WHO'S THERE?"

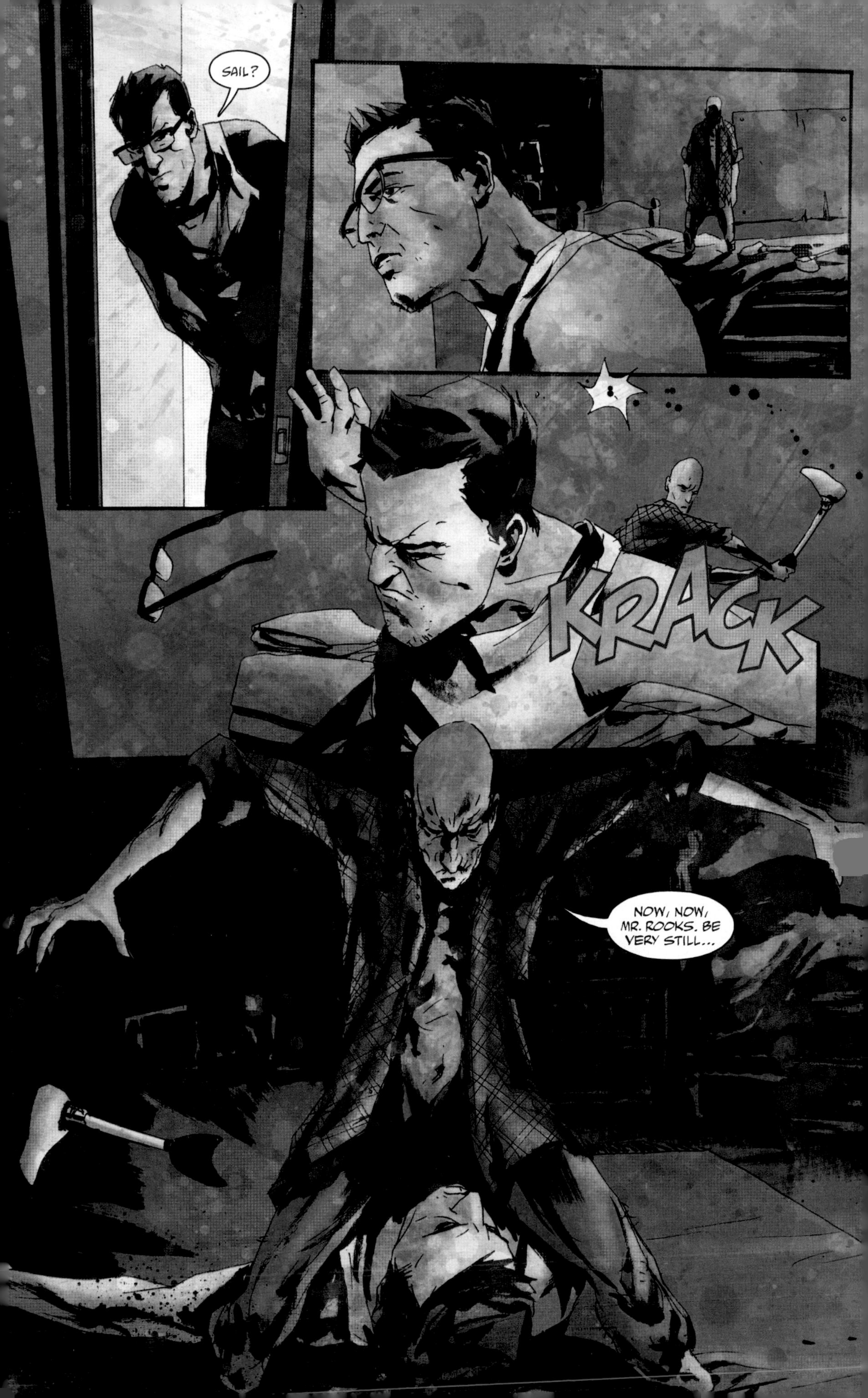
SAIL?
KRACK
NOW, NOW, MR. ROOKS. BE VERY STILL...

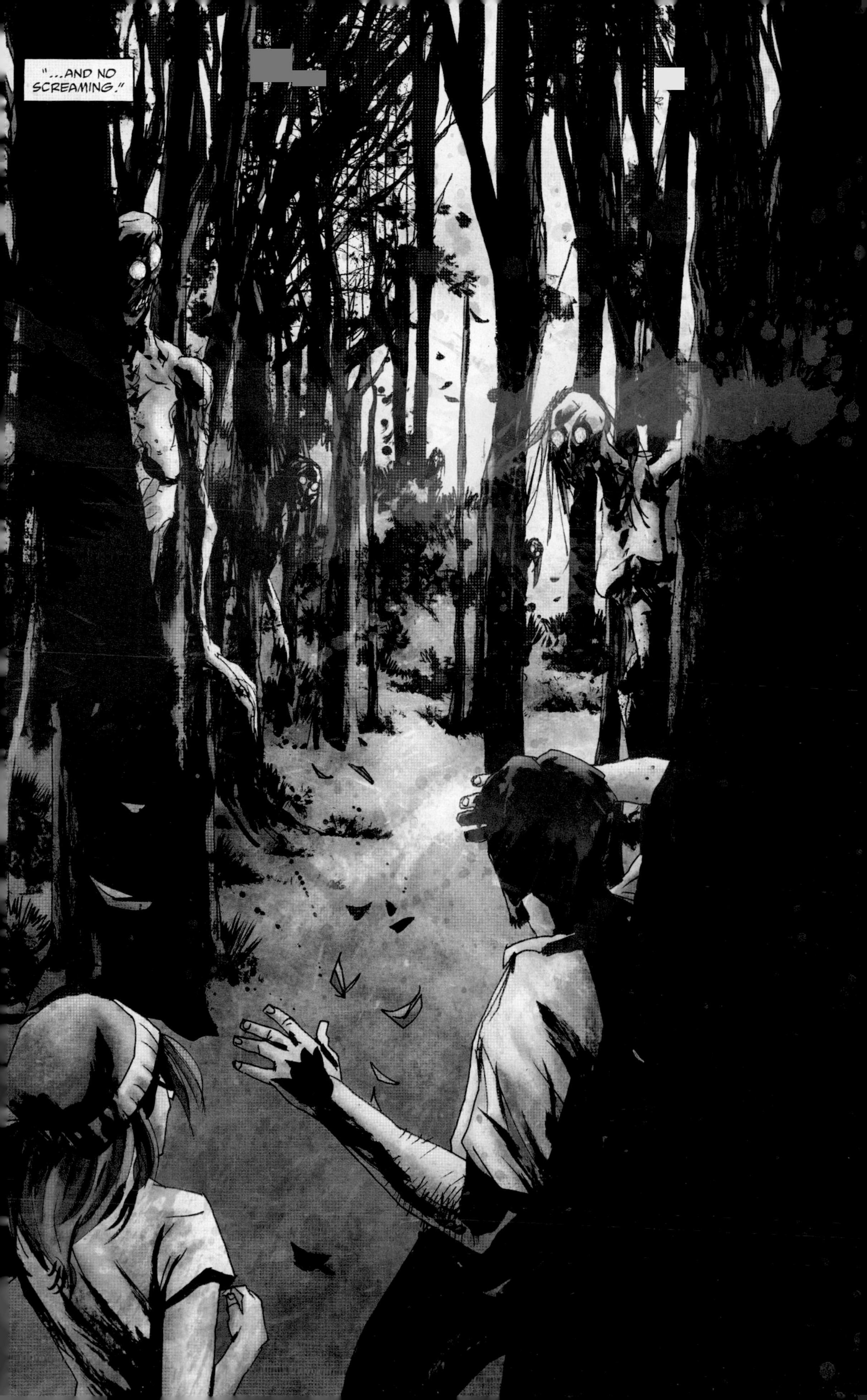
"...AND NO SCREAMING."

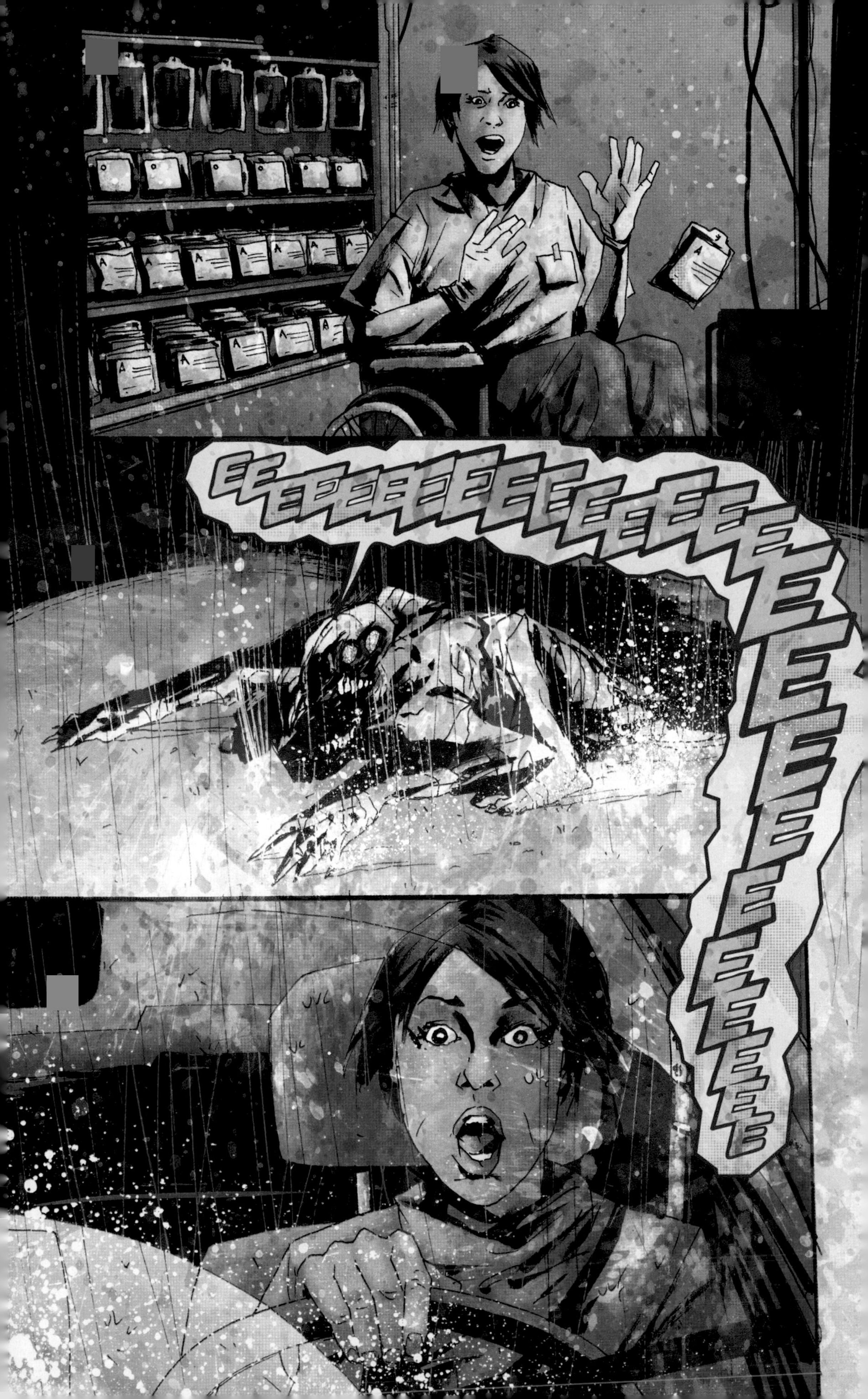
EEEEEEEEEEEEEEEEEEEEEEEEEEEEEE

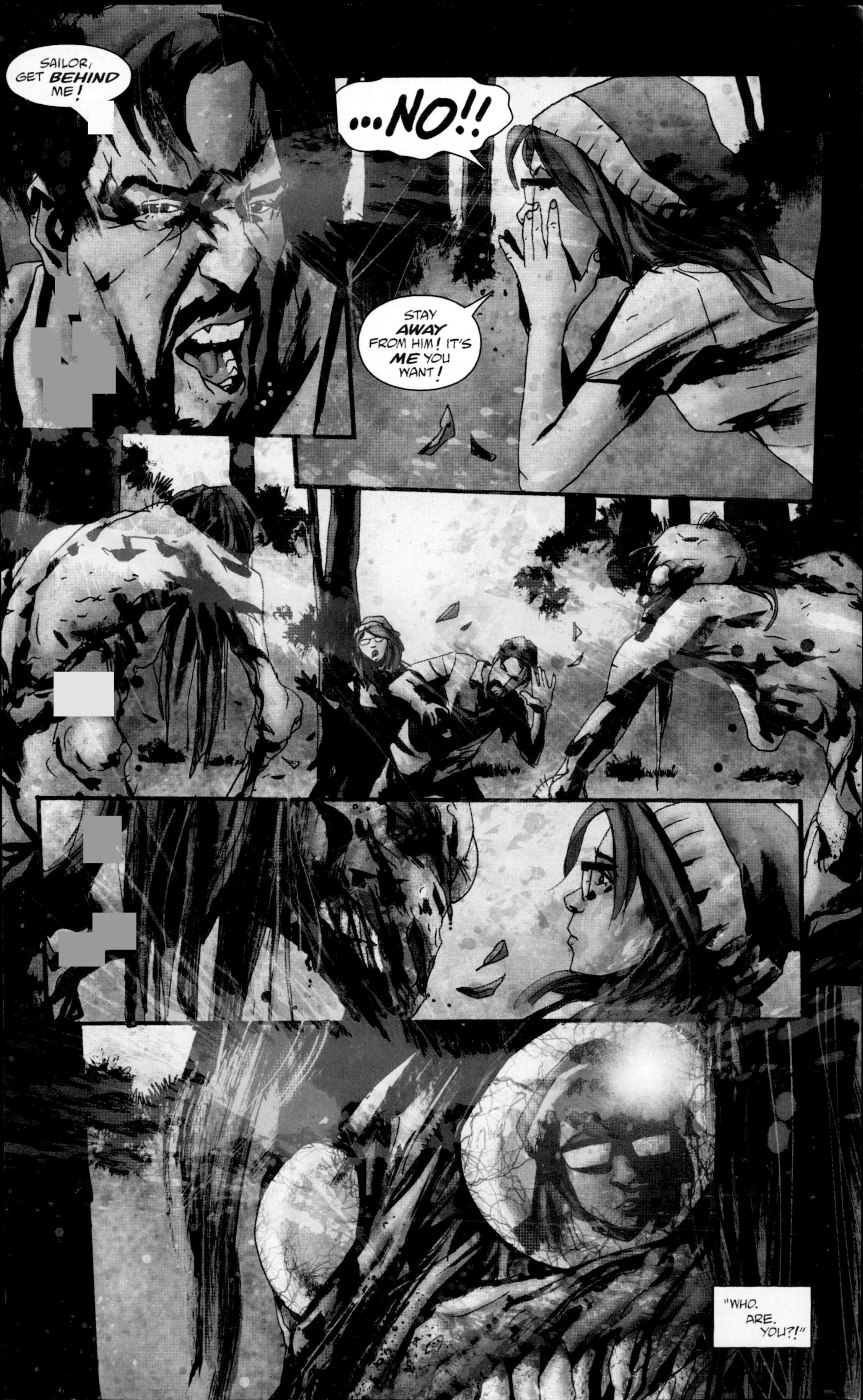
SAILOR, GET BEHIND ME!
...NO!!
STAY AWAY FROM HIM! IT'S ME YOU WANT!
"WHO. ARE. YOU?!"

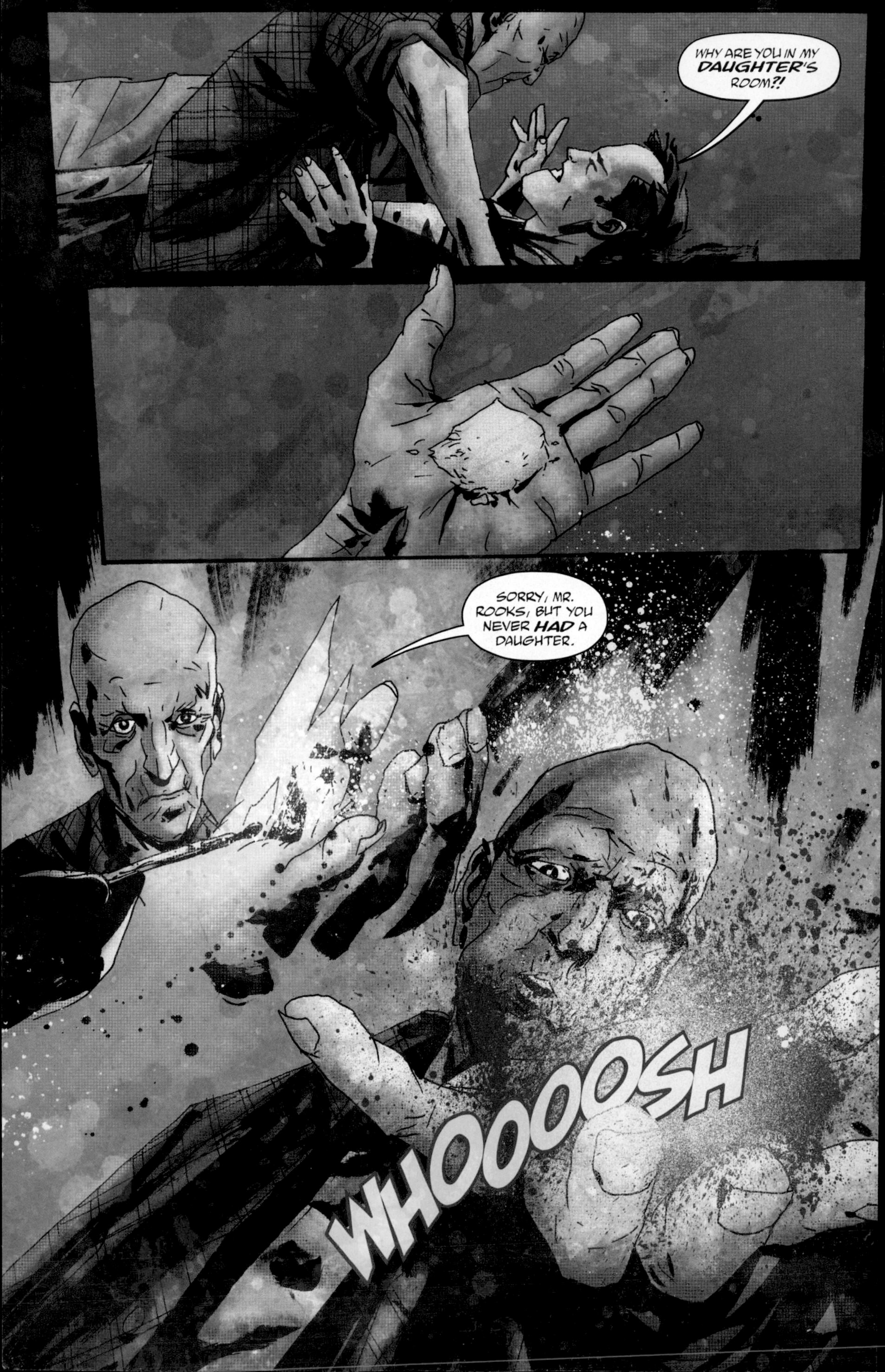
WHY ARE YOU IN MY DAUGHTER'S ROOM?!
SORRY, MR. ROOKS, BUT YOU NEVER HAD A DAUGHTER.
WHOOOOSH

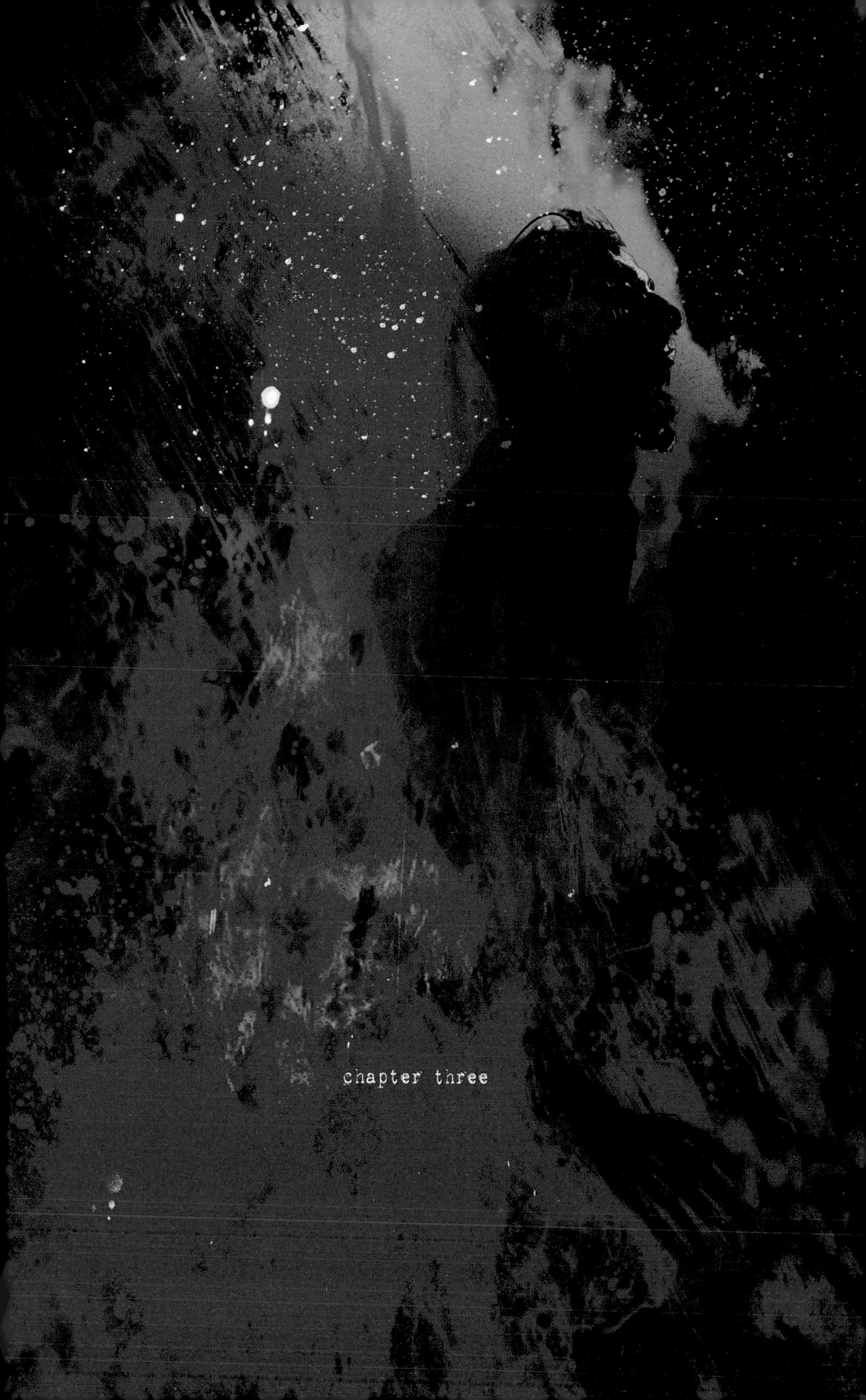

chapter three

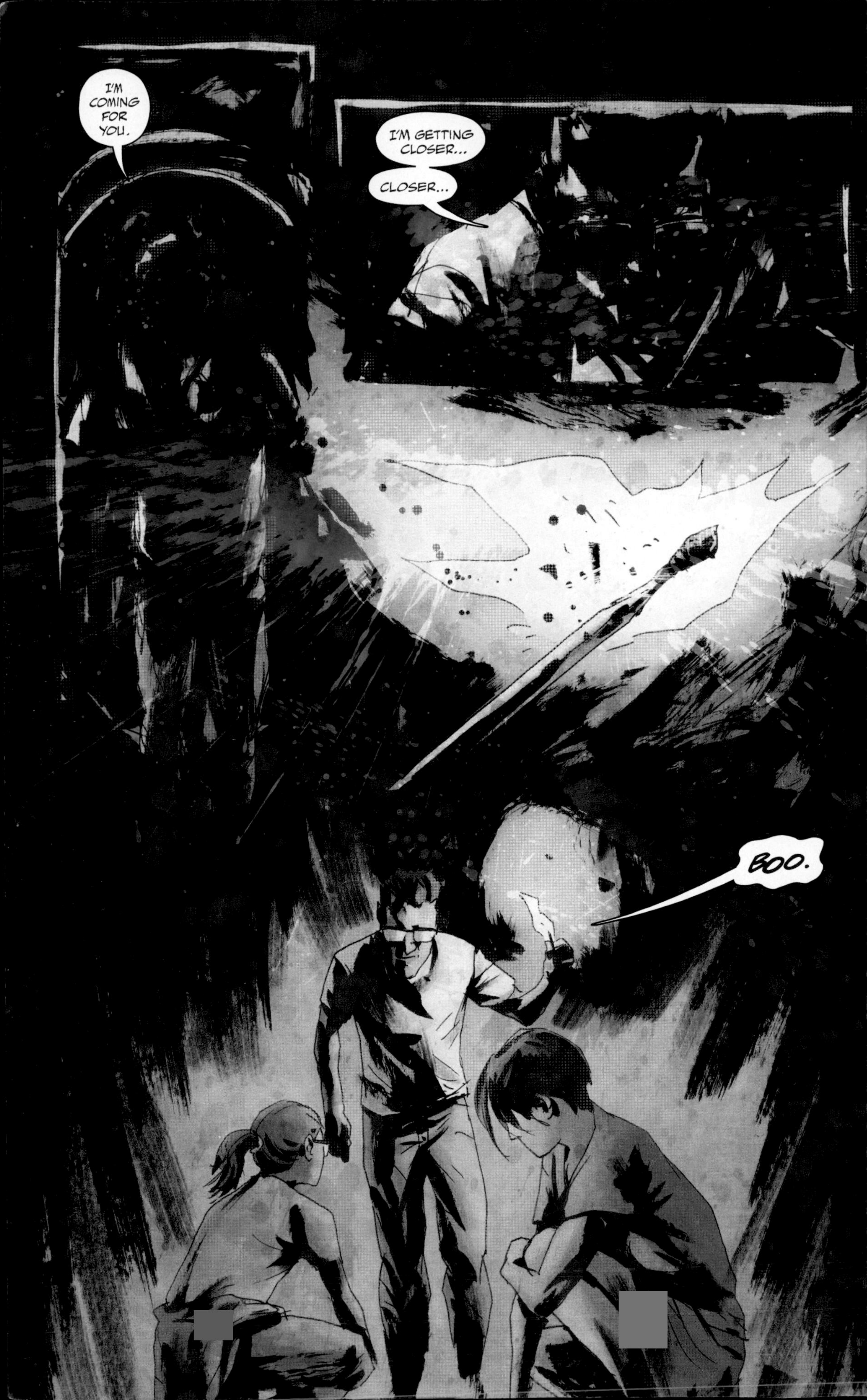
I'M COMING FOR YOU.
I'M GETTING CLOSER...
CLOSER...
BOO.

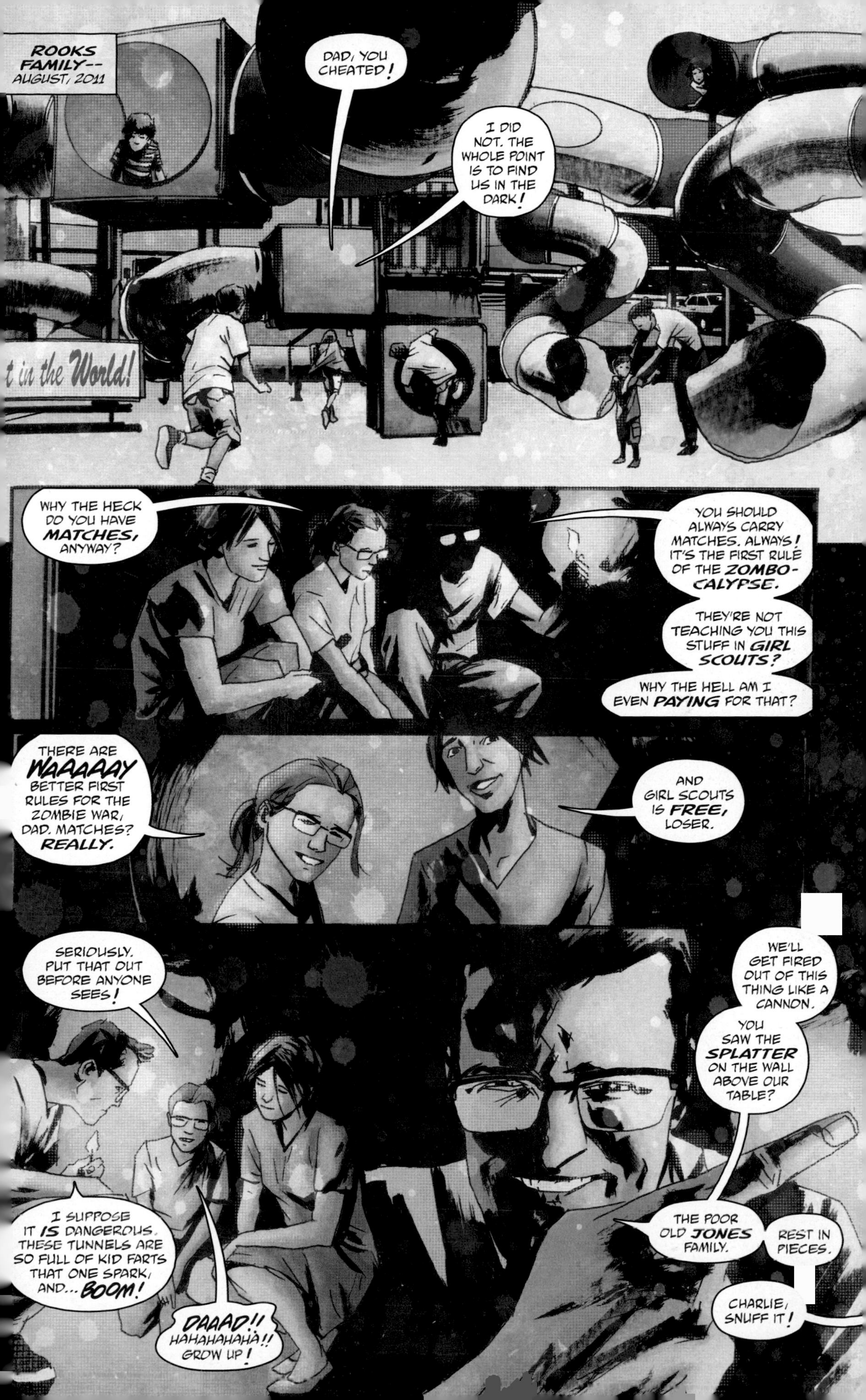
ROOKS FAMILY-- AUGUST, 2011
DAD, YOU CHEATED!
I DID NOT. THE WHOLE POINT IS TO FIND US IN THE DARK!
...t in the World!
WHY THE HECK DO YOU HAVE MATCHES, ANYWAY?
YOU SHOULD ALWAYS CARRY MATCHES. ALWAYS! IT'S THE FIRST RULE OF THE ZOMBO-CALYPSE.
THEY'RE NOT TEACHING YOU THIS STUFF IN GIRL SCOUTS?
WHY THE HELL AM I EVEN PAYING FOR THAT?
THERE ARE WAAAAAY BETTER FIRST RULES FOR THE ZOMBIE WAR, DAD. MATCHES? REALLY.
AND GIRL SCOUTS IS FREE, LOSER.
SERIOUSLY. PUT THAT OUT BEFORE ANYONE SEES!
WE'LL GET FIRED OUT OF THIS THING LIKE A CANNON.
YOU SAW THE SPLATTER ON THE WALL ABOVE OUR TABLE?
THE POOR OLD JONES FAMILY.
REST IN PIECES.
I SUPPOSE IT IS DANGEROUS. THESE TUNNELS ARE SO FULL OF KID FARTS THAT ONE SPARK, AND... BOOM!
DAAAD!! HAHAHAHAHA!! GROW UP!
CHARLIE, SNUFF IT!

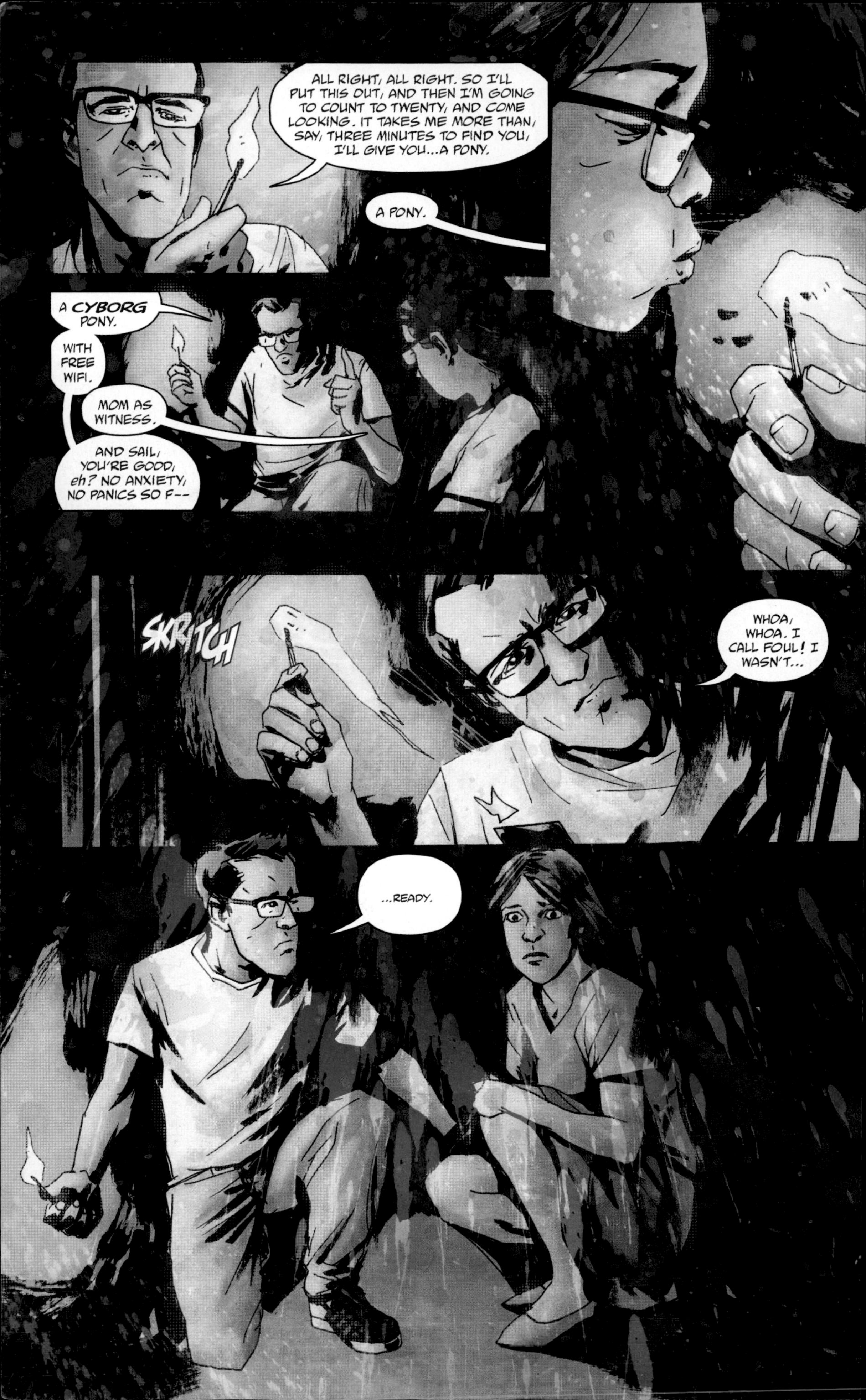
ALL RIGHT, ALL RIGHT. SO I'LL PUT THIS OUT, AND THEN I'M GOING TO COUNT TO TWENTY, AND COME LOOKING. IT TAKES ME MORE THAN, SAY, THREE MINUTES TO FIND YOU, I'LL GIVE YOU...A PONY.
A PONY.
A CYBORG PONY.
WITH FREE WIFI.
MOM AS WITNESS.
AND SAIL, YOU'RE GOOD, eh? NO ANXIETY, NO PANICS SO F--
SKRITCH
WHOA, WHOA. I CALL FOUL! I WASN'T...
...READY.

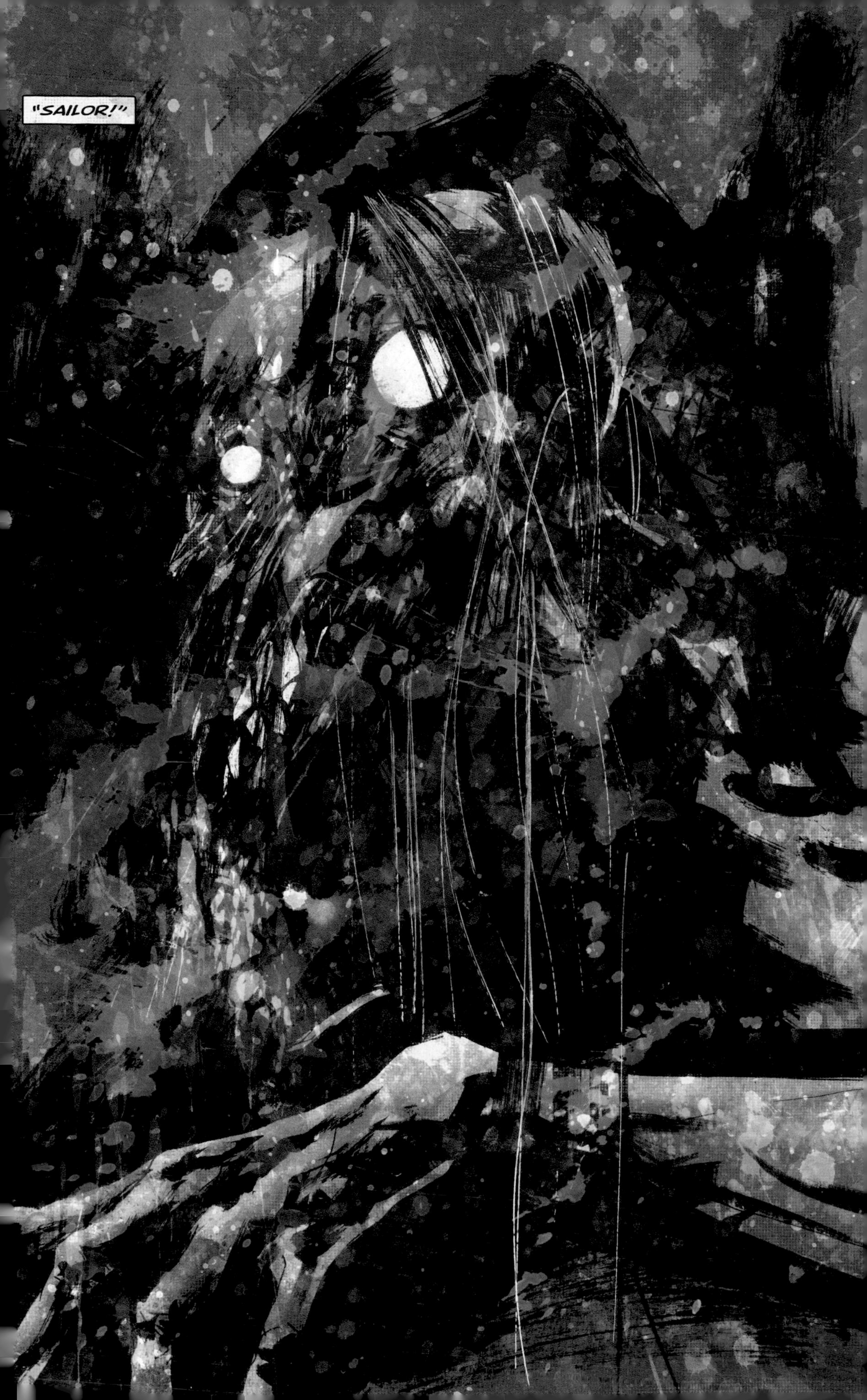
"SAILOR!"

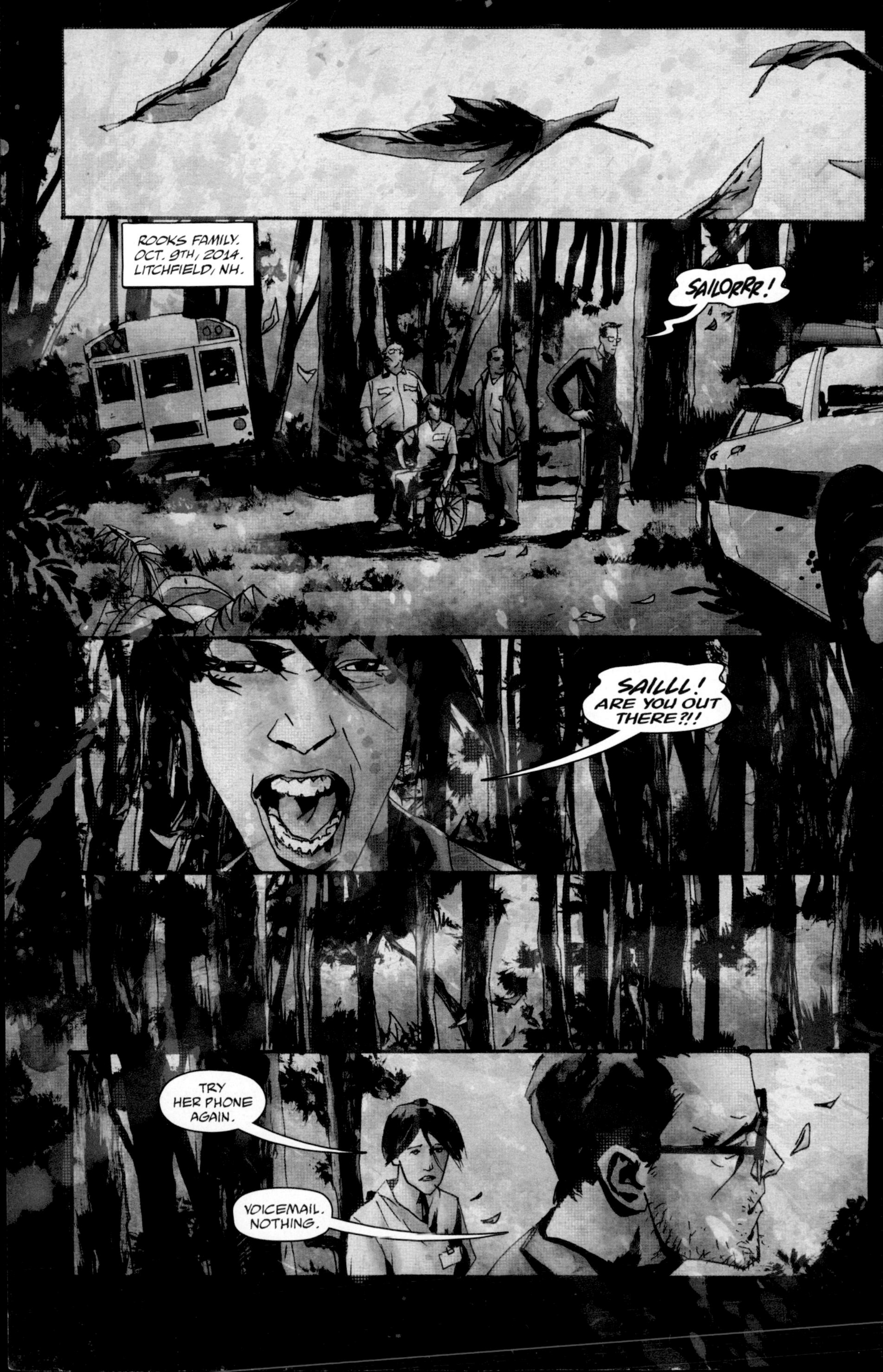
ROOKS FAMILY. OCT. 9TH, 2014. LITCHFIELD, NH.
SAILORRR!
SAILLL! ARE YOU OUT THERE?!!
TRY HER PHONE AGAIN.
VOICEMAIL. NOTHING.

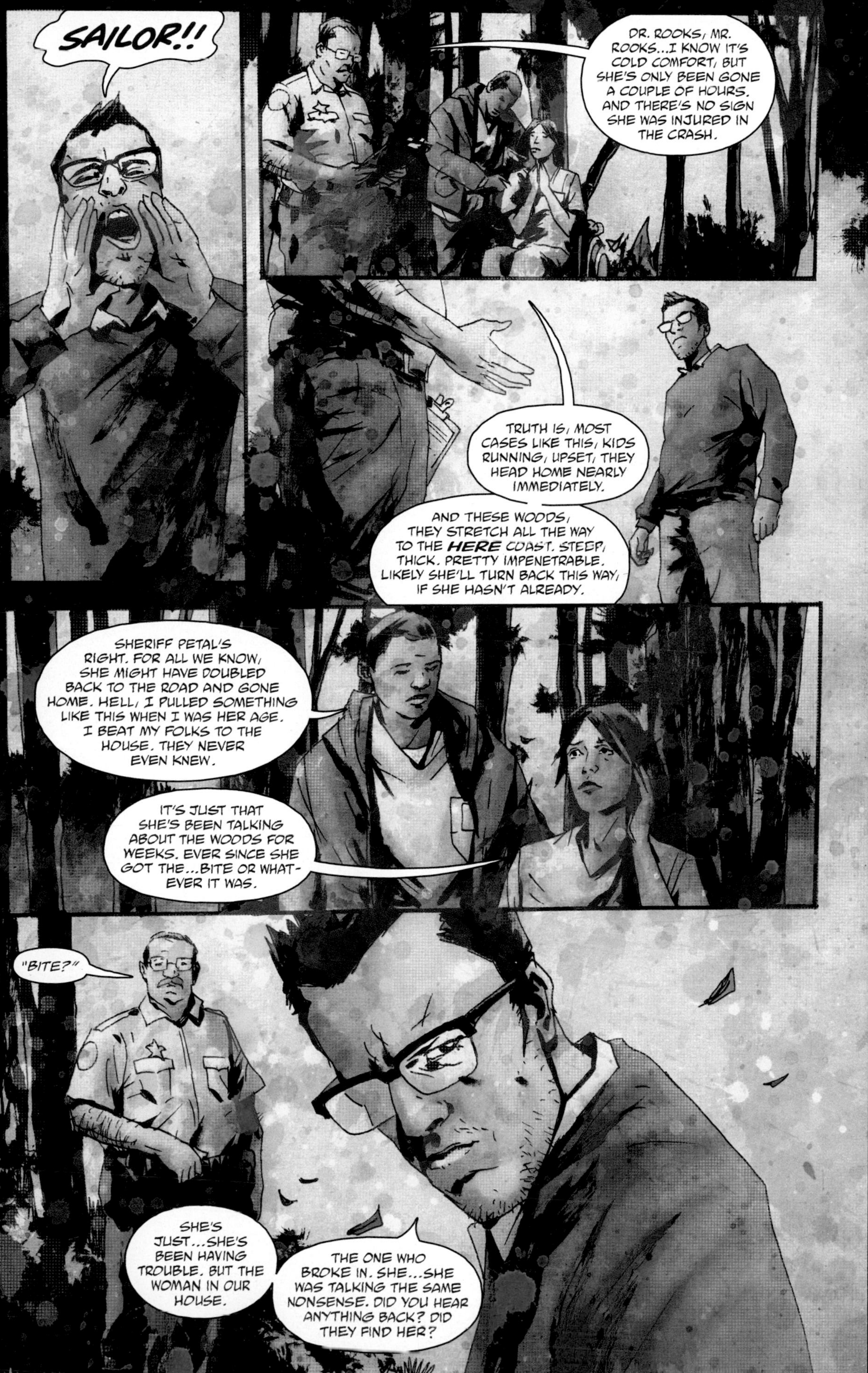
SAILOR!!
DR. ROOKS, MR. ROOKS...I KNOW IT'S COLD COMFORT, BUT SHE'S ONLY BEEN GONE A COUPLE OF HOURS. AND THERE'S NO SIGN SHE WAS INJURED IN THE CRASH.
TRUTH IS, MOST CASES LIKE THIS, KIDS RUNNING, UPSET, THEY HEAD HOME NEARLY IMMEDIATELY.
AND THESE WOODS, THEY STRETCH ALL THE WAY TO THE HERE COAST. STEEP, THICK. PRETTY IMPENETRABLE. LIKELY SHE'LL TURN BACK THIS WAY, IF SHE HASN'T ALREADY.
SHERIFF PETAL'S RIGHT. FOR ALL WE KNOW, SHE MIGHT HAVE DOUBLED BACK TO THE ROAD AND GONE HOME. HELL, I PULLED SOMETHING LIKE THIS WHEN I WAS HER AGE. I BEAT MY FOLKS TO THE HOUSE. THEY NEVER EVEN KNEW.
IT'S JUST THAT SHE'S BEEN TALKING ABOUT THE WOODS FOR WEEKS. EVER SINCE SHE GOT THE...BITE OR WHATEVER IT WAS.
"BITE?"
SHE'S JUST...SHE'S BEEN HAVING TROUBLE. BUT THE WOMAN IN OUR HOUSE.
THE ONE WHO BROKE IN. SHE...SHE WAS TALKING THE SAME NONSENSE. DID YOU HEAR ANYTHING BACK? DID THEY FIND HER?

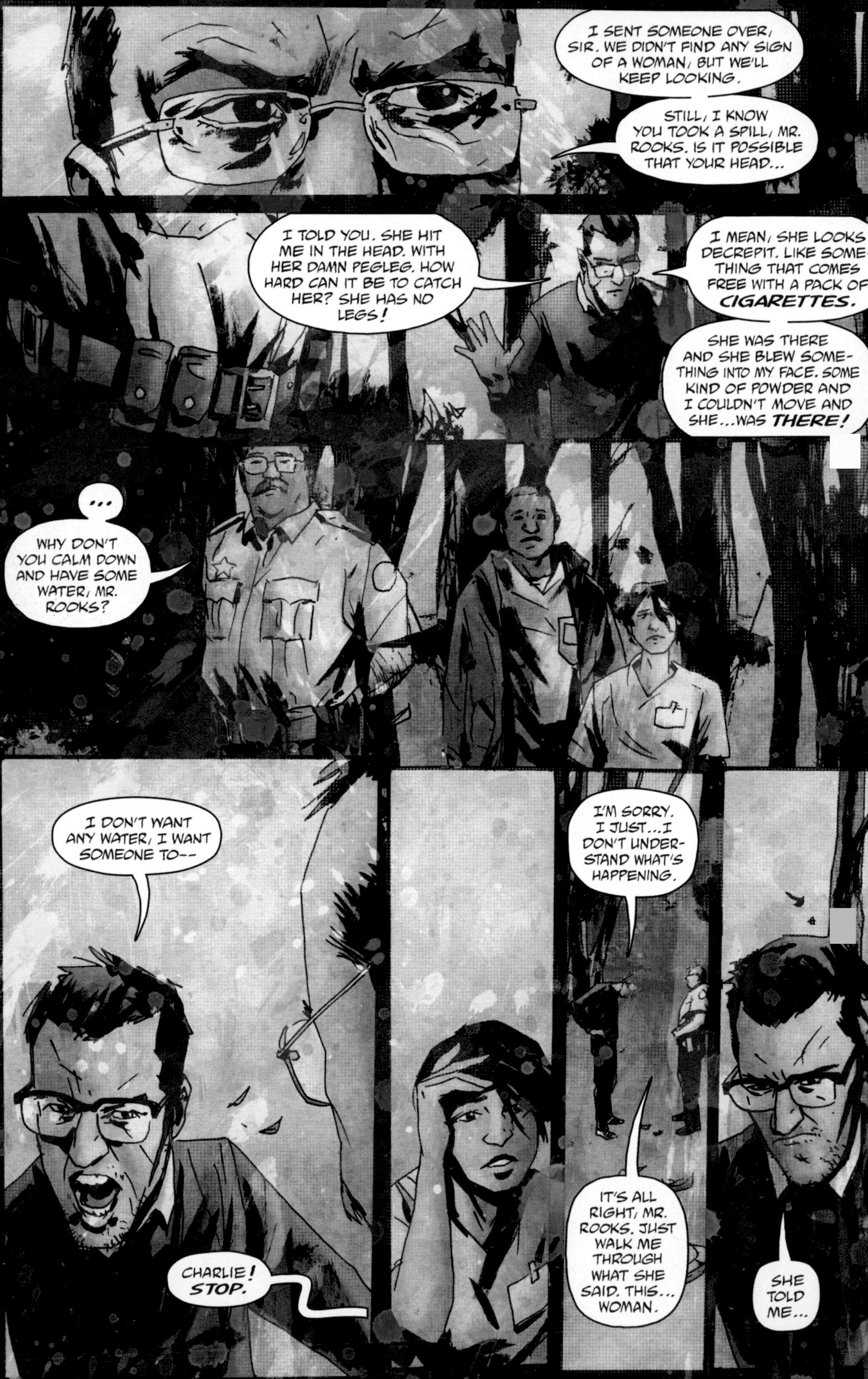

I SENT SOMEONE OVER, SIR. WE DIDN'T FIND ANY SIGN OF A WOMAN, BUT WE'LL KEEP LOOKING.
STILL, I KNOW YOU TOOK A SPILL, MR. ROOKS. IS IT POSSIBLE THAT YOUR HEAD...
I TOLD YOU. SHE HIT ME IN THE HEAD. WITH HER DAMN PEGLEG. HOW HARD CAN IT BE TO CATCH HER? SHE HAS NO LEGS!
I MEAN, SHE LOOKS DECREPIT. LIKE SOMETHING THAT COMES FREE WITH A PACK OF **CIGARETTES.**
SHE WAS THERE AND SHE BLEW SOMETHING INTO MY FACE. SOME KIND OF POWDER AND I COULDN'T MOVE AND SHE...WAS **THERE!**
...
WHY DON'T YOU CALM DOWN AND HAVE SOME WATER, MR. ROOKS?
I DON'T WANT ANY WATER, I WANT SOMEONE TO--
CHARLIE! **STOP.**
I'M SORRY. I JUST...I DON'T UNDERSTAND WHAT'S HAPPENING.
IT'S ALL RIGHT, MR. ROOKS. JUST WALK ME THROUGH WHAT SHE SAID. THIS... WOMAN.
SHE TOLD ME...

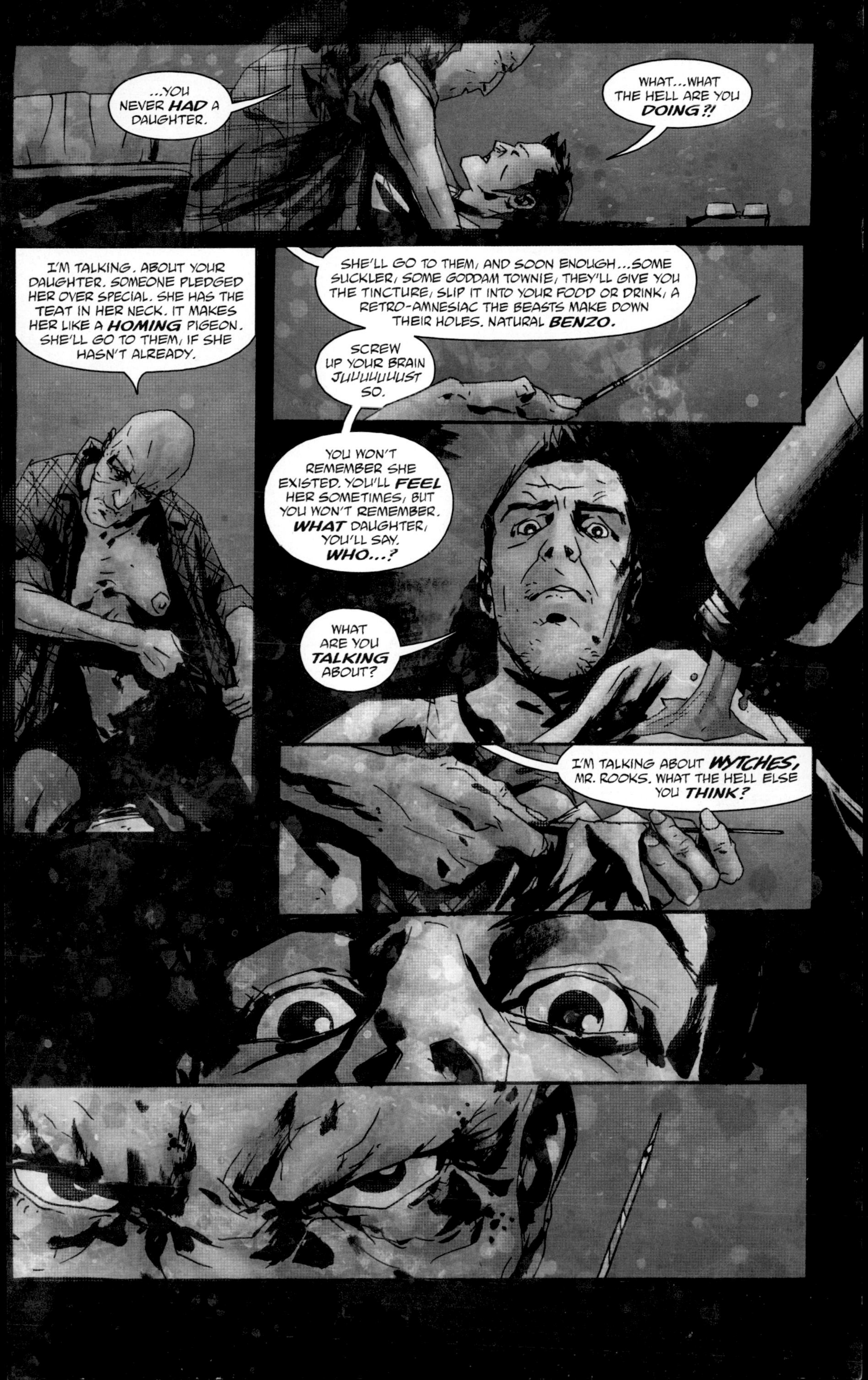
...YOU NEVER HAD A DAUGHTER.
WHAT...WHAT THE HELL ARE YOU DOING?!
I'M TALKING. ABOUT YOUR DAUGHTER. SOMEONE PLEDGED HER OVER SPECIAL. SHE HAS THE TEAT IN HER NECK. IT MAKES HER LIKE A HOMING PIGEON. SHE'LL GO TO THEM, IF SHE HASN'T ALREADY.
SHE'LL GO TO THEM, AND SOON ENOUGH...SOME SUCKLER, SOME GODDAM TOWNIE, THEY'LL GIVE YOU THE TINCTURE, SLIP IT INTO YOUR FOOD OR DRINK, A RETRO-AMNESIAC THE BEASTS MAKE DOWN THEIR HOLES. NATURAL BENZO.
SCREW UP YOUR BRAIN JUUUUUUUST SO.
YOU WON'T REMEMBER SHE EXISTED. YOU'LL FEEL HER SOMETIMES, BUT YOU WON'T REMEMBER. WHAT DAUGHTER, YOU'LL SAY. WHO...?
WHAT ARE YOU TALKING ABOUT?
I'M TALKING ABOUT WYTCHES, MR. ROOKS. WHAT THE HELL ELSE YOU THINK?

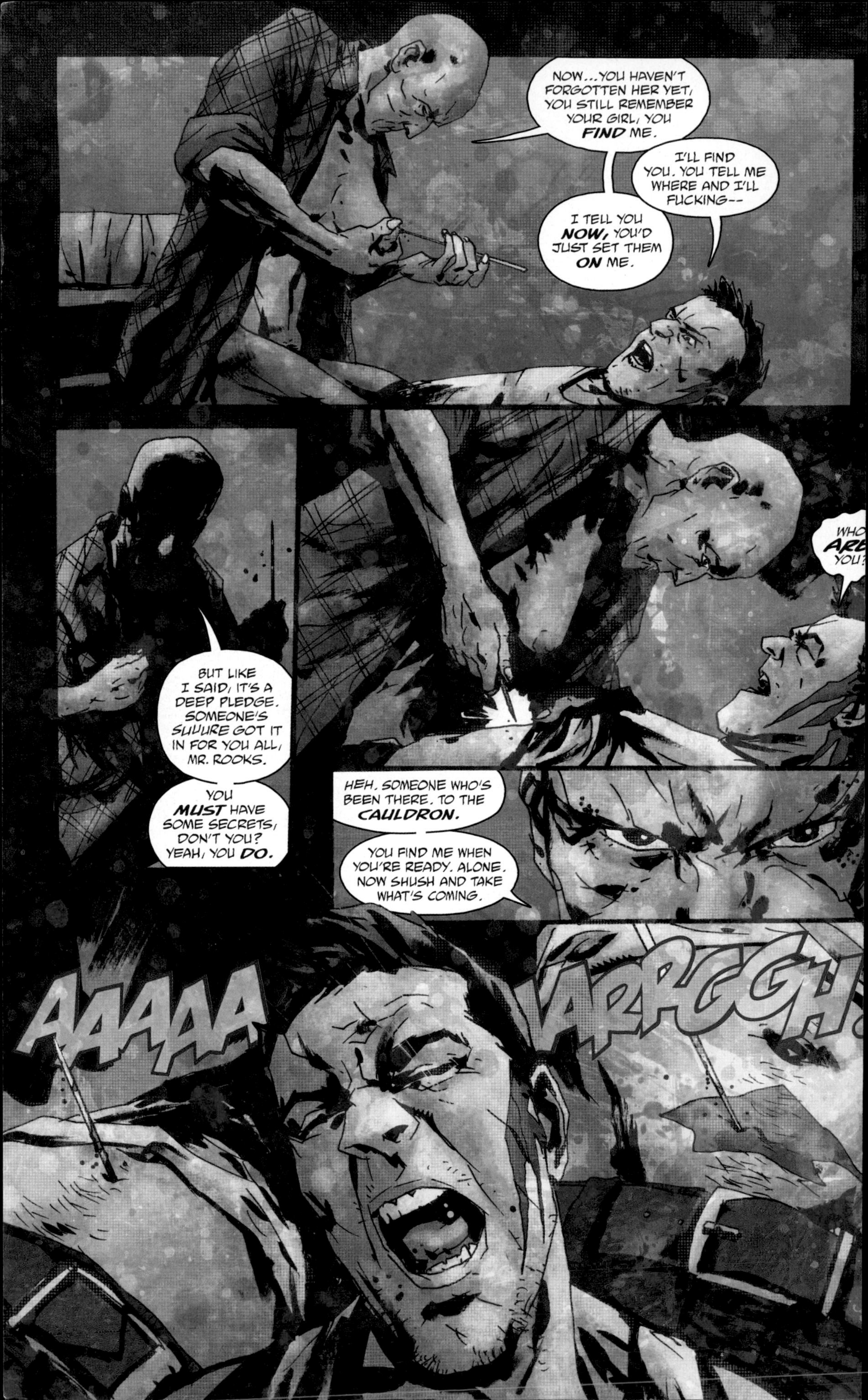

NOW... YOU HAVEN'T FORGOTTEN HER YET, YOU STILL REMEMBER YOUR GIRL, YOU **FIND** ME.
I'LL FIND YOU. YOU TELL ME WHERE AND I'LL FUCKING--
I TELL YOU **NOW,** YOU'D JUST SET THEM **ON** ME.
BUT LIKE I SAID, IT'S A DEEP PLEDGE. SOMEONE'S SUUURE GOT IT IN FOR YOU ALL, MR. ROOKS.
YOU **MUST** HAVE SOME SECRETS, DON'T YOU? YEAH, YOU **DO.**
WHO ARE YOU?
HEH. SOMEONE WHO'S BEEN THERE. TO THE **CAULDRON.**
YOU FIND ME WHEN YOU'RE READY. ALONE. NOW SHUSH AND TAKE WHAT'S COMING.
AAAAARRGGH!

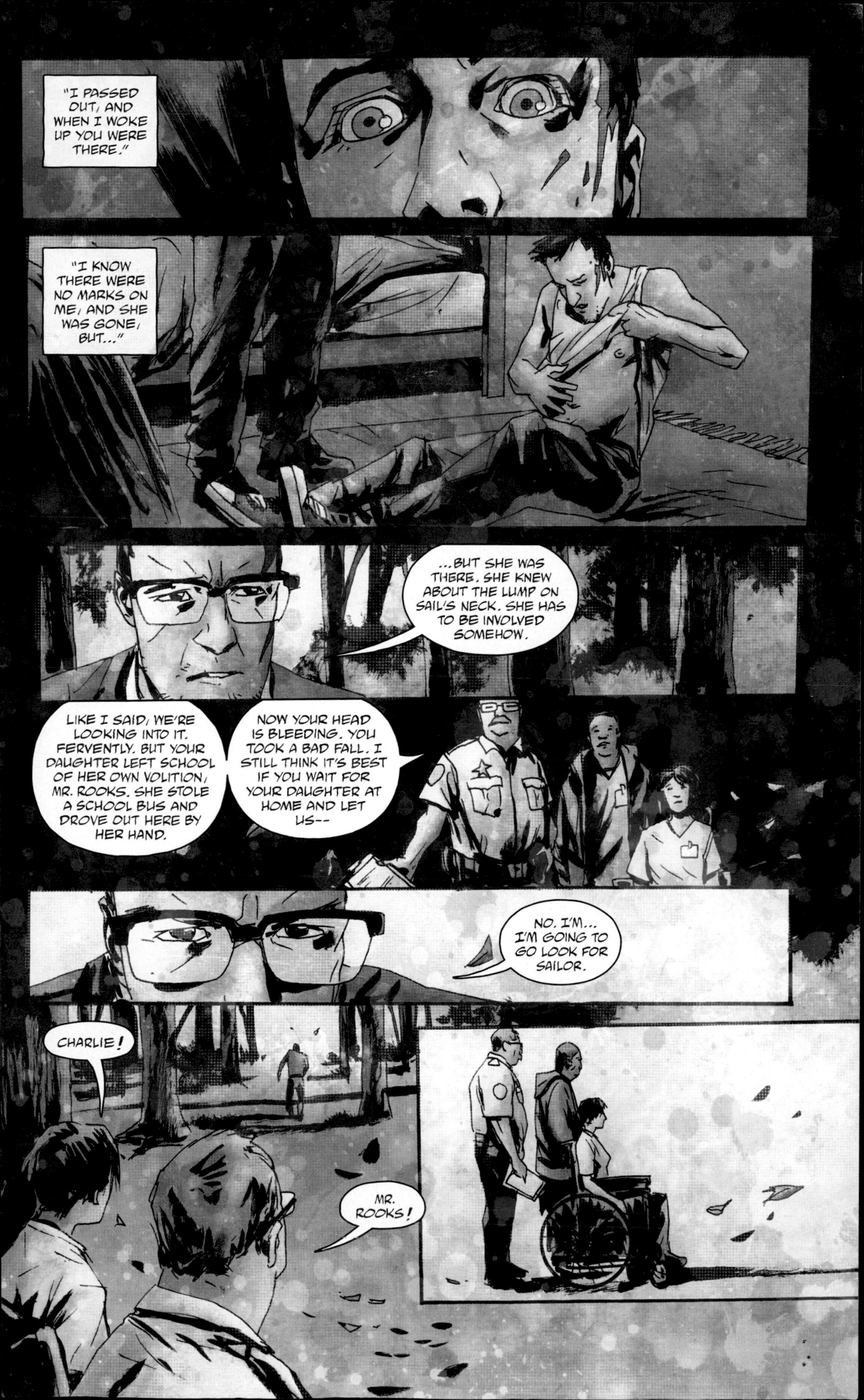
"I PASSED OUT, AND WHEN I WOKE UP YOU WERE THERE."
"I KNOW THERE WERE NO MARKS ON ME, AND SHE WAS GONE, BUT..."
...BUT SHE WAS THERE. SHE KNEW ABOUT THE LUMP ON SAIL'S NECK. SHE HAS TO BE INVOLVED SOMEHOW.
LIKE I SAID, WE'RE LOOKING INTO IT. FERVENTLY. BUT YOUR DAUGHTER LEFT SCHOOL OF HER OWN VOLITION, MR. ROOKS. SHE STOLE A SCHOOL BUS AND DROVE OUT HERE BY HER HAND.
NOW YOUR HEAD IS BLEEDING. YOU TOOK A BAD FALL. I STILL THINK IT'S BEST IF YOU WAIT FOR YOUR DAUGHTER AT HOME AND LET US--
NO. I'M... I'M GOING TO GO LOOK FOR SAILOR.
CHARLIE!
MR. ROOKS!

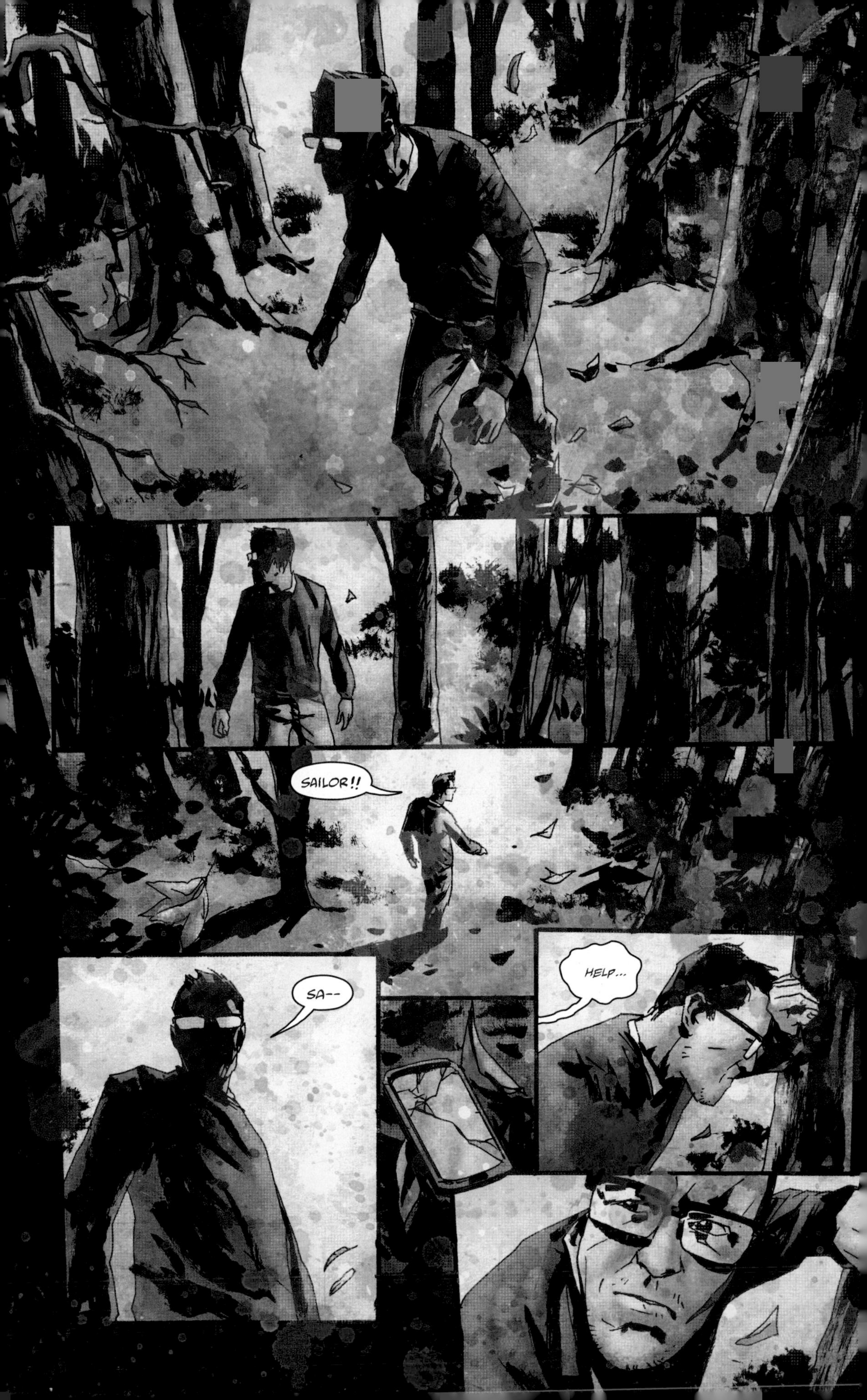
SAILOR!!
SA--
HELP...

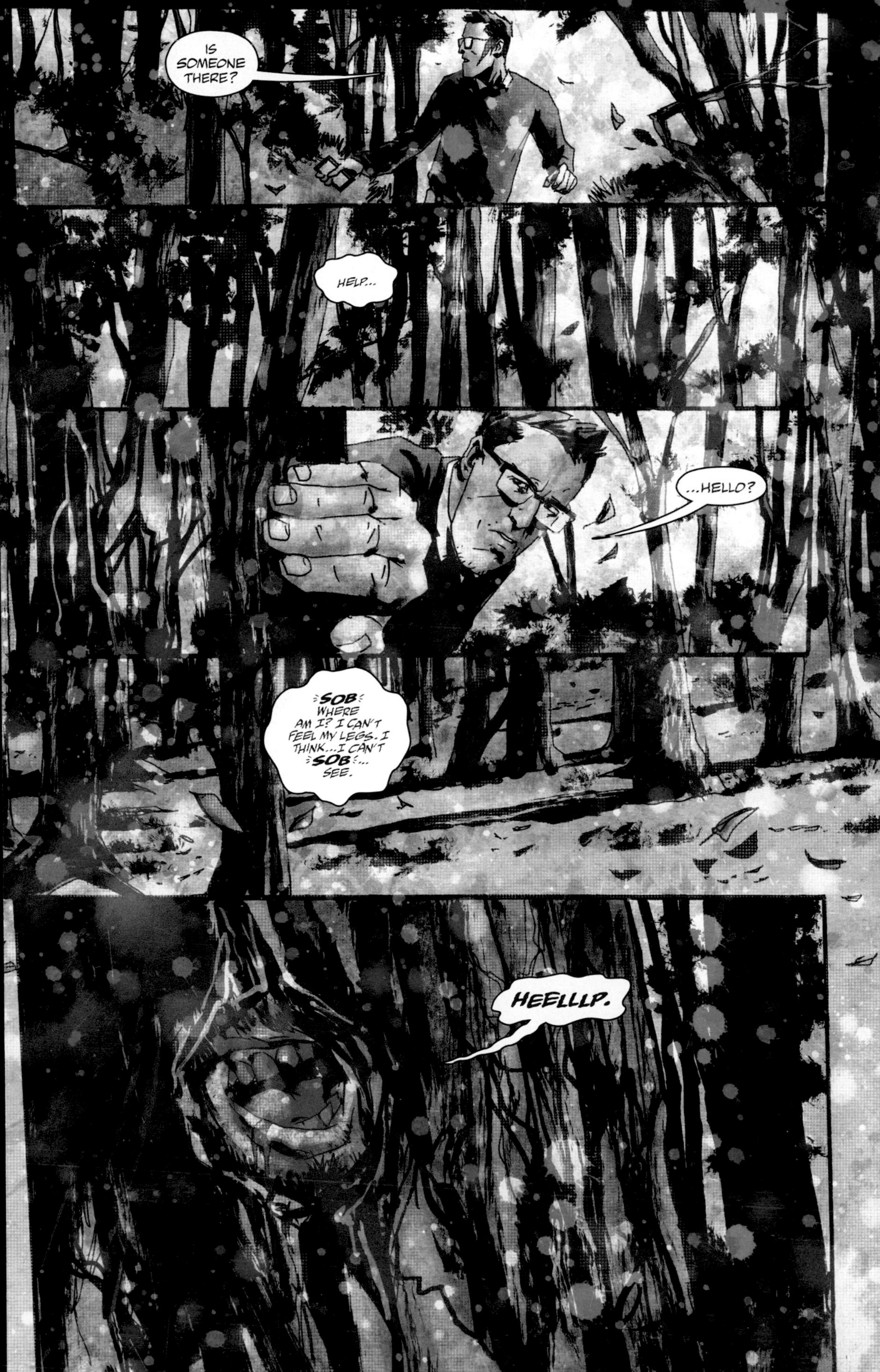
IS SOMEONE THERE?
HELP...
...HELLO?
SOB WHERE AM I? I CAN'T FEEL MY LEGS. I THINK...I CAN'T SOB... SEE.
HEELLLP.

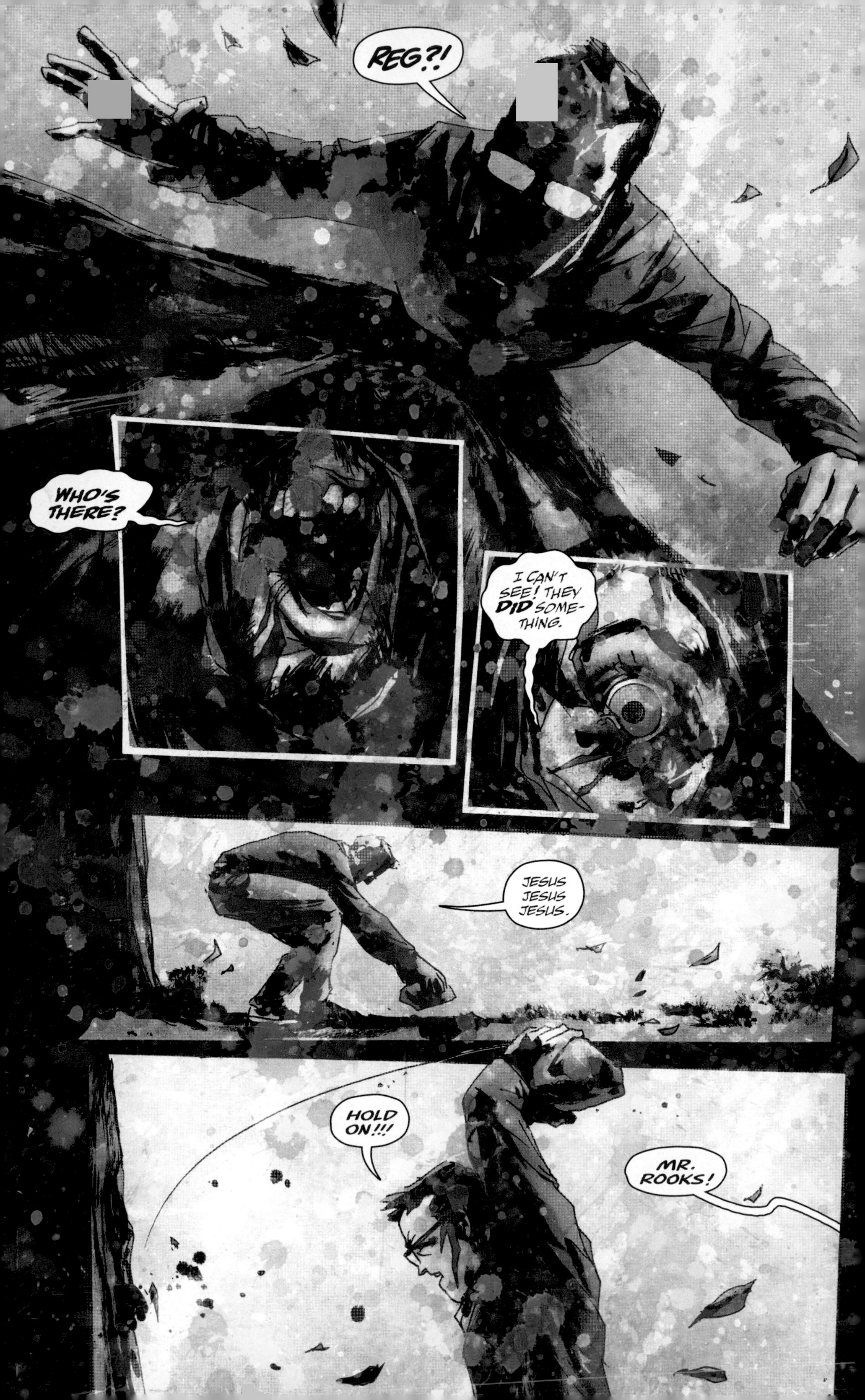
REG?!
WHO'S THERE?
I CAN'T SEE! THEY **DID** SOMETHING.
JESUS JESUS JESUS.
HOLD ON!!!
MR. ROOKS!

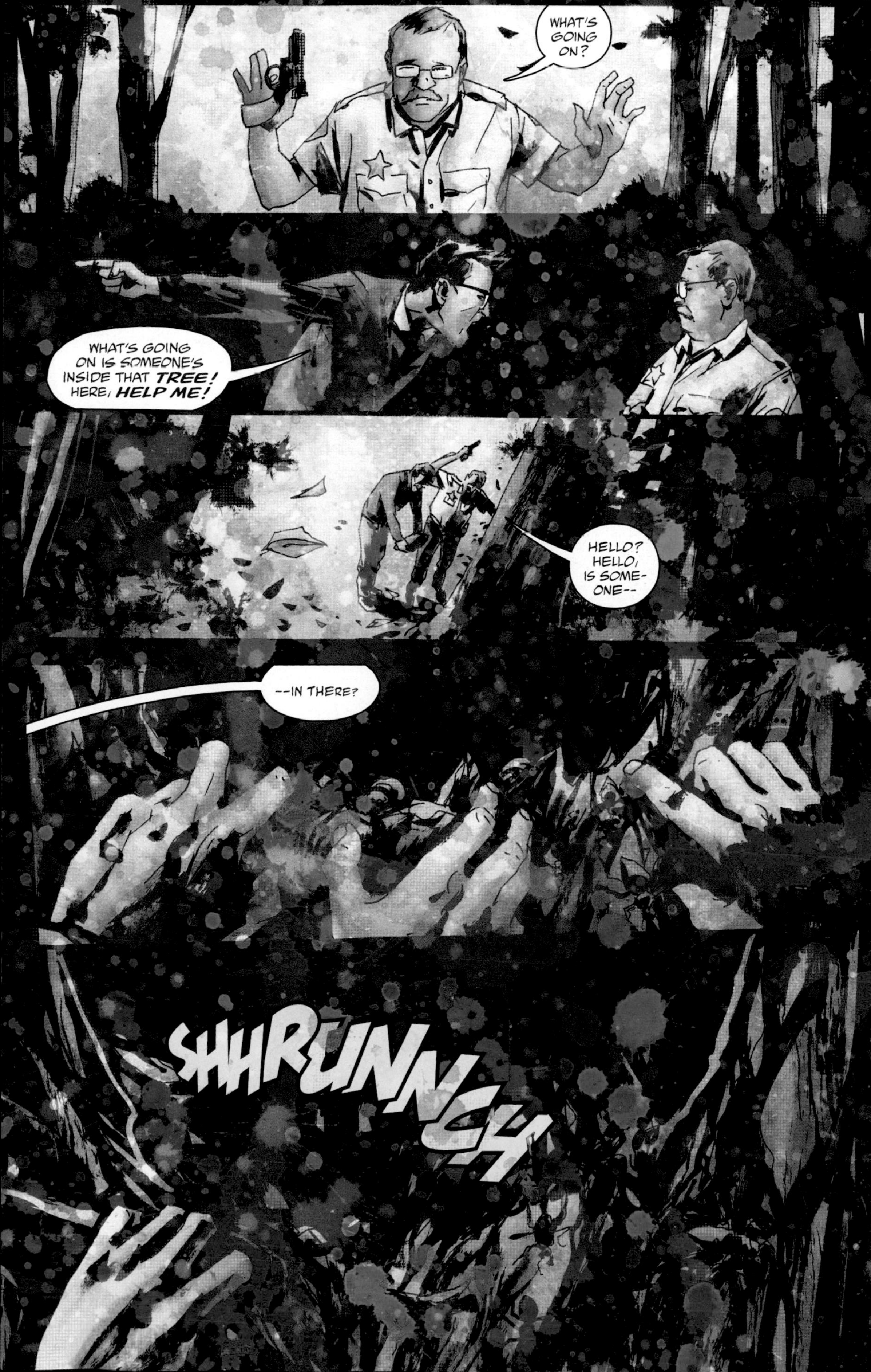
WHAT'S GOING ON?
WHAT'S GOING ON IS SOMEONE'S INSIDE THAT TREE! HERE, HELP ME!
HELLO? HELLO, IS SOME-ONE--
--IN THERE?
SHHRUNNCH

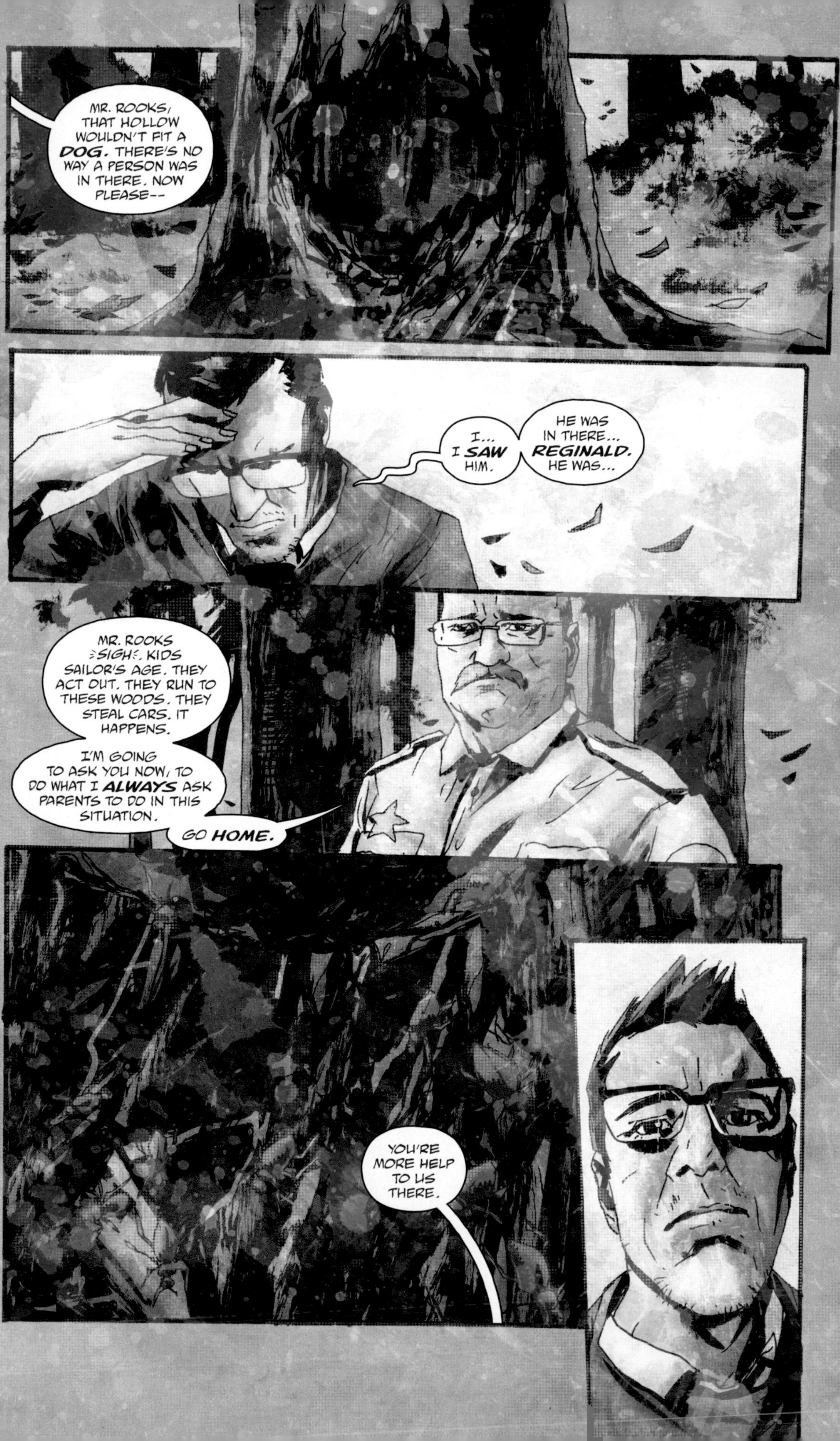
MR. ROOKS, THAT HOLLOW WOULDN'T FIT A DOG. THERE'S NO WAY A PERSON WAS IN THERE. NOW PLEASE--
I... I SAW HIM.
HE WAS IN THERE... REGINALD. HE WAS...
MR. ROOKS *SIGH*. KIDS SAILOR'S AGE. THEY ACT OUT. THEY RUN TO THESE WOODS. THEY STEAL CARS. IT HAPPENS.
I'M GOING TO ASK YOU NOW, TO DO WHAT I ALWAYS ASK PARENTS TO DO IN THIS SITUATION.
GO HOME.
YOU'RE MORE HELP TO US THERE.

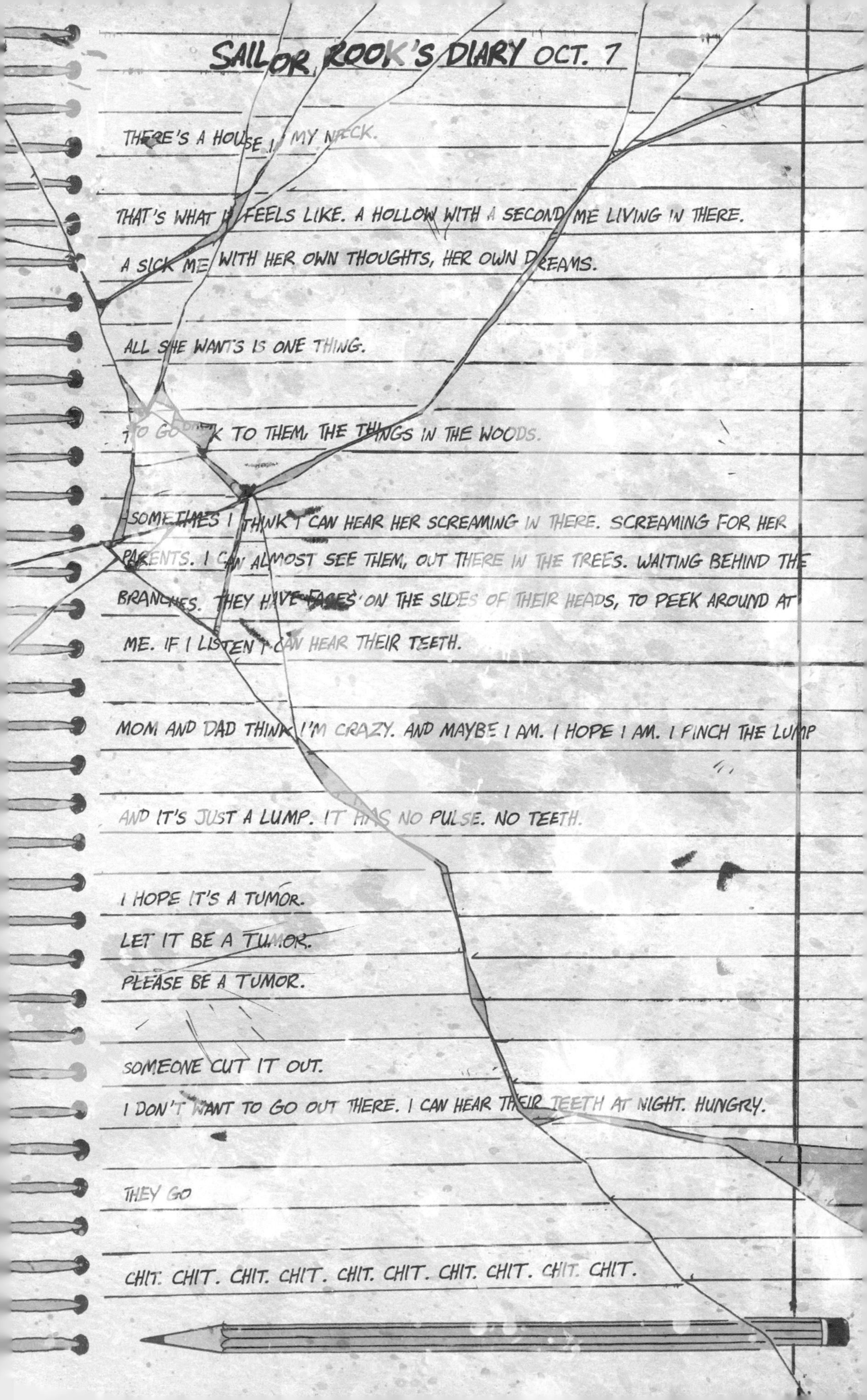
SAILOR ROOK'S DIARY OCT. 7
THERE'S A HOUSE IN MY NECK.
THAT'S WHAT IT FEELS LIKE. A HOLLOW WITH A SECOND ME LIVING IN THERE.
A SICK ME, WITH HER OWN THOUGHTS, HER OWN DREAMS.
ALL SHE WANTS IS ONE THING.
TO GO BACK TO THEM, THE THINGS IN THE WOODS.
SOMETIMES I THINK I CAN HEAR HER SCREAMING IN THERE. SCREAMING FOR HER PARENTS. I CAN ALMOST SEE THEM, OUT THERE IN THE TREES. WAITING BEHIND THE BRANCHES. THEY HAVE FACES ON THE SIDES OF THEIR HEADS, TO PEEK AROUND AT ME. IF I LISTEN I CAN HEAR THEIR TEETH.
MOM AND DAD THINK I'M CRAZY. AND MAYBE I AM. I HOPE I AM. I PINCH THE LUMP
AND IT'S JUST A LUMP. IT HAS NO PULSE. NO TEETH.
I HOPE IT'S A TUMOR.
LET IT BE A TUMOR.
PLEASE BE A TUMOR.
SOMEONE CUT IT OUT.
I DON'T WANT TO GO OUT THERE. I CAN HEAR THEIR TEETH AT NIGHT. HUNGRY.
THEY GO
CHIT. CHIT. CHIT. CHIT. CHIT. CHIT. CHIT. CHIT. CHIT. CHIT.

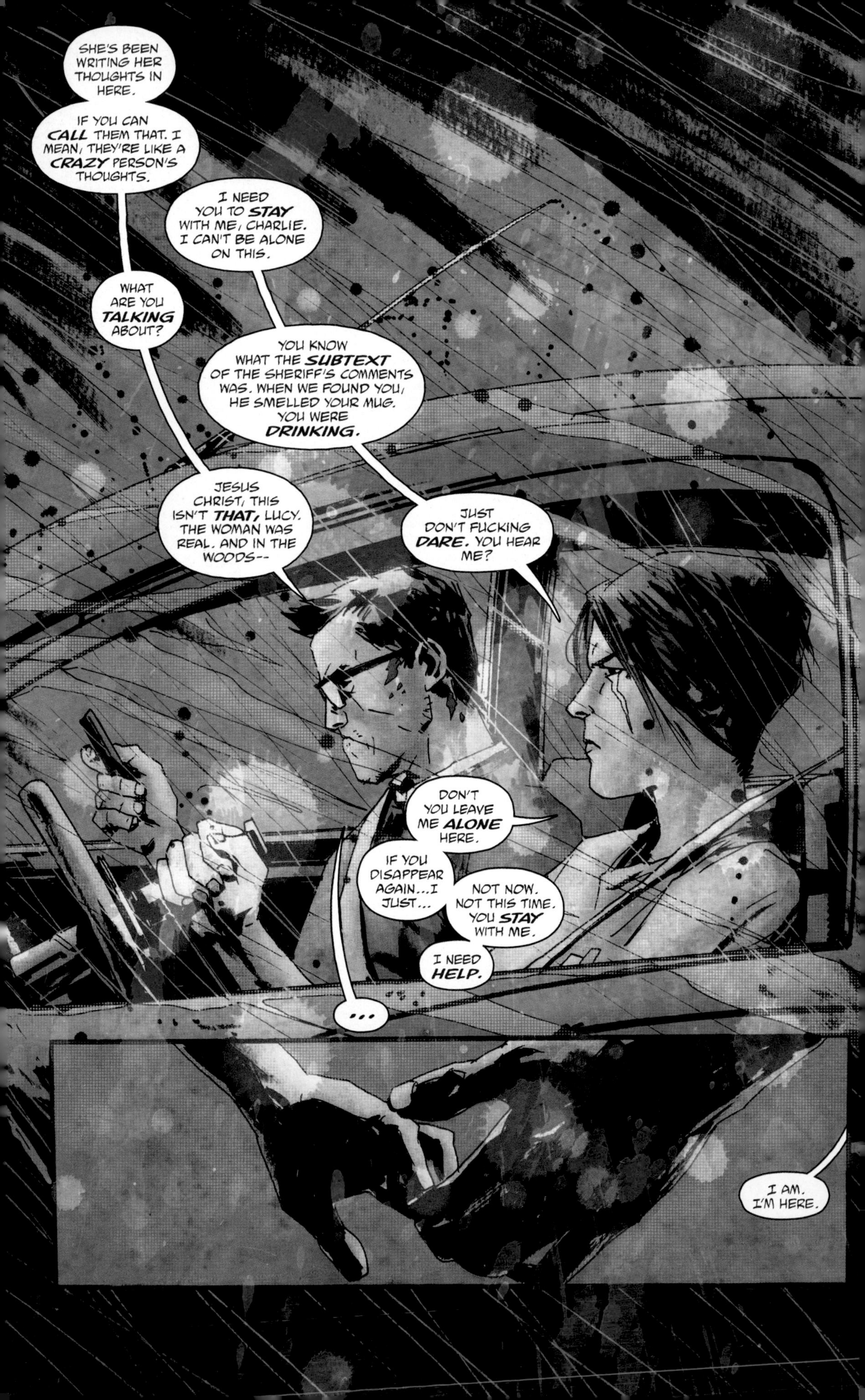
SHE'S BEEN WRITING HER THOUGHTS IN HERE.
IF YOU CAN CALL THEM THAT. I MEAN, THEY'RE LIKE A CRAZY PERSON'S THOUGHTS.
I NEED YOU TO STAY WITH ME, CHARLIE. I CAN'T BE ALONE ON THIS.
WHAT ARE YOU TALKING ABOUT?
YOU KNOW WHAT THE SUBTEXT OF THE SHERIFF'S COMMENTS WAS. WHEN WE FOUND YOU, HE SMELLED YOUR MUG. YOU WERE DRINKING.
JESUS CHRIST, THIS ISN'T THAT, LUCY. THE WOMAN WAS REAL. AND IN THE WOODS--
JUST DON'T FUCKING DARE. YOU HEAR ME?
DON'T YOU LEAVE ME ALONE HERE.
IF YOU DISAPPEAR AGAIN...I JUST...
NOT NOW. NOT THIS TIME. YOU STAY WITH ME.
I NEED HELP.
...
I AM. I'M HERE.

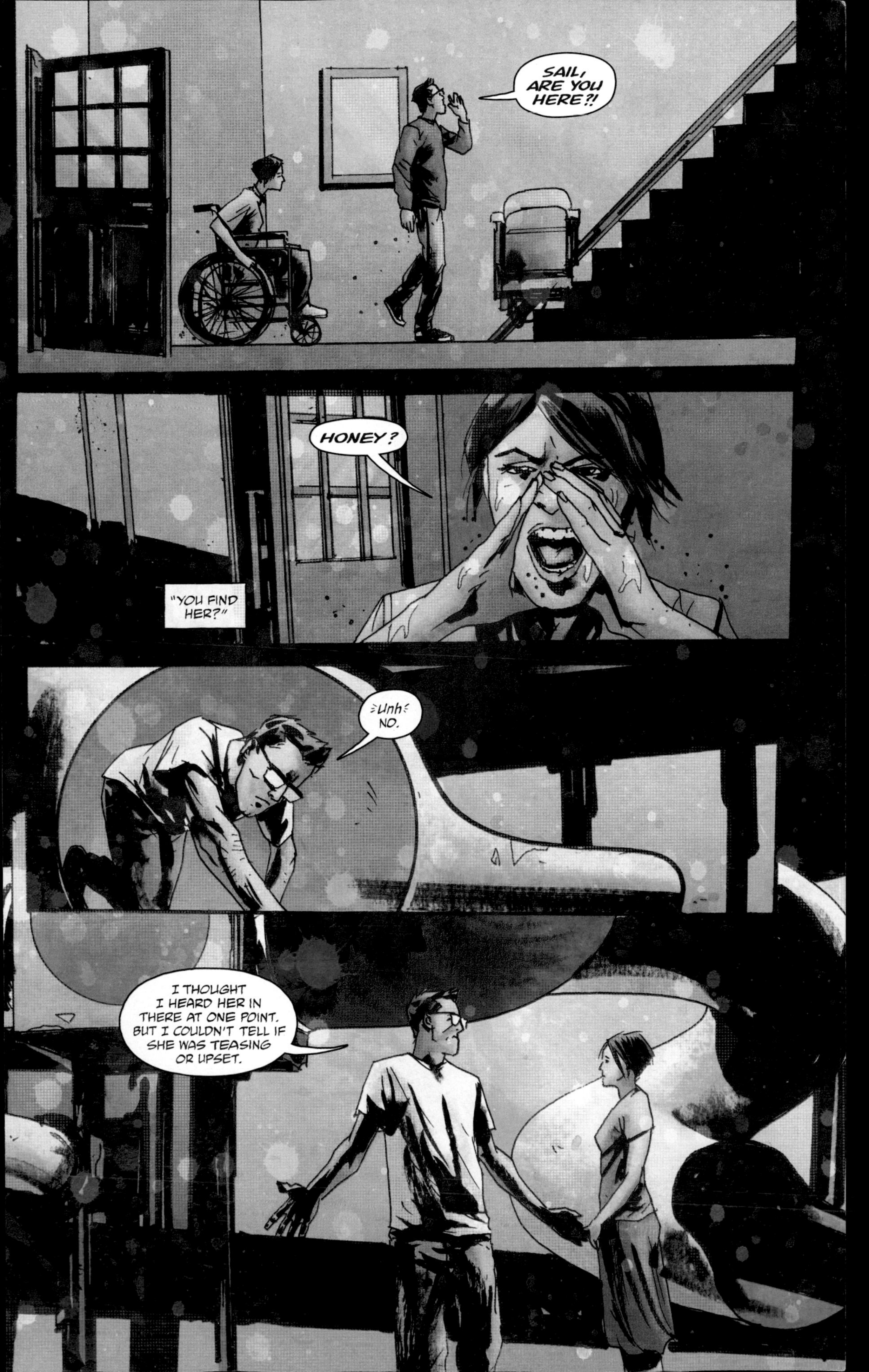
SAIL, ARE YOU HERE?!
HONEY?
"YOU FIND HER?"
Unh NO.
I THOUGHT I HEARD HER IN THERE AT ONE POINT. BUT I COULDN'T TELL IF SHE WAS TEASING OR UPSET.

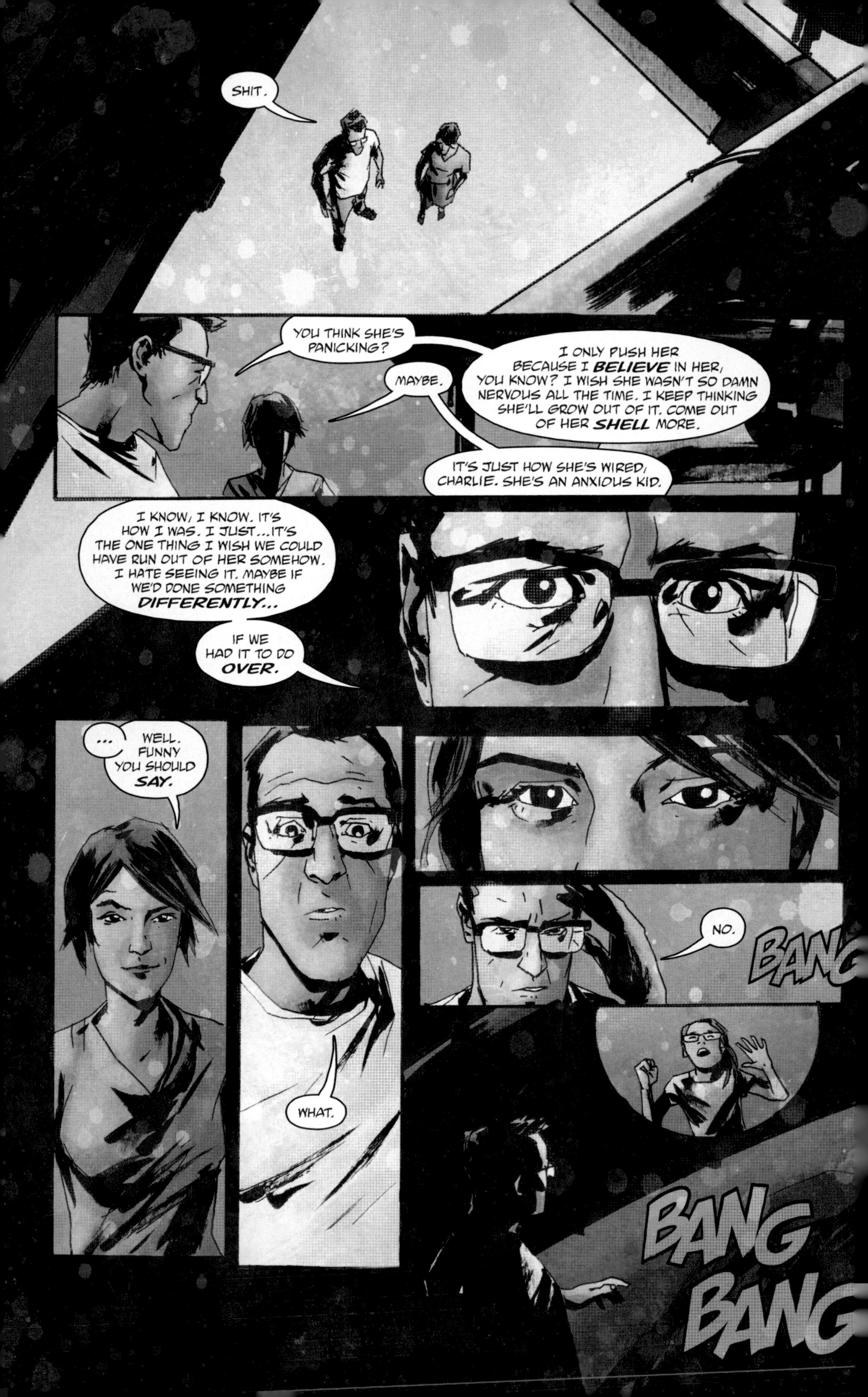
SHIT.
YOU THINK SHE'S PANICKING?
MAYBE.
I ONLY PUSH HER BECAUSE I BELIEVE IN HER, YOU KNOW? I WISH SHE WASN'T SO DAMN NERVOUS ALL THE TIME. I KEEP THINKING SHE'LL GROW OUT OF IT. COME OUT OF HER SHELL MORE.
IT'S JUST HOW SHE'S WIRED, CHARLIE. SHE'S AN ANXIOUS KID.
I KNOW, I KNOW. IT'S HOW I WAS. I JUST...IT'S THE ONE THING I WISH WE COULD HAVE RUN OUT OF HER SOMEHOW. I HATE SEEING IT. MAYBE IF WE'D DONE SOMETHING DIFFERENTLY...
IF WE HAD IT TO DO OVER.
...
WELL. FUNNY YOU SHOULD SAY.
WHAT.
NO.
BANG
BANG
BANG

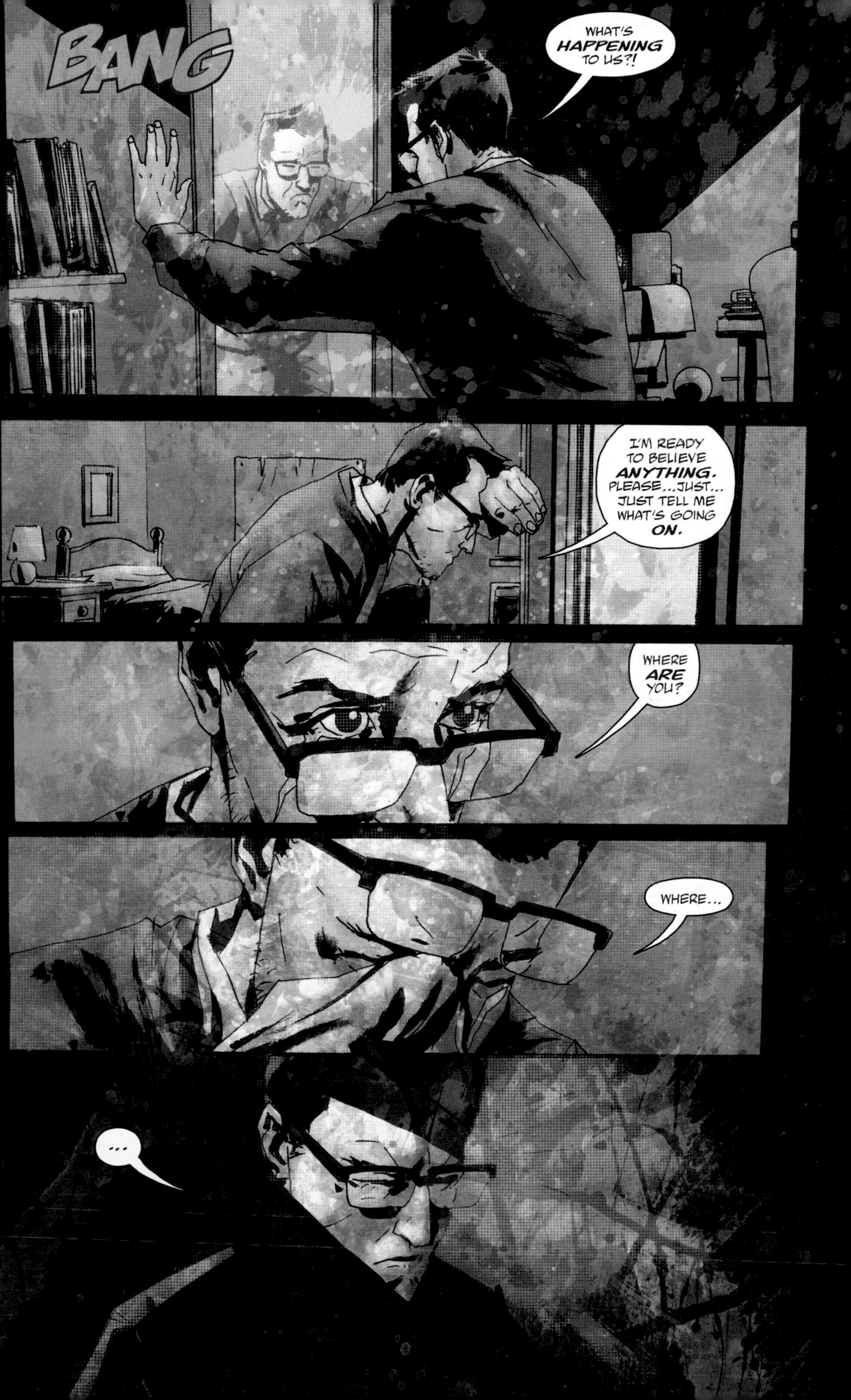
BANG
WHAT'S HAPPENING TO US?!
I'M READY TO BELIEVE ANYTHING. PLEASE...JUST... JUST TELL ME WHAT'S GOING ON.
WHERE ARE YOU?
WHERE...
...

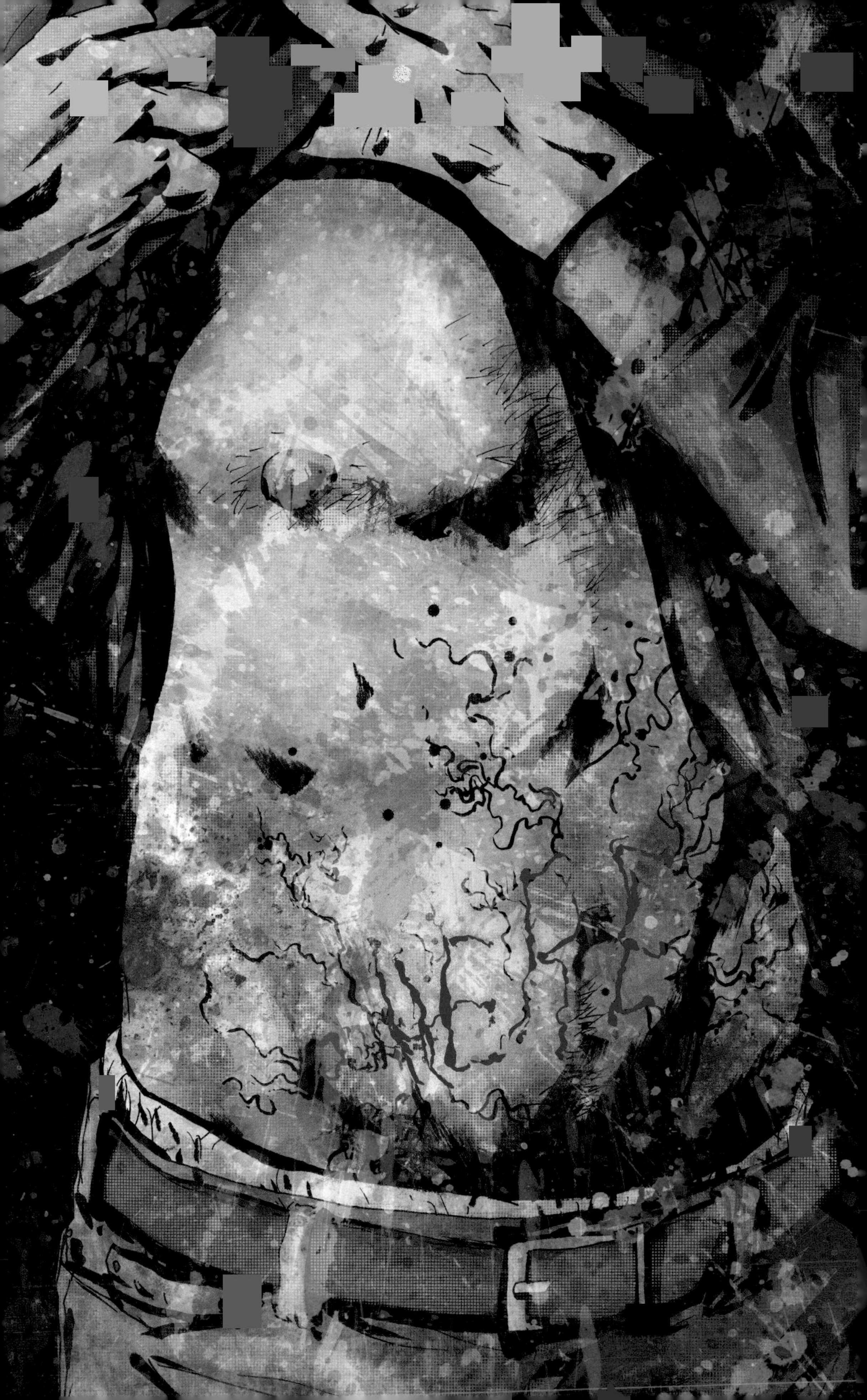

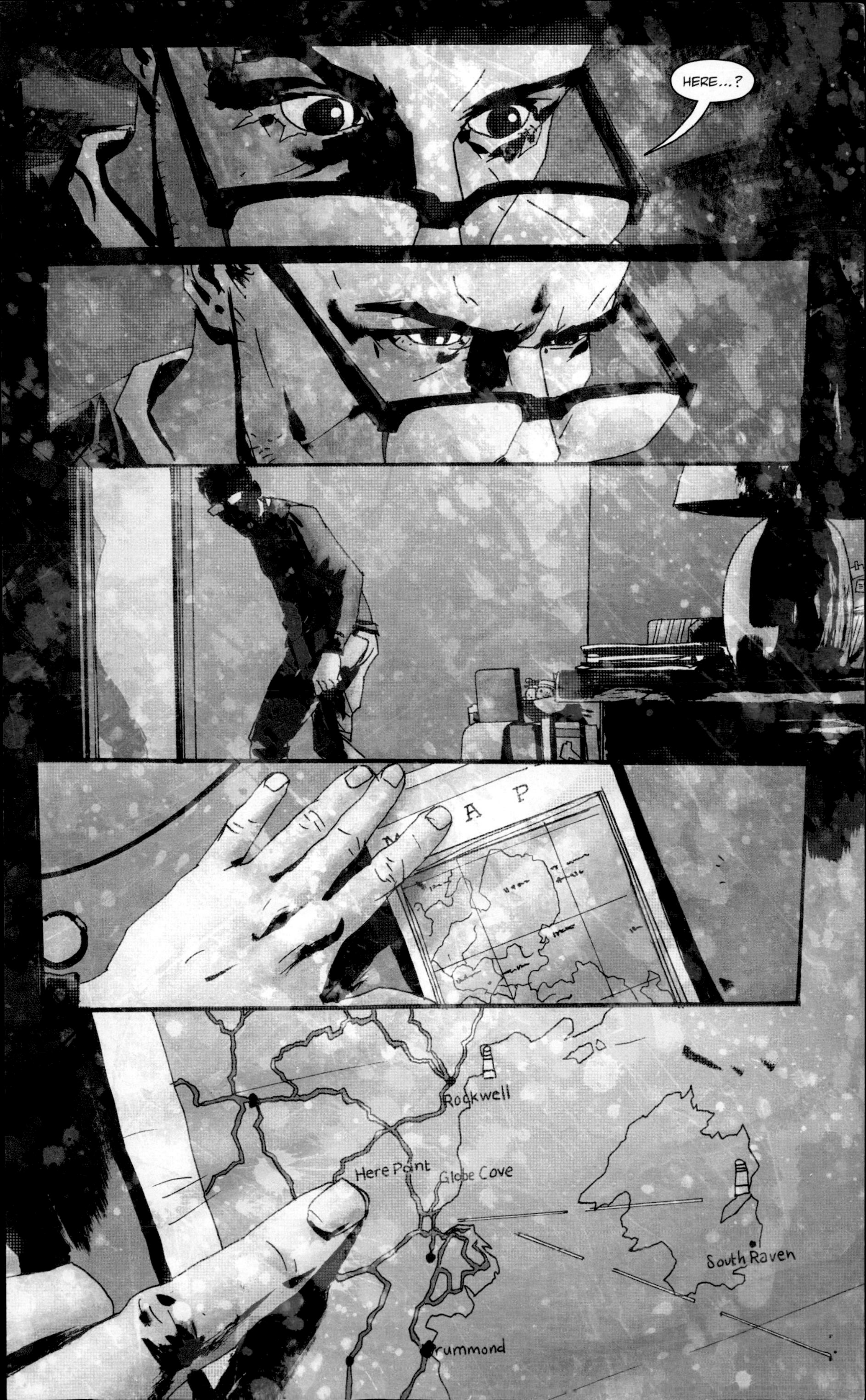
HERE...?
M A P
Rockwell
Here Point
Globe Cove
South Raven
Drummond

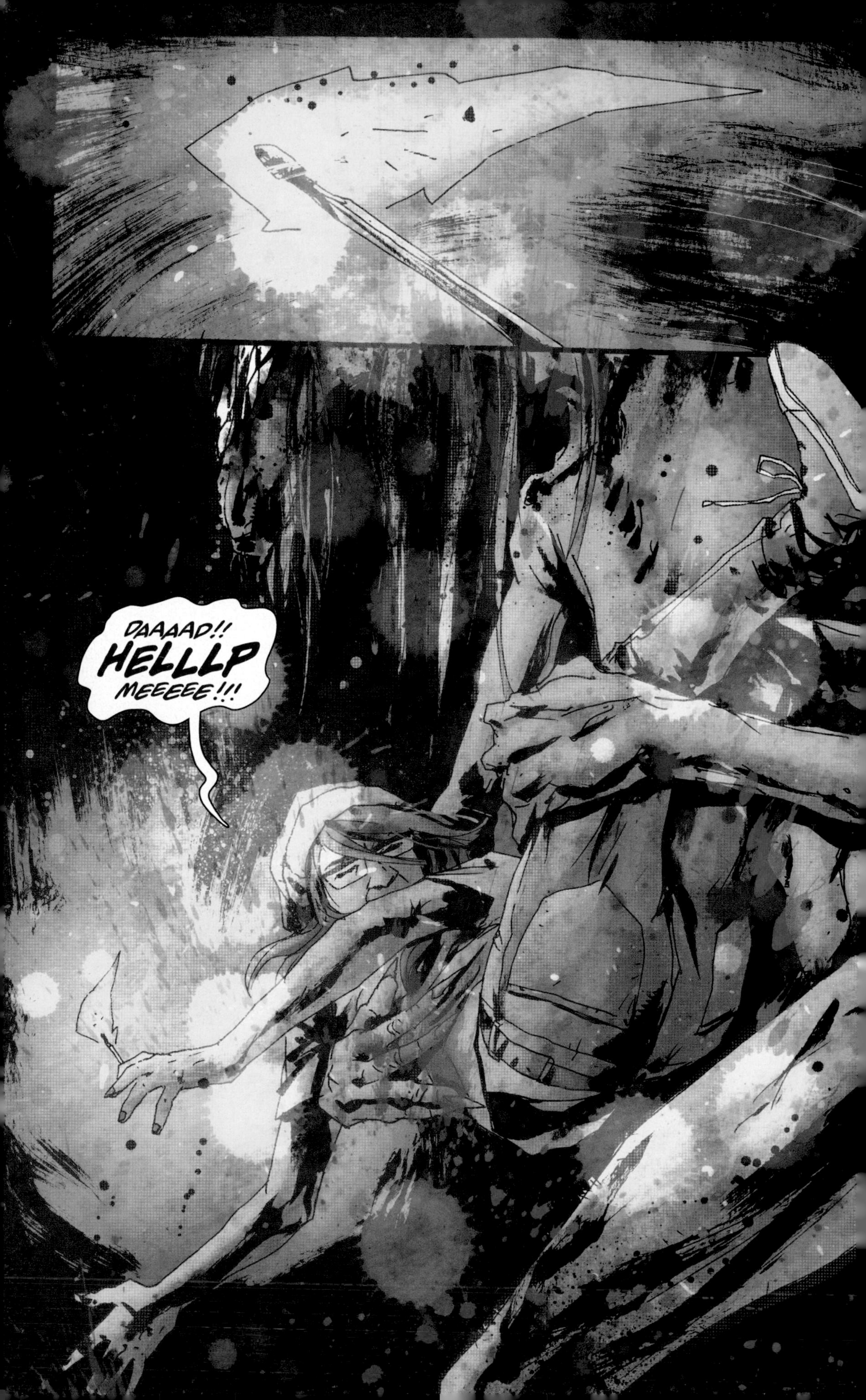
DAAAAD!! HELLLP MEEEEE!!!

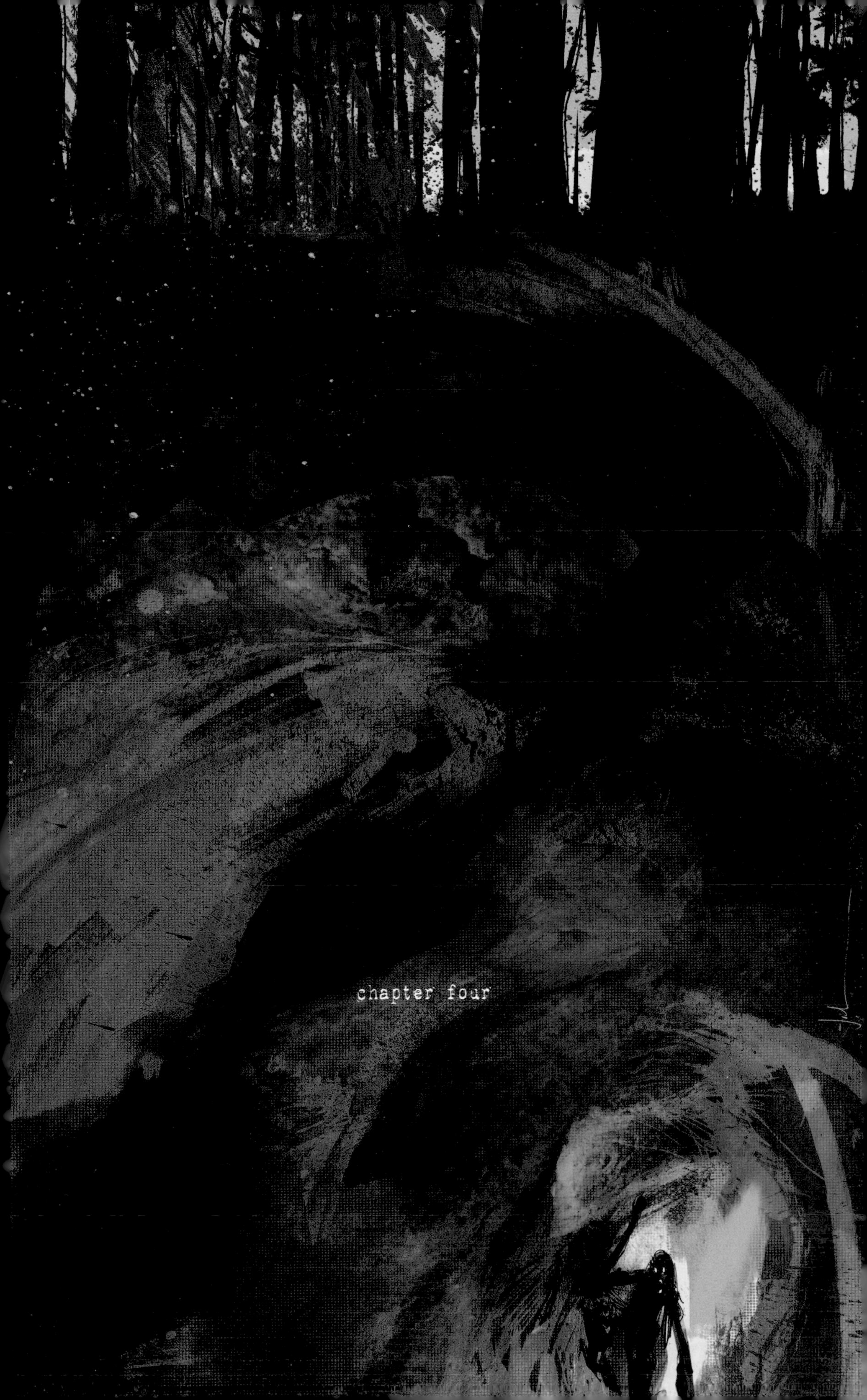
chapter four

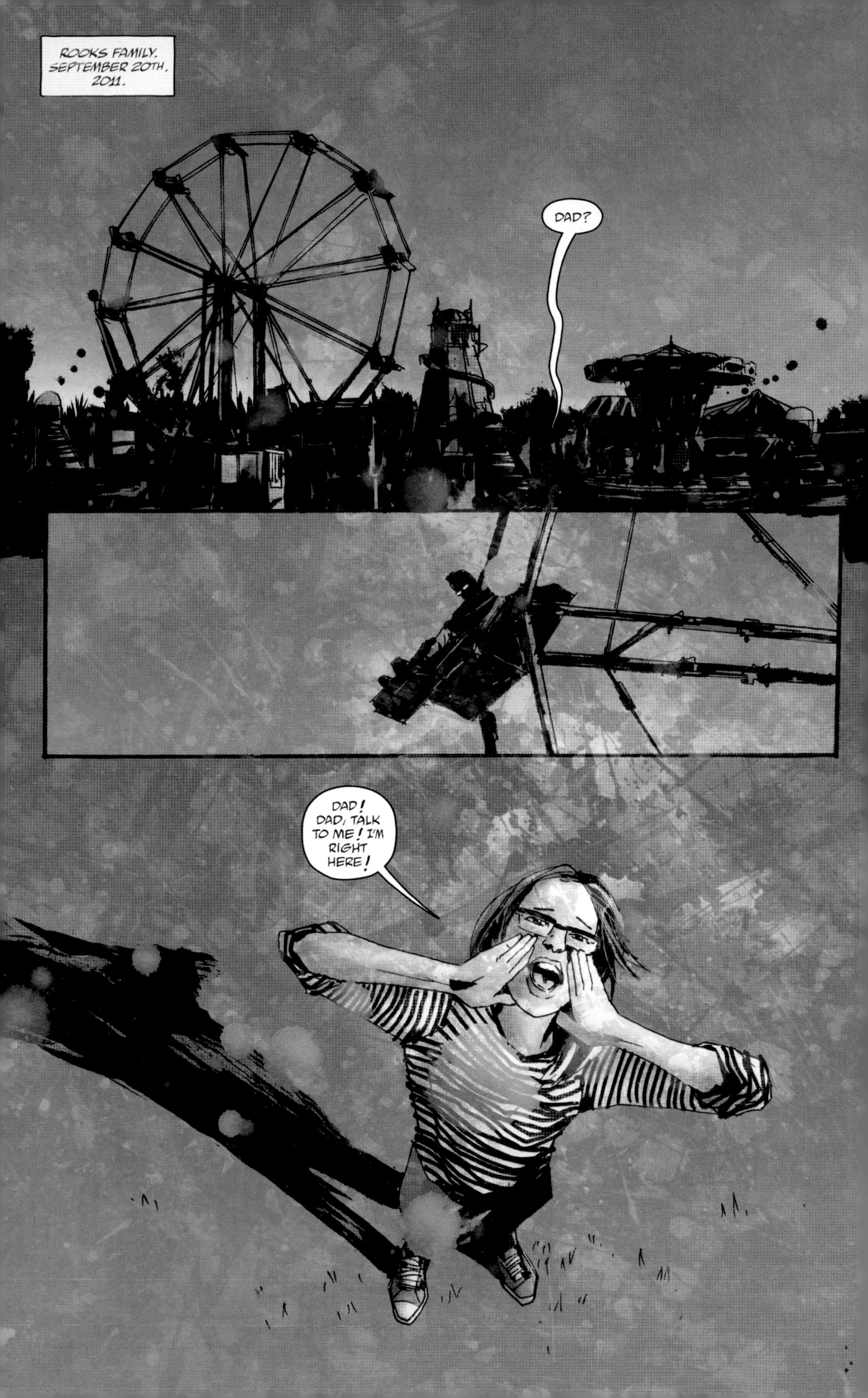
ROOKS FAMILY. SEPTEMBER 20TH, 2011.
DAD?
DAD! DAD, TALK TO ME! I'M RIGHT HERE!

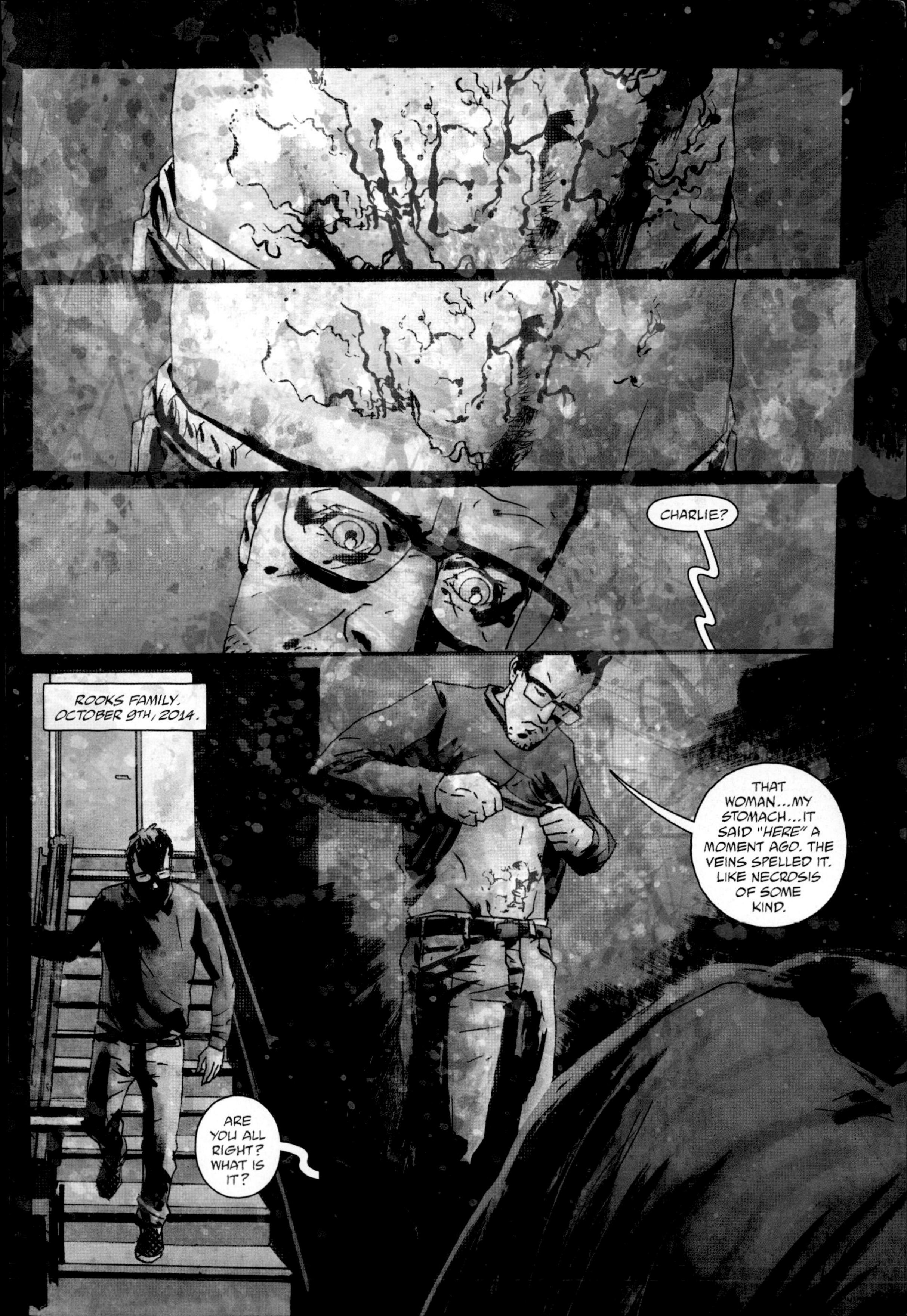
CHARLIE?
ROOKS FAMILY. OCTOBER 9TH, 2014.
ARE YOU ALL RIGHT? WHAT IS IT?
THAT WOMAN...MY STOMACH...IT SAID "HERE" A MOMENT AGO. THE VEINS SPELLED IT. LIKE NECROSIS OF SOME KIND.

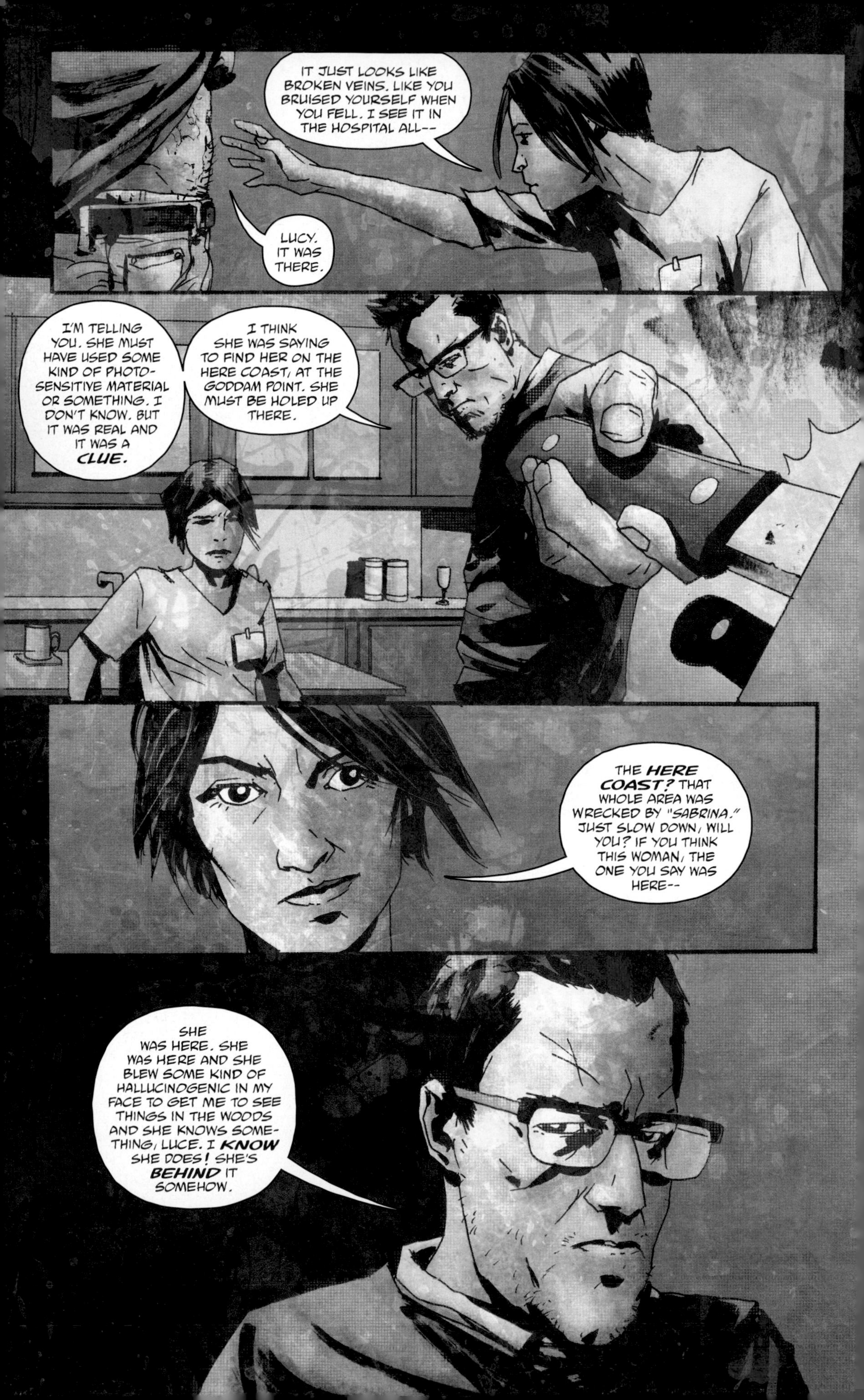
IT JUST LOOKS LIKE BROKEN VEINS. LIKE YOU BRUISED YOURSELF WHEN YOU FELL. I SEE IT IN THE HOSPITAL ALL--
LUCY. IT WAS THERE.
I'M TELLING YOU. SHE MUST HAVE USED SOME KIND OF PHOTO-SENSITIVE MATERIAL OR SOMETHING. I DON'T KNOW. BUT IT WAS REAL AND IT WAS A CLUE.
I THINK SHE WAS SAYING TO FIND HER ON THE HERE COAST, AT THE GODDAM POINT. SHE MUST BE HOLED UP THERE.
THE HERE COAST? THAT WHOLE AREA WAS WRECKED BY "SABRINA." JUST SLOW DOWN, WILL YOU? IF YOU THINK THIS WOMAN, THE ONE YOU SAY WAS HERE--
SHE WAS HERE. SHE WAS HERE AND SHE BLEW SOME KIND OF HALLUCINOGENIC IN MY FACE TO GET ME TO SEE THINGS IN THE WOODS AND SHE KNOWS SOME-THING, LUCE. I KNOW SHE DOES! SHE'S BEHIND IT SOMEHOW.

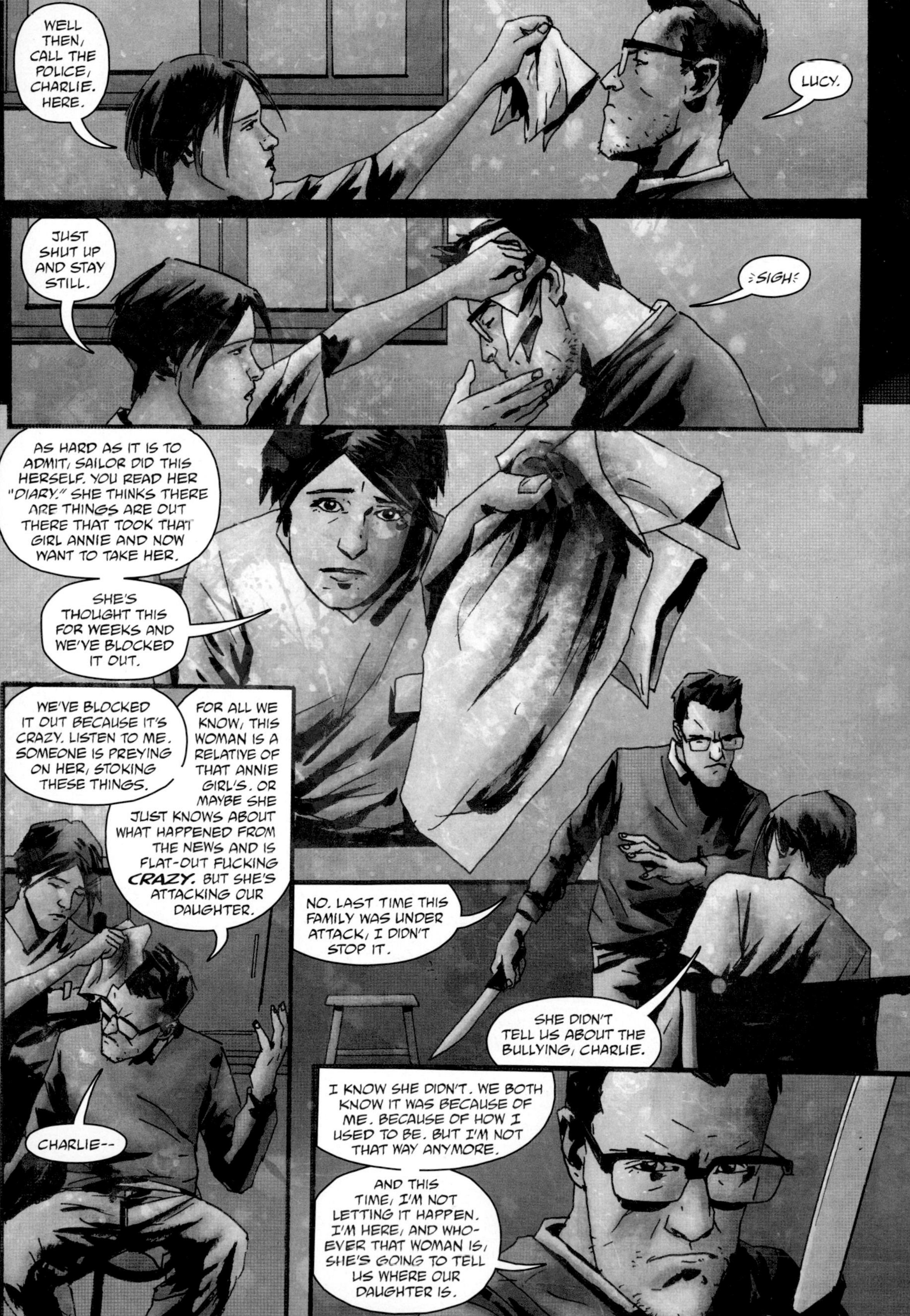
WELL THEN, CALL THE POLICE, CHARLIE. HERE.
LUCY.
JUST SHUT UP AND STAY STILL.
SIGH
AS HARD AS IT IS TO ADMIT, SAILOR DID THIS HERSELF. YOU READ HER "DIARY." SHE THINKS THERE ARE THINGS ARE OUT THERE THAT TOOK THAT GIRL ANNIE AND NOW WANT TO TAKE HER.
SHE'S THOUGHT THIS FOR WEEKS AND WE'VE BLOCKED IT OUT.
WE'VE BLOCKED IT OUT BECAUSE IT'S CRAZY. LISTEN TO ME. SOMEONE IS PREYING ON HER, STOKING THESE THINGS.
FOR ALL WE KNOW, THIS WOMAN IS A RELATIVE OF THAT ANNIE GIRL'S. OR MAYBE SHE JUST KNOWS ABOUT WHAT HAPPENED FROM THE NEWS AND IS FLAT-OUT FUCKING CRAZY. BUT SHE'S ATTACKING OUR DAUGHTER.
CHARLIE--
NO. LAST TIME THIS FAMILY WAS UNDER ATTACK, I DIDN'T STOP IT.
SHE DIDN'T TELL US ABOUT THE BULLYING, CHARLIE.
I KNOW SHE DIDN'T. WE BOTH KNOW IT WAS BECAUSE OF ME. BECAUSE OF HOW I USED TO BE. BUT I'M NOT THAT WAY ANYMORE.
AND THIS TIME, I'M NOT LETTING IT HAPPEN. I'M HERE, AND WHOEVER THAT WOMAN IS, SHE'S GOING TO TELL US WHERE OUR DAUGHTER IS.

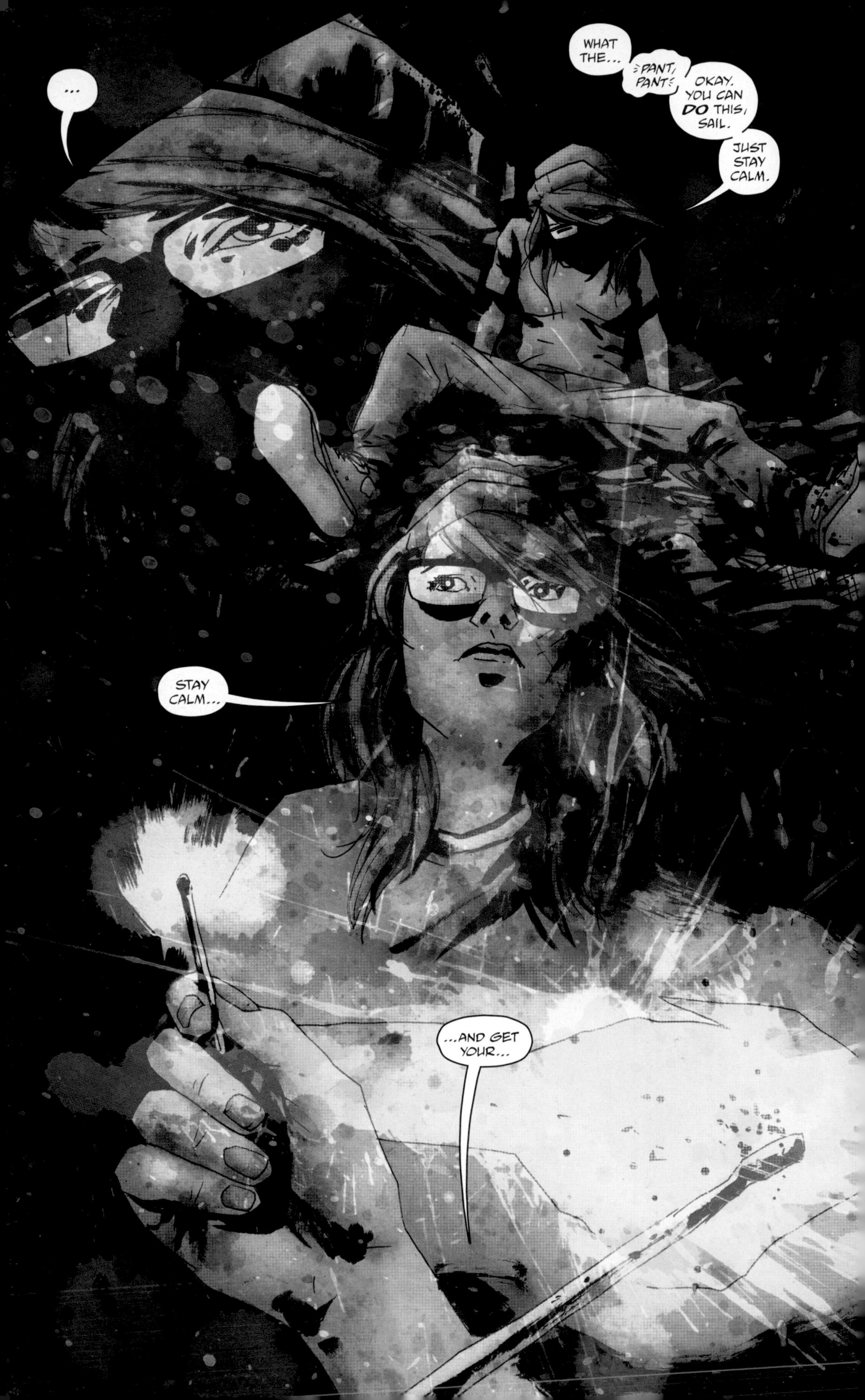
...
WHAT THE...
PANT, PANT
OKAY. YOU CAN DO THIS, SAIL.
JUST STAY CALM.
STAY CALM...
...AND GET YOUR...

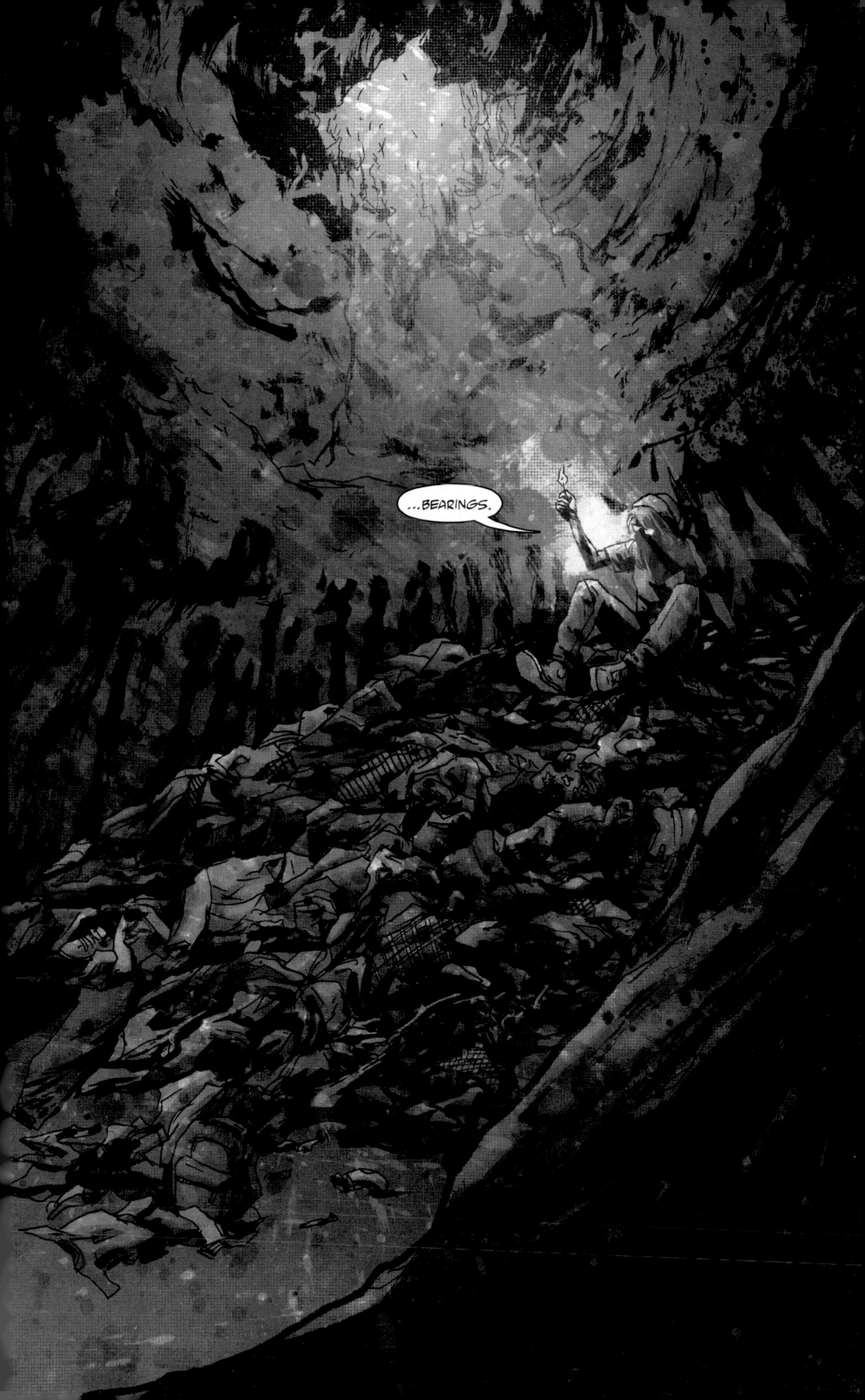
...BEARINGS.

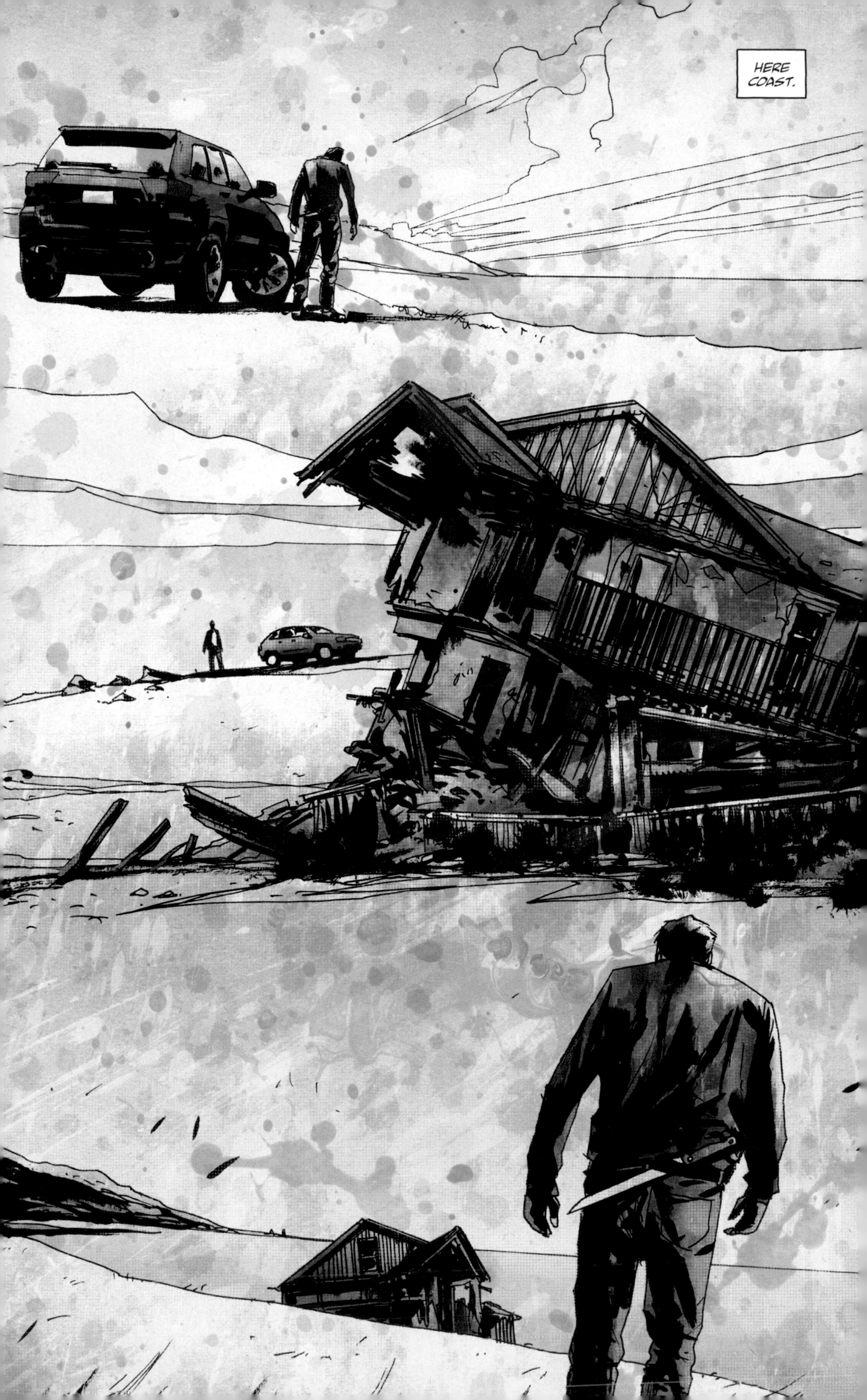
HERE
COAST.

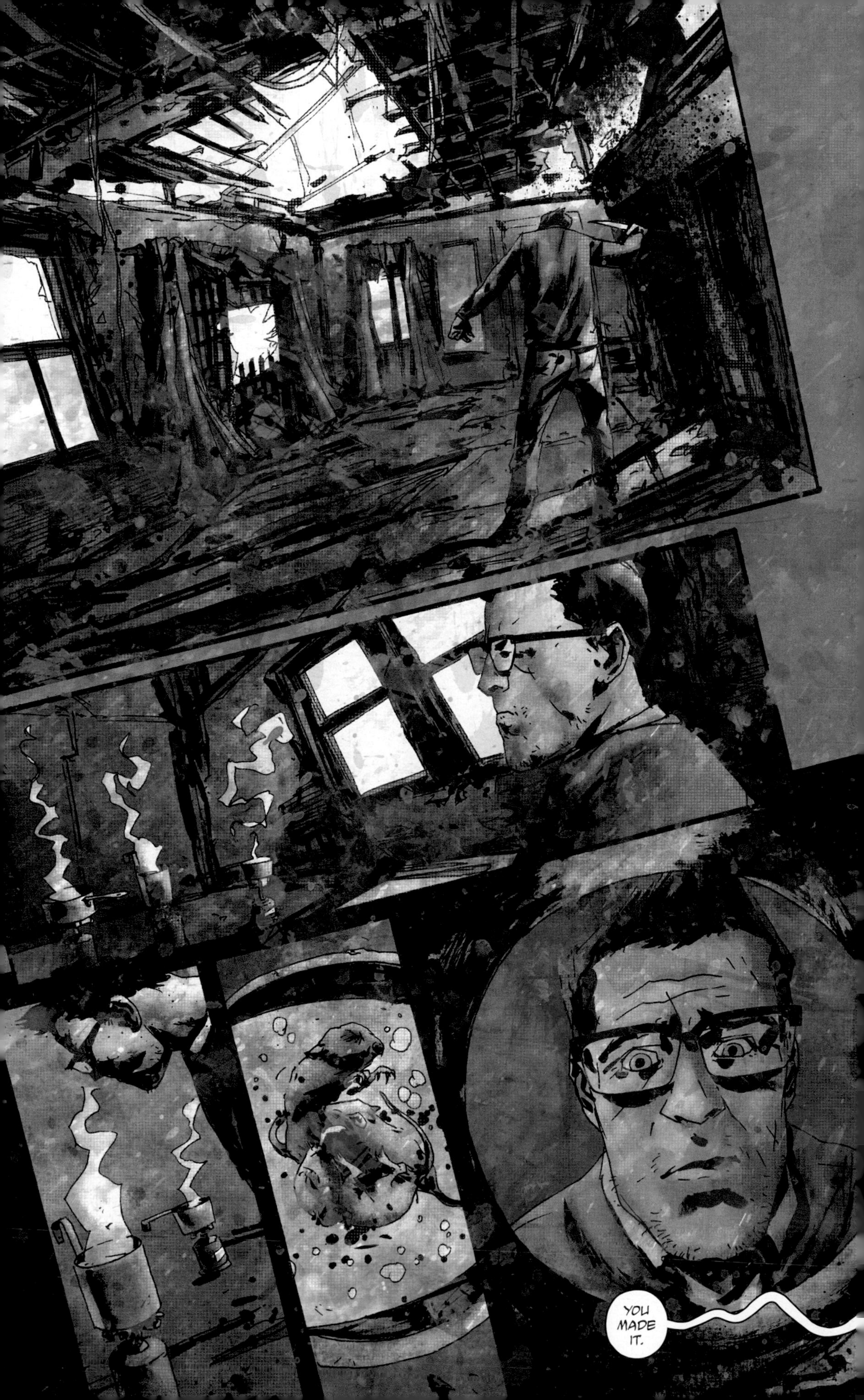
YOU MADE IT.

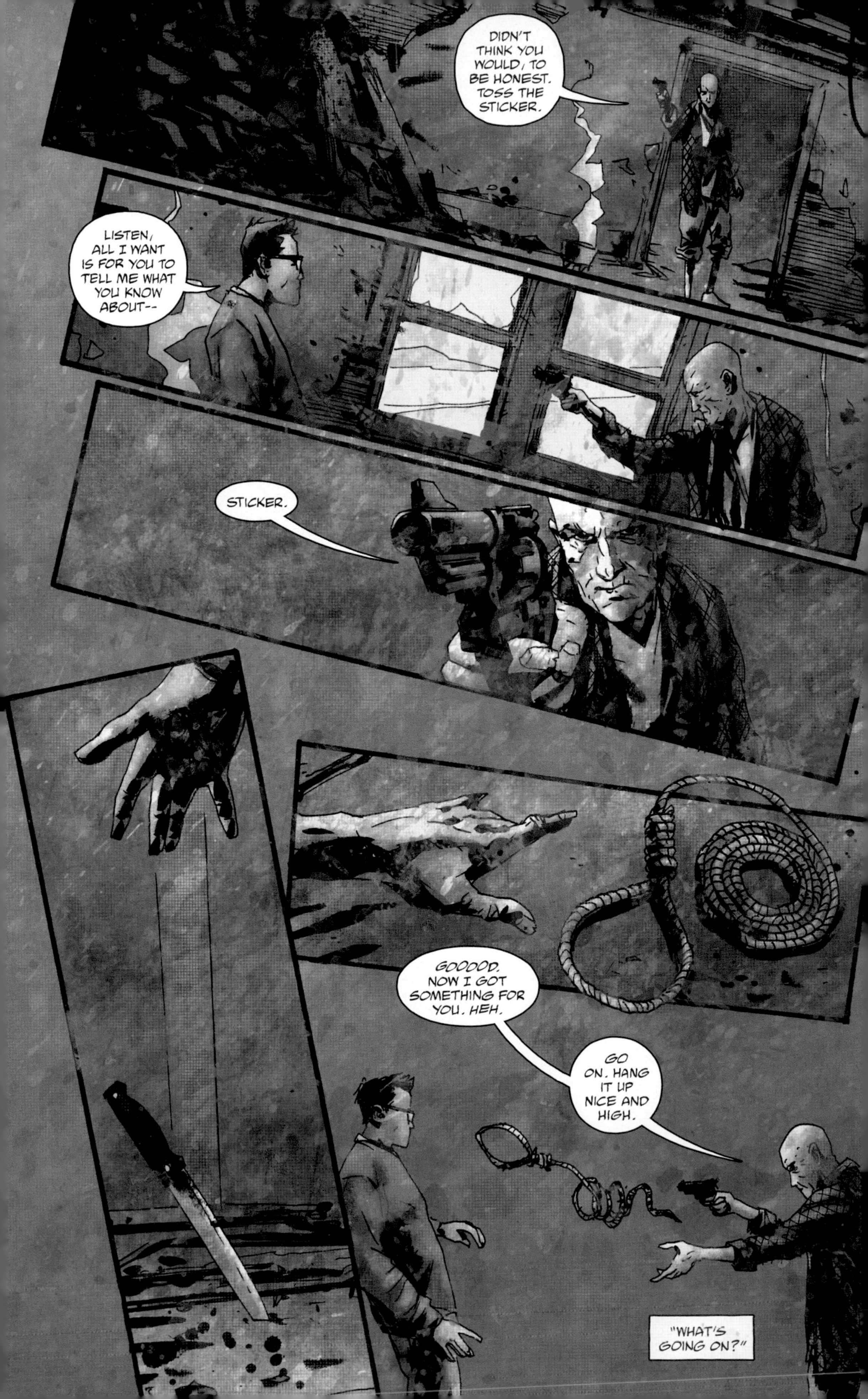
DIDN'T THINK YOU WOULD, TO BE HONEST. TOSS THE STICKER.
LISTEN, ALL I WANT IS FOR YOU TO TELL ME WHAT YOU KNOW ABOUT--
STICKER.
GOOOOD. NOW I GOT SOMETHING FOR YOU. HEH.
GO ON. HANG IT UP NICE AND HIGH.
"WHAT'S GOING ON?"

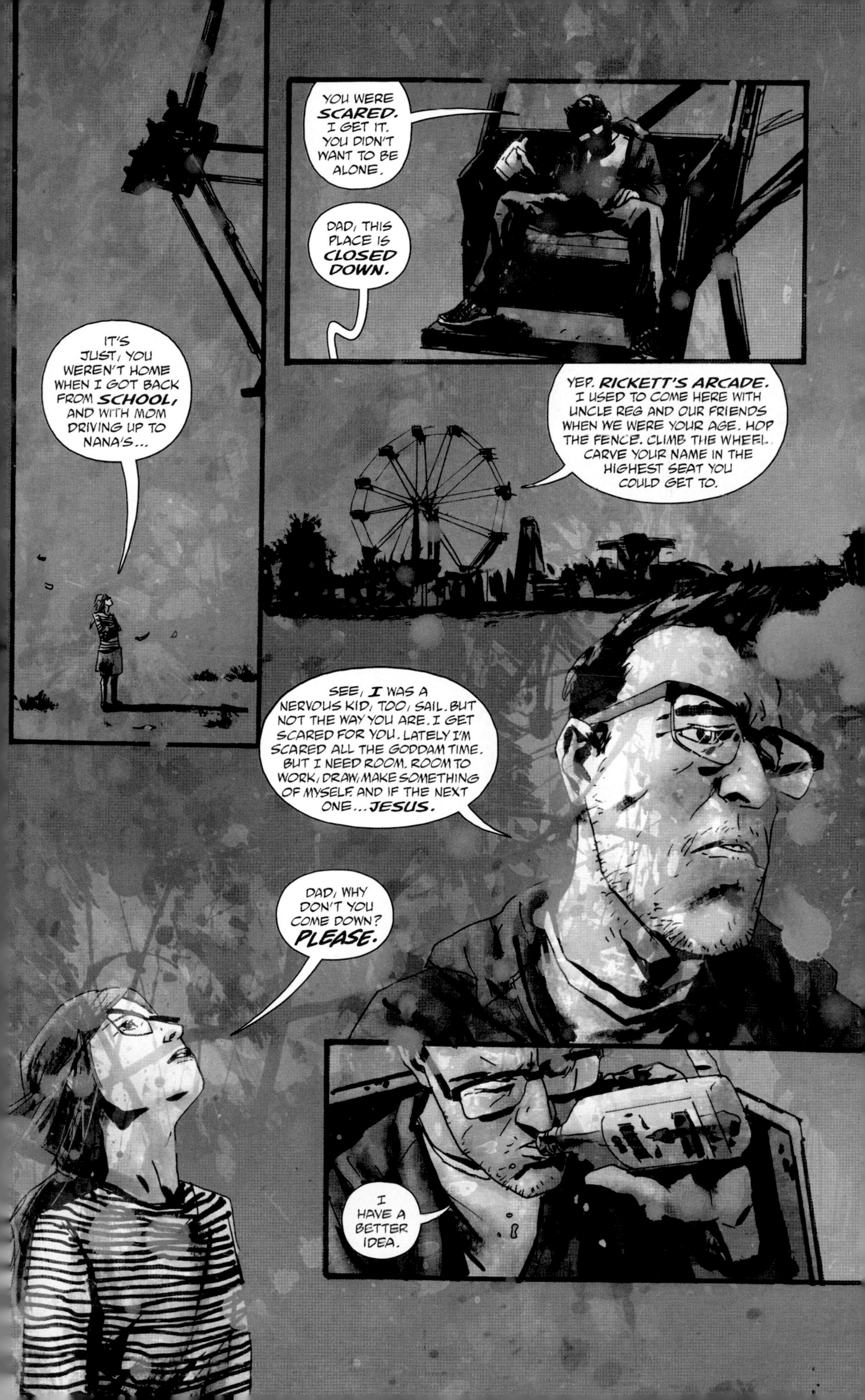
YOU WERE SCARED. I GET IT. YOU DIDN'T WANT TO BE ALONE.
DAD, THIS PLACE IS CLOSED DOWN.
IT'S JUST, YOU WEREN'T HOME WHEN I GOT BACK FROM SCHOOL, AND WITH MOM DRIVING UP TO NANA'S...
YEP. RICKETT'S ARCADE. I USED TO COME HERE WITH UNCLE REG AND OUR FRIENDS WHEN WE WERE YOUR AGE. HOP THE FENCE. CLIMB THE WHEEL. CARVE YOUR NAME IN THE HIGHEST SEAT YOU COULD GET TO.
SEE, I WAS A NERVOUS KID, TOO, SAIL. BUT NOT THE WAY YOU ARE. I GET SCARED FOR YOU. LATELY I'M SCARED ALL THE GODDAM TIME. BUT I NEED ROOM. ROOM TO WORK, DRAW, MAKE SOMETHING OF MYSELF. AND IF THE NEXT ONE... JESUS.
DAD, WHY DON'T YOU COME DOWN? PLEASE.
I HAVE A BETTER IDEA.

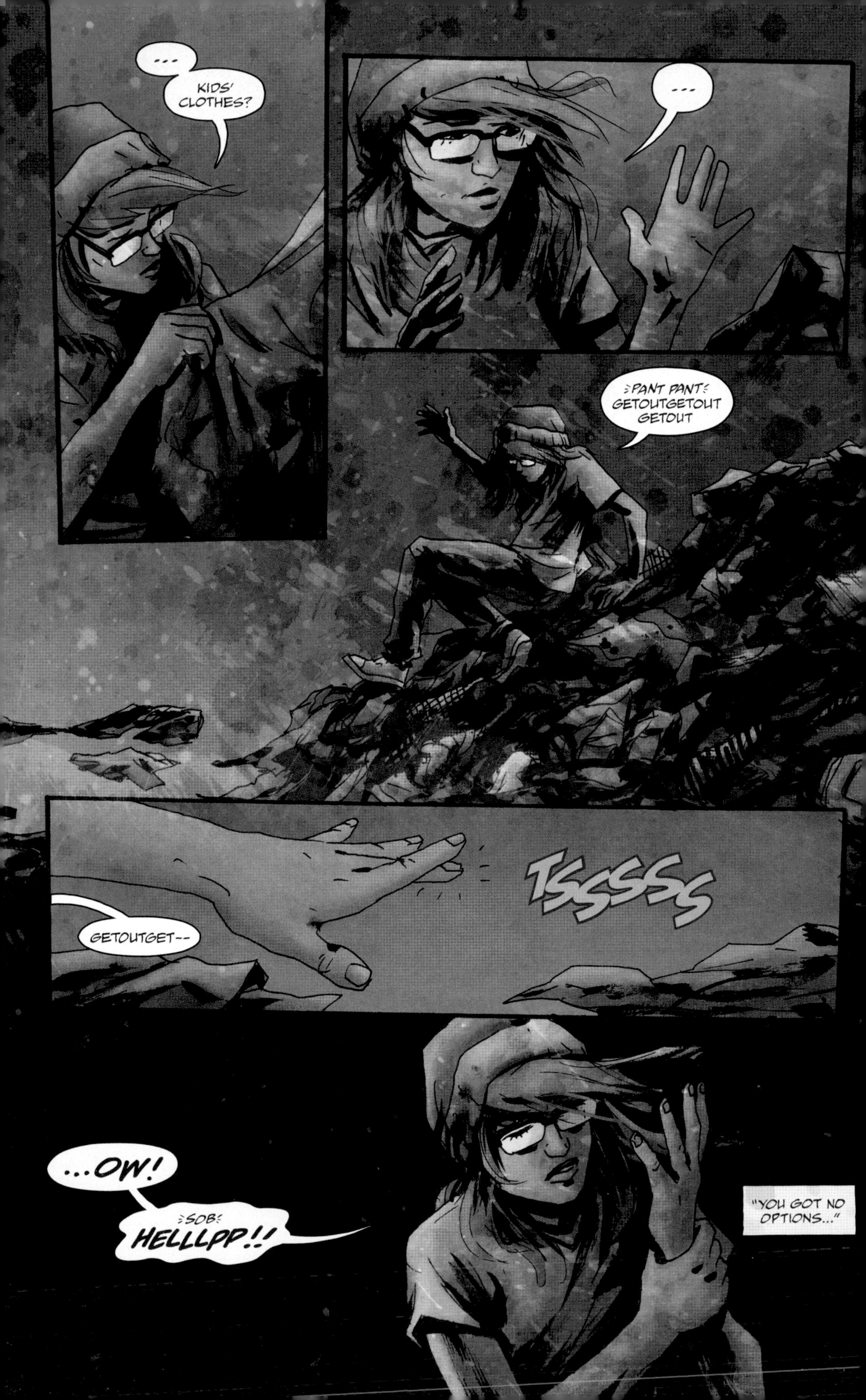
...
KIDS' CLOTHES?
...
PANT PANT
GETOUTGETOUT GETOUT
TSSSSS
GETOUTGET--
...OW!
SOB
HELLLPP!!
"YOU GOT NO OPTIONS..."

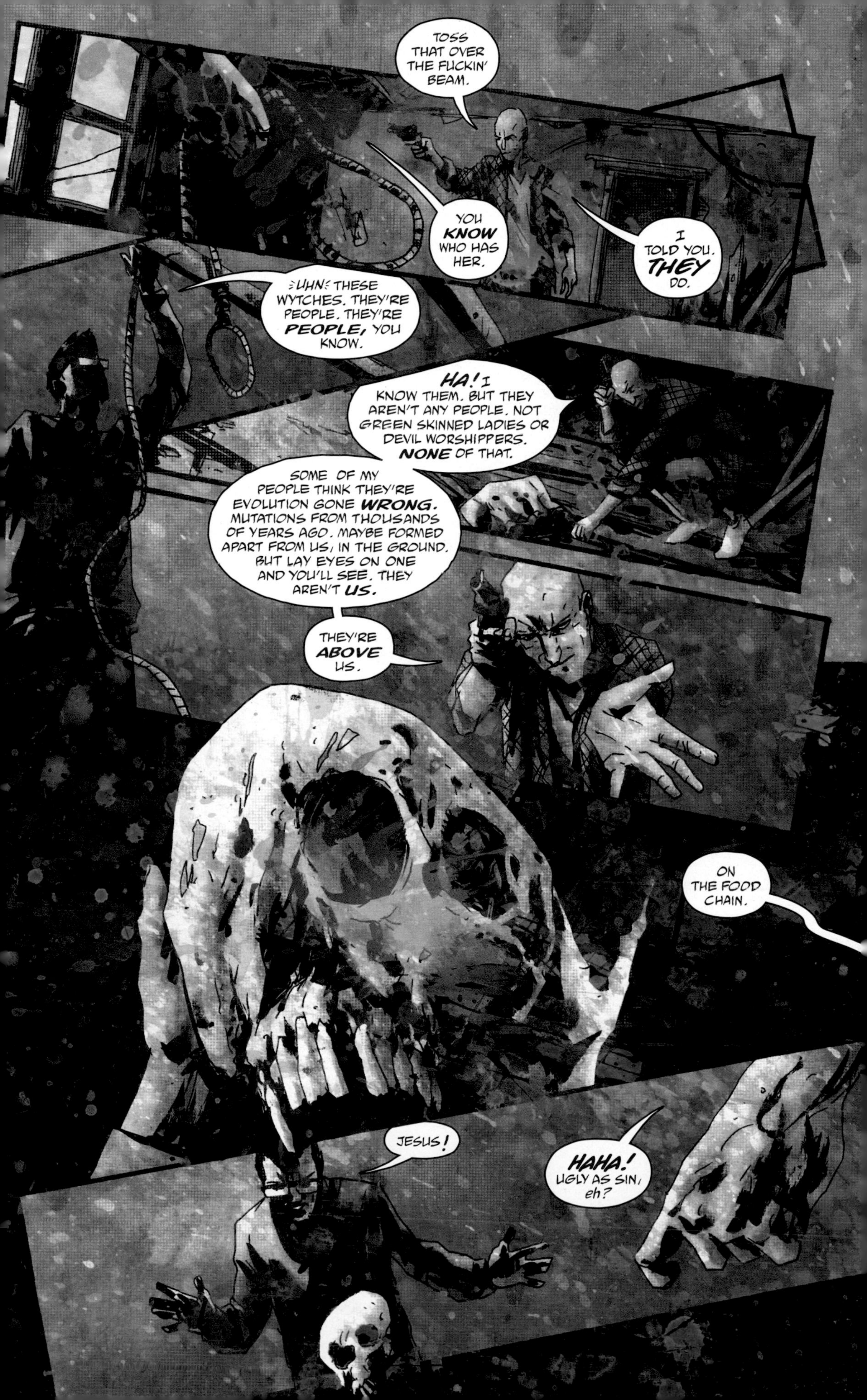
TOSS THAT OVER THE FUCKIN' BEAM.
YOU KNOW WHO HAS HER.
I TOLD YOU. THEY DO.
UHN THESE WYTCHES. THEY'RE PEOPLE. THEY'RE PEOPLE, YOU KNOW.
HA! I KNOW THEM. BUT THEY AREN'T ANY PEOPLE. NOT GREEN SKINNED LADIES OR DEVIL WORSHIPPERS. NONE OF THAT.
SOME OF MY PEOPLE THINK THEY'RE EVOLUTION GONE WRONG. MUTATIONS FROM THOUSANDS OF YEARS AGO. MAYBE FORMED APART FROM US, IN THE GROUND. BUT LAY EYES ON ONE AND YOU'LL SEE. THEY AREN'T US.
THEY'RE ABOVE US.
ON THE FOOD CHAIN.
JESUS!
HAHA! UGLY AS SIN, eh?

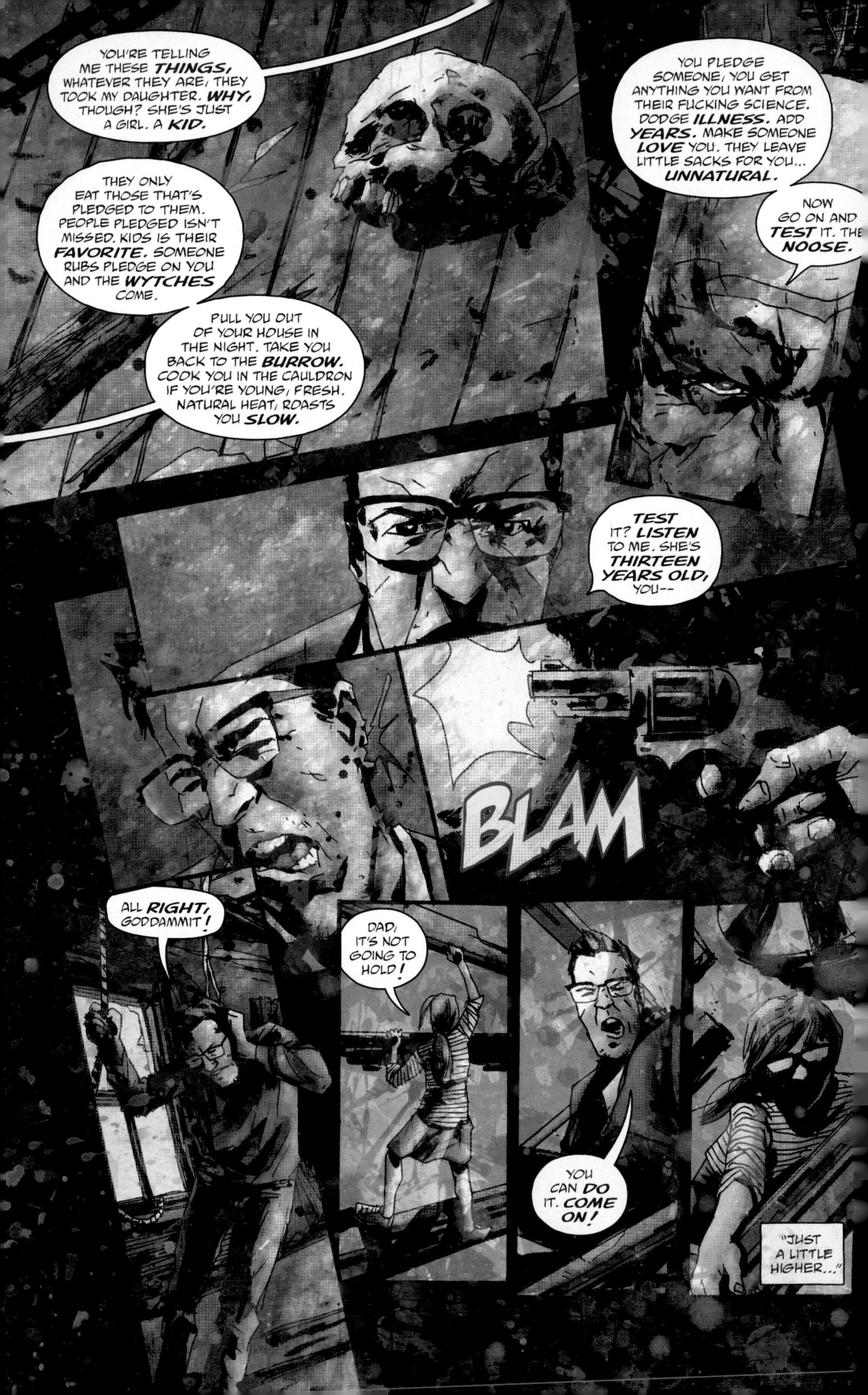
YOU'RE TELLING ME THESE THINGS, WHATEVER THEY ARE, THEY TOOK MY DAUGHTER. WHY, THOUGH? SHE'S JUST A GIRL. A KID.
THEY ONLY EAT THOSE THAT'S PLEDGED TO THEM. PEOPLE PLEDGED ISN'T MISSED. KIDS IS THEIR FAVORITE. SOMEONE RUBS PLEDGE ON YOU AND THE WYTCHES COME.
PULL YOU OUT OF YOUR HOUSE IN THE NIGHT. TAKE YOU BACK TO THE BURROW. COOK YOU IN THE CAULDRON IF YOU'RE YOUNG, FRESH. NATURAL HEAT, ROASTS YOU SLOW.
YOU PLEDGE SOMEONE, YOU GET ANYTHING YOU WANT FROM THEIR FUCKING SCIENCE. DODGE ILLNESS. ADD YEARS. MAKE SOMEONE LOVE YOU. THEY LEAVE LITTLE SACKS FOR YOU... UNNATURAL.
NOW GO ON AND TEST IT. THE NOOSE.
TEST IT? LISTEN TO ME. SHE'S THIRTEEN YEARS OLD, YOU--
BLAM
ALL RIGHT, GODDAMMIT!
DAD, IT'S NOT GOING TO HOLD!
YOU CAN DO IT. COME ON!
"JUST A LITTLE HIGHER..."

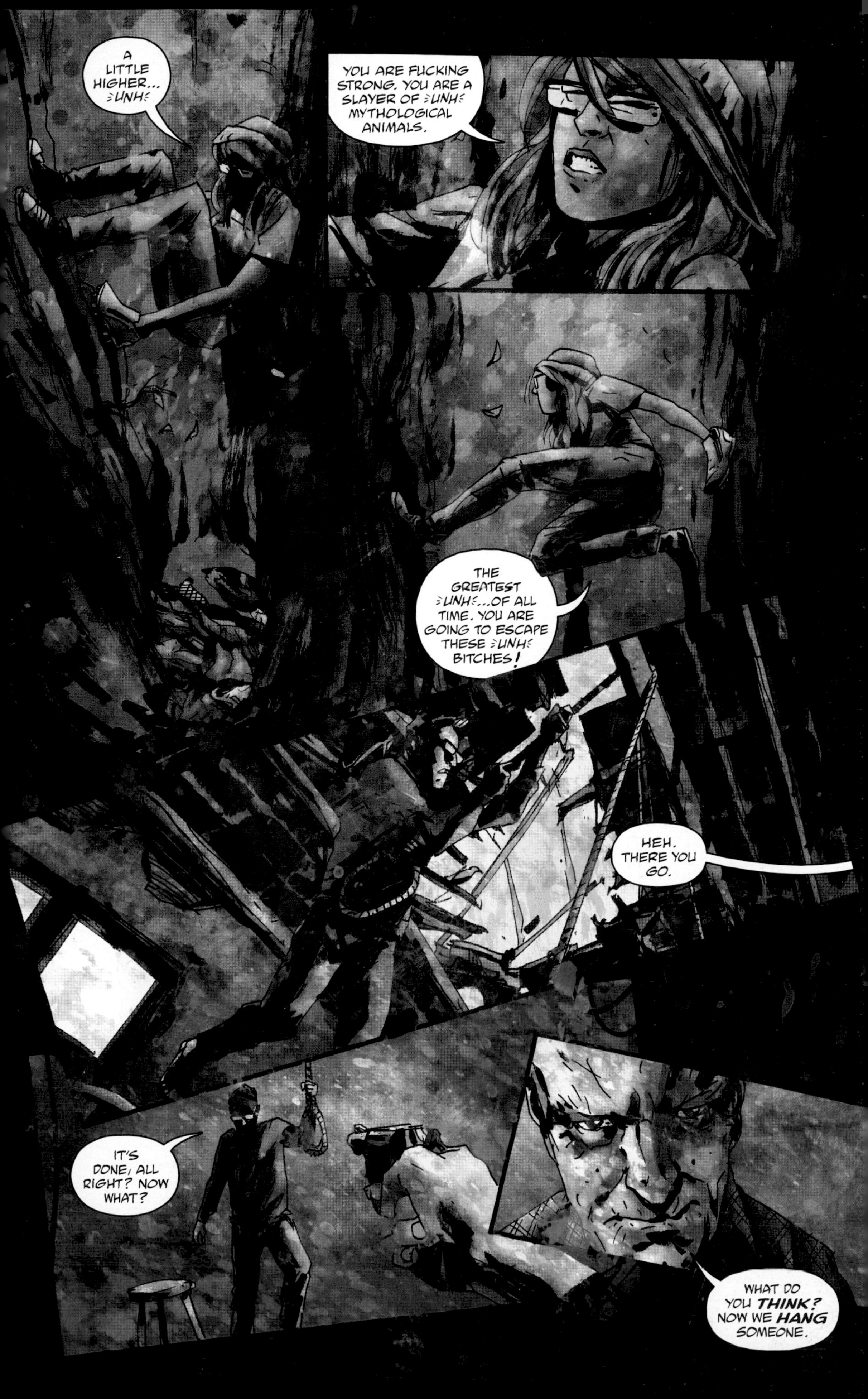
A LITTLE HIGHER... ⪢UNH⪡
YOU ARE FUCKING STRONG. YOU ARE A SLAYER OF ⪢UNH⪡ MYTHOLOGICAL ANIMALS.
THE GREATEST ⪢UNH⪡...OF ALL TIME. YOU ARE GOING TO ESCAPE THESE ⪢UNH⪡ BITCHES!
HEH. THERE YOU GO.
IT'S DONE, ALL RIGHT? NOW WHAT?
WHAT DO YOU THINK? NOW WE HANG SOMEONE.

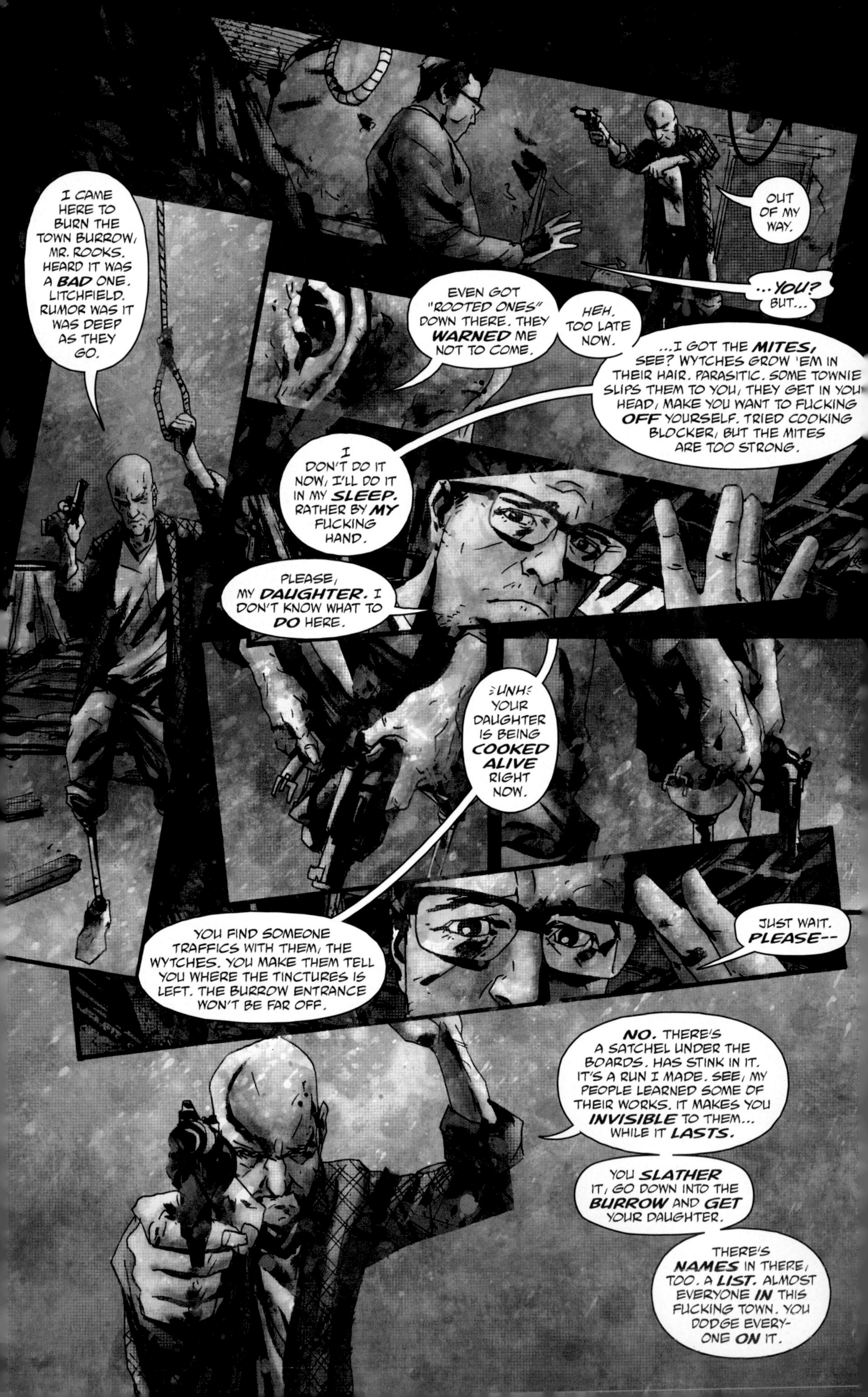
OUT OF MY WAY.
...YOU? BUT...
I CAME HERE TO BURN THE TOWN BURROW, MR. ROOKS. HEARD IT WAS A BAD ONE. LITCHFIELD. RUMOR WAS IT WAS DEEP AS THEY GO.
EVEN GOT "ROOTED ONES" DOWN THERE. THEY WARNED ME NOT TO COME.
HEH. TOO LATE NOW.
...I GOT THE MITES, SEE? WYTCHES GROW 'EM IN THEIR HAIR. PARASITIC. SOME TOWNIE SLIPS THEM TO YOU, THEY GET IN YOU HEAD, MAKE YOU WANT TO FUCKING OFF YOURSELF. TRIED COOKING BLOCKER, BUT THE MITES ARE TOO STRONG.
I DON'T DO IT NOW, I'LL DO IT IN MY SLEEP. RATHER BY MY FUCKING HAND.
PLEASE, MY DAUGHTER. I DON'T KNOW WHAT TO DO HERE.
UNH YOUR DAUGHTER IS BEING COOKED ALIVE RIGHT NOW.
YOU FIND SOMEONE TRAFFICS WITH THEM, THE WYTCHES. YOU MAKE THEM TELL YOU WHERE THE TINCTURES IS LEFT. THE BURROW ENTRANCE WON'T BE FAR OFF.
JUST WAIT. PLEASE--
NO. THERE'S A SATCHEL UNDER THE BOARDS. HAS STINK IN IT. IT'S A RUN I MADE. SEE, MY PEOPLE LEARNED SOME OF THEIR WORKS. IT MAKES YOU INVISIBLE TO THEM... WHILE IT LASTS.
YOU SLATHER IT, GO DOWN INTO THE BURROW AND GET YOUR DAUGHTER.
THERE'S NAMES IN THERE, TOO. A LIST. ALMOST EVERYONE IN THIS FUCKING TOWN. YOU DODGE EVERY-ONE ON IT.

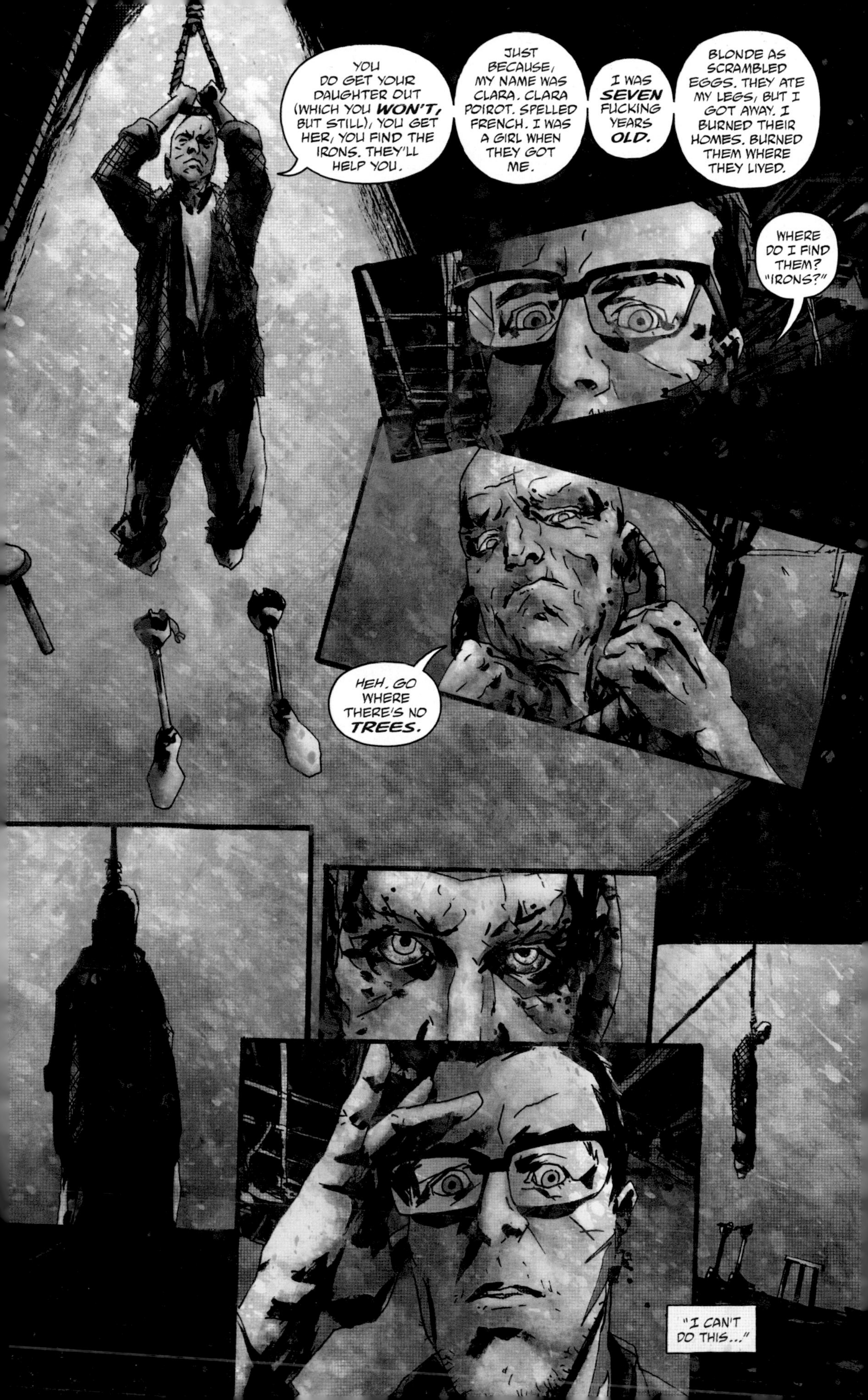
YOU DO GET YOUR DAUGHTER OUT (WHICH YOU **WON'T,** BUT STILL), YOU GET HER, YOU FIND THE IRONS. THEY'LL HELP YOU.
JUST BECAUSE, MY NAME WAS CLARA. CLARA POIROT. SPELLED FRENCH. I WAS A GIRL WHEN THEY GOT ME.
I WAS **SEVEN** FUCKING YEARS **OLD.**
BLONDE AS SCRAMBLED EGGS. THEY ATE MY LEGS, BUT I GOT AWAY. I BURNED THEIR HOMES. BURNED THEM WHERE THEY LIVED.
WHERE DO I FIND THEM? "IRONS?"
HEH. GO WHERE THERE'S NO **TREES.**
"I CAN'T DO THIS..."

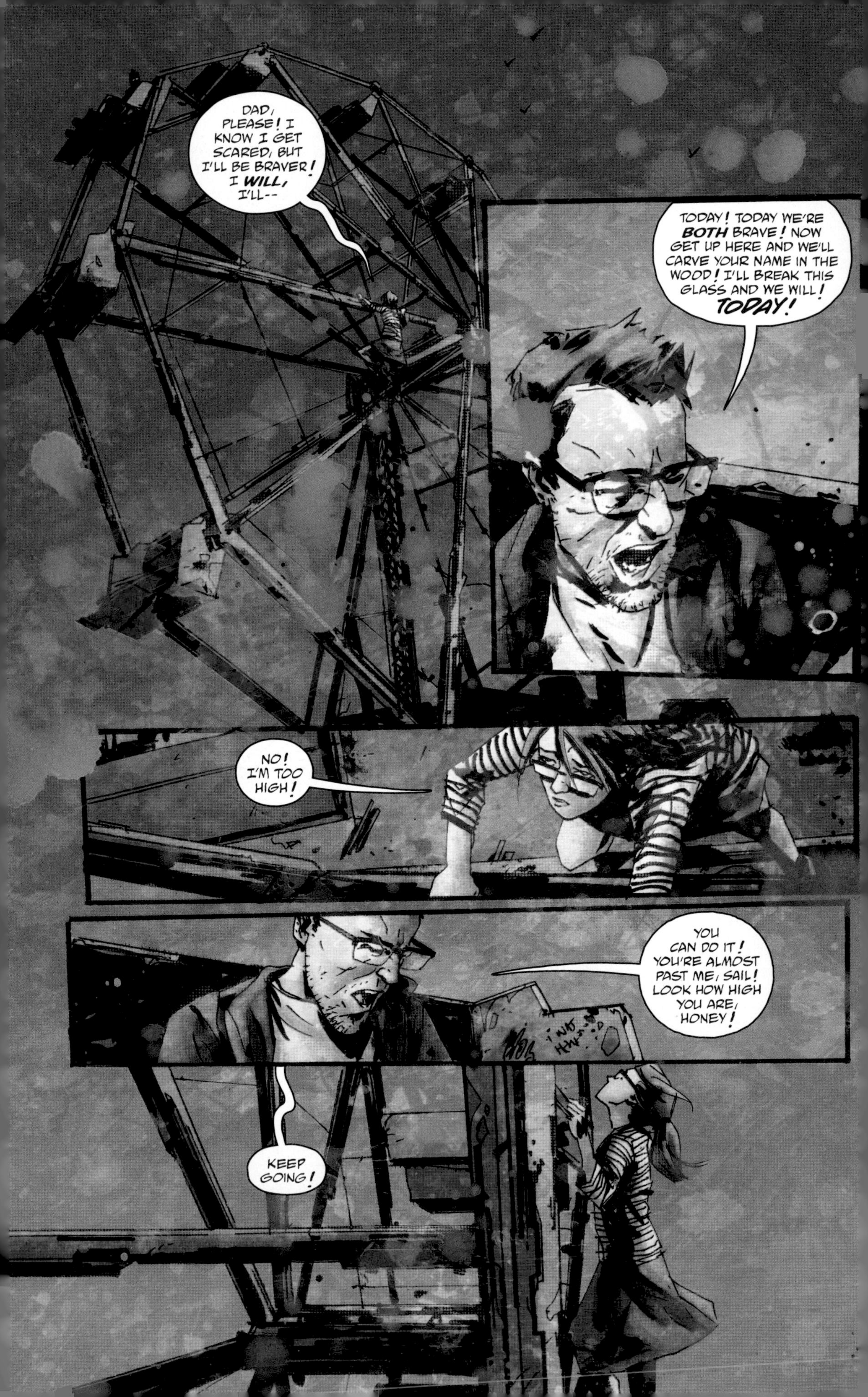
DAD, PLEASE! I KNOW I GET SCARED, BUT I'LL BE BRAVER! I WILL, I'LL--
TODAY! TODAY WE'RE BOTH BRAVE! NOW GET UP HERE AND WE'LL CARVE YOUR NAME IN THE WOOD! I'LL BREAK THIS GLASS AND WE WILL! TODAY!
NO! I'M TOO HIGH!
YOU CAN DO IT! YOU'RE ALMOST PAST ME, SAIL! LOOK HOW HIGH YOU ARE, HONEY!
KEEP GOING!

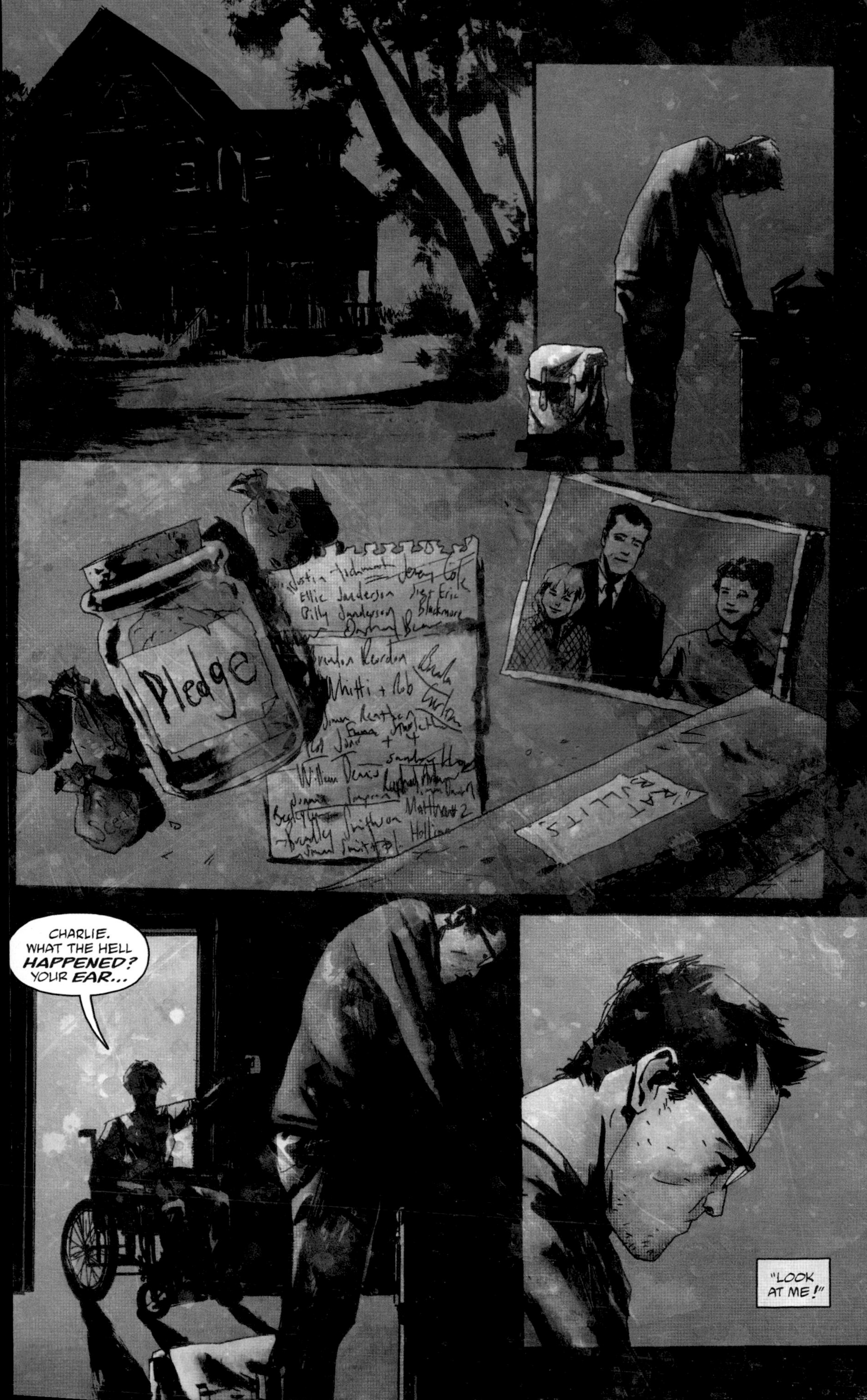
Pledge
CHARLIE. WHAT THE HELL *HAPPENED?* YOUR *EAR...*
"LOOK AT ME!"

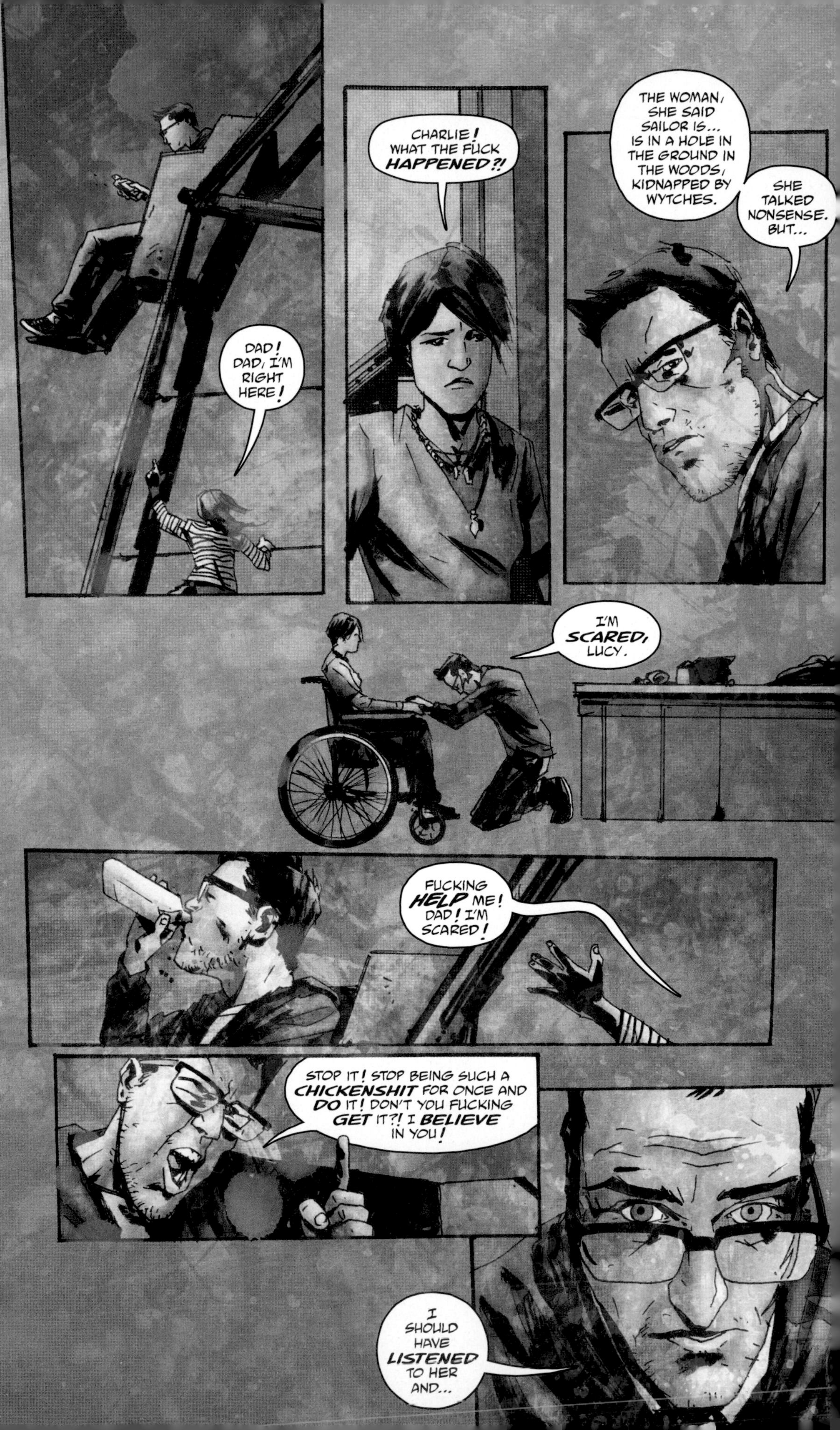
DAD! DAD, I'M RIGHT HERE!
CHARLIE! WHAT THE FUCK HAPPENED?!
THE WOMAN, SHE SAID SAILOR IS... IS IN A HOLE IN THE GROUND IN THE WOODS, KIDNAPPED BY WYTCHES.
SHE TALKED NONSENSE. BUT...
I'M SCARED, LUCY.
FUCKING HELP ME! DAD! I'M SCARED!
STOP IT! STOP BEING SUCH A CHICKENSHIT FOR ONCE AND DO IT! DON'T YOU FUCKING GET IT?! I BELIEVE IN YOU!
I SHOULD HAVE LISTENED TO HER AND...

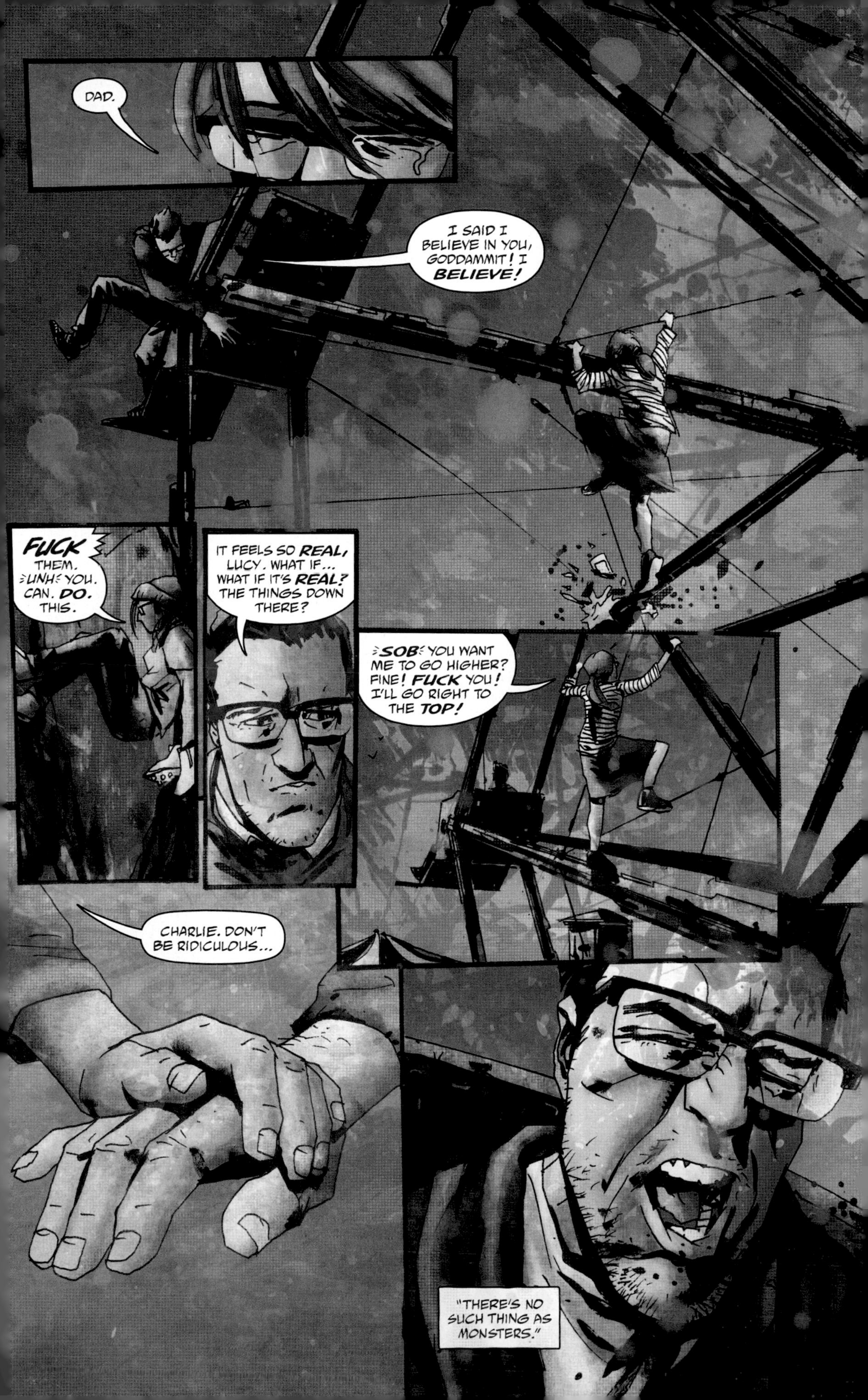
DAD.
I SAID I BELIEVE IN YOU, GODDAMMIT! I BELIEVE!
FUCK THEM. UNH YOU. CAN. DO. THIS.
IT FEELS SO REAL, LUCY. WHAT IF... WHAT IF IT'S REAL? THE THINGS DOWN THERE?
SOB YOU WANT ME TO GO HIGHER? FINE! FUCK YOU! I'LL GO RIGHT TO THE TOP!
CHARLIE. DON'T BE RIDICULOUS...
"THERE'S NO SUCH THING AS MONSTERS."

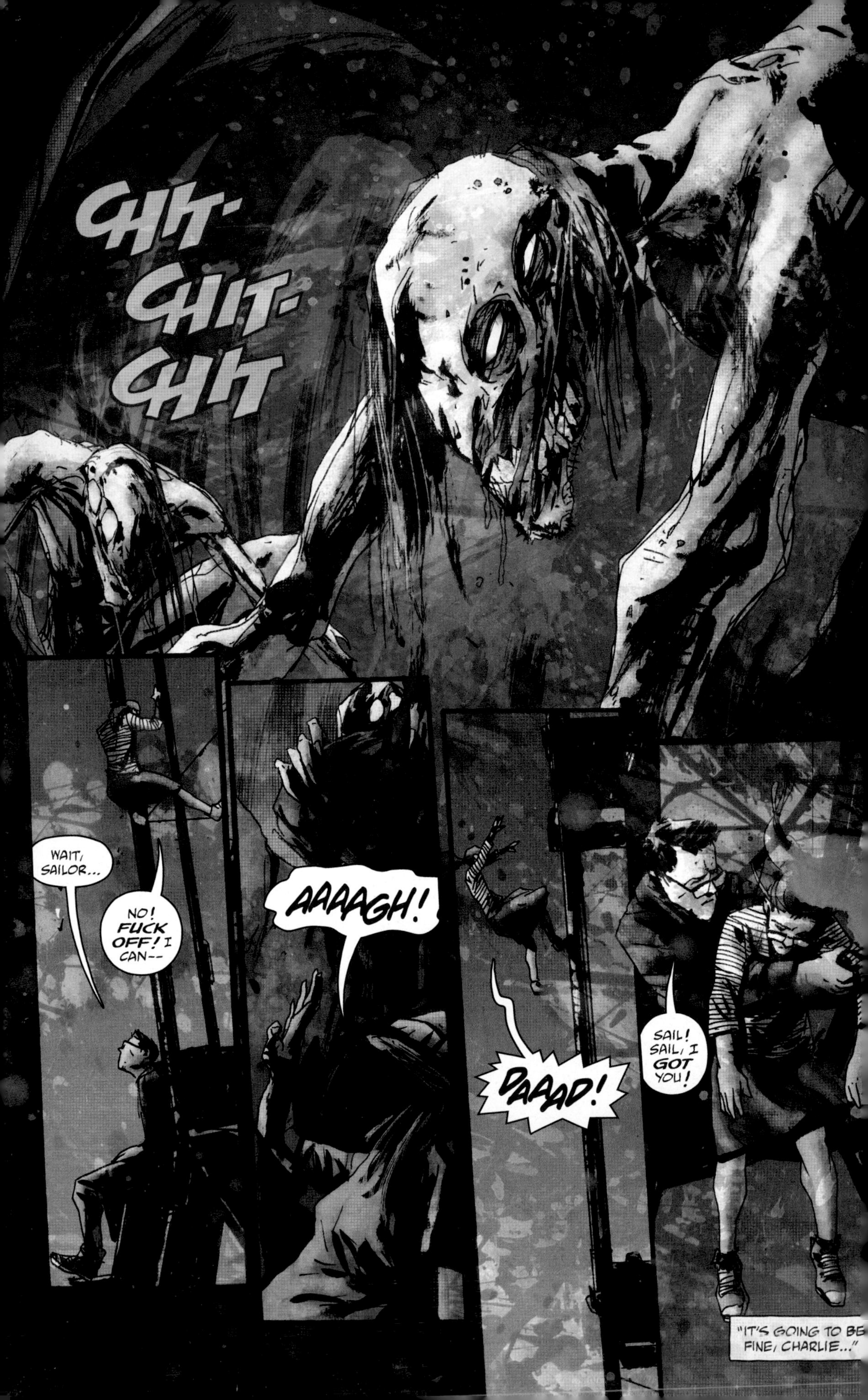
CHIT-CHIT-CHIT
WAIT, SAILOR...
NO! FUCK OFF! I CAN--
AAAAGH!
DAAAAD!
SAIL! SAIL, I GOT YOU!
"IT'S GOING TO BE FINE, CHARLIE..."

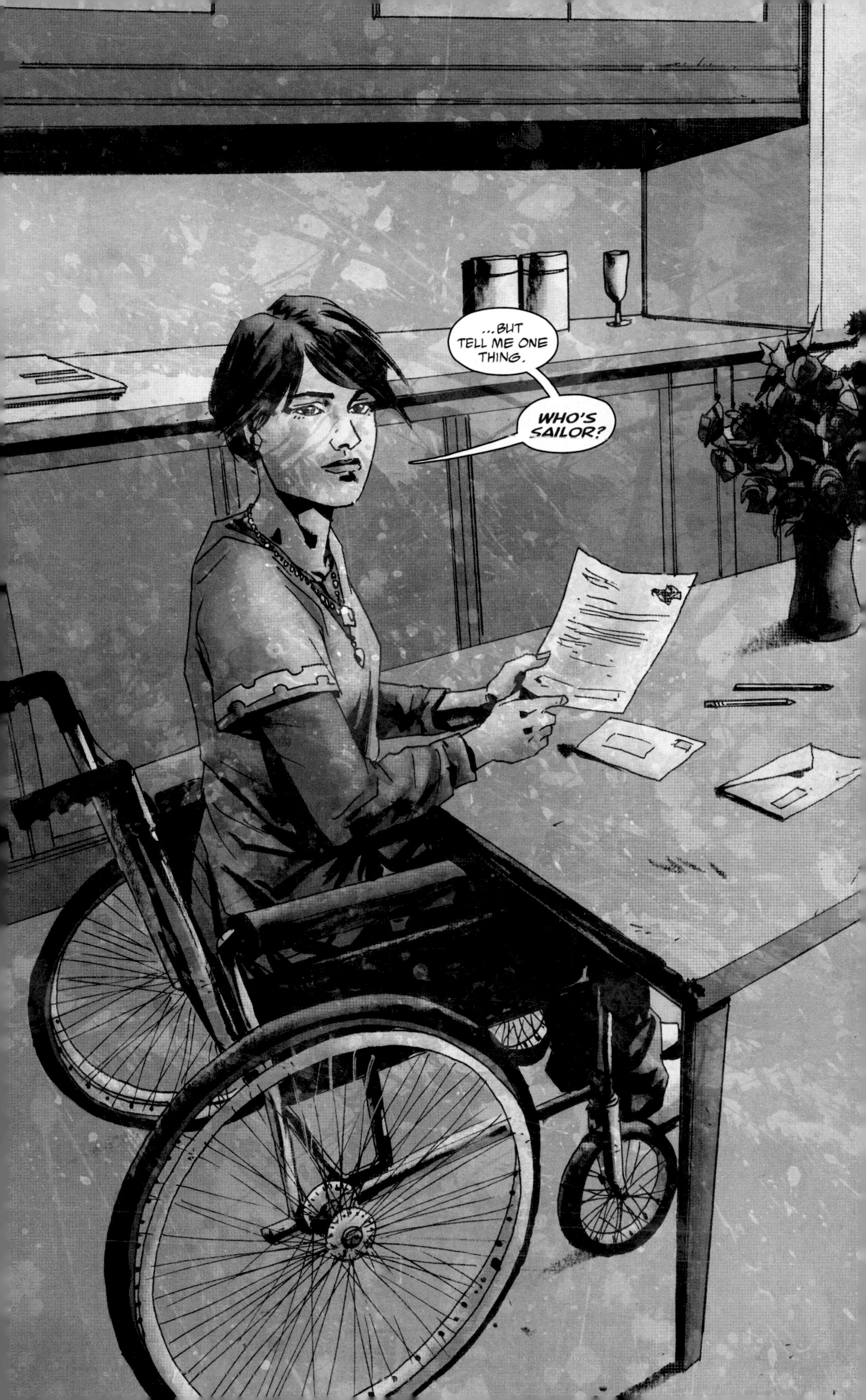
...BUT TELL ME ONE THING.
WHO'S SAILOR?

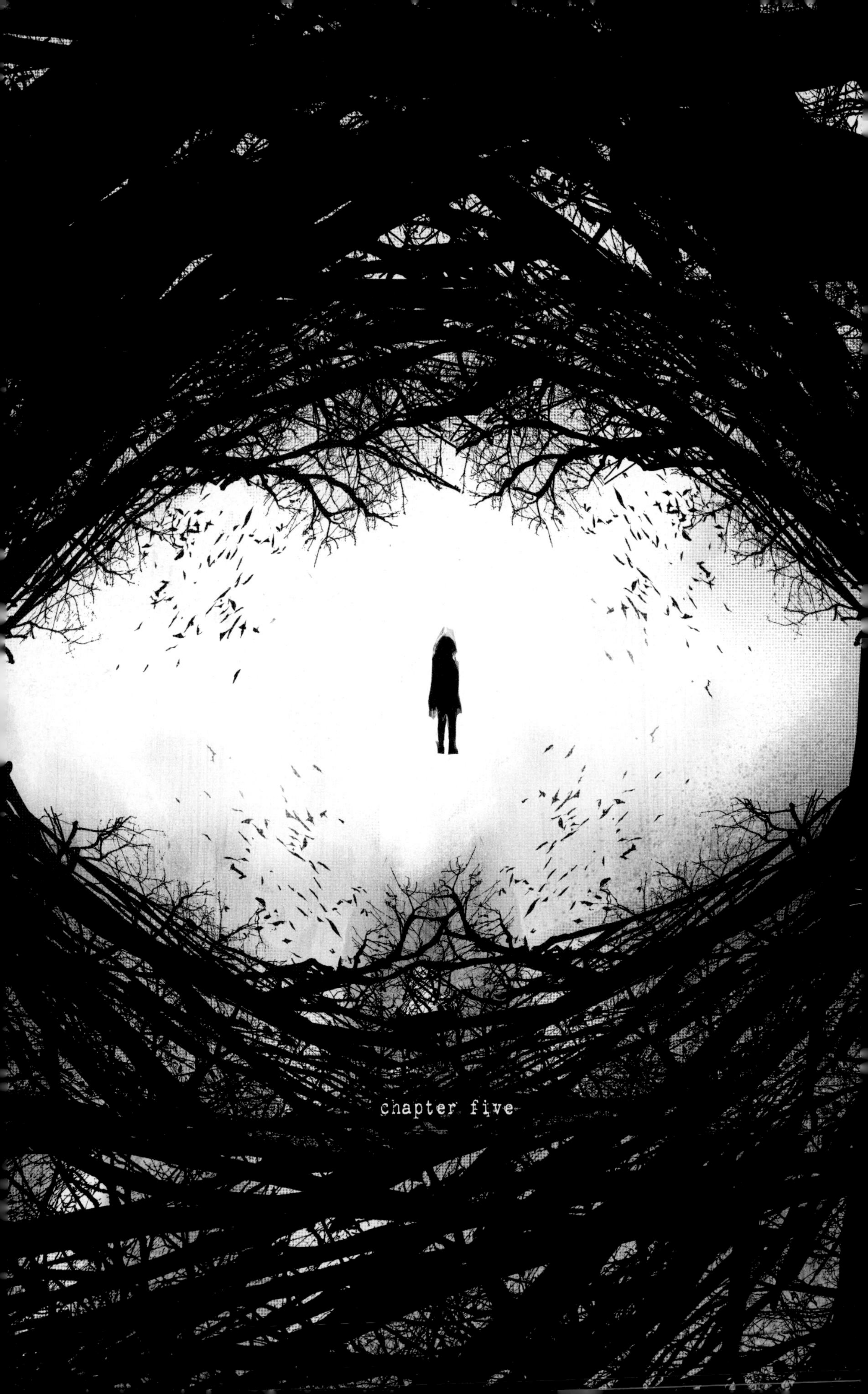
chapter five

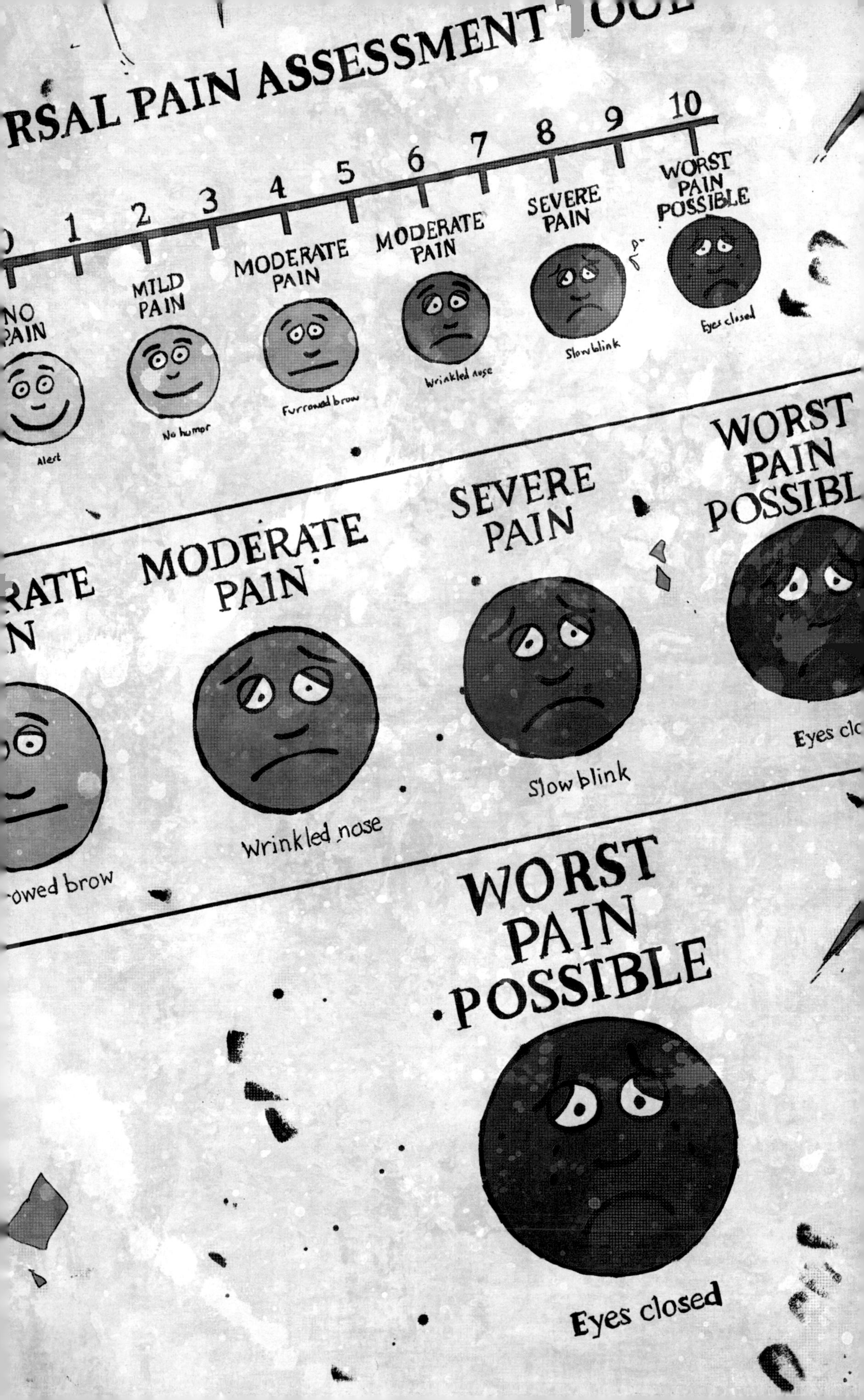

RSAL PAIN ASSESSMENT
1 2 3 4 5 6 7 8 9 10
NO PAIN
MILD PAIN
MODERATE PAIN
MODERATE PAIN
SEVERE PAIN
WORST PAIN POSSIBLE
Alert
No humor
Furrowed brow
Wrinkled nose
Slow blink
Eyes closed
RATE
MODERATE PAIN
SEVERE PAIN
WORST PAIN
owed brow
Wrinkled nose
Slow blink
WORST PAIN POSSIBLE
Eyes closed

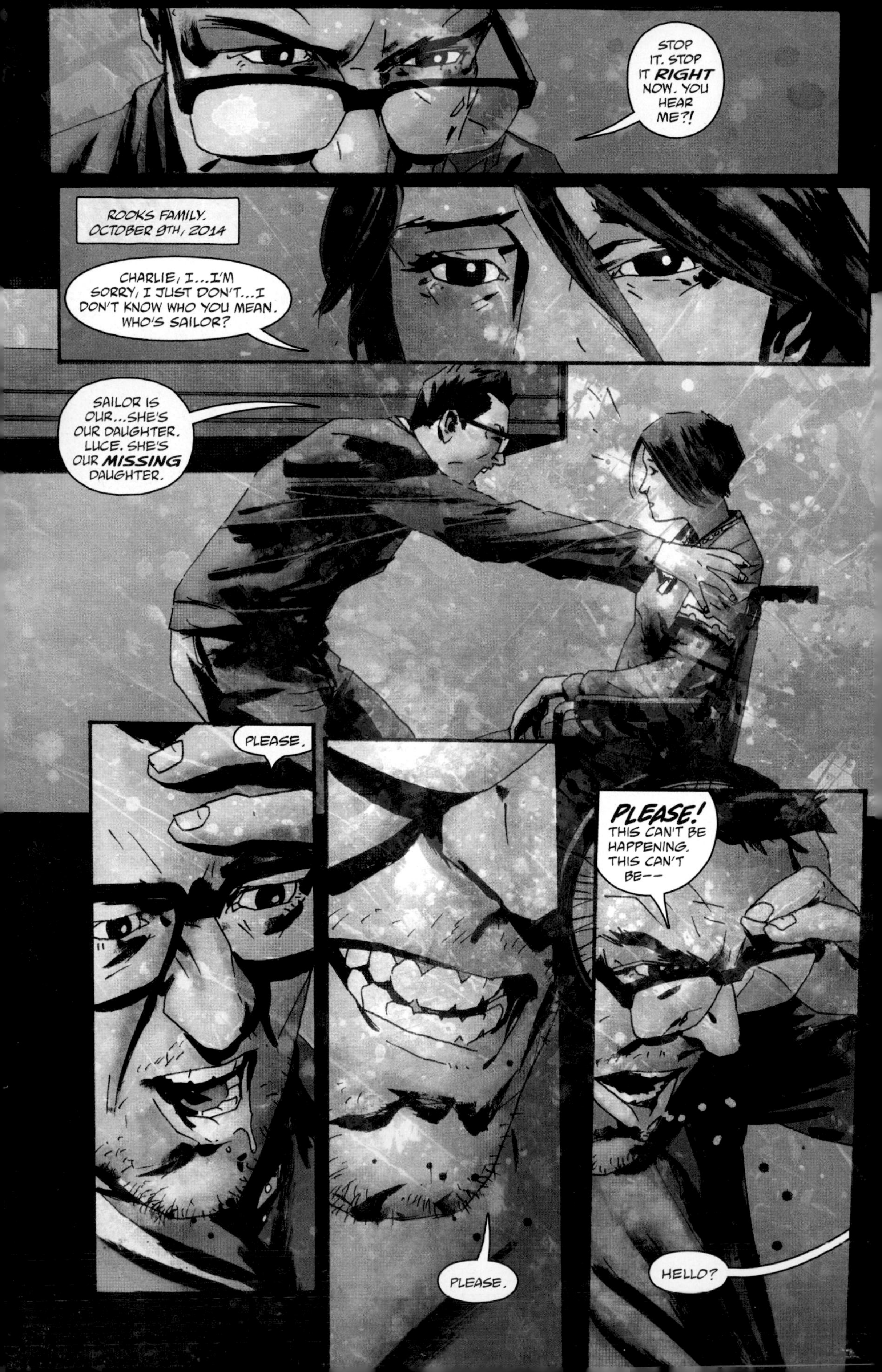

STOP IT. STOP IT **RIGHT** NOW. YOU HEAR ME?!
ROOKS FAMILY. OCTOBER 9TH, 2014
CHARLIE, I...I'M SORRY, I JUST DON'T...I DON'T KNOW WHO YOU MEAN. WHO'S SAILOR?
SAILOR IS OUR...SHE'S OUR DAUGHTER. LUCE. SHE'S OUR **MISSING** DAUGHTER.
PLEASE.
PLEASE! THIS CAN'T BE HAPPENING. THIS CAN'T BE--
PLEASE.
HELLO?

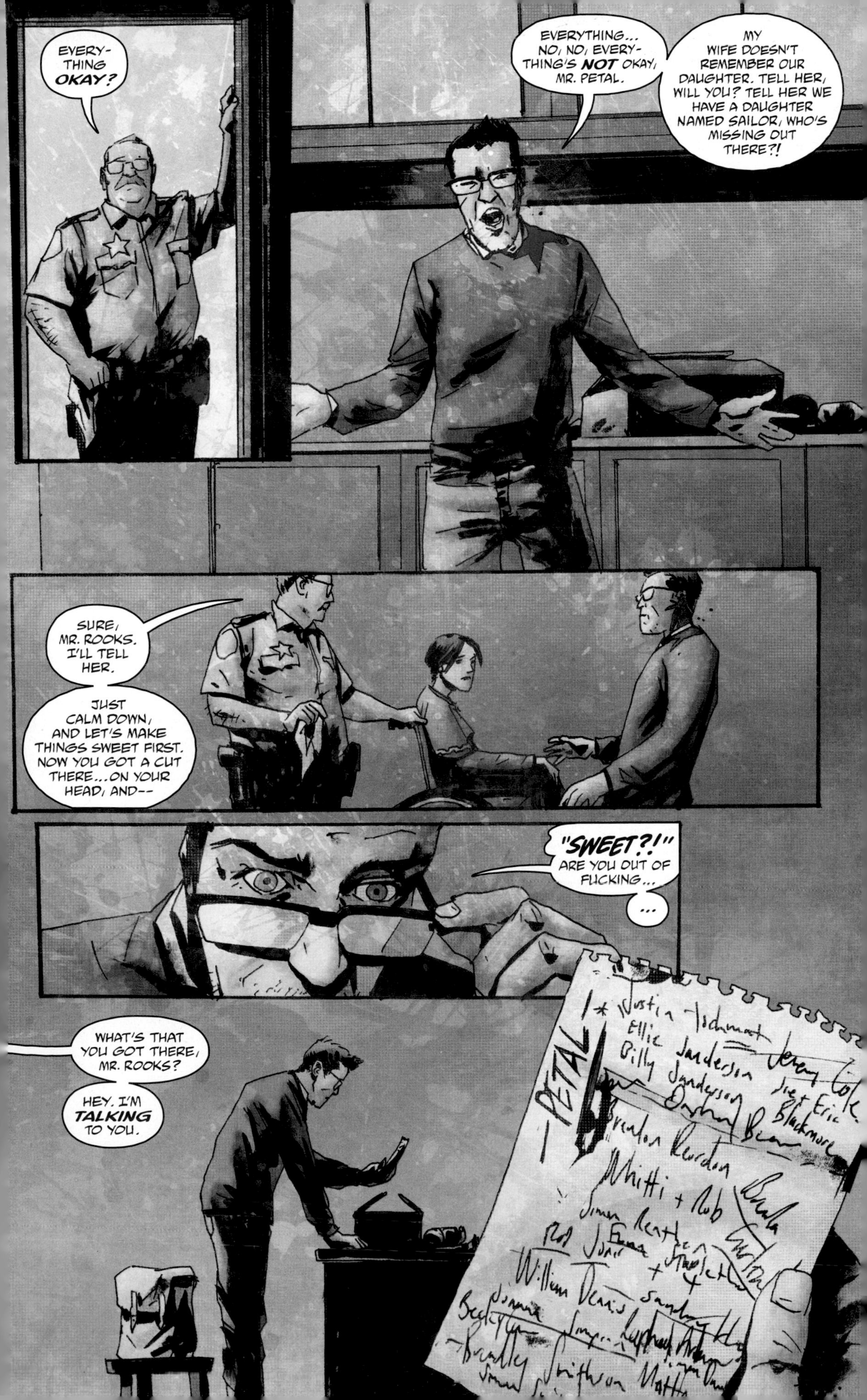
EVERY-THING OKAY?
EVERYTHING... NO, NO, EVERY-THING'S NOT OKAY, MR. PETAL.
MY WIFE DOESN'T REMEMBER OUR DAUGHTER. TELL HER, WILL YOU? TELL HER WE HAVE A DAUGHTER NAMED SAILOR, WHO'S MISSING OUT THERE?!
SURE, MR. ROOKS. I'LL TELL HER.
JUST CALM DOWN, AND LET'S MAKE THINGS SWEET FIRST. NOW YOU GOT A CUT THERE...ON YOUR HEAD, AND--
"SWEET?!" ARE YOU OUT OF FUCKING...
...
WHAT'S THAT YOU GOT THERE, MR. ROOKS?
HEY. I'M TALKING TO YOU.

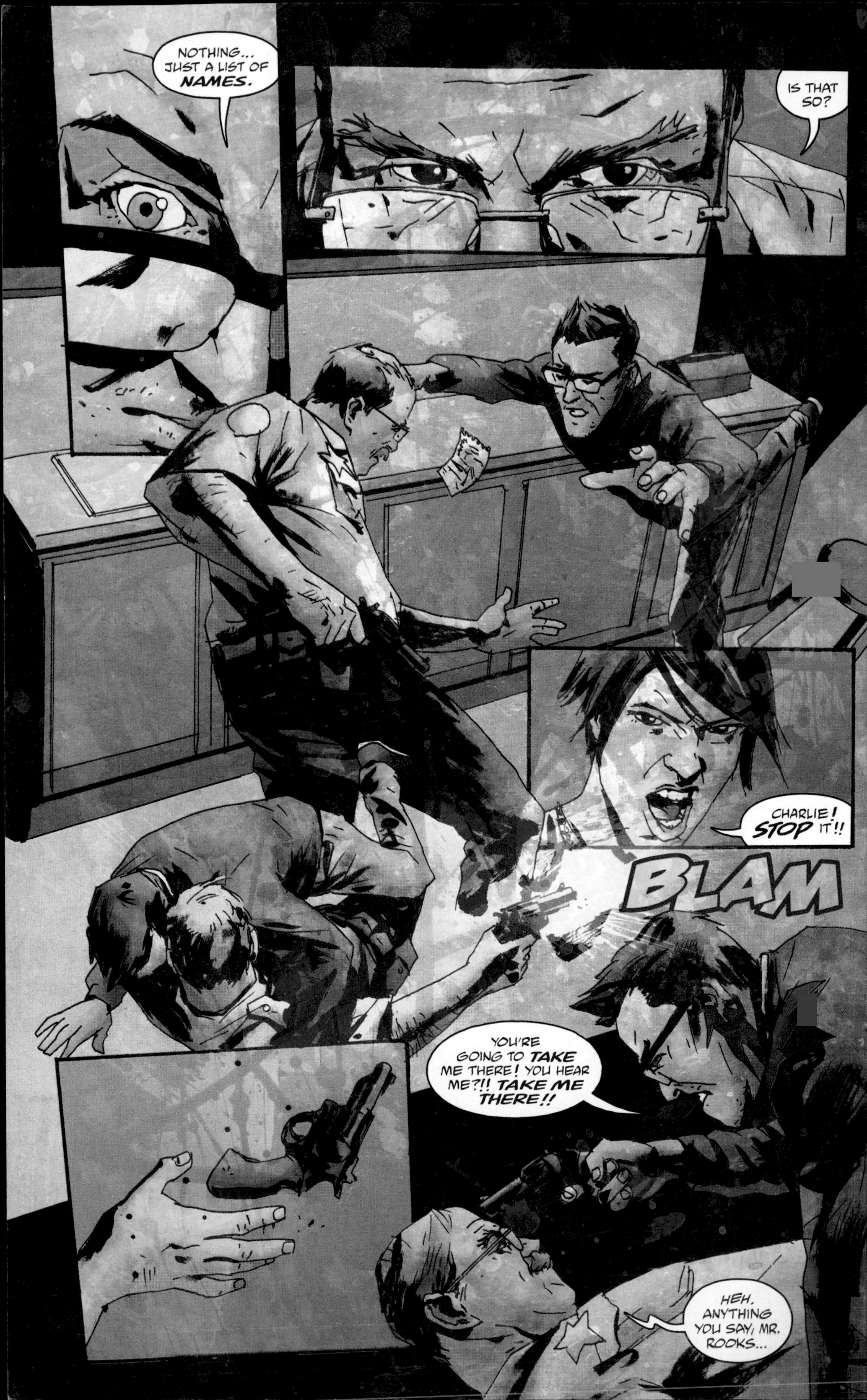
NOTHING... JUST A LIST OF NAMES.
IS THAT SO?
CHARLIE! STOP IT!!
BLAM
YOU'RE GOING TO TAKE ME THERE! YOU HEAR ME?!! TAKE ME THERE!!
HEH. ANYTHING YOU SAY, MR. ROOKS...

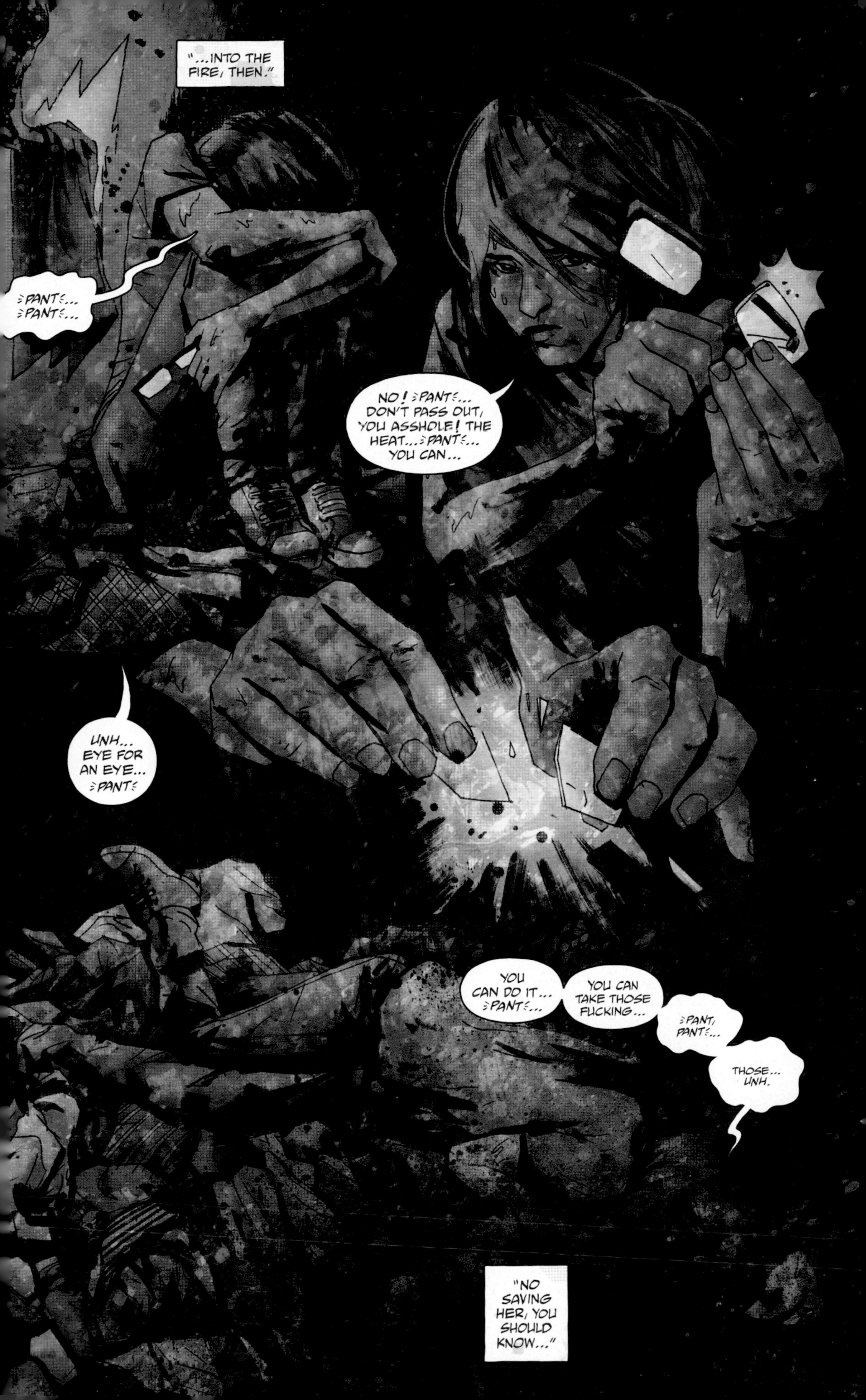
"...INTO THE FIRE, THEN."
PANT... PANT...
NO! PANT... DON'T PASS OUT, YOU ASSHOLE! THE HEAT... PANT... YOU CAN...
UNH... EYE FOR AN EYE... PANT
YOU CAN DO IT... PANT...
YOU CAN TAKE THOSE FUCKING...
PANT, PANT...
THOSE... UNH.
"NO SAVING HER, YOU SHOULD KNOW..."

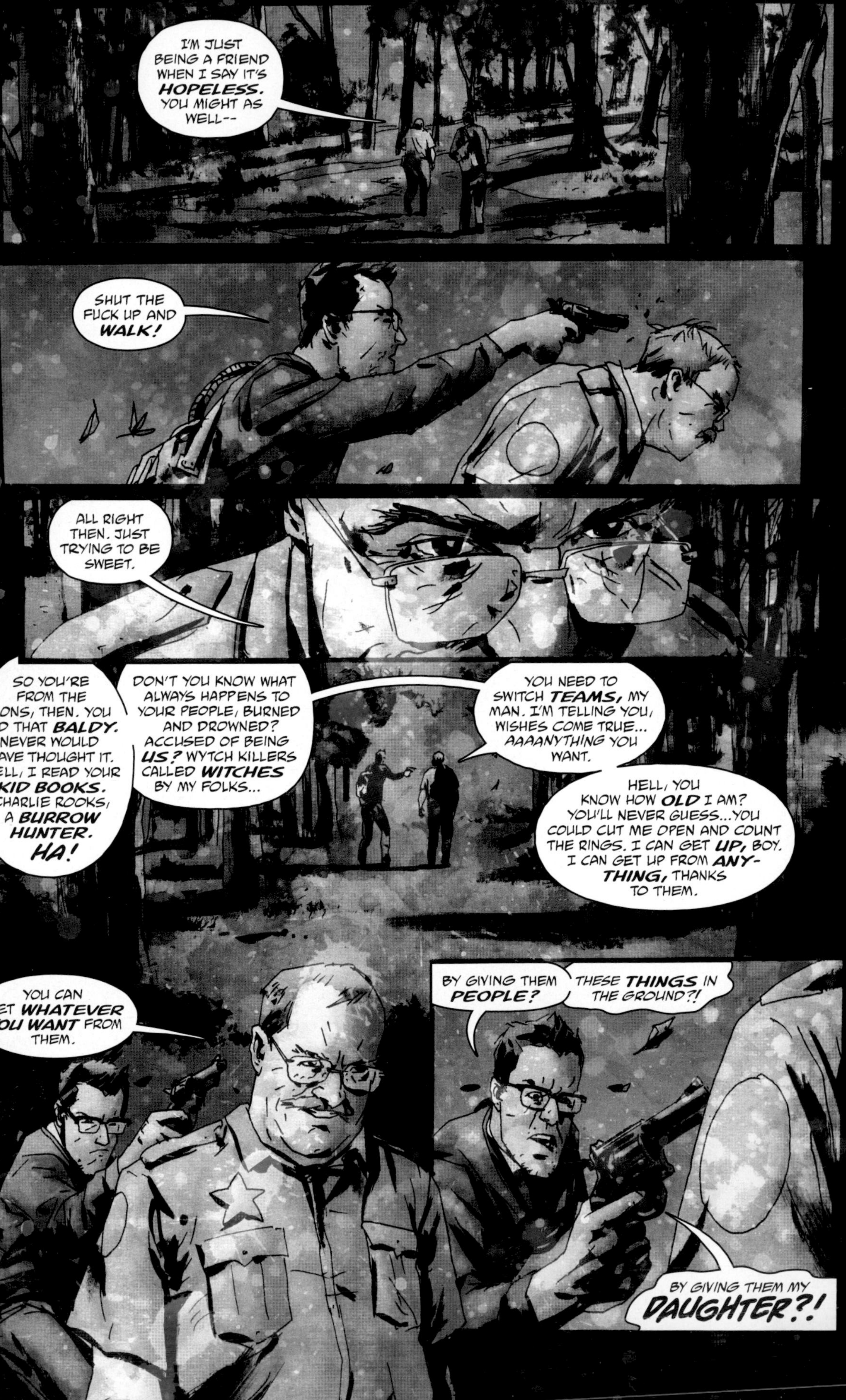
I'M JUST BEING A FRIEND WHEN I SAY IT'S HOPELESS. YOU MIGHT AS WELL--
SHUT THE FUCK UP AND WALK!
ALL RIGHT THEN. JUST TRYING TO BE SWEET.
SO YOU'RE FROM THE IRONS, THEN. YOU AND THAT BALDY. NEVER WOULD HAVE THOUGHT IT. HELL, I READ YOUR KID BOOKS. CHARLIE ROOKS, A BURROW HUNTER. HA!
DON'T YOU KNOW WHAT ALWAYS HAPPENS TO YOUR PEOPLE, BURNED AND DROWNED? ACCUSED OF BEING US? WYTCH KILLERS CALLED WITCHES BY MY FOLKS...
YOU NEED TO SWITCH TEAMS, MY MAN. I'M TELLING YOU, WISHES COME TRUE... AAAANYTHING YOU WANT.
HELL, YOU KNOW HOW OLD I AM? YOU'LL NEVER GUESS...YOU COULD CUT ME OPEN AND COUNT THE RINGS. I CAN GET UP, BOY. I CAN GET UP FROM ANY-THING, THANKS TO THEM.
YOU CAN GET WHATEVER YOU WANT FROM THEM.
BY GIVING THEM PEOPLE?
THESE THINGS IN THE GROUND?!
BY GIVING THEM MY DAUGHTER?!

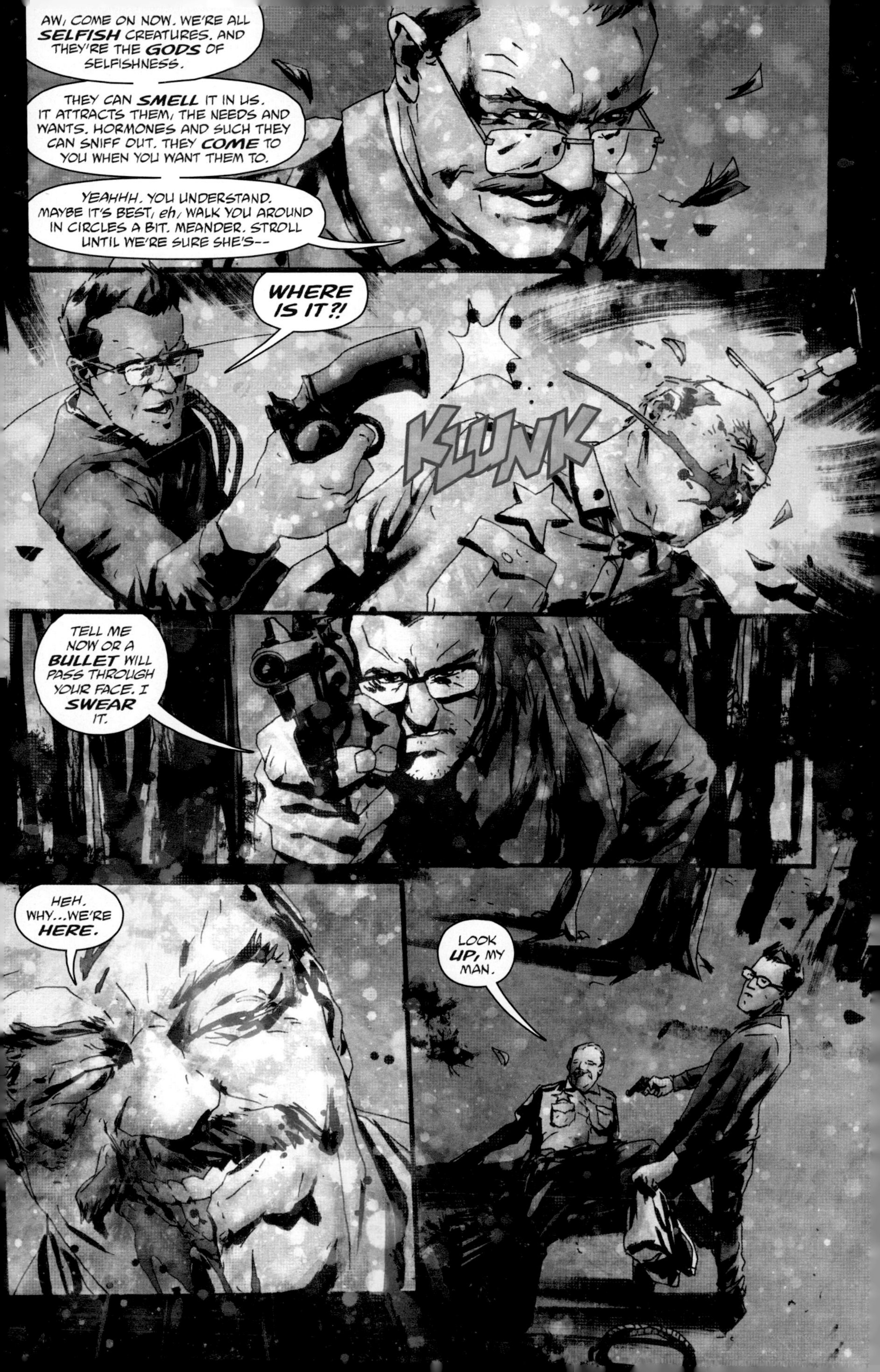
AW, COME ON NOW. WE'RE ALL SELFISH CREATURES. AND THEY'RE THE GODS OF SELFISHNESS.
THEY CAN SMELL IT IN US. IT ATTRACTS THEM, THE NEEDS AND WANTS. HORMONES AND SUCH THEY CAN SNIFF OUT. THEY COME TO YOU WHEN YOU WANT THEM TO.
YEAHHH. YOU UNDERSTAND. MAYBE IT'S BEST, eh, WALK YOU AROUND IN CIRCLES A BIT. MEANDER. STROLL UNTIL WE'RE SURE SHE'S--
WHERE IS IT?!
KLUNK
TELL ME NOW OR A BULLET WILL PASS THROUGH YOUR FACE. I SWEAR IT.
HEH. WHY...WE'RE HERE.
LOOK UP, MY MAN.

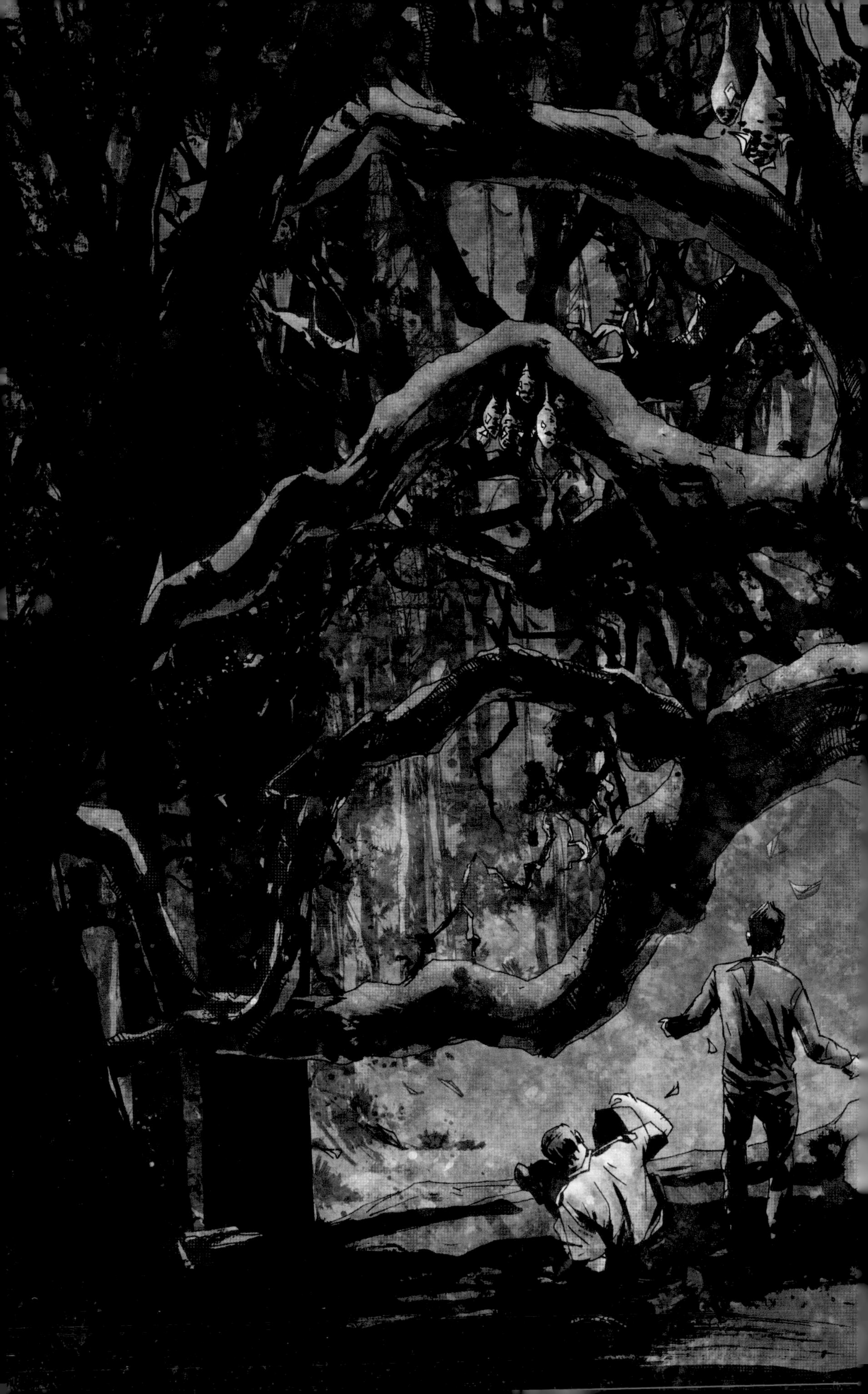

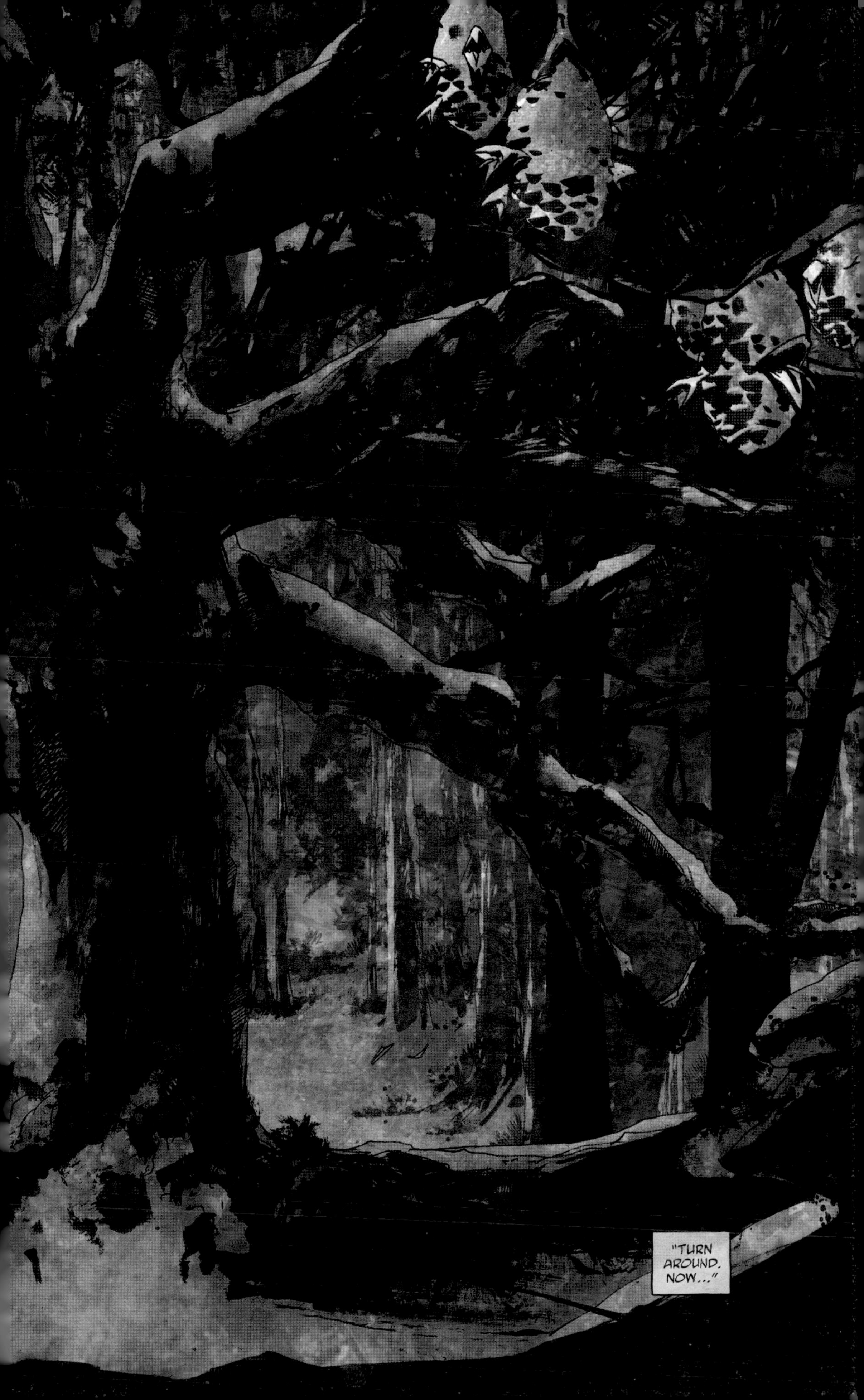
"TURN AROUND, NOW..."

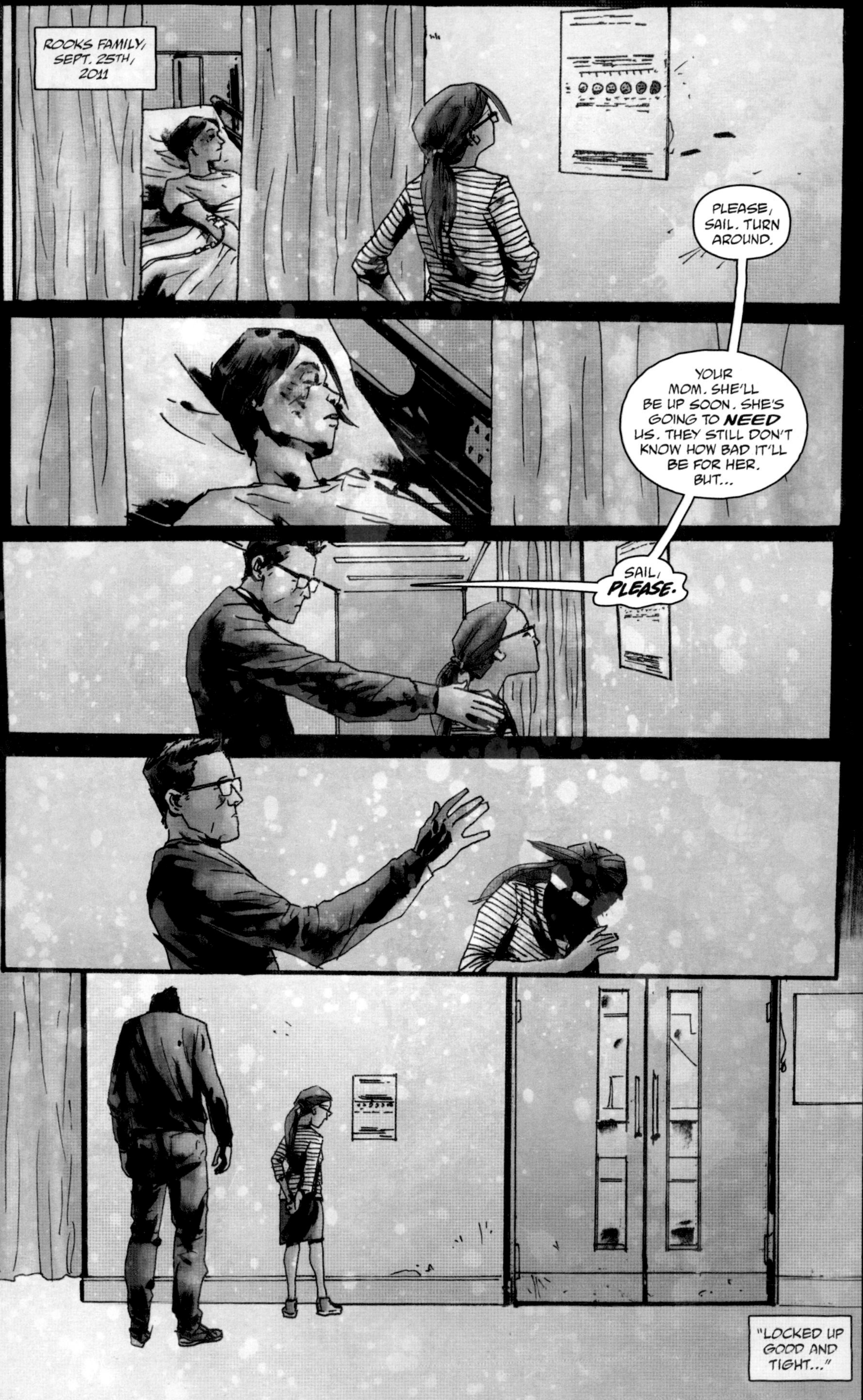
ROOKS FAMILY, SEPT. 25TH, 2011
PLEASE, SAIL. TURN AROUND.
YOUR MOM. SHE'LL BE UP SOON. SHE'S GOING TO **NEED** US. THEY STILL DON'T KNOW HOW BAD IT'LL BE FOR HER. BUT...
SAIL, **PLEASE.**
"LOCKED UP GOOD AND TIGHT..."

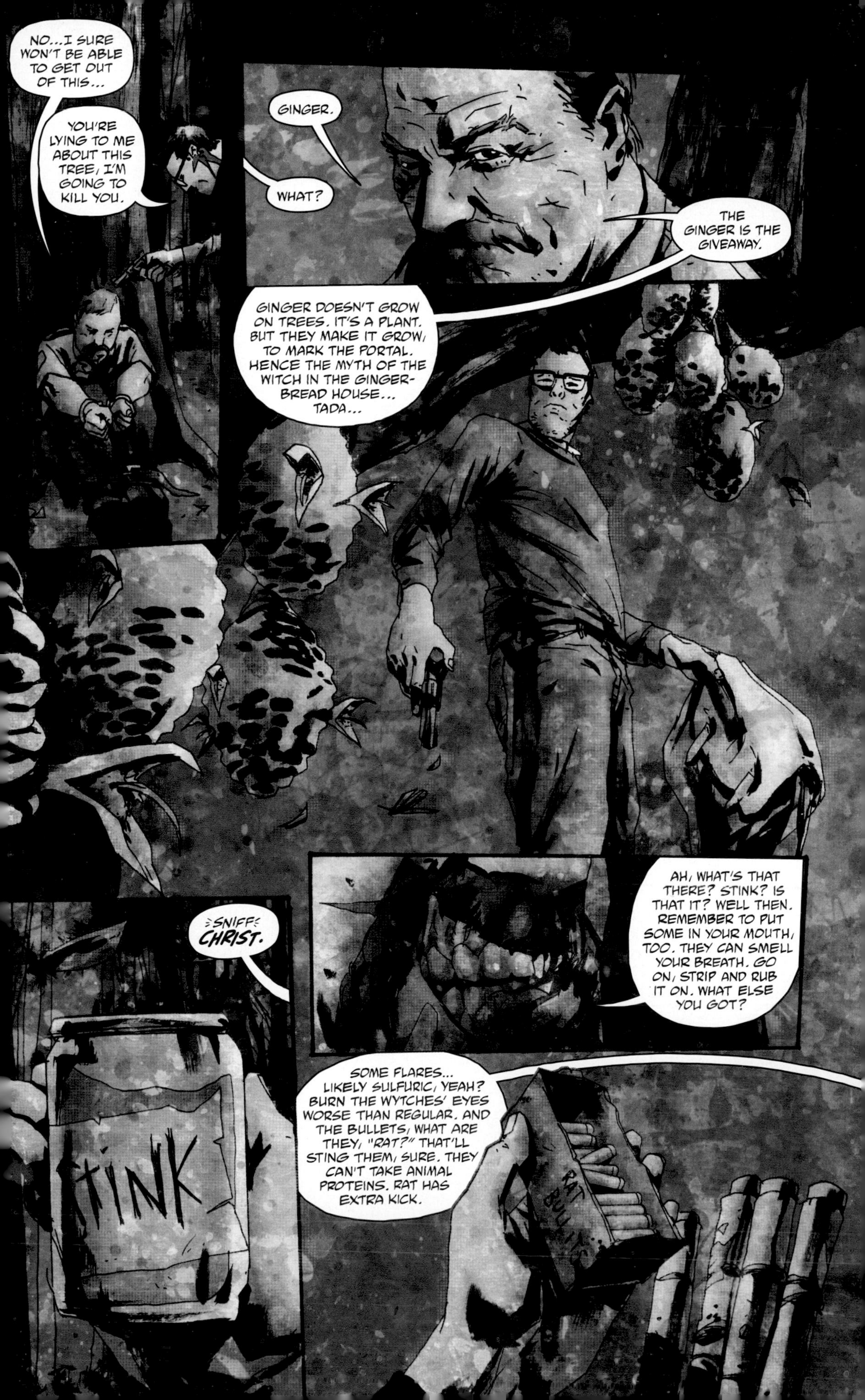
NO...I SURE WON'T BE ABLE TO GET OUT OF THIS...
YOU'RE LYING TO ME ABOUT THIS TREE, I'M GOING TO KILL YOU.
GINGER.
WHAT?
THE GINGER IS THE GIVEAWAY.
GINGER DOESN'T GROW ON TREES. IT'S A PLANT. BUT THEY MAKE IT GROW, TO MARK THE PORTAL. HENCE THE MYTH OF THE WITCH IN THE GINGER-BREAD HOUSE... TADA...
SNIFF CHRIST.
AH, WHAT'S THAT THERE? STINK? IS THAT IT? WELL THEN. REMEMBER TO PUT SOME IN YOUR MOUTH, TOO. THEY CAN SMELL YOUR BREATH. GO ON, STRIP AND RUB IT ON. WHAT ELSE YOU GOT?
STINK
SOME FLARES... LIKELY SULFURIC, YEAH? BURN THE WYTCHES' EYES WORSE THAN REGULAR. AND THE BULLETS, WHAT ARE THEY, "RAT?" THAT'LL STING THEM, SURE. THEY CAN'T TAKE ANIMAL PROTEINS. RAT HAS EXTRA KICK.
RAT BULLETS

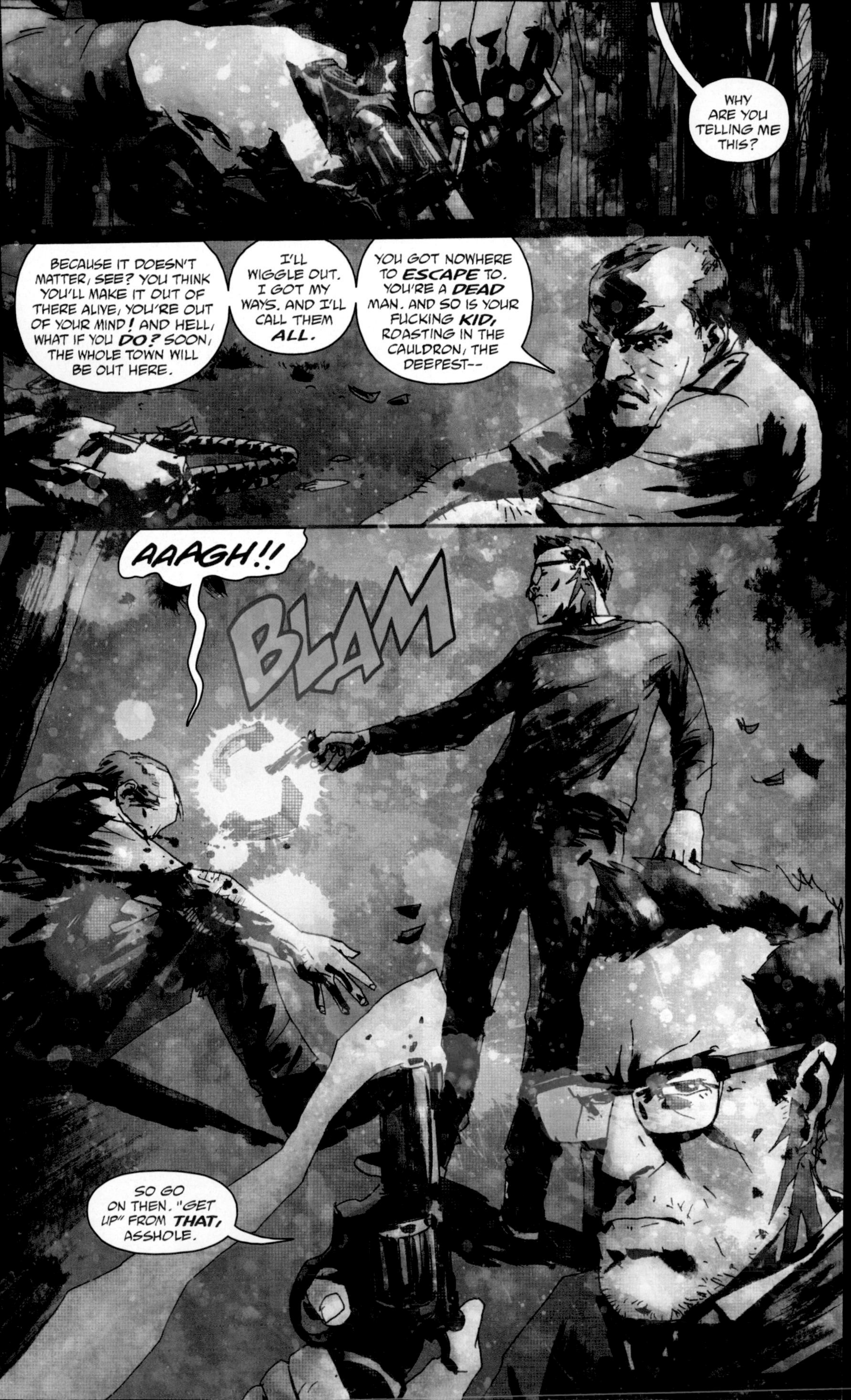
WHY ARE YOU TELLING ME THIS?
BECAUSE IT DOESN'T MATTER, SEE? YOU THINK YOU'LL MAKE IT OUT OF THERE ALIVE, YOU'RE OUT OF YOUR MIND! AND HELL, WHAT IF YOU DO? SOON, THE WHOLE TOWN WILL BE OUT HERE.
I'LL WIGGLE OUT. I GOT MY WAYS. AND I'LL CALL THEM ALL.
YOU GOT NOWHERE TO ESCAPE TO. YOU'RE A DEAD MAN. AND SO IS YOUR FUCKING KID, ROASTING IN THE CAULDRON, THE DEEPEST--
AAAGH!!
BLAM
SO GO ON THEN. "GET UP" FROM THAT, ASSHOLE.

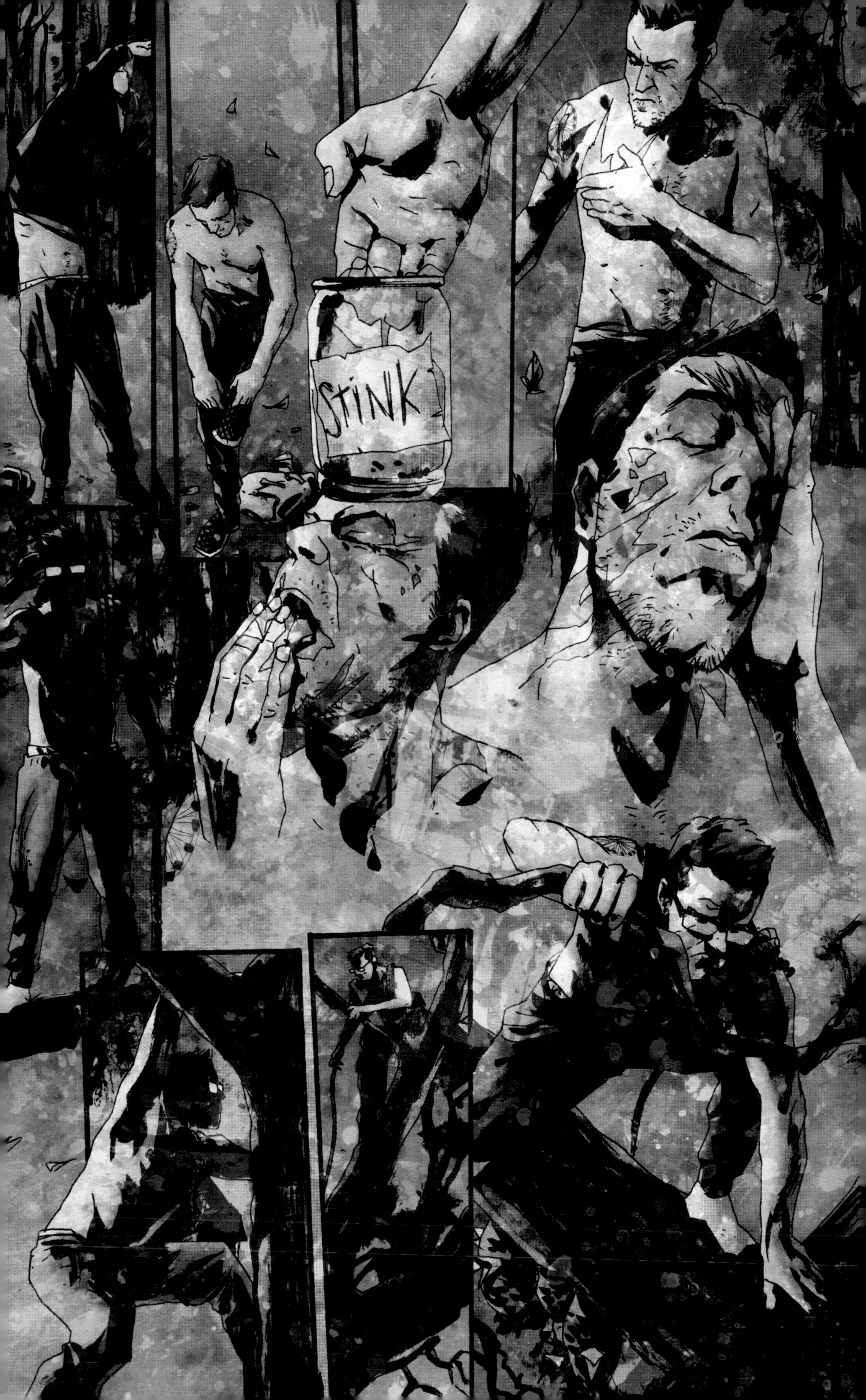
STINK

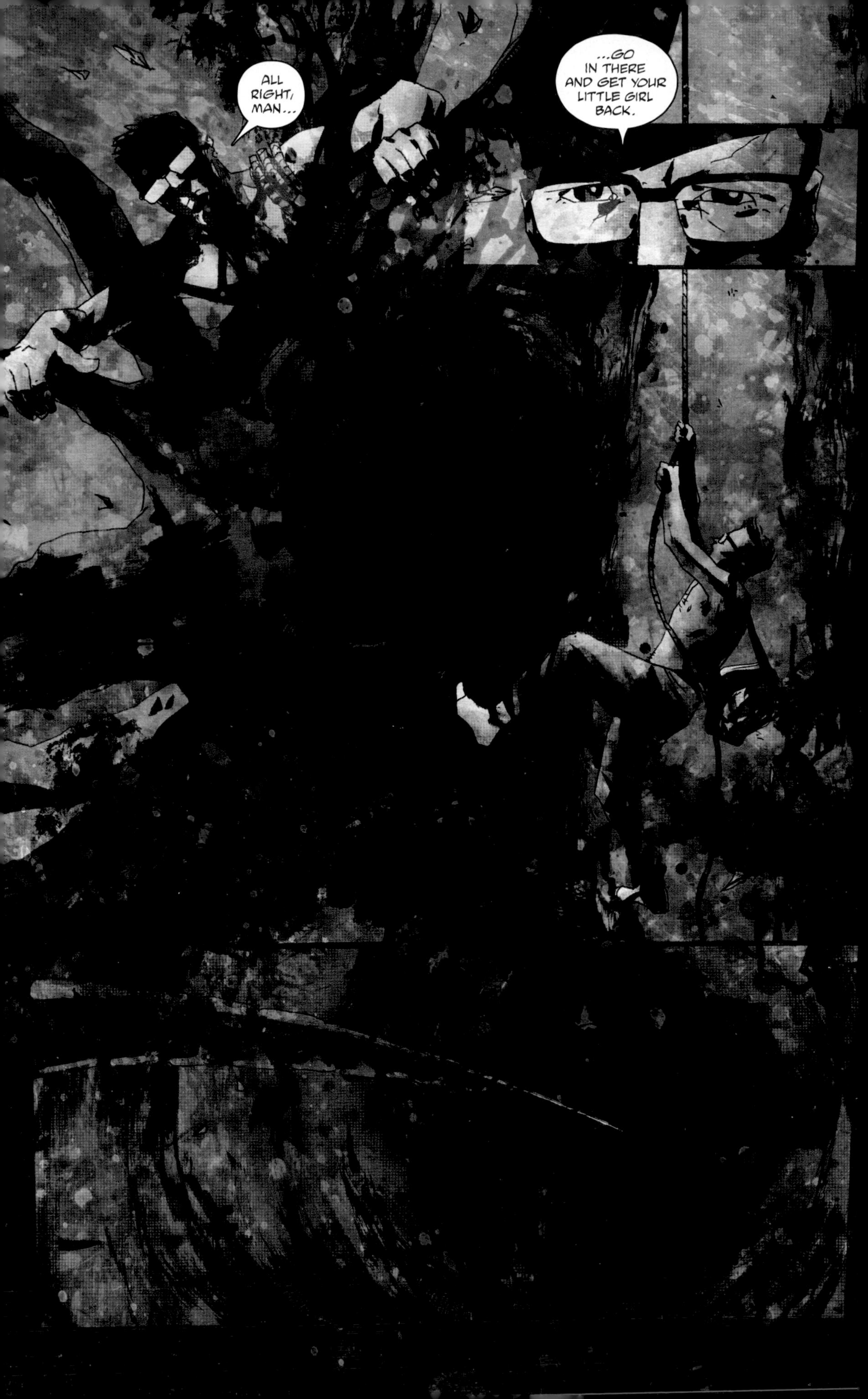
ALL RIGHT, MAN...
...GO IN THERE AND GET YOUR LITTLE GIRL BACK.

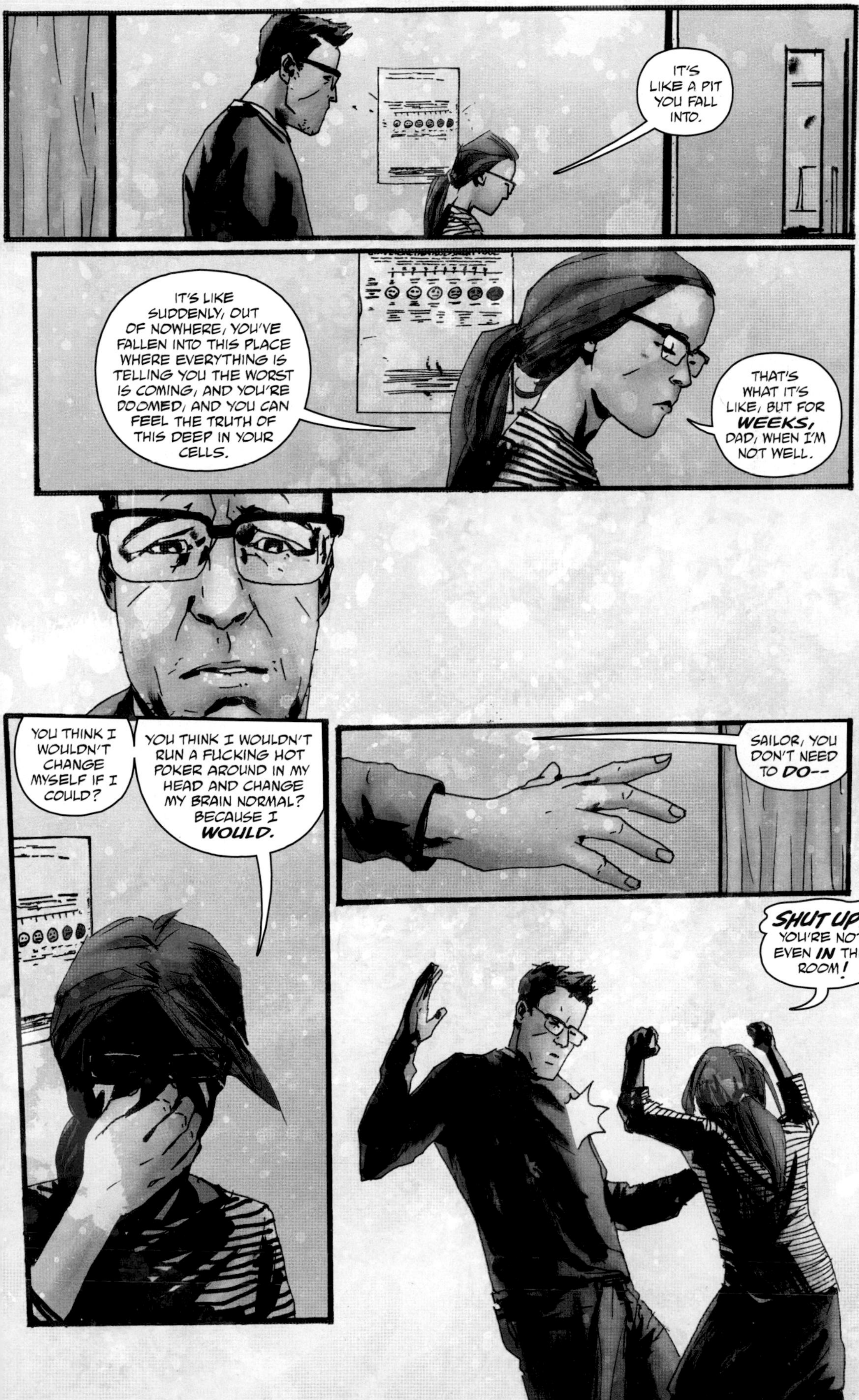

IT'S LIKE A PIT YOU FALL INTO.
IT'S LIKE SUDDENLY, OUT OF NOWHERE, YOU'VE FALLEN INTO THIS PLACE WHERE EVERYTHING IS TELLING YOU THE WORST IS COMING, AND YOU'RE DOOMED, AND YOU CAN FEEL THE TRUTH OF THIS DEEP IN YOUR CELLS.
THAT'S WHAT IT'S LIKE, BUT FOR WEEKS, DAD, WHEN I'M NOT WELL.
YOU THINK I WOULDN'T CHANGE MYSELF IF I COULD?
YOU THINK I WOULDN'T RUN A FUCKING HOT POKER AROUND IN MY HEAD AND CHANGE MY BRAIN NORMAL? BECAUSE I WOULD.
SAILOR, YOU DON'T NEED TO DO--
SHUT UP! YOU'RE NOT EVEN IN THIS ROOM!

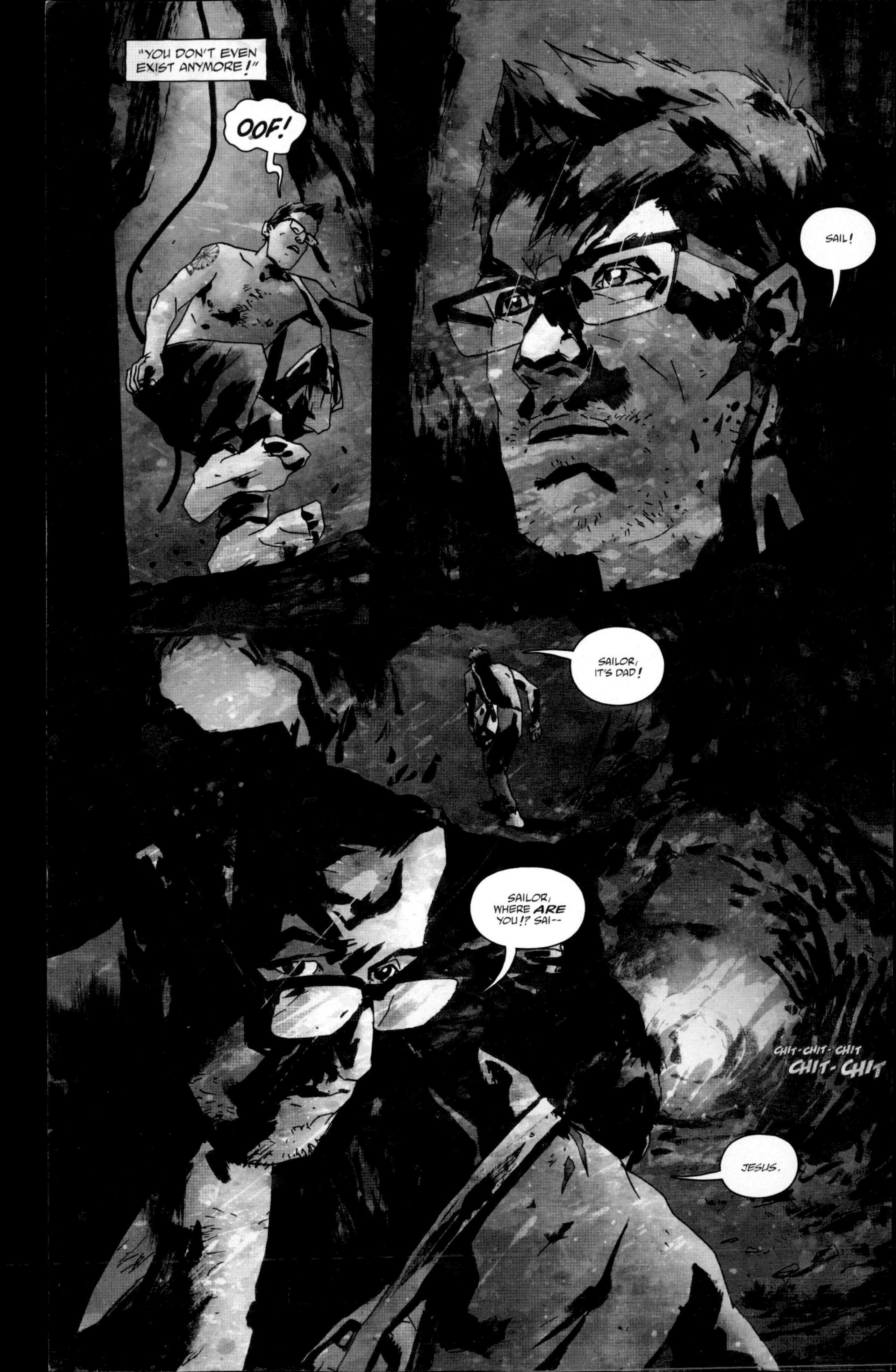
"YOU DON'T EVEN EXIST ANYMORE!"
OOF!
SAIL!
SAILOR, IT'S DAD!
SAILOR, WHERE ARE YOU!? SAI--
CHIT-CHIT-CHIT
CHIT-CHIT
JESUS.

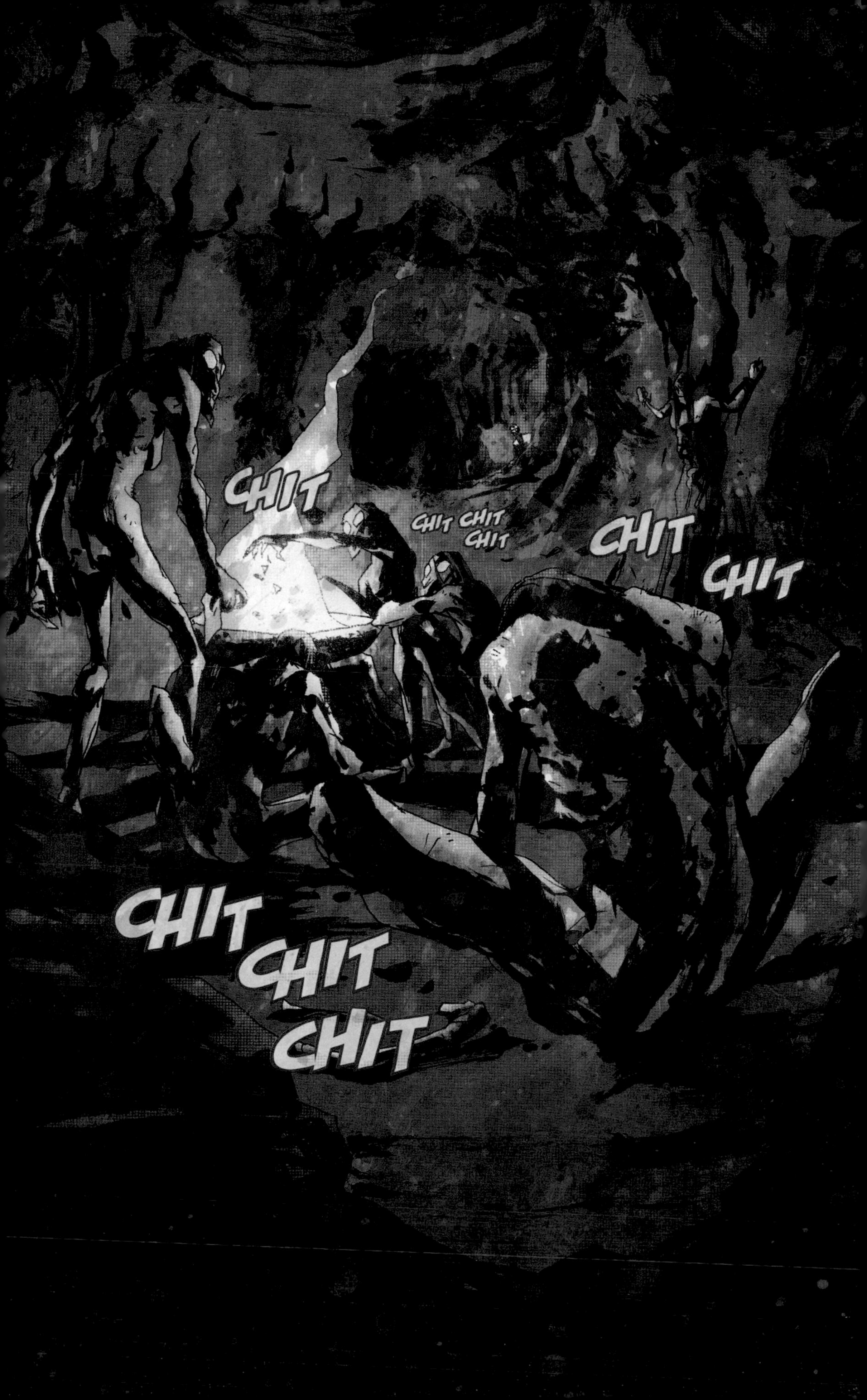
CHIT
CHIT CHIT
CHIT
CHIT
CHIT
CHIT
CHIT
CHIT

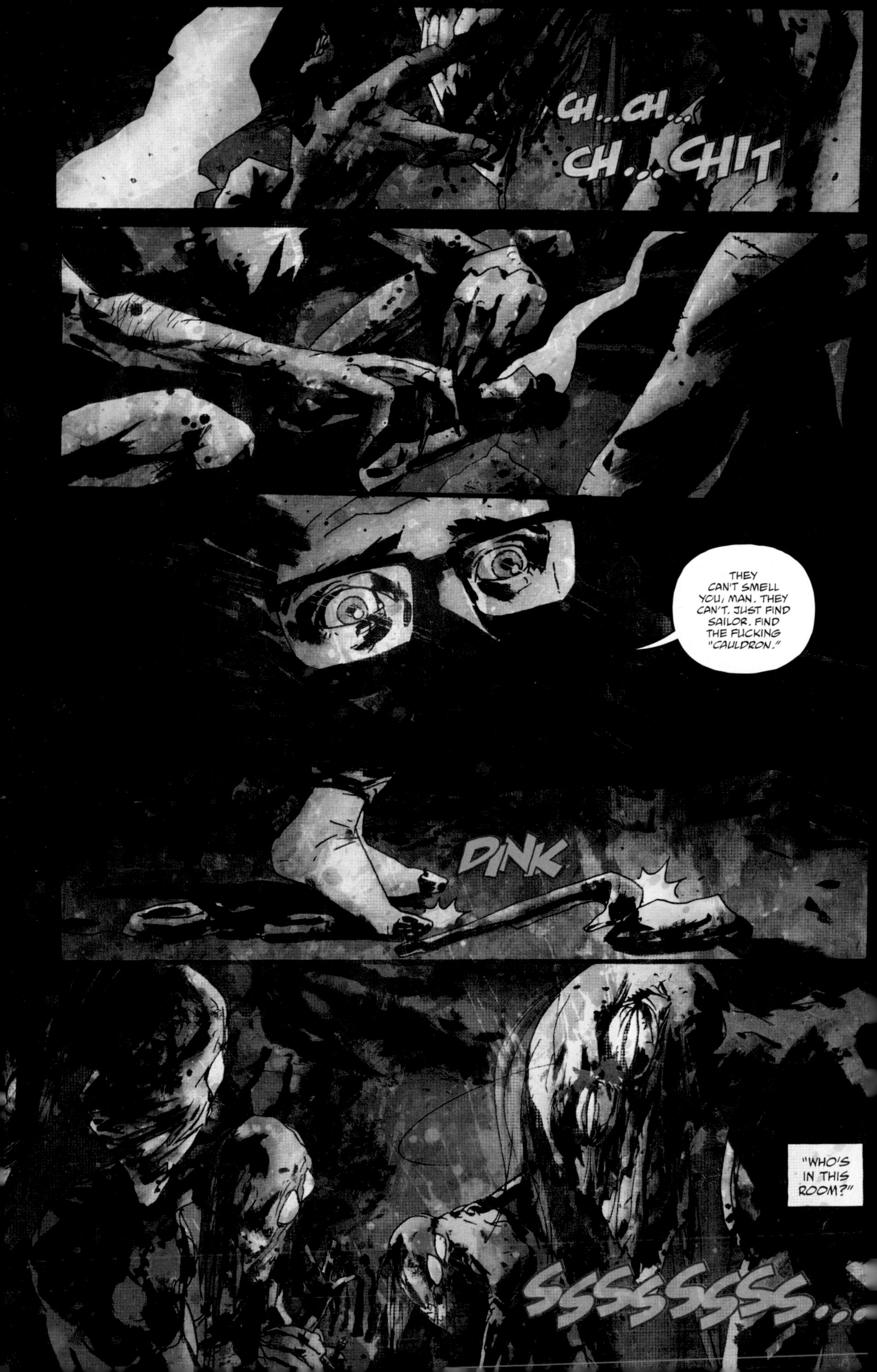
CH...CH...
CH...CHIT
THEY CAN'T SMELL YOU, MAN. THEY CAN'T. JUST FIND SAILOR. FIND THE FUCKING "CAULDRON."
DINK
"WHO'S IN THIS ROOM?"
SSSSSSSS...

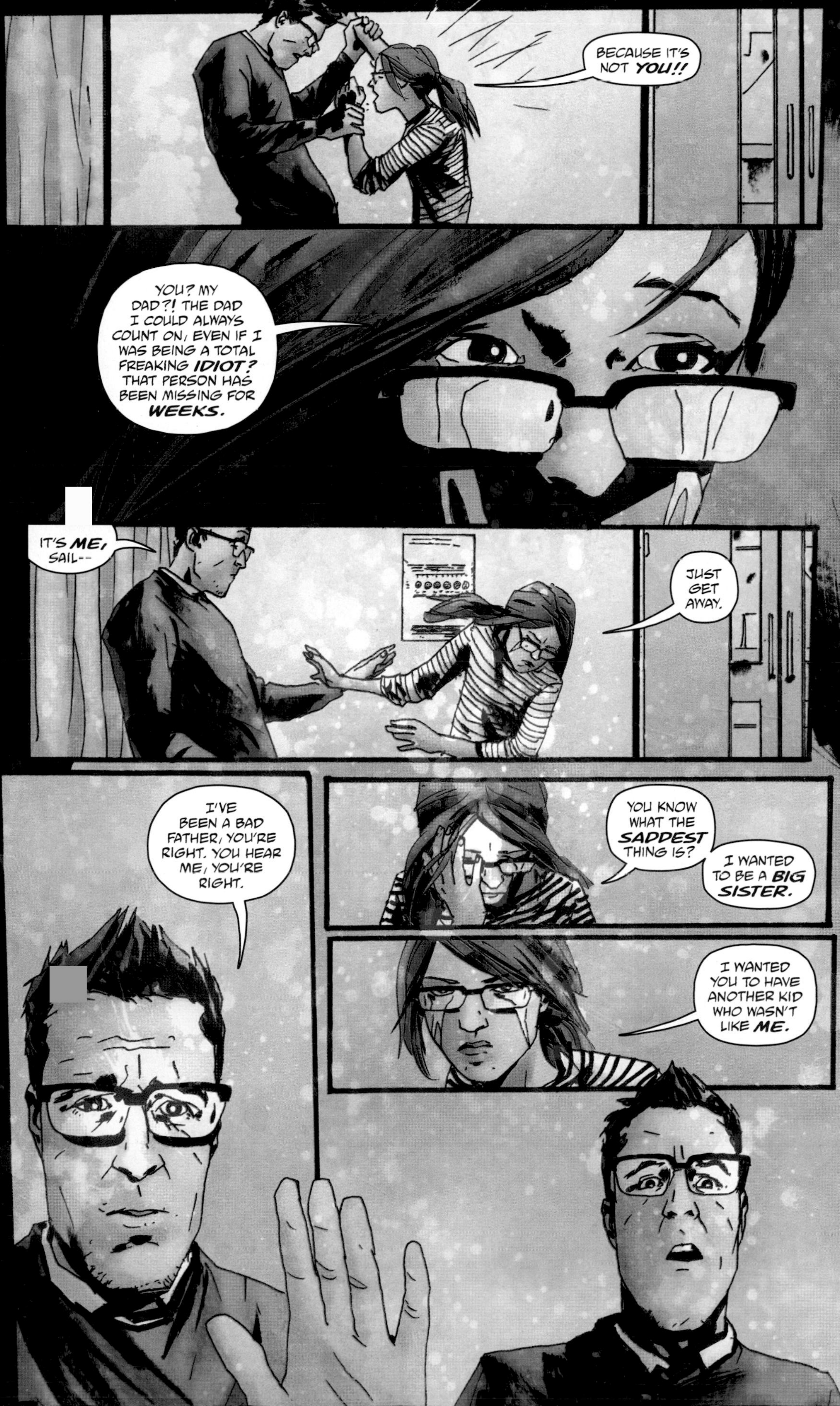
BECAUSE IT'S NOT YOU!!
YOU? MY DAD?! THE DAD I COULD ALWAYS COUNT ON, EVEN IF I WAS BEING A TOTAL FREAKING IDIOT? THAT PERSON HAS BEEN MISSING FOR WEEKS.
IT'S ME, SAIL--
JUST GET AWAY.
I'VE BEEN A BAD FATHER, YOU'RE RIGHT. YOU HEAR ME, YOU'RE RIGHT.
YOU KNOW WHAT THE SADDEST THING IS?
I WANTED TO BE A BIG SISTER.
I WANTED YOU TO HAVE ANOTHER KID WHO WASN'T LIKE ME.

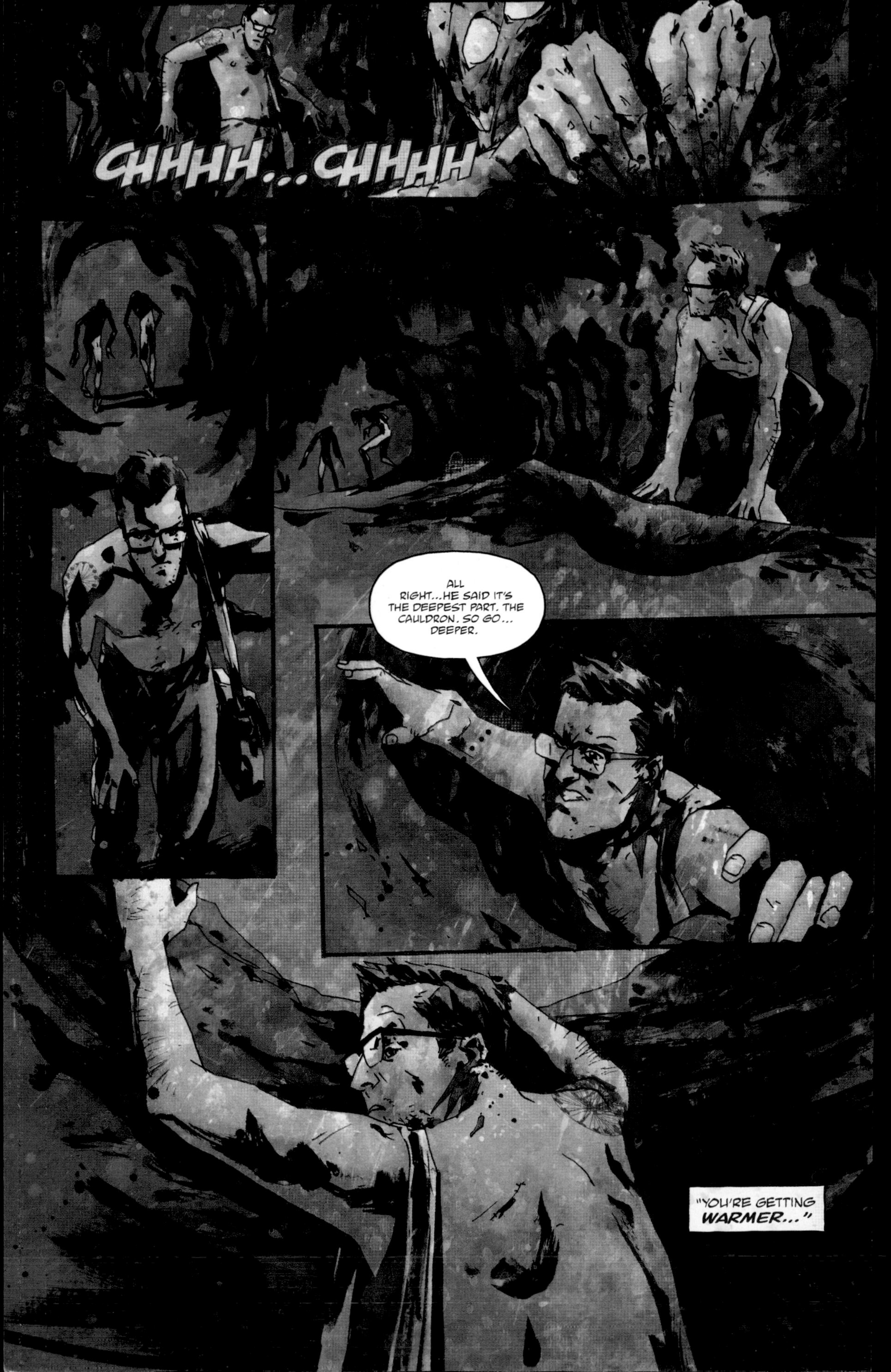
CHHHH...CHHHH
ALL RIGHT...HE SAID IT'S THE DEEPEST PART. THE CAULDRON. SO GO... DEEPER.
"YOU'RE GETTING WARMER..."

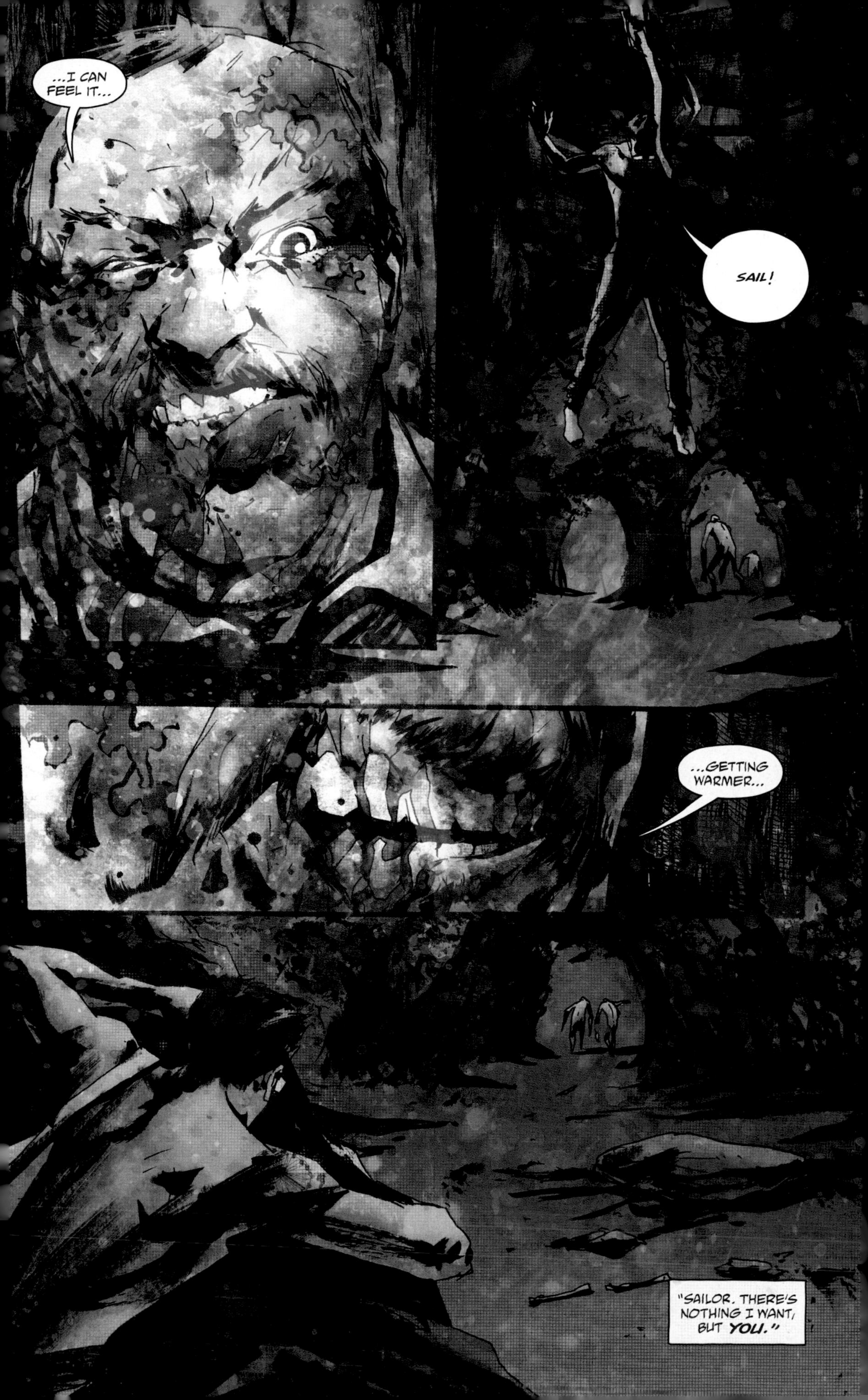
...I CAN FEEL IT...
SAIL!
...GETTING WARMER...
"SAILOR. THERE'S NOTHING I WANT, BUT YOU."

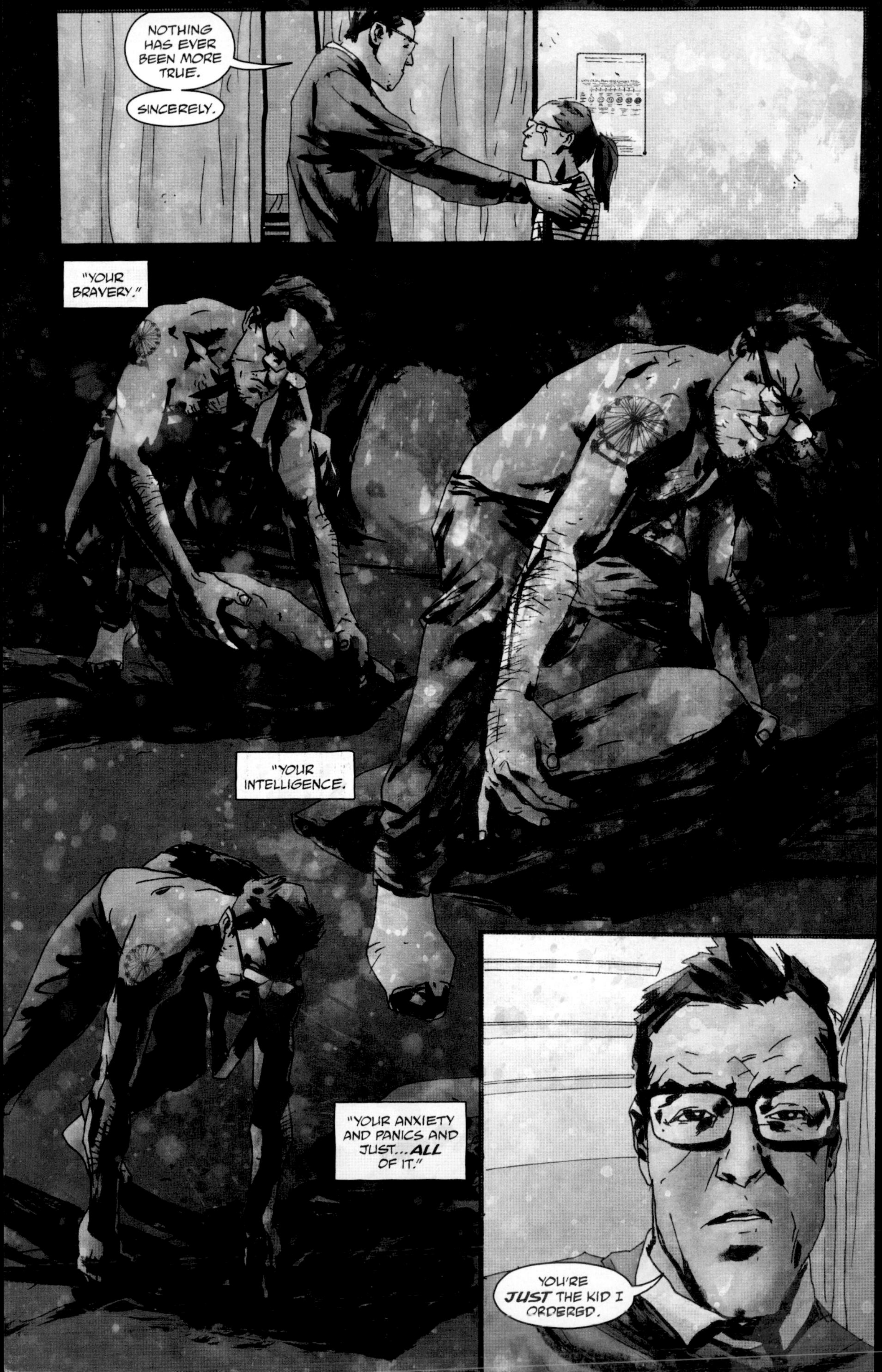
NOTHING HAS EVER BEEN MORE TRUE.
SINCERELY.
"YOUR BRAVERY."
"YOUR INTELLIGENCE.
"YOUR ANXIETY AND PANICS AND JUST... ALL OF IT."
YOU'RE JUST THE KID I ORDERED.

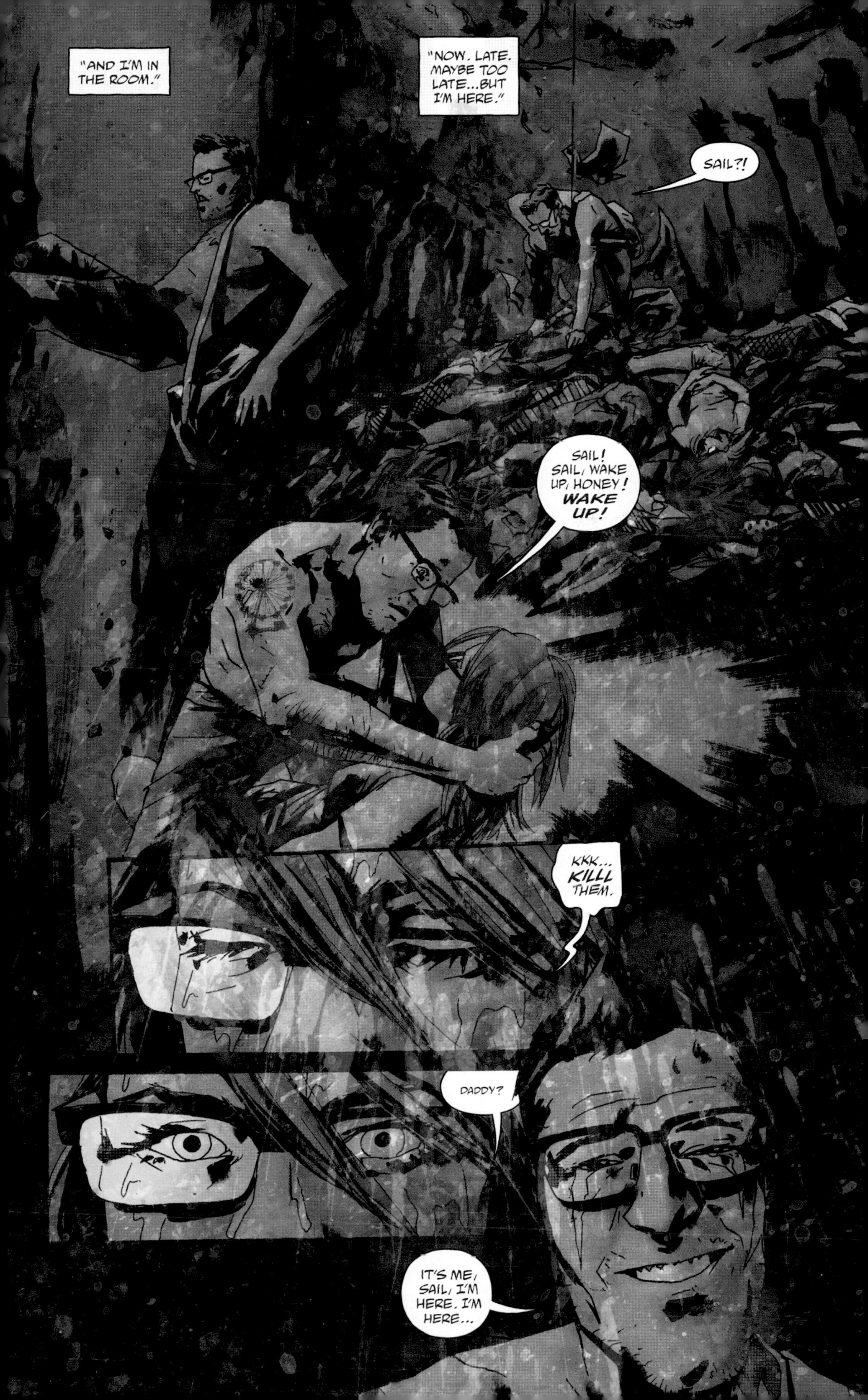
"AND I'M IN THE ROOM."
"NOW, LATE. MAYBE TOO LATE...BUT I'M HERE."
SAIL?!
SAIL! SAIL, WAKE UP, HONEY! **WAKE UP!**
KKK... **KILLL** THEM.
DADDY?
IT'S ME, SAIL, I'M HERE. I'M HERE...

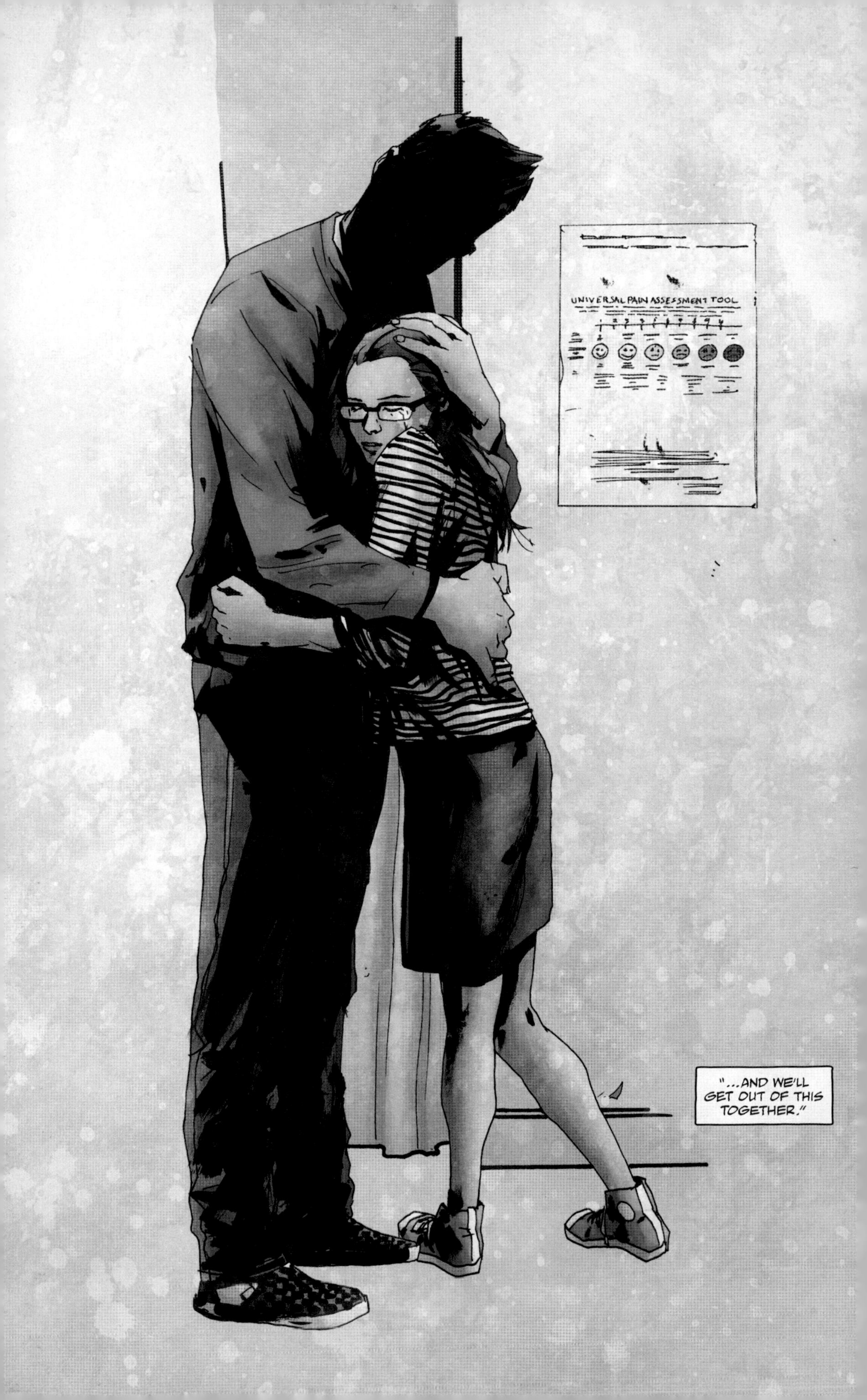
UNIVERSAL PAIN ASSESSMENT TOOL
"...AND WE'LL GET OUT OF THIS TOGETHER."

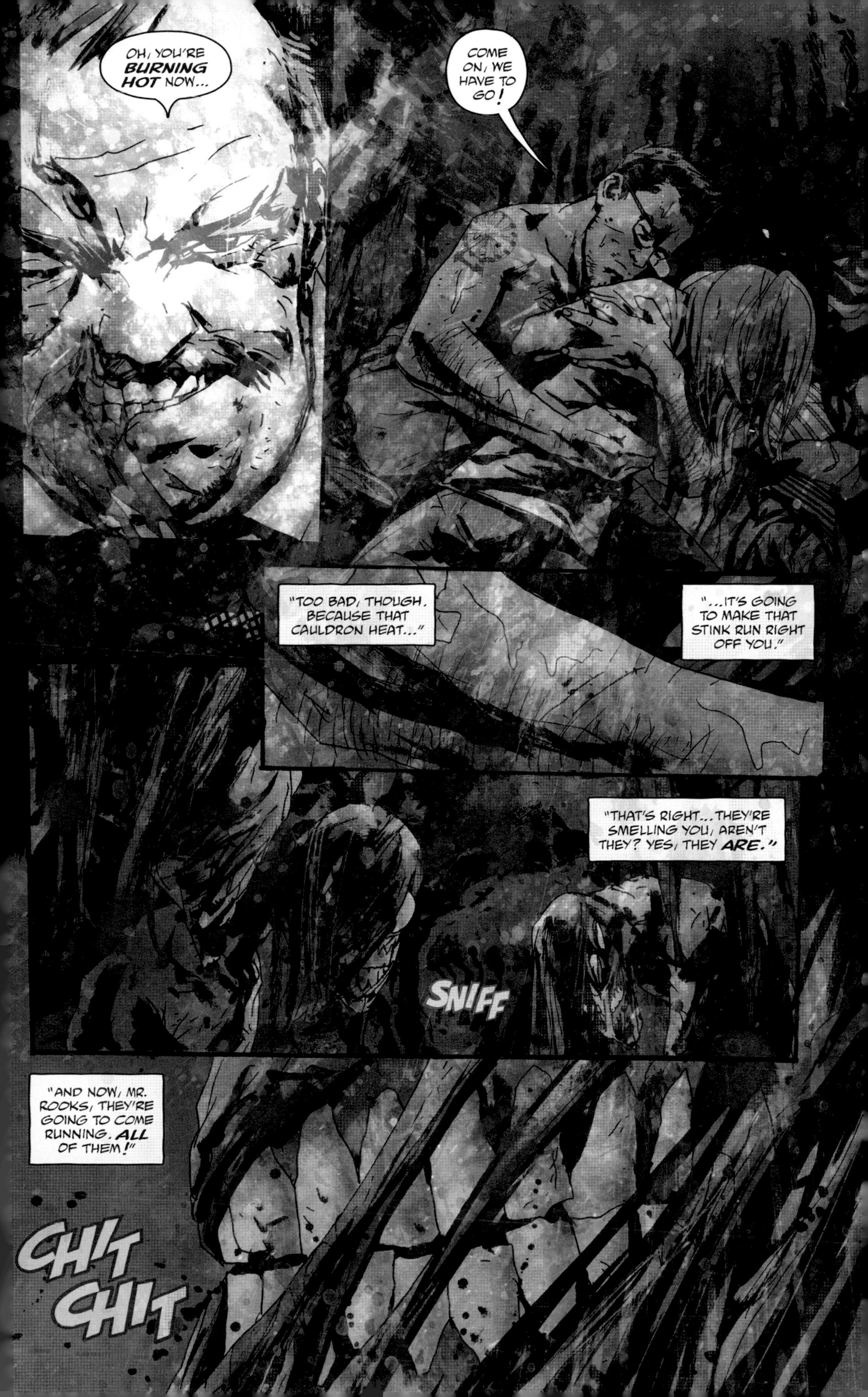
OH, YOU'RE **BURNING HOT** NOW...
COME ON, WE HAVE TO GO!
"TOO BAD, THOUGH. BECAUSE THAT CAULDRON HEAT..."
"...IT'S GOING TO MAKE THAT STINK RUN RIGHT OFF YOU."
"THAT'S RIGHT... THEY'RE SMELLING YOU, AREN'T THEY? YES, THEY **ARE**."
SNIFF
"AND NOW, MR. ROOKS, THEY'RE GOING TO COME RUNNING. **ALL** OF THEM!"
CHIT CHIT

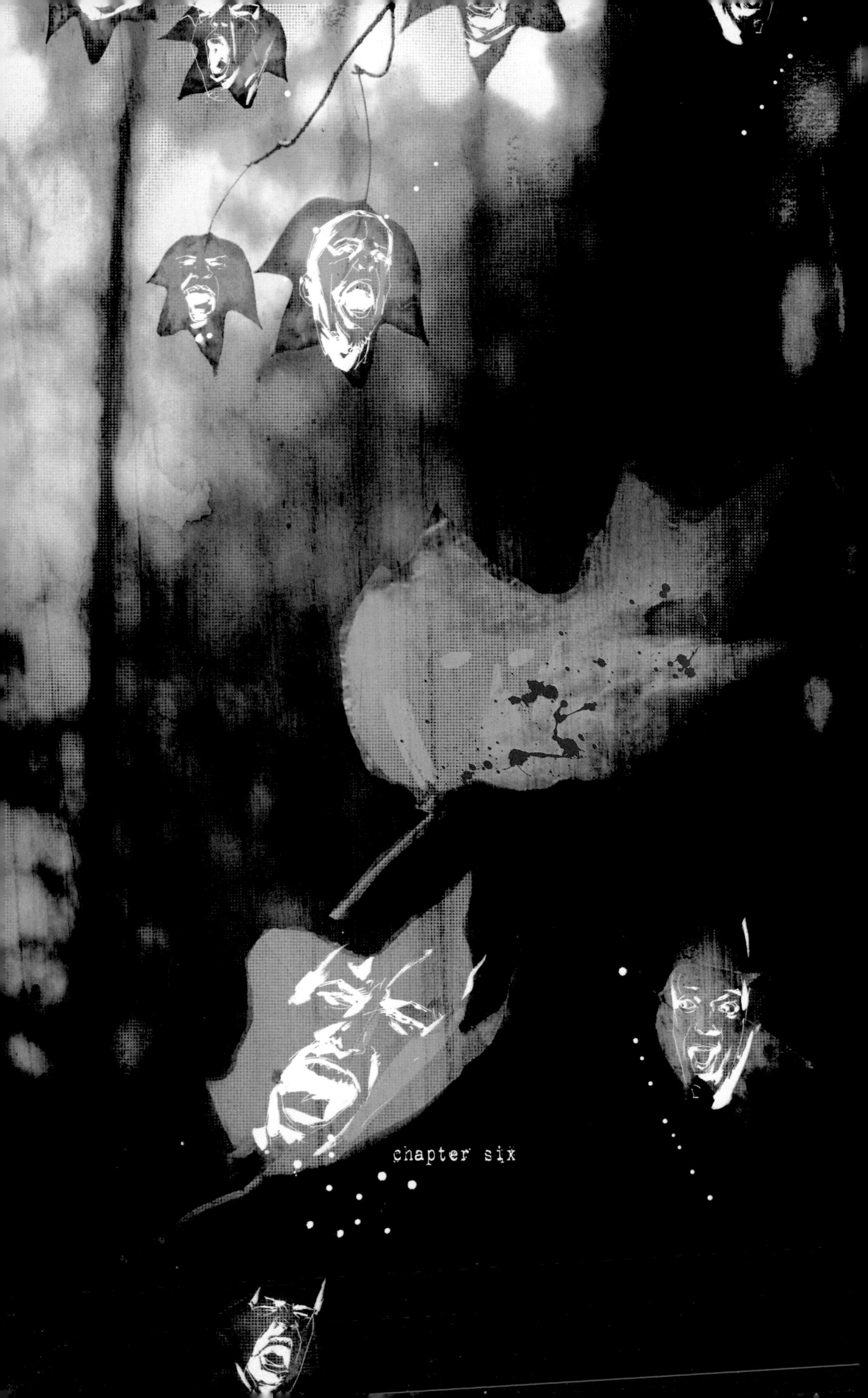

chapter six

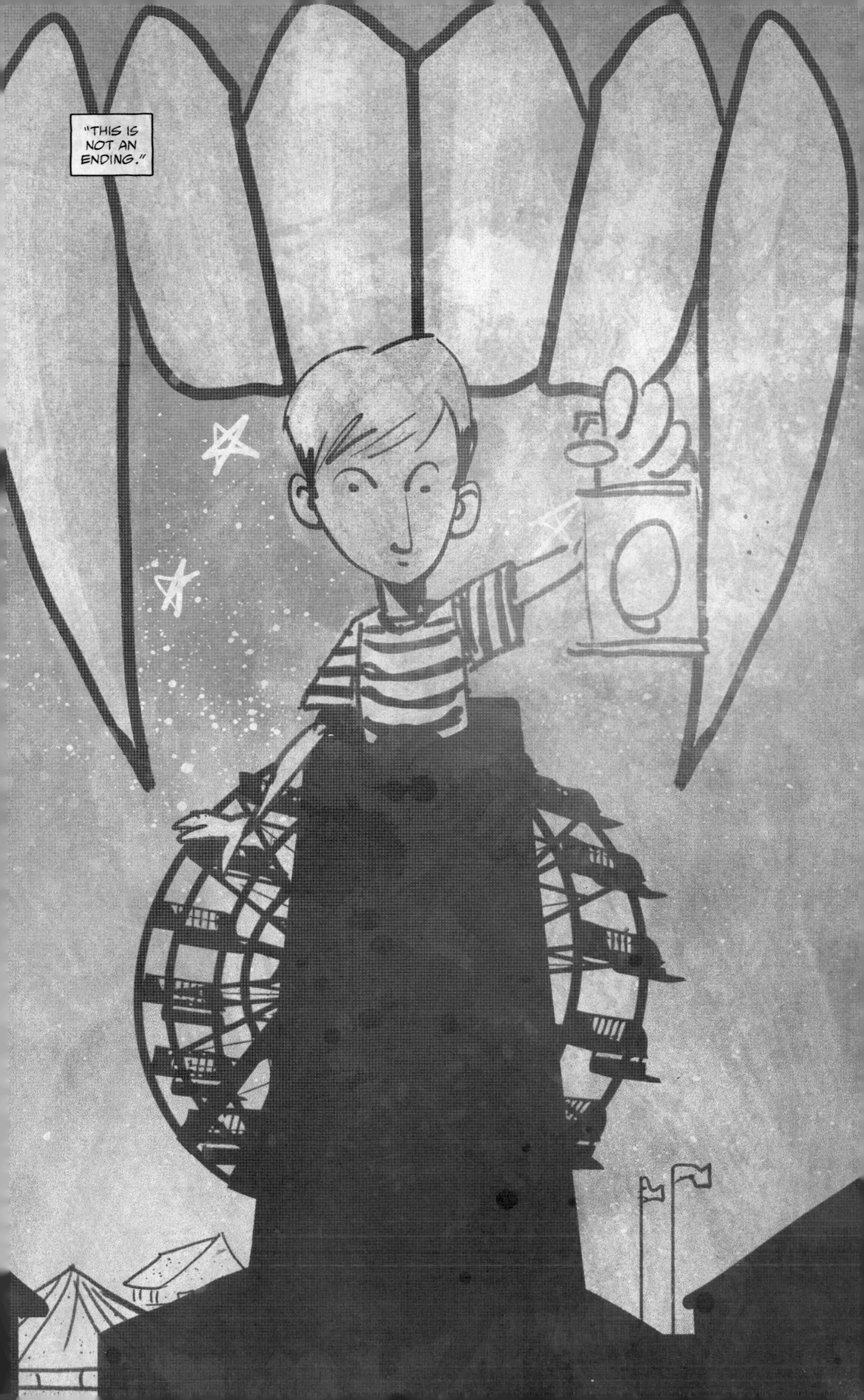
"THIS IS
NOT AN
ENDING."

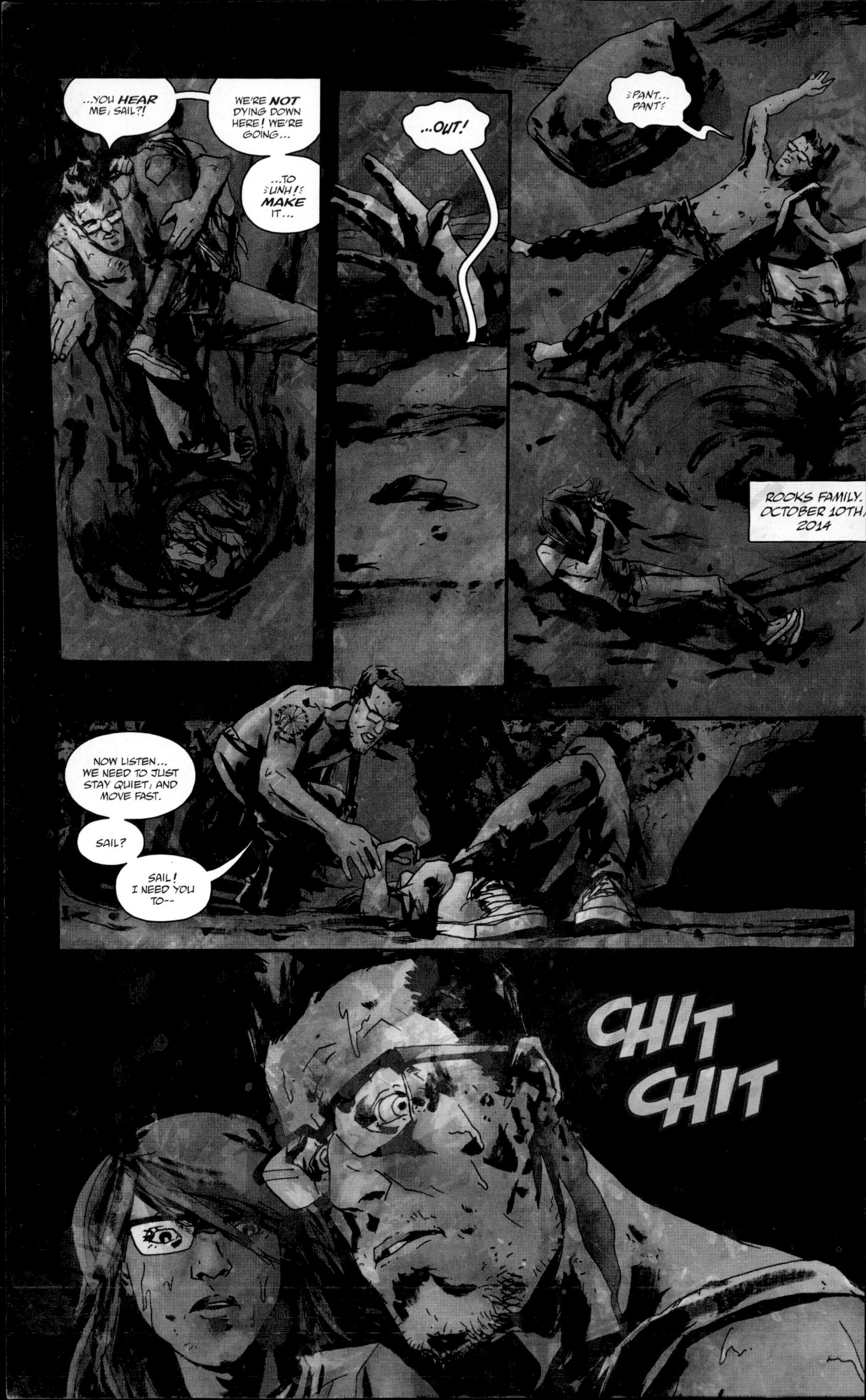
...YOU HEAR ME, SAIL?!
WE'RE NOT DYING DOWN HERE! WE'RE GOING...
...TO UNH! MAKE IT...
...OUT!
PANT... PANT
ROOKS FAMILY. OCTOBER 10TH, 2014
NOW LISTEN... WE NEED TO JUST STAY QUIET, AND MOVE FAST.
SAIL?
SAIL! I NEED YOU TO--
CHIT
CHIT

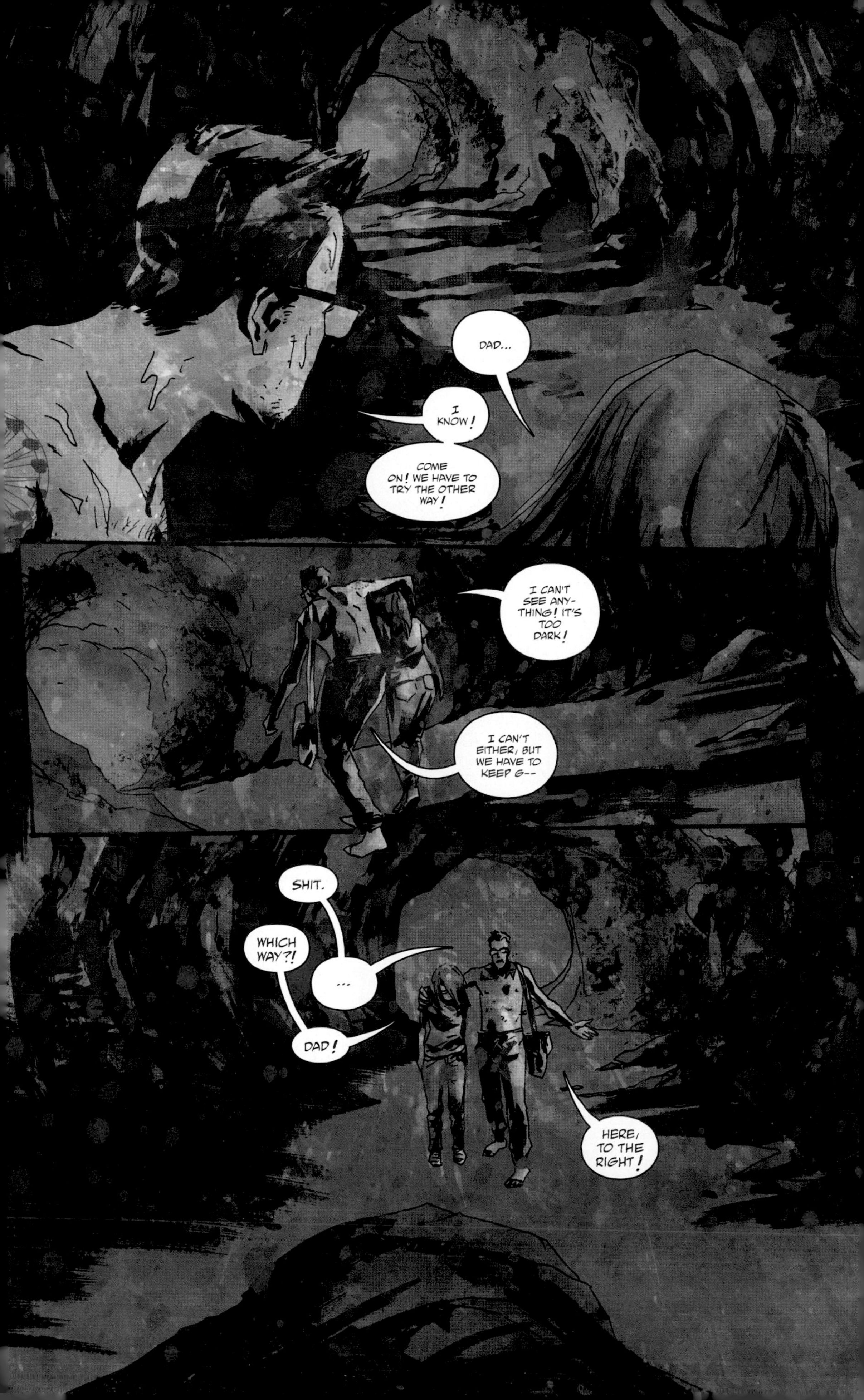
DAD...
I KNOW!
COME ON! WE HAVE TO TRY THE OTHER WAY!
I CAN'T SEE ANY-THING! IT'S TOO DARK!
I CAN'T EITHER, BUT WE HAVE TO KEEP G--
SHIT.
WHICH WAY?!
...
DAD!
HERE, TO THE RIGHT!

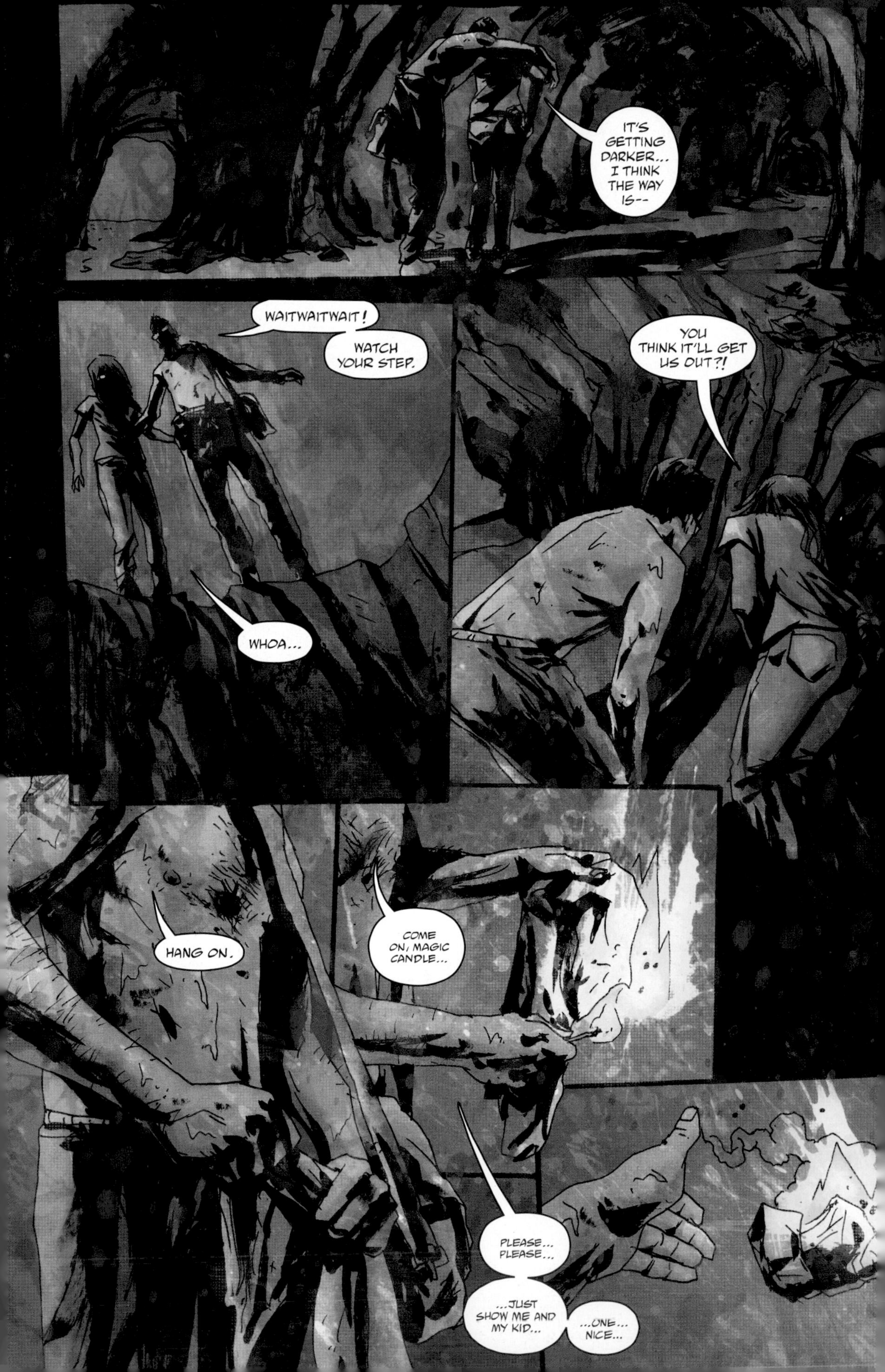
IT'S GETTING DARKER... I THINK THE WAY IS--
WAITWAITWAIT!
WATCH YOUR STEP.
WHOA...
YOU THINK IT'LL GET US OUT?!
HANG ON.
COME ON, MAGIC CANDLE...
PLEASE... PLEASE...
...JUST SHOW ME AND MY KID...
...ONE... NICE...

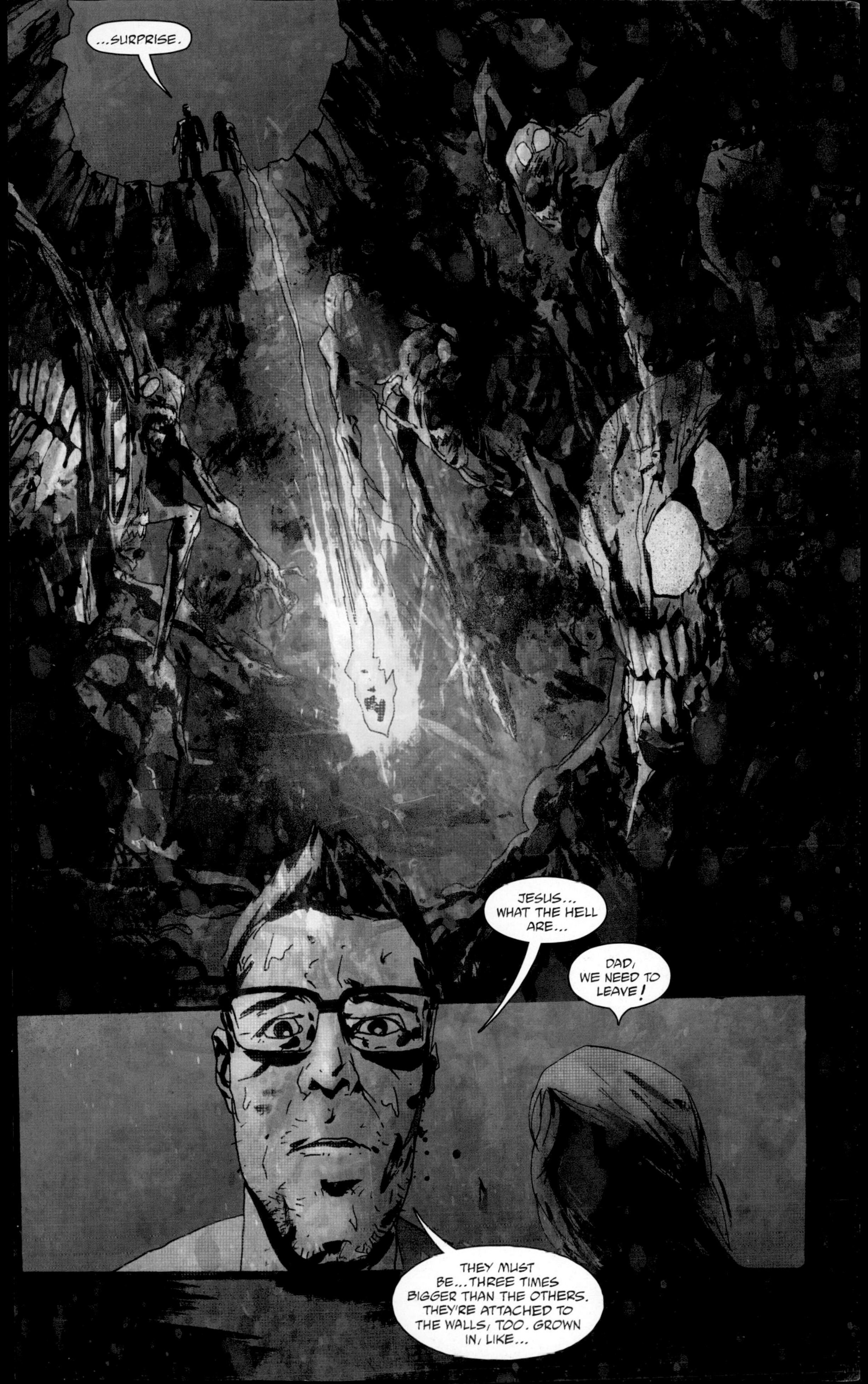
...SURPRISE.
JESUS... WHAT THE HELL ARE...
DAD, WE NEED TO LEAVE!
THEY MUST BE...THREE TIMES BIGGER THAN THE OTHERS. THEY'RE ATTACHED TO THE WALLS, TOO. GROWN IN, LIKE...

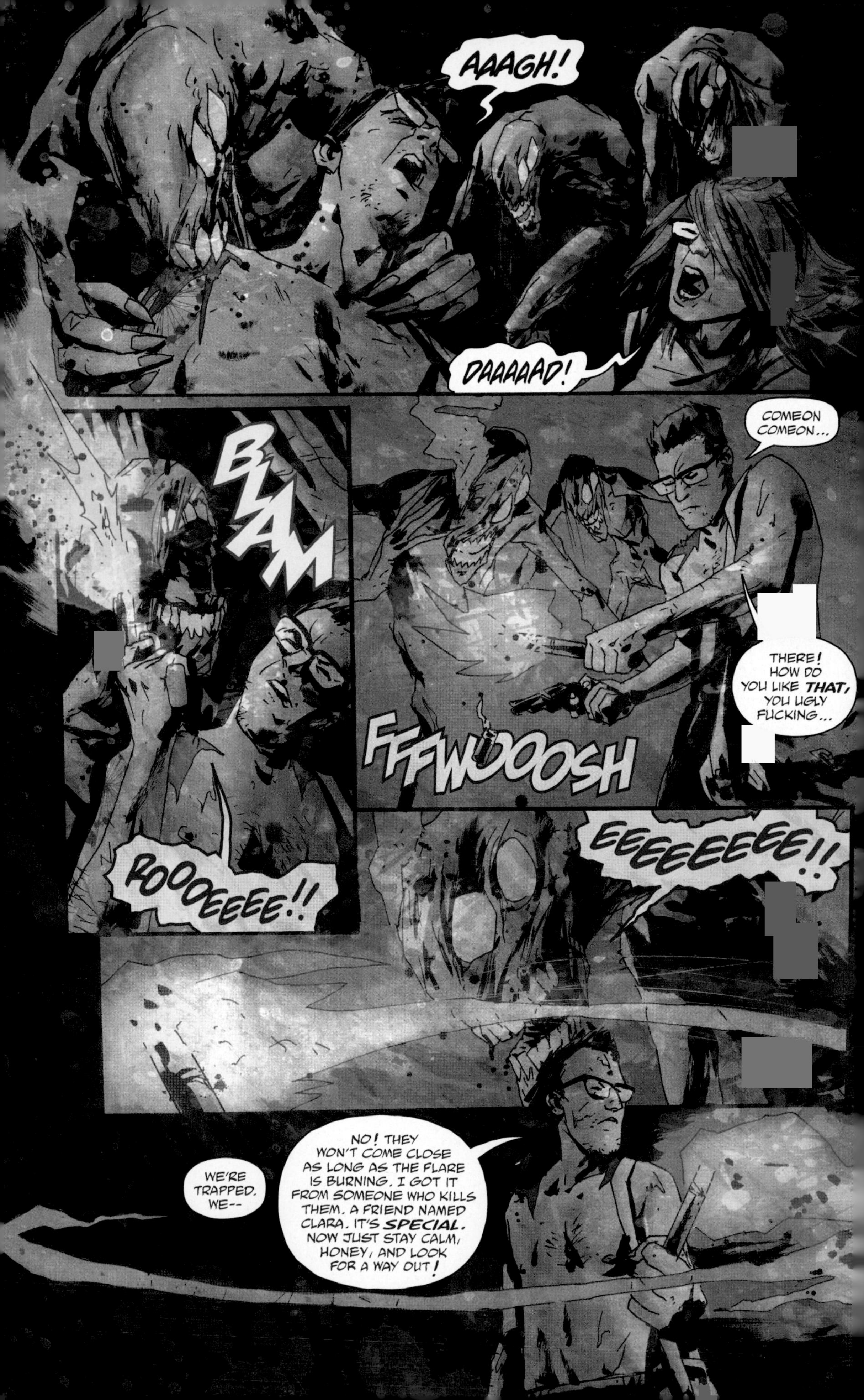
AAAGH!
DAAAAAD!
BLAM
ROOOEEEEE!!
COMEON COMEON...
FFFWOOOSH
THERE! HOW DO YOU LIKE THAT, YOU UGLY FUCKING...
EEEEEEEEE!!
WE'RE TRAPPED. WE--
NO! THEY WON'T COME CLOSE AS LONG AS THE FLARE IS BURNING. I GOT IT FROM SOMEONE WHO KILLS THEM. A FRIEND NAMED CLARA. IT'S SPECIAL. NOW JUST STAY CALM, HONEY, AND LOOK FOR A WAY OUT!

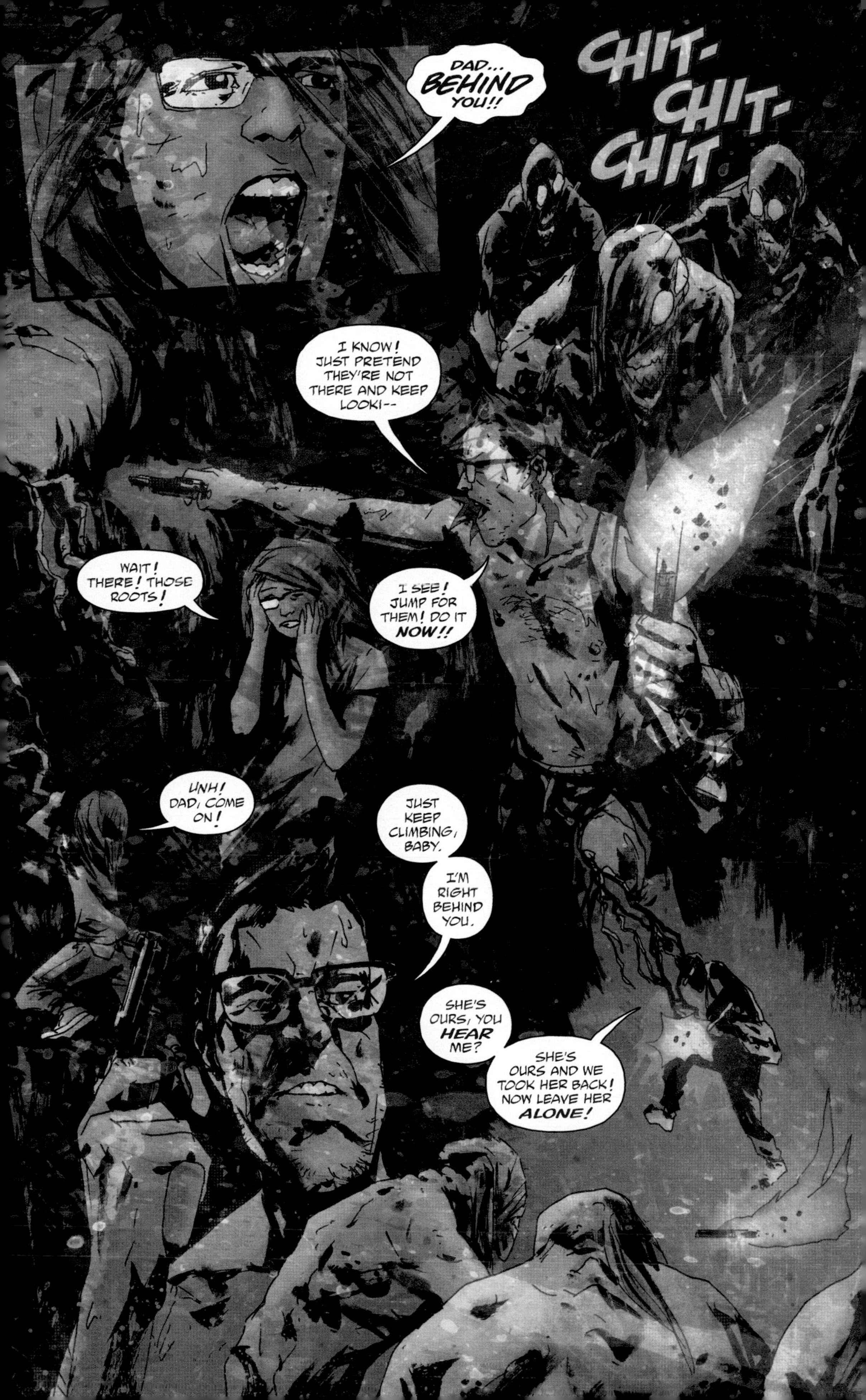
DAD... BEHIND YOU!!
CHIT-CHIT-CHIT
I KNOW! JUST PRETEND THEY'RE NOT THERE AND KEEP LOOKI--
WAIT! THERE! THOSE ROOTS!
I SEE! JUMP FOR THEM! DO IT NOW!!
UNH! DAD, COME ON!
JUST KEEP CLIMBING, BABY.
I'M RIGHT BEHIND YOU.
SHE'S OURS, YOU HEAR ME?
SHE'S OURS AND WE TOOK HER BACK! NOW LEAVE HER ALONE!

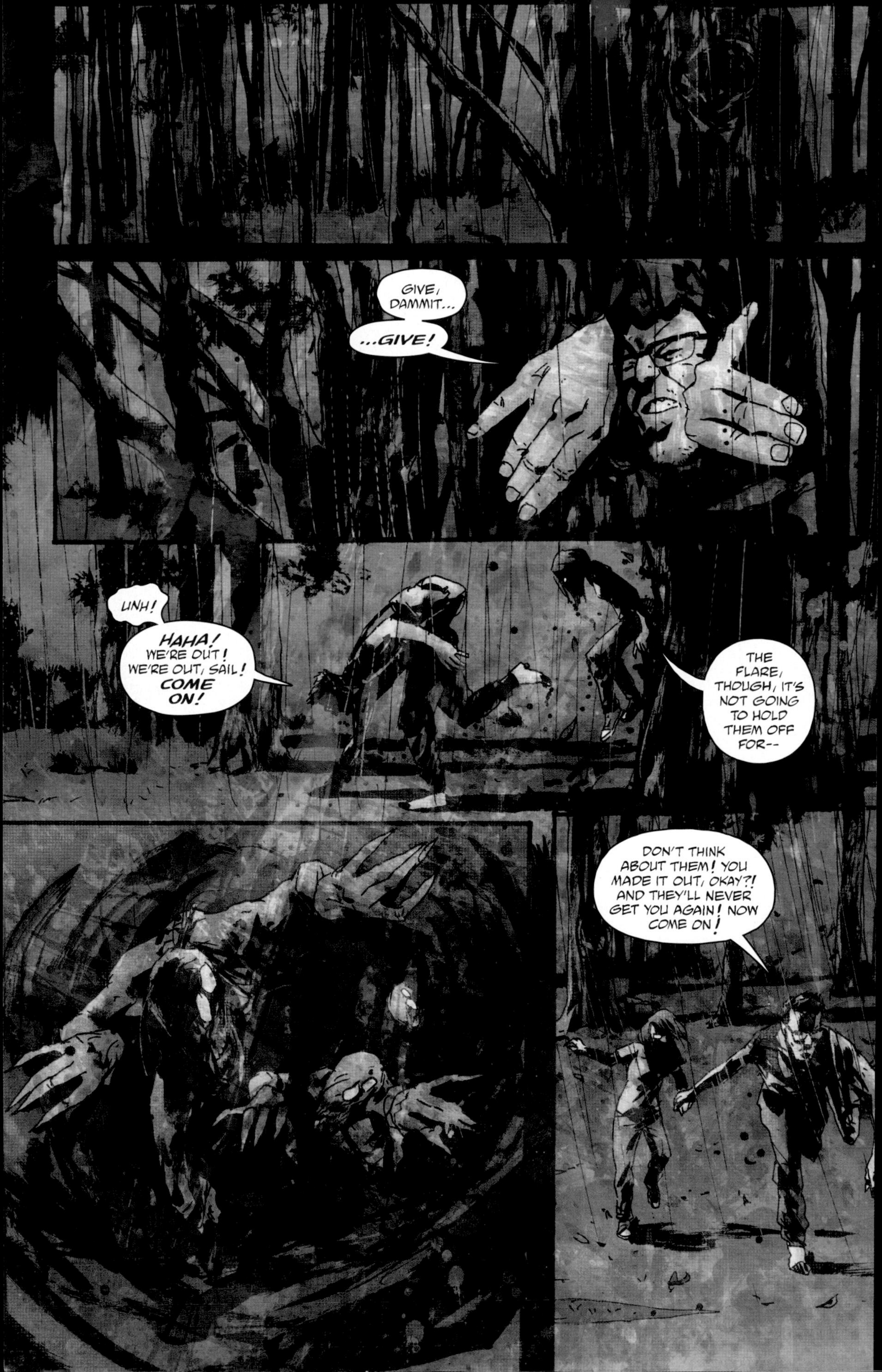
GIVE, DAMMIT...
...GIVE!
UNH!
HAHA! WE'RE OUT! WE'RE OUT, SAIL! COME ON!
THE FLARE, THOUGH, IT'S NOT GOING TO HOLD THEM OFF FOR--
DON'T THINK ABOUT THEM! YOU MADE IT OUT, OKAY?! AND THEY'LL NEVER GET YOU AGAIN! NOW COME ON!

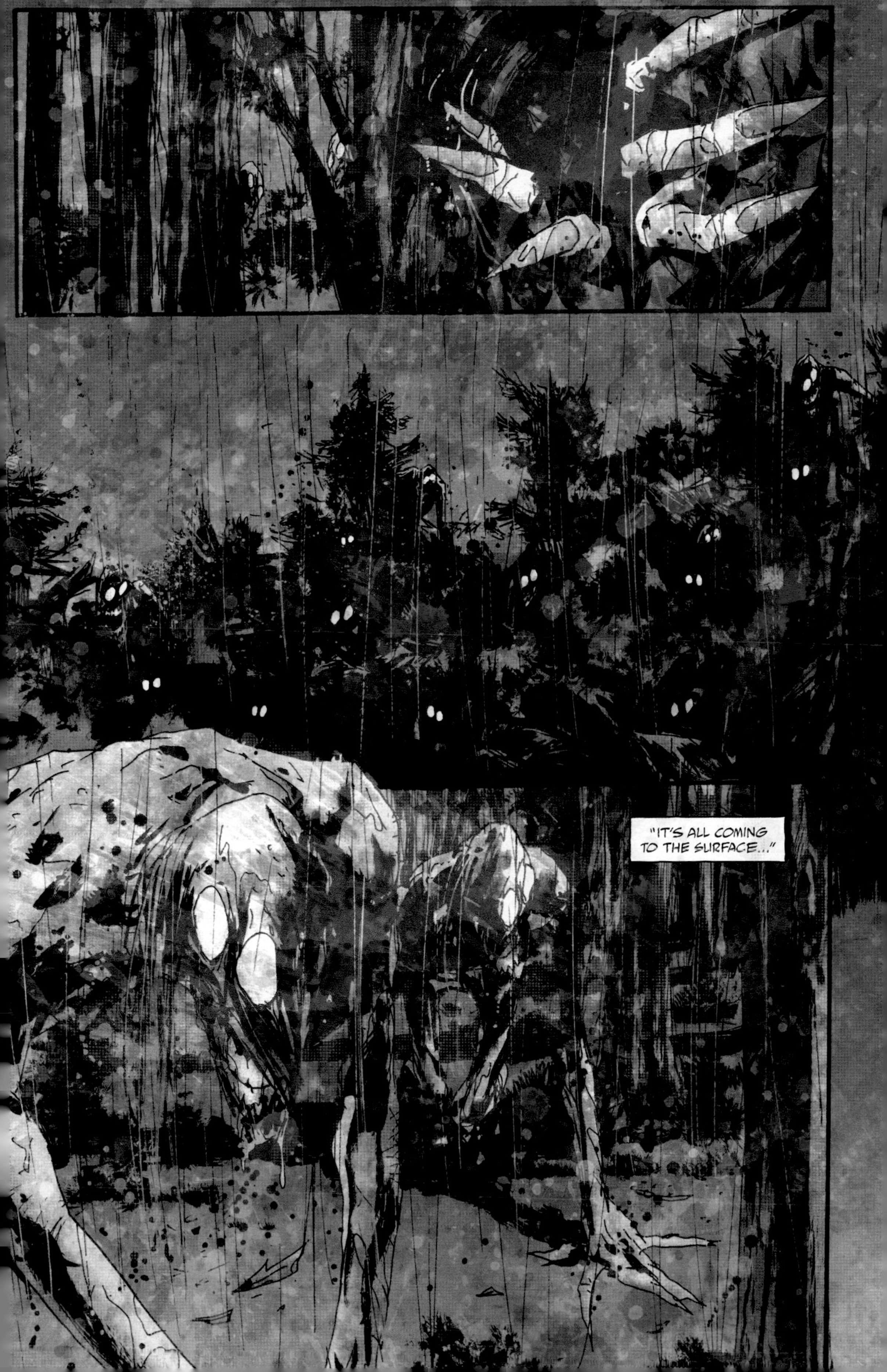
"IT'S ALL COMING TO THE SURFACE..."

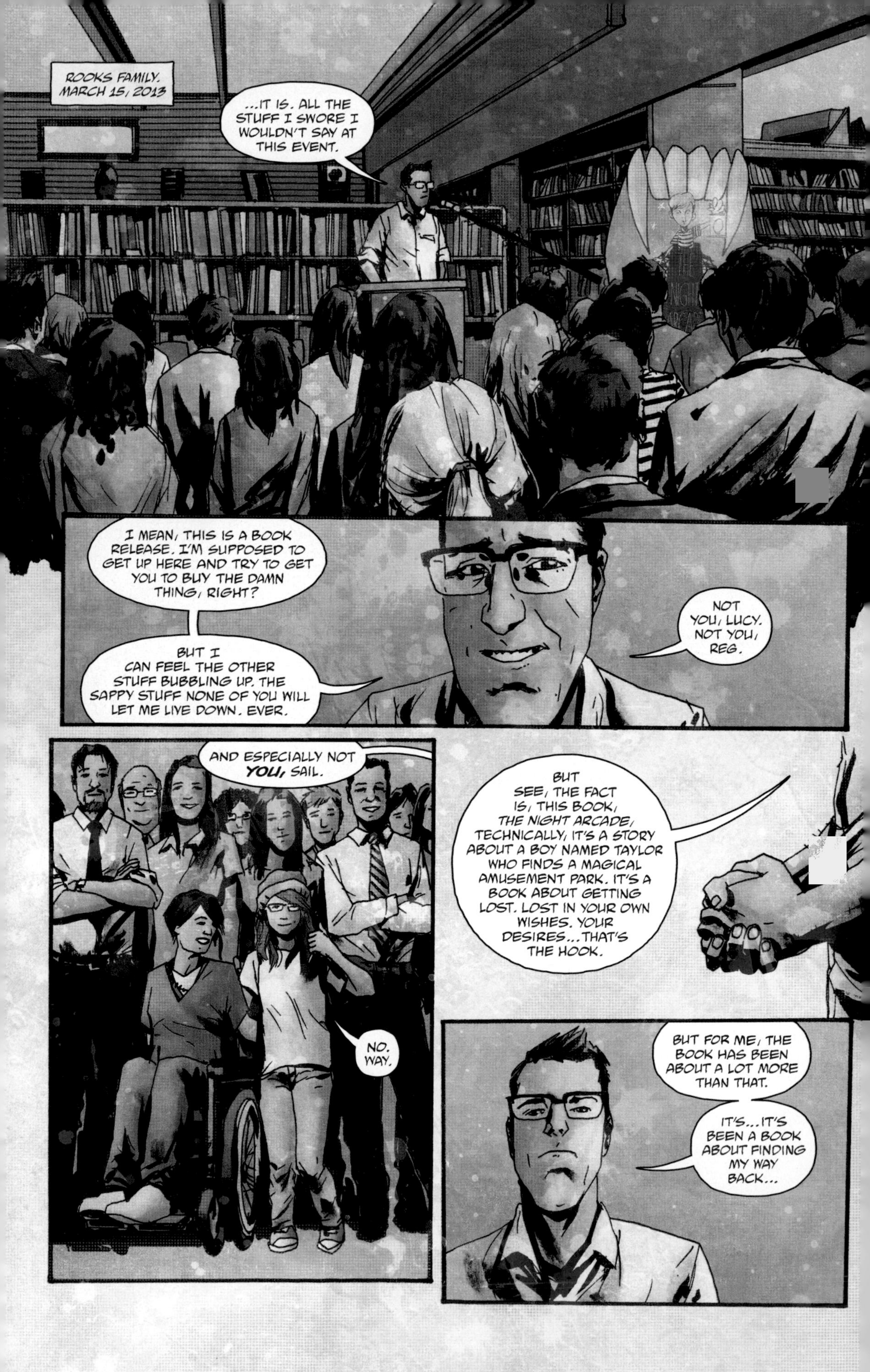
ROOKS FAMILY. MARCH 15, 2013
...IT IS. ALL THE STUFF I SWORE I WOULDN'T SAY AT THIS EVENT.
I MEAN, THIS IS A BOOK RELEASE. I'M SUPPOSED TO GET UP HERE AND TRY TO GET YOU TO BUY THE DAMN THING, RIGHT?
BUT I CAN FEEL THE OTHER STUFF BUBBLING UP. THE SAPPY STUFF NONE OF YOU WILL LET ME LIVE DOWN. EVER.
NOT YOU, LUCY. NOT YOU, REG.
AND ESPECIALLY NOT YOU, SAIL.
NO. WAY.
BUT SEE, THE FACT IS, THIS BOOK, THE NIGHT ARCADE, TECHNICALLY, IT'S A STORY ABOUT A BOY NAMED TAYLOR WHO FINDS A MAGICAL AMUSEMENT PARK. IT'S A BOOK ABOUT GETTING LOST. LOST IN YOUR OWN WISHES. YOUR DESIRES...THAT'S THE HOOK.
BUT FOR ME, THE BOOK HAS BEEN ABOUT A LOT MORE THAN THAT.
IT'S...IT'S BEEN A BOOK ABOUT FINDING MY WAY BACK...

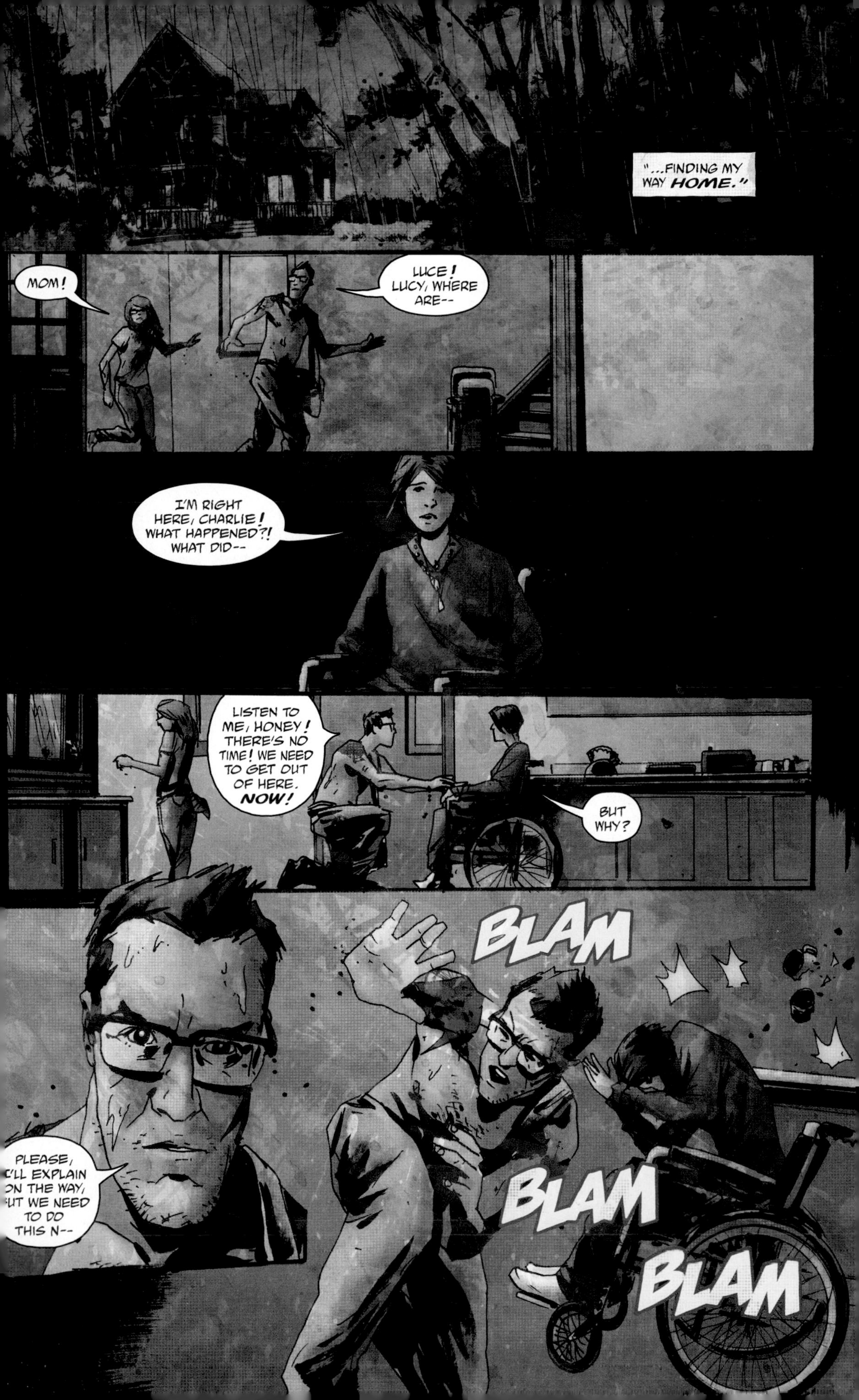
"...FINDING MY WAY HOME."
MOM!
LUCE! LUCY, WHERE ARE--
I'M RIGHT HERE, CHARLIE! WHAT HAPPENED?! WHAT DID--
LISTEN TO ME, HONEY! THERE'S NO TIME! WE NEED TO GET OUT OF HERE. NOW!
BUT WHY?
PLEASE, I'LL EXPLAIN ON THE WAY, BUT WE NEED TO DO THIS N--
BLAM
BLAM
BLAM

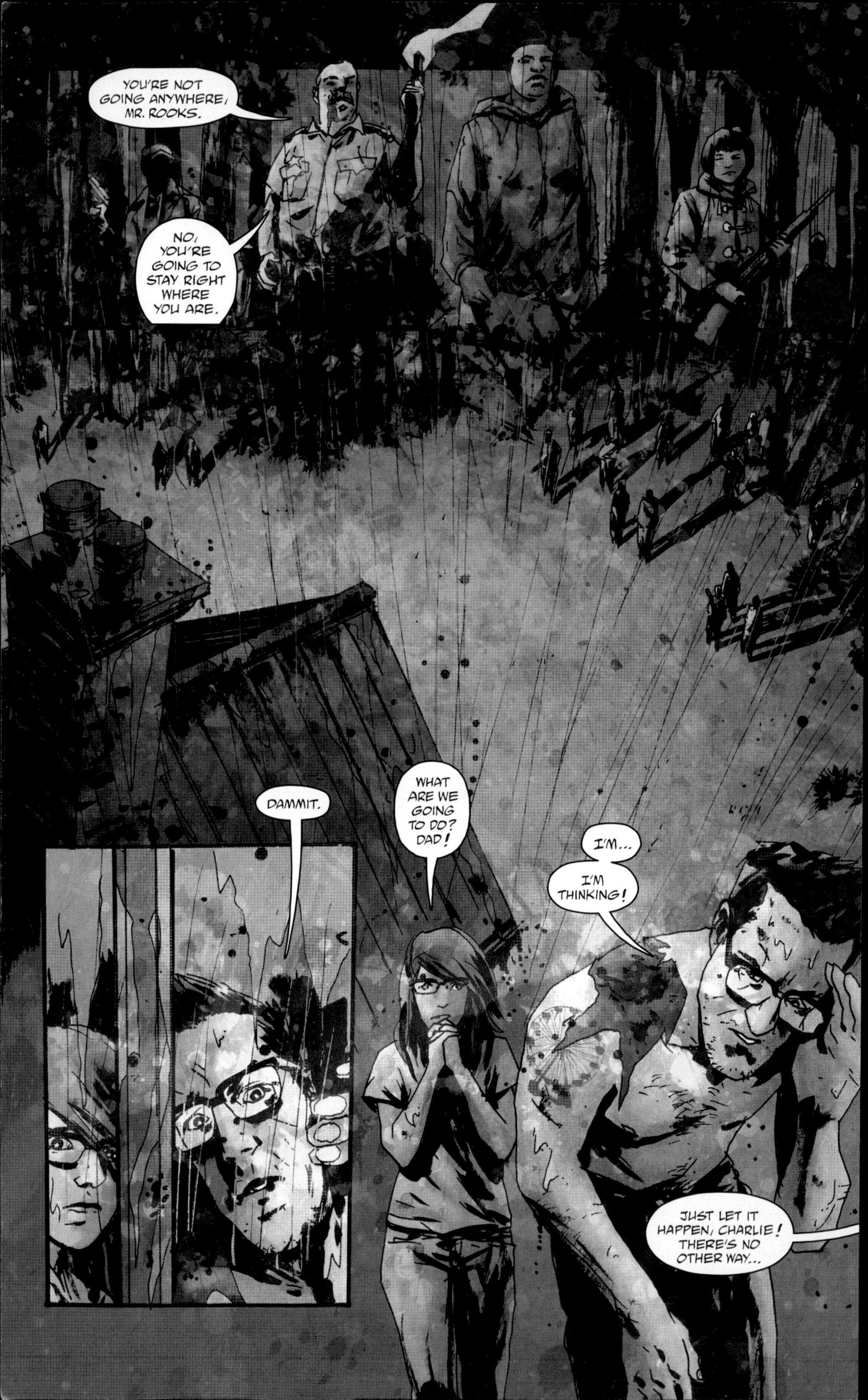
YOU'RE NOT GOING ANYWHERE, MR. ROOKS.
NO, YOU'RE GOING TO STAY RIGHT WHERE YOU ARE.
DAMMIT.
WHAT ARE WE GOING TO DO? DAD!
I'M...
I'M THINKING!
JUST LET IT HAPPEN, CHARLIE! THERE'S NO OTHER WAY...

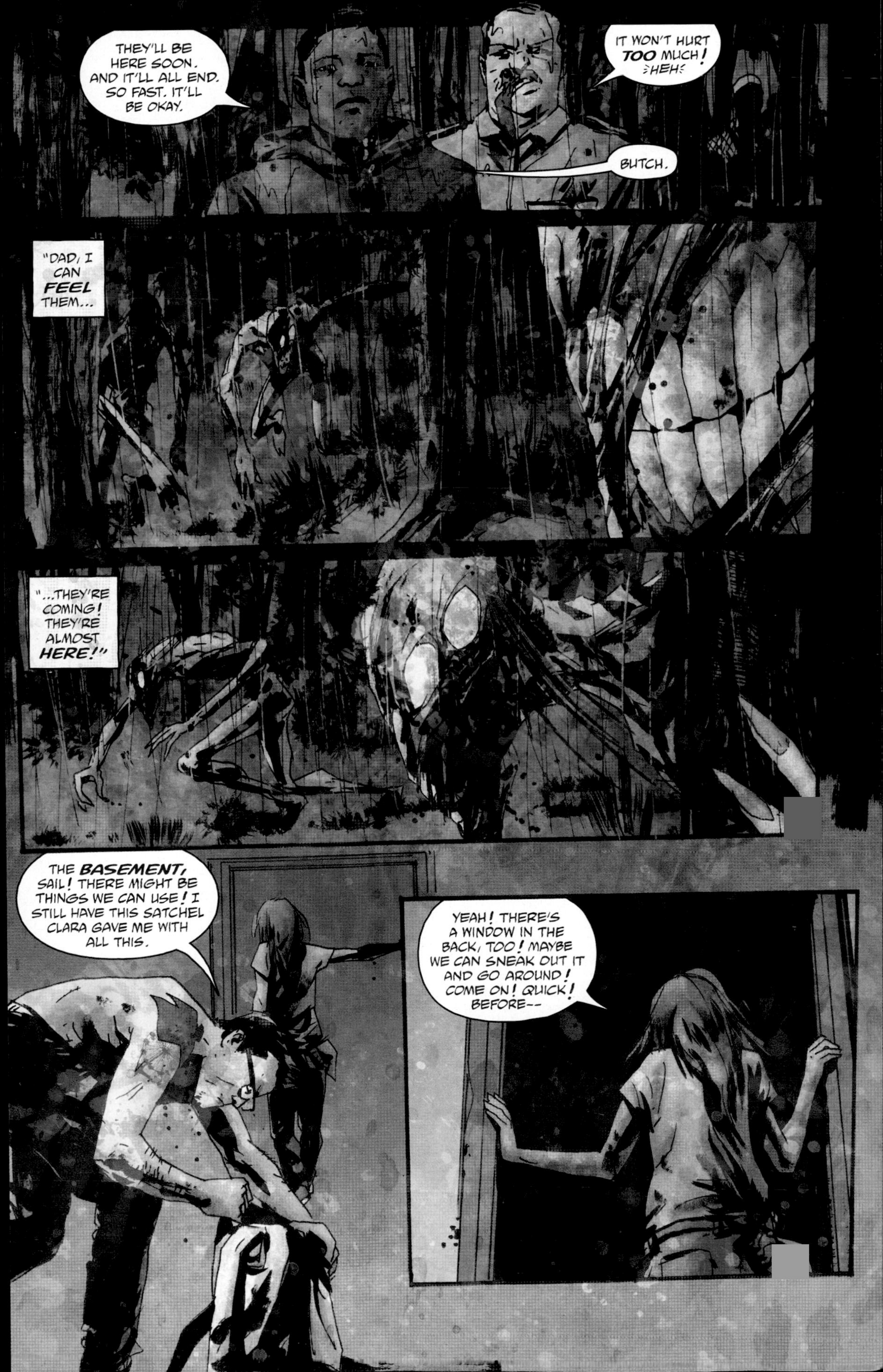
THEY'LL BE HERE SOON. AND IT'LL ALL END. SO FAST. IT'LL BE OKAY.
IT WON'T HURT TOO MUCH! HEH
BUTCH.
"DAD, I CAN FEEL THEM...
"...THEY'RE COMING! THEY'RE ALMOST HERE!"
THE BASEMENT, SAIL! THERE MIGHT BE THINGS WE CAN USE! I STILL HAVE THIS SATCHEL CLARA GAVE ME WITH ALL THIS.
YEAH! THERE'S A WINDOW IN THE BACK, TOO! MAYBE WE CAN SNEAK OUT IT AND GO AROUND! COME ON! QUICK! BEFORE--

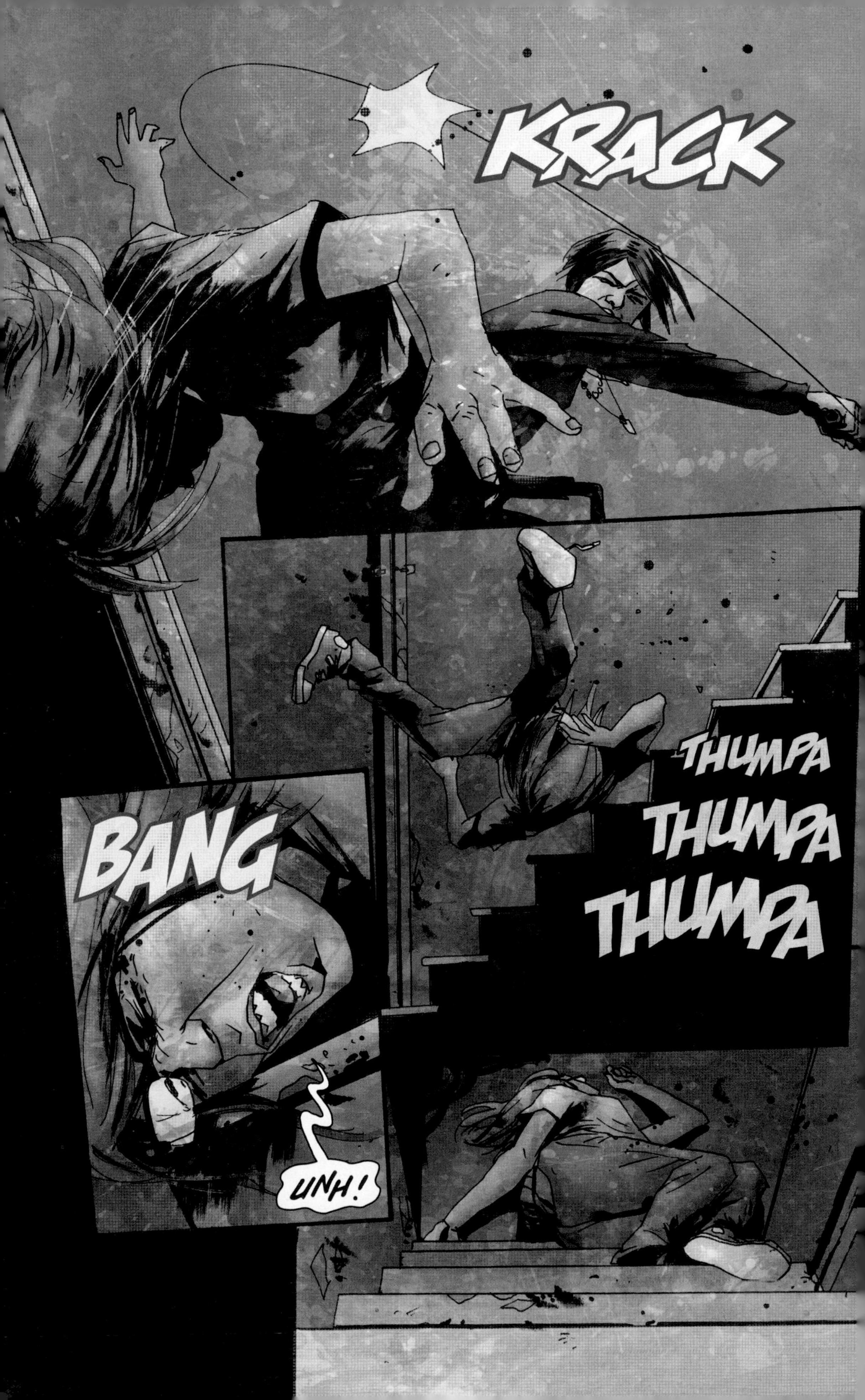
KRACK
THUMPA
THUMPA
THUMPA
BANG
UNH!

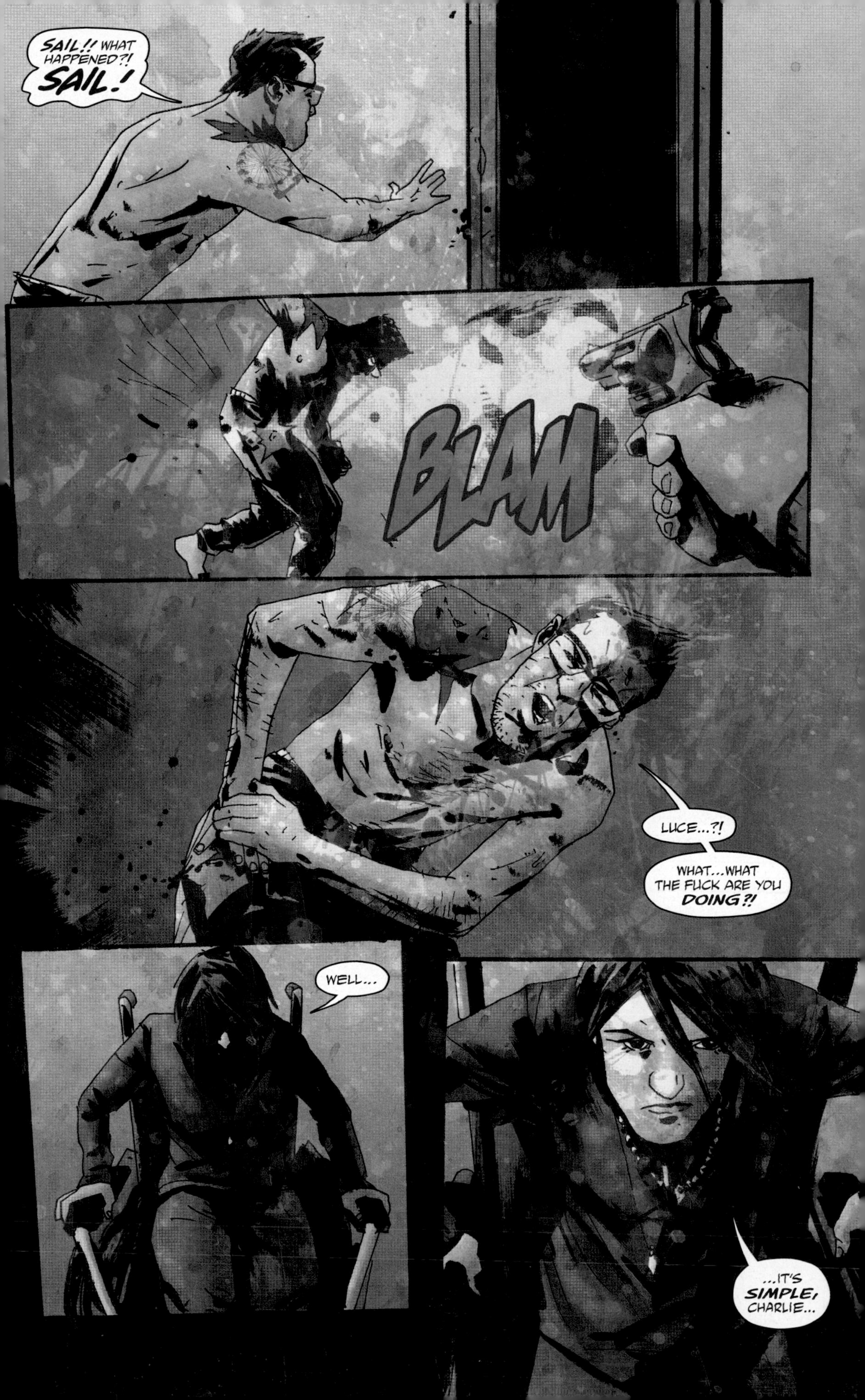
SAIL!! WHAT HAPPENED?! SAIL!
BLAM
LUCE...?!
WHAT...WHAT THE FUCK ARE YOU DOING?!
WELL...
...IT'S SIMPLE, CHARLIE...

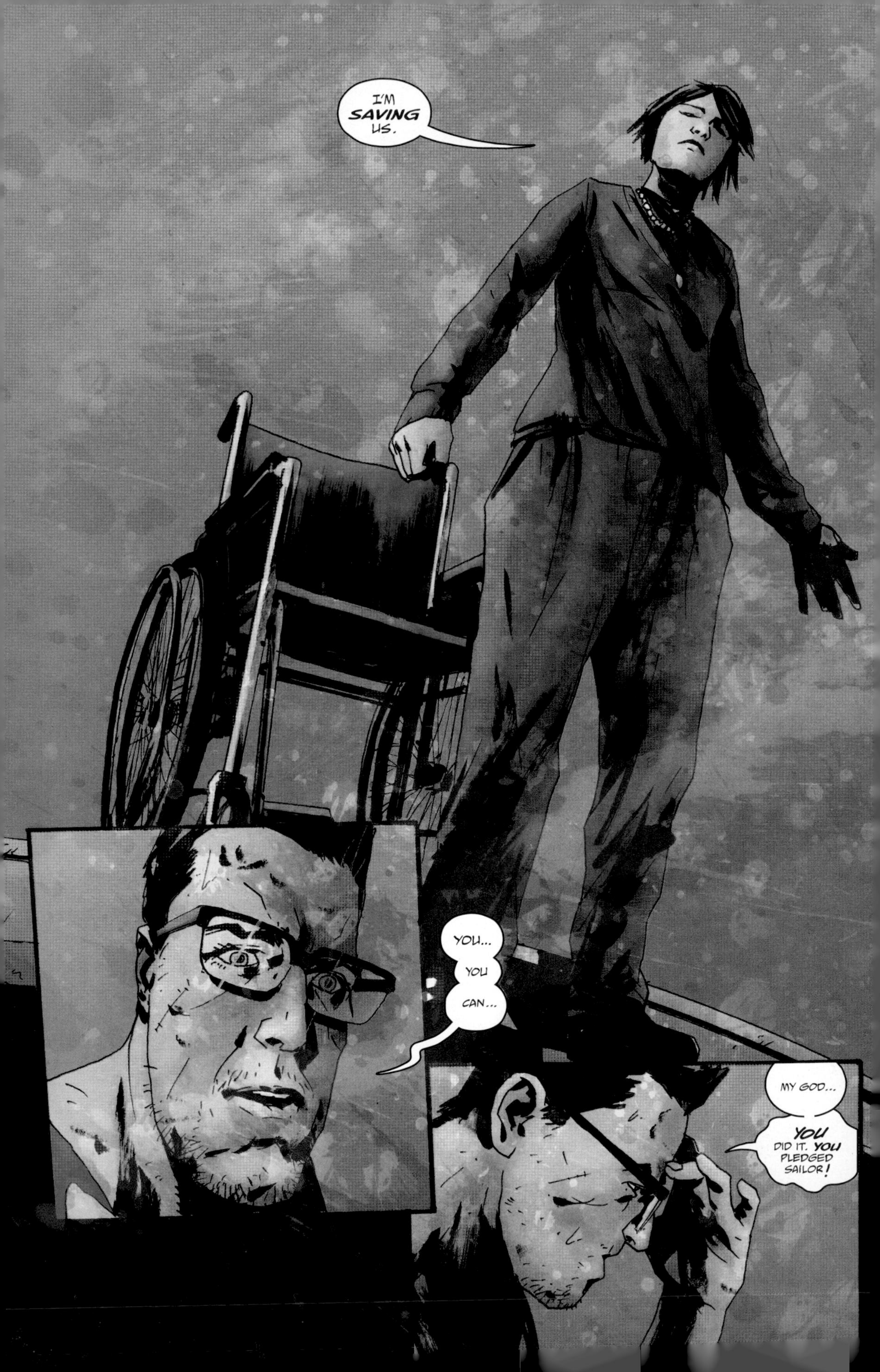
I'M *SAVING* US.
YOU...
YOU
CAN...
MY GOD...
YOU DID IT. *YOU* PLEDGED SAILOR!

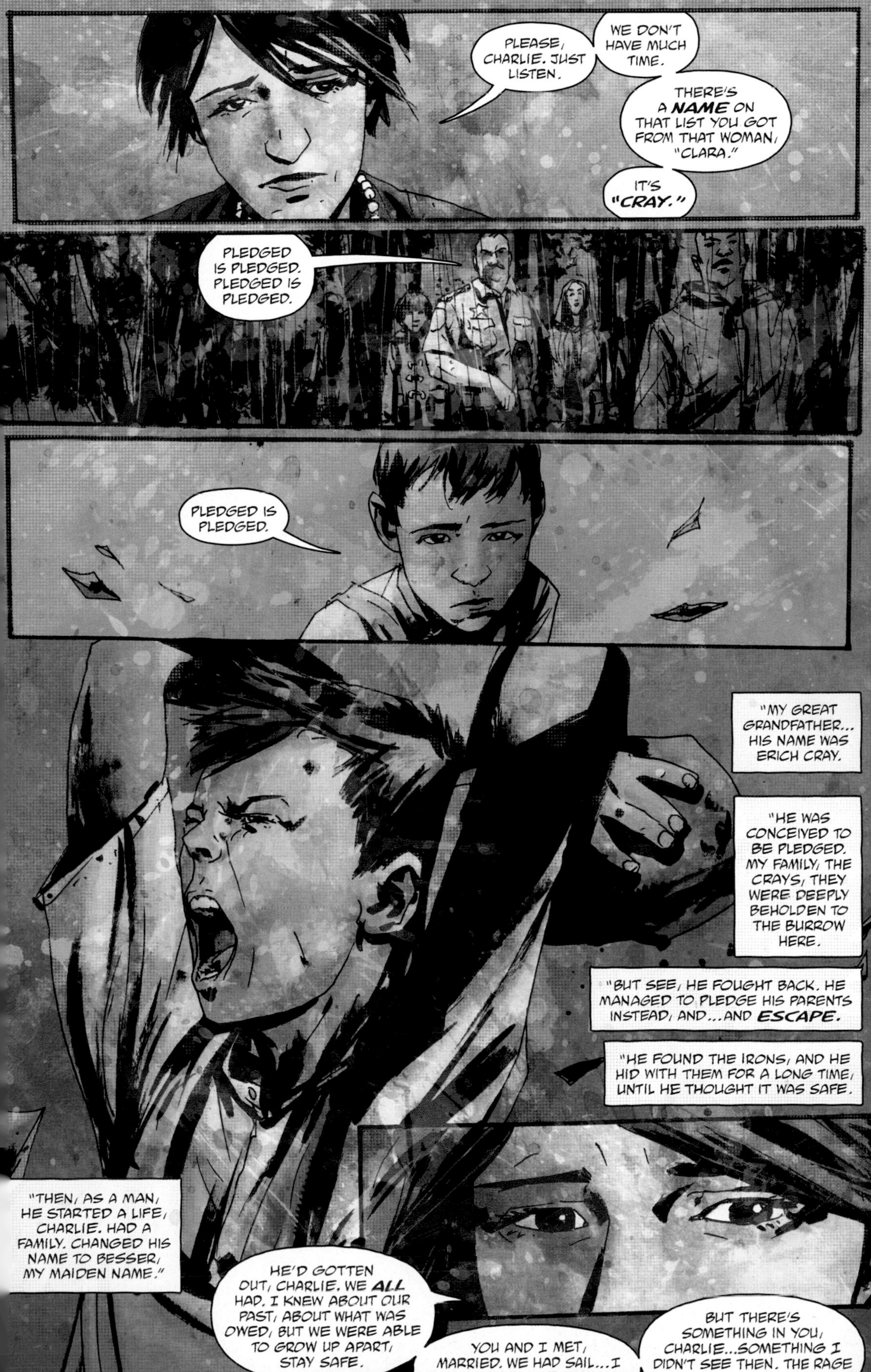

PLEASE, CHARLIE. JUST LISTEN.
WE DON'T HAVE MUCH TIME.
THERE'S A **NAME** ON THAT LIST YOU GOT FROM THAT WOMAN, "CLARA."
IT'S **"CRAY."**
PLEDGED IS PLEDGED. PLEDGED IS PLEDGED.
PLEDGED IS PLEDGED.
"MY GREAT GRANDFATHER... HIS NAME WAS ERICH CRAY.
"HE WAS CONCEIVED TO BE PLEDGED. MY FAMILY, THE CRAYS, THEY WERE DEEPLY BEHOLDEN TO THE BURROW HERE.
"BUT SEE, HE FOUGHT BACK. HE MANAGED TO PLEDGE HIS PARENTS INSTEAD, AND...AND **ESCAPE.**
"HE FOUND THE IRONS, AND HE HID WITH THEM FOR A LONG TIME, UNTIL HE THOUGHT IT WAS SAFE.
"THEN, AS A MAN, HE STARTED A LIFE, CHARLIE. HAD A FAMILY. CHANGED HIS NAME TO BESSER, MY MAIDEN NAME."
HE'D GOTTEN OUT, CHARLIE. WE ***ALL*** HAD. I KNEW ABOUT OUR PAST, ABOUT WHAT WAS OWED, BUT WE WERE ABLE TO GROW UP APART, STAY SAFE.
YOU AND I MET, MARRIED. WE HAD SAIL... I HAD A HAPPY LIFE. ***WE*** HAD A HAPPY LIFE.
BUT THERE'S SOMETHING IN YOU, CHARLIE...SOMETHING I DIDN'T SEE THEN. THE RAGE AT IT ALL. THE SECRET WANTS...

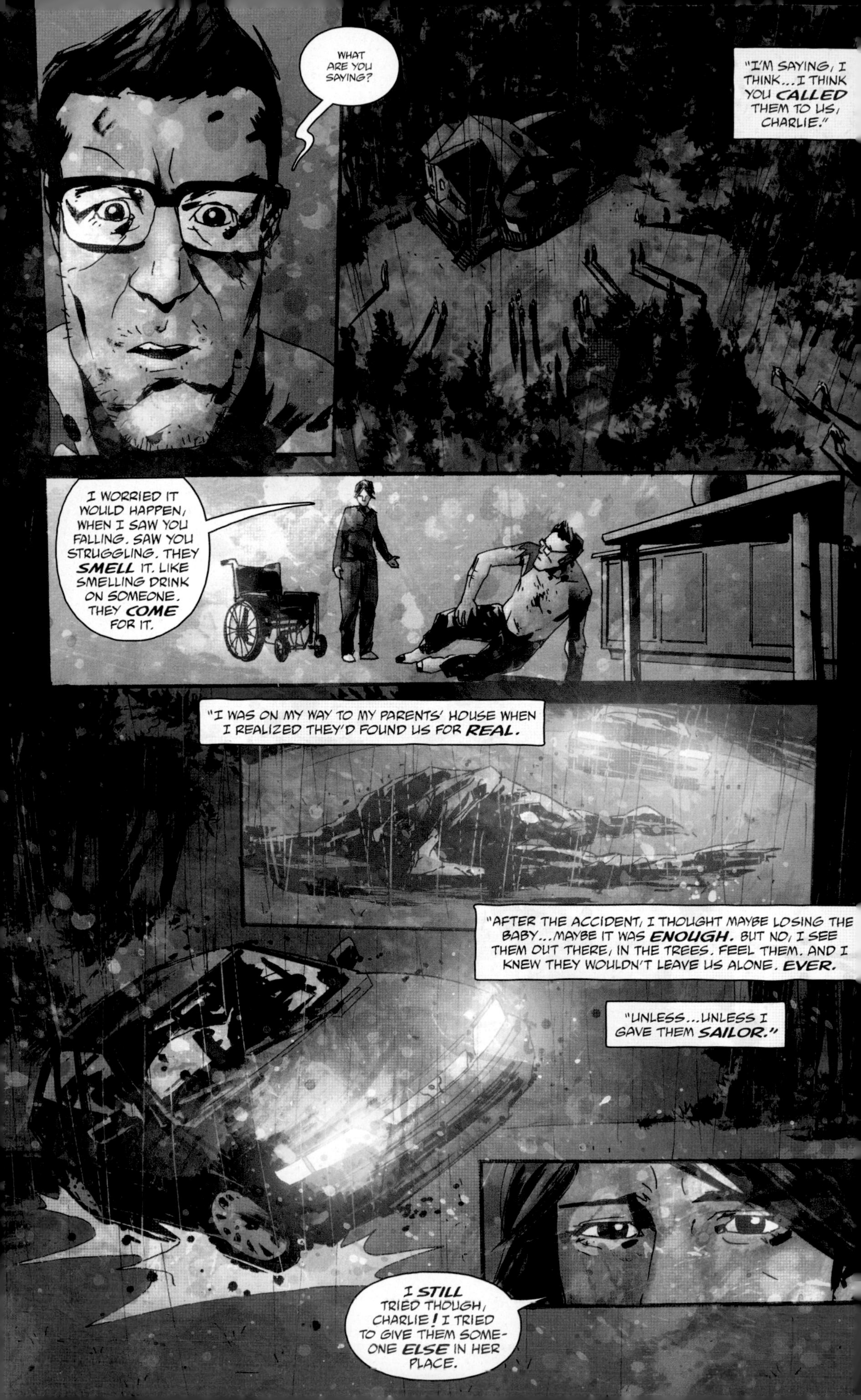
WHAT ARE YOU SAYING?
"I'M SAYING, I THINK... I THINK YOU CALLED THEM TO US, CHARLIE."
I WORRIED IT WOULD HAPPEN, WHEN I SAW YOU FALLING. SAW YOU STRUGGLING. THEY SMELL IT. LIKE SMELLING DRINK ON SOMEONE. THEY COME FOR IT.
"I WAS ON MY WAY TO MY PARENTS' HOUSE WHEN I REALIZED THEY'D FOUND US FOR REAL.
"AFTER THE ACCIDENT, I THOUGHT MAYBE LOSING THE BABY... MAYBE IT WAS ENOUGH. BUT NO, I SEE THEM OUT THERE, IN THE TREES. FEEL THEM. AND I KNEW THEY WOULDN'T LEAVE US ALONE. EVER.
"UNLESS... UNLESS I GAVE THEM SAILOR."
I STILL TRIED THOUGH, CHARLIE! I TRIED TO GIVE THEM SOME-ONE ELSE IN HER PLACE.

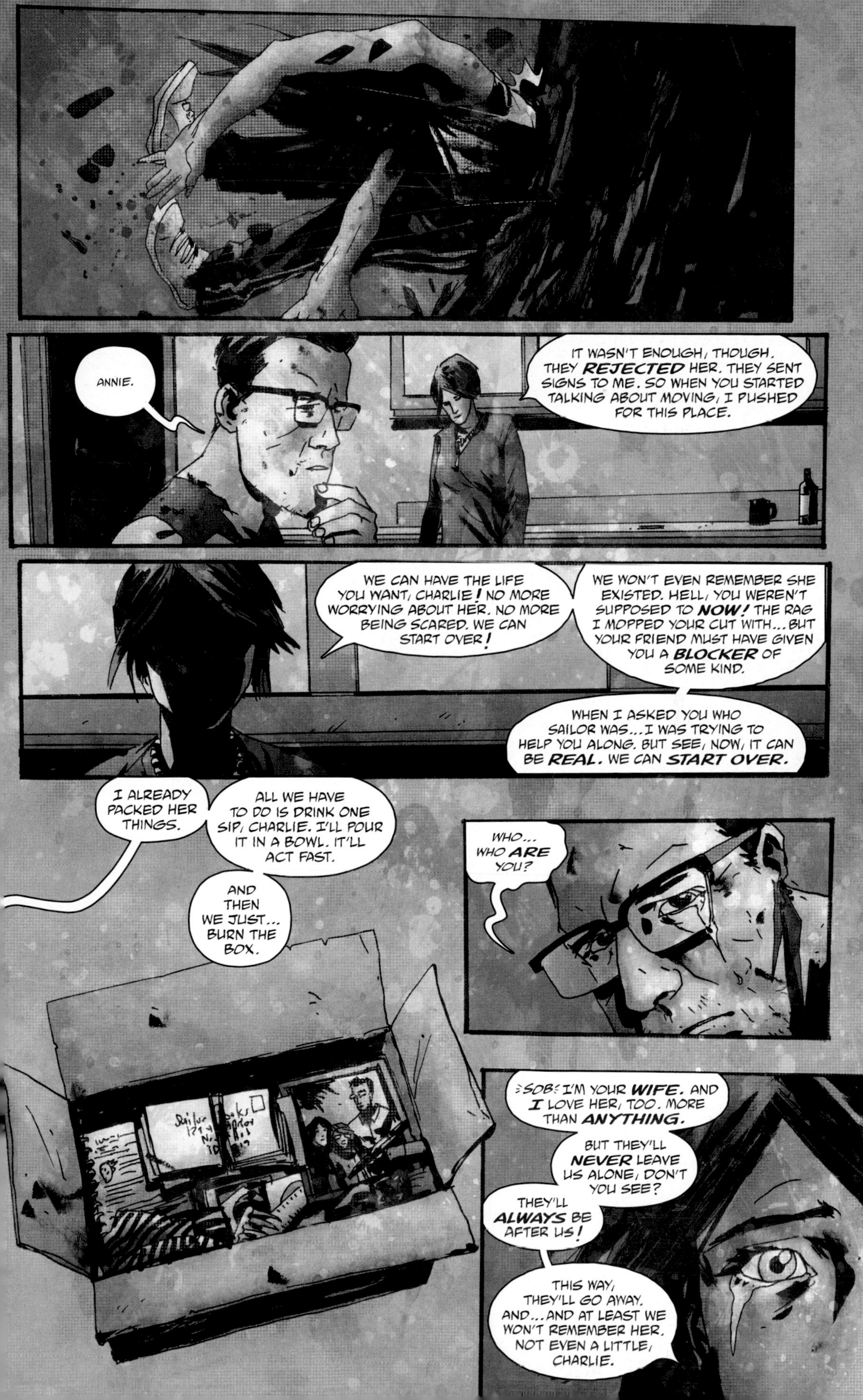
ANNIE.
IT WASN'T ENOUGH, THOUGH. THEY REJECTED HER. THEY SENT SIGNS TO ME. SO WHEN YOU STARTED TALKING ABOUT MOVING, I PUSHED FOR THIS PLACE.
WE CAN HAVE THE LIFE YOU WANT, CHARLIE! NO MORE WORRYING ABOUT HER. NO MORE BEING SCARED. WE CAN START OVER!
WE WON'T EVEN REMEMBER SHE EXISTED. HELL, YOU WEREN'T SUPPOSED TO NOW! THE RAG I MOPPED YOUR CUT WITH... BUT YOUR FRIEND MUST HAVE GIVEN YOU A BLOCKER OF SOME KIND.
WHEN I ASKED YOU WHO SAILOR WAS... I WAS TRYING TO HELP YOU ALONG. BUT SEE, NOW, IT CAN BE REAL. WE CAN START OVER.
I ALREADY PACKED HER THINGS.
ALL WE HAVE TO DO IS DRINK ONE SIP, CHARLIE. I'LL POUR IT IN A BOWL. IT'LL ACT FAST.
AND THEN WE JUST... BURN THE BOX.
WHO... WHO ARE YOU?
SOB I'M YOUR WIFE. AND I LOVE HER, TOO. MORE THAN ANYTHING.
BUT THEY'LL NEVER LEAVE US ALONE, DON'T YOU SEE?
THEY'LL ALWAYS BE AFTER US!
THIS WAY, THEY'LL GO AWAY. AND... AND AT LEAST WE WON'T REMEMBER HER. NOT EVEN A LITTLE, CHARLIE.

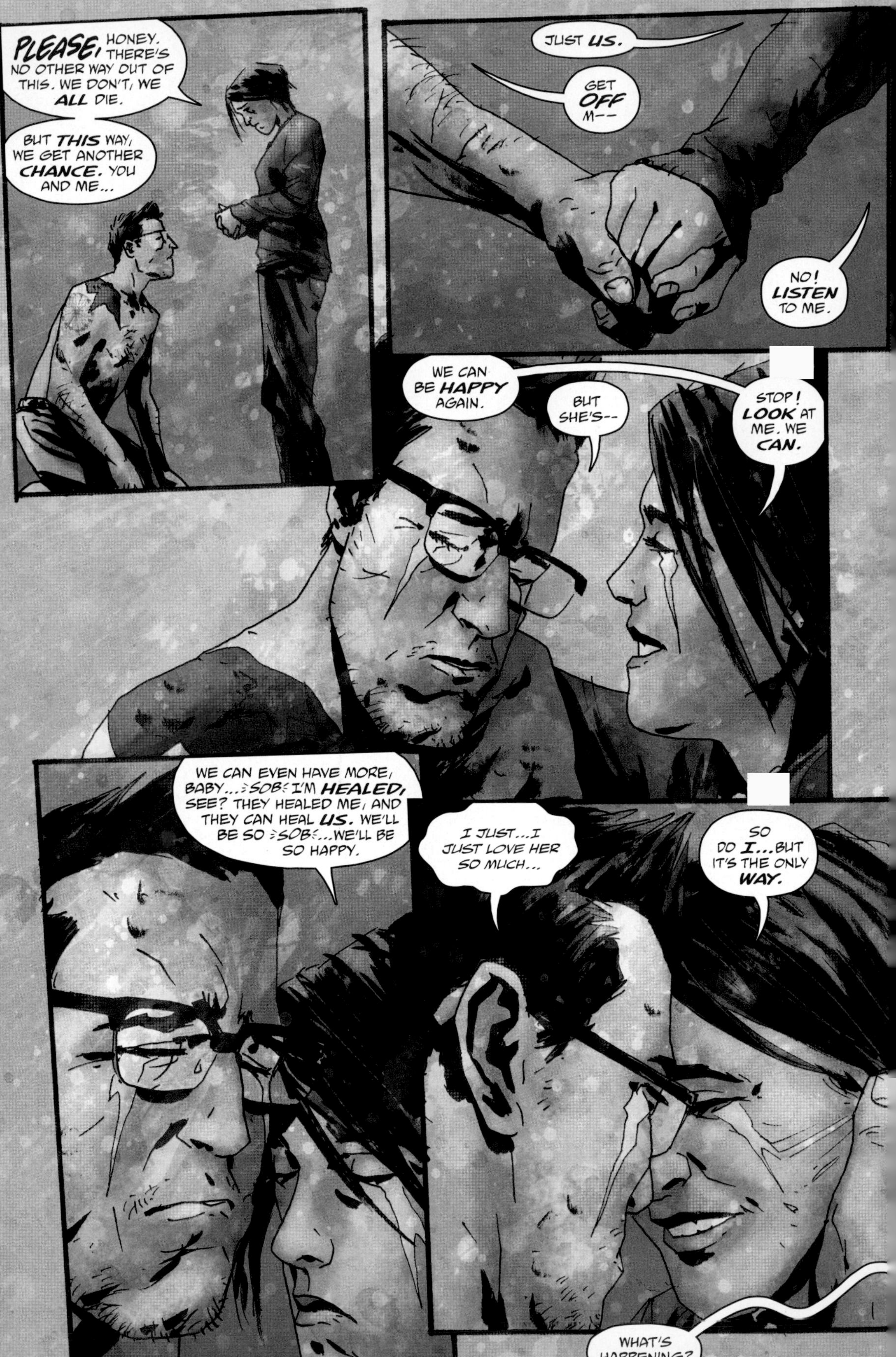
PLEASE, HONEY. THERE'S NO OTHER WAY OUT OF THIS. WE DON'T, WE ALL DIE.
BUT THIS WAY, WE GET ANOTHER CHANCE. YOU AND ME...
JUST US.
GET OFF M--
NO! LISTEN TO ME.
WE CAN BE HAPPY AGAIN.
BUT SHE'S--
STOP! LOOK AT ME. WE CAN.
WE CAN EVEN HAVE MORE, BABY... SOB I'M HEALED, SEE? THEY HEALED ME, AND THEY CAN HEAL US. WE'LL BE SO SOB... WE'LL BE SO HAPPY.
I JUST... I JUST LOVE HER SO MUCH...
SO DO I... BUT IT'S THE ONLY WAY.
WHAT'S HAPPENING?

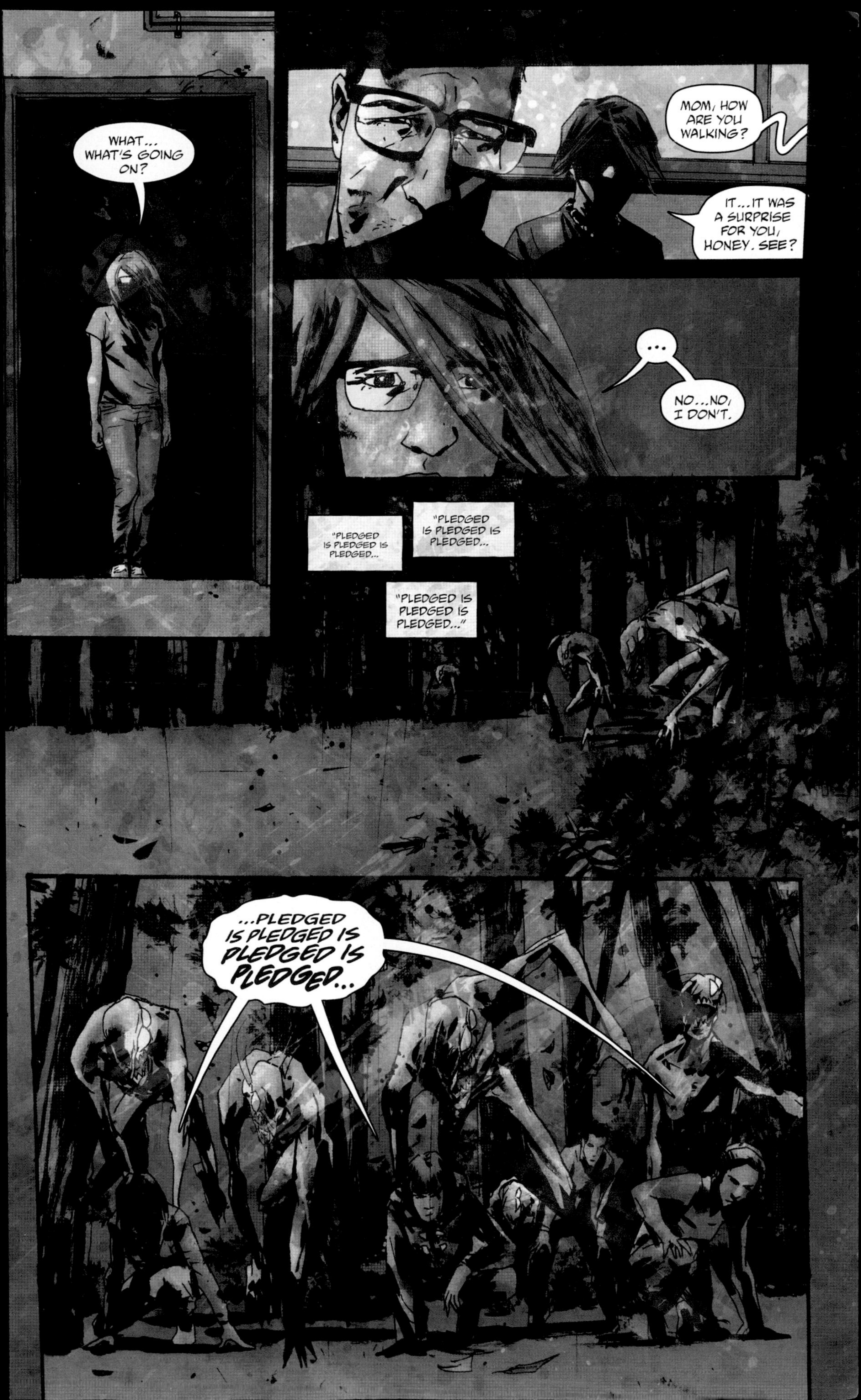
WHAT... WHAT'S GOING ON?
MOM, HOW ARE YOU WALKING?
IT...IT WAS A SURPRISE FOR YOU, HONEY. SEE?
...
NO...NO, I DON'T.
"PLEDGED IS PLEDGED IS PLEDGED...
"PLEDGED IS PLEDGED IS PLEDGED...
"PLEDGED IS PLEDGED IS PLEDGED..."
...PLEDGED IS PLEDGED IS PLEDGED IS PLEDGED...

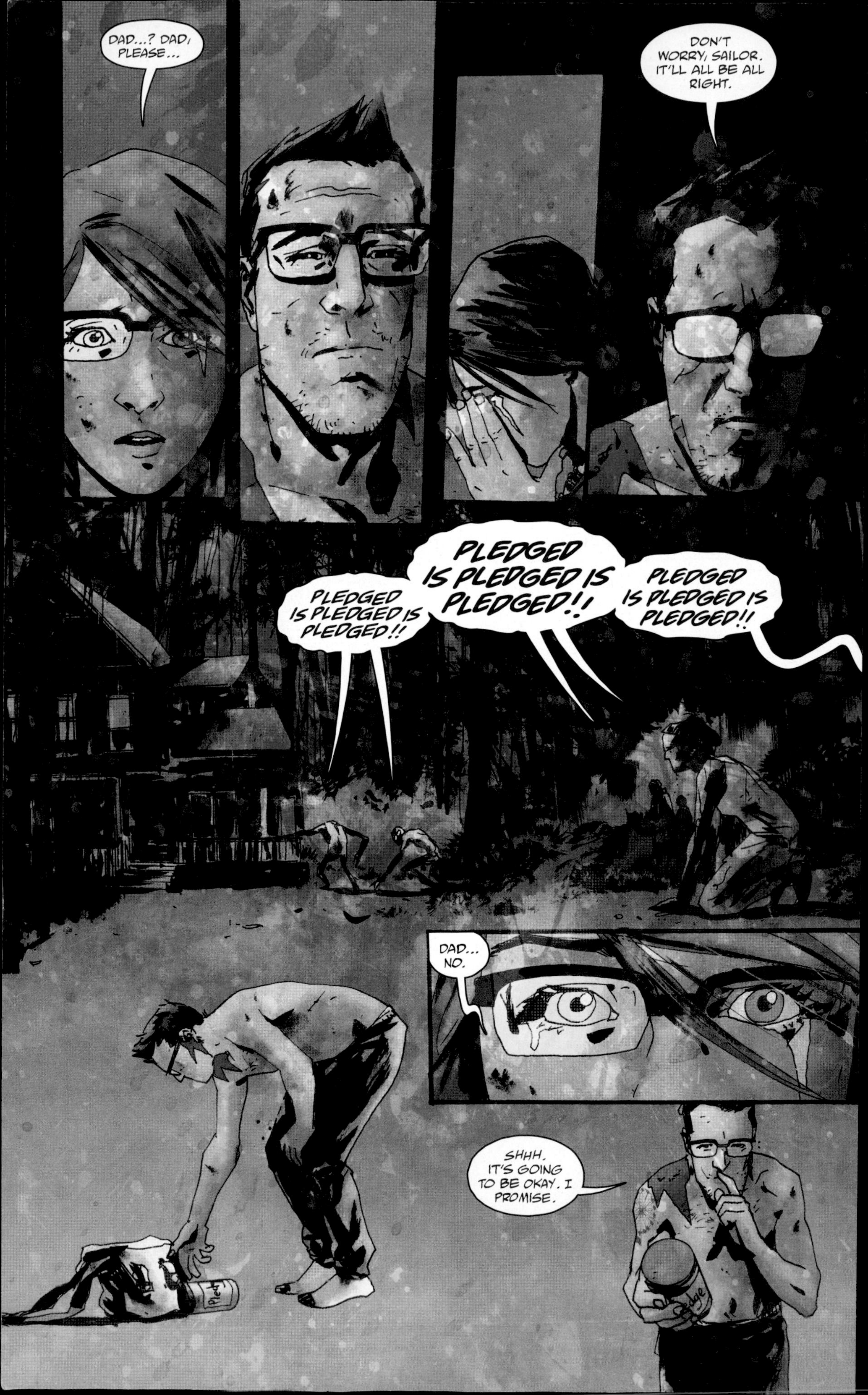
DAD...? DAD, PLEASE...
DON'T WORRY, SAILOR. IT'LL ALL BE ALL RIGHT.
PLEDGED IS PLEDGED IS PLEDGED!!
PLEDGED IS PLEDGED IS PLEDGED!!
PLEDGED IS PLEDGED IS PLEDGED!!
DAD... NO.
SHHH. IT'S GOING TO BE OKAY. I PROMISE.

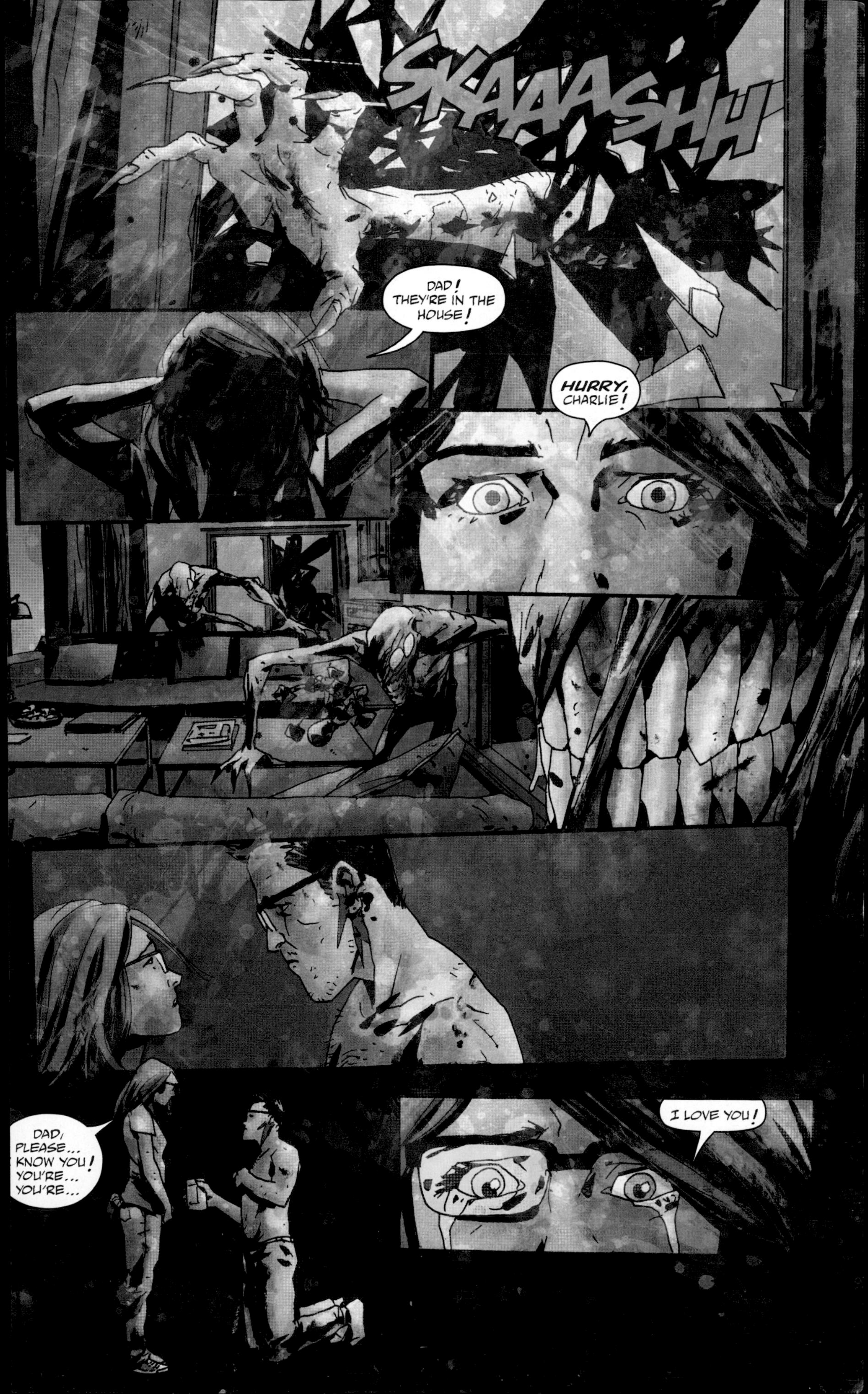
SKAAASHH
DAD! THEY'RE IN THE HOUSE!
HURRY, CHARLIE!
DAD, PLEASE... KNOW YOU! YOU'RE... YOU'RE...
I LOVE YOU!

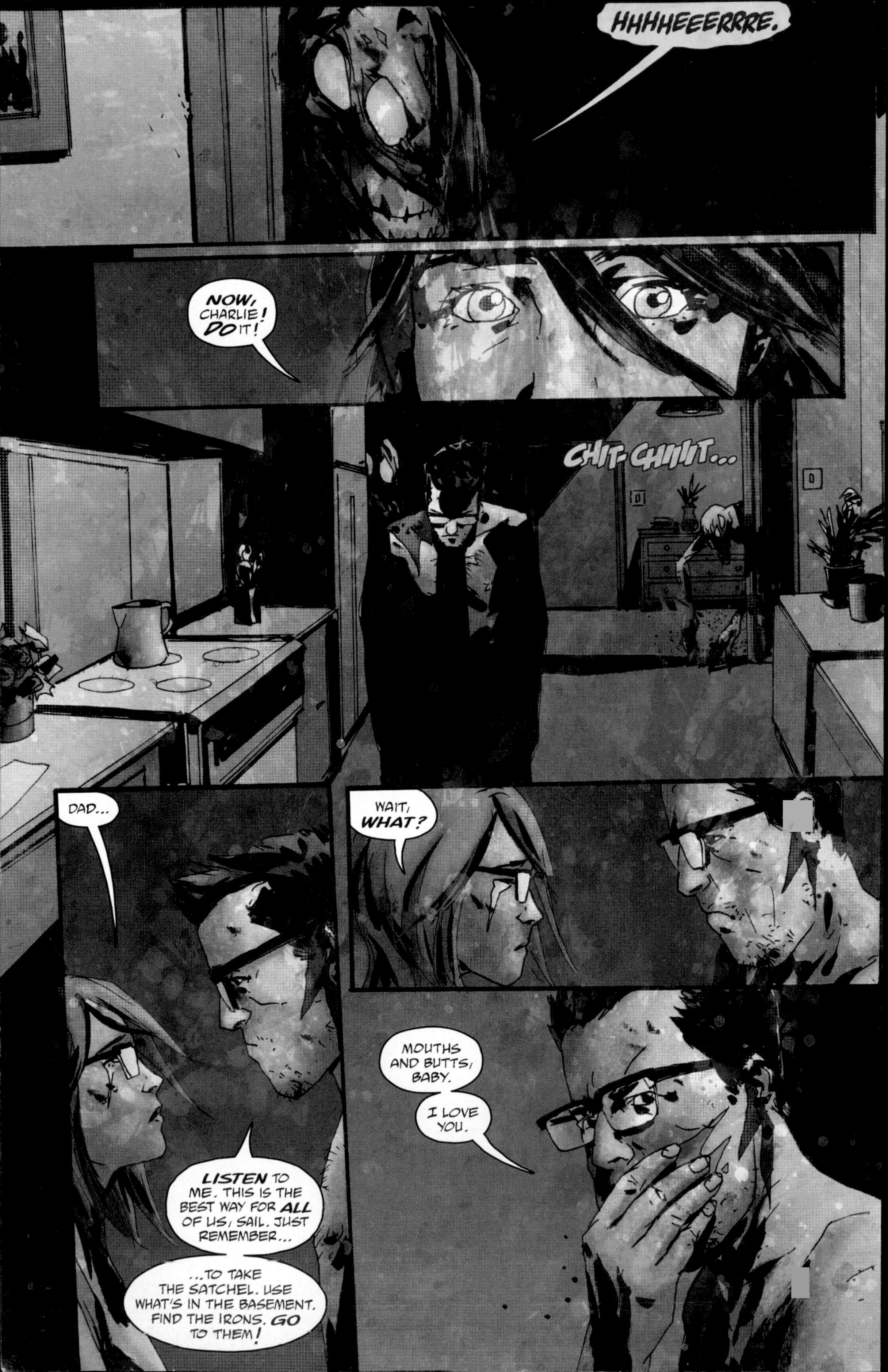
HHHHEEERRRE.
NOW, CHARLIE! DO IT!
CHIT-CHIIIT...
DAD...
LISTEN TO ME. THIS IS THE BEST WAY FOR ALL OF US, GAIL. JUST REMEMBER...
...TO TAKE THE SATCHEL. USE WHAT'S IN THE BASEMENT. FIND THE IRONS. GO TO THEM!
WAIT, WHAT?
MOUTHS AND BUTTS, BABY.
I LOVE YOU.

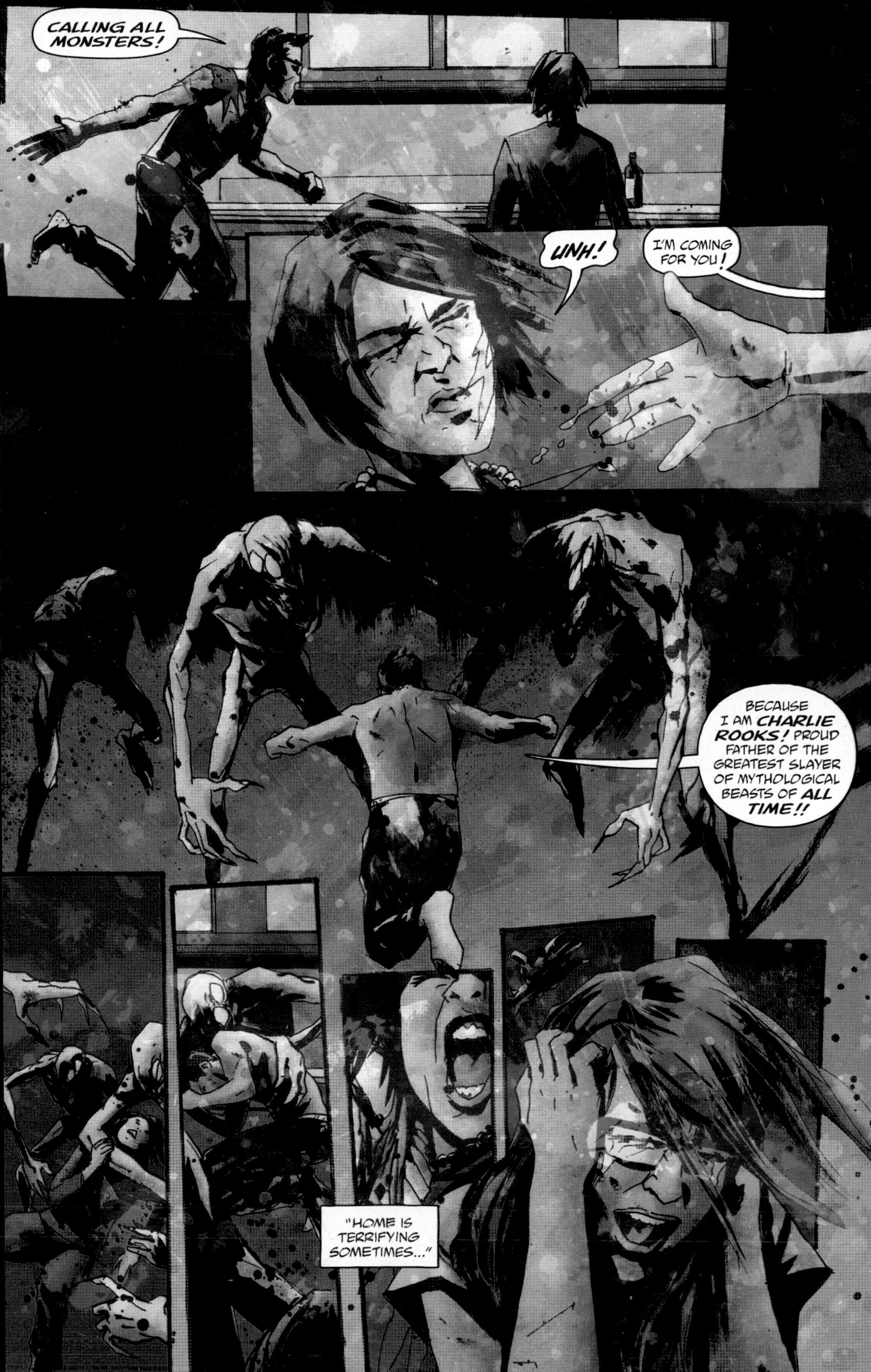
CALLING ALL MONSTERS!
UNH!
I'M COMING FOR YOU!
BECAUSE I AM CHARLIE ROOKS! PROUD FATHER OF THE GREATEST SLAYER OF MYTHOLOGICAL BEASTS OF ALL TIME!!
"HOME IS TERRIFYING SOMETIMES..."

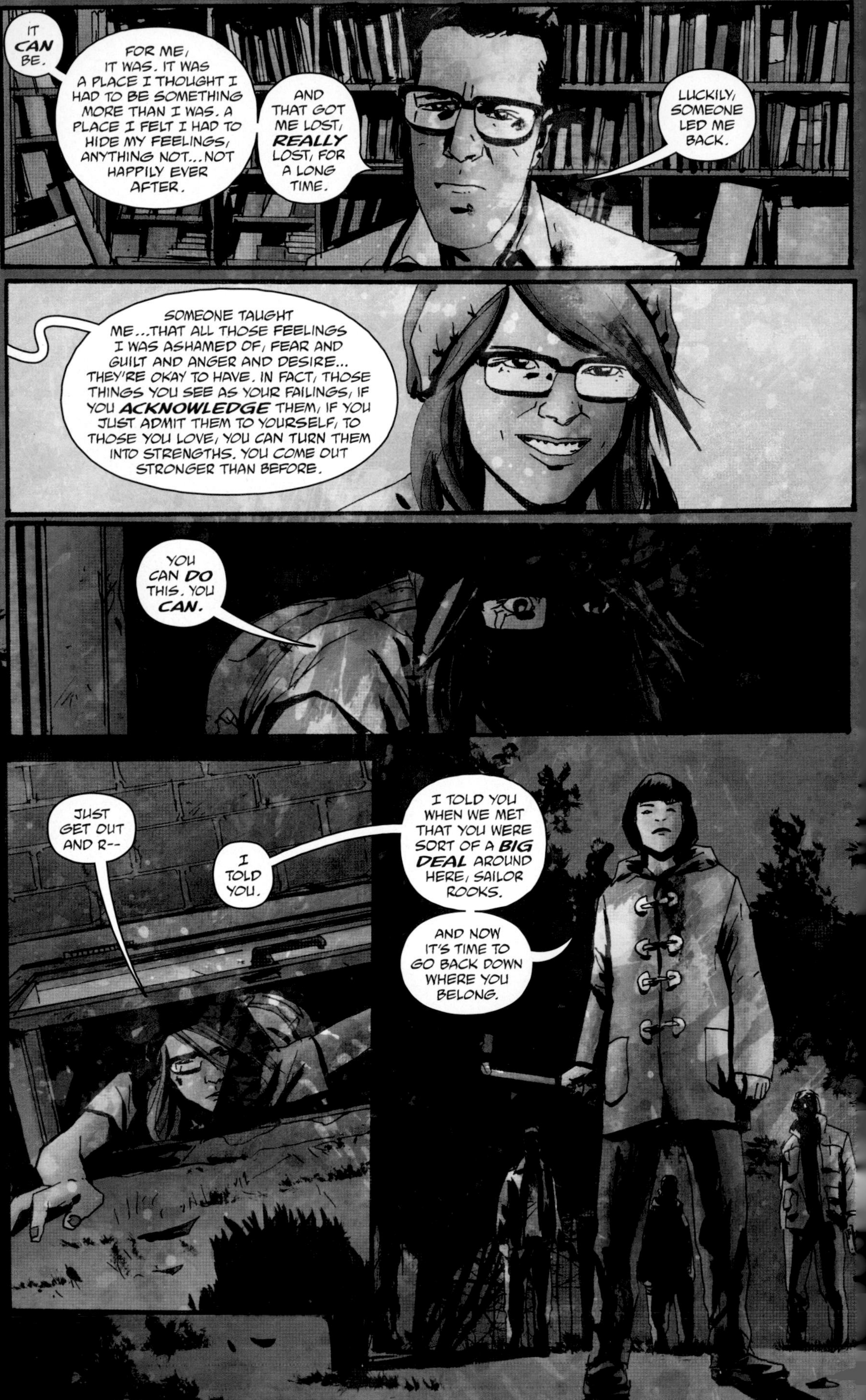
IT CAN BE.
FOR ME, IT WAS. IT WAS A PLACE I THOUGHT I HAD TO BE SOMETHING MORE THAN I WAS. A PLACE I FELT I HAD TO HIDE MY FEELINGS, ANYTHING NOT...NOT HAPPILY EVER AFTER.
AND THAT GOT ME LOST, REALLY LOST, FOR A LONG TIME.
LUCKILY, SOMEONE LED ME BACK.
SOMEONE TAUGHT ME...THAT ALL THOSE FEELINGS I WAS ASHAMED OF, FEAR AND GUILT AND ANGER AND DESIRE... THEY'RE OKAY TO HAVE. IN FACT, THOSE THINGS YOU SEE AS YOUR FAILINGS, IF YOU ACKNOWLEDGE THEM, IF YOU JUST ADMIT THEM TO YOURSELF, TO THOSE YOU LOVE, YOU CAN TURN THEM INTO STRENGTHS. YOU COME OUT STRONGER THAN BEFORE.
YOU CAN DO THIS. YOU CAN.
JUST GET OUT AND R--
I TOLD YOU.
I TOLD YOU WHEN WE MET THAT YOU WERE SORT OF A BIG DEAL AROUND HERE, SAILOR ROOKS.
AND NOW IT'S TIME TO GO BACK DOWN WHERE YOU BELONG.

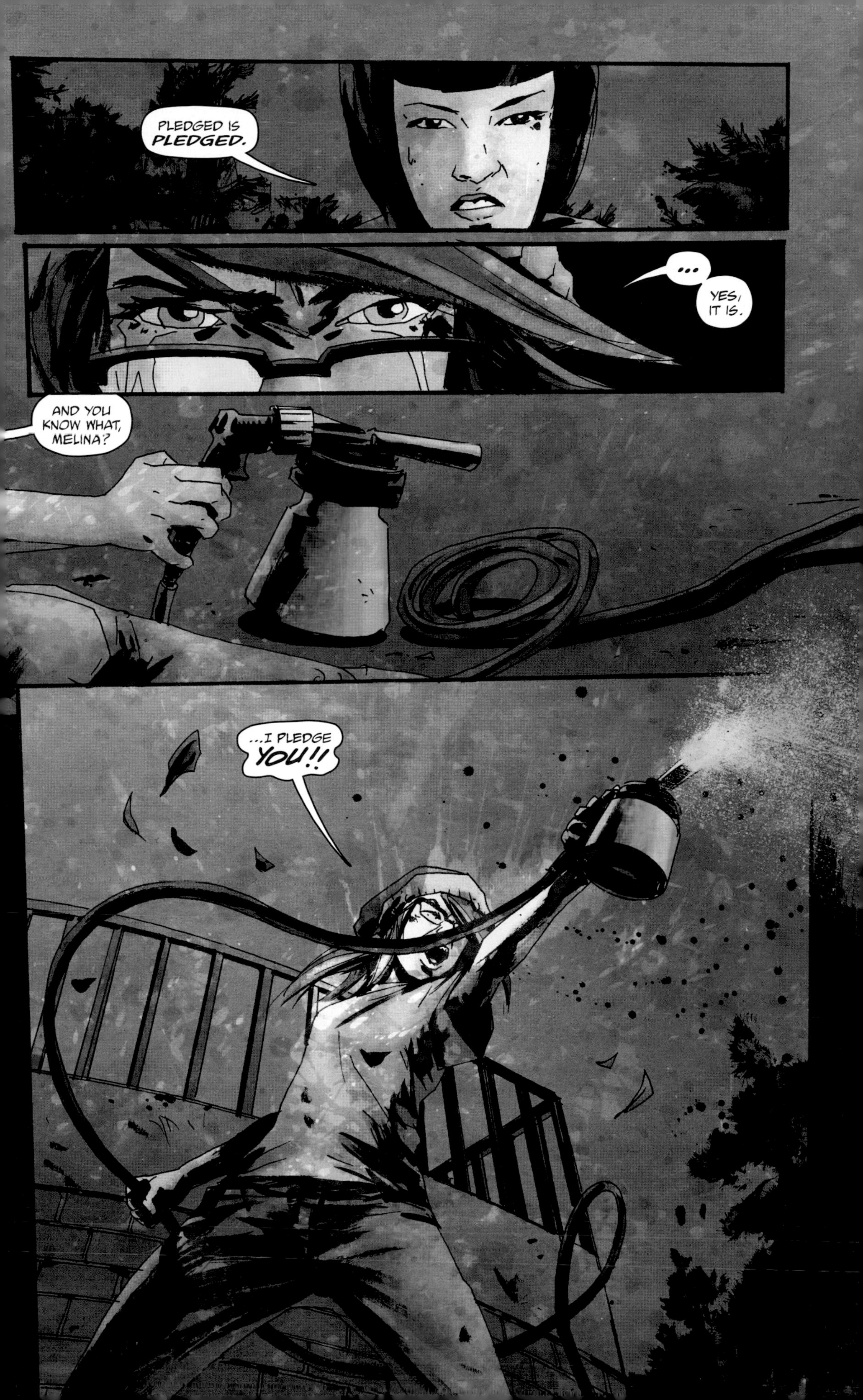
PLEDGED IS PLEDGED.
...
YES, IT IS.
AND YOU KNOW WHAT, MELINA?
...I PLEDGE YOU!!

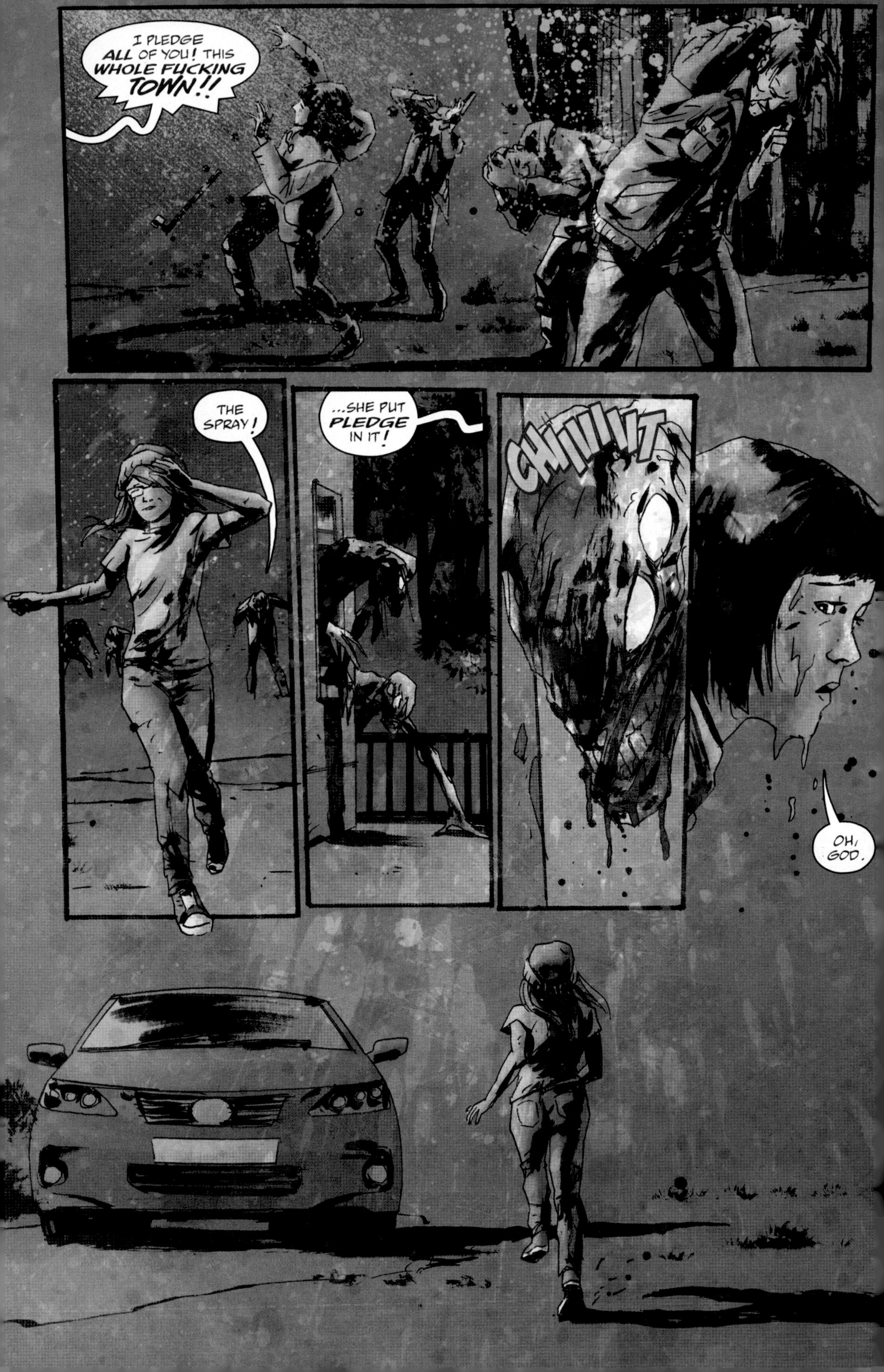
I PLEDGE ALL OF YOU! THIS WHOLE FUCKING TOWN!!
THE SPRAY!
...SHE PUT PLEDGE IN IT!
CHWIIIIT
OH, GOD.

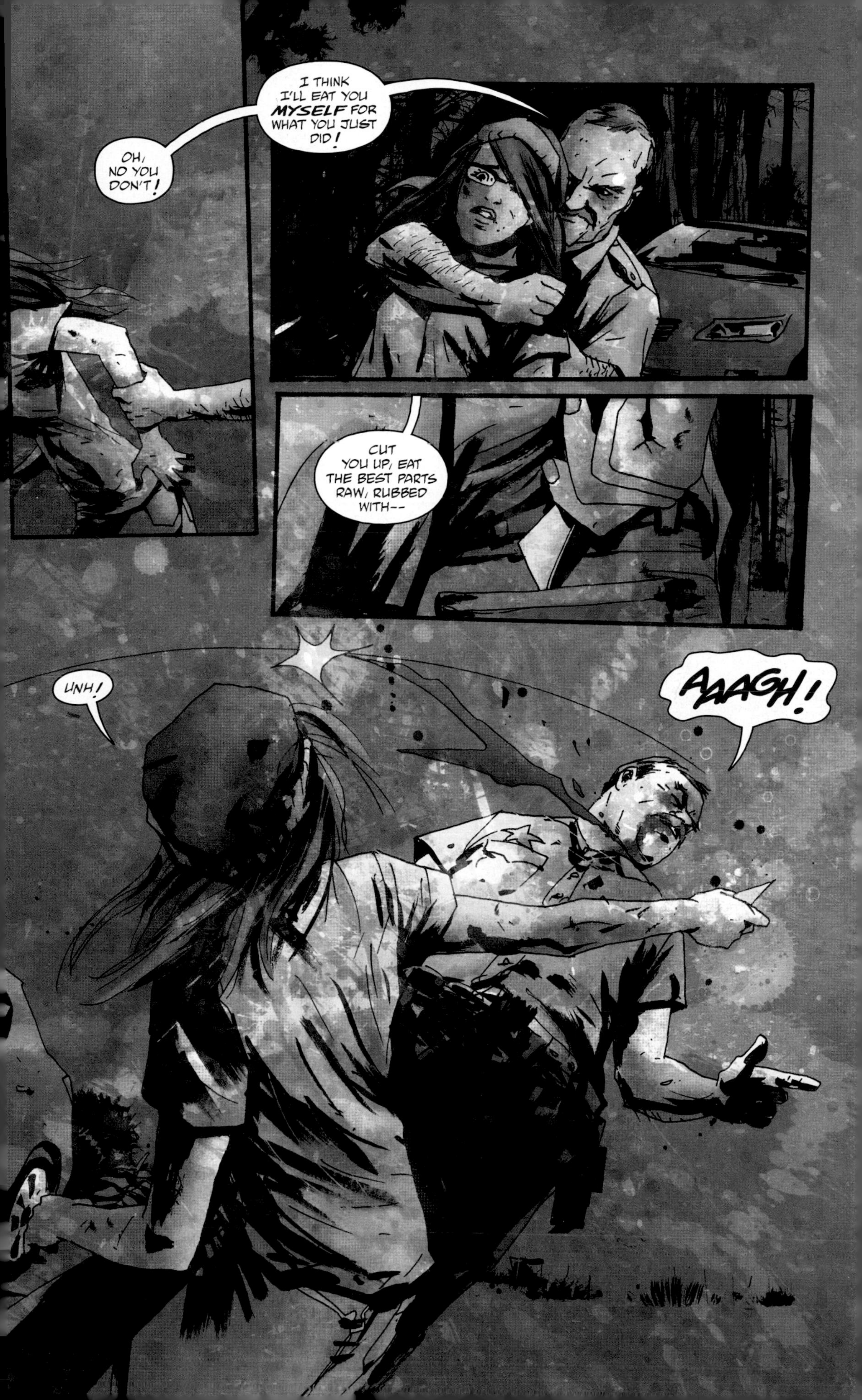
OH, NO YOU DON'T!
I THINK I'LL EAT YOU MYSELF FOR WHAT YOU JUST DID!
CUT YOU UP, EAT THE BEST PARTS RAW, RUBBED WITH--
UNH!
AAAGH!

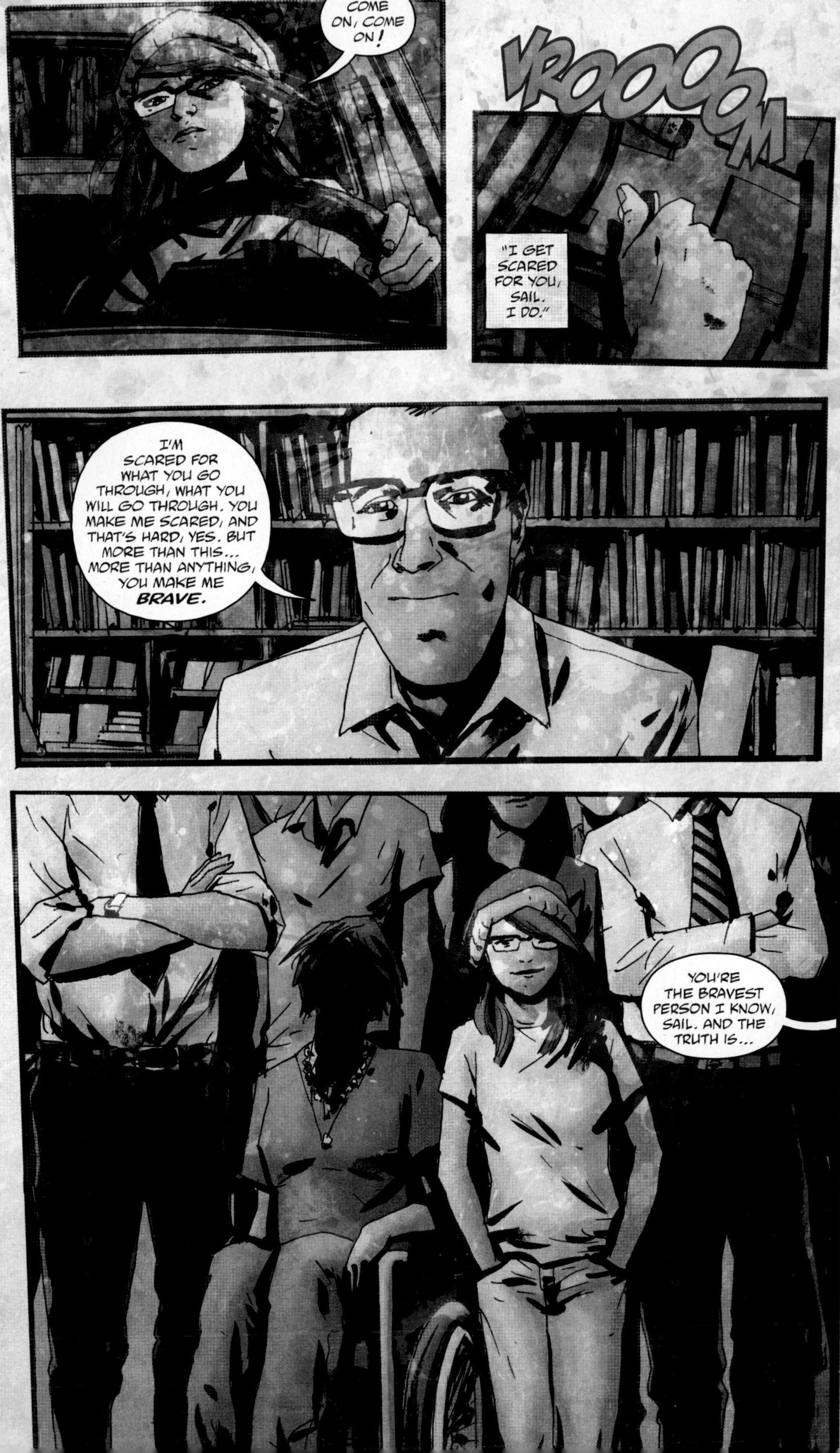
COME ON, COME ON!
VROOOOOM
"I GET SCARED FOR YOU, SAIL. I DO."
I'M SCARED FOR WHAT YOU GO THROUGH, WHAT YOU WILL GO THROUGH. YOU MAKE ME SCARED, AND THAT'S HARD, YES. BUT MORE THAN THIS... MORE THAN ANYTHING, YOU MAKE ME **BRAVE.**
YOU'RE THE BRAVEST PERSON I KNOW, SAIL. AND THE TRUTH IS...

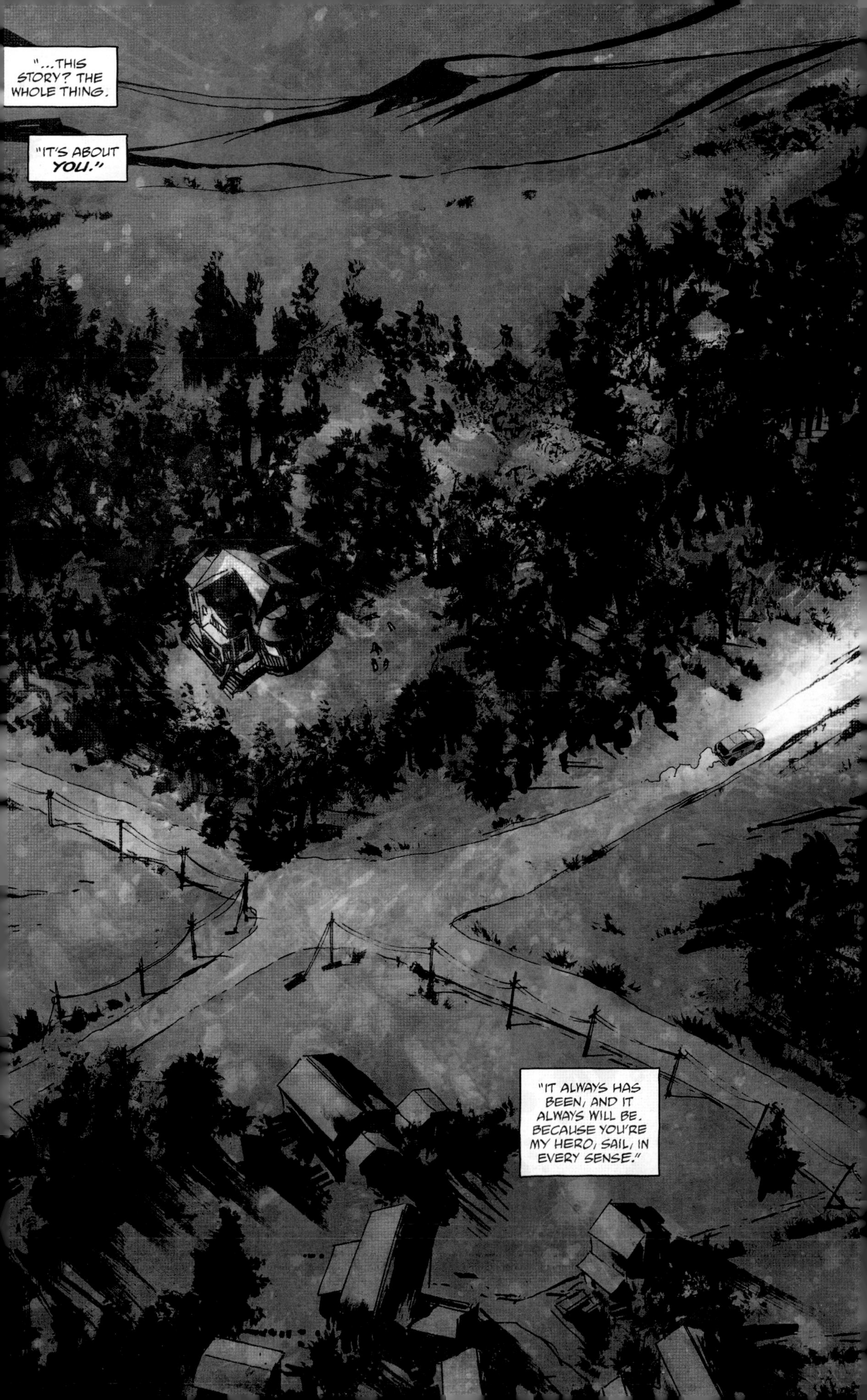
"...THIS STORY? THE WHOLE THING.
"IT'S ABOUT *YOU.*"
"IT ALWAYS HAS BEEN, AND IT ALWAYS WILL BE. BECAUSE YOU'RE MY HERO, SAIL, IN EVERY SENSE."

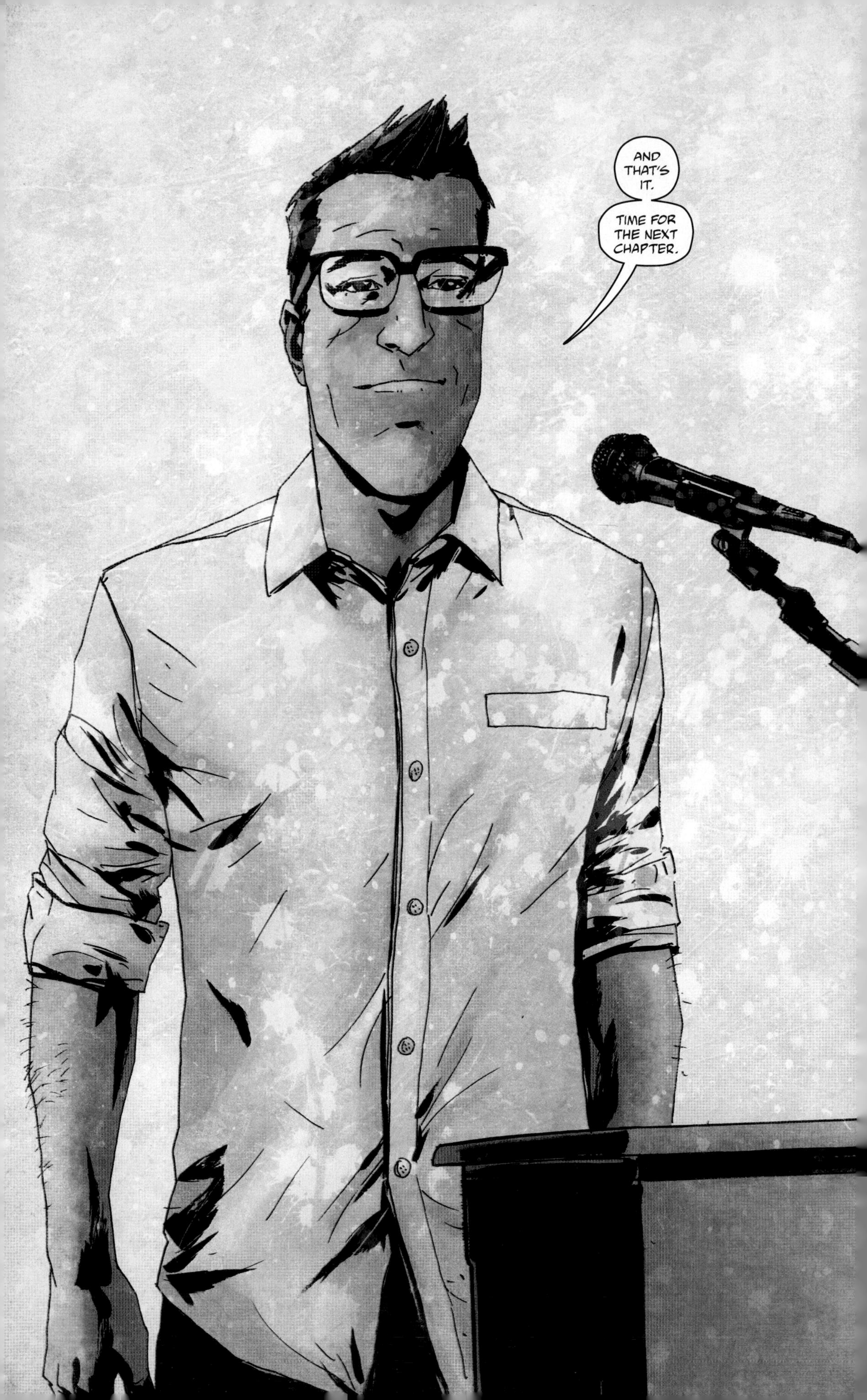
AND THAT'S IT.
TIME FOR THE NEXT CHAPTER.

issue 1:

WHO WOULD YOU PLEDGE?

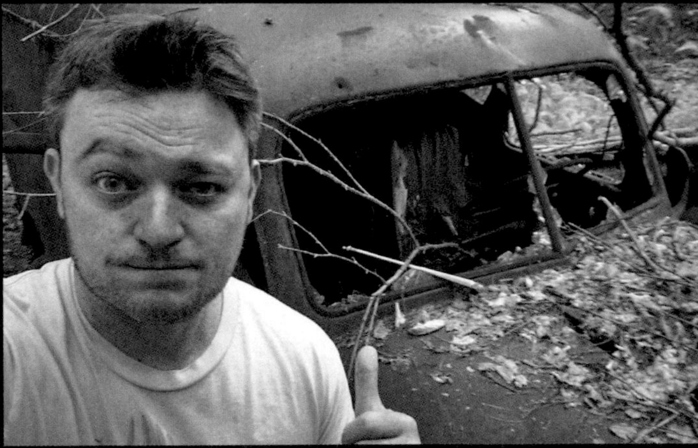

When I was a boy, I used to go witch hunting in the woods across the road from my house. It was one of my favorite activities, witch hunting. I would go with my neighbor, Ryan. Together we'd head out into the woods with a Polaroid camera (mine), and two bats with nails in them (his), in search of witches hiding out there.

This all happened in rural Pennsylvania. I was a city kid, but when I was about six, my parents – worried about raising kids in the city – managed to buy a small weekend house in southern Pennsylvania. The house was rustic, built in the 1940s – more like an expanded cabin, tucked deep in the woods, on a small lake. We'd go there every weekend possible, and spend long weeks there in the summer.

Our neighbors had a boy my age, Ryan, and we became fast friends. I'd cross the woods to his house and we'd play Nintendo, D&D, we'd trade comics... we were both geeks, imaginative kids. It was around age eleven that we started going monster hunting in the woods.

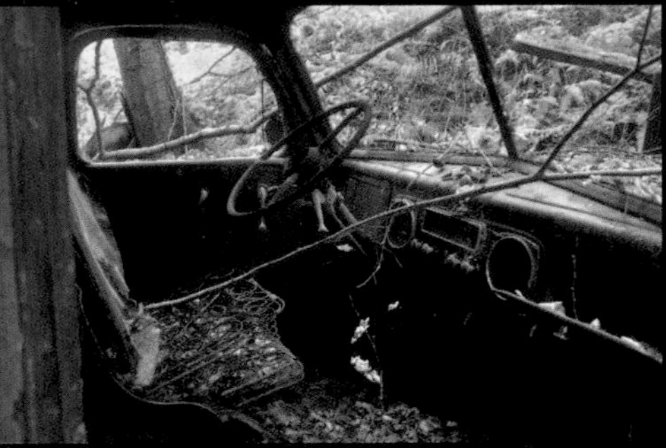

The woods were thick and deep and we concocted all sorts of stories for ourselves about the creatures that lived out there. But, having both recently read Roald Dahl's The Witches, we were both particularly interested in the notion of witches living in the woods. Men and women who worshipped Satan! Sacrificing animals and worse, deep in the trees across the road! Other monsters fell away and we became all about witches and warlocks. They were out there and we would find them.

To be fair, these woods were pretty rich with things we could cite as witch "evidence." Once we found an old graveyard – seriously, a graveyard. We found a box of false teeth another time. And on one trip, deeper in the woods, we found an old car, a meat truck from the 1940s. From then on, the truck became our base, and we would walk out to it with lunch, and then explore the woods in various directions. We marked areas we'd explored with tape. We put pieces of string across paths, to detect witch crossings. Any old bone was a sign of witchcraft.

One windy day, we were hanging out by the car, eating and joking around and all of a sudden, Ryan jumped to his feet. "Who the hell are you?" I remember him saying, literally reaching for his bat. Terrified, I turned and looked and didn't see anything. I asked him what was the matter and he said he saw someone, or something, peeking out from behind a tree. But the person was big, he said, like taller than a normal man or woman. Way taller than we'd thought a witch would be. "It was huge," he said, "just watching us."

Nervously, we explored the area but of course found nothing. The witch must have been a tree, swaying in the wind, and we laughed about it afterwards, on the way out of the woods, how he'd nearly shit himself over nothing, what a pussy, and so on, but I think both of us walked a little faster than normal that day.

Ryan and I didn't make many trips in to the woods after that. For one, his mother found his nail-riddled bat. And soon after that, the district built a school across the road, which blocked the old path we took into the woods. We're still friends though, Ryan and me. He's married now with kids, and lives in Ohio, but still. We actually joke about going back there, witch hunting in the woods. My folks kept the house all this time. We came here through my teenage years. I brought friends during college. I got engaged here, down by the lake. Now my wife and I bring our kids up here.

Anyway, about a year ago, I went for a run along the road by our house, and I decided to take a peek into the woods. I hadn't been back there in fifteen, maybe twenty years, but for some reason, I figured I'd just take a look to see if our old trail was still there.

I stepped off the main road, started walking through the ferns and brush towards the taller trees and that's when I saw the witch. I kid you not, something leaned out from behind the trees — something tall and skeletal and dark and I froze. I froze and that strange hot chill of terror shot through me and I was a kid again, deep in the woods, and that thing was looking at me through the trees. It had been waiting here all along, hadn't it? It had known I'd come back and it had been patient...

Of course, a moment later, the sun shifted and the witch vanished, somehow changed into a tree, a freakishly human looking tree, but still, and my body relaxed and I turned and walked away.

Later that night, I found myself haunted by the image of the witch, peeking out from the behind the tree. I knew what had really frightened me wasn't the "witch" in the trees — sure the sight had scared me — but what had really gotten me spooked was the idea that this witch had ALWAYS been there. That all the years in between were nothing to it. Because it knew... it knew one day I'd come back and it would be waiting. And why had it waited? What did it want?

For hours that night, I kept on with these questions. I knew that there was a story here for me. Something more than scary, something personal, something terrifying in that special way that gets at the deeper fears, the fears below.

And so the next day, I started working on Wytches, a story about an ancient evil waiting out there in the woods. Now as you may have guessed, our witches aren't the kinds you've seen before. No brooms or pointy hats. In fact, forget everything you know about witches, because in our world, all the people assumed to be witches, the people burned and drowned for witchcraft, all of them were just the human worshippers of witches. The witches themselves — the wytches — are more like that thing Ryan and I saw in the woods. They're huge and ancient and primal and deeply evil. They have a knowledge of natural science that surpasses the limits of modern medicine. They have great power. They can give you almost anything you want. And they're out there, waiting for you to come ask. But first, you have to give them what they want... They have to eat, after all. So who would you give them to get what you want? To cure a sick loved one? To cure yourself? To get what you've always wanted? A neighbor? A loved one? Who would you pledge?

Now as a final note, just before starting this essay, I decided to head back into those woods once and for all and see if our old car was still there. I had to cross the school property and make my way over a fence and hedge, but still, I managed to do it, and though it was less pronounced, I did find the old path Ryan and I always took in to the woods. I walked back there, a quarter mile, a half, the trees growing thicker and taller, and there it was: our old car. Still there, twenty years later. I've included some pictures here.

So, if you've read this far, just give me a chance to say thank you. Not just for following me down memory lane here, but for giving this book a chance. I hope you can see that Wytches is a deeply personal book for me, and I'm deeply grateful to Jock, Matt, Clem, David, Eric, and Image for giving it a home. More than this, I'm grateful to you for picking it up. In the end, for me, it's a book that's been in the making for a long time. A book that has waited for me to write it. And in the end, sitting here writing this — in the upstairs room of my parent's lakehouse, the woods right outside this window — I like to think that if this book waited, maybe the wytches are out there waiting, too.

So... who would you pledge?

Scott Snyder
August 2014

Inks

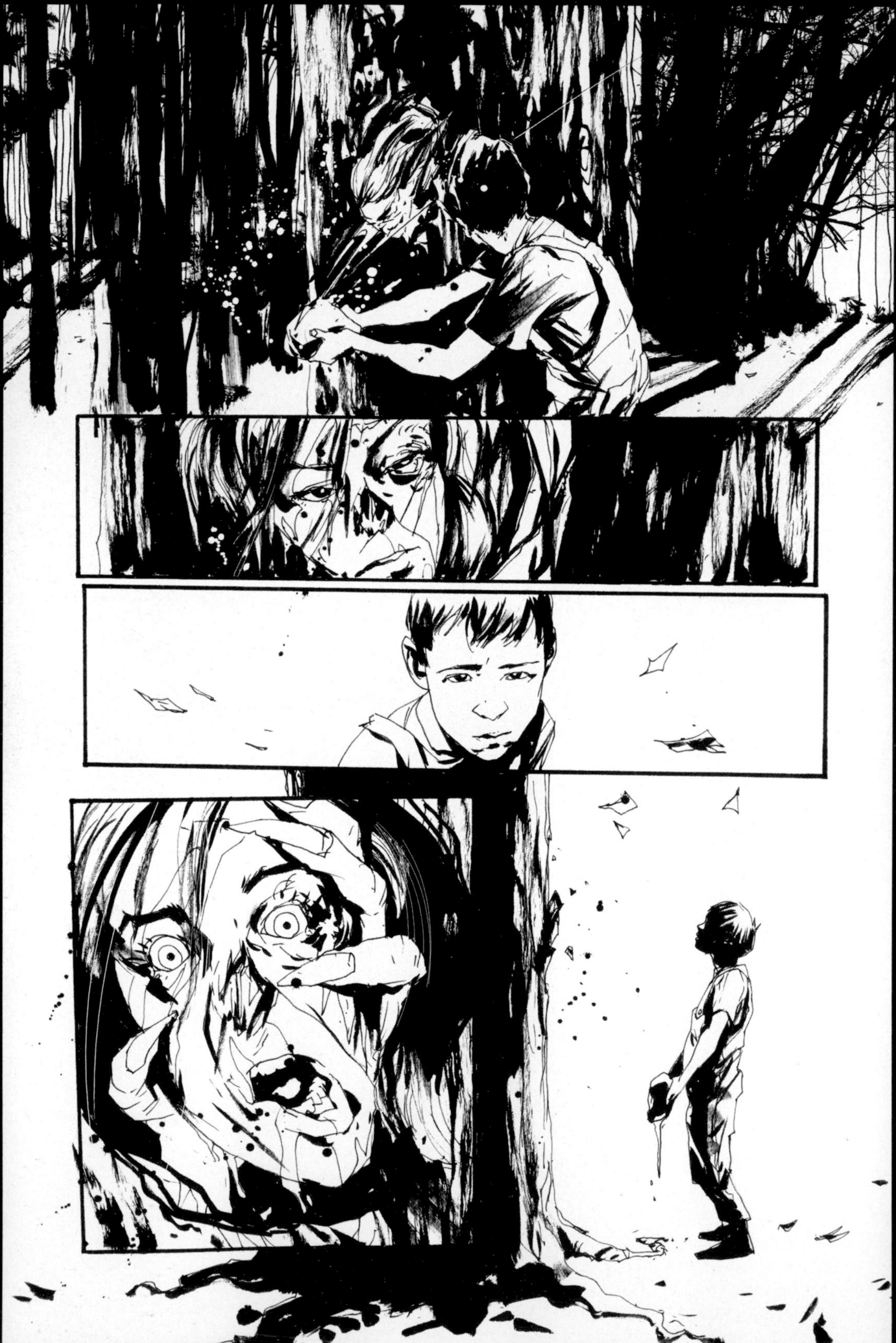

To Colors

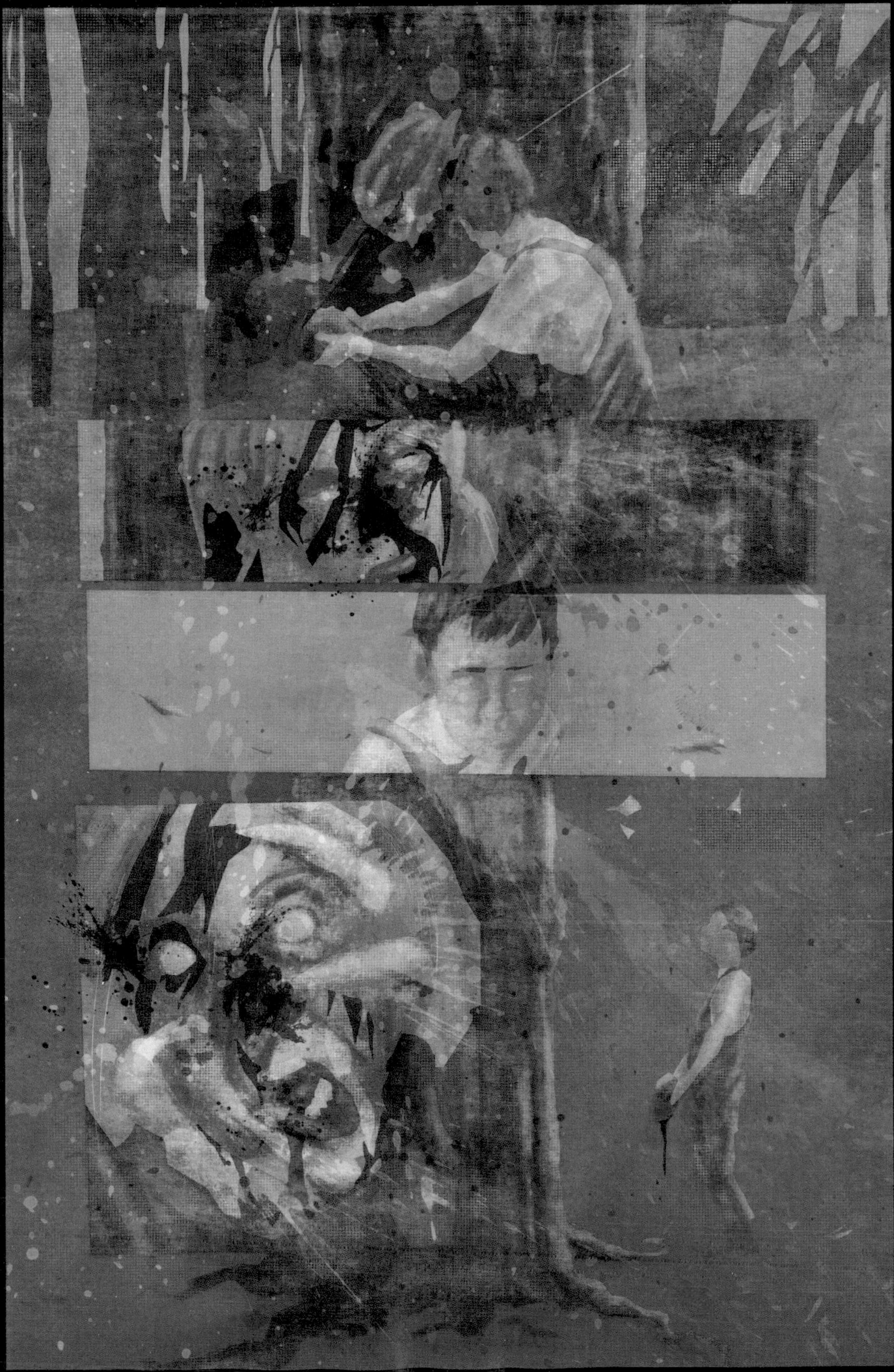

issue 3:

WHO WOULD YOU PLEDGE?

Before we get started, I just wanted to extend a note of sincere thanks from everyone on the Wytches team to you guys. As I write this, Wytches #1 and #2 are going back to press, and there really is no way to explain to you how overwhelmed (and stunned) we all are by your support.

The truth is, this is NOT a book that should do what it's doing. It's a mean little book. It's black and twisted and cruel and imperfect and above all, personal. In #1, I wrote a piece about where the idea for Wytches came from. But here, by way of thanking you guys, let me speak a little to what it's about.

Not long ago, my 7-year-old son lost a tooth. It was his second tooth to go and I was a little apprehensive about what his reaction would be; with his first tooth to fall out, he'd suffered some real fears about the tooth fairy. He'd always had nightmares, been the type of kid to come into the room in the middle of the night and ask to sleep in our room or have me sleep in his (to be fair, I try to keep my office free of faceless clowns and vampires as possible, but still...). Anyway, he was a nervous kid, and he had not been cool with this idea that she was going to climb in his window and over his bed. "Wait, so she breaks into my room, like home invasion?" he'd asked me. I'd tried to explain it was less nefarious than that, but still, he'd been unnerved. I could see his little brain working as he held the tiny tooth in his hand: conjuring images of this spindly creature climbing over his face with its dirty feet, a bag of bloody teeth in its hand...

But this time he seemed more relaxed, more confident. I asked him if he was excited for the tooth fairy to come and bring him money. "Yeah," he said, wrapping the tooth in paper. "She only has power if you believe in her anyway. And I only believe in her part way."

I cannot tell you how great I found this answer. So he believed in her enough to get the money, but not enough for her to be powerful enough to scare him. I remember telling my wife about his comments later that night, after he was asleep. And I remember how strange it was to think that he was passing out of a phase of these kid fears. Soon there'd be no more worries about monsters in the closet or under the bed. No more questions about "ghosties" in the garage. I was relieved all of sudden. Maybe this was the end of the nightmare phase. He was becoming a little man.

Anyway, he got his few dollars for his tooth and we spent it at the comic store and all was good. And then, about a week later, I got a call from Jack's teacher while he was at school. Apparently, the school had something called a lockdown drill that day. (When I'd first heard about these drills I wasn't sure what they were—fire drills? I remember asking the mother of a friend of Jack's one morning and her grimacing and explaining in a whispered tone: "school shooter drills."

I know.)

Anyway, Jack's teacher explained to me that, unfortunately, he'd been outside the classroom when the drill had happened. He'd been getting a drink of water and the alarm had gone off and he'd been out there, in the hallway, alone. To be fair, his teacher was great about it, sympathetic and apologetic, nurturing.

But when he got home that day, Jack was clearly rattled by the experience. Tight lipped. Quick to start. I took him to the comic store; we got treats. But it'd shaken him. And that night, before bed, he asked me if he could take a thermos to school from then on so he wouldn't have to leave the classroom for water. I told him sure. But that it was just a mistake and he shouldn't worry. There was nothing to be afraid of. It was just a loud bell. "But there are shooters, aren't there?" he said. "Like school invasion?"

...

What could I say, except yes, there were. And suddenly I wished I could go back to the kid fears. The tooth fairies and monsters. Because these NEW fears—fears concerning the evil that people do to one another—they are justified and potent and terrifying. And worse than this, there is no protecting your child from them. From the dirty, black-footed tooth fairy, sure. But from a gunman... And this helplessness engenders its own evil feelings; I worry about my children and I can't protect them. I wish I could stop worrying. I want a moment's peace. And so on. It's like your child has just entered this realm of human monsters and you're one, too.

The truth is, this is largely what Wytches is about. The Wytches are monsters, but they're monsters that only act when we give them permission to. When we go to them and pledge each other, then they come with their teeth bared. And their favorite things to eat are children. Get rid of your weakness. Get rid of your fear. Kill your love.

Yes, it has a high concept, sure. "Wytches: forget everything you thought you knew about them." But ultimately, it's a book about the terrifying parts of ourselves we don't like looking at. The funhouse mirror parts. The ugly parts, and how those ugly parts lie just beneath the skin.

So, let me say it again: this is NOT a book that should be selling 90,000 copies. It's a book we figured MIGHT sell half of that, if we were lucky and really pushed. But the fact that you all have pushed books like this, and Outcast and Wicked + Divine and Saga and East of West and Lazarus so high on the charts... you're changing the landscape of comics. Really and truly. You're giving creators incentive like never before to take risks, to go out and tell the stories they want to tell, without reservation. The personal stories. The risky stories. The ugly stories. It's truly inspiring. So thank you from all of us.

And I promise we'll get back to letters next week - there've been some great ones! Don't forget to email us your darkest thoughts and deepest fears at askthewytches@gmail.com and mark your letters "okay to print!"

-Scott Snyder, November 2014

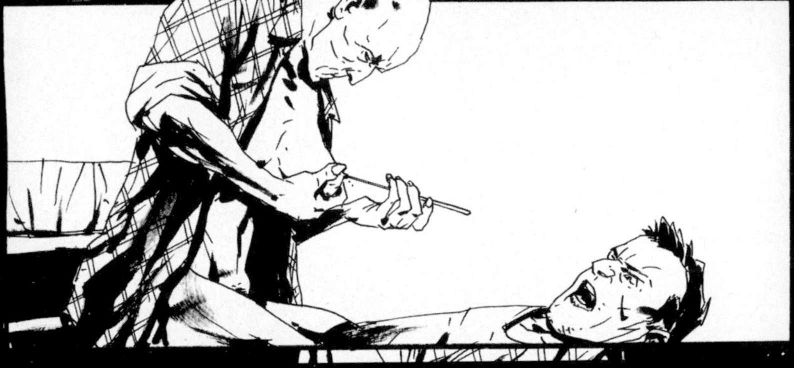

lat colors.
t dark,
paint is
ned ahead.

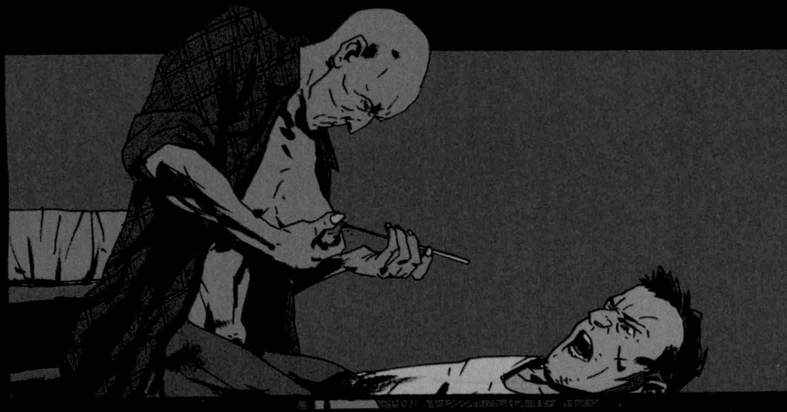

3. Basic paint in Photoshop.

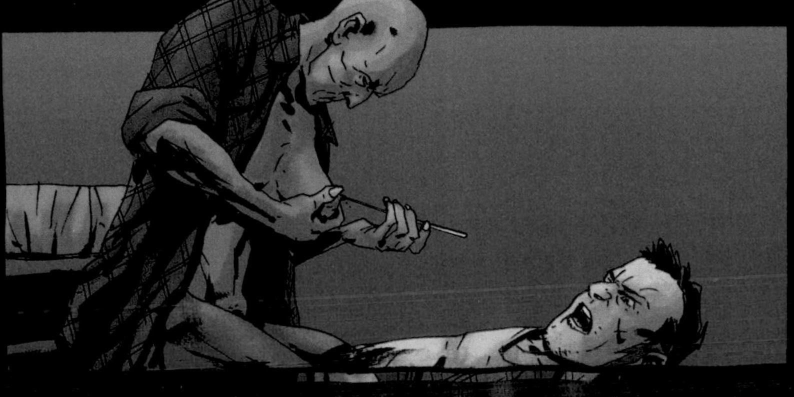

4. Zip and paper added.

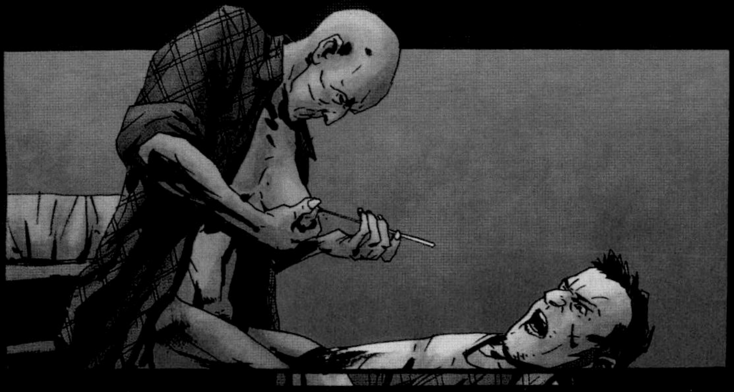

5. First spatter sets and letters from Clem Robins added. Spatters manually painted, watercolor on paper.

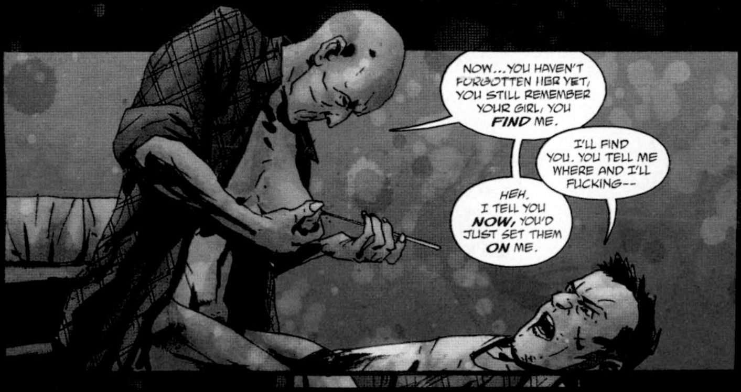

NOW... YOU HAVEN'T FORGOTTEN HER YET, YOU STILL REMEMBER YOUR GIRL, YOU **FIND** ME.
I'LL FIND YOU. YOU TELL ME WHERE AND I'LL FUCKING--
HEH. I TELL YOU **NOW,** YOU'D JUST SET THEM **ON** ME.

. The hero spatter. atercolor and liquid crylic on watercolor aper.

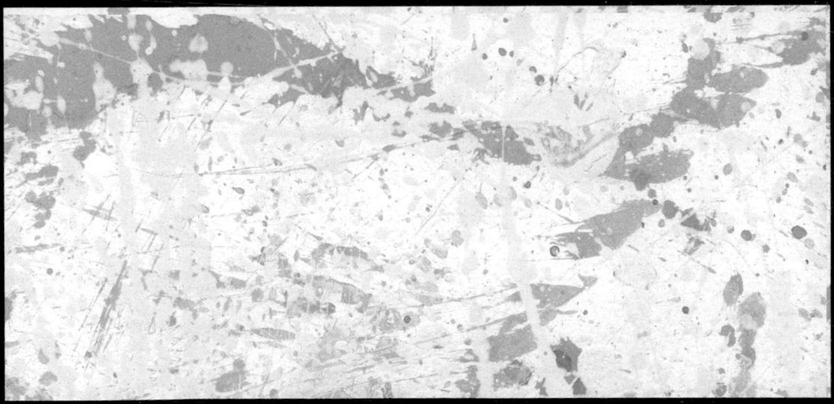

7. Final painted and composited image..

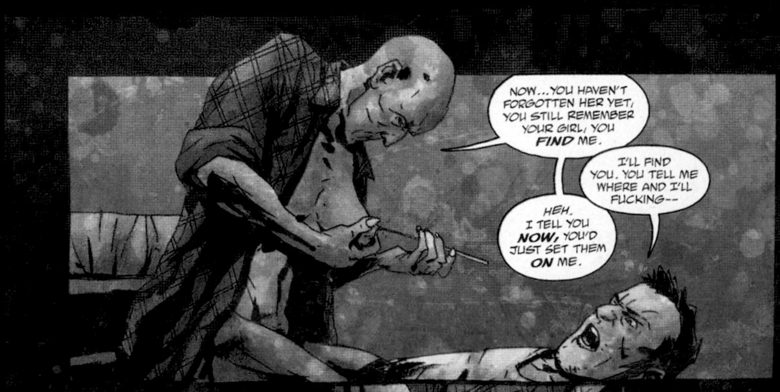

NOW... YOU HAVEN'T FORGOTTEN HER YET, YOU STILL REMEMBER YOUR GIRL, YOU **FIND** ME.
I'LL FIND YOU. YOU TELL ME WHERE AND I'LL FUCKING--
HEH. I TELL YOU **NOW,** YOU'D JUST SET THEM **ON** ME.

The spatter is all painted by hand, with watercolor and liquid acrylic and other paint on paper. That is then scanned and composited in Photoshop with other layers, which are mostly digitally painted, for a mixed media approach.

issue 4:

WHO W[redacted]U[redacted]D YOU [redacted]L[redacted]E?

I was nine years old when I fell in love with horror. I actually remember the exact day—the exact moment—it happened. It was summer, and I was away at sleep-away camp for the first time. The place was this an all-boys, super competitive sports camp located in upstate New York on a remote lake - all pine tries and dark log cabin bunks. To be clear, sports were like the religion of the place. First thing in the morning, we played a sport, then another, then lunch, then rest, then afternoon sports, then evening sports. We were on all sorts of teams with all sorts of rankings and all of it was very important in the day to day.

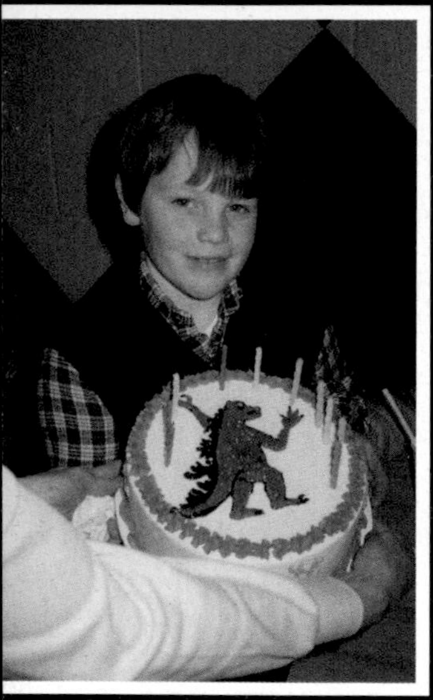

Me, I was a pale, chubby, nervous kid from the city. I was into videogames, drawing superheroes (I wanted to be a comic book artist back then, not writer - writer? Fuck that), and not much else. I'd followed a friend to the camp, and quickly lost him in the maw. My parents still have my first letter from that summer, in which I ask them to come get me, right above a spot on the page showing a tear stain, circled in red with the words "ACTUAL TEAR" written above in caps.

It was the kind of place, for example, where color war was taken extremely seriously. There were two teams; Green and Gray and once you were chosen for a team you were that team for life. For life. No matter what. The process by which you were chosen for a team was something in and of itself, too. On the night color war started, older boys would set off alarms and come running into the younger boys bunks' and wake us all up. Then they'd take us up to the cafeteria, which had a porch about twenty feet off the ground with lights pointed at it. One by one, boys new to the camp - unpicked by a team - would walk nervously out on to this porch in front of the whole camp and two counselors, one representing each team, would pretend to play tug of war with the boy, until one of them pulled him over to the appropriate side and he would be ushered down the steps by his new (lifelong) teammates.

I was terrified of this prospect. What if no one wanted me? What if my arms got ripped off? I mean ripped the fuck off?! How would I be a comic book artist then?! The night this all did happen for me, I made the unfortunate choice of wearing green Hulk pajamas. Unfortunate because I was subsequently picked for the gray team. And so as I went down the steps, the pajamas were pulled off me, leaving me in my underpants in front of my new teammates. (Full disclosure: the underpants were actually—I shit you not—Batman-themed, and gray, which went over great with the older boys. And so it's wholly possible all my writing for Batman is just some attempt on my part to repay him for saving me from DEFCON 1-level boyhood mortification had my underpants been green. I love you, Bruce.)

To be fair, the camp wasn't a bad place; it was just extremely competitive, with this very intense macho energy that I couldn't tap into. I was bullied over my weight, my shitty sports skills, but the thing that really made me anxious was how foreign it all felt to me. There was only strangeness. I didn't understand the rules. Everything was scary in that regard. And I remember very quickly becoming very panicky and very nervous... then developing these little habits to make myself feel better, odd little behaviors and such. Counting, walking certain ways. I took to spending time hiding out at the arts and crafts center—really just a small, meager cabin at a remote end of camp where they kept some paints for making team posters. I remember pouring a lot of time into designing elaborate and imaginary team floats I would one day build to win all my teammates over. Floats. Like parade floats.

So what does any of this have to do with horror?

Well, there was one thing I loved about camp that summer, the thing I remember most vividly, and it has to do with horror. We had this counselor, Ted, in our bunk, and for some reason, he'd decided that he was going to read us a book that summer. He was a bit of an oddball counselor. Pudgy, a bit awkward, artistic... Anyway, he'd picked a book and he'd mapped it all out so that he'd start the book on the first night and end pretty much on the last. The book was Stephen King's Eyes of the Dragon.

When I heard this, I was terrified. I knew Stephen King by reputation, and was sure the book would only make things worse for me. The truth is, I'm teasing my nine-year-old self here, but I was really scared that summer. Not simply because camp wasn't for me. But because I was experiencing my own unhappiness in a way I hadn't before. Somehow, it felt different, like a constant state of nervousness. I was having trouble calming down, ever. My mind wouldn't let go of particular worries unless I performed particular tasks... It was all very scary and all I wanted was NOT to be scared anymore.

I tried not to listen that first night, when Ted began the book. It was just after lights out, not long after I'd written that tear-stained letter home), and I viscerally remember lying in the dark, under the covers, but, trying not to hear, but hearing him say: "Once, in a kingdom called Delain, there was a king with two sons..." The

Kingdom of Delain. Roland the Good. Peter. And Flagg...

From go I was transported. And while the book isn't straight-up horror, the horror parts are what I remember being most captivated by, even on that first night. The cut made to Sasha so she bled to death. The twisted poisoning of Roland... It made NO goddam sense to me. If I felt scared all the time, why would being more scared feel...good?

Still, it got so all day I'd look forward to lights-out so I could hear what happened next. Soon I was asking my parents for Pet Semetery, Cujo... I was reading Tomb of Dracula. Swamp Thing...

As I got older, I continued to be a nervous kid—later an anxious kid—and yet over and over, for some reason, horror always made me feel calmer, better. The stories (the good ones), the ones I loved best, cut right to the core of my childhood fears. Losing family. Being alone. A world transformed around you. Experiencing them made me feel...good.

It wasn't until much later I began wondering about the weird paradox inherent in my own relationship to horror. I've said before, but I don't mind saying again here, I've had troubles with anxiety and depression over the years. Looking back, I can see the precursors in moments like that first stretch at camp—the panics and odd behaviors... I've had about nine or ten bad bouts with it over the years, give or take, and when it comes on strong (usually a result of a combination of factors, some preventable, some not), it puts me in a dark way. It starts with a kind of low-frequency nervousness about a topic (the ones that come up most often for me are illness, or loss through aging)—a nervousness that won't quite go away, that seeps into everyday life in ways it shouldn't, and if I'm not careful, it can spiral very quickly into a kind of crippling and fearful obsession with that topic.

For me, when I'm down in this way, everything I look at is a reflection of myself, but an ugly, funhouse mirror reflection telling me my fear about the topic at hand is true. If the topic is illness: see that poster for a cancer center? You have cancer. It's in you. Or: going for a run, Scott? Why bother, you're already sick. Feel that lump in your throat? No, better check and check and check and... I end up avoid looking at newspapers for fear I'll see something about illness that will trigger a panic. Or watching TV. Or talking with friends. All these things I find comfort in most times become monstrous. I don't know how to explain it except to say that nothing is safe to encounter, because it all points back at me in a menacing way.

The thing is, the best horror, in my opinion at least, does this, too. Great horror takes the things we find safety in and turns them menacing. Your friendly neighbors plotting against you. Your own child coming back evil. Sleep being a place you can die. A road-trip with friends suddenly becoming a nightmare. The world you know turning on you. Classic monsters are enduring, I think, because they offer ways of expressing this. Zombies are your friends and loved ones come back to kill you. Vampires too. Werewolves. The people you know turning murderous. Your own body changing, becoming unfamiliar...

That's the funny thing: even when I'm at my worst, one of the few activities I really like doing is experiencing horror stories. When I'm not well, and I see a horror film or read a horror book dealing with the fears I'm experiencing in my own exaggerated, obsessive ways, it makes me feel less alone with these fears; someone else has them, too. But for another thing, the book ends, the movie ends, and just by ending, the story suggests that the depression will end. Great when the hero survives and triumphs, but honestly, even in stories where the monster wins, where everyone dies, the story ends and I am released from it. In the end, the truth is, when I'm well or not well, horror helps me explore the things I'm sometimes afraid to look at in real life in piercing and true ways that somehow make me feel better.

That's the trick of horror for me. I love reading it to feel less alone with my fears. To experience them acutely and then be set free. I love writing it to explore them in ways that are probing and difficult for me and well, scary too, but controlled. Not controlled because those fears are less potent, but controlled because I decide how far to go with them, where they lead...

So: Wytches. It gives me a place to go as dark as I can, talk about my fears now – fears about being a bad parent, about being selfish, about anxiety in children, about losing myself in my own head when I'm anxious or depressed, about losing a child... about all of it in a way that allows me to go as dark as I can, and then, when it's done, close the laptop and walk away.

At the end of the day, I guess I love horror because at its best, horror scares me into not being...well, so damn scared.

To close, a quick thanks to all the friends and family who help me when things get bad and watch horror movies with me. (Some of you even work on this book). And thank to you all for reading.

[Also, as a quick epilogue... I actually kept going back to camp. I ended up liking it more than I thought I would. And in my third year at this camp color war came down to just a few points, and this year they decided for some reason that the arts and crafts point would be THE deciding factor. And—no bullshit—that year, I had made a float. Yes, a float. A big-ass gray dragon out of wire and papier-mâché and crappy clay and all that. And my team WON because of this point—the arts and crafts point – and from that moment on, no one ever teased me about my geekiness ever again. I just became that kid who made the floats. They all left me alone to do my weird art thing.

Which is pretty much how things are now, too... no?]

Scott Snyder, January 2015

issue 5:

WHO WOULD YOU PLEDGE?

First, I'd like to say thanks for reading these little pieces I've been doing in the back of the book. When we started, I figured I'd do one for fun, about the genesis of the series, and that would be it. But your (surprising) enthusiasm for them encouraged me to do more, and honestly, they've been a real joy for me to write. For one, it's a thrill to write prose again in any form, and also, they've given me a place to explore my own thoughts on the book, my own fears, my love of horror. They've become a place for personal disclosure—a scary place, but a bit wondrous, too, and I appreciate the opportunity. So thank you.

And, speaking of places scary and wondrous... I confess that I am actually writing this one from Disney World in Orlando. And, in the spirit of disclosure, I admit that was never the plan. Honestly, I'd intended to write this piece before I took this vacation with my family, but weather and school closures prevented that. So here I am, writing about horror at Disney World. The kids are asleep in the other room, surrounded by plush Olaf's and antenna toppers of hitchhiking ghosts. Cinderella's castle is visible from the hotel window. I can just make out the marching lights of the electric parade. In a lot of ways, there's no place less inspiring for a horror piece than this.

Still, I do have one Disney World memory that reminds me of this book—this issue even—and I'll tell it to you here. This story I'm thinking of, it happened while I was actually working at the Disney parks. I did this for the better part of a year, right after college. I was twenty-two, and I wanted to be a writer and was all about having experiences far away from New York or anything familiar.

Anyway, the story I want to tell happened when I was just starting as a character. Maybe a couple days in. I was hired for custodial at the Magic Kingdom and had worked in that department for a number of months before getting a chance to audition for characters. Custodial had been hard work, pushing a massive garbage trolley around in the sun—thirty-six cans worth of trash—so I was ecstatic to be a character now.

On this particular day, I was Buzz Lightyear. Out of all the characters I played—Eeyore, Pluto, among others—Buzz was far and away my favorite. For one, he was foam and mesh, so way less hot than the other characters. Don't get me wrong, they were all VERY hot—hell, our coach, Bob, on the first day of training, he suggested we newbies sit in the parking lot in our cars with the engines off to train. But with some characters, like Rafiki, you were wearing huge ass pads and chest pads, tights, full fur, and carrying a fruit staff to boot. But Buzz...foam and mesh and he also had great visibility. With certain characters, you only saw through the mouth or nose, which was like looking out at the world through a foggy periscope. On days I was those characters, I learned to swing my head from side to side as I walked to scan the way ahead and avoid stepping on kids.

I'm there as Buzz, stamping books, acting the super-hero, and I feel something hit my leg. I try to swing around, and I look down through the neck of the suit and I see a boy, about six years old, giving me a hug. I hugged him back and tried to gently direct him to the line but he stayed beside me, telling me how much he loved me, and so on. Buzz was his favorite and he had a toy of me at home and on he went, adorably. My handler, an older man named David, asked him where his mother was, and the boy said he didn't know, so David began the process of calling this in. In the meantime, the boy—whose name was Chester, he said—hung out by my side, copying my actions, laughing. This little tow-headed guy making muscles and jumping around. I pretended he was my sidekick.

It was only about a minute into this that his mother showed up. She came running over, arms wide, and he ran to her, happy, telling her he'd found Buzz! He'd found him! And I was just about to wave when she smacked his face. I mean I heard it in my costume—SMACK—the clap of her fingers against his little cheek.

I was stunned. She was yelling at him now. Yelling right into his face—HOW COULD HE DO THAT?! HOW COULD HE RUN OFF?!!!

I wanted to go over and say something, but there were kids I was interacting with, and before I knew it Chester and his mother were gone. Lost in the crowd. I told David after about it, about how angry the mom had been at Chester, and to my surprise he looked at me and said, "Yeah. Get used to it."

And he was right. Not about the smack.

I rarely saw any form of hitting again. But the fury parents displayed toward lost children, now found...that I saw play itself out over and over again. A parent bearing down on a child, rage in the parent's eyes as he or she grabbed the little shoulders...

At the time, I didn't really understand it. There were systems in place for lost children at Disney. Nothing terrible could really happen, could it? So, why the rage? But typing this now, my kids asleep in the next room, that electric parade snaking slowly along, I completely get it. Because there is no worse feeling than failing to keep your child safe—especially when you're right there with them, in a place that's supposed to be as safe as can be. A place you've taken them yourself. You're at the playground, holding your kid's hand and he falls and scrapes his chin to shreds. Your kid is standing next to you on the steps of a pool and you turn for a moment—less than five seconds—to say hello to your friend and you turn back and your child is underwater, the little hands flailing above the surface.

Bad things shouldn't happen when you're there next to your child. It's upsetting. But maybe what's most upsetting about incidents like these is the notion that your child now knows you can't keep them safe. You can't keep them from getting lost or hurt, not if they're not careful themselves, and maybe not even then. It's all an illusion. You can't stand between them and the monster. All the rides here, all the pretending things are going dangerously wrong—you're in a train in a mine that's caving in! You're trapped in haunted house with no way out!—are all reinforcing the opposite sentiment, leading to the safe landing on the other side. They turn danger into something to be laughed at. So how infuriating when danger finds its way (on your watch) into your child's life.

Admittedly, I've been that furious parent. I've never hit my kids, but I've certainly wanted to when they've put themselves in danger while I was watching them. I've wanted to shake them until they could somehow promise me they'd always stay safe. Promise me that I hadn't failed them and would never fail them, nor would they fail me. They'd never get hurt, never get sick, never die.

The thing that I try to remember is that other side of it, too. Because the fear you feel as a parent in those situations is awful. The rage and guilt. But what I saw as a cast member—the only part I really saw and understood—were the kids' faces when their parents came at them that way. Chester looking back at his mother as she yelled into his face...the horror there. A child looking up and seeing that his parent has become the danger... the monster lurking there all along.

As a late night postscript: Because you sat through that, I will tell you my favorite moment working at Disney. It happened the final day of training for characters. I was in a group of three other young people, and all week we'd been practicing. Learning how to move like our characters. Learning how to have fun with the guests, but get off-stage quickly. All of the practical stuff. I was Pluto, the young man in my group was Chip, and the young woman was Mickey. They were both actors, and they were unequivocally great at their characters. This guy got Chip perfectly. He was all hyped-up energy and joy. And the girl just WAS Mickey. She had the friendly, modest pomp down pat. We were in this gymnasium we'd practiced in most of the week. So now it was the last day and our coach, Bob, was congratulating us, telling us to go out and knock them dead and so on. But, he said...he had a treat for us.

Then pulled out this boom box and put a CD in (this was 1998). Bob looks at us and he says conspiratorially: "They don't like it when I do this, but I think it's crucial. So keep it between us, but for the duration of this song, you dance however you want." Mickey looked at Chip who looked at me. I could barely see through my fogged dog eyes. "Well go on," Bob said. "Get it out of your darn system now, because you'll never get to do it again. For this moment on, you'll always be in character when you put that costume on. But right here, right now, this is a moment out of time and space."

He pushed the button. "Rumpshaker" came on. That saxophone. The record scratching, the beat... Chip began to dance. Mickey began to dance. I shuffled around, trying not to pass out. I moved around a couple seconds, turning and such, and then I saw Mickey... Mickey was not just shaking it, but like... working it. Dancing up on Chip, grinding... it was like a car wreck. I couldn't look away, and then Mickey turned to me. I looked away, dancing sheepishly. I looked back, and Mickey was still coming, like stripper dancing coming. And that image, Mickey Mouse working it, coming toward me to the sounds of ""Rumpshaker"...it is one of my most cherished memories.

-Scott Snyder, March 2015

issue 6:

WHO WOULD YOU PLEDGE?

WE PLEDGE YOU...

There's a conversation that sometimes comes up with friends. It usually happens after a whiskey or two, and when the mood is light, and it involves admitting one's greatest parent fail. Someone will be talking about some misstep they made with their kids that day—"I accidentally sent Joey into school wearing a costume when the costume party was tomorrow"—and then, laughing, someone will top that story, like: "Oh yeah, last wee[redacted] I was watching the Super Bowl with friends and my[redacted]hree-year-old, Becca, walked by the living room a[redacted] smiled and said, 'Hi, Daddy,' and she was carrying a hacksaw." And invariably, little by little, the conversation will become this kind of conspiratorial game of one-upmanship.

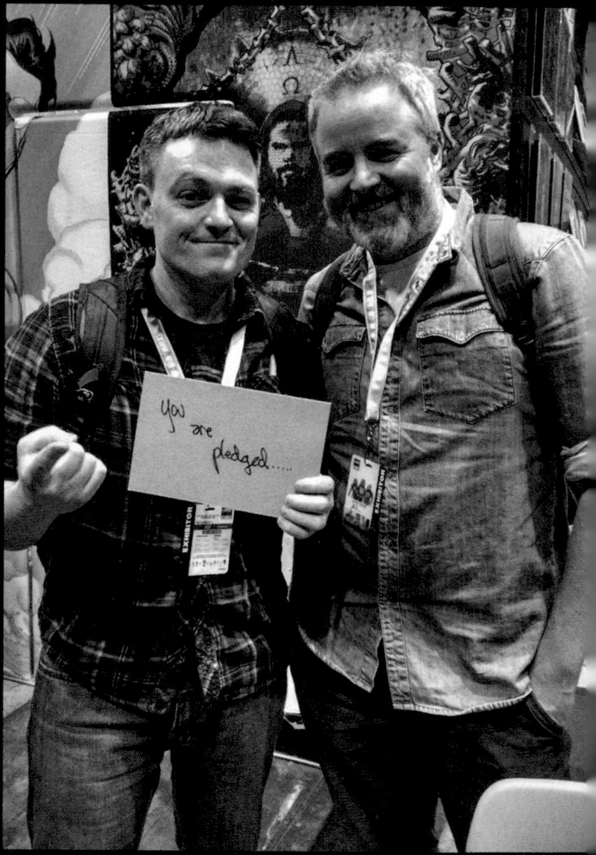
you are pledged.....

As for my possible contributions, I'm afraid I have plenty to choose from. There was the time I took baby Jack to see Saw IV. Yes, Saw IV ("It's a Trap."). To be fair, he was in the bjorn, facing me, so he couldn't see the screen, but even so, I took my baby to see Saw IV. And I ate popcorn over his head and dropped some in his ear and I watched people tortured and killed over his little head and I loved it. Another time, when he was three[redacted] was in a pool with him, and a friend came out onto the patio and I let go of his hand to wave, and when I looked back, Jack had slipped off the steps and was underwater, his little hands waving above the surface—an image I will take with me to my grave.

Parent fails. The thing about these conversations is that they d[redacted]t feel bad to have. Instead they feel strangely good. [redacted]athartic. Which is the oddest thing, because

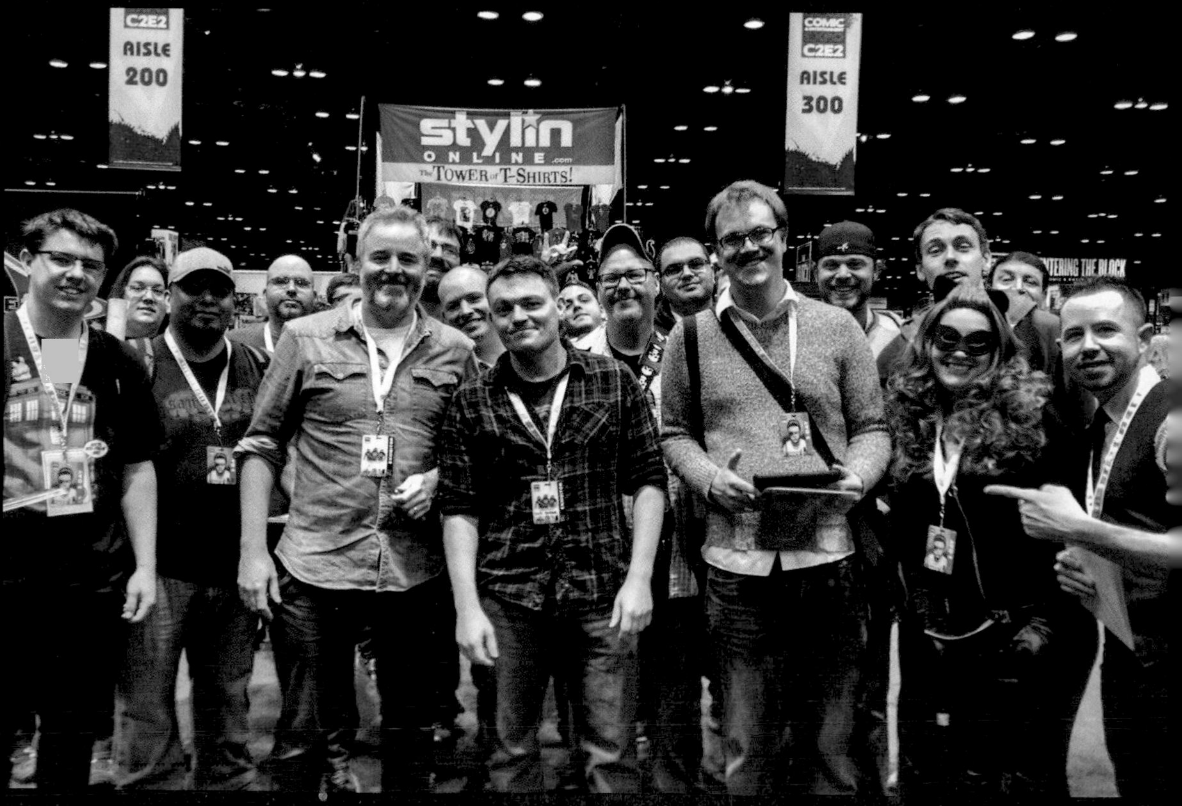
C2E2
AISLE
200
stylin
ONLINE.com
The TOWER of T-SHIRTS!
COMIC
C2E2
AISLE
300

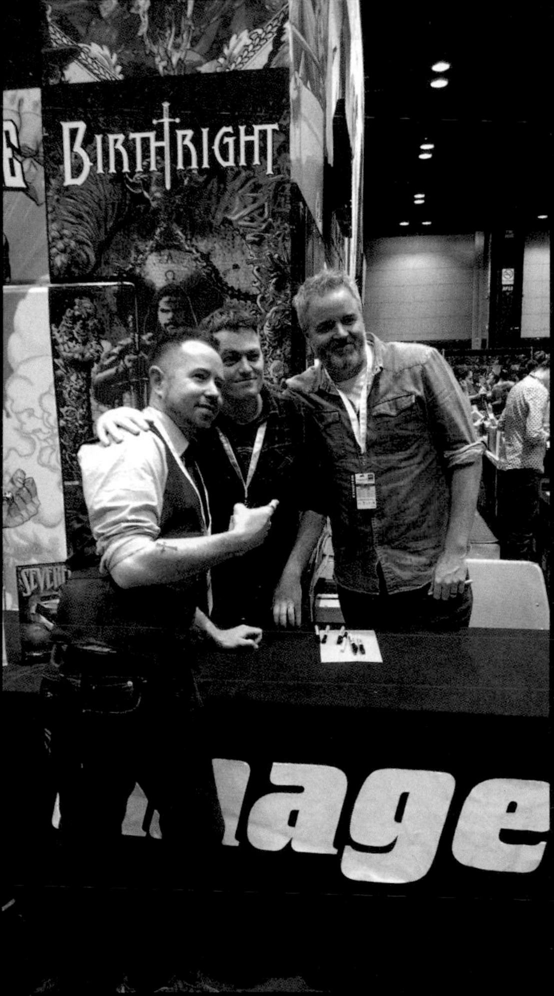
BIRTHRIGHT

really, no matter how small the admission, each one does speak to some larger failing on the part of the teller. For example, I took my kid to horror movies because I was going stir crazy in the house, and because I was feeling trapped by my new dad role and I needed to do something adult. With Jack at the pool, I was so excited to see my friend I forgot about my son for a moment. Laughable as some are, parent fails speak to moments of selfishness or neglect, of desire and longing. And so these incidents are tough things to admit, even in the generally humorous context of the conversation. But the thing is, you leave these conversations much better friends than you came in. That's the strangest part of all.

Which brings us to Wytches. By now I hope it's clear that this book is intensely personal to me and the rest of the team. For me, it's been a place I can explore some pretty deep fears about myself, my kids, explore some things I'm extremely proud of, some things I'm ashamed of. Like Sailor, I do struggle with anxiety and with my own mental health. Like Charlie, I do struggle with my fears for my kids, and I have gone through bad periods during those struggles.

And when we started this book, I remember telling Jock that this was going to be a dark one. That it was unlikely we'd have a sizeable readership. That the ugliness of the book might scare people off. But the thing is, to our amazement, you guys didn't get scared off. Not by the story, not by the essays. Instead you embraced the book to a degree we never expected. Having Wytches #6 clock in where it has in sales...we're all just floored. And more than sales, the Sailor cosplay, the letters you wrote, the stories you told us about your own struggles, your own fears... The way you took to this book and made it yours...answered it with your voices and made this a conversation bigger than any parent fail talk, but a conversation about our vulnerabilities, our humanity... We truly feel like we're leaving this first arc with a lot of new friends. We simply can't thank you enough.

So before I close I just want to say that as a way of thanking you, all of us on Wytches—Jock and Matt and Clem and David and I—we're going to pledge you. We're going to pledge—to you, all of you—that we could not be more committed to this book, and that we will come back even stronger than we left (Jock and I just plotted out the second arc in Chicago this past weekend, where we took the pics included here). We pledge that we will never take your support for this book for granted, as we have been stunned and humbled by it. And we pledge to keep the book true to its nature. The next arc will focus on Sailor, and the Irons, but at its core it will be about issues as personal as this arc has been—no spoilers, but that I can promise you. And lastly, we pledge you our thanks. You have made this book what it is, and for that, we are indebted to you.

Pledged is pledged.

Scott Snyder

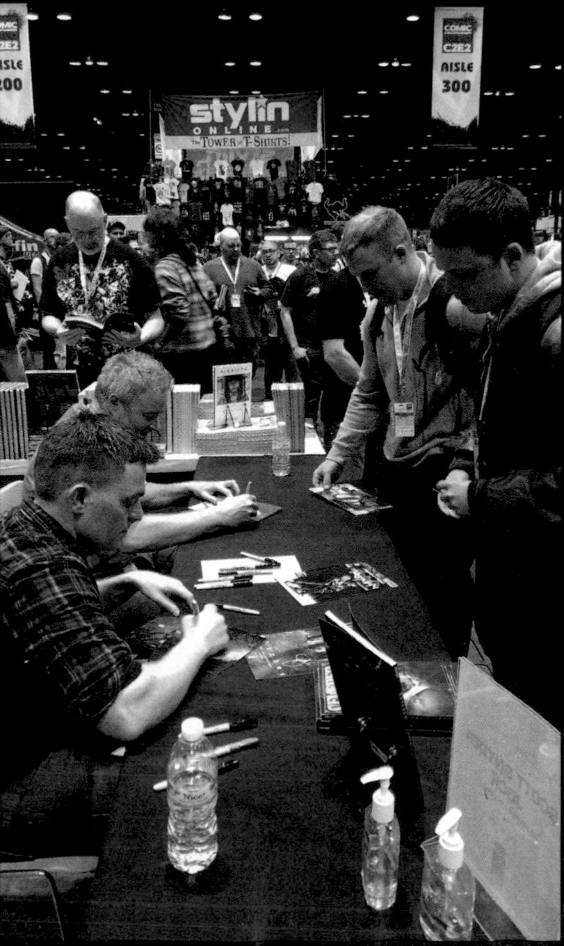
C2E2
AISLE
300
stylin
ONLINE .com
The TOWER of T-SHIRTS!

Process:
Evolution of the Wytches

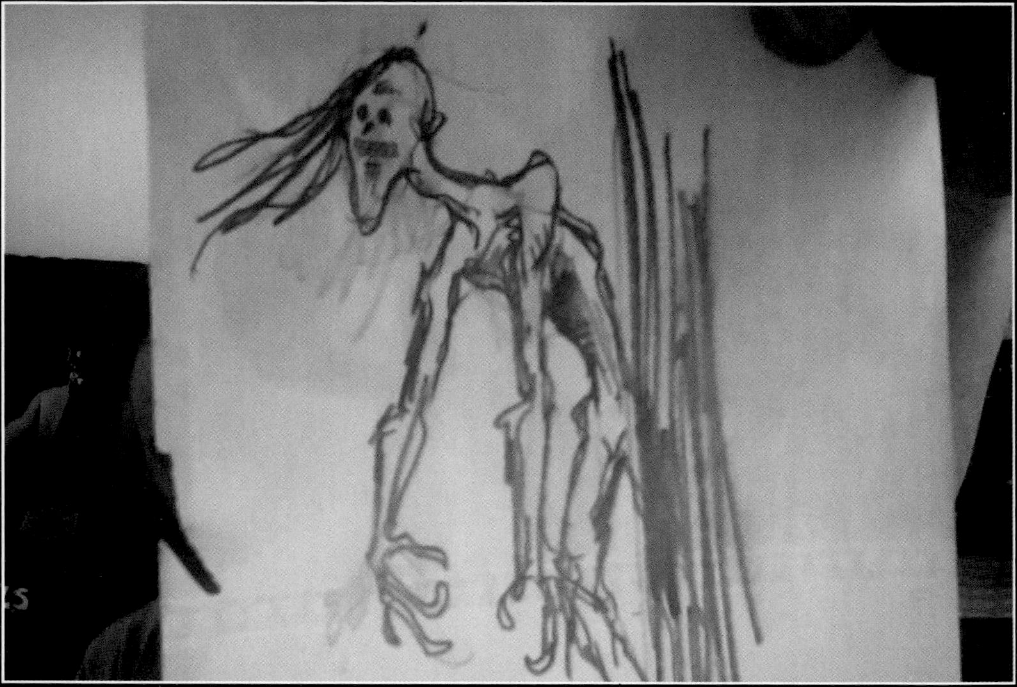

Scott's original concept

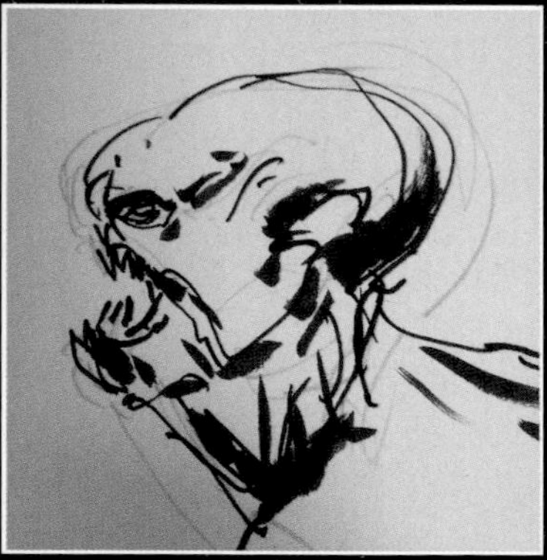

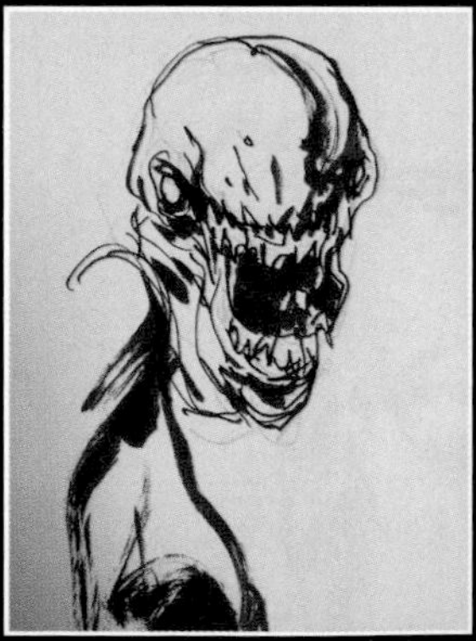

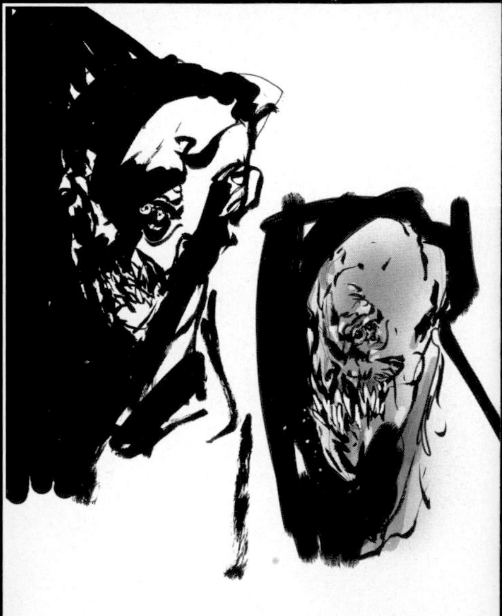

Jock's various concepts

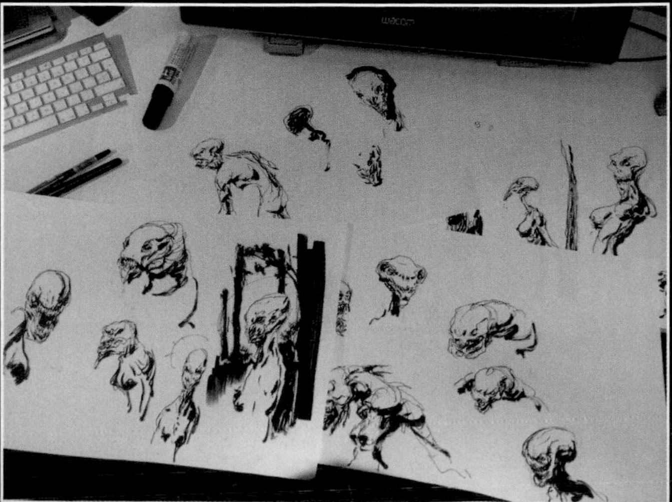
wacom

Unused Promotional Art

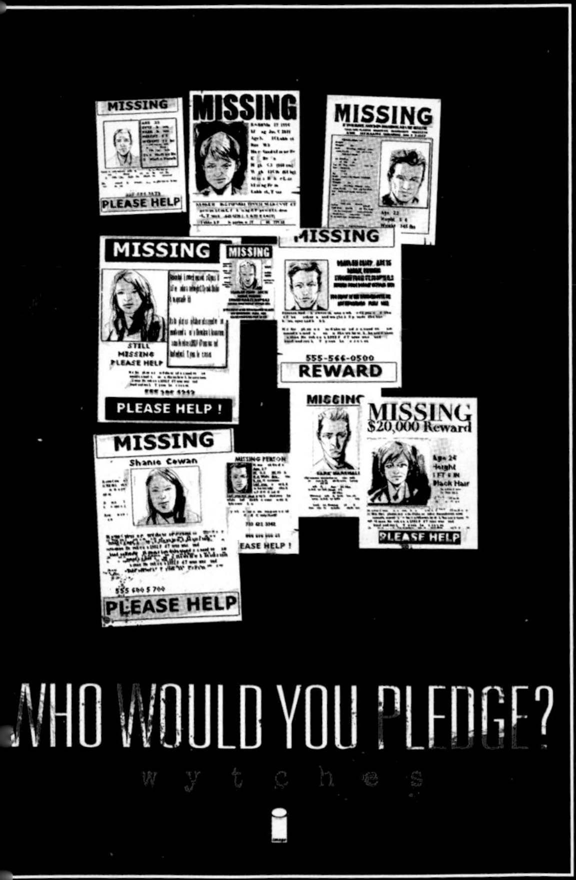
MISSING
PLEASE HELP
MISSING
MISSING
MISSING
MISSING
STILL MISSING PLEASE HELP
PLEASE HELP !
MISSING
555-566-0500
REWARD
MISSING
Shanie Cowan
PLEASE HELP
MISSING
$20,000 Reward
PLEASE HELP
WHO WOULD YOU PLEDGE?
wytches

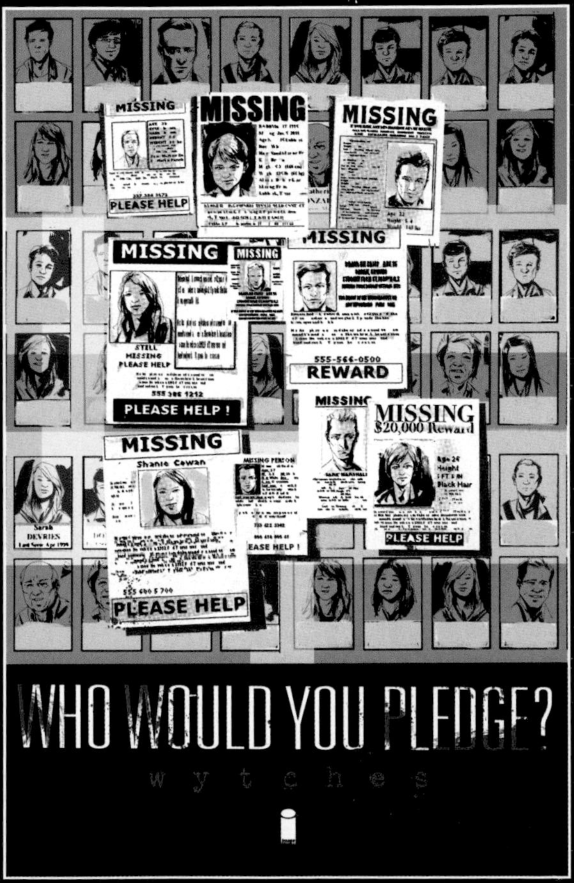
MISSING
PLEASE HELP
MISSING
MISSING
MISSING
MISSING
STILL MISSING PLEASE HELP
PLEASE HELP !
MISSING
555-566-0500
REWARD
MISSING
Shanie Cowan
PLEASE HELP
MISSING
$20,000 Reward
PLEASE HELP
WHO WOULD YOU PLEDGE?
wytches

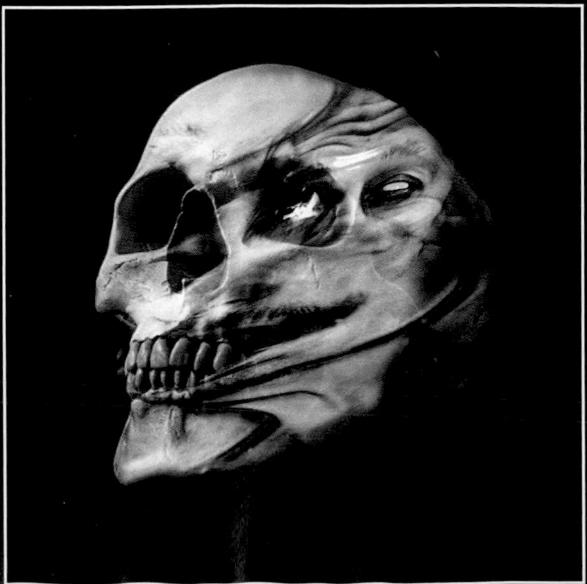

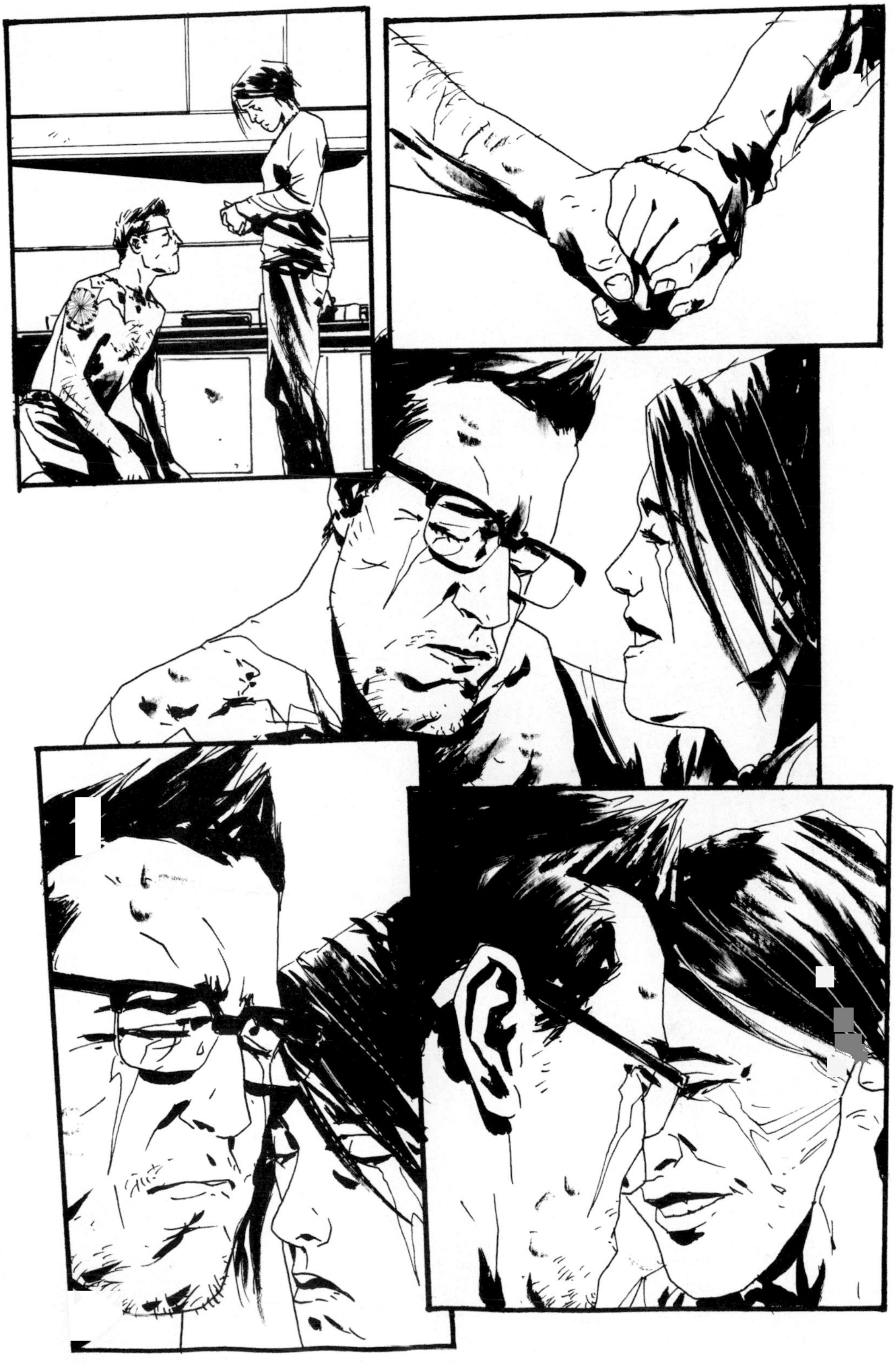

wytches

witch (wich) *n.* [ME *wicche* < OE *wicce*, fem, of *wicca*, sorcerer, akin to NDu *wicken*, to use ~~magic~~ < IE base *weik*, to separate (hence se~~t~~ aside or religious matters~~s~~) ~~cf. both weihs, holy. OB~~ *v~~ig.~~* *id~~e.~~*] 1 a per~~son, esp. a wo~~man having supernatural power as by a ~~com~~pact ~~with the devil~~ or evil spirits, so~~rc~~eress 2 an ugly and ill tempered ol~~d woman, hag~~ 3 a ~~priestess~~ ~~or~~ follower of white magic or of WICCA 4 ~~In~~form. ~~a~~ b~~e~~witching or fascinating woman or girl 5 short for WATER WITCH ~~sense~~ 2 —*vt.* 1 to put a magic spell o~~n~~, bewitch 2 [A~~rch.~~] to charm, fascinate —*vi.* DOWSE —**wit~~ch~~'~~like'~~** *adj.* —**wit~~ch~~'~~y~~** *adj.* **wit~~ch~~'ier, witch'-iest**

number one

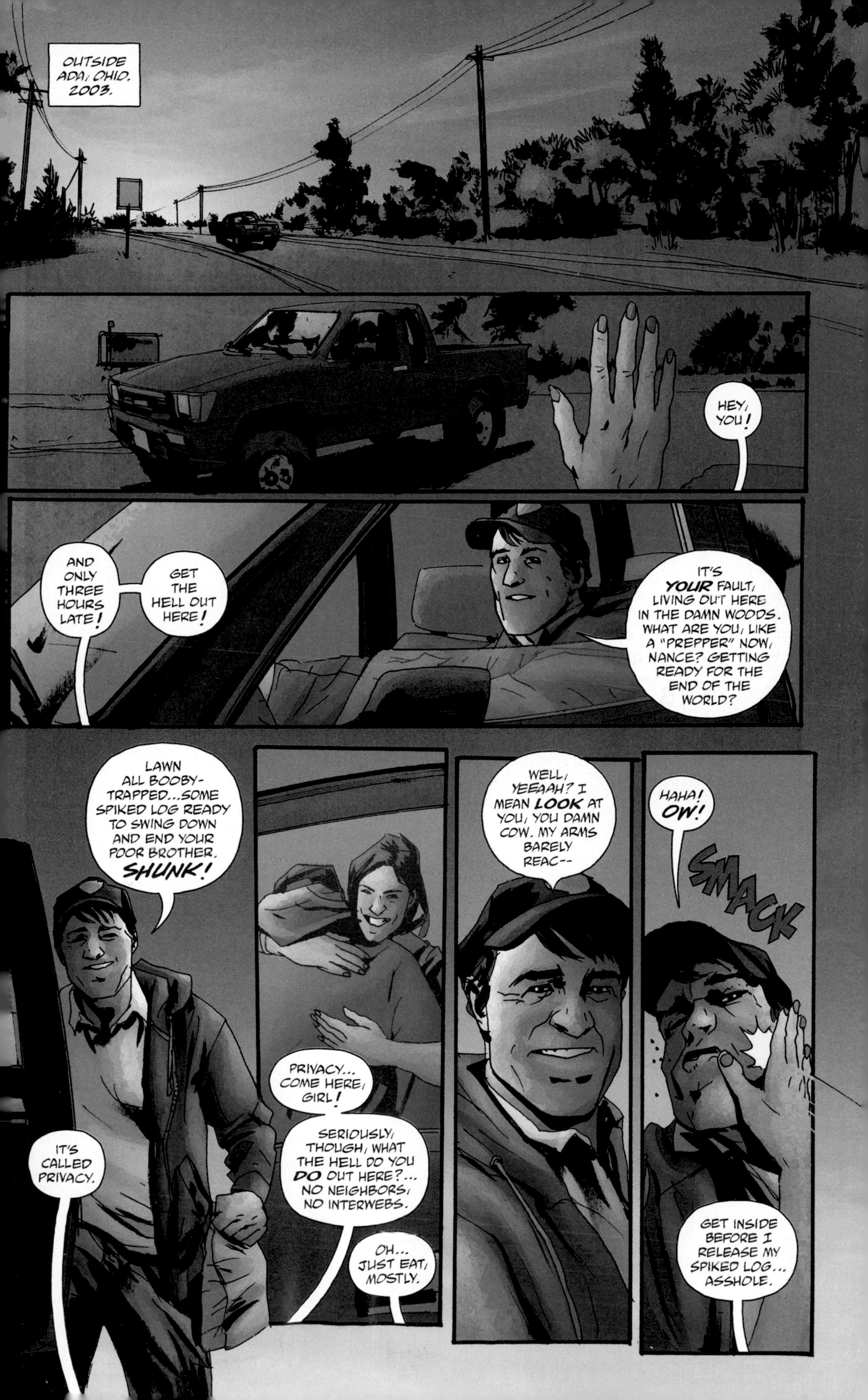
OUTSIDE ADA, OHIO, 2003.
HEY, YOU!
AND ONLY THREE HOURS LATE!
GET THE HELL OUT HERE!
IT'S YOUR FAULT, LIVING OUT HERE IN THE DAMN WOODS. WHAT ARE YOU, LIKE A "PREPPER" NOW, NANCE? GETTING READY FOR THE END OF THE WORLD?
LAWN ALL BOOBY-TRAPPED...SOME SPIKED LOG READY TO SWING DOWN AND END YOUR POOR BROTHER. SHUNK!
IT'S CALLED PRIVACY.
PRIVACY... COME HERE, GIRL!
SERIOUSLY, THOUGH, WHAT THE HELL DO YOU DO OUT HERE?... NO NEIGHBORS, NO INTERWEBS.
OH... JUST EAT, MOSTLY.
WELL, YEEAAH? I MEAN LOOK AT YOU, YOU DAMN COW. MY ARMS BARELY REAC--
HAHA! OW!
SMACK
GET INSIDE BEFORE I RELEASE MY SPIKED LOG... ASSHOLE.

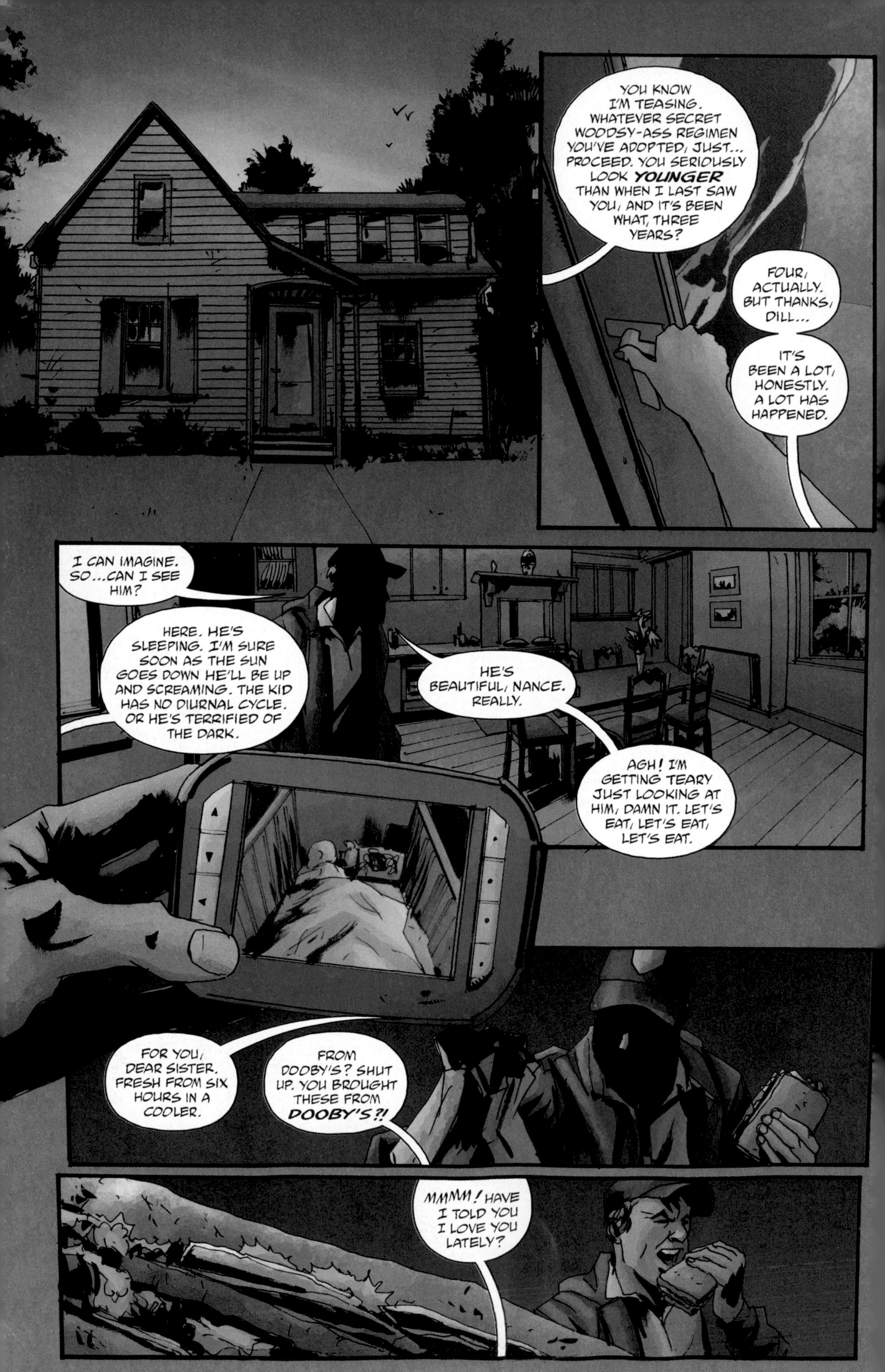
YOU KNOW I'M TEASING. WHATEVER SECRET WOODSY-ASS REGIMEN YOU'VE ADOPTED, JUST... PROCEED. YOU SERIOUSLY LOOK YOUNGER THAN WHEN I LAST SAW YOU, AND IT'S BEEN WHAT, THREE YEARS?
FOUR, ACTUALLY. BUT THANKS, DILL...
IT'S BEEN A LOT, HONESTLY. A LOT HAS HAPPENED.
I CAN IMAGINE. SO...CAN I SEE HIM?
HERE. HE'S SLEEPING. I'M SURE SOON AS THE SUN GOES DOWN HE'LL BE UP AND SCREAMING. THE KID HAS NO DIURNAL CYCLE. OR HE'S TERRIFIED OF THE DARK.
HE'S BEAUTIFUL, NANCE. REALLY.
AGH! I'M GETTING TEARY JUST LOOKING AT HIM, DAMN IT. LET'S EAT, LET'S EAT, LET'S EAT.
FOR YOU, DEAR SISTER. FRESH FROM SIX HOURS IN A COOLER.
FROM DOOBY'S? SHUT UP. YOU BROUGHT THESE FROM DOOBY'S?!
MMMM! HAVE I TOLD YOU I LOVE YOU LATELY?

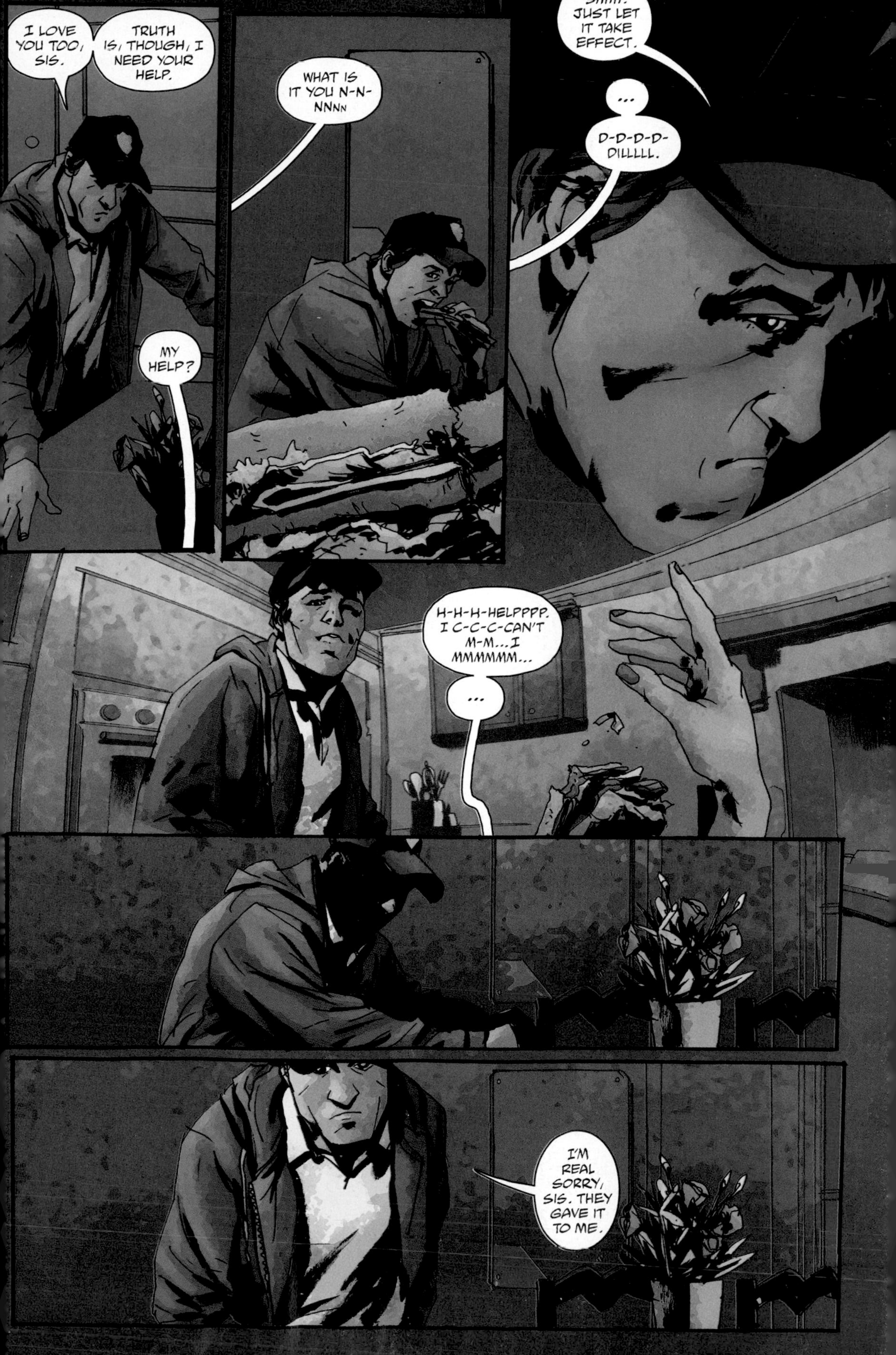
I LOVE YOU TOO, SIS.
TRUTH IS, THOUGH, I NEED YOUR HELP.
MY HELP?
WHAT IS IT YOU N-N-NNNn
Shhh. JUST LET IT TAKE EFFECT.
...
D-D-D-D-DILLLLL.
H-H-H-HELPPPP. I C-C-C-CAN'T M-M...I MMMMMM...
...
I'M REAL SORRY, SIS. THEY GAVE IT TO ME.

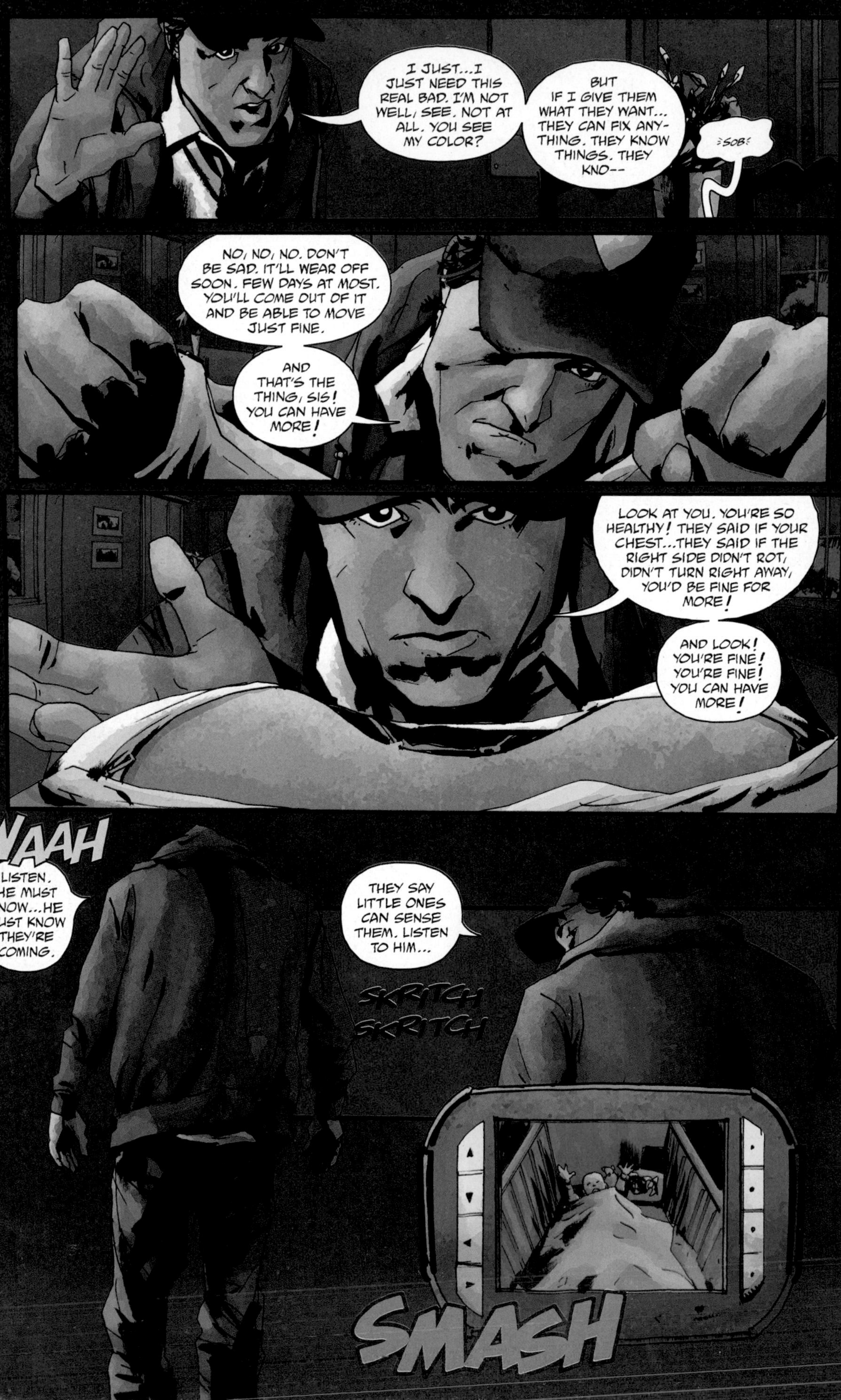
I JUST...I JUST NEED THIS REAL BAD. I'M NOT WELL, SEE. NOT AT ALL. YOU SEE MY COLOR?
BUT IF I GIVE THEM WHAT THEY WANT... THEY CAN FIX ANYTHING. THEY KNOW THINGS. THEY KNO--
SOB
NO, NO, NO. DON'T BE SAD. IT'LL WEAR OFF SOON. FEW DAYS AT MOST. YOU'LL COME OUT OF IT AND BE ABLE TO MOVE JUST FINE.
AND THAT'S THE THING, SIS! YOU CAN HAVE MORE!
LOOK AT YOU. YOU'RE SO HEALTHY! THEY SAID IF YOUR CHEST...THEY SAID IF THE RIGHT SIDE DIDN'T ROT, DIDN'T TURN RIGHT AWAY, YOU'D BE FINE FOR MORE!
AND LOOK! YOU'RE FINE! YOU'RE FINE! YOU CAN HAVE MORE!
WAAH
LISTEN. HE MUST KNOW...HE MUST KNOW THEY'RE COMING.
THEY SAY LITTLE ONES CAN SENSE THEM. LISTEN TO HIM...
SKRITCH
SKRITCH
SMASH

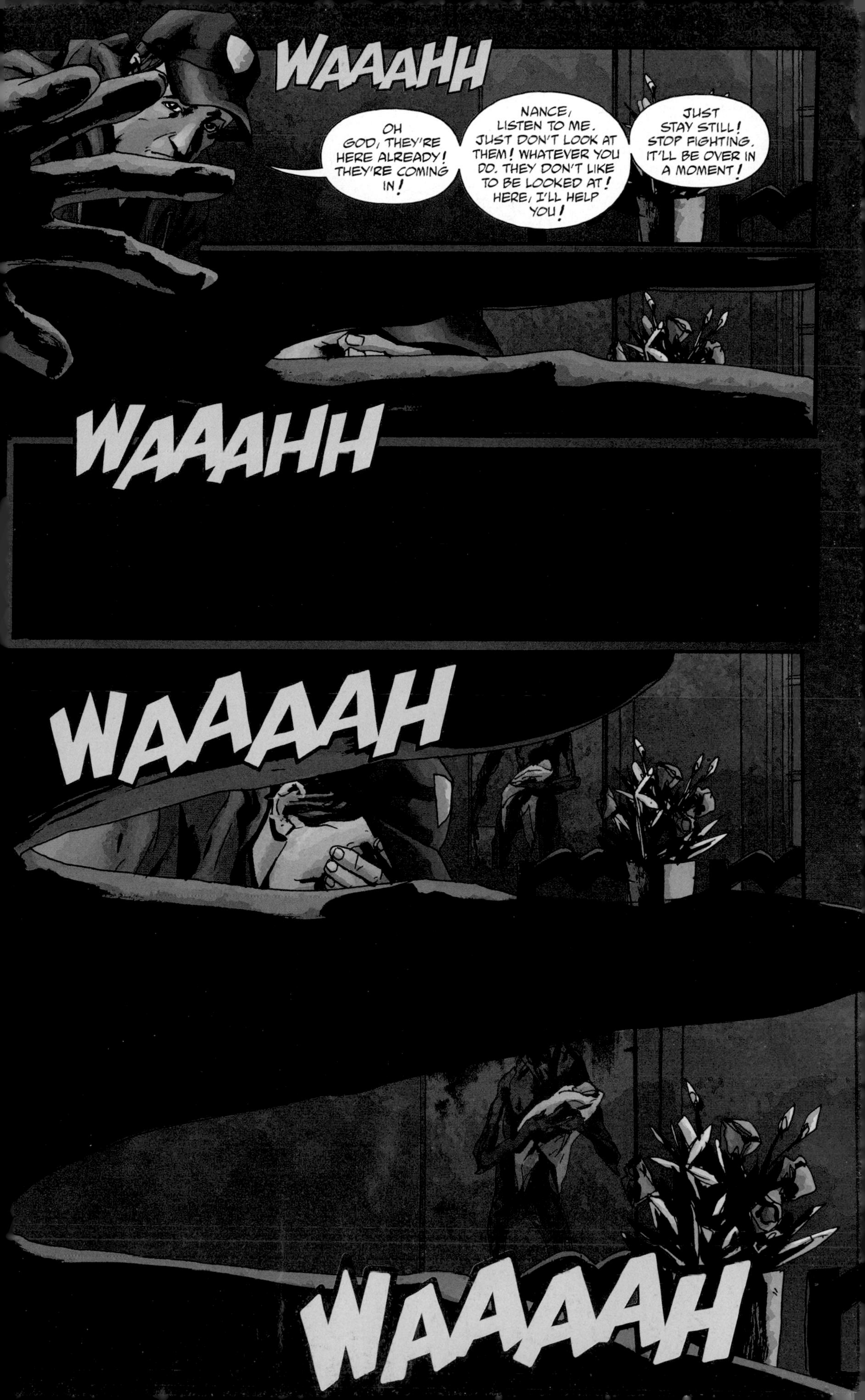
WAAAHH
OH GOD, THEY'RE HERE ALREADY! THEY'RE COMING IN!
NANCE, LISTEN TO ME. JUST DON'T LOOK AT THEM! WHATEVER YOU DO. THEY DON'T LIKE TO BE LOOKED AT! HERE, I'LL HELP YOU!
JUST STAY STILL! STOP FIGHTING. IT'LL BE OVER IN A MOMENT!
WAAAHH
WAAAAH
WAAAAH

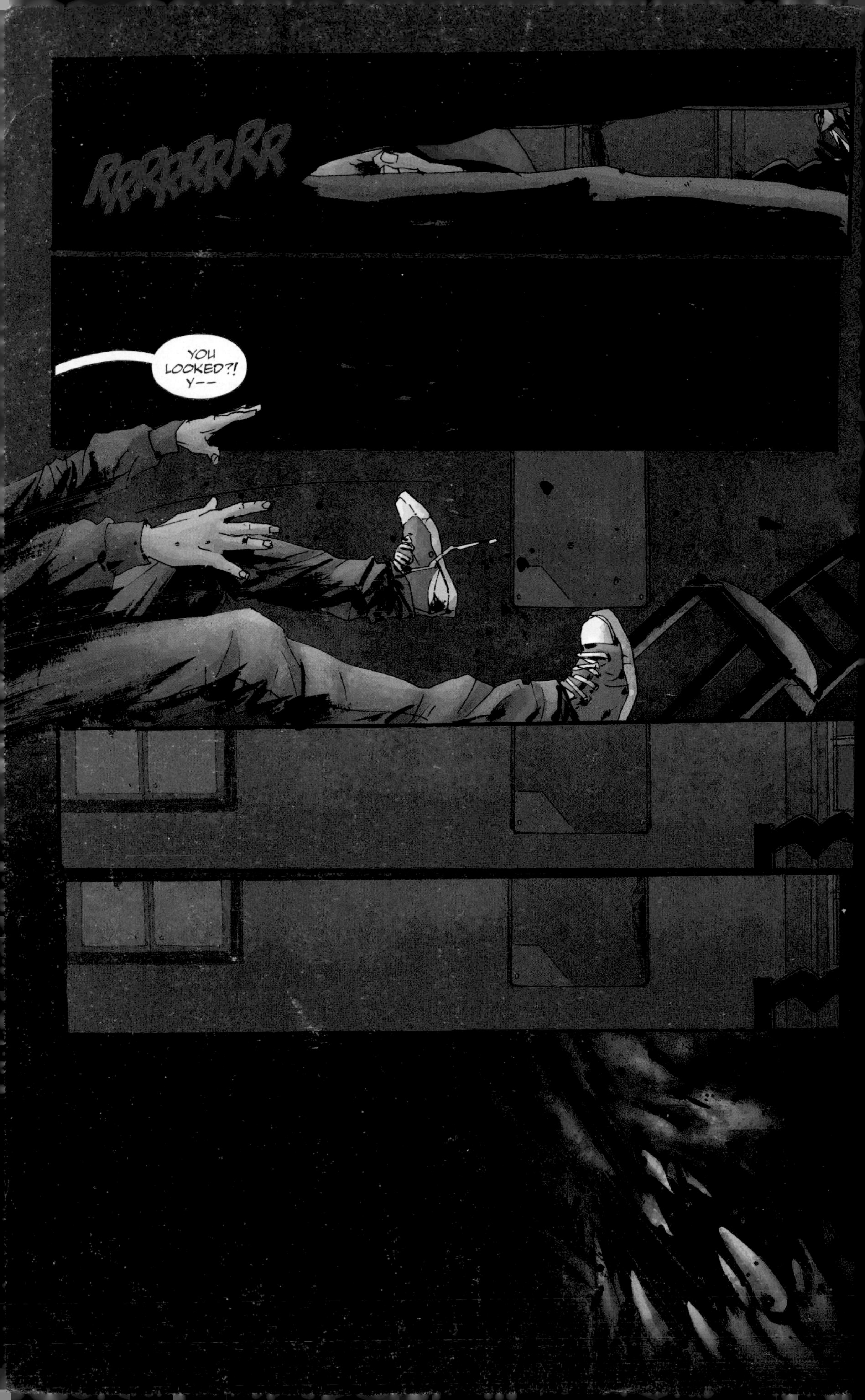
RRRRRRRR
YOU LOOKED?! Y--

Multicultural Issues in the Criminal Justice System

Marsha Tarver

California State University, Fresno

Steve Walker

California State University, Fresno

P. Harvey Wallace

California State University, Fresno

Allyn and Bacon

Boston • *London* • *Toronto* • *Sydney* • *Tokyo* • *Singapore*

Editor in Chief: *Karen Hanson*
Series Editor: *Jennifer Jacobson*
Editorial Assistant: *Tom Jefferies*
Marketing Manager: *Jude Hall*
Editorial-Production Administrator: *Bryan Woodhouse*
Editorial-Production Service: *Chestnut Hill*
Composition and Prepress Buyer: *Linda Cox*
Electronic Composition: *Peggy Cabot, Cabot Computer Services*
Manufacturing Buyer: *Joanne Sweeney*
Cover Administrator: *Kristina Mose-Libon*

A Pearson Education Company
75 Arlington Street
Boston, MA 02116

Internet: www.ablongman.com

Between the time Website information is gathered and then published, it is not unusual for some sites to have closed. Also, the transcription of URLs can result in unintended typographical errors. The publisher would appreciate notification where these occur so that they may be corrected in subsequent editions.

Library of Congress Cataloging-in-Publication Data

Tarver, Marsha.
Multicultural issues in the criminal justice system / Marsha Tarver, Steve Walker, Harvey Wallace.
p. cm.
Includes bibliographical references and index.
ISBN 0-205-31879-7
1. Criminal justice, Administration of—United States—Cross-cultural studies. I. Walker, Steve (Steven Douglas) II. Wallace, Harvey. III. Title.

HV9950 T36 2002
364—dc21 2001046134

Printed in the United States of America

10 9 8 7 6 5 4 3 06 05 04

To my Parisian roommate, and to The Beetle and Taffy—MT

To Ben S. Walker and Mae Pitzer—SW

To Randa—HW

Contents

Preface

Effective criminal justice systems rely upon the correct interpretation of accurate data about the populations they serve. Using these interpretations, they seek to develop appropriate policies and procedures governing how they will perform such functions as law enforcement, victim assistance, crime prevention, community service, and treatment of deviance. Some concepts are central to our basic understanding of human interaction across racial, ethnic, and cultural lines. Others are central to our understanding of the current American milieu in which criminal justice systems must function effectively. This text seeks to define and characterize the dynamics of cross-cultural interaction, and to provide a brief explanation of the circumstances that have brought American criminal justice into the twenty-first century.

Any understanding of population data affecting cross-cultural interaction must first include descriptions and brief explanations about the concepts of race, ethnicity, and culture. Some anthropologists combine these concepts under the umbrella of the term *peoplehood*. After establishing the importance to our discussion of concepts of peoplehood, we must then discuss briefly the cultural-historic circumstances that give us our modern-day nation. Finally, those circumstances combined with their historic settings build the governing philosophies that define the roles of the criminal justice system in a culturally diverse and complex society.

This is a fairly tall order for any textbook, and the reader should expect that our treatment of complicated issues surrounding anthropology and history will be geared to summarize and significantly generalize many concepts, while relating them to the emergence of the modern criminal justice system. Although it does not address every nuance of culture or every issue and question about cultural interaction that might influence the criminal justice system, this textbook is designed to direct our thoughts toward those nuances, issues, and questions.

Acknowledgments

The authors would like to acknowledge and thank a very supportive group of people from Allyn & Bacon and their team of editors: Karen Hanson, Jennifer Jacobson, Tom Jefferies, Bryan Woodhouse, and Myrna Breskin. We appreciate their assistance, direction, and invaluable comments and suggestions in the development of this text.

In every endeavor there are pioneers, and so it is true for cultural diversity education. I would like to acknowledge Senior Consultant Dave Spisak of the California Commission on Peace Officer Standards and Training for his vision and for giving me so many "green lights" to develop diversity education for law enforcement personnel over the past decade. Thanks to the efforts of Suzanne Foucault and the San Diego Regional Training Center for providing a vehicle for delivery of diversity training throughout the state. Finally, thanks to the Fresno City College Peace Officers Academy which has been the proving ground for much of the curriculum, theories, and ideas that are reflected in this text. Thanks to my department chair, P. Harvey Wallace, for a variety of opportunities, support, and encouragement throughout the process.

MLT

I would first like to acknowledge all of my victimology course students, whose projects on their own victimization keep me focused clearly each semester. I want to acknowledge my parents, Ben and Irene Walker, who taught me the patience and commitment to finish this project. Thanks to the Pitzer family for teaching me that we all should endeavor to make a difference; to my best friend and brother, Charles Wilson, for his consistent support in keeping me grounded; to Harvey Wallace for his continual encouragement, without which this project would have gone unfinished.

SDW

Thanks to my colleagues in the Criminology Department, California State University, Fresno, for their support and understanding during this process.

HW

1

The Impact of Culture on the Criminal Justice System

Learning Objectives

After reading this chapter you should be able to do the following:

1. Compare and contrast the three waves of immigration and their effect upon society.
2. Distinguish among race, ethnicity, and culture.
3. Define civil rights legislation and identify key legislative acts.
4. Generalize the relationship of peoplehood to the criminal justice system.

Understanding Peoplehood

Peoplehood refers to the social-psychological core that connects individuals through an ancestral and future-oriented identification with a group (Gordon, 1978, 1996). Each group entering America brings a culture and ethnicity that represents its peoplehood. These groups are comprised of populations sharing collective identities, as well as cultural and racial heritage. People receive a sense of belonging and personal strength as they identify with others. That sense, that peoplehood, unifies groups. The value of keeping alive our traditions and customs can provide us with a sense of ancestry and a past.

The notion of peoplehood in the United States incorporates concepts of culture, race, and ethnicity, along with the status derived from being immigrants, refugees, or colonialized, indigenous subjects. This incorporation is a salient part of our diversity. Theorists find it difficult to characterize the prototypical American according to appearance, trait, or background. And while terms such as *culture, race,* and *ethnicity* can be defined, they are far from exclusive of each other in modern times. They are, in fact, dependent upon each other, as any study of peoplehood in complex society reveals.

Examples of this abound throughout the literature, including Kneller's (1965) allegory of an encounter along the river ten thousand years ago between two people from primitive cultures. Each was unfamiliar to the other, so they approached with caution. After establishing some form of communication, the first question that would pass between them is "Who are you?" Ten thousand years ago, peoplehood was far more simple than today. The answer, "I am Arapesh," would be adequate to describe one's self. If you, the questioner, knew anything about the Arapesh people, then you knew most everything significant to your transactions with that person on the river.

However, as history progressed, different peoples began trading with each other, they intermarried, they specialized in vocations and professions, and caste divisions and class distinctions began to form. "Who are you?" became a complicated question requiring some detailed explanation. Our differences as humans were accentuated as interaction increased. This change gave rise to intergroup tension. Kneller (1965) noted that "the more tightly knit the culture the greater its resistance to change." He explains that, since change is inevitable in this highly technical and advanced world, groups that are not open to

---

FOCUS BOX • *Primitive Cultures*

The term *primitive culture* tends to conjure up negative images. Individuals often mistake "primitive" for "low functioning" or somehow "inferior." Such distinctions are inaccurate and unproductive in discussions about diversity.

Primitive cultures differ from complex societies in many ways. They generally do not synthesize chemicals to find vaccinations for polio, they don't invent florescent lighting, nor do they mine ore from the earth to build machines that fabricate the electrophoresis plates used for DNA research. Complex societies tend to be better at these things than are primitive cultures.

However, primitive cultures tend to excel at such things as group and family cohesiveness, the transmission of community values and learning to young persons, and self-reliance borne of the ability to manage available resources to survive without dependence upon such things as foreign oil.

change will experience a collapse. Alternatively, groups that are more loosely integrated and that can more readily absorb a range of innovations are less likely to perceive change as threatening the foundations of their peoplehood. Kneller's theory is still relevant today.

Peoplehood is an interesting, complex concept. Among the many facets of peoplehood are race, ethnicity, culture, age, and gender. While the basic definitions of age and gender are simple, their roles in the overall composition of our peoplehood can be complicated. On the other hand, terms such as *race, ethnicity,* and *culture* require some basic definitions before the discussion can proceed. Additionally, much of our sense of peoplehood depends upon relationships between groups, and those relationships require definition as well.

Race, Ethnicity, and Culture

These are terms that anthropologists and sociologists regard as "primarily social constructs." In other words, categorizing groups of people is generally considered a method by which to label differences.

The traditional definition of *race* is separated into three categories, and they are labeled Caucasoid, Negroid, and Mongoloid. These categories are based on genetic traits that differentiate physical characteristics such as hair types, skin color, and bone structure.

FOCUS BOX • *Race*

When we discuss geographic origins of races, some clarification is appropriate. We generalize for the sake of discussion and understanding when we identify Europe as the geographic origin of Caucasians, Africa as the geographic origin of Negroid people, or Asia as the geographic origin of Mongoloid people. That generalization carries the potential of reductionism and oversimplification.

Let's look at some examples.

Africa is the world's second largest continent, and over 70 percent of its people are black (Negroid). However, within the designation of Negroid there is terrific diversity. This diversity is oversimplified if we consider race alone, and to understand it we must also consider ethnicity and culture. Therefore, to say that a person is African is to be very general indeed. Americans of African ancestry who have a heritage rooted in slavery often have difficulty tracing their actual ethnicity because of the lack of reliable records available to them.

Caucasians are thought to have originated in Europe, and depending upon how we define "Europe" this designation too can lead to an oversimplified view of diversity. The statement that "whites come from Europe" tells us nothing about the individual. Again, this is a concept of ethnicity.

Finally, we might assume that Mongoloid peoples originate from Asia. Asia is the world's largest continent and has over 60 percent of the world's population. The Asian continent has a vast diversity of people, language, culture, and ethnicity. The physical characteristics that are associated with Mongoloid peoples are often designated "Oriental." Oriental is a term usually reserved for things (such as artifacts), so the correct designation for people who fit the morphology might be "Far Eastern."

Detailed discussions regarding these terms are the purview of anthropology rather than criminology, but some clarification is important. Statements and ideas that are reductionistic and oversimplify our origins can sometimes foster tension, prejudice, and discrimination.

The Caucasoid label (from which we derive the term *Caucasian*) is associated with European ancestry. The Negroid label (from which we derive the term *Negro*) is associated with ancestry from parts of the African Continent. The Mongoloid label is associated with ancestry from parts of Asia (Gordon, 1978, 1996; Walker, Spohn, & DeLone, 2000).

These three traditional designations of race have blurred over the last several centuries. As groups intermarry (Kneller's [1965] term "amalgamation") and have children of mixed racial backgrounds, new race designations are certainly plausible. Even so, the three racial categories are used as the basis for the categorization and collection of demographic data about people.

Concepts surrounding *ethnicity* are complex, and explanations about ethnicity can vary depending upon one's frame of reference. For our discussions, it is sufficient to limit definitions of ethnicity to family heritage. Your ethnicity as an American might be Italian (from Southern Europe), Cantonese (from Eastern China), Ibu (from Africa), Palestinian (from the Near East), or Yocut (Native American from the West). American peoples are noted for ethnic mixtures in individual families. For instance, it is common for American families to have Mexican national heritage with ethnic mixtures of several European and Native American groups.

Defining *culture* involves understanding the elements that combine to create a culture. We will list several concepts that are generally included in the elements of culture, and define them in very general terms. They are:

- Common history. People who share cultures in common usually share or are from families that share a historic past.
- Common geographical basis. Geography is important because the elements of where you live shape much of your life and that of your ancestors.
- Some political agreement. Not that everyone in your cultural group need be either a Democrat or a Republican, but there is usually agreement about the political process.
- Common beliefs. There are shared general religious or philosophical beliefs, such as Judeo-Christianity, the Islamic faith, and so forth.
- Shared customs. These can include attire, culinary customs, and celebrations such as Thanksgiving, Rosh Hashanah, or Ramadan.
- Similar artistic basis. This would embrace music and performing arts, sculpture, and the like.
- Morals, mores, and folkways. These three related concepts follow in an order of descending formality.
  - Morals are usually considered to be formalized, and are usually common to different groups. For instance, nobody wants to live with a murderer in the village, have a thief in his or her midst, or transact business with a liar.
  - Mores might be very different, depending upon the group. For instance, the marriage of a 14-year-old girl to a 38-year-old man is acceptable in some groups, and might be a crime in others. Mores include cultural notions of childhood, sexual taboos, family responsibilities for the elderly, and so forth.
  - Folkways describe specific behaviors that are loosely coupled to mores and represent the preferred interaction between members of the group. Folkways are less

formalized, and can be very different between groups. Folkway practices include shaking hands, bowing, eye contact, and expressions of endearment. Proxemics, the study of the spatial distance between individuals during social and interpersonal situations, is an example of a culturally bound activity.

- Law by consensus. As in political agreement, this does not suggest that we enjoy speed limits and tax regulations. However, cultural groups understand the necessity of laws and agree upon the processes by which they are made. This stands in contrast to conflict-coercion theories of lawmaking.

- Common linguistic bonds. With some leeway for dialect, people who share culture in common usually share language skills sufficient for communication.

- Common racial background. While racial background is a hallmark of shared culture, this can sometimes be supplanted by strong common beliefs or political consensus.

This listing offers some good points for understanding and discussion. Although it is not all inclusive, and there are certainly some exceptions that some scholars would note, these elements do in fact blend together to help create a group's culture (Gordon, 1978, 1996; Kneller, 1965; Spindler & Spindler, 1987). "We may regard culture as the learned and shared behavior (thoughts, acts, and feelings) of a certain people together with their artifacts (art, houses, tools)—learned in a sense that this behavior is transmitted socially rather than genetically, shared in that it is practiced either by the whole population or by some part of it" (Kneller, 1965, p. 4). The social system of shared values aids in the adaptation to the environment and ensures that traditions and beliefs are systematically shared with the next generation. The sense of commonality and behaviors that support this need for identity and historical connection is partly due to our psychological need of "belongingness." The strength of groups enduring difficult transitions lies in the security of the traditional culture. Groups that feel secure in their identity tend to be more open and to have greater freedom and flexibility when they confront new cultural groups. On the

FOCUS BOX • *Nationality*

We often seek information about ethnicity by asking, "What is your nationality?" The answer we expect might be, "Well, my mother was German and my dad was Italian-Swiss." By definition, that is the incorrect answer for questions concerning nationality.

Although racial and ethnic groups might be associated with particular countries, race, ethnicity, and nationality are different. Race refers to categories based on defining characteristics. Ethnicity refers to categories based on ancestral origin around the world. Nationality is a term that defines the country of a person's citizenship. An individual either is born in that country or applies for citizenship and becomes naturalized.

Some people may have dual citizenship. For example, a child born in Canada to Laotian parents who are naturalized Canadians might become a naturalized citizen of the United States as an adult.

Nationality is a term sometimes misused in conversation. For the sake of our discussion in this chapter, your nationality is defined by the cover of your passports and the country in which you may register to vote.

other hand, groups who are not secure in their cultural identity or are confronted with extreme levels of prejudice and discrimination might experience a distorted sense of self that impinges on their well-being.

Relationship among Groups

The history of the Western Hemisphere gives us the basis for modern-day relationships among groups in the United States. For our discussion, it is adequate to categorize these groups according to the following general criteria:

- Indigenous persons are those who were present in the Western Hemisphere upon the arrival of European explorers. *Native Americans* or *First Nations* are familiar terms.
- Immigrants are those who came to the United States to explore economic or political opportunity. The Spanish and French had a formidable early presence in what would be the United States, and the English and Germans were among the first immigrants to this country.
- Refugees leave their homes abroad under circumstances beyond their control. These circumstances might be political, military, or economic. Irish persons fleeing the potato famine were early refugees, and Hmong people fleeing "The Killing Fields" were refugees in recent years.
- Colonialized subjects are either indigenous people who have been militarily conquered or slaves who were brought here against their wills. Native Americans and African slaves are among examples of colonialized subjects.

John Ogbu (1992) notes that the four groups each have very different relationships with "the establishment."

- *Indigenous persons* and *colonialized subjects* view the establishment as dominating and oppressive, and note a history of military conquest, annihilation, and oppression as part of official U.S. policy. The relationship arising from this history is strained, and further harmed by ongoing instances of discrimination.
- *Immigrants* share more positive historical context with the establishment. The United States is a land of opportunity, and the same government policies that displaced Native Americans gave land grants to early immigrant settlers.
- *Refugees* often view the United States as a sanctuary from the circumstances surrounding their flight from their homelands. No matter what the problems in America, at least it holds the promise of deliverance from those circumstances. Some refugees hold to the notion that they will return to their homelands after the circumstances are resolved, but historically this is not often the case.

Peoplehood in America: The Challenges for Government

The divisions and specialization that developed through history resulted in the establishment of "pecking orders," with groups striving for elevated status. An unfortunate part of human history, these instances of domination and imperialism are common to most groups in most nations, regardless of race or culture.

Highly visible cases in the news bring to us the realization that conflicts arising from race, ethnicity, age, gender, and culture still occur in America. Institutional segregation, discrimination, sexual harassment, racial profiling, and hate crimes fill the news long after the passage of laws intended to eliminate these unfortunate artifacts of the human need for a "pecking order."

Growth, economics, and immigration are among the dynamics of all national histories. The same holds true for the United States, but in many ways our history is exclusive because of our stated philosophy encouraging immigration and diversity. One must emphasize *stated* American philosophy because, in spite of our Declaration of Independence and the lovely words on our Statue of Liberty, coming to—and being accepted in—America has been and continues to be more difficult than we would like to believe. This difficulty is based partly upon the necessity of laws and immigration control to ensure stability and security, and partly upon society's attitudes toward both indigenous and immigrant groups. The result is that social controls are imposed by government and enforced by government agencies.

Many of the agencies that share responsibility for social control fall under the criminal justice umbrella. Since social control is generally encouraged by majority and minority populations, government assumes its rightful place as the active agent in the balance between immigration control and civil rights.

Early work by Lambert (1981) offered a useful explanation of this balance and the stages of American governmental involvement in these issues. He characterizes five concepts:

1. Government as an agent of social control by the majority
2. Government as a guarantor of evenhanded treatment of minorities in its own process
3. Government as a guarantor that public behavior will be non–ethnic- and non–racial-specific
4. Government as a guarantor that group affiliation will not affect an individual's life chances

FOCUS BOX • *Melting Pot*

The idea that it will be easy to govern a country that is homogeneous (all peoples generally similar in culture, race, and ethnicity) is too simplistic. The "melting pot" theory, whereby all immigrants and natives can "boil and become one," does not fit the individualistic image of what American citizens want.

While individuals and individual groups are definitely affected by the influence of the whole, the passage of centuries and various circumstances are necessary to create the result that we know as a true "melting pot." Assimilation and acculturation are real phenomena, but other factors such as cultural identity and pluralism play important roles.

R. Roosevelt believes that the idea of "melting pot" is "the wrong metaphor in business because not only is it impossible to melt down the many diverse groups that make up the American workforce, but most individuals are no longer willing to be melted down" (Workforce 2000, p. 19).

5. Government as an active agent to redistribute and to equalize the current social and, particularly, economic, status of ethnic/racial groups as a whole by redistribution of social rewards (p. 201)

This government involvement in social issues creates opportunities and challenges for the criminal justice system as an active agent for social control. The enforcement of laws that are designed to protect individual civil rights from racist actions actually brings society into more contact with police. While protection of individual civil rights is a positive concept, much of this contact is nontraditional policing and might have some negative implications for individual officers. On the other hand, the added exposure to police activities can create tension for citizens who are intended to be beneficiaries of those activities. Many people in this field hope that, as the architects of the criminal justice system become more aware of the challenges posed by our multicultural society, we will be able to more effectively respond to these issues.

Cultural History and Patterns of Change

Perhaps the relevance of what has preceded us is illusive, or perhaps our electronic and information age is too forward-thinking and often fails to recognize the value of the past. Whatever the reasons, given a choice between the History Channel or HBO, or between a Crichton novel or John Redpath, it seems that HBO and fiction novels are often the American preference.

What we risk is the failure to recognize the connection between this evening's news and such events as the European settlement of the Western Hemisphere, Nelson's victory at Trafalgar, the American Civil War, the fall of the Soviet Empire, and the return of Hong Kong to China. These events, from the most distant to the most recent, shape our government, our criminal justice system, and how we do business each day.

Cause and Effect: A Historic Context

Events beginning around the end of the Crusades have shaped the character of modern life in the Western Hemisphere (Viola & Margolis, 1991). Events surrounding the colonial period of world history (such as the partitioning of Africa and the European occupation of the Americas) have left an indelible mark on the United States. The first, second, and third "great waves" of immigration to the United States have created a multiethnic mosaic of peoples. The historic assimilation of cultures, and terms such as Angloconformity, the melting pot, world view, and cultural pluralism, are related to such issues as urban decay and the emergence of adolescent gangs in the inner city. As we briefly review the cultural history of America and the resulting patterns of change, we will discuss only a few of the many circumstances that brought us to the modern-day criminal justice system and its relationship to American communities. We will seek to illustrate how that system is a product of our history.

Our psychology and cultural "peoplehood" is based upon information learned from our environment, and in the contexts of primary group relationships. The criminal justice system utilizes cultural studies involving historic context, seeking to define the relationships of persons to their past and how the past relates to their present behavior. It is through this awareness of the congruence between our thoughts and actions that we gain an understanding of ourselves and of our interactions with others. This understanding does not mitigate the responsibility for or effects of deviant behavior, but it does provide some explanations. Such explanations might alleviate frustration and stress felt by people working in the criminal justice system as they serve victims, witnesses, and suspects who are different from themselves.

The study of American history is interwoven with groups of people that are immigrants, refugees, indigenous persons, and colonialized subjects. While demographers recognize that these terms encompass very distinct groups of people coming to America, very often the term *immigrants* is used in a more global fashion to define all categories save indigenous persons. Unless otherwise noted, this discussion will use the term *immigrant* to include refugees.

In the late 1980s, two-thirds of the world's immigration came to the United States. Half of that number, or one-third of the world's immigration, came to the Los Angeles Basin and the San Joaquin Valley of California (Kotkin & Kishimoto, 1988). This trend seems to have continued through subsequent years, and this flood of immigrants (many from primitive cultures) has a significant impact upon social services resources in the involved regions. Minority groups who have been present in certain areas for generations find themselves being economically and geographically displaced, and the resulting economic strain and political uncertainty create tension in neighborhoods and communities.

Such changes in America's demographics result in stress upon the government in general and the criminal justice system in particular. On the other hand, the influx of new groups of people brings creative approaches to business management, senses of responsibility for family, the willingness to work hard to improve their lives, and the desire to achieve the "American dream."

It is against this backdrop of demographic changes that a brief review of American history will relate the impact of the past upon the present and future of the criminal justice system in America.

The Rediscovery of America: Settlement by Europeans

The rediscovery of America is a phrase that more correctly reflects European settlement of this hemisphere in the fifteenth century. The original discovery of what would later be named for Columbus's cartographer probably occurred when groups of hunters migrated from Siberia across the Bering Strait via the Beringia, or land bridge, during the Pleistocene period of natural history. The descendants of these first migrants populated what are now North, Middle, and South America. Over thousands of years, linguistically and culturally distinct bands of people developed societies that were considered parallel to sixteenth-century Spanish social organization. Archeologists report evidence of their advancements in astronomy, mathematics, architecture, and agricultural technology. These Native Americans are considered indigenous people, meaning that they were the original inhabitants, or aboriginal people, of the land.

In the late 1400s these indigenous populations were discovered and colonialized by the Spanish. Through force, fear, and enslavement, the complexion of America changed.

The Spanish and the Portuguese saw the "New World" as a continent to be conquered, people to be subdued, and land to be controlled. Native Americans were enslaved and pressed into service, first on large sugar plantations in the Caribbean, and slavery soon expanded to tobacco and cotton farming in what would become the tidewater South of the United States. The exploitation and mistreatment of slaves has left an enduring legacy of tension and resentment that shapes race relations today.

The "Great Waves" of Immigration

The New World became part of the economic world market. Opportunities for wealth inspired new generations of European descendants to come to the Americas. Europeans were coming to the New World as entrepreneurs, as adventurers, and to seek freedom from religious persecution (Viola & Margolis, 1991). It is this group of Europeans that comprise what theorists call the first great wave of immigration.

The First Great Wave.   The first great wave of immigration is associated with what some call the Founding Fathers of our country. This group of people became the new settlers of a European America. They brought their cultures from England, Spain, France, Holland, and Germany to this new land.

Colonies of people developed different patterns of social and economic organization as they adapted to the geography and climate of this new land. Our early history was heavily influenced by German settlers, and German nearly became our official language, but the English established the majority of the colonies so they imposed their language and government practices upon the region. Between 1620 and 1642, 20,000 English immigrants arrived. In 1775 there were 40,000 people in Philadelphia, the largest city in colonial America, which was second in size among all English-speaking cities to London (Linton, 1975).

In 1783, George Washington proclaimed that the "bosom of America is open to receive not only the opulent and respectable stranger, but also the oppressed and persecuted of all nations and religions, whom we shall welcome to a participation of all our rights and privileges" (Paludeine, 1998, p. 14). A population census in 1790 recorded 3,929,214 people, and though slaves accounted for one-fifth of the population, neither blacks nor Native Americans were included in the census.

FOCUS BOX • *Founding Fathers*

The Founding Fathers were actually the founders of the American government. They were not necessarily the European explorers who "discovered" the Americas. The discovery of the United States was very much a French, Spanish, and (in the West) Russian enterprise. The Spanish were in Yellowstone long before the Lewis and Clark Expedition, Florida was originally "New Spain," and France laid claim to the center of the United States until Napoleon sold it in 1802 to finance his adventures in Europe.

FOCUS BOX • *The First Police Force*

After the "discovery" of the New World, it would take another 100 years before an actual colony was established in America. The English are noted for the formal establishment of the Virginia Colony. The First Charter of Virginia was the first government document to set policies and laws for the settlers to follow. A historian noted that the early settlers had plans to come to America, dig for gold, become rich, and return to England. They saw America as strictly an economic enterprise. In 1609, 500 immigrants came to America and the governor left to return to England. Without a leader to enforce the laws and policies of the First Charter, the settlers were left to themselves to become "idle and riotous." By 1610, only 60 people were left from the new colony. The early recognition of needing a "civilized society" led to the development of police and court systems fashioned after England.

The English officials had difficulty using English enforcement procedures in the rural wilderness of America. As cities grew, hiring watchmen (the early police officers) to protect citizens and property was part of the American landscape. Each colony organized and operated its own court system, which was the impetus to keep the concept of sovereignty of states in the Declaration of Independence.

In 1782 in *Letters from an American Farmer*, the French-born writer and agriculturalist J. Hector St. John Crèvecoeur posed the question, "What is an American?" He wrote

> He is either European, or the descendent of an European, hence that strange mixture of blood, which you will find in no other country. I could point out to you a family whose grandfather was an Englishman, whose wife was Dutch, whose son married a French woman, and whose present four sons have now four wives of different nations. He is an American, who leaving behind him all his ancient prejudices and manners, receives new ones from the new mode of life he has embraced, the new government he obeys, and the new rank he holds. He becomes an American by being received in the broad lap of our great Alma Mater. Here all individuals are melted into a new race of men, whose labors and posterity will one day cause great changes in the world. (Kneller, 1965, p. 116)

At that time, 90 percent of immigrants were Protestants from England and Scotland. The number of immigrants coming to America was growing at a substantial rate. Population counts indicate that, between 1789 and 1819, 250,000 immigrants called America their home. This first great wave was filled with people settling a new land, developing a government, and establishing a new world power in the western hemisphere. There was an expectation that immigrants would "melt together" and create a new cultural synthesis "merging the individual life . . . to the promise of world brotherhood."

The Second Great Wave.   The 1860 census records 31,443,321 people in the United States. Again, this count excluded slaves and Native Americans. Nine out of ten immigrants were from northern or western Europe, specifically, the United Kingdom, Germany, and the Scandinavian countries. Between 1882 and 1891 the total number of immigrants to the United States was 5,137,601. In 1890, over half of all immigrants were from the United Kingdom of England, Scotland, and Ireland, and one-third of immigrants were from Germany. Tens of thousands of Irish came to America fleeing racism of the English and the economic devastation of Ireland due to the potato famine in the1840s. Many more thousands of Germans came to the United States fleeing the despotic government of Germany, and they became known the "Pennsylvania Dutch" (actually a misspelling of "Pennsylvania Deutsche").

The largest record to date of immigrants in United States history was 8,795,386, and they came to this country between 1901 and 1910. More immigrants came to America in 1907 than in any other year until 1990. Toward the end of the nineteenth century, the changing faces of immigrants represented the changes in southern and eastern Europe. These new immigrants were from Italy, Greece, Poland, Portugal, Spain, Russia, and Turkey, and many were less skilled in responding to the technological advances of the industrialized America. Immigration control acts increased during the first part of the twentieth century because of the influx of "excludable classes" into America. Anti-immigration attitudes were prevalent and name-calling proliferated. Immigrants were referred to as "lawless, immoral, vicious, criminal, social dregs, rogues, and vicious scourings."

In that time, as now, the negative attitude toward immigrants was in conflict with actual practice. On one hand, we needed workers for factories, railroad and subway construction, and the establishment of city infrastructure. On the other hand, the immigrants were imagined to be incapable of assimilating into the "American way of life." The idea of a melting pot had mixed reviews. One playwright of the time, Israel Zangwill, wrote a play entitled *The Melting Pot,* in which his character delivers a speech about America. The character proclaims that "America is God's crucible, the great Melting Pot where all the races are melting and reforming . . . God is making the American . . . where all races and nations come to labor and look forward" (Kneller, 1965, p. 121).

The conceptual "melting pot" seemed to be a plausible attempt to merge various groups into one. However, assimilation posed problems as the new immigrants brought their culture, religion, and folkways—many of which were in direct contrast to the existing norms. This, combined with changes in the American economy, the portent of foreign wars that threatened to involve the United States, and fears of new groups of "foreigners" arriving into American cities, fostered reactionary social and political ideas.

An example of one such idea offers some understanding of the time. Popular during this time of history in many parts of the Country, it developed into what would become known as the Anglo Conformity Movement.

The Third Great Wave.   The third great wave of immigration occurred during a time of drastic social and cultural change in America not seen since the impact of social changes of the Civil War. There is some evidence that it continues today.

The 1960s and 1970s saw dramatic changes in civil rights, broad domestic reforms, fears of communism, concerns about U.S. border control, and military conflict in the Asian-Pacific triangle. These events prompted the United States to enact additional restrictions on immigration. However, in the late 1970s and 1980s the Refugee Act and the Immigration Reform and Control Act of 1986 reflected relaxed attitudes toward legalizing entrance into the country by refugees from the Vietnam War, as well as easing regulations regarding immigration by agricultural workers.

The result of this easing of regulations was the greatest influx of immigrants into America since the first decade of the twentieth century. Between 1981 and 1990 the influx of immigrants jumped to 7,338,062 people, The number of immigrants from Mexico was estimated at 1,655,842, and from Latin America and the Caribbean at 1,802,444. Record immigration from Asia was estimated at 2,738,157 people during that decade (Paludeine, 1998).

Immigrants from these areas continue to comprise what is perhaps the most significant immigration impact on American culture. In addition, people from the former Communist-bloc countries are now calling America home. This third great wave is expected to continue for the next twenty years, with projections for the twenty-first century showing vast regions of immigrant communities. It is estimated that 95 percent of all Americans "are descended from people that didn't live on this continent in the eighteenth century, and nearly 10% of current American citizens were not born in the US" (Paludeine, 1998, p.128). The national identity continues to change, and the need for a multicultural philosophy seems to be warranted more than ever.

Key Issues: Angloconformity, Cultural Pluralism, and Peoplehood

The expression that "there is nothing new under the sun" seems to be revalidated with each epoch of history. Modern debates over closing our borders, and discontinuing multilingual education programs, as well as fears about the subversion of America by multiculturalism, sound all too familiar to the student of American history. Philosophies that, inasmuch as "they" (foreigners) come here to live, they should acculturate and assimilate in short order, speak and transact only in English, and abandon the ways of the old country are not new to this generation of Americans. Such philosophies can probably be collected together under the heading of Angloconformity, and the concept of Angloconformity has it roots in the American public school system during the early part of the twentieth century.

The mission and purpose of the public school system has been to provide "students with the explicitly necessary academic, social, and civic skills for negotiation with life in the dominant mainstream society" (Ovando & Collier, 1985). While this is a valid goal, some theorists believe that it can happen only when children are assimilated into the "American culture" with the help of the school system. It was this assimilation that fostered Angloconformity.

The Angloconformity process involved the absorption of ethnic minority groups into the mainstream culture by encouraging minority students to disown their own cultural identities and accept the national identity. The implicit message of the school system was the "homogenization of children" to build a better national character. The "homogenized children" then would become better workers and be less deviant as adults. The idea was to cement this multiethnic America into one dominant culture, with some theorists believing that the Anglo-Saxon culture of mainstream America was superior to other cultures represented by immigrant groups.

This philosophy then led the school system to practice Angloconformity. Such forced assimilation changed how America perceived and treated immigrants. Sue and Padilla (1986) reported that advocates for assimilation believed that this philosophy would keep America from becoming too fragmented, would increase the acquisition of functional skills in society, and would promote lower incidents of deviant behavior.

Gordon's early studies on assimilation and Angloconformity found differing perspectives on the "homogenization of society." Wisdom of the day predicted that the school system could aid America in eliminating cultural differences in language, food, dress, and manners. This should then create a more unified America and reduce conflict between cultural groups. In contrast to this approach, some theorists believed that Angloconformity could affect the behavior of children and adolescents in negative ways.

It became clear that separation of persons from their cultural roots could leave a void in place of the values, customs, and identity that they share. An attempt to forcibly transplant people, especially adolescents, from their original peoplehood into the new culture could have poor results. Many of those people had not been in America long enough to accept and be accepted by the mainstream. When told that they must separate from the values of their peoplehood, they were left between two worlds. Adolescents in American public schools were taught to deny their original cultures, yet were not ready to acculturate into their new ones. Lacking clear identity and values, they created their own identities and values, as adolescents are quick to do. The result was a destructive influence that confounded traditional family values among immigrants, and helped create an atmosphere that was conducive to delinquency and formation of gangs. Adolescents were left without the culture of their parents to guide them, but they did not fully possess the culture of the American mainstream. They were then without a firmly identified sense of peoplehood, and without the accompanying morals, mores, and folkways. It was theorized that immigrant children experienced a dysfunctional discontinuity (Kneller, 1965) in the abrupt separation from traditional, stable values as they entered American society from their original culture. Children born to parents who were recent immigrants experienced the effects of life within families in which clear roles and hierarchies no longer existed. Children born to indigenous minorities experienced the resentment of the mainstream and castelike treatment, and assumed the "caste thinking" that Ogbu (1985; 1992) characterizes as pathological to achievement. This identity crisis is generally credited with the beginning of street gang activities in American cities in the early twentieth century.

Healthy personal identities are more likely to develop when school systems and society accept and encourage cultural diversity (Sue & Padilla, 1986; Ogbu, 1992). Children's acquisition of functional skills is not impaired when they are allowed to keep personal ties to their own culture. Some studies actually showed an increase in cognitive skills with multicultural education. Angloconformity fell from favor as a way to promote American unity, and a new philosophy of cultural pluralism took hold.

Cultural pluralism was originally fostered by intellectuals who went into American cities (at approximately the turn of the twentieth century) "to sup with the poor" (Gordon, 1978). Unlike the historical Angloconformity movement, which tried to create "the American culture," these researchers learned an appreciation for various cultures, and felt that different cultural input was good for American society and democracy.

The philosophy of cultural pluralism allows people to keep their cultural identity while they learn and participate in the mainstream social structure of society. Pluralism holds that effective primary group relations true to one's culture are beneficial to society, provided that they don't lead to lack of unity or domination of one group by another.

In trying to understand the impact of immigrants on the dominant American culture, sociologists identified social factors that promoted and maintained independent subcultures within the mainstream culture of America. They found that newly arrived immigrant groups brought their own values, beliefs, and attitudes, which clashed with the dominant value system. For example, their practice of religion, their type of dress, and their style of family discipline played a part in distinguishing them from the mainstream. These "separatist" ideas resulted in *culture conflict* between agents of the middle class and people from poverty-stricken areas. Such cultural phenomena resulted in a subculture of violence.

Though Angloconformity is considered an outdated philosophy and is not the stated mission of modern schools, many groups either have their traditional family cohesiveness supplanted by premature attempts at structural assimilation or are subjected to the world view of teachers who consider them inferior to the mainstream culture (Epstein & Glazer in Ovando & Collier, 1985; Ogbu, 1985; 1992). Many researchers challenge the basic notion that the Anglo-American culture is inherently superior to that of other groups (Ovando & Collier, 1985; Sue & Padilla, 1986). Claiming that a variety of genetic inferiority and cultural deficit theories foster prejudice and discrimination, they believe that there are no differences in the thinking ability of different races, "only differences in what they think about."

Cultural pluralism does not lend itself to the kind notion of the "melting pot" in America. In theory, the "melting pot" requires many generations and much amalgamation (intermarriage) to be fully realized (Gordon, 1978, 1996). Cultures change as they experience contact with each other, and the "key to understanding achievement is the change that occurs because of the interaction between different cultures" (Sue & Padilla, 1986).

The multicultural nature of America has become more pronounced during the past two decades, and projections for the twenty-first century show a vast array of cultural groups. There is value in teaching people to function successfully in a multicultural, multiethnic milieu, and this successful functioning depends largely upon the acceptance between groups. If assimilation fully occurs over time, it will be a comfortable transition that is not forced upon groups to rob them of their "peoplehood." Pluralism is believed to promote such healthy assimilation, and in that role does not pose a threat to American cohesiveness. Angloconformity and resentment of groups (either implied or expressed) can foster caste thinking and promote divisions along ethnic, racial, religious lines. This division, known by theorists as Balkanization, carries the portent of significant racial, ethnic, and religious conflict that is pathological to social systems and public peace.

There is evidence that successful assimilation should not be mistaken as a one-sided process, for it has reciprocal properties. As new groups are influenced by the mainstream, the mainstream is influenced by the new groups. These social interrelationships are continuous, and this process persists in redefining the American culture.

After the Three Great Waves: The Demographics of America

Though we remain in the midst of the third great wave of immigration, we can already see the effects of the three great waves. We can also generalize from our experiences and the latest census and make some predictions about America's population in the first part of the New Millennium.

This country is, and has always been, a mixture of ethnic and racial diversity. The U.S. Census develops data about racial and ethnic categories from political-social anthropological-scientific constructs. The current standard of categories for race that are designated to help label Americans are (1) American Indian or Native, (2) Asian or Pacific Islander, (3) black, and (4) white. These categories are intended to describe the four major broad population groups. Categories of ethnicity are grouped into (1) Hispanic origin and (2) Not of Hispanic origin. Typically, these census groupings are used by schools, medical facilities, and other private and public entities, and rely upon self-reported information. Individuals choose the label that best represents them. This labeling is not designed to identify or designate people as minorities. The minority label is assigned to people based not on their actual numbers, but on their status in society according to their history and relationship to the dominant group. Traditionally, minority and underrepresented group status is associated with populations that have been "objects of collective discrimination," such as blacks, Hispanics, and women. People with disabilities can also be considered among these numbers. Currently, as changes in demographics move nondominant groups into a more dominant status, the minority classification will probably change.

In the decade between 1980 and 1990, the U.S. population increased by 23 million people. Consistent with the 1990 census population base, estimates for May 2000 indicated that the U.S. total population was 274,708,000 people. As of December 2000, the first phase of data available for the 2000 census indicates that the U.S. resident population was 281,421,906. Additional data on specific demographics will become available in 2001 (U.S. Bureau of the Census, 2000).

The current statistics for demographics are based on the U.S. Census Bureau population estimates, which show that 49 percent of the population is male and 51 percent female. The mean age of the population is calculated at 36.5 years. The black/African American population is approximately 12.8 percent of the total, with 48 percent male and 52 percent female. The American Indian/Eskimo/Aleut classification of people are approximately 0.9 percent of the U.S. population. Males and females are evenly represented. Asian/Pacific Islanders comprise 4 percent of the total population; 48 percent are male and 52 percent are female. A very broad category of people that classify themselves as "white" comprise 82.3 percent of the total population, with 49 percent male and 51 percent female. Hispanics in any of the racial categories account for 11.7 percent of the total, and numbers of males and females are roughly equal.

The 2000 census was expected to be higher than 1990. The current figures represent an increase of 13.2 percent over the last census. As predicted, the immigrants that would have the highest impact on U.S. population figures are from Pacific Rim countries and countries with Hispanic populations. Since Asian and Hispanic immigrants tend to be younger and have higher overall birthrates than other immigrant populations, projection for the year 2010 is that minority populations will be the majority (U.S. Bureau of the Census, 2000).

By 2025, projections from the last U.S. Census predict Hispanics to increase in population by 26 percent in Georgia, 22 percent in Florida and 16 percent in California. Asians have an expected increase of 27 percent in New York, 26 percent in Georgia, 25 percent in Texas, 18 percent in California. In addition, blacks have an expected increase of 13 percent in Georgia, 12 percent in Florida, and 11 percent in Texas. In Texas, Florida, and Pennsylvania Native Americans will increase by 13 percent.

The United States Department of Commerce, Economic and Statistics Administration, Bureau of the Census noted in their *Census Brief* that the United States is "warmer, older, and more diverse." Analysts project that, by 2025, the population will increase by 72 million, and the vast majority of Americans will live in the South and the West. They will be older and have Hispanic or Asian/Pacific Islander roots.

It will take several years before specific demographic data from the 2000 census will confirm these projections. However, it is generally accepted that this mixture of people continues to be a challenge for the educational system, private industry, law enforcement, and corrections.

The Impact of Equity and Equality Laws on the Criminal Justice System

American government and legal institutions embrace the philosophy of equality and equity for all persons living under our jurisdiction. And while there is a conceptual leap from the philosophy to the practice, we are constantly striving to be better than we have been.

Included in our history is the unfortunate legacy of prejudice, discrimination, and racism. As the histories of nations go, we are certainly not alone in this regard. It seems that the history of most human political endeavor is filled with injustices against racial, ethnic, cultural, and religious groups. And while the discussions continue about reparations for historic injustices, we seem as a nation to have at least made some significant statements about our present and future behavior. Those statements are reflected both in our laws, and in the role into which the criminal justice system has emerged in the enforcement of those laws.

The practice of segregation in employment, housing, and schools created a society with disadvantaged people facing substantial barriers to advancement. As society struggled with its desire to remove barriers and treat people fairly, government intervention seemed the only plausible method by which to ensure some kind of equality. To rectify injustices and to promote equality, the enforcement of civil rights legislation became the purview of the civil and criminal justice systems.

There currently are numerous laws that address issues of discrimination, and the basis for many of these laws can be traced back to post–Civil War reconstruction in America in 1869. The U.S. Constitution was amended to guarantee equal protection under the law. The Fourteenth Amendment states that "No State shall . . . deny to any person within its jurisdiction the equal protection of the laws." This constitutional mandate is upheld through legislation and other court actions by a process of continuous review and interpretation, and it fostered the beginning of civil rights activities at state levels.

The following are significant examples of laws or acts that address the principles of integration and civil rights.

The Civil Rights Act of 1964

Under the administration of Lyndon B. Johnson, the Civil Rights Act of 1964, Title VII, is considered the most comprehensive civil rights law prohibiting discrimination in employment. The Equal Employment Opportunity Commission (EEOC) was established to ensure compliance with the Civil Rights Act. EEOC was charged with curbing employment discrimination based on race, color, religion, gender, or national origin, and with the promotion of equal job opportunities for all individuals (PL 88-352). In 1972, state and local governments were prohibited from discrimination by the Equal Employment Opportunity Act. This extension of Title VII coverage to other government agencies sought to eliminate employment discrimination in all jobs.

Reverend Jesse Jackson, Sr., states that, "It is important to understand that the movement for civil rights, which took place primarily in the 1960s, was not the product of one man or one organization, but was a people's movement. From the time when Martin Luther King, Jr., led the Montgomery bus boycott in 1955 until today, the Civil Rights Movement lives and is a product of every person who will not bow down to the dehumanization of another person or group of people" (Jackson, 2000, p. 9).

Subsequent amendments such as the Civil Rights Act of 1991 expanded the "remedies for intentional discrimination and unlawful harassment in the workplace . . . by expanding the scope of relevant civil rights statutes in order to provide adequate protection to victims of discrimination" (PL 102-166). This act gave victims the right to seek job reinstatement, back pay, benefits, and previous privileges.

Affirmative Action

Upon passage of the Civil Rights Act of 1964, a concern for "righting the wrongs of the past" came to the forefront. Because of past discriminatory employment practices, enactment of new laws could not rectify lost opportunities for generations of disenfranchised American citizens. The strategy that was developed to help remedy past acts of discrimination was called *affirmative action.* The idea was that all public and private entities receiving federal funding would participate in the hiring of underrepresented groups through a preference system. The affirmative action policy called for "the establishment of programs that involve giving preference, in jobs and college admissions, to members of groups that have been discriminated against in the past." The assumption was that, "with equal education and the full political citizenship ensured by Voting Rights acts, blacks could gain legal rights as individuals in the courts and administrative tribunals" (Lipset, 1999, p. 299).

The concept of affirmative action has two distinct definitions, legal remedy and compensatory opportunity (Glasser, 1999). The definition of "legal remedy" refers to something that is "temporarily imposed or approved by the courts in particular cases to redress the specific effects of past or current discrimination, where such discrimination has been proved." The second definition is broader in scope and suggests a form of moral reparation through a process of temporary compensatory opportunity. This definition refers to an approach that is "designed to make up generally for past injustices and to get things even again before allowing the race to continue on relatively equal terms" (p. 307).

Glasser (1999) notes that there is another concept associated with affirmative action that proposes to "achieve fair and visible representation for minorities for reasons of social or political effectiveness" (p. 307). This visible representation can be applied to law enforcement agencies by having their forces reflect a proportion of minorities represented in their communities. This representation of minorities in leadership roles sets a tone of full membership in society and can inhibit injustices and discrimination against individuals and groups.

In theory, over time, affirmative action would have rectified "the wrongs of the past," and minorities and women would be fully represented in employment. As it was originally intended the policy would no longer be needed. However, lackluster participation by employers, poor policy enforcement, misapplications of the policy, and unfair quota systems inadvertently labeled this employment strategy as harsh and discriminatory. In response to criticism of Affirmative Action, Glasser (1999) states that

> Affirmative Action remedies, properly conceived and implemented, ought only to open up opportunities for the development of skills, opportunities previously closed either by overt racial discrimination or by the habits that flourished in a discriminatory culture . . . advocates for affirmative action do not claim it as a panacea, or cure for all the racial and economic ills we face . . . it is a means of breaking through a reified system of discrimination and of giving people who have long been handicapped by the system a temporary leg up. (p. 317)

After nearly 40 years of affirmative action, full representation of all groups in public and private entities does not exist. Some believe this lack of representation is due to continuing discrimination, while others perceive that this discrepancy is due to minority groups themselves not "doing their part to succeed." These two viewpoints continue to polarize thought on the effectiveness of affirmative action, and seem to move overt discrimination to covert levels.

The current movement for disbanding affirmative action policies is based upon the principle that the United States is more culturally and racially diverse and that "targeting specific minority groups for preference inevitably discriminates against other minorities, which, in part, defeats the purpose of affirmative action." In 1996, the California Proposition 209 initiative received a vote of 54 percent in favor of amending the state's constitution to eliminate preferential treatment. In 1998, the state of Washington approved a ballot measure to end state-sponsored affirmative action. R. Roosevelt Thomas, Jr., former director of the American Institute for Managing Diversity at Atlanta's Morehouse College, states that affirmative action must go beyond emphasis on gaining employment. It must move to an attitude of "affirming diversity." This attitude would create a climate "in which each individual worker, regardless of race or gender, can fully develop and move up in the company" (Workforce 2000, p. 18). Such concepts can move society toward ideals of educational development and preparation for minority groups.

The White House reports that the justification for affirmative action can be found in the continuing need to address discrimination and exclusion for minority groups in America. The report states 'there has been undeniable progress in many areas . . . but evidence is overwhelming that the problems affirmative action seeks to address—widespread discrimination and exclusion and their ripple effects—continue to exist" (Affirmative Action Review, 2000). These "ripple effects" are most noted in housing and job discrimination between white and black applicants.

> The Urban Institute's Employment and Housing Discrimination Studies conducted a study matching "equally qualified" white and black testers who applied for the same jobs or visited the same real estate agents. Twenty percent of the time, white applicants advanced further in the hiring process than equally qualified blacks. In one in eight tests, the white

received a job offer when the black did not. In housing, both black and Hispanic testers faced discrimination in about half their dealings with rental agents. The Justice Department has conducted similar testing to uncover housing discrimination. Those tests also have revealed that whites are more likely than blacks to be shown apartment units, while blacks with equal credentials are told nothing is available. Since the testing began, the Justice Department has brought over 20 federal suits resulting in settlements totaling more than $1.5 million. A particularly graphic case of discrimination occurred during a fair housing test performed by the Civil Rights Division in Wisconsin, which sought to establish whether discrimination existed against the relatively large East-Asian population there. When the Asian tester approached the apartment building, the rental agent stood between the tester and the door to the rental office and refused to allow the tester to enter the building. The tester was told that there were no apartments available and there would not be any available for two months. When the white tester approached two hours later, the individual was immediately shown an apartment and was told he could move in that same day. (Affirmative Action Review, 2000)

Laws and policies will continue to reflect changes in our culture and create a new cultural history.

Sexual Harassment

The Civil Rights Act prohibits gender discrimination in the workplace and, in 1980, the EEOC issued guidelines on what constitutes sexual harassment. Section 703 of Title VII states that harassment on the basis of sex is a violation of law. The guidelines defining sexual harassment are as follows:

> Unwelcome sexual advances, requests for sexual favors, and other verbal or physical conduct of a sexual nature constitute sexual harassment when (1) submission to such conduct is made either explicitly or implicitly a term or condition of an individual's employment, (2) submission to or rejection of such conduct by an individual is used as the basis for employment decisions affecting such individual, (3) such conduct has the purpose or effect of unreasonably interfering with an individual's work environment.

There are two basic categories of legal actions associated with sexual harassment: *quid pro quo* and a hostile work environment. *Quid pro quo,* in its simplest form means "this for that." For example, supervisors offer to give promotions or job opportunities in exchange for some sort of sexual involvement with their subordinates. "Hostile work environment" refers to a work environment punctuated by sexually harassing overtures and innuendo. This may or may not be directed at a particular individual, but the complainant feels threatened and it interferes with her or his ability to do the job.

Generally, sexual harassment complaints are associated with *quid pro quo* issues. Women are sometimes harassed for sexual favors by their supervisors in exchange for job opportunities or continued employment. Often the issues are clouded because women and men in the workplace might differently view sexualized or sexually expressive behavior. Some of those differences are probably based on stereotypic sex roles and perceptions of what constitutes sexual harassment (PennState, 2000). While there might be disagreement on exact definitions of sexual harassment, founded instances of such behavior are prohibited by law. Title VII also protects job status and retention for those who report sexual harassment or hostile work environment.

A survey of women in government employment reported numerous accounts of both kinds of sexual harassment. Seventy percent of women in the military reported being sexually harassed, 50 percent of women who worked in congressional offices believed they were victims of harassment, and 40 percent of women who worked for federal agencies reported instances of sexual harassment (Conway & Conway, 1993).

A review of New York Governor Mario Cuomo's 1993 Task Force on Sexual Harassment noted the following statistics:

> There is an estimate that one out of every two women will be sexually harassed at some point during her academic or working life.
>
> Sexual harassment is virtually an expected event in most women's lives.
>
> In a UCLA Graduate School of Management Survey entitled "Decade of the Executive Women," two-thirds of the 400 top female executives responded that they had been sexually harassed.
>
> The National Law Journal surveyed 900 women from the top 250 law firms in the United States and found that 60% of these women experienced sexual harassment. (PennState, 2000)

The majority of women who participate in surveys on sexual harassment say they have not officially reported specific acts of harassment. The fear of retaliation or being ostracized by fellow employees discourages formal action. Some decide to "just live with it" or they simply quit their jobs.

Sexual harassment charges rose from one in 1980 to 15,618 in 1998 (EEOC, 2000). In addition to women filing sexual harassment charges, the number of men filing rose from 958 in 1992 to 2,015 in 1998. Some researchers theorize that, as more women move into management and supervisory positions, the cases of sexual harassment against subordinate male employees will increase. While such cases might reflect a new sense of "feminine power" in the workplace, the behavior is prohibited by Title VII.

The right to be free from sexual harassment in the workplace is also extended to members of the same sex. In March 2000, the Supreme Court ruled in *Oncale v. Offshore Sundowner* that Title VII of the Civil Rights Act of 1964 makes it illegal, irrespective of sexual orientation, for employers to discriminate on the basis of sex, and the Court considered it same-sex harassment. Justice Antonin Scalia said, "Male-on-male sexual harassment in the workplace was assuredly not the principal evil Congress was concerned with when it enacted Title VII, but statutory prohibitions often go beyond the principal concerns of our legislators."

The Hate Crime Statistics Act

In 1990, the Bush administration required the United States Justice Department to collect and publish data from law enforcement agencies across the nation on crimes that "manifest prejudice based on race, religion, sexual orientation, or ethnicity" (PL 101-275).

A hate crime is any criminal act or attempted criminal act directed against a person(s), public agency, or private institution based on the victim's actual or perceived race, nationality, religion, sexual orientation, disability, or gender, or because the agency or institution is identified or associated with a person or group of an identifiable race, nationality, religion, sexual orientation, disability, or gender. A hate crime includes an act that results in injury, however slight; a verbal threat of violence that apparently can be carried out; an act that results in property damage; and property damage or other criminal act(s) directed against a public or private agency.

In 1991, the FBI documented 4,558 hate crimes that represented 2,800 law enforcement departments from 32 states. By 1996, 8,759 hate crime incidents were reported from 11,355 agencies. The majority of hate crimes, 63 percent, are race-related, with 42 percent of that total crimes against African Americans.

Violent Crime Control and Law Enforcement Act of 1994

The Violent Crime and Law Enforcement Act mandated establishment of a National Commission on Crime Control and Prevention to address issues of controlling and preventing crime through nontraditional approaches. This commission was charged with recommending distinctive responses to crimes against minority groups, to violence in schools, and with developing a comprehensive proposal for preventing and controlling crime and violence in the United States (PL 103-322).

The Violence Against Women Act of 1994

The Violence Against Women Act (VAWA) was passed by Congress to address domestic violence and rape against women. In 1994 VAWA stated "all persons within the United States shall have the right to be free from crimes of violence motivated by gender" (42 USC 13981). VAWA also provided funding for education and training, and for the pursuit of compensatory and punitive damage awards for victims.

The Age Discrimination in Employment Act of 1967

The Age Discrimination in Employment Act (ADEA) prohibits employment discrimination against persons 40 years of age or older. It is the purpose of this act "to promote employment of older persons based on their ability rather than age; to prohibit arbitrary age discrimination in employment; to help employers and workers find ways of meeting problems arising from the impact of age on employment (PL 90-202). This act has increased in relevance with the "graying of the American population."

The Americans with Disability Act of 1990

The Rehabilitation Act of 1973 states that

No otherwise qualified handicapped individual in the United States shall solely by reason of his/her handicap be excluded from participation in, be denied the benefits of, or be

FOCUS BOX • *A Message from the Attorney General Janet Reno*

On July 26, 2000, the Americans with Disabilities Act celebrates its 10th anniversary. And there is so much to celebrate!

Look around. Over the past decade so much has changed. It is no longer unusual to see people with disabilities dining out at restaurants, working in the office, participating in town hall meetings, shopping at the malls, watching a movie or cheering at a stadium. That's because the ADA is making the dream of access a reality.

As Attorney General, I have made enforcement of the ADA one of my top priorities. At the Justice Department we have engaged in extensive educational outreach, and entered into hundreds of agreements ensuring greater access to thousands of businesses and governments. We have also increased the number of attorneys who en-

force the law, and stepped up funding for ADA-related programs across the country. And under the leadership of Acting Assistant Attorney General for Civil rights Bill Lann Lee, and our United States Attorneys across the country, we will continue to build on this past decade of access.

As this Report illustrates, the ADA has made a difference in the lives of so many. But there are many others who still face barriers—barriers that man-made structures create and barriers stemming from people's attitudes. Those barriers took generations to create. It will take continued vigilance and dedication to remove them. But if the past 10 years is any indication, Americans with disabilities are well on their way to experiencing all society has to offer.

subjected to discrimination under any program or activity receiving Federal financial assistance. (PL 93-112)

The Rehabilitation Act set the foundation for the Americans with Disability Act (ADA). The ADA promotes access for and prohibits discrimination against the approximately 49 million Americans with disabilities. The ADA originated and was developed by the National Council on Disability and gives

Civil rights protection to individuals with disabilities that are like those provided to individuals on the basis of race, sex, national origin, and religion. It guarantees equal opportunity for individuals with disabilities in employment, public accommodations, transportation, state and local government services, and telecommunications.

To be protected by the ADA, one must have a disability or have a relationship or association with an individual with a disability. An individual with a disability is defined by the ADA as a person who has a physical or mental impairment that substantially limits one or more major life activities, a person who has a history or record of such an impairment, or a person who is perceived by others as having such an impairment. The ADA does not specifically name all of the impairments that are covered. (PL 101-336)

Summary

Our society has an overwhelming desire to seek civil rights. While many other countries do not have civil rights as a priority, America has a pattern of addressing forms of discrimination by enacting laws, legislative mandates, and acts to eliminate forms of injustice. This philosophy drives waves of people to come to America to seek opportunity and freedom to express a myriad of beliefs and traditions. These people become part of the pluralistic American society that in turn creates laws and legislation that support their freedoms.

Discussion Questions

1. Is there a relationship between early philosophies about the Anglo-Saxon superiority philosophy and hate crimes of today?

2. How does a sense of peoplehood affect interactions with law enforcement?

3. How are the waves of immigration impacting the criminal justice system?

2

African Americans and the Criminal Justice System

Learning Objectives

After reading this chapter you should be able to do the following:

1. Explain the historical perspective of African Americans and how it relates to the criminal justice system.
2. Identify the "ties that bind" African Americans and discuss the components.
3. Identify the elements of worldview and compare the relationship to gangs, crime, and sense of trust.

As with every cultural, ethnic, and racial group in America, the present-day relationship between African Americans and the United States is historically driven. From the first introduction of indentured servants and slaves into the New World in the 1500s, to the American Civil War in the 1800s, to the Civil Rights Movement in the 1960s, African Americans have been an integral part of the economic, political, and social development of America. Their experiences are replete with struggles for survival, acceptance, and equality in American society. And while the events that surround this struggle have affected the lives of all Americans by forging the Civil Rights Movement, African American history in the United States generally stands in sharp contrast to the social ideals that we claim to foster. If this history provides any lessons, the most profound are the value of determination, persistence, and courage.

This chapter provides an overview of the historical relationship of African Americans or blacks (this name will be used interchangeably) to American society. No other group's history has had such a dynamic impact on present-day events. Interwoven into a tapestry that reflects our emergence as a nation, the black experience is an archetype of racial issues, prejudice, discrimination, stereotyping, and crime on the one hand, and integration, achievement, and resilience on the other.

While African Americans are identified by checking the box on a census form, they are not all alike. While much of the black community might be tied together because of race and a sense of peoplehood, they also represent a cross-section of society as it relates to education, economics, and status. The worldview of blacks has several aspects that describe their relationship to society, based largely upon historical influences of status. These relationships are discussed—as well as the demographics, the community, and cultural attitudes. The relationship to the criminal justice system and issues concerning the building of relationships follow.

Numbers

As discussed earlier, African Americans comprise nearly 12.8 percent of the American population. Out of approximately 281 million people, 35 million are African Americans (U.S. Bureau of the Census, 2000). By 2010 this number is expected to reach 40 million, and by 2025 there is an expected increase of 14 million, occurring mostly in Texas, Florida, Georgia, and California. The U.S. Census Bureau predicts that approximately 59 percent of the expected increase of 14 million will be added to the South. Recent trends show that Atlanta is home to a new migration of middle- and upper-class blacks between the ages of 25 and 45. This reverse migration of African Americans to an area once thought of as the "Old Confederacy" is the result of reasonable real estate, warm climate, employment opportunity, and a slower pace of life (Pedersen & Smith, 1997). While the division between black and white still seems to exist, the "newcomers" are confident and prepared to meet the challenge of overcoming the historical attitudes in the South toward blacks (Pedersen & Smith, 1997). These newcomers are interested in their "roots" and feel their journey home is "the chance to start something new, to remake the South in a different image." Pedersen and Smith summarized this migration as a "deeply American irony, that the ground burdened by slavery and exploitation becomes at the end of the century, the real land of opportunity" (p. 39).

Historical Perspective

The relationship of African Americans to American history is one of labor and, specifically, free labor through slavery. The contributions of blacks in developing the New World are numerous. Generally, when historians discuss the makings of America they "throw in" that blacks were slaves and worked on plantations in the South. This account is perpetuated through films and such books as *Gone with the Wind,* portraying slavery as natural, necessary, and generally a benevolent institution (Robinson, 1997). Between 1929 and 1941 over 75 films portrayed the South in this way, continuing the depiction of blacks as having less value than the dominant culture. Media messages accepting racial disparity as part of the American culture hindered race relations for decades. Sloan (1971) proposed that this limited view of the contributions made by blacks perpetuates the problems of race in our country. He purports that a different perspective about achievement, contributions, and significant events can reduce the discrimination characterizing "historical scholarship."

An example of this occurs in the historical account of Columbus "discovering" the New World. While the 1492 discovery is generally recognized as exclusively a Spanish-European event, scholars have identified one of Columbus's pilots as Pedro Alonzo Nino, an African native. In addition, in 1513, Balboa's expedition to the Pacific included thirty blacks who were instrumental in his success.

People from Africa became the backbone of success in the New World. Their contributions range from clearing and cultivating the virgin lands to being heroes during the American Revolution and Civil War. From the early years, the inventive genius of Whitney with his cotton gin, McCormick with his field reaper, and Blair with his corn harvester have changed working conditions for blacks and the entire labor industry of America. Perhaps most paradoxical is the history of blacks defending and supporting the freedom of America through numerous wars. Over 5,000 blacks fought in the American Revolution to secure freedom from the British Empire, and over 200,000 fought during the Civil War to secure freedom from the South. All the while they were a people without freedom. This is a testament to the true character of a community fighting against the odds in hopes for a better tomorrow.

While many have fought and won against the odds, there are many that did not fare so well. Currently, African Americans are overrepresented in the criminal justice system, and over 43 percent of African American children live in poverty (Siegel, 1999). In a society that has outlawed discrimination and racism, racial lines still divide America. The following history of blacks and their worldview is divided into the Slave and Colonialized Era, Reconstruction after the Civil War, the Civil Rights Era, and present day.

The Slave and Colonialized Era

The history of the slave trade has a direct impact on the worldview of many African Americans. While slavery was abolished over 100 years ago, that impact of 400 years of slavery still lingers. The historic institutions that utilized a race of people as free labor and chattel property still influence the mindset of our nation today. Blacks were seen as people who were inherently inferior to whites, and there are groups in our society who still feel this way. For centuries, blacks were not afforded the opportunities to excel in society. When change did occur, many people became threatened and hung on to old stereotypes about the role of blacks in America. These attitudes continued to reinforce racial animosity between blacks and whites.

In the early 1500s, the colonization of the New World was often a violent enterprise. When the Spanish and the Portuguese sailed to this new land, dreams of fortune and glory dominated their motives. They found in the Caribbean rich landscapes with soil and climate ideal for a thriving sugar industry. They conquered the original peoples of the New World and enslaved them as their first workforce. Disease and violence claimed the lives of thousands of Native Americans, and presented the need for a new workforce. The colonialized lands on the African continent provided the opportunity to export captured persons for labor, and so the slave trade began. Tribal peoples were captured from West and Central Africa and taken against their will to the Caribbean islands to work in the sugar industry. There was no concern for bringing specific ethnic groups or keeping family units together during the slave trade, and so Africans brought to the New World represented a myriad of ethnic, cultural, and language groups with distinct customs, beliefs and traditions. Some accounts suggest that slave traders purposely divided families and groups so that the resulting fragmentation of peoples would eliminate the threat of organized rebellion.

A literate slave recalls his journey from slavery to freedom in his autobiography from 1789. Olaudah Equiano was from an Ibu village located in modern-day Nigeria. He was captured and became a shipmate to an English naval officer. He found favor with his master and received English lessons. His command of the English language and high intellect endeared him to various masters along the journey. He eventually won his freedom, but he recounts the sense of horror as people lost their freedom during "the round up of slaves."

> I have often seen slaves, particularly those who were meager, in different islands, put into scales and weighed; and then sold from three pence to six pence or nine pence a pound. My master, however, whose humanity was shocked at this mode, use to sell such by the lump. And at or after a sale it was not uncommon to see Negroes taken from their wives, wives taken from their husbands, and children from their parents, and sent off to other islands, and wherever else their merciless lords chose; and probably never more during life to see each other! Oftentimes my heart has bled at these partings; when the friends of the departed have been at the waterside, and, with sighs and tears, have kept their eyes fixed on the vessel till it went out of sight. (Equiano, 1988, p. 73–74)

This policy of separating family members and moving people from plantation to plantation was practiced well into the 1800s. The rationalization of such treatment rested in the notion of blacks as property. Between 1500 and 1888, more than 10 million Africans were brought to the New World as slaves. Some estimates of the number of Africans removed from the continent are as high as 15 million (Levine, 1996; Viola & Margolis, 1991). They were forced into slavery by first the Spanish and the Portuguese, then the Dutch, and later the English and French to aid in the production of sugar and the building of the New World. Of all the African slaves taken to the New World, only 5 percent actually were brought to the United States. Approximately 40 percent were taken to Brazil and another 40 percent to the Caribbean. The other Spanish colonies accounted for the remaining 10 to 15 percent (Levine, 1996).

Reconstruction after the Civil War

By the 1800s the slave trade was becoming less profitable, and existing slaveholders could depend on their own supply of slaves instead of buying new ones. Humanitarian groups in European countries spearheaded a movement to end slavery. By 1807 Britain had abolished it, but this did not affect British colonies until 1833. The French colonies abolished slavery in 1848, and the Portuguese in 1871. Brazil, a former Portuguese colony, practiced slavery until 1871. Cuba stayed active until 1886. The last slave ship unloaded its "cargo" in Mobile, Alabama, in 1859.

Abraham Lincoln became president in 1860 and used his position to move toward abolition of slavery. The ensuing Civil War is considered one of the most crucial events in American history, and while slavery was a collateral issue, it would have one of the greatest impacts on the American landscape. Between 1861 and 1865 the Civil War claimed over 600,000 lives, and over 1 million people suffered war casualties. The South's economy was devastated and its way of life destroyed. The approximate population during this time was 40 million people, and the loss of 600,000 had an enormous impact on society in general and specifically on the culture and worldview of the South. After 135 years, there are states that still fly the Confederate flag as a symbol of protest against losing the war.

Several amendments specifically addressed the change in status for African Americans. In 1863, the Thirteenth Amendment abolished slavery. In 1868, the Fourteenth Amendment, the Civil Rights Act, established due process and equal protection for all citizens. In 1870, the Fifteenth Amendment gave the right to vote to all citizens regardless of race, color, or previous condition of servitude. These amendments had direct connections to the relationship between Blacks and the criminal justice system.

After the end of the Civil War, the time of addressing the needs of former slaves and the rebuilding of the South became known as the Reconstruction Period. Twenty years after the Civil War, legislation was still being enacted to address rebuilding the South. Whites found the rebuilding process difficult because they depended on the free slave labor to make a living. Blacks also had a very difficult existence trying to survive in a country in which land ownership and credit was an integral component of citizenship. The devastation experienced by blacks included the deaths by starvation and disease of tens of thousands due to lack of resources to care for themselves (Cook, 1998). Billingsley (1968) summarizes the ravages of slavery and the temporary and limited support for blacks during Reconstruction as a testament to a group of people. He states,

> The survival of the [African American] people after such a holocaust can be attributed primarily to the resiliency of the human spirit. It most certainly cannot be attributed in large measure to the efforts of [their] society to help [them] survive. For the ingredient most absent to make freedom meaningful was the ingredient that has been most useful to other depressed people, namely opportunity. (Billingsley, 1968, p. 70)

The rising tensions between the former southern states and Washington, and between blacks and whites, were the impetus for legislation to address racial issues. Jim Crow was a slave who entertained people from his plantation through song and dance. White performers imitated his speechmaking, singing, and dancing style, and dressed with clothing and makeup to appear to be black while they performed minstrel shows. Entertainers who mimicked black slaves became known as Jim Crows and were welcomed in white communities. The term *Jim Crow* soon became a label for the separation of whites from blacks in all aspects of society (Abrahams, 1992; Free, 1996).

By 1896 the U.S. Supreme Court decision in *Plessy v. Ferguson* legitimized this form of segregation, allowing for a "separate but equal" doctrine for blacks. Homer Plessy filed a lawsuit challenging segregation aboard passenger trains. He lost his action, which opened the doors for Jim Crow policies that affected schools, restaurants, hotels, and jobs. This segregation had a major impact on the education of black children. Cook (1994) noted that the educational standards for African Americans significantly lagged behind the rest of society up to the 1950s. He found in Mississippi that black children consisted of 57 percent of the school-age population and received only 13 percent of the state's education budget. This "separate but equal" philosophy was very separate but usually unequal, and continued the disenfranchisement of blacks.

To ensure that the implicit social caste system of the South continued, any blacks who disobeyed the segregation laws were treated as criminals. In the deep South, between 1882 and 1930 the number of lynchings reached 1,844. Reconstruction of the South had a deconstructing effect on African Americans. Estimates indicate that nearly 1 million blacks left for the North between 1914 and 1920. However, seeking industrial jobs and opportunities, the majority met with the same kind of racism they had experienced in the South (Free, 1996; Viola & Margolis, 1991). The only available places to live were in the inner slum areas, and they became yet another manifestation of discrimination. Segregation continued in America until the 1960s, and that awakened a new interest in Civil Rights.

The Civil Rights Era

The massive changes that took place during the civil rights era in the 1960s are related to the political and social climate of America during and after World War II. In hopes of receiving a sense of honor and respect, African Americans volunteered in vast numbers to defend America; over 1 million blacks served in the military during the war. While their efforts were noble, it was soon realized that discrimination would be part of the military world also. Troops were separated by color. Training was minimal and assignments were menial. Segregation and discrimination in the armed forces continued to disenfranchise blacks. In fact, Levine (1996) noted an absurd example of racism during the war when the Red Cross decided to segregate white from black blood. He explains that this policy seems "especially ridiculous because Dr. Charles Drew, medical director of the Red Cross blood program, whose research in blood preservation had made blood banks possible, was black" (p. 167).

Many racial incidents were recorded between whites and blacks in America and overseas. The level of violence increased as more soldiers of both races were in close quarters. Word about the continued discrimination toward black soldiers who were putting their lives on the line for America angered blacks everywhere, and some historians believe that racial violence in the ghettos was due in part to the anger they felt toward the discrimination of black soldiers in the war. Several riots were directly related to this issue, perhaps the worst in urban Detroit. On June 20 and 21, 1943, 25 blacks and 9 whites were killed. In August of the same year, someone heard that a black soldier had been killed by a white police officer and a riot raged in Harlem, New York. Riots were becoming part of the landscape of America as a reaction to discrimination (Levine, 1996).

Segregation continued after World War II, although the technological boom in industry created numerous opportunities for white society. Urban areas felt the crush of overcrowding as people rushed to the cities for jobs. Schools were brimming with the Baby Boom generation and housing was limited. The courts continued to hear cases opposing segregation, and the most important civil rights ruling in the twentieth century focused on the education of black children.

In 1909 the National Association for the Advancement of Colored People (NAACP) was established by sympathetic whites, and it sought to educate blacks to promote racial change, acceptance, and complete equality under the law between the races. The NAACP was the leader in promoting equal education for blacks. In the 1930s legislation was enacted that allowed integration in the country's state colleges. But it was not until 1954 when the U.S. Supreme Court case, *Brown v. Board of Education of Topeka,* declared that "separate educational facilities are inherently unequal" and therefore violated the Fourteenth Amendment. This decision abolished the Jim Crow laws and superceded *Plessy v. Ferguson.*

The rights of black children to attend white schools were met with massive resistance. In 1957, in Little Rock, Arkansas, nine black high school students had to be escorted to school by federal troops because of the mob violence that included white citizens and local police officers. The reactions to integration increased the Ku Klux Klan's membership, and school and church bombings became commonplace. In protest to integration, the state of Georgia changed its state flag and added the "stars and bars" of the Confederacy. The beginnings of the Civil Rights Movement were met with violence and much discrimination as the status quo was being altered.

Grassroots movements continued the fight for civil rights under the law. One most notable event involved a 42-year-old seamstress from Tuskegee, Alabama. Raised by her mother, grandmother, and aunt, Rosa Parks was living and working in Montgomery and felt discrimination daily. The rules for blacks riding city buses required that they go to the front of the bus, pay the fare, then enter the bus through the back door. The seats up front were saved for white patrons. City bus drivers had police powers to enforce segregation and the laws stated that blacks could not sit with or across from whites. On December 1, 1955, after a long day at work, Parks rode the bus in her appropriate "Colored section" as she always had. But, a white man came on the bus and the bus driver asked her to move back one more row in the Colored section so the white man could have the row to himself. She decided that she would not move back. She was arrested, thrown in jail, and eventually fined. Through court appeals and extensive publicity her fine was dismissed and the Montgomery Bus Boycott became the next logical sequence of events (Cook, 1998; Levine, 1996). Rosa Parks was already active in black civic affairs and was involved with the NAACP. She commented that she was not on the bus to get arrested, but simply to go home. She had not planned on making history, but was just tired of giving in to the injustices. In her book, *Quiet Strength,* she discusses her concerns about being treated fairly.

FOCUS BOX • *Quiet Strength*

Human dignity must be respected at all times. I would have compromised my dignity if I had buckled one more time to the white establishment and relinquished my seat. The mistreatment would have continued. I also would have compromised my dignity if I had resisted violently. Not standing up on the bus that night was a matter of self-respect. Every day of my life, I have wanted to be treated with respect, and I have wanted to treat others with respect. I had expected and hoped that others would feel the same. But because of my race, I was denied that respect. In many ways, that still happens among us today. (Parks, 1994, p. 43)

The Montgomery Bus Boycott was led by the 26-year-old pastor of the Dexter Avenue Baptist Church in Atlanta, Martin Luther King, Jr. He was a well-educated, charismatic speaker who promoted a Gandhi-like approach to eliminating segregation and discrimination. His nonviolent, direct-action campaign for civil rights and to change the status quo received worldwide attention. On December 5, 1955, the bus boycott began as the first organized action by southern blacks to defeat the legacy of Jim Crow. The boycott lasted 381 days and secured a place in history for a nonviolent approach to rectify the wrongs of the past. Martin Luther King, Jr., continued his involvement with civil rights and became the leader in southern reforms. The Southern Christian Leadership Conference (SCLC) became an additional organization that ignited grassroots movements to eliminate segregation.

Individuals asserted their new sense of identity and independence and were not always respected by whites or blacks for their social stand. In February of 1960, two black college students entered F.W. Woolworth store in Greensboro, North Carolina, and purchased school supplies. They next decided it was time to help move their hometown forward. They sat at the "whites only" food service counter and ordered lunch. The waitress was shocked and embarrassed and refused to give them service. The manager's response was similar. Two white elderly women encouraged them and wished them well. White male patrons called them derogatory names and told them they need to go to the basement with the rest of the "niggers." The black female dishwasher told them that this counter had always been for whites and they should leave. Cook (1998) summarizes that such outward black conformity is one reason for the persistence of the caste system. After years of discrimination and negative treatment by society, many blacks accepted the status quo. As grassroots movements began to spring up across college campuses and in urban areas, many blacks felt threatened and vulnerable to the possible retaliations of the dominant culture. Their lives existed under the umbrella of "clientship," and government programs provided an odd sense of safety and security. To live with the status quo seemed easier. Black activism meant personal danger for oneself and one's family.

With continuing civil rights protests, the focus centered on voting rights for blacks. Although African Americans had received the right to vote with the Fifteenth Amendment in 1870, due to segregation and discrimination most southern blacks were refused their rights. Not until the Voting Rights Act of 1965 did they receive guarantee from the government that made it illegal for anyone to interfere with another's right to vote. This act was considered a political revolution that affected the lives of millions, and voter registration for blacks increased substantially in southern states. In Georgia it jumped from 27 percent to 60 percent, and in Mississippi—where only 7 percent were registered to vote prior to 1965—the number increased to 67 percent. The South was experiencing enormous changes in the social and political climate of the times. As the Civil Rights Movement unfolded, the media carried images to all cities in the United States. Television chronicled society's changes and became the carrier of the concept of Black Power to all urban areas.

The Black Power movement did not always embrace nonviolent protests against discrimination. Years of frustration and anger came into sharp focus for residents in inner-city Los Angeles after they received no response from officials regarding complaints of police brutality. In 1965, violent protests that became known as the Watts Riots in Los Angeles claimed the lives of 34 people, with over 1,000 injured and $2 million in property damage. In 1966, demonstrations against segregated housing turned into three nights of rioting in Chicago's predominately black neighborhood. In the same year, 14 people were shot during the 1,500-member youth riot in Buffalo, New York. Detroit incurred a death toll of 36 people when rioting required President Johnson to send in 4,700 army paratroopers to handle the situation. With a growing sense of empowerment, extremists felt that the Martin Luther King, Jr., philosophy of nonviolence would not be enough.

King did not support the Black Power movement. He tried to reduce racial tensions through interracial cooperation, and was committed to rectify the past through nonviolence and total integration. His direct-action approaches led him to receive the Nobel Peace Prize and the unending support of millions of Americans and political leaders of all races. His "I Have a Dream" speech is recognized as one of the most significant orations in our history, and his work for reducing poverty and increasing employment rights was fundamental to achieving economic justice. On April 4, 1968, while in Memphis, Tennessee, to support the striking black sanitation workers, King was assassinated. It is ironic that the assassination of a man who stood for nonviolence and peace caused 125 cities across the United States to erupt in violence. A total of 46 people were killed and over 20,000 people were arrested. President Johnson deployed more than 50,000 federal and state troops to assist local law enforcement during the rage (Billingsley, 1968; Cook, 1998; Levine, 1996). Martin Luther King, Jr.'s, dream is still part of the worldview of many African Americans and whites. For many, his vision remains one in which "Black men and White men, Jews and Gentiles, Catholics and Protestants . . . will sing. . . . Free at last, free at last; thank God Almighty we are free at last." The message that he sent and the life that he lived permeated the movement for equality.

The Present Day

The United States experienced enormous social and political changes during the 1960s and 1970s stemming from the Civil Rights Movement. These social changes did not accomplish as much as people expected. Blacks experienced frustrations with the gap between promise and performance, and by 1970 over 29 percent of blacks lived below the poverty line, compared to 8 percent of whites. Advancements have continued to move through society over the last twenty years. Affirmative action increased the enrollments of blacks into colleges, and some employment opportunities improved. Black influence in politics helped to create a middle class that represents roughly one-third of the U.S. African American population (Cook, 1998). African American self-image increased with a sense of black pride, but hundreds of years of disenfranchisement prevented total change in the lives of blacks in the 30 years after the Civil Rights Movement. High rates of unemployment, poverty, and crime within the black culture demonstrate their lack of full assimilation in, and acceptance by, the dominant culture. This lack of assimilation is partly due to the racism that still exists in America.

Ties That Bind

Religion

For the majority of African Americans, the church is the historic center of spiritual, community, and political life. The church was a place to come together as a people, experience leadership roles, and enjoy fellowship with one another. It was the starting point for much of the Civil Rights Movement. The belief system of African Americans incorporated aspects of their native African culture with orthodox, Protestant, and European religions, which provided a sense of escape from the oppression of slavery. Blacks believed that God would take them to that "Promised Land" and out of bondage. Since there was no single black church, there was a variety of beliefs, worship, and songs. The beginnings of a formalized Black church date to the mid 1700s. The black Baptist churches were the most common in the South. By the beginning of the 1800s, expansion of more liberal Methodist and Episcopal churches occurred in the North. Robinson (1997) notes that "Black Christianity was at once the dominant social and moral philosophy, the centering source of collective and personal identity, and the conceptual marking device for the historical past and political destiny of Blacks" (p. 98). This source of centering was aided by music, which became the outlet and the voice for African American peoplehood.

A review of slave songs indicates that the tempo, cadence, and rhythm are correlated with West African harmonic patterns of music. The musical styles included body movement, expressions, and verse that told stories, proverbs, tales, and anecdotes. The antiphonal style, with the call and response, brought people together as one group. They used spiritual or secular songs as a way to preserve communal values and create a sense of solidarity. The purpose of religious expression through song provided occasions for people "to transcend, at least symbolically, the inevitable restrictions of [their] environment and society by permitting [them] to express deeply held feelings which ordinarily could not be verbalized" (Levine, 1977, p. 10). Religion and music were used as a method to cope with their experiences. During slave times, Frederick Douglass stated that songs were an "expression of intense feelings as they were experienced by the whole group moving together in common purpose." This expression united the group in a spiritual sense (Abrahams, 1992, p. 85). Such themes of music are similar today. Rap music tells a story in a musical style involving a particular tone and cadence that have their roots in African American folk music. In addition, the rich expression of Gospel music is associated with African American churches, and jazz music and the blues have their roots in African American folk music.

Religious beliefs continue to sustain families as well as the larger black community. Religious leaders such as the late Martin Luther King, Jr., and Reverend Jesse Jackson, both Baptist ministers, urged reconciliation between the races and work toward harmony.

FOCUS BOX • *Million Man March*

Another famous black religious leader was Malcolm X. His father was a Baptist minister, though Malcom X chose another approach to unifying blacks through religion. Originally, he joined an unorthodox Muslim group called the Nation of Islam or Black Muslims. Founder Elijah Muhammad focused his teachings on the principle that whites are racists and blacks need to separate and form their own nation. Malcolm X found that belief plausible at the time. He gave up his last name and selected the letter *X* to represent his unknown roots to the African continent. He spoke out against the Civil Rights Movement, integration, and thought Martin Luther King, Jr.'s, message of nonviolence was cowardly. It was after his visit to Mecca in 1965 that he had a spiritual awakening. He no longer advocated against civil rights or saw all whites as racist. He still called himself a black nationalist but viewed America through "new eyes." He was shot and killed by militant members of the Nation of Islam. The current leader of the Nation of Islam, Louis Farrakhan, continues to bolster Black Pride with an anti-white and anti-reconciliation message. In 1995, he initiated the "Million Man March" in Washington, D.C., that drew over 500,000 black men and boys. While the idea was worthy and notable, some say his message against the wealthy, the Jews, and people in power seemed to polarize more than cement relationships (Cook, 1998; Levine, 1996).

They emphasized using the church as an avenue for reducing racial tensions and increasing a sense of ethnic pride.

Family

A family is generally defined as a group of people related by ancestry or marriage and living in one household. A nuclear family is defined as a mother, father, and their offspring living together in one household. Extended families include various members related by ancestry or marriage, such as in-laws or grandparents, who share the same household as the nuclear family. Augmented families have people who are not related but reside with the nuclear family.

In general, more African American households are of the extended family or augmented family structure. This sense of kinship recognizes that family is more than immediate relatives. There also tend to be fewer sex-linked roles than with other cultural groups. Studies indicate that sharing of household responsibility has been higher for black than white males. The acceptance of women working outside the home by African American men reflects the strong roles women have had in black families (Sue, 1981; Free, 1996).

Families can generally be characterized as either patriarchal or matriarchal. Billingsley (1968) found that black females were heads of 21 percent of families, whereas white females were heads of 6 percent of families. By 1991, figures indicate that black female-headed households were 46 percent while white female-headed households were 15 percent (Free, 1996). Some researchers say that others misinterpret the strong roles of African American women as heads of households. In actuality, the power structure of families is more related to social class than race (Sue, 1981). By 1996, the Joint Center for

Political and Economic Studies reported that approximately 85 percent of African American children were living in single, female-headed homes that were impoverished (Children's Defense Fund, 1996). In addition, rate of poverty for African Americans is three times higher than that for whites. While whites constitute the largest group of people living in poverty, minorities are overrepresented per capita in the poverty category. Over 43 percent of black children live in poverty compared to 17 percent of white children. However, the poverty rate for Hispanics rivals that of African Americans, and their economic conditions are worsening.

White middle- and lower-class families may share with blacks the same social status, but they generally will not share the same sense of peoplehood. Black middle- and lower-class families experience not only a sharing of similar social status but also a "historical identification" or a sense of peoplehood. This sense of peoplehood seems to transcend social and economic status (Billingsley, 1968; Levine, 1996). However, the sense of peoplehood can not make up for the high numbers of unemployed and underemployed blacks.

Economic Factors

Unemployment is a gauge for understanding the economic well-being of the country. At the time of this writing, unemployment rates are at an all time low, in some areas as low as 5 percent. However, the unemployment rates for young African Americans indicates that they are "no better off today than 20 years ago" (Free, 1996). Free (1996) reports that there are several factors that contribute to African American unemployment. Some of these factors are related to the influx of immigrant populations that are willing to work for lower wages, and to the increasing number of women in the workforce. A large percentage of African Americans live in economically depressed inner cities where jobs are limited, making attractive many profitable but illegal activities.

A poll by the Anti-Defamation League showed that Americans feel more prejudice against blacks than other racial groups and view them as more violence-prone. This attitude of prejudice and discrimination further hinders the prospects of employment for black youth. While headlines state that the "American family is in trouble," the headlines for black families could read "the struggle continues."

Relationship to the Criminal Justice System

A key issue for the criminal justice system is understanding crime causation and its relationship to specific groups. Many theories have evolved in an attempt to explain this relationship. Theories range from sociological to biological to integrated approaches, and each seeks to help explain, predict, and eventually to prevent crime. Free (1996) proposes that, to understand black crime, theories should focus on understanding concepts of poverty, illiteracy, unemployment, selective law enforcement, discrimination, segregation, inadequate housing, and nutrition. This approach would consider the minority perspective on crime with emphasis on the exploitative structural system. While there are challenges to this theory as a means to explain all criminal behavior, the approach is a valid alternative to many other existing rationales.

Given an overrepresentation of African Americans in the criminal justice system, three questions can be asked to reveal the historical and structural factors that foster the distribution of black crime. Free (1996) suggests

1. To what extent do laws (e.g., drug legalization) differentially impact black populations?
2. Under what structural conditions are blacks more (or less) likely than whites to be officially processed by the system and receive stiffer penalties?
3. What effect does institutional racism have on the distribution of crime?

In addition, he suggests that questions directed to individuals and groups involved in crime would also aid in the understanding of this overrepresentation.

One theory that attempts to explain criminal behavior conceptualizes the problem within a socioecological framework. Social structure theorists see crime as a factor of one's place in the socioeconomic structure of society. Social stratification in American society primarily consists of three divisions that can be expressed as upper, middle, and lower classes. While there is a broad range of characteristics within each class, the members in each strata generally have similar values, attitudes, norms, and lifestyles. For the most part, people in the lower strata are concentrated in inner cities and in deteriorated sections of urban areas. People who live in poor, urban areas where neighborhoods are socially disorganized, poverty is abundant, and community and social services are weak or nonexistent experience high levels of crime. Crime rates are higher in lower-class areas than in middle- and upper-class parts of cities. Adolescents in poor, deteriorating neighborhoods have a higher incident of dropping out of school and engaging in deviant behaviors than do adolescents in prospering neighborhoods.

Economically disadvantaged groups who generally live in deteriorating neighborhoods also experience more social problems that can inhibit the "road to success." Members of the lower-class culture experience poor housing, inadequate health care, and more social problems than do middle- or upper-class groups. In the 1960s, sociologists found evidence that people living in America's slums develop what he calls a *culture of poverty*. This culture of poverty can undermine the traditional connection that people will make with norms and values of the mainstream. People living in the lower classes can develop a sense of apathy, cynicism, helplessness, and mistrust of social institutions and of the police. Recent studies indicate that the lower classes continue to experience more social ills than do other groups. Living in socially disorganized neighborhoods, the disenfranchised youth become America's "real crime problem."

Crime is associated with the lower class, specifically with the youth that are involved in violent destructive gangs, and with marginally employed young adults. Approximately 50 million people live in poverty conditions—defined as a family of three earning less than $18,000 a year. While whites represent nearly 70 percent of the people living in poverty and minorities are approximately 30 percent, statistical analyses indicate that minorities are significantly overrepresented per capita. Their numbers indicate that about 45 percent of African Americans and about 42 percent of Hispanics live in poverty.

Worldview

The worldview of African Americans has been shaped by our history and our socio-political system. The success and failure experienced by many blacks can be understood through the theories that describe the locus of control and responsibility. Researchers theorize that our understanding of our abilities, whether we are successful or not, is based on our past experiences; and our perceptions of our abilities influence our behaviors. In addition, our expectations of our ability to control the reinforcements we receive are related to two facets of internal and external locus of control.

People with internal locus of control believe that they can shape their own fate. They perceive that rewards or punishments they receive are a result of their own behaviors. People with external locus of control feel that rewards or punishments are beyond their control. Good and bad events are related to luck, fate, and other people. Using an example of someone who steals a car, we find two different perspectives on the event, depending upon whether the thief's locus of control is internal or external. A typical response for someone with internal control might be, "I stole the car, now I'm going to jail." A person with external control might perceive the event differently as, "The cops are always picking on me; that is why I am in jail."

In addition, locus of responsibility is related to the degree of responsibility or blame that people place on themselves or the system. If you have internal locus of responsibility you perceive your success or failure as related to your ability, effort, and success in society. If you have external locus of responsibility, your view of success or failure is related to something outside your own personal attributes. The socioeconomic and sociocultural systems, in your perception, dictate your success and failures.

Due to their history of slavery and discrimination, many African Americans experienced external locus of control and external locus of responsibility. Many blacks see their sense of identity and self as a function of the "system." There is a sense of blaming the system for the severe obstacles they have faced. After years of discrimination, prejudice, and oppression from the dominant culture, a form of learned helplessness can result. Theories of motivation conceptualize this sense of helplessness as occurring when individuals believe that they are powerless to overcome problems. This attribution of personal helplessness lowers self-esteem and can contribute to feelings of depression. These feelings can then be globalized to other areas of people's lives and might become a learned response to conditions in society, blocking paths to success. Seligman believed that "humans exposed to helplessness (underemployment, unemployment, poor quality of education, poor housing) via prejudice and discrimination may exhibit passivity and apathy . . . and learn that their responses have minimal effects" (Sue, 1981, p. 86). There is a feeling that life is "relatively a fixed" phenomenon and the best one can do is "suffer the inequities in silence for fear of retaliation." Coping mechanisms learned by blacks during much of their history in America focused on getting by and doing what they could, while engaged in indirect expressions against the oppressive society.

Many blacks have experienced "minimal effects" as a result of changes in segregation and discrimination. The large migration from the South to the North during the first part of the twentieth century pushed the majority of African Americans to the inner cities. The ghettoization of black America became the dominant organizing principle for housing and residential patterns, which linger today. The isolation of tens of thousands of African

Americans in segregated areas during that time has continued to be a problem in this century. Massey and Denton (1993) refer to this culture of segregation and note that it

> arises from the coincidence of racial isolation and high poverty, which inevitably occurs when a poor minority group is residentially segregated. By concentrating poverty, segregation simultaneously concentrates male joblessness, teenage motherhood, single parenthood, and alcoholism and drug abuse, thus creating an entirely black social world in which these oppositional states are normative. (p. 170)

They further state that black street culture moved from American middle-class values that seemed impossible to obtain and lowered individuals' self-esteem to a culture that relies on the system for survival. The sense that there is little control over personal conditions in life, disengagement from society, and the development of a tough, cynical attitude toward others and life in general all create a permanent underclass and an autonomous cultural system. This cultural system continues the ghettoization of black Americans, leaving racial segregation as a "fundamental cleavage in American society." This cleavage creates disenfranchised people that search for meaning and acceptance through alternative sources of criminal activity. The net result is inner cities that are home to violence, drugs, deterioration, and blocked goals.

In order to dismantle disparity in housing and segregated neighborhoods, social policy must address race and class issues. Programs that empower neighborhoods toward self-sufficiency and provide resources for economic independence must be addressed. Raising educational levels through quality public education, creating employment opportunities, strengthening the family, and reducing crime are a beginning to breaking the cycle of poverty that is deeply rooted in the American ghetto (Massey & Denton, 1993).

Researchers have also identified the worldview of many African Americans as internal with regard to their locus of control, and external with regard to their locus of responsibility. This dimension helps explain the focus of many blacks on securing identity within the dominant culture in spite of the discrimination and prejudice that they experience. They do actually have a sense of greater personal efficacy and higher aspirations, and believe that they can make a difference. They also recognize that achieving success has been both influenced and inhibited by the system. Recognizing this fact, they work together by participating in social and political activism to achieve their goals.

Such activism was prominent during the 1960s and 1970s as movements centered around racial pride and identity provided a symbol of positive self-identification within the dominant culture. While some chose to declare racial pride using civil rights methods, others took a more militant approach. These two approaches clearly identified that collective social action was necessary to gain national recognition of the existence of overt and covert racism in society.

Many social and behavioral theorists believe that, to bolster racial pride, one must strengthen the black identity. Strengthening that identity sounds positive and beneficial. However, Levine (1996) notes that lack of a strong national commitment to combat racial problems in general and discrimination, poverty, injustice, and resentment in particular will result in racial polarization's becoming a "part of the fabric of American life."

The combination of external locus of control and internal locus of responsibility helps explain how individuals might feel responsible for their own success but have little control over how they are characterized by the dominant culture. This combination creates a sense of powerlessness over one's fate. The term "marginal man" or marginal people defines groups that accept the dominant culture's sense of responsibility while having very little control over how they are perceived in society. Many avenues of success are inhibited due to discrimination and racism. *Marginality* refers to living on the margin between your original culture and the new dominant culture. Many reject their original culture, believing it is a handicap to success, while being unable to fully acculturate in the dominant culture due to perceptions of status. Some even experience a sense of racial hatred and feel powerless to control their sense of self-worth (McGoldrick, Pearce, & Giordano, 1982; Sue, 1981). They then might be viewed by the dominant culture as too "ethnic," that they "don't fit in," and therefore "are not welcomed."

African Americans were historically considered to be "three-fifths of a person" due to their status in society and the color of their skin. This has helped establish an attitude that these minority groups are less valued than are members of the dominant culture. Children growing up this environment embrace the dominant culture's standards but find that personal success is unattainable. Their locus of control becomes external, they believe that their failure is due to the system, and they cannot obtain success in conventional approaches. Many turn to deviance as their "quick fix" avenue to success, and this brings them into contact with the criminal justice system. When groups are fully acculturated, meaning that the dominant-subordinate relationship between groups is eliminated, the sense of marginality disappears.

African American Gangs

The emergence of African American gangs was first noted in the 1920s in the large cities of the North. The emergence corresponds with the large migration of blacks from the South between 1914 and 1920, in search of job opportunities and less discrimination. However, the large influx of poor southern blacks into the inner cities was met with more discrimination than they had anticipated. The Great Migration of over 1 million blacks to New York changed the city's demographics from 92,000 to 153,000, a 67 percent increase in the population. In Chicago, there was a 150 percent increase in blacks to the inner city, from 44,000 to 109,000. Philadelphia experienced similar racial changes with a 59 percent increase and Kansas City, Kansas, had an increase of 55 percent. Detroit experienced a 600 percent increase, from 6,000 to 42,000.

African Americans were still restricted to live in certain areas of each city, creating monumental problems with housing. The substandard housing, high rents, and overcrowded conditions created neighborhoods that continued to separate blacks from whites, rich from poor, and created a culture of segregation (Levine, 1996). Black gang membership was not related to defending turf, since blacks were limited to specific areas of cities, but gang activity was related to street crime.

In the 1920s the work of Shaw and McKay defined gang involvement as an inner-city phenomenon. The migration of blacks recurred together with movement of tens of thousands of immigrants to the inner cities searching for housing and job opportunities. The overcrowded conditions were apparent, with over 50 percent of these families living in one-room dwellings. Poor living conditions in substandard housing, long work hours, and limited access to viable opportunities for achieving the American dream created a sense of frustration and stress for families. Children experienced weak family controls, poverty, and a lack of social identity within traditional society. Competition between new immigrant groups and migrant blacks for housing and job opportunities left many children from these families experiencing a sense of marginality. Struggling to survive in a competitive world without normal access to achievement created black neighborhoods that grew into ghettos, locking people into a particular way of life. This sense of frustration and blocked goals compelled groups of boys to separate from their families as their source of social control and to join together to achieve economic success. Many of these children turned away from parental ties to seek attachments with other youths. Conflicts within their families supplanted parental influence and placed aggressive youth in control of families. Gang membership was also viewed as a way to satisfy personal needs of love, and recognition, and to provide avenues toward middle-class economic goals.

Between 1920 and 1950 black gang membership continued to grow across America as black youths continued to feel disenfranchised by society. The 1960s created other opportunities for African American youths to express their concerns over racism, and discrimination and gang activity declined on a national level. However, the 1970s saw a reemergence of gang activity due to the proliferation of the drug culture. In Los Angeles the two largest gangs to emerge during that time were the Bloods and the Crips, both using violence and drugs as their base of power. By 1996 an estimated 846,000 youths were involved in gang membership in the United States, with over 31,000 identifiable, separate gangs (Moore & Terrett, 1998).

Across the United States, gang activity is linked with drugs and violent crimes. A National Institute of Justice survey indicated that gang membership is comprised of 35 percent African American, 44 percent Hispanic, 5 percent Asian, 14 percent Anglo/ Caucasian, and 2 percent other ethnic groups (Moore & Terrett, 1998). Gang formation is generally racially homogeneous and based on geography. However, some studies indicate that certain violent gangs actually do include diverse ethnic and racial groups.

Over the last several decades the reemergence of gangs has led to a reevaluation of why youth join them. The increases in use, distribution, and sales of illegal drugs, combined with strained economic conditions and the disorganization of the American family, give us some explanations for increased gang activity.

Race and Crime

In 1962 research by Louis Lomax noted that there is a direct correlation between black crime and the inability of blacks to get jobs. He further noted that this "economic straitjacket has everything to do with the breakdown of family life and general morality in the [black] community; it is the basic explanation for the inordinate [black] crime rate" (p. 80). This economic straitjacket is fundamentally linked to discrimination in our society. In 1966 Lerone Bennett wrote an essay on *The White Problem in America,* asserting that discrimination and prejudice against blacks is really a problem with whites. He suggested that many whites experience high levels of personal and social disorganization, which include feelings of insecurities, anxieties, and frustrations that can lead to irrational ideas of race and can influence negative assumptions about groups. This in turn leads to an accepted rationale that blacks are inferior. This assumption is used as a rationale for "giving Blacks poor schools, poor jobs, and poor housing, then, we will sooner or later create a condition which confirms our assumptions and justifies additional discrimination" (p. 272). Discrimination against African Americans becomes accepted practice and actually becomes sanctioned by the system, creating a larger division between blacks and whites in society and increasing racial tensions. One view of overt and covert racial discrimination in the criminal justice system can be seen as a problem that whites have in coping with race.

Almost forty years after the research by Lomax, race and crime are in the forefront of criminal justice issues. While overt racial discrimination is illegal and prohibited by law, there still exists some form of covert discrimination in society. Cook (1998) suggests that discrimination in some form continues inasmuch as high numbers of African Americans are overrepresented in the criminal justice system, creating a self-fulfilling prophecy that blacks cannot trust the system. Whites then receive confirmation that blacks are to be feared.

Bureau of Justice statistics (Beck, 2000) indicate that, while only 12.8 percent of the nation is categorized as African American, 45.7 percent of state and federal inmates are black males. This can be compared to whites, who comprise 82 percent of the population but account for 33 percent of prisoners, and Hispanics, who comprise approximately 12 percent of the population but account for 17.9 percent of prisoners. In addition, black males between 25 and 29 years of age account for 9.4 percent of prisoners, compared to Hispanics and whites at 3.1 percent and 1 percent, respectively. Blacks had the highest rates of violent crimes including murder, robbery, rape, and assault, and had the highest incarceration rates for drug offenses. The incarceration rate is seven times higher for black men than for white men. In addition, intraracial crime (crime that involves the same race for victim and suspect) is the highest for blacks. The Bureau of Justice statistics for 1998 found that blacks were six times more likely to be murdered than any other group. In fact, 94 percent of black victims were killed by blacks, while 85 percent of white victims were killed by whites. Hacker (1992) referred to this intraracial phenomenon of black homicide as "a self-inflicted genocide, reflecting both bravado and despair" (p. 188). Approximately 40 percent of the inmates on death row are black and 53 percent of all people executed since 1930 were black (Walker, Spohn, & DeLone, 2000).

This overrepresentation of one particular group in our society should be a concern for everyone. What drives such a large number of blacks into the criminal justice system? How will this trend affect society generally and, specifically, an entire race of people? This alarming trend of "black crime" fuels society's beliefs that victimization at the hands of blacks is inevitable for all people. Bennett concludes that this creates a condition of fear, which then confirms our assumptions that criminals are black. This then justifies additional discrimination; this suspicion and fear is a factor that drives discrimination in police and court practices.

Historically, inequities in police discretion toward minority groups pervade the system. Studies indicate that blacks are more likely than whites to be shot and killed by officers, to experience excessive physical force more often, and to have higher arrest rates than other groups. In court proceedings, African Americans are more likely to receive harsher penalties and sentencing for similar crimes than whites. In addition, some characterize the War on Drugs as a war on African Americans. This is fostered by differential penalties for certain street drugs such as crack cocaine that permeate inner city areas. Crack cocaine is relatively inexpensive compared to designer drugs, steroids, and narcotics. Its use is concentrated in inner cities among the poor and the lower classes (Free, 1996; Walker, Spohn, & DeLone, 2000; Weitzer & Tuch, 1999). The crack-cocaine–mandated "federal sentencing guidelines are substantially harsher than the penalties provided by many state statutes . . . suggesting that state prosecutors are more likely to refer crack cases involving racial minorities to the federal system for prosecution" (p. 143).

Such differential efforts to combat crack cocaine might be explained in part by the racial threat hypothesis, that the dominant culture feels more vulnerable to victimization by minorities and fear of crime motivates punitive actions. Increased punitive actions toward crack cocaine users correlate with the media's highlighting the movement of crack from the ghettos to suburbia. This fosters fears that "our neighborhoods are under attack" (Crawford , Chiricos, & Kleck, 1998). The fear of drugs too close to home then translated into fear and anger toward minority groups who are envisioned as the source of the original drug problem. In contrast, no fear was expressed toward the $1 billion-a-year market for steroids that are generally associated with middle- and upper-class nonminority groups.

Sentencing Factors

A number of studies indicate that court proceedings sometimes exhibit racial disparities. Data suggest that whites receive a higher proportion of plea bargains and "better deals" than do blacks. As cited in Walker, Spohn, and DeLone (2000) Weitzer's California study concluded that "Whites were more successful in getting charges reduced or dropped, in avoiding enhancements or extra charges, and in getting diversion, probation, or fines instead of incarceration" (p. 147). However, other studies indicate that there are inconsistent results of the effect of race on plea bargaining and prosecution strategies.

Some theorists indicate that the discrepancies are related to geographic areas with high concentrations of minorities, high percentages of minorities in social or political positions, and historical connections of discrimination to minority groups. Free (1996) proposes that an understanding of the historical and structural factors that aid in the distribution of black crime yields data to support that laws do differentially impact black populations, processing of them by the system, and sentencing.

A Sense of Trust

A history of negative experiences with the criminal justice system can discourage positive interactions and promotes distrust between officers and the public. Unfortunately, there are incidents that contribute to such notions. Though isolated when compared to thousands of daily police contacts across the country, these cases usually become infamous.

The televised beating of Rodney King by Los Angeles police officers in 1991 encapsulated and galvanized the historic fears and mistrust of the system by African Americans. The subsequent trial of the police officers who clubbed and kicked King fifty-six times found the white officers not guilty. The verdict resulted in two days of rioting across Los Angeles as the African American community protested against what they believed was a racist jury decision. A year later, a federal trial found two of the officers involved in the beating guilty and sentenced them to two and a half years in prison, which was considerably less than the sentencing guidelines.

In 1997 the beating and sodomizing of a Haitian immigrant by New York police officers provided another incident that fueled community alienation from the system. Abner Louima was brutally beaten by two white officers while a precinct of people heard him cry out for help. Although these events do not represent the actions of a vast majority of law enforcement officers, they are reminders that historical attitudes about racism exist, are sometimes validated, and can polarize segments of society.

Building Relationships

Historic perceptions about discriminatory enforcement practices have harmed law enforcement relations with the communities they serve. Changing the perceptions of law enforcement toward blacks and vice versa is fundamental in the move toward building trust. Adequate and fair resolution of citizen complaints, good service to minority communities, and interest in minority victimization can go far to reduce tension and build trust between the two groups. Weitzer and Tuch (1999) found that there is a difference in the perceptions of whites and blacks concerning racial disparities in policing. Blacks in general believe that the police are more discriminatory toward them than they are toward whites. Building relationships requires that both groups address these concerns.

The media displays continual reminders of problems between the two groups. At the same time, the media has drawn attention to issues that need to be addressed and helped promote change. An example of this is the issue of racial profiling, "Driving While Black." The ACLU successfully sued the Maryland State Police in 1992 for inappropriately stopping drivers for no reason other than that they were African Americans. Evidence indicated that only 14 percent of all drivers in Maryland were African American, whereas 73 percent of the cars stopped and searched were driven by African Americans. There is evidence that this constituted discriminatory practices by the state police. Media coverage of this event prompted other states to monitor their highways and review traffic stop practices. In 1997 a bill was enacted that required law enforcement agencies to report data on race and traffic law violations. The proactive stand of law enforcement agencies to review their police practices and address issues related to the possibility of racial profiling contributes to building relationships. Community groups are working with agencies to address this concern and others to improve the relationship between the African American population and the criminal justice system.

Another method for building positive relationships is through community-oriented policing. In addition, court liaisons and advocates have helped to bridge the gaps between victims, suspects, and witnesses within the court services. Further studies indicate that recruitment and retention of minority officers rates high in public opinion polls as an effective method to reduce tension between the criminal justice system and ethnic and racial groups.

Community-oriented policing (COP) and problem-oriented policing (POP) are designed to take officers out of their cars and into neighborhoods. They constitute a change from reactive policing to a proactive approach. The philosophy moves police management from a centralized to a decentralized philosophy, establishing substations closer to the communities that officers will serve. Many substations are established in local strip malls to create easy access to officers. Instead of waiting for calls for service, the proactive approach has officers involved in the community setting up special training programs, arranging neighborhood cleanups, and addressing the specific crime-related needs of the community. Prevention of crime requires a combination of ideas from citizens as well as from officers. Reducing the public's fear of crime translates to increased cooperation between the public and law enforcement.

Recruitment of minority officers and women into law enforcement has a positive impact on agencies and the communities they serve. When law enforcement personnel reflect the diversity within the community, then law enforcement becomes a visible affirmation of the acceptance and inclusion of racial and ethnic groups in positions of authority. When there is an absence of diversity within government it seems to "nurture an outsider syndrome that perpetuates an us-versus-them approach to civic affairs" (Alozie & Ramirez, 1999, p. 458). The idea that society experiences reflections of self in the public service arena through "street-level bureaucrats" is directly related to the need to recruit minorities. The presence of minority officers increases the likelihood of police effectiveness in minority communities, and might help reduce police brutality and racial discrimination (Free, 1996).

The first African American police officer was hired in Washington, D.C., in 1861 (Free, 1996). Chicago hired its first African American officer in 1872, and by 1884 23 black officers were on the force (Siegel, 1998); however, recruitment of African American officers did not increase for the next 100 years. Findings from the 1968–69 Commission and from the 1992 Christopher Commission indicated that the lack of black officers contributed to racial unrest within the Black community. As a result of affirmative action, there has been a slow and gradual rise in minority representation in law enforcement agencies. Racial and ethnic minorities accounted for 21.5 percent of full-time sworn officers in 1997, which represented an increase of almost 7 percent in a 10-year period. Blacks accounted for approximately 11.7 percent of all local police personnel, with 9.1 percent male and 2.5 percent female. The largest representation of African American officers are currently found in agencies that serve populations of 500,000 or more (Reaves & Goldberg, 2000).

Large American cities are beginning to reflect equity in the numbers of minority officers they employ. In the city of Los Angeles, blacks represent approximately 14 percent of the general population and 14.1 percent on the police force. However, this upward trend in employment has not been uniform across police jurisdictions. New York has approximately 28.7 percent African Americans in the population but only 11.4 percent on the force. Substantial gains have been made in approximately 45 percent of all local police departments nationwide.

Minority representation in the criminal justice system sends a clear message to the community that agencies are trying to identify with the people that they serve. Larger numbers of minority officers also have an impact on the police subculture. Perhaps minority officers can provide different perspectives regarding police and community issues. Some studies indicate that black officers have been more effective in bridging the gap between the police and the black community. Police support organizations can create opportunities for officers to become mentors and role models for their communities and to develop strategies for the reduction of crime in ethnic neighborhoods. Special programs can increase the likelihood of building trust between the community and law enforcement agencies.

Another strategy for building relations between the criminal justice system and African Americans is related to bringing the "black experience" into the comprehension and etiology of minority crime (Free, 1996). This will aid in understanding crime causation theories that take into account historical, political, social, and economic differences between blacks and whites in the American society. These theories might consider social factors instead of skin color, focus on black achievement and contributions, and emphasize the power of role models among black officers.

Summary

This chapter provides an overview of the historical relationship of African Americans to the American society. No other group's history has had such a dynamic impact on present-day events. Interwoven into a tapestry that reflects our emergence as a nation, the black experience is an archetype of racial issues, prejudice, discrimination, stereotyping, and crime on the one hand, and integration, achievement, and resilience on the other.

The black community is tied together because of race and a sense of peoplehood and represents a cross-section of society as it relates to education, economics, and status. Several aspects of the worldview of blacks describe their relationship to society, based largely upon historical influences of status. African Americans comprise nearly 12.8 percent of the American population. Out of approximately 281 million people, 35 million are African Americans.

Building relations with the criminal justice system involves components of community relations and equal employment opportunity. Addressing these concerns could help to minimize racial bias in all aspects of the criminal justice system. Programs that focus on job and housing parity could reduce poverty, and educational programs that target African American children could better prepare them for higher education and help provide employment opportunities within the system. Such inclusive efforts might go far to mend the historic divisions between African Americans and the criminal justice system, as well as promote the perception that police are a legitimate part of the entire American community.

Discussion Questions

1. What are some ways that the historic relationship between African Americans and the dominant culture affect their worldview?

2. What are key issues in building trust between the African American community and the criminal justice system?

3. What are some examples of racial stereotyping and its impact on the system?

4. How do the concepts of locus of control and responsibility apply to the African American culture?

3

Hispanic Americans and the Criminal Justice System

Learning Objectives

After reading this chapter you should be able to do the following:

1. Explain the historical perspective of Hispanic Americans and how its relates to the criminal justice system.
2. Identify the ties that bind Hispanic Americans and discuss the components.
3. Identify the elements of worldview and compare the relationship to gangs, crime, and sense of trust.

Understanding Hispanic groups in the United States requires a comprehension of the relationships between historic events, government policies, and immigration cycles. Because the label *Hispanic* includes many different ethnic and national groups, these relationships differ across those groups. Our discussion will cover three within Hispanic culture—Mexican Americans, Puerto Ricans, and Cubans.

The historic relationship for Mexican Americans is one of a social policy related to labor. The relationship for Puerto Ricans involves a social policy that defines the group as an American possession, and for Cuban Americans there is a social policy punctuated by asylum for political refugees. As with other groups in the United States, their individual and corporate worldviews, their individual and corporate senses of self, and the resulting relationship with America all drive their involvement in the criminal justice system.

Hispanic Diversity

In America, over 25 different ethnic groups use the label of Hispanic. The ethnic and cultural origins of Hispanics are from a myriad of countries. The predominant countries of origin for Hispanics in the United States—Mexico, Cuba, and Puerto Rico—contribute 85 percent of the American Hispanic population. Specifically, people of Mexican descent account for 65 percent of the Hispanic population in the United States.

The modern use of the Hispanic label was a product of the 1970s, when the American government sought, for census purposes, to address all groups with Spanish origins and/or surnames under one category. "Hispanic" continues to appear on state, local, and federal forms. Other terms with which some members of these groups identify are *Latino* and *Chicano*. *Latinos* refers to the whole population and males, while the feminine form *Latina* refer specifically to women. The terms Chicano and the feminine form Chicana originate from Native American dialects, but modern usage generally refers to people who were involved with the political and Civil Rights Movement in the 1960s. It is usually adopted as the result of issues surrounding Mexican American identification and recognition. These issues related in part to young people who lived along the U.S. and Mexican border, and who were a part of two worlds. Though living in Mexico, many of these children attended schools in America and adapted American customs. Often they were considered to be *Norte Americanos* by their Mexican peers and *Mexicanos* by persons in the United States. The Chicano movement was about bridging the gap between these two worlds and providing opportunities for thousands of Mexican American young people and for future generations (Flores, 1990; Portes, 1996).

Hispanic does not adequately reflect the various ethnic and cultural groups under this broad umbrella. Each of these groups has its own distinct culture, heritage, religion, and traditions. However, the ethnic and cultural roots of Hispanic Americans can be traced to Spain and its influence on North and South America. The focus of this chapter is on people whose ancestry and language is Spanish in origin, and on the many labels they use for self-identification. Some labels are a hyphenation of the country of origin and adding *American*—for example, Mexican American or Puerto Rican American. Other labels such as *Chicano* or *Latino* were designed to better reflect changes in status and political awareness. Whatever the label, the fact remains that the Hispanic population is one of the fastest-growing minority groups in America.

FOCUS BOX • *The Rays of Light*

Some Native Americans attribute the ancient origins of the label *Chicano* to intermarriage between ethnic and cultural groups in Middle America during the Colonial Period of history in the Western Hemisphere. Anthropologists refer to such intermarriage as amalgamation, and the result is transculturated societies.

When Cortez arrived near what would later be known as Vera Cruz on the Gulf Coast of modern Mexico, he brought no European women in his cadre. It took relatively little time for amalgamation between Native American women and European men to propagate generations of children who shared each ethnicity. These generations were considered by Native Americans to be European and by Europeans to be Native American.

The resulting identity issues caused the new generations to adopt for themselves the Native American term *Xico* (pronounced and spelled Chico). Xico is defined by some groups as a term depicting rays of light streaming from the beard of the sun. The sun is characterized as a wise old man overseeing the Earth. It is from Xico that we derive the word *Mexico,* and the term *Chicano.*

Modern Mexico is fully transculturated, with mixtures of ethnic and racial groups from throughout the world. It is this transculturation and the resulting diversity that *Mexicanos* celebrate as *La Dia de la Raza Nueva* (Day of the New Race). In North America *La Dia de la Raza Nueva* is known as Columbus Day.

Numbers

As mentioned earlier, people who use the Hispanic label can be the ancestors of a variety of different racial, ethnic, and national groups. People who describe themselves as having a Hispanic origin account for 12 percent of the U.S. population of approximately 281 million people (U.S. Bureau of the Census, 2000b). More specifically, Mexican Americans account for approximately 65 percent of the Hispanics living in the United States. Puerto Ricans account for 15 percent of the Hispanic population while Cuban Americans total 6 percent. By 2010 Hispanics will account for 15 percent of the population and for 24 percent by 2025. By 2025 the United States will have 335 million people, and the states with the largest expected increases in numbers of Hispanics are California, with an additional 12 million, and Texas and Florida, with an additional 8 million each. Additionally, New York is the favored destination for many Hispanics from Latin America and the Caribbean. The Hispanic population has nearly doubled since 1990, and it currently accounts for nearly 25 percent of all New Yorkers. The largest Hispanic population in New York after Puerto Ricans is the Dominicans. In 1960 they accounted for 1.7 percent of the Hispanic population, and by 1990 they represented 18.7 percent (Flores, 2000; Portes & Rumbaut, 1996).

These expected increases in migration are from Mexico and Central and South America, as well as increases in birth rates. The median age of the U.S. population is 36 years, while the Hispanic median age is 27 years. Nearly 58 percent of the Hispanic population is under 30, while only 42 percent of non-Hispanics are under 30. In addition, 35 percent of the Hispanic population is under 18 years of age. Demographers predict that the population growth will continue to escalate. Sociologists attribute these increases to the cultural factors involving Catholicism and the religious tradition of having large families.

The educational attainment levels for Hispanic Americans tend to be lower than the national average but higher than for their countries of origin. Nationally, 77 percent of the population are high school graduates and 20.3 percent completed 4 years of college or more. Only 24.3 percent of Mexican Americans attained a high school education and 3.5 percent completed 4 or more years of college. Cuban Americans have a higher number of high school graduates and college graduates compared to Mexican Americans—54.1 percent and 15.6 percent, respectively (Portes & Rumbaut, 1996). In general, over the last 10 years, more Hispanics are completing high school and going to college than in previous years. These numbers are expected to increase with continued emphasis on academic programs that specifically target Hispanic students.

The Ties That Bind

Although several ethnic groups exist under the Hispanic label, as we have said, there are three traditions that most of these groups share. These are language, *la familia* (the family), and religion. The historic influences of Spain and the Catholic Church helped create these ties that bind.

Language

The first tie that binds Hispanics together is language, of which Spanish is predominant in countries with primarily Hispanic populations. Immigrants naturally bring their first language with them to the United States, and through acculturation and assimilation processes they eventually learn English. While acquisition of a national language is just one dimension in the acculturation process, in the United States, when groups do not learn English, they are often perceived as resistant to assimilation. Portes and Rumbaut (1996) record a comment by Stonequist that summarizes America's attitude toward bilingual persons. "What do you call a person who speaks two languages?" "Bilingual." "And one who knows only one?" "American" (p. 195). The idea that to be "American" you must speak only English impacts society's attitude toward different ethnic groups. Conflicts arise due to the myth that groups come to America and never learn the language, and this myth has more of an impact on Hispanics than on any other ethnic group in America.

Statistics indicate that only 20 percent of the population having origins in Cuba, Mexico, and Puerto Rico show a preference to Spanish, but it is not their exclusive language. The language shift toward English has been adopted by 96 percent of the U.S.-born adults. Research into generational patterns of language indicates that, by the third generation, English is dominant and the use of Spanish begins to diminish. A study of Mexican American couples from Los Angeles showed that 85 percent of first generation women spoke Spanish in the home, 14 percent used both languages, and 2 percent used English only. By the third generation, 4 percent of women from these families used Spanish in the home, 12 percent used both languages, and 84 percent used English only. The men in these families exhibited similar generational language patterns (Portes & Rumbault, 1996). These and other data support the notion that monolingual and bilingual skills are directly tied to generational patterns of language acquisition.

La Familia

The second tie that binds Hispanics together is the basic unit of family. The family is hierarchical and patriarchal; the father is the head of the household and will pass down the responsibility of managing the family to his eldest son. The role of women is subordinate to men, although they might exercise considerable influence behind the scenes. The sense of individuality, identity, and worldview is shaped through the concept that responsibility to the family is more important than to friends, coworkers, or to "manmade" institutions. The development process of children involves the whole family—meaning that parents, grandparents, and other extended family members participate in the rearing and disciplining. Many family celebrations are tied to the Catholic Church (see the following section) and include religious ceremonies for births, deaths, weddings, and other rites of passage.

Hispanic families also experience what some call a *double standard of morality* for men and women. It is expected that women should be faithful and loyal wives, mothers, and daughters. Daughters are expected to help their mothers to take care of the family and meet the needs of the men in the household. While women are expected to keep a pure and chaste life until marriage, it is commonplace to expect the opposite of men. It is considered a sign of machismo for them to express sexual freedom (Heyck, 1994).

Generally, daughters are expected to marry and have children and not get an education or have a career. Since the responsibility is on the sons to be the family providers of the future, they are encouraged to go to school and gain employment. If they are not good providers, they disgrace the family.

Conflicts arise when traditional Hispanic values and norms come into contact with generational patterns of families in America. The opportunities for women in this culture to become independent, educated, and self-sufficient people is in direct conflict with traditional Hispanic culture, where the father is the authority figure and provider. Hispanic women routinely report the difficulties of trying both to be successful and to still fulfill the needs of the family. In her book *Chiquita's Cocoon,* Flores (1990) writes of conflicts within families that many Hispanic women face when considering the balance between having careers versus having children. Many men also express difficulties with the traditional values of their parents. They value personal freedom more than responsibility and tradition.

FOCUS BOX • *Rites of Passages*

Cultures abound with ceremonial rites of passage. They encompass the lifespan from celebrations of birth to rites of death. Between these are acknowledgments of life-changing events such as marriage or retirement, and especially rites of passage into adulthood. One such rite of passage in the Hispanic tradition is the *quinceanera*. The quinceanera (from the Spanish word for fifteen) recognizes the transition through puberty when girls enter adulthood. Quinceaneras are often elaborate celebrations in honor of these young women and, like so many cultural rites, they cement a sense of kinship between family and friends.

Religion

Religious beliefs are an important part of the Hispanic culture. Individuals might not claim a religious belief, but collectively the culture is based on Christian belief systems, more specifically Roman Catholicism. Many Hispanics consider themselves religious but that does not "necessarily mean going to church or being active in an organization; rather it means belonging to a religious people . . . it is more emotionally based than theologically based . . . and represents the character of the practitioner more than that of the rule makers" (Heyck, 1994, p. 94).

The religious experience is intertwined with family events and celebrations. While there are variations in the religions practiced among Hispanics, they generally subscribe to Catholicism. In fact, Mexican Americans account for 65 percent of all Catholics in the southwestern part of the United States. Approximately 80 percent of Puerto Rican Americans are Catholics. Catholic beliefs among Hispanics are often mixed with African spiritualism and Native American traditions.

Catholicism is a monotheistic belief system practiced throughout the world and promotes an individual relationship with God, and his son, Jesus. It also promotes the honoring of the Virgin Mary, who gave birth to Jesus here on Earth, and to various saints who intercede for individuals to God. The head of the Catholic Church is the Pope, who lives in the Vatican City in Rome, which is the spiritual and administrative center of the Roman Catholic church. Priests or Fathers are the religious leaders of individual churches. The church doctrine promotes following the teachings of Jesus as outlined in the New Testament of the Holy Bible, children are a blessing from God so contraception is forbidden, and confession of one's sins to a priest is required. The majority of Hispanic Catholics practice iconography, which includes wearing crosses and pins of saints and angels, the use of rosary beads in prayer, and the presence of icons and altars for personal devotion in the home.

Language, family, and religion are at the core of the Hispanic culture, but these core values can be expressed differently among peoples with origins from Mexico, Cuba, and Puerto Rico. The waves of immigration and the generational patterns experienced by people with Mexican, Cuban, and Puerto Rican origins help explain their relationships to American society and to the criminal justice system. Therefore it is helpful to distinguish between several predominant groups within the Hispanic mosaic.

Mexican Americans

Mexican Americans have a rich cultural heritage that dates back to 10,000 B.C., when humans are thought to have migrated across the Bering Strait and down to the tip of South America. These people, whom we now call Native Americans or First Nations, are the "founding fathers" of the great Olmec and Mayan civilizations of present-day Mexico, Guatemala, and Honduras. By the 1300s the Aztecs, successors to the Mayans, developed complex societies that spanned present-day Mexico and the western United States. The heritage of Mexican Americans is from these great Indian civilizations and three periods of Mexican history: the Spanish Conquest, Northwest Expansion, and the Revolution.

Likewise, the Mexican American culture in the United States is based upon these three periods of Mexican history. The politics of immigration, border patrol, labor, and law enforcement can be better understood if considered within this historical context.

Three Periods

As Europe began voyages of exploration into the Americas in the 1400s, the conquering of the indigenous populations was inevitable. Between 1510 and 1522 the Spanish sent Hernán Cortes to the New World, and he invaded the Aztec Empire (Mexico) and colonialized the native people—known as the Spanish Conquest. Cortes brought with him 200 islanders from Cuba, several slaves from Africa, a few Indian women, and sixteen horses. Because horses had been extinct for over 10,000 years, their reintroduction to the Western Hemisphere from Spain influenced the development of human culture and the advancement of the New World. The introduction of African and Spanish peoples forever changed the history of the indigenous people of Mexico. In fact, some estimates indicate that 30 million Latin Americans and millions more Hispanics are descended from Africans brought to the New World as slaves.

When the Spanish Conquest began in Mexico in the early 1500s, population estimates for the indigenous people were between 1,500,000 and 3,000,000. By 1600, there were approximately 70,000. In the end, the Aztecs were outnumbered by the power of Spanish guns and the devastation of European diseases. This land was forever changed along with its people. The Spanish brought their religion, art, culture, and colonial government to Mexico. The first university in the New World was established in Mexico in 1551. New ethnic groups were formed through the unions with the Indians, Spanish, and the Africans. These new groups were called *mestizos,* people with mixed European and American Indian blood.

The Spanish continued their colonial adventures in what is known by historians as the Northwest Expansion. By 1800 they had colonialized the area that is now present-day California, Nevada, Utah, Arizona, Colorado, Wyoming, New Mexico, and Texas. The majority of these new settlers were the mestizos.

FOCUS BOX

An Aztec poet mourns the loss of his world:

Broken spears lie in the roads
we have torn our hair in our grief
the houses are roofless now, and their walls
are red with blood.
Worms are swarming in the streets and plazas
and the walls are splattered with gore
the water has turned red, as if it were dyed
and when we drink it
it has the taste of brine.
We have pounded our hands in despair
against the adobe walls
for our inheritance, our city, is lost and dead.
the shields of our warriors were its defense
but they could not save it.
(Viola & Margolis, 1992, p. 41)

By 1810 the New World colonies began to revolt against the Spanish government. In 1821, a revolution led by Father Miguel Hidalgo helped bring about the independence of Mexico from Spain. In 1824, the Mexican constitution was accepted by the territories of California, New Mexico, and Arizona. In 1836, Texas Mexicans (the Tejanos) lost control of their region when Anglo Texans joined the United States. The war that followed between the two countries ended in 1848 with the Treaty of Guadalupe Hidalgo. Mexico agreed to cede Texas, California, Utah, Nevada, and parts of New Mexico, Arizona, Colorado, and Wyoming for $15 million and guaranteed land rights for existing Mexican landowners. The guarantees were not respected for long, and many Mexicans lost entire farms that had been in their families for several hundred years. By 1853, James Gadsden, the U.S. Minister to Mexico, created the Gadsden Purchase whereby 45,000 square miles of land was acquired from Mexico for another $10 million. At this time thousands of Mexican citizens with generations of history in the same regions were considered foreigners living in the United States.

Social Policy

Between 1848 and 1900, there was practiced an informal and open immigration policy across U.S. and Mexican borders. Between 1900 and 1910, the Mexican Revolution was the impetus for large masses of people to flee Mexico and come to the United States. Between the years of 1918 and 1930, the United States experienced a labor shortage brought about in part by World War I. During this time, 500,000 Mexican immigrants were encouraged to come to work in this country. At the beginning of the Depression, fears of the unemployed created an anti-immigrant movement, and immigration laws were modified to deport the "undesirables" and restrict the numbers of foreign-contract laborers. The tide turned once again with the start of World War II; thousands of men were involved with the war effort, and a significant labor shortage existed. The United States Congress enacted the Bracero Program, which brought in thousands of agricultural workers to help with the labor shortage. *Bracero* is a Spanish term that was used to describe guest workers coming from Mexico to the United States. By the end of the Bracero Program in 1964, 5 million Mexican workers were imported into this country.

By the 1950s the Immigration and Naturalization Service documented the increases in both legal and illegal immigration from Mexico. In 1952, 500,000 illegal aliens were apprehended along the southern border and sent back to Mexico. The rising numbers of displaced war survivors from Europe flooded the shores of America and created new employment concerns. Sharing America's apprehension over too many immigrants were people from Mexico living in the United States. In 1954, a program called "Operation Wetback" was started to repatriate Mexican workers. This "sweep of illegal aliens" along the Texas-to-California border drove 1 million people—Mexicans and many U.S. citizens—across the border and out of their U.S. jobs (Paludeine,1998). Immigration policies continued to fluctuate with economic tides. Border patrols increased and deportations of illegal aliens continued. Significant legislation on immigration, called the Immigration Reform and Control Act of 1986, occurred during the Reagan administration. This act authorized temporary resident status, which became permanent resident status for all aliens who had lived in the United States since January 1, 1982. This amnesty act also provided special agricultural workers (SAW) temporary and later permanent status, which applied to all illegal alien farm laborers who worked at least 90 days in seasonal agricultural work during the year ending May 1, 1986. This act had an enormous impact on Mexican immigration, with 1,655,842 people entering the United States during the decade of the 1980s. Since the first decade of the twentieth century, this was the largest number of immigrants from a single country. An interesting fact is that, by 1990, 5 percent of all people born in Mexico were living in the United States (Massey, Arango, Hugo, Kouaouci, Pellegrino & Taylor, 1998).

During the 1990s, estimates indicate that between 2 to 12 million undocumented workers were entering the United States from Mexico; over 95 percent of apprehended illegal aliens were from Mexico (Portes & Rumbaut, 1996). These migrants face tremendous risks crossing the borders, but they continue nevertheless in their search for work. A study of documented and undocumented Mexican workers from two rural agrarian towns and two urban industrial communities determined that the majority of workers were undocumented. Statistics indicate that 73.2 percent of the workers from the town of Altamira were undocumented, while the remaining numbers were either formally documented, part of the Bracero program, or tourists. Similar numbers were present in the study of three other towns (Massey, Alarcon, Durand, & Gonzalez, 1987).

Concern over the large numbers of illegal workers flooding the job market and public assistance programs was the impetus for the Clinton administration to enact the Illegal Immigration Reform and Immigrant Responsibility Act of 1996. This increased border patrols and barriers along the southwest border between California and Texas. It also increased the number of investigators monitoring workplace employment of aliens, passport fraud, and alien smuggling.

The policy that best describes the relationship between the United States and Mexico is a labor policy. When the economic conditions in America are good, issues surrounding immigration, legal resident status, work visas, and undocumented workers have less of an impact on society. On the other hand, when America experiences economic stress, society views Mexican immigrants in a more negative light. In turn, many people will express hostility and negative attitudes toward the immigrant population, as well as toward anyone of Hispanic origin.

Puerto Rican Americans

The cultural heritage of Puerto Ricans can be divided into three time periods—the pre-Spanish, Spanish colonialization, and U.S. territory.

The Pre-Spanish Period

The pre-Spanish period dates back to 120 A.D., when a tribal group of aboriginal people called the Igneri came from modern-day Florida to settle the land in the eastern end of the Caribbean Sea. The European discovery of Puerto Rico was by the Spanish in the late 1400s, and it became a Spanish colony in 1508. The indigenous people that inhabited the island at the time of the Spanish discovery were the Arawak Indians, also called the

Tainos. The Tainos created a complex society of religious beliefs, rituals, and social organization on this small island that measures 100 miles in length and 35 miles wide. The majority of these native people were killed or died of European diseases (Fitzpatrick, 1987).

Spanish Colonialization

Spanish colonialization began when Ponce de Leon became governor of this island. Originally he called this land the Island of San Juan Bautista and the harbor Puerto Rico. The island was a strategically placed colony for the Spanish in the New World. The harbor's name soon became the island's name and the capital became San Juan. The island took the lead in the production of sugar cane for the Spanish Empire and came to be home to African slaves that replaced the Tainos as a labor force. By 1530, Africans outnumbered the Spanish and the Tainos, and to this day the influence of Africa is woven into the physical features of Puerto Ricans and into their traditions and beliefs.

From 1510 to 1812, the Spanish colony of Puerto Rico became an influential agricultural island in the New World. Sugar, tobacco, corn, coffee, and cattle created a strong economy for the Spanish. During the latter part of the Spanish rule, sugar plantations began to dominate the agricultural landscape to the extent that they produced 57,000 tons per year. The Spanish declared Puerto Ricans citizens of Spain in 1812, and this new citizenship status increased the numbers of immigrants to the island and set the stage for the upcoming revolts for independence. Spain abolished slavery in 1873, creating a new autonomy for the vast majority of its citizens. By 1897, Spain granted a degree of autonomy to Puerto Rico after its nearly 400 years as a colony.

U.S. Territory

When the Spanish-American War broke out in 1898, Puerto Rico was occupied by American troops. The United States seized the island, and Spain ceded Puerto Rico to the United States with the signing of the Treaty of Paris. At that time, there were approximately 1 million people on the island, the majority of whom were laborers for the few wealthy families. By 1917, the United States replaced military rule with a civilian code of government and appointed a governor. Soon after the establishment of the formalized government, the Jones Act was enacted, granting United States citizenship to Puerto Ricans. Some historians conclude that citizenship was granted "just in time so Puerto Ricans could be military fodder for World War I" (Garza, 1977). Some found this act to be another form of colonization, that American citizenship was forced on Puerto Ricans whether they wanted it or not. These issues were at the forefront when sugar production was increased to 200,000 tons per year; however, concerns over loss of cultural and national identity ranked higher than those over economic security.

The positive aspects of citizenship increased the ease of movement from Puerto Rico to the mainland and substantiated political status. While not allowed to vote in U.S. presidential elections, Puerto Ricans did receive congressional representation that could observe and report on conditions and concerns of the island.

By the 1930s, sugar production continued to climb to 900,000 tons per year, however, this economic boom was felt by only a relatively few wealthy U.S. investors. The vast majority of the people were poor laborers who experienced little difference between the past systems and this increased political and civil autonomy. The sugar production required an enormous of amount of labor for approximately 5 to 6 months a year, but the other 6 months left the majority of the island people without jobs. By the 1940s, the poor economy forced over 100,000 people off the island to look for work in the mainland United States.

Under the leadership of Puerto Rican Luis Munoz Marin and the Truman administration's "New Deal for Puerto Rico," Operation Bootstrap inaugurated a program of economic development. The industrial growth of the country brought about sweeping changes in its infrastructure. By one estimate, over 1,066 new factories were opened between 1947 and 1970. This directly created over 68,000 jobs and indirectly created between 60,000 and 70,000 service industry jobs (Fitzpatrick, 1987). On July 25, 1952, a commonwealth known as the Free Associated State was established, and Puerto Rico had its own constitution granting autonomy from the United States. This allowed Puerto Ricans to keep their cultural identity, to coexist with English and Spanish, and to have many social program benefits through the close identity with the United States. This new relationship between the United States and Puerto Rico still recognized their citizenship and their participation in the military and gave them access to federal assistance such as welfare and Social Security. Constitution Day celebrates this reform, and is considered one of the most important civil holidays of the country. However, Puerto Ricans do not pay federal taxes, they still are not allowed to vote in presidential elections, and their congressional representatives remain observers only.

While the commonwealth status had positive impacts on the island's economic base, many Puerto Ricans emigrated to the United States under the Contract Farm Labor Program, and others chose to come to the mainland for "better" opportunities. Over 600,000 people left Puerto Rico for the United States between 1940 and 1960. In the 1960s, nearly 70 percent of all Puerto Rican immigrants lived in and around New York City, and due to their vast numbers, the term "Nuyoricans" was informally adopted. Currently, the Northeast is still the destination for over 80 percent of all Puerto Ricans, with the largest percentages going first to New York City; the next largest percentages locate in Chicago.

At the heart of Puerto Ricans' experiences living in America is their struggle to keep their own identity, language, culture, traditions, and political recognition while becoming part of American life. This struggle has helped create a sense of cultural pluralism that continues to aid in the movement toward social, economic, and political security. Many Puerto Ricans see themselves in a crossroads of culture and experiences that make them uniquely American. Aurora Levins Morales, a Jewish Puerto Rican poet, expresses the pluralistic reality of new generations of Puerto Ricans in her book *Getting Home Alive*. She describes the blending of cultures through intermarriage, which creates a peoplehood that is distinct and unique. Historical factors help develop crossroads of change that affect future generations (Heyck, 1994).

Cuban Americans

Cuban Americans have a similar ancestral heritage to that of Puerto Ricans, and this heritage can be divided into periods of history that reflect pre- and post-colonization. In the precolonization period, the earliest inhabitants were thought to be an aboriginal group that came from South America in approximately 3500 B.C. The indigenous Arawaks, known also as the Tainos, later joined these groups. Over thousands of years, the early indigenous culture created a sophisticated society of cultural traditions and trade systems. This society was vastly altered when Christopher Columbus and the Spanish discovered the island in 1492.

Colonialization

The Spanish exploration and conquering of new lands and people dominated the Americas. Cuba is the largest Caribbean island in the Antilles Archipelago and is only 90 miles south of Florida. Today it ranks as the fifteenth largest island in the world. It is understandable that Cuba would be considered one of the most strategic Spanish outposts as it was the gateway to South America and to controlling trade in the New World. By 1515 a colony was established in Havana, and excellent harbors provided an outpost for Spanish treasure ships. The land was rich and fertile and supported great plantations of sugar cane, tobacco, and coffee. By 1524 the indigenous population was nearly decimated by exploitation and European diseases, so the Spanish imported African slaves to continue with agricultural production. Contributing to the survival of the African culture in Cuba were attempts by the Spanish to keep together African tribal groups. Tens of thousands of African slaves were imported to work the large plantations, the colony continued to flourish, and it became one of the largest producers of sugar in the world (Heyck, 1994; Portes & Bach, 1985).

Between the 1600s and 1700s many Caribbean islands changed colonial hands from the Spanish to the British and the French. As other islands were occupied by foreign troops, thousands of Spaniards fled to Cuba. By 1825, Spain's colonial holdings in the Caribbean were reduced to Puerto Rico and Cuba. By 1868 the Creole community—people with Spanish and African blood—rose up against the Spanish oppression and declared independence. After ten years of war and 200,000 deaths, Cuba was still ruled by the Spanish. Rebel groups continued to fight for independence and solicited the United States for help. The U.S. involvement began in 1898 when an explosion of unknown origin destroyed the U.S. warship *Maine* while it was anchored in Havana Harbor. America promptly declared war on Spain. The Spanish-American War lasted only 3 months, mostly because the Spanish colonial forces were so weakened by sustained rebel conflicts over the years. Spain ceded Cuba, Puerto Rico, Guam, and the Philippines to the United States. Through the Platt Amendment, the United States gave Cuba the right to self-determination but retained the right to intervene militarily in domestic affairs. In 1903, Guantanamo Bay became an American military holding, and is considered by some to be a symbol of U.S. imperialism.

U.S. Involvement

American companies invested heavily in farmland and other Cuban holdings. By the 1920s, two-thirds of the island's farmlands were owned by American companies. The majority of Cuban people were poor laborers who lived under the rule of dictators and corrupt politicians who practiced discrimination and social injustice to further their own economic goals. By the 1950s civil unrest plagued the island and a three-year guerilla campaign led by a young lawyer named Fidel Castro ousted the Cuban president. Castro seized power and immediately moved the country into a socialist state. The communist government nationalized all U.S. holdings, clashing with U.S. politics and trade interests. As relationships deteriorated, America placed trade restrictions upon sugar and tobacco imports. Fearing the Castro regime, approximately 64,000 people left Cuba for America, with most residing in Miami. Cubans had had a presence in Miami for nearly 100 years, but the migration between 1959 and 1960 was the largest in Cuban-American history. In 1961 the Kennedy administration supported an invasion to overthrow Castro with a CIA-trained counterrevolutionary army of Cubans exiles. Many of these people lost their lives and blame the debacle on the Kennedy administration. At the time of the invasion, nearly 1,800 Cubans were arriving in the United States each week.

As America was being forced out of Cuba, the USSR supported the struggling communist government. Cuban exports moved from the free market of the United States to the socialist market of the Soviet Union. The USSR became the leading importer of 80 percent of Cuban goods. In 1962, the United States received military photographs indicating that the USSR was developing nuclear missile sites on the island. A U.S. naval blockade turned back Russian ships during a very tenuous time in the history of the Western Hemisphere, and the Cuban Missile Crisis resulted in an unprecedented agreement between the United States, Cuba, and the Soviet Union. In exchange for the withdrawal of Russian missiles, the United States agreed not to invade Cuba. Over 180,000 Cubans fled to the United States during this episode in history. Between the 1960s and the 1980s, a total of 875,000 Cubans left their homeland to settle in this country, again predominately in Miami.

This mass exile from a politically oppressive system to a politically liberating one has changed the face of Miami. Cuban Americans have a strong sense of identity and entrepreneurship. In the 1970s they were known to become naturalized faster than any other ethnic group in history. In addition, over 20 percent of new immigrants were self-employed within 6 years of entry into the United States (Heyck, 1994). By the 1980s, a strong sense of community developed and is reflected in the following comments from the *Miami Herald.*

> The Cubans' presence in Miami has an extraordinary importance. The rapid development achieved by the city is a feat that has no precedent in the history of the country and has been called, in multiple occasions, "the Great Cuban Miracle." For this reason, the exiles who came from the island after 1959 and others who arrived later with the same faith and hope must be proud of what they have achieved for themselves and for the community in general. (Portes & Stepick, 1993, p. 148)

Although great strides have been made by many Cubans, some still have families and friends living under the Castro government.

Communism

The Cuban government is still ruled by Fidel Castro and has been criticized for its human rights record against "political prisoners." Thousands of people have been killed or imprisoned for criticizing the leadership and government policies under the military dictatorship.

The Soviet Union helped ensure relative economic stability in Cuba, but after the fall of Eastern Europe and collapse of communism beginning in 1989, the USSR was no longer able to act in that role. The Soviets withdrew 11,000 military personnel from Cuba, leaving political and economic instability. Castro redesigned the Cuban Constitution to more aptly reflect the loss of Marxism and Leninism and attempted a communistic reform in the fading shadow of the former Soviet Empire. This reform has had little impact on economic growth, and U.S. trade embargoes against Cuban goods continue. U.S. citizens are not allowed to travel to Cuba without a special license, and Cubans are not allowed to move freely to the United States. The Cuban government is the main reason that so many people seek political asylum to America.

Relationship to the Criminal Justice System

A key issue for the American criminal justice system is the understanding of crime causation and its relationship to specific groups. Theories surrounding these relationships include sociological, biological, and integrated approaches, and are intended to help explain, predict, and eventually prevent crime.

One such theory explains criminal behavior within a socioecological framework. Social structure theorists see crime as a result of people's places in the socioeconomic structure of society. Social stratification in American society consists primarily of three classes—upper, middle, and lower—and while there is a broad range of characteristics within each class, members usually have similar values, attitudes, norms, and lifestyles. For the most part, people in the lower strata are concentrated in inner cities and in deteriorated sections of urban areas. People who live in poor, urban areas where neighborhoods are socially disorganized, poverty is abundant, and community and social services are weak or nonexistent experience high levels of crime. Crime rates are higher in lower-class areas than in middle- and upper-class parts of cities. Adolescents in poor, deteriorating neighborhoods have a higher incidence of dropping out of school and engaging in deviant behaviors than do adolescents in prospering neighborhoods.

Many economically disadvantaged groups also experience more social problems that can inhibit the "road to success." The lower-class culture experiences poor housing, inadequate health care, and more social problems than does the middle or upper class. In the 1960s sociologist Lewis identified people living in America's slums as forming a culture of poverty. This culture of poverty can undermine the traditional connection that people will make with norms and values of the mainstream. People living as members of the lower classes can develop a sense of apathy, cynicism, helplessness, and mistrust with social institutions and with the police. Recent studies indicate that the lower classes continue to experience more social ills than do other groups. Living in socially disorganized neighborhoods, the disenfranchised youth become America's "real crime problem."

Crime is associated with the lower classes. Specifically, there are significant correlations between high crime rates, youth involved in violent and destructive gangs, and unemployed or marginally employed young adults. Approximately 50 million people live in poverty conditions—defined as a family of three earning less than $18,000 a year. Statistical analysis per capita indicates that minorities are overrepresented as living in poverty, including approximately 42 percent of Hispanics. As large percentages of those groups live in lower-class neighborhoods, this environment increases the likelihood of deviant behavior.

Key issues in the criminal justice system with Hispanics are related to history, trust and respect for "the system," and perceived acceptance in society. Many theorists believe that this is evident in Hispanic gang activity and the growing numbers of Hispanics in correctional settings.

The System and Hispanics

Many Hispanics have a worldview that is different than what has come to be known as the "traditional mainstream." While generally hard working, some Hispanics report that achievement in American life is beyond their grasp and out of their control.

As previously discussed, persons who experience internal locus of control and responsibility are likely to attribute success or failure to personal endeavor and industry. They believe success and the reinforcements from success are the result of hard work and determination. They also tend to hold the same mindset with failure, believing that failure is the result of missed opportunities and lack of sufficient endeavor. In contrast, persons who experience external locus of control and responsibility hold a view that is quite different, attributing success to luck and the intervention of others. As forces outside oneself drive success, failure is the fault of others and the fault of circumstances beyond one's control. For example, incarcerated individuals who take little personal responsibility for their situations instead blame the system and claim persecution rather than accepting their just deserts.

Many groups that exhibit external locus of control and responsibility have experienced historic disenfranchisement, such as colonialization or slavery. This is true for many Hispanics who have such a heritage, as it is true for many former Eastern Europeans who lived for decades under the oppression of communism. While there can be established no direct correlation between crime and external locus of control and responsibility, there is a correlation between economic development and the latter. And the correlation between economic development and crime is fairly well established.

In addition to issues surrounding control and responsibility, the disenfranchised heritage of many Mexican Americans and Puerto Ricans often leads to what some theorists call "marginality." As discussed in the previous chapter, this marginality can interfere with minority people participating fully in their own culture or in the dominant culture. People living on this cultural margin are often rejected by their own cultural group and can be discriminated against by the dominant culture. Their sense of worth is marginalized and it often interferes with personal success.

Mexican American and Puerto Rican history might cast those persons as victims of military conquest and second-class citizens, fostering the notion that these groups are somehow less valuable than others within the dominant culture. Children growing up with an alternative cultural heritage might learn distrust for the establishment, that success is unattainable, and the oppressive system is to blame. Related to Rotter's work, their locus of control and responsibility becomes external, and they believe that failure is due to the system. Success will not occur within conventional approaches controlled by the system, so many feel the right to turn for success to alternative behaviors of deviance. Worldviews built upon external control, external responsibility, and marginality can easily run head-long into the criminal justice system.

The erosion of the family that pervades America also affects Hispanic families living here. Values and traditions within families are challenged by outside social forces, and many adolescents express their own autonomy through disrespectful attitudes that negate those values and traditions. These youths easily become disenfranchised from the family unit and many join gangs.

Studies from the National Institute of Justice (NIJ) confirmed that gangs are formed along racial and ethnic lines. In 1996, NIJ estimated that there were 555,181 gang members with 47.8 percent African American, 42.7 percent Hispanic, 5.2 percent Asian, and 4.4 percent whites. Los Angeles is considered the "gang capital" of the United States and has the largest percentage of Hispanic gang members. These gang members have changed their sense of loyalty from their families to their peer group. The traditional role of La Familia is becoming distorted with the influences of drugs, gangs, teenage pregnancies, and poverty. Many believe survival of the Hispanic culture will be through the return of the foundation of family values.

Puerto Ricans became part of America just over a 100 years ago. They are, as a whole, one of the poorest ethnic groups in America. Originally working as farm laborers, they experienced discrimination at the economic and political levels that inhibited opportunities for advancement. Many researchers still site discrimination as the biggest problem facing Puerto Ricans in America. However, there is an increasing rise in the middle class, with 2.7 percent holding technical jobs. The movement for more economic and social independence is changing generationally (Haslip-Viera, 1996; Hernandez, 1996). The economic struggle has pitted many Puerto Ricans against other ethnic minority groups as they compete for limited resources in large urban areas. In addition, many Colombians, Ecuadorians, and Dominicans living in large urban areas will view Puerto Ricans as people who are part of an American possession but not truly part of the Latino culture (Flores, 2000; Heyck, 1994). This lack of identity with other Hispanic groups interferes with cultural acceptance and economic progress. There are also conflicts between many blacks and Puerto Ricans as both groups try to survive with discrimination, high unemployment rates, and poor living conditions.

Historic associations between Cuban Americans and the establishment are related to their status as political refugees. In the 1960s Congress passed legislation allowing refugee status to any Cuban who manages to land on American soil. As stated earlier, Cubans fleeing an oppressive government came to America seeking freedom. Their internal locus of control and responsibility motivate them to become actively involved with political movements and civil rights issues. They believe that, within the American system, they can become designers of their own fate. This is evident in the fact that, during the 1970s when large groups migrated to Miami, 20 percent became self-employed within months. Their ethnic group reached the national median for household earnings. Some researchers also believe that the rapid advancement of Cuban Americans was due to sympathetic attitudes among Americans for persons fleeing the great evils of Communism. Portes and Stepick (1993) noted that between 1968 and 1980 the Small Business Administration of Dade County, Florida gave business loans to 46 percent of Cuban Americans and only 6 percent of blacks. Unfortunately, this enhanced the Cuban American view of American society as a positive influence; no such enhancement occurred for blacks.

Given the Cuban American experience that was borne of history and politics, one can easily differentiate between their situations and those of Mexican Americans or Puerto Ricans. Cubans learned that they were welcome, and that they could shape their own environments and opportunities. They became known as industrious and talented. They were also cognizant of that fact that, as an ethnic group new to the area, discrimination and prejudicial attitudes from the dominant culture were unavoidable. Yet with the positive influences at work, many Cubans saw this as an opportunity to express their ethnic pride and to strive for their own cultural identity within the framework of the dominant culture. Their political activities for social action are well-known (Heyck, 1994). However, while they generally fare better as a group, many Cuban American families have felt the strain of cultural differences, and some children have experienced marginality and the resulting deviant behavior patterns.

Hispanic Gangs

Early studies among social theorists and criminologists indicated that gangs were originally an inner-city phenomenon. In the 1920s the work of Shaw and McKay found that gang involvement was a mechanism of empowerment for hundreds of poor immigrant children. These children experienced marginality, weak family controls, and poverty and lack of social identity within traditional society. This was further amplified as new immigrant groups moved into the inner cities to compete for housing and job opportunities. The history, family structures, and ethnic and cultural traditions came into direct conflict with the mainstream. Many of these children turned away from parental attachments to seek them with other youths. Conflicts within families widened the gap between parental and

FOCUS BOX • *Mexican American Children*

Many Mexican Americans seem to lack cohesiveness in community and in family life. This can be associated with wide status disparities within the Mexican ethnic group. The levels of economic and social standards separate the farm laborer from the professional. Many with professional status do not want to identify with lower-status groups, and young Mexican American youths seek status and positive ethnic identity. Traditional approaches to gaining status in the dominant culture sometimes conflict with fast routes to economic and occupational mobility. Struggles between existing groups and new immigrants create distrust for each other and for the system, conflicts affect relationships within families, and discord abounds. Discord within the Mexican American family makes it more difficulty to protect children from discriminatory practices and attitudes of the majority group. These children can become alienated, not only from the majority, but from their own parents. Such alienation inhibits personal development, and affects school achievement and work behaviors. The peer group becomes an escape from family tensions and removes parental authority and discipline. Joining the "gang" gives a sense of status and power. (De Vos, 1982) adolescent control of youthful activities. In addition, conflict between ethnic groups competing for resources advanced gang membership as lower-class boys asserted power for authority to control their own ethnic neighborhoods and to keep rival groups out. Gang membership was also viewed as a way to satisfy personal needs such as love and recognition, and provided an avenue toward middle-class economic goals.

Over the last several decades the reemergence of gangs has led to a reevaluation of the gang phenomenon. The increases in use and sales of illegal drugs, strained economic conditions, and the disorganization of the American family are some reasons to explain the increases in gang activity. Hispanic families are not immune to these forces, and their risk for marginality enhances the effects.

Hispanic gangs have evolved over time to include numerous groups of immigrants from Spanish-speaking countries. As families move into the barrios of inner cities, children seek to identify with the new culture. They are exposed to gang activity and are recruited for membership as a way to achieve status in this new culture. The gang becomes an alternative family, and loyalty to the gang is above loyalty to their family. Hispanic gang members account for 42.7 percent of the estimated 555,181 gang members in the United States (Curry, Ball, & Fox, 1994).

The violence of gang-related incidents has increased over the last 10 years, and law enforcement has expanded efforts to control gang activity. The increase in drug use and manufacturing is correlated with the increase in gang violence, and with growing methamphetamine production in the western states. While the major production and transport of such drugs is done by Mexican nationals, the accessibility and ease of manufacturing are finding their way into rural areas of the United States and bolstering the economic bases of Hispanic gangs.

Drug Use

The National Institute of Justice studied over 1,000 jailed meth users and found a link between drug use and violent and destructive behaviors. The majority of meth users are white males, with the second highest number being Hispanic males. Reducing drug trafficking has been difficult due to the nature of how drugs are sold. Most drug sales take place in homes or in hotel rooms—not on the streets, as with cocaine. Most law enforcement agencies have special gang units that are combined with narcotics units to detect and reduce gang and drug activities. Special gang units also focus on gang member identification, specific policies that focus on controlling activities, and laws designed to inhibit gang activity. In addition, many criminal justice agencies have joined together to control gang activity.

In 1997 in Fresno, California, the Multi-Agency Gang Enforcement Consortium (MAGEC) was formed to "expand our war against criminal activity." The operation involves over thirty law enforcement agencies, including the police and sheriff departments, California Highway Patrol, Federal Bureau of Investigation, Drug Enforcement Administration, Internal Revenue Service, State Parole, Fresno County Probation, California Department of Corrections, the Immigration and Naturalization Service, and the district attorney's office. Combining resources and efforts has helped to suppress criminal activity. It is recognized as the "largest long-term consolidation in law enforcement history . . .

and is the most comprehensive and effective method in existence" (Fresno County Sheriff's Department, 2000).

A Sense of Trust

The history of Hispanics is also related to their sense of trust of the criminal justice system in their countries of origin. Mexican Americans, Puerto Ricans, and Cuban Americans have had similar experiences with the criminal justice systems in their home countries. For example, Mexicans know that the Mexican government, in general, and law enforcement, in particular, are corrupt enterprises. Civil rights abuses are common within their system. Dan Rather interviewed the Attorney General of Mexico on a *60 Minutes* segment, and he stated that he has a very difficult job trying to uncover and control the rampant corruption in his country. Immigrants from Mexico do not automatically trust the criminal justice system in America when they cross the border. They approach law enforcement contacts with fear, and assume the worst. Many will take evasive actions to avoid contact with law enforcement, which in turn creates more conflict.

Many Hispanics who have lived in America most of their lives also lack trust in the system. Historic accounts of police brutality against Mexican Americans in the years between 1845 and 1947 show that negative attitudes about Mexican people pervaded the dominant culture. In his book, *The Texas Rangers,* Webb records that Mexicans were murdered because they were perceived to be "treacherous, cowardly, and diabolical . . . and must be dealt with cruelly" (Viola & Margolis, 1991). These attitudes from the dominant culture instilled lack of trust in the system. Also, conflicts between ethnic groups of Mexican descent foster feelings of social and personal distrust. There are a variety of internal class and status conflicts between these groups, driven by prejudices over a mixture of European and Indian heritages. Individuals who identify as "la raza" feel superior to groups of Mexican Indian heritage. Many do not want to be identified with the "lower class of Mexican Americans." Such social distrust of people from their own ethnic group, poverty, and feelings of government oppression combine to create an attitude of suspicion and envy. De Vos (1982) noted that some in the Mexican American community feel that they must defend themselves against their neighbors and the system. Many find it difficult to conceive of the economic success of others without feeling that they themselves have been deprived of something to ensure that success. This attitude affects whole communities in their relationship with the system.

The Civil Rights Movement in the 1960s gave Puerto Ricans confidence to establish organizations that could impact the poverty and police brutality that they experienced while living in America. As large groups continued to move into New York, they were accused of causing housing shortages, escalating unemployment, and of coming to America to collect welfare. Garza (1977) reported that "they were charged with responsibility for all the ills of society . . . and Puerto Ricans 'naturally' resort to violence when they participate in politics" (p. 35). The police reacted to their new-found pride and expression of self-identity with brutality. Puerto Ricans' lack of trust of the criminal justice system continued to be reinforced, as were external locus of control and responsibility.

This lack of trust also affects the reporting of crimes and differential treatment. Experiences from past contacts with the criminal justice system discourage many Hispanic

victims from reporting crimes. Many Hispanics fear reporting because they feel they do
not have adequate police protection. Conclusions from a report on Hispanic victimization
from the Bureau of Justice Statistics indicated that Hispanics perceive recriminalization
and lack of police response as the major concerns of reporting crime. The report also highlights perceived stereotypes by law enforcement agencies about Hispanics, and stereotypes that Hispanics have about law enforcement personnel continue to inhibit effective
interactions.

The growing numbers of Hispanics in the correctional system can promote stereotypic perceptions by the public as their "being a dangerous group of people." While Hispanics account for nearly 12 percent of the current population, statistics indicate that the
number of Hispanic prisoners in state or federal facilities is 219,500, or 17.9 percent of all
prisoners. Between 1990 and 1998, Hispanics committed the highest number of violent
crimes, accounting for 56 percent of total offenders. Though black males between 25 to 29
have the highest rates of incarceration, at 9.5 percent, Hispanic males accounted for 3.1
percent of those incarcerated. White males accounted for 1 percent. Female incarceration
rates indicate that 212 per 100,000 blacks, 87 per 100,000 Hispanics, and 27 per 100,000
whites are in prison. The Bureau of Justice Statistics found male and female incarceration
rates to be consistent across age groups (Beck, 2000). By 2025, the expected increase in
Hispanic population is 26 percent in selected states. With the continued increases in population, incarceration rates will climb. Hispanics' experiences in prison will continue to
promote external locus of control and responsibility because the correctional setting does
not generally reward initiative and creativity. The system rewards those who are external
in their approach to life in prison.

As with other groups, the level of population of Hispanics in prison is driven by
recidivism rates. Between 1990 and 1998, the largest increase in prison population was
related to recidivating offenders. Approximately 54 percent of the increase in prison populations is related to parole violators, with 59 percent of the violators returning because of a
new conviction.

Building Relationships between Hispanic Americans and the System

Many methods exist to improve the relationship between the Hispanic population and the
criminal justice system. Community-oriented policing has had a positive impact on building relationships between law enforcement and Hispanics. In addition, court liaisons and
advocates have helped to bridge the gaps between victims, suspects, and witnesses within
the court services. Further studies indicate that recruitment and retention of minority officers is rated high in public opinion polls as an effective method to reduce tension between
the criminal justice system and ethnic and racial groups.

As previously stated, community oriented policing (COP) and problem-oriented policing (POP) are designed to take officers out of their cars and into neighborhoods, and this
change from reactive policing to proactive community involvement can only improve relations between law enforcement and the Hispanic community. These programs move police management from a centralized to a decentralized philosophy, establishing substations
closer to the communities that officers will serve. Many substations have been established

in Hispanic communities in local strip malls for easy access to officers. Instead of waiting for calls for service, the proactive approach has officers actively involved in the community, setting up special training programs, arranging neighborhood cleanups, and addressing the specific crime-related needs of the community. The programs are combinations of ideas from citizens as well as from officers. In addition to prevention of crime, reducing the public's fear of crime is related to increased cooperation between the public and law enforcement.

Providing Spanish-speaking liaisons and advocates for people involved in the court system has a positive impact on groups. It is hard to trust a system that speaks another language. Saltzburg (1998) points out that the numbers of non-English-speaking witnesses are on the rise. He suggests that such modern rules as the Federal Rule of Evidence 604 recognize the need for assistance with non-English-speaking court participants. Saltzburg states that the "rules of evidence must be flexible enough and trial judges must have sufficient discretion to permit non-English speaking witnesses to provide a trier of fact with their testimony." Asking leading questions of a non-English-speaking witness might be unfair.

Recruitment of minority officers and women into law enforcement can have a positive impact on agencies and the communities they serve. When law enforcement personnel reflect the growing numbers of diverse groups, then law enforcement becomes a visible connection to the acceptance and inclusion of racial and ethnic groups in positions of authority. When there is an absence of diversity within government positions it seems to "nurture an outsider syndrome that perpetuates an us-versus-them approach to civic affairs" (Alozie & Ramirez, 1999, p. 458). The idea that society experiences self-reflections in the public service arena through "street-level bureaucrats" is directly related to the need to recruit minorities. The increasing numbers of Hispanics in society seem to have an influence on recruitment efforts by law enforcement agencies to recruit Hispanic officers. When Hispanics attain positions within local governments as council members, mayors, and other highly visible positions of authority, political pressure to educate and employ minorities rises to the forefront. Alozie and Ramirez (1999) found that there is a direct correlation between education and employment for Hispanic officers. Stokes and Scott (1996) reported that Hispanic police officers as a group had more college degrees than European American officers. They note that, while minorities and women still seem to be underrepresented in law enforcement agencies, Hispanics have been more successful in gaining employment than women. If the mission and goals of law enforcement are to work effectively with diverse groups in their communities then it is imperative that the workforce become diverse (Stokes & Scott, 1996).

Racial and ethnic minorities in law enforcement increased from 14.6 percent in 1987 to 21.5 percent in 1997. Hispanic officers increased from 5 percent in 1987 to 8 percent in 1997. In calculating percentages for cities with a population of 1 million or more, Hispanics represent 15.6 percent of the officers, which is twice the overall average (Reaves & Goldberg, 2000).

These numbers are expected to increase over the next 10 years, and to provide a good basis for improved relationships between the criminal justice system and the Hispanic community. A sense of value and participation are necessary to bring together various groups, and inclusion in the process holds the promise of improved relationships in the American mosaic.

Summary

The label *Hispanic* includes many different ethnic and national groups, and relationships differ across those groups. The ethnic and cultural origins of Hispanics include myriad countries. This chapter discussed three groups within Hispanic culture, Mexican Americans, Puerto Ricans, and Cubans. In America, over 25 different ethnic groups use the label of Hispanic. The historic relationship for Mexican Americans is one of a social policy related to labor. The relationship for Puerto Ricans involves a social policy that defines the group as an American possession, and for Cuban Americans there is a social policy punctuated by asylum for political refugees. As with other groups in the United States, their individual and corporate worldviews, their individual and corporate senses of self, and the resulting relationship with America drive their involvement in the criminal justice system.

Many methods exist to improve the relationship between the Hispanic population and the criminal justice system. Community-oriented policing has had a positive impact on building relationships between law enforcement and Hispanics. In addition, court liaisons and advocates have helped to bridge the gaps between victims, suspects, and witnesses within the court services. Further studies indicate that recruitment and retention of minority officers is rated high in public opinion polls as an effective method to reduce tension between the criminal justice system and ethnic and racial groups.

Discussion Questions _____

1. What are some ways that the historic relationship between Hispanic Americans and the dominant culture affect their worldview?

2. What are key issues in building trust between the Hispanic American community and the criminal justice system?

3. What are some examples of racial stereotyping and its impact with in the system?

4. How do the concepts of locus of control and responsibility apply to the Hispanic American culture?

4

American Indians and the Criminal Justice System

Learning Objectives

After reading this chapter you should be able to do the following:

1. Explain the historical perspective of American Indians and how it relates to the criminal justice system.
2. Identify the specific issues that impact the system as it relates to American Indians.
3. Identify the elements of worldview and compare the relationship to gangs, crime, and sense of trust.

The broad term *Native Americans* might incorrectly promote the idea that there is one ethnic group that represents this population. Though such terms as *Indian, American Indian, First Nation,* and *Native American* do represent the indigenous people of the Americas, these terms do not adequately represent the vast physical, cultural, and social characteristics of the various communities.

The Bureau of Indian Affairs (BIA) (2000) reported that the term *Native American* came to be used in the 1960s to denote the groups served by their agency: American Indians and Alaska Natives (Indians, Eskimos, and Aleuts of Alaska) and, at a later date, Native Hawaiians and Pacific Islanders. The BIA reported that *Native American* came into disfavor among some Indian groups that preferred the term *American Indian.* However, Eskimos and Aleuts in Alaska are two culturally distinct groups that are historically resistant to being included under the "Indian" designation. They prefer to be called "Alaska Natives."

Any labeling for purposes of demographic identification tends to be a social construct based upon cultural, political, and social factors at any given time. Therefore, many Indian and non-Indian scholars use these terms interchangeably.

While the term *tribe* is generally accepted to refer to American Indian communities, some scholars feel this term has negative connotations representing "white creations used by Indians to survive." On the other hand, American Indians commonly refer to their communities with tribal designations and use the term as part of their official names. The labeling of tribal groups in some ways provides ethnic identity and a sense of cultural identity with other Indians. There are 556 federally recognized tribes that range from the Aleuts and Inuit in Alaska to the Navajo and Hopi in the Southwest to the Seneca and Mashantucket Pequot in the East (Bureau of Indian Affairs, 2000).

While diverse in culture, these tribal groups have similar histories in relationship to federal, state, and local governments. This history must be explored to better understand the relationship of Native Americans/American Indians to the dominant culture and to the criminal justice system.

The Historical Perspective

The historical perspective of Native Americans is based on periods of interactions with groups of people coming to the New World. As with African slavery, this history is marked by the oppressive, military colonialization of the Western Hemisphere. Historic Indian colonial policies range from early relationships with Europeans in the 1500s to federal policies in the newly developed United States.

The period of this history that is perhaps most germane to our discussion came between the late 1700s and early 1800s, and involved treaty development and removal of Indians to reservations away from the emerging cities of America. Subsequently, between the 1860s and the early 1900s the policies of the federal government were built upon allotment of land and assimilation into "mainstream" culture. This presented a new approach to "dealing with the Indian problem." The 1920s through the 1940s were a time of Indian reorganization that halted the allotment and assimilation processes, and was followed by a termination period between the 1940s and early 1960s that attempted to further dismantle

Indian culture and landholdings. It was during this time that the movement for self-determination promoted reforms toward greater powers of tribal self-government to the exclusion of state authority. The last thirty years are recognized as a period of renewal for Indian affairs.

The Paleo-Indians

Native Americans and their current relationships to social policy are firmly based on the early inhabitants of the Western Hemisphere. It is theorized and generally accepted that American Indians today are descendants of the Paleo-Indians, the early residents of the Western Hemisphere. Theory holds that the Bering Sea contained a land bridge connecting Siberia and Alaska during the Pleistocene glacial period of natural history (approximately 28,000 to 10,000 B.C.). The land bridge provided the opportunity for migration, and the ultimate result was human population in the Western Hemisphere from Alaska to El Tiera Del Fuego. The migrations occurred as people traveled north and south along the various corridors.

Examples of this early human presence abound in the natural record. Obsidian and flint-crafted tools were first found in Clovis, New Mexico, indicating that humans were in that area in approximately 25,000 B.C. Early Paleo-Indian sites in Colorado indicate that humans were a nomadic group collecting wild plants and hunting large game animals in approximately 11,000 B.C. Human remains from 10,000 B.C. were discovered in Teotihuacan, near Mexico City. Other remains have been uncovered throughout North and South America, indicating large migrations of people throughout the New World. As the final Ice Age subsided and glaciers receded in approximately 10,000 to 7,000 B.C., the Bering Land Bridge disappeared into the ocean and the large migrations of animals and people ended. Changes in climate and geography eventually altered nomadic lifestyles of many inhabitants to more sedentary, agriculturally based settlements (Nies, 1996; Taylor,1997; Viola & Margolis, 1991).

Archaeological records are replete with human settlements comprised of relatively sophisticated societies. Inhabitants of the Great Lakes region mined copper and hammered

FOCUS BOX • *The Spirit Caveman*

Though these *early people* are presumed to be from Northeast Asia, controversial new discoveries indicate that they might have also come from Eurasia. The 9,300-year-old Kennewick Spirit Caveman was uncovered in 1996 in Kennewick, Washington. Kennewick Man appears to have the morphology of the indigenous Ainus people of Japan, and looks more Caucasoid than Asian (Morell, 1998). The skeletal remains indicate that there might have been several waves of migration from the Old World to the New World instead of the theorized one or two. It is probable that there were many groups of people migrating using the land bridge, following herds of large mammals, traveling along the edges of land that meet the oceans, and populating this hemisphere. While new information emerges from the archaeological and anthropological records regarding the early peoples, the fact remains that these inhabitants were directly tied to the land.

it into tools. In Florida and Georgia, advanced food-storage systems utilizing specialized pottery created a society that could plan for surplus crops instead of moving from place to place. The Olemecs in Mexico were known for their sophisticated horticulture that developed over centuries creating corn, beans, legumes, chili peppers, cocoa, and cotton. Centuries of experimentation led to agricultural accomplishments and, when Europeans came to the New World in the late fifteenth century, they returned with ideas and seeds that changed the agricultural practices of Europe.

Historic accounts and the natural record indicate that the Western hemisphere flourished during the pre-colonial period, with complexity demonstrated in sophisticated societal systems of architecture, astronomy, metal working, urban planning, extensive trade routes, and political structures. By 700 A.D. Teotihuacan was the sixth-largest city in the world, with Constantinople and Alexandria ranking only slightly above. Population estimates at the time of the arrival of Columbus range from 70 million to 110 million people living in the Western Hemisphere (Nies, 1996; Viola & Margolis, 1991).

Some historians acknowledge the idea of "discovering the New World" as European arrogance typical of the colonial period of history. Nies (1996) writes, "How can you 'discover' a hemisphere that has over 70 million people? Why couldn't the European Christians see the Native peoples as fellow human beings?" (p. 2). But, it was more than their arrogance that changed the indigenous populations of this hemisphere. The Europeans assaulted these populations with disease, most notably smallpox, measles, influenza, bubonic plague, cholera, and tuberculosis, and this first contact changed the landscape of the Americas forever. Between 1492 and 1918, grand-scale epidemics of disease decimated indigenous populations that had no natural resistance to Old World illnesses. According to Dobyns, "an estimated 95% of [the Native American] population decline occurred between 1519 and 1617, and one Native American lived in the Twentieth Century where about 72 had existed four centuries earlier" (Nagel, 1996, p. 61).

Other estimates indicate that between 50 percent and 90 percent of all indigenous peoples perished as European diseases naturally spread throughout the environment, and that most of the victims never actually saw a European. This is evident in the history of Puerto Rico where, in three years, over 180,000 natives died after contact with Columbus and his men. In other parts of the Caribbean more than 3 million Arawaks died during some 30 years that followed contact with Columbus. These numbers continued to escalate as Spanish, Portuguese, English, French, and Dutch explorers invaded the New World. During 1659 over 10,000 Florida Indians died of measles brought over from Spanish ships. In 1738 white slave traders brought smallpox to Charleston, South Carolina, and through goods and supplies traded with the Cherokee Indians in Georgia the disease killed over half of the tribe (Dennis, 1971; Nies, 1996).

We mention at some length this devastation of the indigenous population by disease and military conquest to emphasize that the cultures of the New World were dramatically changed by the presence of Europeans. These changes affect modern history, as well as the relationship between Native Americans and the establishment (Nies, 1996; Olson & Wilson, 1984).

In 1570 a League of Six Nations comprised of the Iroquois, Mohawks, Oneidas, Senecas, Cayugas, and Onondagas formed to develop plans to peacefully coexist with each other and with the growing numbers of Europeans in the New York area (Dennis,

1971). Their eventual contact with English colonists became a short-lived peaceful union. The insatiable desire of the settlers for more land for farming and urbanization crushed tribes and pushed them further west and off their original lands.

The Early Years: The Formative Period of America

The early years of interactions between Native Americans and colonists are marked by policies and charters designed by European powers to control the "Indian problem in the Americas." In 1532, charters were established to "respect and guarantee aboriginal rights" and guaranteeing that no European power could acquire existing Indian land or have governmental power over Indians. This charter was ignored and the movement toward land expansion continued. Native American nations were considered "sovereign Indian nations" and Europeans quickly developed treaties—formal agreements between two or more sovereign powers—to establish land rights. Treaties traditionally cover issues concerning trade, tariffs, taxation, economic and technical cooperation, diplomatic relations, land boundaries, and defense matters such as ending wars between nations. Jaimes (1999) notes that there are over 350 formally ratified treaties between Native Americans and the federal government. One of the first was the Treaty of Shackamaxon (The Penn Treaty), signed by Lenape (Delaware) Indians and William Penn in 1682. This treaty allowed Penn to purchase Indian territory so he could build present-day Philadelphia; it represented fifty years of friendship between the two groups.

In spite of numerous treaties, the majority of colonists and Indians experienced major conflicts. Continual disputes over land encroachment, treaty modifications, and wars between the Indians and the settlers continued with major loss of lives on both sides. In 1754 the British established the Superintendent of Indian Affairs to help manage the ongoing problems. After the Revolutionary War, the newly formed United States Congress established itself as the central authority over the Indians to protect them and preserve the peace. The U.S. Constitution set forth a unique relationship between Indians and the federal government that is distinct from that of any other minority group in America. The first federal Indian reservation was established in 1786, and tribes were relocated away from the bulging cities of the new United States. In 1787 the Northwest Ordinance stated

> The utmost of good faith shall always be observed toward the Indians; their land and property shall never be taken away from them without their consent; and their property, rights and liberty shall never be invaded by Congress; but laws founded in justice and humanity shall from time to time be made for preventing wrongs to them, and for preserving peace and friendships with them. (Dennis, 1971, p. 19)

Congress designated Native Americans as members of independent foreign nations so that the government could sign land and boundary treaties with them. This designation excluded Native Americans from the civil protections afforded American citizens, and Indians were subject to the "just and lawful wars authorized by Congress for the purposes of keeping the peace." By 1824 Secretary of War John C. Calhoun created the Bureau of Indian Affairs (BIA); however it took ten years before Congress authorized its establishment. During the congressional discussion regarding establishment of the BIA, five "Civilized Tribes" consisting of peoples from the Chickasaw, Cherokee, Creek, Choctaw, and

Seminole were relocated to new lands west of the Mississippi that would later become Oklahoma. Between 1832 and 1842 14 more tribes were relocated to reservations by military action. These relocations resulted in the deaths of 4,000 Cherokee, or one-fourth of their number (Green & Tonnesen, 1991). These historically independent and distinctly different tribes were moved to a single reservation without regard for their distinct differences. The U.S. government still regards them as a single tribe.

The reservations that resulted from such locations were designed through treaties to be solely under tribal control and separate from state governments. Treaties focused upon cessions of land from the Indian tribes to the United States in exchange for land that would be designated as secure and sovereign. By the late 1850s the westward expansion found the federal government in the middle of rewriting treaties to gain more land from existing tribal reservations. In a period of ten years, over 53 treaties were renegotiated to acquire over 174 million acres of Indian land. The prevailing attitude of the time ignored Indian independence and supplanted it with the notion that Indians should be "wards of the government entitled to its fostering care and protection." This notion had the effect of allowing the nationalization of Indian land holdings. In the final analysis, the removal of Indians to reservations excluded them from the American economy, afforded them no civil or voting rights, and excluded them from the American political system.

Continual conflicts between settlers and Indians prompted the formation of a Congressional "peace commission." Congress "agreed with the commission that the root of the problems lay in the treaty process. The solution, however, according to federal officials, lay not in the improved adherence to the treaties, but in discontinuing treatymaking and solving the Indian problem by absorbing tribes into mainstream America" (Green & Tonnesen, 1991, p. 51).

Allotment and Assimilation

In the late 1880s it became apparent to U.S. policy makers that the reservation system was not the appropriate mechanism to foster the assimilation of Native people into the American mainstream. Assimilation would be possible only if Indians became more like Europeans, so governmental policies shifted toward the eradication of Native American cultural folkways. Various rituals that were key to tribal life were outlawed by the U.S. government, and the resulting resistance from Indian groups led to violent and oppressive incidents. Among those incidents was the famous Wounded Knee Creek Massacre of 1890 that resulted from prohibitions against the Ghost Dance Ritual.

Further attempts to assimilate Native Americans into the mainstream culture involved such tactics as removing children from their parents to be raised in white-run boarding schools, enforcing English-only rules, enforcing the wearing of "American dress," and adopting Christian religious values (Nagel, 1996; Nies, 1996; Olson & Wilson, 1984). The status of Native American tribes rested upon two concepts. First, Indian tribes were wards of the nation, depending upon the federal government for food, protection, and basic survival. Second, they owe no allegiance to the state governments and therefore receive from them no protection. In *United States v. Kagama,* 118 U.S. 375 (1886), the Court noted "because of the local ill feeling, the people of the States where they are found are often their deadliest enemies. From their weakness and helplessness, so largely due to

FOCUS BOX • *The Wounded Knee Massacre*

The Wounded Knee Massacre at the Pine Ridge Reservation is noted as the "last major bloody encounter" between Indians and government troops. On December 29, 1890, U.S. soldiers fearing a resurgence of the Ghost Dance religion massacred 250 Indian men, women, and children at Wounded Knee Creek in the southwestern part of South Dakota. The Ghost Dance religion involved a "vision quest" through prayer, dancing, fasting, and forms of self-mutilation to exemplify dedication and sincerity. The "vision quest" religious ceremony anticipated that one day the earth will be transformed to its original state before the "white man" and the dead buffalo and Indians will return. The ceremony created heightened states of arousal for participants. The government expressed concerns over the resurgence of this "odd form of ritual" and sent in troops to suppress these activities. Sitting Bull, the most famous Chief of Hunkapapa, Western (Teton) Sioux, and the leader of the largest group of Plains Indians in history, was suspected of inciting ceremonial activi-

ties. He was arrested and killed by Indian police. Other Sioux angered over the death of Sitting Bull and frustrated with the reservation system refused to agree to the demands of U.S. troops sent to control the Ghost Dance movement. A skirmish began, and soldiers using rapid-fire Hodgkiss rifles opened fire and killed over 250 Indian men, women and children.

Wounded Knee is considered a holy place and was used as the site for a meeting of over 200 traditional activists, members of the American Indian Movement, in 1973 that occupied the Tribal Council buildings. The Occupation turned in to a 73-day siege with U.S. Marshalls and the FBI. The activists chose this site in remembrance of the tragic loss of life in 1890 and used this venue to draw attention to the declining conditions of reservation life. At the end of the Occupation, two Indians and one FBI agent were dead, and many traditionalists were imprisoned or fled their homes to escape imprisonment. (Olson & Wilson, 1984; Wall & Arden, 1990)

the course of dealing of the Federal government with them, and the treaties in which it has been promised, there arises the duty of protection, and with it the power" (PL 95-608, p. 7536).

Near the end of the nineteenth century there occurred various legislative mandates and government efforts toward assimilation of Native Americans. The Commissioner of Indian Affairs proposed that Indians could not become self sufficient without individual ownership of land, so the Indian Allotment Act or the Dawes Act of 1887 sought to create farming and property ownership opportunities for Indians (Dennis, 1971; Nies, 1996; Olson & Wilson, 1984; Philip, 1999). Selected Native American lands and specific tribal groups deemed appropriate for this plan were allowed to participate in a BIA effort that distributed reservation land into individual allotments for persons having *one-half Indian blood or more.* Each eligible family received 160 acres, single adults over 18 years of age received 80 acres, and other single youth received 40 acres. The allotment process tended to give some of the worst agricultural land to individuals, leaving prime surplus land to be sold to non-Indian investors for development. The Dawes Act conveniently transformed native land holdings in order to dissolve tribal governments so that Oklahoma could become a state in 1907. As a result, the Indian Territory changed drastically in a short period of time. In 1881, Native Americans held 155 million acres, and by 1910 they held only 59 million. Currently, approximately 52 million acres of land are considered Indian country.

The Curtis Act of 1898 terminated tribal sovereignty, abolishing Indian tribal laws and courts with hopes of having Native American culture disappear from history (Jaimes, 1999; Nies, 1996; Olson & Wilson, 1984).

The assimilation process was an enormous failure. This attempt at forced adaptation into the mainstream, the removal of children from families, and the diminishment and elimination of the status of elders and wisdomkeepers did not foster assimilation but did devastate the cultures. Congress followed the effects upon Indian communities of the Dawes Act and found that the allotment process was a debacle. Unemployment, starvation, disease, and poor education and health plagued Indian groups, and the near extinction of Native American culture occurred during this period. Forces sympathetic to the elimination of Indian culture pushed for the Indian Reorganization Act of 1934, and there began changes in allotment and assimilation policies. Tribal governments were reinstituted, and BIA Commissioner John Collier noted that the preservation of Indian heritage was of utmost importance to the survival of that people. He believed cultural pluralism, not assimilation, to be the answer. Nies (1996) notes that "the Indian New Deal did not fundamentally change the relationship between Indians and larger American society, although it did curb some of the worst abuses" (p. 325).

The reform period occurring between 1928 and 1945 is recognized for promoting the exercise of sovereignty for tribal governments and tribal courts. The Indian Reorganization Act provided a framework for the transfer of power from the BIA and state government to tribes.

The Termination Period

The end of World War II provided an opportunity for America to review the sad history of social policy toward Native Americans. The end of the war meant international peace for a time, and promised new social and economic opportunities. Having Native Americans on reservations seemed archaic and oppressive, and came into conflict with prevailing middle-class values. Many Americans recognized that Indian reservations were not "permanent homelands with their own dynamic histories and cultures. Instead, they stereotyped reservations as outmoded concentration camps for captive people, rural slums and backwaters where conquered tribes required outside assistance to obtain their freedom from an antiquated form of colonial rule" (Philip, 1999, p. 172). This encouraged the abolishment of the reservation system to enable Native Americans to join capitalistic models of achievement. Termination of federal services to tribal communities was based on the premise that Native Americans were self-sufficient, had economic stability, and were ready for assimilation into the dominant culture. The rationale was that federal intervention was no longer needed and the practice of wardship was interfering with Indians being absorbed into the population (Nagel, 1996).

During 1945 and 1962, 13 tribes were terminated by Congress. The termination act meant that certain tribes would lose their land base and their right to special services from the federal government. They would lose a trust status with the United States and their tax-exempt status for their lands. While they were compensated for the land loss, it is interesting to note that the termination of tribes corresponds with the discovery of significant mineral deposits on reservation lands. It was estimated that over one-third of mineral resources in America were under reservation control, including 60 percent of America's uranium resources—so vital to an emerging nuclear age (Jaimes, 1999).

The largest tribal community to be terminated was the Menominees in Wisconsin. The Oregon Klamaths lost their tribal identity, and hundreds of rancherias and communities throughout the United States lost federal protection and services. Many had to sell their land to pay taxes and provide health and education services for their communities (Nies, 1996).

Many tribes that were not terminated witnessed their tribal sovereignty diminished. Public Law 280 had the greatest impact on reservations, allowing state court jurisdiction in some specified states on some reservations. It transferred civil and criminal jurisdictions over tribal lands in California, Minnesota, Nebraska, Oregon, and Wisconsin. Health and education services became state responsibilities, thereby removing tribal jurisdiction. The termination policies removed approximately 35,000 Native Americans to urban areas. In 1961, the National Congress of American Indians declared termination to be "the greatest threat to Indian survival since the military campaigns of the 1800s" (Nies, 1996, p. 355). By 1962, termination policies were eliminated, and many of the landholdings and federal services were restored. However, the movements toward self-determination and activism were in a large part based on these termination policies.

The events occurring during the Termination Period of Native American history created new awareness regarding the importance of land trusts between Indians and the federal government. The Bureau of Indian Affairs (2000) now recognizes approximately 275 Indian land areas in the United States, administered as Indian reservations, pueblos, rancherias, or communities. This accounts for approximately 56.2 million acres. The BIA notes that the largest land area of 16 million acres is the Navajo Reservation in the states of Arizona, New Mexico, and Utah. Smaller reservations account for only 100 to 1,000 acres, while the smallest reservation accounts for less than 100 acres. The movement toward self-determination ignited a sense of ethnic pride and promoted autonomy of tribal lands.

Self-Determination

The government's plan to disperse Native Americans into the mainstream of America proved to be a jumpstart for political activism by tribal groups. The 1960s were an era of social unrest and civil rights activism throughout America, and the civil rights era provided a window into the world of underrepresented groups in America's mainstream. A renewal in ethnic pride dominated the American landscape. Terms such as *Black Power, Brown Power,* and *Red Power* revealed militant support of ethnic identity within the dominant culture. It was also a time when urban Indians, many of whom were scattered throughout the American landscape, sought to unite together with small and large tribal communities to form political organizations to reclaim their heritage and land rights. The movement for ethnic identity as a Nation of People promoted vast changes in laws and legislation between 1960 and 1980. President Lyndon Johnson's speech to Congress on "The Forgotten Americans" proposed "a new goal for our Indian programs: A goal that ends the old debate about 'termination' of Indian programs and stresses self-determination as a goal that erases old attitudes of paternalism and promotes partnership and self-help"

FOCUS BOX • *The Occupation of Alcatraz*

On November 20, 1969, as a statement about the federal-tribal relationship, conditions of reservations, and ethnic unrest, 89 Indian college students occupied Alcatraz Island in the San Francisco Bay. The original occupiers claimed the island by "right of discovery" and used an old treaty from 1868 as their foundation for reclaiming all lands originally occupied by Indian tribes once the federal government abandons the property. The occupation lasted 20 months, with thousands of protestors joining in the occupation. Johnson, Nagel, and Champagne (1997) affirmed that the

> Alcatraz occupation and the activism that followed offer firm evidence to counter commonly held views that Indians are powerless in the face of history, are weakened remnants of disappearing cultures and communities . . . and stands as a symbol of long-standing grievances and increasing impatience with a political system slow to respond to native rights. (p. 30–31)

The occupation was suppressed for the most part by the FBI but also through Indian organizations that chose to confront Indian issues through conventional means. The goal to draw national awareness to the plight of Native Americans was met. Changes in national approaches to dealing with Indians came to the forefront. The United Native Americans, the American Indian Movement, and the National Indian Youth Council inspired a sense of nationalistic pride for Indians living on reservations. Other Indian organizations and many traditionalists found the militant approach divisive and disruptive. However, they could not deny that this approach inspired thousands of Native Americans and brought national awareness and new opportunities to Indians (Olson & Wilson, 1984). In 1970 President Richard Nixon stated in a message to Congress that

> The special relationship between Indians and the Federal government is the result of solemn obligations . . . the goal of any new national policy toward Indian people must: strengthen the Indian's sense of autonomy without threatening his sense of community. . . . There is no reason why Indian communities should be deprived of the privilege of self-determination merely because they receive monetary support from the Federal government. (Nagel, 1996, p. 217)

(Green & Tonnesen, 1991). Solutions for Indian problems without compromise of sovereignty rights came to the forefront of the Indian policy debate.

The 1970s are noted for providing Indian tribes and individuals with more legal and policy victories than had occurred during the previous 200 years of federal–tribal relationships (Nagel, 1996). The Alaska Native Claims Settlement Act of 1971 provided a new land settlement for native people of Alaska, transferring 40 million acres in a land grant and $962 million as compensation. The Indian Self-Determination and Education Assistance Act of 1976 lessened Bureau of Indian Affairs control in Indian communities by allowing tribes to make contracts with agencies for specific tribal functions. The Indian Child Welfare Act of 1978 (PL 95-608) set minimum standards for the removal of Indian children from their families through adoption, foster care, or boarding schools, and requires that the majority of adoption and guardianship proceedings be handled through tribal courts with preferences for Indian over non-Indian guardians. Also in 1978, a joint resolution on American Indians' religious freedom was addressed by the 95th Congress (PL 95-341) stating that

> henceforth it shall be the policy of the United States to protect and preserve for American Indians their inherent right of freedom to believe, express, and exercise the traditional

religions of the American Indian, Eskimo, Aleut, and Native Hawaiians including but not limited to access to sites, use and possession of sacred objects, and the freedom to worship through ceremonials and traditional rites.

The 1980s are recognized as the decade of Indian law, strengthened by the Supreme Court's recognition of "fundamental attributes of sovereignty" such as non-Indian taxation of reservation lands. For example, in 1985 the Court ruled that three Indian tribes from Oneida nation could claim damages for property taken in 1795. The Indian Gaming Regulatory Act of 1988 allows Indian gaming operations on reservations. The 1990s are heralded as a time of new tribal sophistication in wielding political power for community resources. Tribal courts are increasing in numbers and professional legal standing, and the accompanying ethnic self-determination creates a sense of national community through personal and collective identity.

Numbers

The best estimates available from the 1600s indicate that between 5 and 10 million Native American people inhabited North America. As was discussed earlier, disease, wars, starvation, slavery, and policies designed to eliminate Native American culture drastically changed the population. By 1890 the Indian population was 248,253 people, and in ten years the population dropped by 1,000 people per year. The 1990 Census indicated there were 1,959,234 American Indians and Alaska Natives living in the United States and, out of that number, 1,878,285 were American Indians, 57,152 were Eskimos, and 23,797 were Aleuts. The current estimate for American Indian, Eskimo, and Aleuts accounts for 0.9 percent of society, with 2,428,000 million people (U.S. Census, 2000). The median age of this diverse ethnic group is 27.8 years, with the population approximately equal for males and females. The expected increase of this population by 2010 is an additional 150,000 people and by 2050 the number will increase to 4.3 million. These figures are expected to represent approximately 1 percent of the total U.S. population. Currently, approximately 50 percent of the population live on or adjacent to federal Indian reservations, with the majority of Native Americans living in the states of Oklahoma, New Mexico, Arizona, and California (Bureau of Indian Affairs, 2000).

The largest number of urban American Indians lives in the Los Angeles area, with a population of approximately 58,000. Oklahoma City has the highest percentage overall for Native Americans, accounting for 4 percent of their population. There are two tribal communities that account for 28 percent of the American Indian population. The Cherokee account for approximately 308,000 people, representing 16.4 percent and the Navajo account for 275,000 people, representing 11.7 percent. Examples of other tribal memberships range from Lumbees of North Carolina with approximately 48,444 members, Choctaw of Philadelphia, Mississippi, with 8,300 members, and Santa Rosa Rancheria of Lemoore, California, with 400 residents. Many tribal communities have had federal recognition for centuries. However, there were many that lost status during periods of our history and wanted recognition. In 1978 the Bureau of Indian Affairs provided the following criteria to officially claim American Indian status and to qualify for federal services. Tribal groups must be recognized as:

FOCUS BOX • *Tribal Recognition Process*

ASSISTANT SECRETARY-INDIAN AFFAIRS ACKNOWLEDGES HURON POTAWATOMI, INC., AS A TRIBE OF AMERICAN INDIANS

Ada E. Deer, Assistant Secretary-Indian Affairs, will formally acknowledge the Huron Potawatomi, Inc., also known as the Nottawaseppi Huron Band and a tribe of American Indians under 25 CFR 83.

An acknowledgment ceremony will be held at the Daughters of the American Revolution (DAR) building, on December 19, 1995, at 9:30 A.M., in the Assembly Room. The DAR building is across 18th Street, from the Department of the Interior building on the east side. Attendees should use the D Street entrance on the DAR at 1776 D Street N.W. This ceremony is being held at the DAR, as opposed to the Department of the Interior, because of the federal government shutdown.

The Huron Potawatomi, Inc., consists of 602 descendants of a band which signed the Treaty of Greenville in 1795 with the federal government.

The Huron Potawatomi community has consistently been identified as a settlement of Michigan Potawatomi Indians in federal, state, and local records. The tribe maintained usage of the Potawatomi language and had a high level of in-group or patterned out-group marriages through 1960. At least through 1934, over 50 percent of the group resided at or near the Pine Creek reservation.

Traditional chiefs led the tribe through 1934. From 1934 to 1970, leadership was by a committee closely associated with the Methodist Indian mission on the Pine Creek reservation. After incorporating in 1970, the tribe elected a chairman and council to administer its affairs. These leaders regularly represented the tribe with the Bureau of Indian Affairs and with the public, as well as supervise internal reservation activities.

ASSISTANT SECRETARY-INDIAN AFFAIRS FINDS THE RAMAPOUGH MOUNTAIN INDIANS, INC.-NEW JERSEY DO NOT MEET FEDERAL STANDARDS FOR ACKNOWLEDGMENT

Ada E. Deer, Assistant Secretary-Indian Affairs, issued a notice today declining to acknowledge the Ramapough Mountain Indians Inc., as a Federally recognized tribe.

A Proposed Finding to decline to acknowledge the Ramapough Mountain Indians Inc., was first published in the FEDERAL REGISTER on December 8, 1993, and the original 180-day comment period was extended until May 8, 1995. The 60-day comment period for the Ramapoughs to respond to third-party comments ended on July 10, 1995.

As a result of this publication, the Bureau of Indian Affairs conducted an extensive review of (1) the Ramapoughs' response to the Proposed Finding, (2) the comments submitted by interested and third parties, and (3) the Ramapough's response to the public comments, and (4) researched additional historic records in order to arrive at a final determination regarding their status.

Based on this review, the Bureau of Indian Affairs has determined that the Ramapough Mountain Indians, Inc., do not meet three of the seven mandatory criteria for acknowledgement as an Indian tribe under Federal law. Specifically, the Ramapoughs failed to meet criteria b, c, and e, of the federal regulations (25 CFR 83.7) because they did not exist as a distinct community from historic times to the present, did not maintain political influence or authority over their members from historic contact to present, and their membership does not descend from a tribe of American Indians or from tribes that combined and functioned as a single autonomous entity.

This decision will become effective in 90 days unless the tribe requests a reconsideration before the Interior Board of Indian Appeals.

a single Indian group which has existed since its first sustained contact with European cultures on a continuous basis to the present; that its members live in a distinct autonomous community perceived by others as Indian; that it has maintained some sort of authority with a governing system by which its members abide; that all its members can be traced genealogically to an historic tribe. (Nagel, 1996, p. 242)

Labels

The label of Native American is dependent upon many factors, from eligibility for federal and state services to claims of racial and ethnic origin. The Census Bureau depends upon self-identification of ethnic and racial categorization. The Indian Health Service provides services to people who are enrolled in recognized tribes. Numerous reasons for people to identify themselves as Indian has changed over the years. There was a 72 percent increase in population for American Indians between the 1970 and 1980 census (Nagel, 1999). Census changes in the 1960s, 1970s, and 1980s correlate with people claiming the "new identification" of being Indian. Some of the increase in population during this "self-identification era" is due to adults' reclaiming their "Indianness." People who either were not comfortable with their status as American Indians or were unaware of their historical roots found a sense of pride in claiming Indian ancestry. Another factor affecting the changes in the American Indian population is racial intermarriage. The 1980 census data indicate that nearly half (48 percent) of American Indians were intermarried with another race, compared to blacks who self-reported intermarriage rates of 2 percent and whites at 1 percent. The rates at which individuals claimed Indian heritage for the mixed-race children vary, depending upon region. Families living in non-Indian areas would claim their children as Indians approximately 33 to 45 percent of the time, while families living in Indian areas would claim their children as Indians 36 to 73 percent of the time (Nagel, 1999).

Another factor related to the official designation of American Indian is related to the degree of ancestry. The concern over "full or mixed blood" as a measurement of ancestry was first noted in the 1740 slave code in South Carolina. Indian women and black male slaves were routinely intermixed. Black male slaves numbered three to one compared to black female slaves, and there was a dramatic decline in numbers of Indian males due to disease, enslavement, and war during the colonial period. This created communities of Afro-Indians through intermarriage. The slave code recognized the growing numbers of the mixture of black and Indian slaves (called mulattos by early Americans), and designated regulations specifically for them.

European, African, and Indian heritage was historically intermixed during the colonial period. Since then, federal policy identifies Indian heritage through the "blood quotient." In order to apply for federal recognition as a member of a tribal group, individuals must complete a Certificate of Degree of Indian or Alaska Native Blood (CDIB). The Bureau of Indian Affairs (2000) requires individuals to show a relationship to "an enrolled member(s) of a federally recognized Indian tribe, whether it is through your birth mother or birth father, or both. A federally recognized Indian tribe means an Indian or Alaska Native tribe, band, nation, pueblo, village, or community which appears on the list of recognized tribes published in the Federal Register by the Secretary of the Interior (25 U.S.C. § 479a-1(a)." The regulations further state that an individual's "degree of Indian blood is computed from lineal ancestors of Indian blood who were enrolled with a federally recognized Indian tribe or whose names appear on the designated base rolls of a federally recognized Indian tribe."

The idea of quantifying a "blood quotient" becomes ominous for many American Indians. During the 1950s, thousands of Native Americans became part of the urban landscape of America through relocation programs. The loss of ethnic identity through assimilation and intermarriage "accelerated the process of biological hybridization" (Jaimes, 1999, p. 161). "Claiming to be Indian" is also a concern with other American Indians. Many reported that this resurgence of identification must be addressed. The Cherokee population increased 300 percent between the 1970 and 1980 census. Questions arose concerning the "racial purity" of those who identified themselves as Cherokee Indians (Nagel, 1996). Some tribal members associate increasing claims of Indian heritage with the lucrative gaming business on tribal lands. They argue that "you can't just turn up and say 200 years ago I had a Mohican great-great-great-great-grandfather. You don't become tribal overnight. Only people who can prove a continuous social and political contact are admitted to the tribe" (Taylor, 1997, p. 93).

Tribal identity and self-reporting issues continue to influence the census data concerning Native Americans. It is reasonable to expect that these numbers will fluctuate by small percentages as people recognize and redefine their American Indian ethnicity.

Worldview and Relationship to the Criminal Justice System

While there are distinct differences between tribal groups, there are some generalizations that can be made about the worldview of American Indians. Their belief systems, culture, religion, attitudes and relationship to the criminal justice system are better understood through their collective worldview.

Most ethnic Indian groups believe that there is no separation between earth, sky, religion, medicine, animals, or people. Some global statements can be made regarding the relationships between American Indian cultural values and those of European Americans and the dominant culture. These statements can define differences in relationships to nature and individual responsibility. For this discussion we can designate five broad cultural philosophies that separate American Indians from the dominant culture. They are:

American Indians	*Dominant Culture*
1. sacred relationship to nature	1. conquering relationship over nature
2. life should be in harmony	2. life should be filled with excitement
3. a sense of community	3. a sense of individuality
4. a reliance on interdependence	4. a reliance on independence
5. cooperation is power	5. competition is power

These comparative worldviews reflect contrasts in beliefs and approaches to life. With these beliefs it is understandable that conflicts and trust issues would have dominated the relationship between these two groups for the last 400 years.

Trust

American Indian individual and collective views about land are based upon their sense of life, Mother Earth, community, and ownership. In general, tribal communities historically viewed land ownership as a foreign and confusing concept. Olson and Wilson (1984) conclude that American Indians believed "land was not a commodity—not a tangible, lifeless item to be measured and sold. It was instead, a living thing in its own right, imbued with a soul and held in trust by all the living for their use and the use of their children" (p. 22). Through the connection to Mother Earth, the belief in sacredness of land and ancestors dictates protection of land and of gravesites that hold "dear ancestors." In an address to the UN Assembly in 1985, Tadodaho Chief Leon Shenandoah Haudenosaunee shared, "These are our times and our responsibilities. Every human being has a sacred duty to protect the welfare of our Mother Earth from whom all life comes. In order to do this we must recognize the enemy—the one within us. We must begin with ourselves. . . ." (Wall & Arden,1990, p. 102). Belief in the value of land and ancestors helped shape the 1990 Native American Grave Protection And Repatriation Act. This act protects Indian gravesites from looting and destruction and requires that all culturally identifiable tribal artifacts and ancestral prehistoric remains must be repatriated.

European colonists believed that land ownership afforded power and influence. This concept was in direct conflict with Native American belief systems, a conflict that created centuries of violence and mistrust between the two groups. The federal government continued to break charters, legislation, and treaties. This further aggravated a historic lack of trust and fear of government among Native American people, and is still present on reservations and among urban Indians today.

Family Structure

There is no single family structure model that applies to the diverse tribal communities within Native American culture. Historic accounts indicate that Indian groups were both matrilineal and patrilineal. Hopi men married into the wife's family and had very passive roles in authority, while other groups followed a pattern of male family structure for discipline and authority. A current example of matrilineal structure as it relates to property occurs in the Pueblo community. Tribal courts in this community recognize that property belongs to females and is divided according to matrilineal definitions in divorce cases (Melton, 2000). There can be separate structures and a blending of gender structures depending on the customs of each tribal group. However, there are common practices among Indian groups regarding their treatment of extended family. What most people in the dominant culture recognize as the nuclear family is defined by Native Americans as the extended family of aunts, uncles, grandparents, and cousins, and all share in the responsibility of child rearing. This culture finds what many family studies have indicated, that extended families can actually strengthen the community's commitment to children. It is common that many children will spend considerable time away from their parents while in the care of extended family members.

Though shared responsibilities for raising children should create a healthy, loving environment for development, Indian communities are not free of instances of reported child abuse. The Bureau of Indian Affairs (2000) reported that child abuse (physical and sexual abuse) is among the top three crimes on reservations. The incidences of suicide among Native Americans between 15 to 24 is approximately three times that of the U.S. rate for other ethnic groups in that age category.

Though there are probably several reasons for the changing American Indian family dynamic, one fact still remains. There is definitive value associated with the roles and positions of individuals in Indian culture, and those individuals wield influence within their communities. For instance, the title of "elder" carries the honor and distinction of wisdom and teaching for the entire community through oral tradition. It is through oral tradition that the history of culture and community is shared among people, and that knowledge of the past is given to future generations. This knowledge includes personal reflections, accounts of events, and stories of incidents that incorporate the experiences of human and nonhuman beings and of their ancestors (Wilson, 1997). The power of sharing stories about the past represents more to Indian culture than simply oral history, it is a way to transmit culture and keep alive traditions, mores, and folkways.

Stories told by elders and other spiritual leaders have tremendous power to create a spirit of community by connecting generations to each other. Peacemaker, the founder of the Iroquois Confederacy in 1000 A.D. and a respected elder, is credited with a simple wisdom that has been faithfully expressed to subsequent generations through the oral tradition. It states, "Think not forever of yourselves, O Chiefs, nor of your own generation. Think of continuing generations of our families, think of our grandchildren and of those yet unborn, whose faces are coming from beneath the ground" (Wall & Arden, 1990, p. 7).

Religion

The sense of community that elders and spiritual leaders profess unites the numerous ethnic groups under the label of American Indian. This sense of community is strengthened by listening and allowing time for the "universal spirit" and for nature to be part of the experience of conversation. This communal connection to each other, to nature, and to their environment is woven into the religious practices of Native Americans.

Religious practices of Native Americans vary greatly, and carry influences of Judeo-Christian beliefs brought by colonists. While many American Indians participate in Christian religious experiences, they incorporate rituals and ceremonial artifacts from their original beliefs. In an effort to preserve religious traditions and connect various ethnic groups, the Native American Church was formed during the first part of the twentieth century. A controversial aspect of this new religion that brought adherents into conflict with the criminal justice system was the ceremonial use of hallucinogenic peyote, which reportedly allows worshipers to enter a spiritual world (Nagel, 1996). The 1994 Native American Free Exercise of Religion Act strengthened the religious rights of American Indians originally outlined in the American Indian Religious Freedom Act of 1978, and allowed the judicious use of peyote by the Native American Church members as part of their religious ceremonies.

The growing desire to recreate an ancestral religious belief system parallels a similar trend to recapture and preserve indigenous languages. Some estimates show that between 200 and 300 distinct language groups were present at the time of the first contact with Europeans. The vast majority of those languages and dialects are lost, and the ongoing gradual loss of native languages is thought by some theorists to be an unfortunate part of the assimilation process.

In 1980, 74 percent of American Indians spoke only English in their homes and, by 1990, that number rose to 77 percent (Nagel, 1999). The largest among Indian nations are more likely to keep their original language and also speak English, and recent trends indicate a popular interest in traditional language preservation. In May 1997 the Fourth Annual Stabilizing Indigenous Languages Symposium met in Arizona. The purpose of that symposium was to recognize and acknowledge the cultural power of language on traditions and beliefs. Presentations and research data focused upon how best to retain and teach tribal languages to future generations. The self-determination movement has helped to create more emphasis on Indian pride and new acceptance of tribal histories. This is associated with changes in locus of control and responsibility.

Specific Issues Related to Crime, Law Enforcement, and Courts

Locus of Control and Responsibility

The concepts of locus of control and locus of responsibility were addressed in previous chapters. The internalization of these concepts is influenced by one's culture. Cultural norms and mores provide a backdrop for learning to be internally or externally motivated. The place of one's personal control and responsibility, either internal or external, plays a significant role in how one responds to the criminal justice system.

The historical review of American Indians reveals a people whose fate has been in the hands of others. Their success or failure has been determined by the system, fostering a tradition of external locus of control and responsibility. However, incredible adaptation, survival, and affirmation of heritage in the face of significant resistance also punctuate this history. In spite of the past, Native Americans have been relatively successful in building bridges between hundreds of tribal groups, reclaiming a sense of history, and building a sense of self-reliance. For these reasons, many researchers have identified a Native American worldview consisting of elements of internal locus of control and responsibility. This dimension helps explain the focus of many Native Americans on securing identity first within their own ethnic group, and then with the dominant culture. This often occurs in spite of the discrimination and prejudice they experience.

Political activism during the 1960s and 1970s united all Native American groups to work toward a national recognition of America's first people, however, this new sense of "ethnic renewal" has come at a cost. Poverty-stricken living conditions, poor schools and health services, and some breakdown in the extended family have contributed to high crime rates in Indian communities. Di Gregory and Manuel (1997) attribute the social and economic conditions in Indian communities to circumstances that are more complex than those in non-Indian areas of the United States. They cite "chronic unemployment, low levels of educational attainment, geographic displacement, and family disruption" as elements that help to foster the rise in all crime categories now confronting Indian communities.

Crime Rates

In their U.S. Department of Justice report recommending criminal justice improvements for Indian communities, Di Gregory and Manuel (1997) outlined the need to ensure basic public safety. Their report found that homicide rates for Indian males are almost three times higher than those for white males. While the nation as a whole experienced a 22 percent decline in violent crime rates between 1992 and 1996, homicides among American Indian lands rose sharply. Some tribal lands report higher crime rates than those found in the most violent of American cities. The report cited a study of the Ft. Peck Reservation in Montana, where the homicide rate is twice that of one of the most violent American cities, New Orleans. In 1996 the Navajo nation had a homicide rate that was equivalent to the 20 most violent cities in the United States. The report also found a steady increase in gang violence on Indian reservations. For example, the Menominee Reservation in Wisconsin showed a 293 percent increase in gang-related juvenile arrests between 1990 and 1994.

The gang activity reported for Indian communities closely follows that reported for urban street gangs in American cities. Shared characteristics include distinctive attire, gang signs, violence, and the use of weapons as a means to create group identity. Gangs among Indian communities differ from those in American cities in that they are not as motivated by economic enterprise, but there is the same tendency to use violence as a way to gain status within groups. Status, recognition, and a sense of belonging among Indian gangs closely parallels the reasoning behind gang membership for youth living at the beginning of the twentieth century as well as for those who join urban gangs today.

The early work of Shaw and McKay in the 1920s focused on gang involvement as a mechanism of empowerment to hundreds of poor immigrant children. Gaining a sense of empowerment is also important to poor Indian adolescents. The early inner-city gang members came from families that experienced weak family controls, poverty, and lack of social identity within traditional society. The traditional society of tribal groups is somewhat fragmented, with many historic interruptions invading American Indian customs and values. This results in self-identity crises for adolescents. Tribal history is filled with ethnic and cultural traditions, but these traditions come into direct conflict with the dominant culture. Children turn away from familial attachments to seek attachments with other youths, and the resulting conflicts within their families widen the gap between parental and tribal control. Gang membership then becomes an avenue to satisfy personal needs for love, recognition, and identity.

Di Gregory and Manuel (1997) described some shocking examples of gang violence in Indian communities in their U.S. Department of Justice report. They noted that in 1996 "a man on the Laguna Pueblo reservation was bludgeoned with a beer bottle, stabbed 72 times, then left with a ritualistic triangle carved on his side." On this same reservation that covers 500,000 acres, the nine police officers that patrol the area were assaulted 34 times by juveniles. In a two-year period between 1992 and 1994, drive-by shootings rose from 1 to 55 in the Salt River Pima-Maricopa community in Arizona. This growing gang problem is exasperated by a growing juvenile recidivism rate due to lack of detention facilities, probation officers, and other social services.

The 1999 Bureau of Justice Statistics report on American Indians and crime followed earlier studies and continues to report a bleak picture of increased criminal activity in Indian country. Bureau of Justice Statistics director Jan Chaiken reported that "The

FOCUS BOX

Richard Littlebear was the keynote speaker at the Fourth Annual Stabilizing Indigenous Languages Symposium in Flagstaff, Arizona, in 1997. One of his ideas for reclaiming indigenous languages suggested the involvement of young people in Indian communities. He noted that more young people are looking to urban gangs for those things that will give them a sense of identity, importance, and belonging, and suggested that they might seek these things from their our own tribal traditions. He stressed the reaffirmation of self-identity through tribal enculturation, noting that tribes have distinctive colors, clothes, music, heroes, symbols, rituals, and "turf." "We American Indian tribes have these too and we need to teach our children about the positive aspects of American Indian life at an early age so they know who they are. This approach could inoculate children against the disease of gangs. This approach could transfer the young people's loyalty back to our own tribes and families, and restore the frayed social fabric of our reservations. We need to make our children see [that] our languages, cultures, traditions and rituals are viable and valuable as anything they could possibly see on television, movies or videos or anyplace else in the dominant culture." (adapted from Littlebear, 1999)

findings reveal a disturbing picture of American Indian involvement in crimes as victims and offenders. Both male and female American Indians experience violent crime at higher rates than people of other races and are more likely to experience interracial violence" (Greenfield & Smith, 1999, p. iii).

Data indicate that, between 1992 and 1996, the average rate for American Indian violent victimization was 124 per 1,000 residents, compared to blacks at 61 per 1,000, whites at 49 per 1,000, and Asians at 29 per 1,000. The report also indicated that alcohol was a major factor in most violent criminal events in Indian communities. The figures revealed that 46 percent of all offenders were drinking prior to the victimization. Self-reports from jailed American Indians indicated that 70 percent were drinking prior to the event that led to incarceration. Arrest rates in Indian communities for driving under the influence (DUI) were more than double those of the total population of America. Alcohol-related crimes are higher per capita on Indian lands than on non-Indian lands, and alcohol appears to be the gateway drug to the use and abuse of marijuana and methamphetamines. Drug and alcohol use is correlated with theft and violent crimes throughout America, and the use of drugs in Indian communities is increasing at an alarming rate. The ability to grow marijuana and to manufacture methamphetamines in secluded rural areas on tribal land contributes to the overall drug trafficking rate and abuse of these illicit drugs.

Law Enforcement and Tribal Courts

The most complicated issues surrounding criminal justice in Indian communities concern jurisdiction of tribal courts. Jurisdictional concerns are related to geography, ethnicity of suspects and victims, types of crimes committed, and provisions within Public Law 280. In 1953 Congress enacted PL 280, which transferred criminal and civil jurisdiction over tribal lands in the states of California, Minnesota, Nebraska, Oregon, and Wisconsin to state and local governments. The Warm Springs Reservation in Oregon, Red Lake Reservation in Minnesota, and Menominee Reservation in Wisconsin were exempt from PL 280. Tribal lands in Alaska that were subject to PL 280 were the communities on the Annette Islands and the Metlakatla tribe. Other provisions of PL 280 affected jurisdiction of tribal courts in Arizona, Iowa, Idaho, Montana, North and South Dakota, and Washington (Vicenti, 1995). This transfer of criminal jurisdiction gave to state and local police the enforcement authority in Indian communities, and cases would be adjudicated in state courts. For areas not affected by PL 280, either the Bureau of Indian Affairs or the tribal councils provide police personnel. In addition, many tribes also contract with local and state police for enforcement support.

This complexity regarding sovereign jurisdiction of tribal councils and courts aggravates further the strained relationship between Native Americans and the criminal justice system. Examples of this strained relationship abound, and often arise from enforcement actions involving non-Indian subjects on Indian lands. Tribal police and courts have no jurisdiction to prosecute non-Indian persons who commit crimes on Indian land. For instance, non-Indian drug traffickers who operate on Indian lands would be prosecuted in state or federal courts. There are two effects that arise from the jurisdiction issues. First, non-Indians are often not prosecuted successfully in state courts because of the perception that crimes on Indian land are Indian issues. Second, Indians who are convicted of crimes by tribal courts are subject to the Indian Civil Rights Act of 1968, which limits tribal criminal sentences to no more than one year in custody and a $5,000 fine, regardless of the crime (Di Gregory & Manuel, 1997). Many Native American liberals and conservatives alike viewed this act as a violation of tribal prerogatives that interferes with their effectiveness to manage their own people (Olson & Wilson, 1984; Vicenti, 1995).

Sponsored by the Office for Victims of Crime (1998), "Upon the Back of a Turtle ... A Cross Cultural Training Curriculum for Federal Criminal Justice Personnel" addressed the complicated issues of jurisdiction in Indian Country. Table 4.1 from their curriculum depicts the relationship between suspect, victim, and jurisdiction in non-PL 280 states.

Current estimates show 2.9 officers per 1,000 citizens in non-Indian communities of under 10,000 population. The Uniform Crime Reports show that an equivalent ratio for Indian communities is 1.3 officers per 1,000 citizens, this despite the higher crime rates in those communities. The approximate 56 million acres of tribal lands in the lower 48 states are patrolled by only 1,600 Bureau of Indian Affairs and tribal uniformed officers. Other tribal lands average less than 1 officer per 1,000 citizens. This shortage is partly due to low pay, poor working conditions, outdated equipment, and vast responsibility without much support (Di Gregory & Manuel, 1997).

To assist in understanding the differences in tribal courts and state and federal court systems Melton (2000) addresses the differences in paradigms. The American justice paradigm has a philosophy of retribution, and is an adversarial process that is guided by codified laws, rules, and procedures. On the other hand, the tribal justice paradigm is based on a holistic philosophy guided by unwritten and customary laws, traditions, and practices. Melton refers to this process as a circle of justice that connects all parties involved, and works towards resolution to attain peace and harmony for the individual as well as the community. Other examples of the differences in paradigms are as follows:

TABLE 4.1 *Indian Country Jurisdiction in Criminal Cases*

Suspect	Victim	Jurisdiction
Indian	Indian	*Misdemeanor: Tribal jurisdiction *Felony: Federal jurisdiction *No state jurisdiction *No federal jurisdiction for misdemeanors
Indian	Non-Indian	*Misdemeanor: Tribal jurisdiction *Felony: Federal jurisdiction *No state jurisdiction
Non-Indian	Indian	*Misdemeanor: Federal jurisdiction *Felony: Federal jurisdiction *Normally not state jurisdiction (the U.S. Attorney may elect to defer prosecution to the state) *No tribal jurisdiction
Non-Indian	Non-Indian	*Misdemeanor: State jurisdiction *Felony: State jurisdiction *Normally U.S. Attorney will decline prosecution *No tribal Jurisdiction
Indian	Victimless	*Misdemeanor: Tribal jurisdiction *Felony: Federal jurisdiction
Non-Indian	Victimless	*Misdemeanor: Usually state jurisdiction *Felony: Usually state jurisdiction *Normally U.S. Attorney will decline prosecution

American Justice Paradigm	Indigenous (native) Justice Paradigm
Vertical power structure	Circular structure of empowerment
Communication is rehearsed	Communication is fluid
Written statutory law derived from rules and procedures	Oral customary law learned as a way of life
Separation of church and state	The spiritual realm is invoked in ceremonies and with prayer
Time-oriented process	No time limits on the process

The tribal courts today are actually based upon the historic institutions utilizing the "normative power of the entire society" to prohibit and correct behavior. The inclusion of family members and elders as well as victims and perpetrators is part of the tribal court process. In spite of PL 280, many tribes have inherent authority over organization of the family and tribal society issues. Carey Vicenti, Chief Judge of the Jicarilla Apache Tribe, noted that, over the last 20 years, tribal courts have made a "sporadic effort to preserve tribal culture," which is at the heart of preserving the traditional way of life. He believes that it is in the "tribal courts that the competing concepts regarding social order, and the place of the individual within the family, the clan, the band and the tribe, will be decided."

Tribal courts vary in their approach to addressing issues of civil and criminal matters. Jurisprudence models incorporate the American court system, traditional courts, family and community forums, the American-traditional hybrid, and models that use combinations of approaches (Melton, 2000; Vicenti, 1995). The tribal court system is a reflection of the concept of human beings that American Indians share across ethnic groups, and dictates that "all aspects of the person and his or her society are integrated. Every action in daily life is read to have meaning and implication to individuals and guides how they interact with tribal society or fulfills obligations imposed by society, law and religion" (Vicenti, 1995).

Incarceration Rates

The 1998 Sourcebook of Criminal Justice Statistics calculated arrest rates for 9,271 law enforcement agencies, with data collected from a 1997 estimated total U.S. population of 183,239,000. The data indicated that whites accounted for approximately 67.1 percent of the arrested population, blacks 30.4 percent, Asian or Pacific Islander 1.2 percent and American Indian or Alaskan Native 1.3 percent. The Native Americans arrested—only 1.3 percent of the total—are equivalent to 132,734 people, or approximately 4 percent of American Indian adult population. The most common categories of offenses charged were violation of liquor laws (3.1%), drunkenness (2.3%), vagrancy (1.9%), and driving under the influence (1.5%). In comparison, whites' most common categories of offenses charged were similar to those of American Indians—driving under the influence (86.3%), liquor law violations (83.5%), and drunkenness (80.3%. For blacks the highest offenses were in the category of robbery (57.1%) and for Asian/Pacific Islanders the category was offenses against family and children (1.9%).

The actual number of American Indians incarcerated as of June 1999 was reported at 19,679. The majority of those were in state or federal prisons (12,858) and in county jails (5,200). The incarceration rates for federal and state prisons and county jails is 797 Indians per 100,000 Indian residents, compared to an average of 682 per 100,000 for other groups. A Bureau of Justice Statistics report on jails affiliated with 53 American Indian tribes in 18 states found 1,621 people incarcerated in the month of June 1999 (Ditton, 1999). This report indicated an 8 percent increase in incarceration rates over the previous year. The study also found that 40 percent of all Native Americans were incarcerated in Arizona, which houses the ten largest facilities.

There are a total of 70 jails and detention centers located on 55 reservations. Most of the facilities were built in the 1960s and 1970s and are in disrepair, are unsafe, and do not meet the basic code requirements. The vast majority of these facilities were designed to hold 10 to 30 inmates and now are operating at 155 percent capacity (Di Gregory & Manuel, 1997; Ditton, 1999). More funding is needed for renovation and repairs, staffing (which is below levels required to operate facilities safely), inmate supplies, education and treatment programs, and staff training. Many facilities reported not having enough blankets, mattresses, and basic hygiene supplies. There are limited opportunities for training and advancement for the officers, and poor working conditions and low pay contribute to the high turnover rate and "burnout" of staff.

Rebuilding Relationships

Building relationships between Native American communities and the criminal justice system must begin with fundamental rebuilding of Native American communities. Issues of poverty and limited resources are associated with criminal activity, and self-identification and self-renewal are key to the health of these communities. Some theorists believe that such phenomena as the financial independence found in the gaming industry will provide some relief from the circumstances associated with crime in Indian communities. While some research shows that only a few tribes are actually benefiting from the gaming industry, the National Indian Gaming Association reported Indian gaming revenue at $8.26 billion in 1999 (10% of total gaming industry in America). The number of tribal governments engaged in gaming is 198, with 326 total gaming operations. Out of 198 tribes involved in gaming, 22 tribal operations account for 56 percent of the total revenue. Out of that number, almost one-third of the gaming revenue comes from two tribes, the Mashantucker Pequots and Shakopee Sioux.

In spite of the impressive gaming dollar amounts, poverty still abounds on reservations. The gaming industry on tribal lands is in the early stages of economic development. Nagel (1996) noted that social and cultural revitalization holds much promise from the gaming income, and that gaming does provide an avenue for economic development of reservation lands. Over 200,000 people are employed in the Indian gaming industry and that number is increasing as more tribes seek gaming operations.

Building relationships with the criminal justice system has improved with the establishment of the Office of Tribal Justice under the Department of Justice (DOJ), Office of the Deputy Attorney General, in 1995. The Office of Tribal Justice has improved communication between DOJ and Indian tribes, maintaining relations with elected tribal officials, coordinating policies, promoting funding, and addressing issues "that are of importance to the Nation's first Americans with renewed effectiveness."

The Department of Justice has also worked at improving law enforcement in Indian communities. The Community Oriented Policing Office has provided assistance to reduce crime rates in tribal lands, and the Federal Bureau of Investigation has dedicated resources to reduce violent crimes and to increase the level of investigation so that criminals can be fully prosecuted. Significant progress is being made toward commitment to law enforcement, to custodial training and development of new training facilities, and to resources that are more accessible to tribal agencies. The attrition rate of new officers is nearly 50 percent, and low pay and poor working conditions drain talented personnel from these agencies within an average of two years.

The need for more personnel and better training facilities continues. Bureau of Indian Affairs officers currently attend the Police Academy at Artesia, New Mexico. This is a satellite facility of the Federal Law Enforcement Training Center (FLETC) in Atlanta. There is an expected need for 4,290 sworn officers to provide minimum coverage to tribal lands. Fostering productive relationships between communities and the criminal justice system requires that this need for uniformed officers be met (Di Gregory & Manuel, 1997).

More programs are being funded to help tribal communities train in-house community members to address social problems of crimes and drugs. New programs have addressed rehabilitation of substance abusers, which in turn lowers recidivism rates. An example of these new approaches to solving crimes in Indian country is the Alaska Native Technical Assistance and Resource Center, coordinated by the Anchorage Justice Center and the University of Alaska. This center is helping natives analyze and solve local crime problems, and it is working with the Substance Abuse and Mental Health Services Administration to implement a comprehensive drug and health treatment program (Di Gregory & Manuel, 1997).

The emergence of recognition for tribal governments and sovereign autonomy will do much to increase opportunities for improving lives and reducing crime. The establishment of positive relationships between the criminal justice system and Indian communities is one of many steps needed to restore a nation of people. Such restoration will have a significant impact on America's future, and the future of generations to come.

Summary

The term *tribe* is generally accepted in refererence to American Indian communities. Some scholars feel this term has negative connotations representing "white creations used by Indians to survive." On the other hand, American Indians commonly refer to their communities with tribal designations and use the term as part of their official names. The labeling of tribal groups in some ways provides ethnic identity and a sense of cultural identity with other Indians. The label of Native American is dependent upon many factors, from eligibility for federal and state services to claims of racial and ethnic origin. There are 556 federally recognized tribes, ranging from the Aleuts and Inuit in Alaska to the Navajo and Hopi in the Southwest to the Seneca and Mashantucket Pequot in the East. While diverse in culture, these tribal groups have similar histories in relationship to federal, state, and local governments.

Discussion Questions _____

1. What are some ways that the historic relationship between American Indians and the dominant culture affect their worldview?

2. What are key issues in the building of trust between the American Indian community and the criminal justice system?

3. What are some examples of racial stereotyping and its impact within the system?

4. How do the concepts of locus of control and responsibility apply to American Indian culture?

5

Asian and Pacific Islander Americans and the Criminal Justice System

Learning Objectives

After reading this chapter you should be able to do the following:

1. Explain the historical perspective of Asian and Pacific Islander Americans and how it relates to the criminal justice system.
2. Differentiate between the various Asian and Pacific Islander groups and identify their waves of immigration.
3. Identify the elements of worldview and compare the relationship to gangs, crime, and sense of trust.

The terms *Asians* and *Pacific Islanders* are broad categories describing various groups of people who have separate worldviews incorporating distinct cultures, traditions, beliefs, and languages. These groups are not homogenous and encompass a great variety of differences that have evolved over centuries. Their histories are replete with conquest, political struggles, and struggles with nature. As with numerous other groups, the development of their cultures is directly related to geography, climate, and the Pacific Ocean. The isolated mountainous terrain from the Philippines to the lowland areas of China helped create variety within each group, and rich cultural heritages were carried forth to the Americas during the course of immigration during many centuries. These very separate worldviews continued to change with influences of American society, and the Asians were often considered the "unwelcome immigrants" in American history.

American immigration practices and policies toward Asian Americans reflect an "antiforeigner stance" that is present throughout American history. Over the last 160 years, Asian and Pacific Islanders have flourished in spite of racial ideologies that limited their access to participation in the dominant culture. Their historical struggle toward acceptance embodies the American ideal of "surviving against the odds."

Labels

The label *Asian* that is used to refer to Asian Americans and Pacific Islanders is a term that represents people from all of Asia. By the mere fact that Asia is the world's largest continent and covers more than 17 million square miles (which accounts for nearly one-third of the earth's landmass) and has over 60 percent of the world's population, one might expect to find a terrific diversity of cultures, ethnicity, and race. The topography of the Asian continent is as varied as its climate. This continent contains Mt. Everest (the world's highest mountain at 29,028 feet) and the Dead Sea (the lowest point on earth at 1,294 feet below sea level). The climate ranges from polar to tropical, and the vegetation ranges from tundra to grasslands to tropical forests. This vast diversity of land is also represented in a great mixture of people who use this broad term of *Asian.*

Historically, Asians were considered Orientals, meaning people from the Far East or the Orient. Asians were also associated with physical features such as a skin color of "yellow" and eyes that were "slanted." The curious use of racial coloring to identify groups of people is common, and Lee (1999) suggests that this mode of placing cultural meaning on physical features is a method that creates separateness and allows one to view people as aliens. Such separation of "white" from "nonwhite" creates a boundary crisis in society. These boundaries in turn affect the assimilation and acculturation processes of immigrant groups into the dominant culture. Socially defined markers of racial differences are symbolic of a society that stereotypes and discriminates. Lee suggests that "Only the racialized Oriental is yellow; Asians are not. Asia is not a biological fact but a geographic designation. Asians come in the broadest range of skin color and hue" (p. 3).

Categorizing people with labels and terms can devalue their existence, exaggerate their differences, and ignore similarities. The terms and labels used to identify Asian Americans for the purposes of this text are used with the utmost respect for all ethnicity and racial groups. The categories used are from the U.S. Census, which states that "all Asian groups, regardless of their size, are important and make contributions to the diversity of the U.S." Generally, discussion about Asians and Pacific Islanders focuses on the largest groups in America. Labels and terms for groups of people consistently change over time due to sociopolitical forces, and the use of *Asian Americans* and *Pacific Islanders* reflects the current trend of identification for this population.

The U.S. Census uses the label *Asian Americans* to refer to people from the Far East, Southeast Asia, and the Indian subcontinent. The *Pacific Islander* label refers to people who have their origins in any of the original peoples of Hawaii, Guam, Samoa, or other Pacific Islander groups (Humes & McKinnon, 2000). While people in these categories would be included in the racial category of Asian, designation of a specific ethnic group or country of origin is common in census data. Some of the countries that are commonly associated with the Far East are China, Japan, Korea, and the Philippines. Some Southeast Asian countries are Thailand, Cambodia, Laos, Malaysia, Indonesia, and Vietnam. Some countries associated with the Indian subcontinent are India, Pakistan, Burma, Sri Lanka, Bangladesh, Bhutan, and Nepal. Some countries associated with Pacific Islanders are Tonga, Samoa, Guam, Tahiti, Northern Mariana Islands, and Palau; the American State of Hawaii is home to the largest Pacific Islander group. The variety of countries represented here reveals the difficulty in stereotyping Asian individuals as looking or acting all alike. Our discussions will designate trends and patterns in demographic changes for ethnic groups under the broad category of Asian American.

Numbers

There is an estimated 10.9 million people under the category of Asian and Pacific Islander. This constitutes nearly 4 percent of the U.S. population, representing a 1 percent increase since 1990 (Humes & McKinnon, 2000). Pacific Islanders represent approximately 6 percent of this category. The western region of the United States accounted for 53 percent of all Asians and Pacific Islanders. The South has the next largest number with 20 percent of the population; the Northeast has 18 percent and the Midwest accounts for 10 percent of the population. California has more Asians than any other state, with 3.9 million people, and it had the largest increase (990,000) of all states, occurring between 1990 and 1998. New York had the second-largest number of Asians, with 995,000 people, while Hawaii had 757,000, Texas 556,000, and New Jersey 453,000. Over 96 percent of this group lives in urban areas with concentrations in Los Angeles–Riverside–Orange County, California (1.8 million); New York–Northern New Jersey–Long Island (1.3 million); San Francisco–Oakland–San Jose, California (1.3 million); Honolulu, Hawaii (566,000); and Washington–Baltimore (373,000). Interestingly, states that had the fastest-growing Asian populations were Nevada, which had a 106 percent increase, Georgia, which had a 95 percent increase, and North Carolina with an 87 percent increase. Separating out the Asian Americans from the Pacific Islanders, California has the largest concentration of both populations. Next for the Asians is New York, and then Hawaii. For the Pacific Islanders, California is followed by Hawaii and Washington State with the largest populations.

The expected population by 2050 is 37.6 million people. The growth is expected to represent 9 percent of the U.S. population. Immigration rates are expected to be part of this increase, with five countries continuing to contribute the largest numbers: Philippines, China, India, Vietnam and Korea (U.S. Census Brief, 2000). In 1997, the U.S. Census determined that 6 out of 10 Asians and Pacific Islanders were foreign born, with the vast majority from the Asian category. The largest increase in population growth is due to birth rates of Asians and Pacific Islanders. Between 1990 and 1998 this group had a higher birth rate than any other racial or ethnic group in America. Birthrate projections for whites and non-Hispanics are approximately 0.6, blacks at 1.3, Hispanics 2.9, American Indians at 1.4, and Asians and Pacific Islanders at 3.8. Statistically, Asian Americans have larger families than whites with 23 percent of married families having five or more members. Only 13 percent of married white couples have five or more members in their family. Approximately 29 percent of Asian American children are under 18 years of age, compared to 24 percent of white children. In addition, the elderly population for whites is 14 percent while for Asian Americans it is 7 percent.

The approximate population percentage for individual ethnic groups in the Asian American category is as follows:

Chinese	24.0%
Filipino	20.0%
Japanese	12.0%
Asian Indian	12.0%
Korean	12.0%
Vietnamese	9.0%
Laotian	2.0%
Cambodian	2.0%
Thai	1.0%
Hmong	1.0%
Other Asian	5.0%

The approximate population percentage for individual ethnic groups in the Pacific Islander category is as follows:

Hawaiian	58.0%
Samoan	17.0%
Guamanian	14.0%
Tongan	5.0%
Fijian	2.0%
Palauan	0.4%
All other groups	4.0%

Language Issues

The majority of Americans with historical roots from the Far East have been here for many generations. This is in contrast to people with roots from Southeast Asia and who are relatively new Americans. No matter the length of their history in America, language issues seem to affect interaction between Asians and the dominant culture. In 1993 the U.S. Department of Commerce reported that over two-thirds of Asian and Pacific Islander people spoke their ethnic language rather than English in the home (Palsano, 1993a,b).

The report indicates that 56 percent of Asians five years and older did not speak English "very well," and 35 percent were linguistically isolated. Linguistic isolation "refers to persons in households in which no one 14 years old or over speaks only English and no one who speaks a language other than English speaks English very well." The most recent of the Asian groups to populate the Americas are the Hmong, Cambodians, and Laotians. They, too, speak predominantly their native language at home, and tend not to "speak English very well" (Palsano, 1993a,b). Asian American groups such as the Chinese, who have been in the Americas for the longest period of time, also have a high percentage of native language use in the home, and people within the home who do not speak English "very well." (See Table 5.1.)

The lack of English skills among groups of people presents many complications for the criminal justice system. Language issues are an overriding problem when conducting effective interviews and investigations in the field of law enforcement. While criminal justice workers often find that many Asian groups speak fluent English, they should respect the fact that native languages are the natural forms of communication for a large majority of Asian Americans.

The use of native language in the homes by Asian Americans is partly due to generations of forced isolation from the dominant culture. Many Chinese and Japanese immigrants were forced into certain sections of cities and considered foreigners. Many laws were designed to control and limit the influence of Asian culture on the dominant culture, and created an "us versus them" mentality that prevented Asians from effectively assimilating into the dominant culture. Such laws often extinguished any thought of citizenship or rights as new Americans, illustrated by an 1854 law prohibiting Chinese and Japanese

TABLE 5.1　*Asian or Pacific Islander Language Spoken at Home and Ability to Speak English: 1990 (Percent)*

	Speak Asian or Pacific Islander Language at Home	*Do Not Speak English "Very Well"*	*Linguistically Isolated*
Total Asian	65.2	56.0	34.9
Chinese	82.9	60.4	40.3
Filipino	66.0	35.6	13.0
Japanese	42.8	57.7	33.0
Asian Indian	14.5	31.0	17.2
Korean	80.8	63.5	41.4
Vietnamese	92.5	65.0	43.9
Cambodian	95.0	73.2	56.1
Hmong	96.9	78.1	60.5
Laotian	95.6	70.2	52.4
Thai	79.1	58.0	31.8
Other Asian	21.0	49.9	30.2

Note: Linguistic isolation refers to persons in households in which no one 14 years old or over speaks only English and no one who speaks a language other than English speaks English "very well."

from testimony in courts against whites. By 1880 California's Civil Code refused marriage licenses to mixed-race couples, and in 1882 the Chinese Exclusion Act suspended immigration of Chinese laborers and declared Chinese people ineligible for citizenship (Wu & Song, 2000). Exclusion and isolation were not limited to nineteenth century America. In 1927, Gong Lum, a Chinese immigrant, petitioned the court on behalf of his daughter, who was denied access to an all-white school. Lum lost the discrimination suit against the State Superintendent of Education of Mississippi (Kim, 1994).

During World War II, President Franklin D. Roosevelt signed Executive Order 9066 that became Public Law 503, requiring the internment of Japanese Americans. Thousands of people lost their citizenship in reaction to the Japanese attack on Pearl Harbor, and the result was exclusion and isolation of an entire group based not upon citizenship but ethnicity. In the 1970s the San Francisco Unified School District had approximately 3,000 Chinese students, of which 1,000 needed help with English. A class action lawsuit was filed that claimed the school district denied an equal education to Chinese limited-English students. The Supreme Court found that the school district did not provide equality of education for limited-English speaking students. Justice Douglas stated that if students cannot understand English, "which is the basic language of instruction in all schools in California, as stated in the California Education Code, then they are unable to receive any meaningful education" (Kim, 1994, p. 170).

Isolation and exclusion by the dominant culture had an effect on the persistence of native language use. In addition, Asian cultural norms also contributed to this isolation. In the 1970s desegregation changed the complexion of neighborhood schools to include a racial mix of each city's school-age children. During this time, San Francisco Unified School District was concerned with desegregating schools that had a majority of Chinese students. However, Chinese American parents feared desegregation for their children as a development that would destroy their language, community, and culture (Kim, 1994). Language binds a culture together against prevailing winds of discrimination and prejudice. For many Asian Americans, keeping their native language alive contributes to their moral order of respect for their heritage, elders and culture.

The Historical Perspective

As with other ethnic groups, the relationship of past experiences with the dominant culture affects present interaction with the dominant culture and with the criminal justice system. Attitudes toward Asian Americans are entwined with stereotypes, sanctioned prejudice, immigration laws, historical events, and discrimination. Political structures historically viewed Asian Americans as an inferior group and as foreigners. Foner and Rosenberg (1993) noted that "no variety of anti-European sentiments has ever approached the violent extremes to which anti-Chinese agitation went in the 1870s and 1880s" (p. 3). However, in spite of historical attitudes of discrimination, Asian Americans survived and continue to contribute to the mosaic of America.

The historical perspective is divided into four broad categories of Asian Americans from the Far East, Southeast Asia, Indian subcontinent, and Pacific Islanders. Understanding the history of Asian groups can increase our understanding of their relationship to society in general and the criminal justice system in particular. Many of the groups came from countries that were colonialized by European powers. This colonialization process and its effects upon groups of people are similar across racial lines. European powers that colonialized groups had an ideology that set themselves apart from the newly "discovered" people. Viewing themselves as superior to the new groups and building a structured society that subordinates the native people, the Europeans created a wedge between the natural development of two cultures. Racist attitudes and behavior, in turn, create "habitual suspicion" among the native groups and ensure their subordination (Foner & Rosenberg, 1993). Albert Memmi, the twentieth century Tunisian philosopher and author, regarding his belief about the effects of colonialization states

> The colonialist stresses those things which keep him separate, rather than emphasizing that which might contribute to the foundation of a joint community. . . . In those differences, the colonized is always degraded and the colonialist finds justification for rejecting his subject. . . . The colonialist removes the factor [the colonized] from history, time, and therefore possible evolution. What is actually a sociological point becomes labeled as being biological or, preferably, metaphysical. It is attached to the colonized's basic nature. (Wu & Song, 2000, p. 11)

This ideology is present today when people stereotype groups and apply individual traits or characteristics to everyone within the groups. These stereotypes evolve into the sociopolitical climate, and become entrenched in people's thinking. At the turn of the century, Asian immigrants were considered sexual deviants, representing "forbidden desire" and characterized as the "yellow peril." In an ironic turn of events during the 1960s they became stereotyped as the "model minority." While sounding positive, this stereotype compared the "quiet, nonmilitant, nonpolitical, Asian Americans" to the militant, political, criminal behaviors of African Americans and Hispanics. The "model minority" label was predicated upon how well nonwhite groups assimilated and became aligned with the U.S. economy and traditions. The post–Vietnam War and postliberal American popular culture of the 1970s found Asian Americans emerging as the invisible enemy threatening the social structure and economic stability American society (Foner & Rosenberg, 1993; Lee, 1999; Wu & Song, 2000).

Understanding stereotypical race-based thinking, and recognizing the pathological nature of discrimination, we can appreciate "historical discourse of race that is embedded in the history of American social crisis" (Lee, 1999, p. 12). When one understands the powerful influence of social events and their effects upon ethnic and racial groups in American, then can one seek to deconstruct stereotypes and move toward reconciliation, acceptance of alternative visions of American identity, and the benefits of valuing diversity in a complex racial society.

Far East Asian Americans

The Far East Asian immigrants have historical roots in China, Japan, Korea, and the Philippines. The Chinese and Filipino Americans are some of the first Asian groups to immigrate to America. Like European immigrants, Asian immigrants came in loosely established waves of immigration seeking opportunities, economic achievement, security, and social acceptance.

Filipinos

The 1.5 million Filipino Americans living in the United States account for approximately 20 percent of the Asian and Pacific Islander population (Paludeine, 1998). Their relationship with America dates back to 1898, when the Treaty of Paris ended the Spanish-American War and the Philippines became the first U.S. colony. After World War II the Philippines were granted independence from the United States, with economic and military strings attached. Agreements were made that allowed military bases on the Philippine Islands for 99 years in exchange for U.S. military protection from neighboring countries. The special relationship that was forged between the former colony and America was seen as proof that America was concerned with the welfare of the Filipino people (Karnow, 1989).

The Philippines is an archipelago of 7,100 islands located in the western Pacific Ocean between Taiwan and Indonesia. Only about 700 of the islands are inhabited, with 11 accounting for most of the population. Their location has historical significance as the gateway to mainland Asia. The original indigenous people were the Aetas, and remnants of this group still live in some of the mountainous islands. In approximately 300 B.C., the mainland people from Indonesia and Malaysia arrived on the islands, intermarried, and became the ethnic group that we know as modern-day Filipino. For nearly 12 centuries the Filipino people evolved as a culture and were influenced by merchants from China, Japan, and India. While the culture evolved to the predominant use of the Tagolog language, formalized political structures and practices were loosely coupled. This is partially because the islands extend for over 1,000 miles along the Eastern Pacific.

This loosely coupled group of islands and people were vulnerable to the colonial expansion of Portugal and Spain. By 1521 the first Portuguese explorers began to colonize this area. By the late 1500s the Spanish people invaded the islands and named the area in honor of King Philip II of Spain. For the next 350 years, Spanish language, culture, traditions, and government influenced the Philippines. The sound of *f* does not occur in the language of the Philippines, so the native people called themselves Pilipinos. The uses of Pilipino and Filipino are commonly accepted today. In typical colonial fashion, exploitation of the native people and the subordination of the indigenous population created a hierarchical system that remained in effect until the end of the nineteenth century. In actuality, the Spaniards who were sent to organize and establish Spanish rule in the Philippines came from colonial Mexico (Karnow, 1989). They brought their governing style, city planning, and many Mexican Indians to the Philippines. This mixture of cultures is seen in the blending of religious beliefs from Catholicism and ancient beliefs from Mexican Indians and native groups from the Philippines.

Filipino Americans are associated with three waves of immigration. These waves correspond with social and political events in America. The earliest record of Filipino immigrants in America was in 1763, when sailors on Spanish ships decided to settle in the trading ports of southeast Louisiana. Marian Espina, a first-generation Filipina librarian from New Orleans, recently found archival evidence of this early community of Filipinos that intermarried with Native Americans (Jacinto & Syquia, 1995). This is the earliest record of an Asian community in the Americas.

The Spanish colonial rule of the Philippines ended in 1898 and America became the new ruler through the Treaty of Paris. In 1901 America sent 600 teachers to reeducate the

Filipinos to the American way of life, language, and government. Within fifty years the American influence rapidly changed the culture of the Philippines.

The first wave of Filipino immigrants came to America between 1906 and 1940. They became known as "Pinoy," a slang term for Filipinos. Approximately 85 percent were young, unmarried men who worked in agriculture in Hawaii and California. Their presence in American agriculture became significant when Filipino labor leaders were the first farm workers to help organize the famed grape protest and strikes in California during the 1970s. In addition to farm workers, a small group of Filipino students came to America for advanced education. They were known as the "pensionados," and their goal was to become educated as future leaders of the Philippines. While in America, the pensionados developed a worldview as zealous advocates for democracy and the American way of life (Jacinto & Syquia, 1995; Wu & Song, 2000).

The second wave of immigration was after World War II and up to 1965. The second wave, unlike the first, consisted of educated and skilled workers and their families. Filipino servicemen who had served in American units during World War II brought their families and called America home, and American servicemen who married Filipina women joined Filipino communities in the United States.

The third wave of immigration occurred after the Immigration and Nationality Act was amended in 1965. This law allowed immigration for over 170,000 people from the Eastern Hemisphere, and 120,000 from the Western Hemisphere (Paludeine, 1998). There was a 700 percent increase in Filipino immigrants between 1960 and 1990. These immigrants were male and female professionals, with the majority making California their home. The largest Filipino communities are in Los Angeles County and the Bay Area. Recent immigrants are progressive and more mobile than in the past, and the 1990 census indicated that approximately 75 percent of the Filipino population are in the workforce. While there are many urban professionals in this group, the majority of Filipinos remain in low-paying service or manufacturing jobs.

The values that these immigrants bring to America reflect mores and folkways of their homeland. It is difficult to accurately generalize values shared by groups, but for the Filipinos such values seem to include respect for elders, a sense of a shared identity of belonging to a group, and a sense of shame when one member fails to conform to group norms. They also experience a sense of fatalism or resignation that life is in the hands of God or fate. Such resignation helps form worldview, and enables individuals within groups to face disaster or tragedy with serenity.

Over the last fifty years, the Philippines experienced corrupt government, civil rights abuses, and civil unrest. Insurgents currently seek to supplant the government, and this instability suggests the prospect of more immigrants and refugees seeking homes in America.

Chinese

Chinese Americans account for nearly 20 percent of the U.S. Asian American population of approximately 1.5 million people. The majority of Chinese Americans live in the Northwest and West, with over 40 percent living in California. Generally, the historical perspective of Chinese Americans conjures images of the westward expansion during the middle to late 1800s. However, the first European encounters with the Chinese were by traders, missionaries, and diplomats from the East Coast between 1780 and 1840. These early American visitors to China returned with stories of a "peculiar people, with strange beliefs, and cuisine." Missionaries reported that the character of the Chinese was deficient because of their "lechery, dishonesty, xenophobia, cruelty, despotism, filth, and intellectual inferiority" (Kim, 1994, p. 43). Negative images and stories about eating dogs, drinking blood from young girls, and engaging in strange herbal medicines heightened racial animosity. Newspapers, minstrel shows, and popular folklore perpetuated these images. In an effort to counteract negative portrayals of the Chinese, Canton merchant Nathan Dunn opened the Chinese Museum in Philadelphia in 1838. He used articles of clothing, artifacts from the Chinese culture, and artwork to expose Americans to another side of the Chinese people. His goal was to promote a positive image of the Chinese (Kim, 1994; Lee, 1999). Before finances caused the museum to close, more than 100,000 people visited the attraction.

The American desire for things unusual, and for exotic and rare oddities, created a market for Chinese collections and curiosities in museums and attractions. One of the best-noted attractions during the mid 1800s was Chang and Eng, physically conjoined Chinese twins from Siam (Thailand). This nationally known exhibit presented curious aspects of the worldview of Americans of the era. Such attractions as the "Chinese Lady" sitting among yards of silk, the naked Hottentot woman, and Chang and Eng performing with their conjoined bodies reinforced stereotypical attitudes toward immigrants. By the time the Chinese immigrants became part of the labor force in the western United States, stereotypes, prejudice, and discrimination were entrenched in American thinking.

Chinese immigration is associated with many major sociopolitical changes in the industrialized world. By the end of the 1830s the British Empire was seeking cheap labor to replace their now defunct slavery industry. The British used force to open trade relationships and ports with China in exchange for cheap labor. Soon to follow was the United States, modeling its contract labor system after the British. Before 1851, official records indicate that only 46 Chinese people lived in America. By the 1870s approximately 151,000 Chinese immigrants were here, with 116,000 of that number living as laborers in California (Kim, 1994; Paludeine, 1998). In 1849 California recorded 715 Chinese people working in the gold mines. One year later, 4,000 Chinese were working in mining towns. By 1851 the Chinese population jumped to 25,000 people, and in many California counties over half of the population was Chinese. The number of Chinese actually recorded as immigrants to America before the 1880 census was 300,000. The census in that year recorded approximately 100,000, and it was common for many Chinese to complete their labor contracts and return to China (Daniels, 1988).

Many miners and townspeople believed that the dramatic growth of the Chinese population would unfavorably affect their ways of life. Fear of this new group precipitated laws and regulations that were designed to limit or remove Chinese influences in American culture, and, therefore, limit Chinese success in American society. In the 1880 census California listed 70,000 Chinese men and 4,000 Chinese women. The Chinese immigrants were considered a "bachelor society," and interracial relationships with the existing groups were common. In New York between 1820 and 1870, 25 percent of Chinese men were married to Irish women (Daniels, 1988; Kim, 1994; Lee, 1999). By a ratio of three to one more Irish women survived the potato famine than did Irish men, leaving Irish women to intermarry with other ethnic and racial groups.

In San Francisco in the late 1800s, one out of every three people was born in Ireland, Germany, China, or Italy. The population jumped from 57,000 residents to over 100,000 in a few years after the Civil War (Lee, 1999). The changes in demographics created opportunities for relationships between predominately male Chinese immigrants and single Irish women. Intermarriage in California was illegal at the time, and Lee (1999) noted that "the marriage of Chinese immigrant men to Irish immigrant women, while not significant in a demographic sense, occurred with sufficient frequency to present itself as an imagined threat to working-class whites whose class and status was precarious and to immigrants whose amalgamation into whiteness was not yet complete" (p. 76). The Chinese, seen as threats to the "blurring of races" quickly became targets of racial animosity and acts of discrimination. Having experienced significant discrimination at the hands of their former British rulers, the Irish felt the threat of the Chinese more than any other group. The sentiment of the time saw Irish immigrant workingmen "as no different between the enslaved Africans and proletarianized Chinese laborer" (p. 70). Both groups were competing for the same low-wage jobs, their collective status in society was not favorable, and they both were considered to be expendable. However, the Irish could eventually blend into mainstream American society while the Chinese still "looked different." Members of the working classes in American society were the biggest opponents of Chinese "incursion." They claimed that the Chinese workers were lowering wages and "thereby lowering the standard of living . . . were inassimilable and that their 'heathen' customs were disgusting and tended to debauch and degrade those around them" (Daniels, 1988, p. 47). Additional propaganda against the Chinese can be reduced to a short phrase that was popular at the time. "The Chinese worked cheap and smelled bad" (Daniels, 1988, p. 53). Conditions in San Francisco's Chinatown were typical of the ghettoization of America's inner cities during the late 1800s. Ethnic neighborhoods experienced great levels of poverty and poor sanitation. While inner cities experienced this across the nation, the labeling of the Chinese as more deplorable than any other group spurred the efforts of legislation focused on exclusion.

Ironically, however, industrialized labor needed workers in the late 1800s, and the Chinese "coolies" were an essential component of that labor force. They were instrumental in running mining towns and providing support services related to cooking, laundry, restaurants and construction. The term "coolie" became synonymous with hard-labor jobs, and is actually from two Chinese words. Roughly translated, "koo" means "to rent," and "lee" suggests "strength" (Daniels, 1988; Paludeine, 1998). Not only did Chinese labor support the mining operations in the West, they are noted for being the backbone of the railroad system that crosses the western United States today.

The Chinese labor force that built the Central Pacific Railroad did so in inhospitable conditions that left thousands dead. Chinese laborers are noted for laying a previously unprecedented 10 miles of track in rough terrain in one single day, though this record did not come without great loss of lives. An ironic twist of fate occurred when more "coolies" were needed in the quickly expanding West. In 1862 while labor contractors were making special efforts to bring more Chinese to America, one of the first laws was passed limiting immigration from China. Over the next 20 years, laws and legislation limiting citizenship, levying additional taxes for foreigners, prohibiting interracial marriage, and prohibiting business license issuance affected the relationship between the dominant culture and the Chinese. Anti-Chinese sentiment continued throughout the Pacific Northwest and the mountain states. The ultimate prohibition on Chinese immigrants was the 1882 Chinese Exclusion Act, which suspended Chinese immigration for 10 years. This act also barred naturalization and set up procedures to deport all illegal immigrants. In 1910, an immigration facility was set up at Angel Island in the San Francisco Bay. It was termed "the Ellis Island of the West," and was a port of entry into the United States where immigrant health status was evaluated.

The separation and exclusion of Chinese immigrants from politics and the assimilation process caused many to form social organizations to promote their own economic welfare. The forming of tongs—secret groups to promote legal and illegal activities—was based on the clan ancestry principle from China. These clans were generally associated with villages. In addition to clan membership, Chinese people also belonged to regional districts within the country of China. The majority of immigrants were from the Kwangtung Province, which had many regional districts. New social organizations developed in America to help and protect immigrants and to maintain control within the Chinese community. In addition to these social organizations that worked within the establishment, social organizations that were anti-establishment also flourished. In China, secret societies formed to retaliate against oppressive governmental demands. This practice of creating secret societies (the tongs) to achieve economic and social goals transferred to Chinese communities living in America, and affected the relationship of Chinese Americans with the criminal justice system. These groups were patterned after the Triad Society that rose against the Manchu Dynasty. They were a minority within the Chinese community, but exercised power with violence. Tongs were involved in illegal activities—including prostitution, gambling, drugs, and protection rackets—victimizing Chinese business owners. The tongs and Triads still operate in cities across America today (Daniels, 1988; Lee, 1999).

The Chinese Exclusion Act of 1882 was in effect until 1943. Sentiment toward the Chinese changed during World War II, when they became our allies. Immigration from China was reopened, but continued to be limited, and during the 1940s approximately 16,709 Chinese people immigrated to America. The Korean War and the founding of the People's Republic of China brought 14,000 refugees to America during the 1950s, and a renewed attitude of prejudice against Chinese Americans emerged with the communist scare that characterized the era. Events of the 1970s and 1980s such as the Tiananmen Square massacre redefined American sentiment toward Chinese immigrants, and thousands of Chinese entered the country as political refugees. In the 1990s, economic, political, and social changes in our relationship with China opened doors for further immigration, and people from Taiwan and the former British Hong Kong are calling America home.

Chinese Americans persevered through early years of discrimination and prejudice to become active members of the labor force and advocates for democracy in the homeland. Over 40 percent of the Chinese population participated in World War II, and they hold the record as the most drafted (into military service) of any ethnic group in America (Espiritu, 2000). Gallup polls of the time reported that Americans expressed a different, more favorable view about Chinese Americans, labeling them as "hardworking, honest, brave, religious, intelligent and practical" people in 1942 (Espiritu, 2000, p. 148).

Religious practices among immigrants to America vary from Buddhism to Christianity, and are related to specific waves of immigration. Variations in cultural identity are related to ties with clans and language dialects. China is a vast nation, with extensive diversity among its people. While Mandarin is China's official language, there are various regional dialects that unite groups of people. In Hong Kong, Cantonese is the common dialect, but Chinese American "old timers" speak a version of Cantonese called Toi San. Because of the great variation in educational practices in urban and rural China, recent immigrants might have little or no English training.

Because of the diversity inherent in Chinese culture, any theories of common worldview among Chinese Americans are mistaken. The American-born Chinese see new immigrants as foreigners and do not identify with them. In fact, some Chinese Americans might join the dominant group and thereby separate themselves from the new immigrants (Wong & Lopez, 1995).

Historic relationships between cultural groups and the mainstream of society certainly affect the present worldview of those groups. New Chinese immigrants will arrive in American society with less opposition than did their ancestors. They will hopefully encounter fewer stereotypes and more opportunities to participate in the American dream, with resulting positive, cross-cultural relationships.

Koreans

Korean Americans have historic roots in a country that has been a center of struggle for economic, political, and social independence. Korea is roughly the size of Minnesota, and is bordered by China to the north and Japan to the east. Koreans are a distinctly different ethnic group from Chinese and Japanese, possessing a blend of cultures ranging from nomadic tribes of Mongolia to Caucasian people from southwestern Asia. Their history is one of forced invasions and political struggles for power with neighboring countries. The most notable historic event in Korean–American history is the Korean War, which occurred from 1950 to 1953 and divided Korea into North and South. North Korea is ruled by a communist regime supported by China, and South Korea by a democratic-approach government supported by the United States. Korean Americans account for approximately 12 percent of the Asian American population. While rich in culture and contributions, Korean Americans tend to be grouped as Asians without recognition of the distinctiveness of their population.

Some of the earliest recorded American contacts with Koreans occurred in 1883 and involved American diplomats. The first wave of immigration to the United States happened from the early 1900s to the 1930s. Generally, the first intake of Koreans into the United States was in Hawaii, where they worked in the sugar cane industry. As was true of other labor-based immigration patterns, the majority of immigrants were male, and over 7,000 Korean immigrants lived in Hawaii by 1905. In 1910 the Japanese invaded Korea, thereby limiting any and all immigration. Between 1910 and 1924, approximately 500 Koreans secretly fled their occupied country (Wu & Song, 2000). While smaller in number than the Chinese, Koreans first worked in the mines and railroad industry of the West. The

1924 Naturalization and Immigration Act limited Korean immigrants for the next 30 years. As a result of their identification with the Asian race, they experienced discrimination similar to that directed at the Chinese in jobs, pay, and living conditions.

The second wave of Korean immigration to the United States is associated with the end of the Korean War in 1953. This wave continued into the 1980s. Immigration was open to thousands of Koreans fleeing communist North Korea, Korean wives of U.S. military personnel, and war orphans and college students. It was estimated that over 15,000 Korean students came to America during this time. Between 1962 and 1983 over 45,000 Korean children were adopted by white, middle-class, Protestant families. An estimated 50,000 Korean women are married to U.S. servicemen. The second wave of immigrants located throughout the United States (Kim & Kim, 1994).

The third wave of immigration to the United States from Korea is still occurring and consists of urban, middle-class professionals; an estimated 50 percent have college degrees. They come to America for business and educational opportunities and a higher standard of living. In 1970 there were 69,000 Korean Americans living in the United States. The 1980 census placed that number at 350,000, and the 1990 census at 800,000. Korean Americans are categorized as entrepreneurial minorities, many of whom start businesses and professional services. They generally tend to live and work in ethnic enclaves, and Los Angeles is home to one of the largest in the United States. On the East Coast, New York and Washington have the next highest populations, followed by Philadelphia and Baltimore (Portes & Rumbaut, 1996).

Korean Americans, more than any other ethnic Asian group, came to America as Christians. American missionary efforts began with a medical missionary who served the royal family in 1884. Missionaries opened education to all and exposed the country to democratic ideals. Christian philosophy continued to blossom in spite of the expulsion of missionaries in 1940. Over 25 percent of the current population of Korea are Christian, and the remainder are divided between Buddhism and Confucianism. Over 70 percent of Korean Americans are Protestant Christians (Daniels, 1988; Kim & Kim, 1994).

Koreans place traditional values on family interdependency, discipline via shame and punishment, and kinship bonds. They have a life philosophy of stoicism and fatalism, success through self-discipline and will, and saving the face of the family at all cost. The traditional worldview of Korean Americans is changing as the children become more Americanized, and parents are concerned that children are losing their sense of family and respect for their elders. Parents have high expectations for their children's academic success, which sometimes creates pressures and conflicts, and generation gaps in language, culture, and communication create conflict between traditional norms and the acculturation process.

Generation gaps and conflicts are not new to American immigrants. Cultural clashes between racial and ethnic groups strain neighborhood and community relationships. Some of the most publicized cultural clashes occurred between African Americans and Korean Americans in the inner cities, most notably Los Angeles. In the late 1950s and early 1960s inner-city South Central Los Angeles changed from a "white" neighborhood to predominately black. Prompted by the Watts riots, white business owners sold their stores to blacks. By the late 1970s and early 1980s, blacks experienced poor profit margins and sold businesses to Korean Americans. While whites moved from the neighborhood after selling

FOCUS BOX

Peter Jennings and Todd Brewster noted in their book, *The Century,* that the attitude of American servicemen was naïve at best as they confronted the North Koreans. Many figured they would be but a week in Korea, "settle the gook thing," then head home. They believed President Truman when he described their mission as a "police action," as if they were going to Asia not for war, but to bang the heads of a few delinquents discovered breaking into the corner drugstore. In fact, three years would pass before the fighting in Korea was done, leaving that nation ravaged—but divided politically, much as it had been when the conflict began. And for that outcome, 54,000 Americans and over 2 million Koreans would die. (p. 381)

off their businesses, the majority of black business owners did not move after the sale of theirs. Clashes between the relatively new Korean population and the established black population began. In 1986 African American robbers killed four Korean merchants. Criminal acts against storeowners continued, and between 1990 and 1992 another 12 Korean merchants were killed in Southern California. In March of 1991 Korean merchant Soon Ja Du, in what police called a justifiable homicide, shot and killed fifteen-year-old Latasha Harlins. Hostilities, anger, frustration, and violence continued to grow between the two groups. After a jury found four Los Angeles Police officers not guilty of beating black motorist, Rodney King, over 700 Korean businesses in South Central Los Angeles were damaged and looted by African Americans (Kim, 2000; Ong, Park, & Tong, 1999). Hispanics also attacked Korean-owned stores in other parts of Los Angeles. Over 40 percent of those business have closed their doors permanently.

Although conflicts continue in various neighborhoods, there seems to have been some reconciliation between groups that has mitigated the violence of the past. The Black-Korean Alliance, along with the Los Angeles County Human Relations Commission, are building relationships between the two groups. Kim (2000) notes that, while violent incidences are portrayed furiously in the media, church-sponsored activities, cultural events, community education, and crime prevention programs designed to bring groups together are not being shared similarly with the public. Changes in attitudes are taking place and the acculturation process of blending of two distinct ethnic enclaves has great promise.

Japanese

Japanese Americans account for approximately 12 percent of the Asian American population, representing approximately 866,000 people in America. Approximately 75 percent of Japanese Americans live in either California or Hawaii, and 68 percent were born in America (Portes, 1996).

The story of Japanese immigrants in Hawaii sets the stage for the movement of Japanese people to North America. Prior to 1869 there were a few Japanese seamen, diplomats, and students who made their way to America. In 1869, 141 Japanese workers came to Hawaii, and by 1890 nearly 30,000 sugar cane workers were Japanese (Daniels, 1988).

In the first wave of immigration between 1890 and 1908, 150,000 Japanese contract laborers came to the mainland United States. They mainly located in California, and over 95 percent of this number were men. Due to the ebb and flow of Japanese immigration, by the 1920 census 110,000 Japanese were living in America, with over 71,000 of that number living in California (Daniels, 1988; Portes & Bach, 1985; Portes & Rumbaut, 1996). The Japanese contract laborers worked with the railroads and other industrial enterprises, but the vast majority of Japanese immigrants came from rural areas as commercial farmers and became the bulk of the agriculture labor market in California. San Francisco was home to Japanese commercial enterprises, with the setting up of ethnic enclaves similar to the Chinese. The bulk of labor activity was related to farming.

In 1900, approximately 40 Japanese farmers combined their resources and farmed 5,000 acres. Over 6,000 Japanese farmers controlled over 210,000 acres in 1909. Resources were again combined, and by 1919 47 percent of all hotels and 25 percent of grocery stores in Seattle were owned and operated by Japanese immigrants. By 1940 the total acreage controlled by Japanese Americans in the Pacific West states were 250,000, with a value of $72.6 million. These farms supplied California with more than 50 percent of all fruits and vegetables, and anti-Asian sentiment promoted the notion that Japanese Americans were displacing white farmers. However, the lands that were developed were new agricultural lands on which were used high-yield practices instead of traditional low-yield American methods of the era (Daniels, 1988). Nevertheless, concerns over the success of Japanese Americans in America and Japanese invasions of countries near Japan created more anti-Japanese sentiment.

In the early 1900s, the California legislature limited Japanese immigration in a bill which stated, in part:

> Japanese laborers, by reason of race habits, mode of living, disposition, and general characteristics, are undesirable. . . . They contribute nothing to the growth of the state. They add nothing to its wealth, and they are a blight on the prosperity of it, and a great impending danger to its welfare. (Portes & Bach, 1985, p. 44)

Additional anti-sentiment from Stanford University professor E. A. Ross characterized the struggles between American society and Japanese immigrants as similar to those with the Chinese. His argument held that "The Japanese are starting the same tide of immigration which we thought we had checked twenty years ago [The Chinese Exclusion Act of 1882] . . . Chinese and Japanese are not the stuff of which American citizens can be made" (Daniels, 1988, p. 112). Headlines in the San Francisco Chronicle in 1905 read

JAPANESE A MENACE TO AMERICAN WOMEN

THE YELLOW PERIL—HOW JAPANESE CROWD OUT THE WHITE RACE

BROWN ARTISANS STEAL BRAINS OF WHITES

CRIME AND POVERTY GO HAND IN HAND WITH ASIATIC LABOR

(Daniels, 1988, p. 116)

Anti-Japanese sentiment continued to rise after the invasion of Korea. Japanese farm workers were routinely being forced from their farms, loaded onto trains, and told "if they came back they would be lynched." The 1924 Immigration Act barred Japanese immigrants from entry into America (Wu & Song, 2000). Japan had become a "first-class power" and was not taken lightly by the American government. Acts against Japanese people seemed to be related to the willingness to work for "less than the Chinese coolies." President Theodore Roosevelt characterized the policy of keeping Japanese children from going to school in San Francisco as "a wicked absurdity," and attributed the "hostility toward Japanese to fears about their efficiency as workers" (Daniels, 1988, p. 122).

The first generation of Japanese immigrants is designated by the Japanese term *Issei*. The Issei wanted their children, the *Nisei* (first generation born in America) to become Americanized as quickly as possible, and many changed their beliefs from Buddhism to Christianity. A Japanese Christian group in Los Angeles in the late 1930s made a statement that "Americanization can only be realized through Christianity . . . we who are in the United States are to be, first of all, loyal to our land of adoption" (Daniels, 1988, p. 170). These parents wanted their children to learn English and become like other Americans, but they also wanted their children to preserve Japanese language and culture. Japanese language schools and organizations reflected this desire to foster Japanese culture and traditions, and also fueled resentment and gave credibility to the internment of Japanese Americans during World War II.

The bombing of Pearl Harbor by Japan on December 7, 1941, created hysteria that targeted Japanese Americans. In 1941, approximately 125,000 Japanese Americans lived in the United States. Out of that number, 110,000 lived on the West Coast and 70,000 had actually been born in the United States. The largest numbers at that time lived in Los Angeles County and the next largest population center was in Seattle. San Francisco was home to approximately 5,000 Japanese Americans but was considered the cultural capital and headquarters for the Japanese American Citizens League. Fears of Japanese American collusion with Imperial Japan were promoted by the geographic location of their populations along the West Coast of the United States and the subsequent proximity to the war in the Pacific. The media helped promote the hysteria against Japanese Americans, suggesting that they were "spies for Imperialist Japan." Over 120,000 Japanese Americans were forced from their homes and interned in dismal camps surrounded by barbed wire and

FOCUS BOX

Peter Jennings and Todd Brewster (1998) recall the attitudes of Americans after the attack on Pearl Harbor in 1941 in their book, *The Century*. The attack of December 7 was a singular moment in modern American history, a penetration of our borders by a hostile force, and it had the effect on the country that a burglary has on the family home: People never felt quite safe again. The surprise had been largely an illusion (leaders on both sides had expected a war and it was assumed that an attack on Pearl Harbor was one of the scenarios the Japanese were considering). Still, for the public at large the news jangled the nerves and helped to create a sense of paranoia that prompted regular "sightings" of hostile aircraft, the cruel and unconstitutional incarceration of Japanese Americans . . . and in part the witch hunt mentality that would survive into the Cold War. Americans simply did not want to be tricked again. (pp. 239–240) troops. Many of those families had sons serving in the armed forces of the United States in European and North African theaters. On March 27, 1942, Japanese Americans had 48 hours to evacuate their homes and businesses to move to "relocation centers." Korn (1969) noted that in California Japanese Americans were

> deprived of nearly a half billion dollars in yearly income, some $70 million worth of farms and farm equipment, $35 million worth of fruit and vegetable produce, and lifetime savings and assets that no one bothered to calculate . . . bank accounts were frozen, banks refused to cash their checks, milkmen refused to deliver their milk, grocers refused to sell them food, insurance companies canceled their policies, licenses were revoked for practicing law or medicine and dismissed people from civil service jobs. . . . No specific charges were made against these people; no hearings were held to determine whether there was evidence of subversion. (p. 201)

The majority of internment camps were on federally owned land, primarily Native American reservations. Each family was given a space of 20 by 25 feet called "apartments," with no partitions between adjoining families (Espiritu, 2000). Environments were harsh and facilities were poor. In Puyallup, Washington, over 100 families were forced to use one bathroom. In Santa Anita, California, thousands of people lived in the horse stalls at the Santa Anita racetrack. In spite of these harsh conditions and "un-American" acts by the government, internees supported the war effort. Residents of the camps made camouflage nets for the Army and worked on scientific projects for the War Production Board. In fact, over 8,000 Japanese Americans, the Nisei generation, served in the military with great distinction. The Nisei 442nd Regiment won numerous awards and citations, including 3,600 Purple Hearts with 500 Oak Leaf Clusters.

At the end of World War II in 1945, there were still over 44,000 Japanese Americans incarcerated in internment camps. Executive Order 9066 by then Democratic President Franklin Roosevelt set a legal precedent in the discrimination of Asian Americans by granting the implementation of the *Final Report: Japanese Evacuation from the West.* This Executive Order still haunts our society as an example of unethical and illegal treatment of American citizens, based on the color of their skin. In 1988, Congress allocated $1.25 billion to approximately 60,000 Japanese Americans displaced during World War II. This compensation, while significant, does not fully reimburse Japanese Americans for their financial, social, and psychological losses.

The 1940s were characterized by antagonistic attitudes and racist sentiment against Japan and Japanese Americans. After World War II and in the 1950s, negative attitudes shifted from Japan and Japanese Americans to China and Chinese Americans, with panic over the threat of communism. Ronald Takaki summarized this new threat by stating that "the new peril was seen as yellow in race and red in ideology" (Wu & Song, 2000, p. 473).

After World War II America invested in Japan's infrastructure to accomplish several goals. The Marshall Plan sought first to discourage expected attempts at incursion by communist countries in the Pacific Rim, and second to reconcile the devastation of dropping two atomic bombs on the Japanese cities of Hiroshima and Nagasaki. The fear of communism in the Far East and the onslaught of the Cold War combined to forge a strong relationship with the Japanese. A new economic relationship between Japan and America increased the acceptance of Japanese Americans after the war. Once fearful of Japanese customs and language, America forged a positive postwar relationship between the two nations. American universities promoted student exchange programs, and Japanese language courses have become the fourth most popular among language programs (Census Bureau Facts, 2000).

Japanese Americans were able to cope with anti-Asian sentiment that they experienced between the 1900s and 1940s by employing several unifying approaches. The development of a Japanese American worldview is partly due to the connection of members of this group through cultural organizations. Early Japanese American immigrants came from over 46 different prefectures (districts) in Japan. These prefectures had associations called *ken-jins,* which had more importance in America than in Japan as they promoted economic success and served a social function in uniting immigrants. The natural response to "fit-in" and belong became the major goal of *ken-jins.* They functioned as mutual aid societies, provided social events, and sponsored immigrants from Japan. While *ken* organizations provided a sense of peoplehood for Japanese Americans, the immigrant press became the "umbilical cord to the culture and politics of the motherland or, conversely, served as a focal point of resistance to the political and cultural aspirations of the homeland" (Daniels, 1988, p. 167). Newspapers unified Japanese Americans in the Pacific west states by providing local, state, and world news to thousands of the Issei generation who spoke Japanese as their primary language. The unifying experience of the internment camps continued to cement the role of community with Japanese Americans. Upon release from the camps the majority of Japanese Americans "were anxious to rebuild their lives and livelihoods and reluctant to relive their experience" (Lee, 1999). The focus became centered on rebuilding families and obtaining success through the education of their children.

The 1950s and the 1960s were a time during which Japanese Americans "remained remarkably silent" about the horrific experience of detainment. In the 1970s and 1980s a movement toward Asian American cultural awareness opened the discussion about the internment of World War II. Lee (1999) reported that social psychologists studying latent behaviors of many former internees likened their behaviors to that "of victims of rape or other physical violation. They demonstrated anger, resentment, self-doubt, and guilt, all symptoms of post-traumatic stress syndrome" (p. 152). However, their sense of community and their desire for achievement set them apart as one of the most successful and educated ethnic groups in America.

Asian Indians

Asian Indians, also called South Asians, account for approximately 11.8 percent of the Asian American population, representing 1,786,000 people. The countries of origin are India, Pakistan, Bangladesh, Sri Lanka, Nepal, Tibet, and Bhutan. The 1990 census indicates that only 25 percent of Asian Indians are born in the United States (Portes, 1996). The majority of the current population came to America between 1980 and 1990. While immigrants from the Indian subcontinent are represented in the American landscape, the majority of Asian Indians are from India, the world's second most populous country. Immigrants from India account for approximately 816,000 people, immigrants from Pakistan represent 81,000, Bangladesh accounts for nearly 12,000, Sri Lanka for almost 11,000, and smaller numbers from additional Asian Indian countries live in America (Leonard, 1997).

The history of Asian Indians involves a complex ethnic composition resulting from invasions and intermarriage between ethnic and national groups. The influences of Hinduism, Buddhism, and Jainism are interwoven into the cultures of South Asia, and issues surrounding religion impact political and social policies. In India, "religion is not a 'Sunday thing'—as it is to many people in the West—but an all-pervasive aspect of every facet of one's existence" (Dave, Dhingra, Maira, Mazumdar, Shankar, Singh, & Srikanth, 2000, p. 70).

Buddhism and Jainism are sects that separated from the ritualistic Veda religion. Buddhism's founder was Siddhartha Gautama Buddha (the awakened one), while the founder of Jainism was Mahavira, a saint who taught the doctrine of the sacredness of all living things. These two founders were from king-warrior castes of people. Jainism stressed nonviolence and respect for living and nonliving things, everything from people to stones. Buddhism stressed understanding the suffering in the world and elimination of that suffering. Desires must be moderated through "turning the wheel of *dharma* [religious duty] to achieve *nirvana* [the highest state of existence that involves freedom from self]" (Leonard, 1997, p. 7).

Hinduism involves *dharma* and *varnas* (ranked categories) and a caste system that divided people into five categories. The highest category is priests and scholars, called *Brahmans,* then the warrior ruler caste of *Kshtriyas,* followed by merchants known as *Vaisyas.* Artisans, peasants and workers are known as *Sudras,* and the *Untouchables* are a caste of people responsible for disposal of human excrement, washing clothes, delivering babies, working with dead animals, creating leather products, and cutting hair. This caste system is based on levels of purity and pollution (Dave et al., 2000; Leonard, 1997). Individuals of high purity intercede with the gods, while those persons having jobs associated with "pollution" could be barred from studying their religion. People marry within their caste system and are not allowed to eat, live, or marry outside. Women in all castes rank well below men "because they could not prevent the bodily production of polluting substances, such as blood from menstruation and childbirth" (Leonard, 1997, p. 7). Hinduism is more of an individual worship experience that focuses on respect for all life and belief in Brahman, the One that is the All. Many Hindus are vegetarians and revere the sacredness of the cow in their religious beliefs. The transmigration of souls (reincarnation) continues unless one practices religious duty, respects and values knowledge, and shows a devotion to God.

Islam became part of the Indian subcontinent around the eighth century A.D., when Muslim traders made contact with Asian Indians. By the 1500s Mongol Genghis Khan founded the Mughal Empire, which brought the Muslim religion and influenced Indian religious practices. The blending of religious practices between Muslim, Hinduism, and Buddhism is reflected in dress, food, language, and caste systems. Sects combining their own ethnic cultural practices with various ethnic groups became common.

The Punjabis, from the Punjab territory in Northern India near Pakistan, followed Guru Nanak, who developed the Sikh religion in the late 1500s. Gobind was the last guru who set the stage for modern Sikhism. Guru Singh (meaning lion) would require outward vestiges to honor belief. Some of these vestiges were unshorn hair and turban, the comb, steel bracelet, short undergarment, and sword (*kirpan*). Men who became disciples would adhere to the visible remnants of religion and take the title of Singh. Sikh religion has elements of the principal Asian Indian religions, but has no official priesthood or caste system. The monotheistic belief stresses equality, land ownership, family honor, independence, willingness to take risks, and courage (Angelo, 1997; Leonard, 1997).

In the late 1700s, the British brought Christianity to Asian Indians. After 300 years of existence, the Mughal Empire succumbed to British colonialism in 1857. In addition to Christianity, the British Crown introduced the English language, government, and education practices as it ruled India and other portions of the subcontinent until 1948.

Immigration Patterns

The earliest Asian Indian immigrants were Punjabis who came to California to work in agriculture in the late 1800s. Between 1899 and 1914, nearly 7,000 peasant men came to farming communities as laborers. They were Sikhs, but the existing groups made no distinctions in eastern religions or people and labeled all as Hindus. Over 85 percent of Asian Indians were Sikhs, 10 percent were Muslim, and another 5 percent were Buddhists and Hindus. The Punjabis experienced similar anti-Asian sentiments in the early 1900s as other Asian groups. An immigration commission noted that "Hindus are regarded as the least desirable, or better the most undesirable, of all the eastern Asiatic races which have come to share our soil . . . between one-half and three-fifths of them are unable to read and write" (Leonard, 1997, p. 42). The small number of early immigrants worked farms side by side with Mexicans. They traveled in small groups from farm to farm and began to marry Mexican women. The Punjabi-Mexican communities became known as "Mexican-Hindus," which of course, was wildly inaccurate.

Immigration patterns remained relatively static between 1900 and 1960. In 1970, Asian Indians totaled nearly 14,000 in America. In 1980, that number grew to 387,000 and, by the 1990 census, to 815,000 people. While many are refugees and people seeking political asylum from wars and uprisings on the subcontinent, the majority of the newest immigrants are seeking economic opportunities. In 1994, approximately 62 percent of the Indian-born population living in the United States had an average household income of $40,000. While new groups experience more unemployment than did previous immigrants, the move to involve themselves in family-owned businesses and in self-employment opportunities is seen by Asian Indian business people as the "best opportunity" for status and success (Leonard, 1997).

Southeast Asian Americans

Immigration from Southeast Asia is directly related to our country's concern over the threat of communism and the Vietnam War. Tensions between the former Soviet Union, their communist allies, and the U.S. government became known as the Cold War. This war of words, warnings, and ideologies began after World War II and continued until the 1990s, when the Soviet-bloc countries were dismantled. During the 1950s, America had an enormous concern about the growing threat of communism in Pacific Rim countries. In 1953, Korea was divided into the communist North and the democratic South, and the influence of Communist China was looming over Southeast Asian countries. America's efforts to contain communism led to the arrival in the United States of thousands of Vietnamese, Cambodian, Laotian, and Hmong refugees.

Waves of Immigration

Demographers describe four waves of immigration of people from Southeast Asia, occurring from 1975 to 1996. These waves are related to immigration laws and refugee status of people fleeing war-torn countries. A small percentage of Vietnamese, Cambodian, and Laotian people left their countries and came to America prior to 1964, but the majority of immigration was after the Vietnam War, between 1980 and 1990 (Chuong, 1994; Lucas, 1993; Paludeine, 1998; Portes & Rumbaut, 1996; Walker, 1994).

The history of Southeast Asian countries is rich in culture, traditions, and beliefs. Over 90 percent of the people from Vietnam are ethnic Vietnamese, whereas the remainder are ethnic Chinese and Hmong. Cambodia is now called Kampuchea, and over 85 percent of the population are ethnic Khmer. Smaller groups of ethnic Vietnamese, Chinese, Malaysian, and tribal people populate the country. The population of Laos is mostly ethnic Lao, ancestrally from Thailand. Several tribal groups are also represented, among them the Hmong, Yao, and Kha. All of these groups came together in the early 1860s under the broad label of Indochina as the French colonized the region. By 1859 the French influence on language, government, and industry pervaded Indochina. The French Michelin Corporation is noted for developing some of the largest industrial rubber manufacturing plants in Indochina. French colonialism ended in 1954 with civil wars and communist takeovers. In 1954, America sent 16,000 military advisors and support personnel in an effort to prevent communism from taking over the struggling new South Vietnam. By 1962 our involvement increased to bombings and air strikes and the use of elite American forces. By 1964 a Harris poll indicated that 85 percent of Americans supported the actions of the government to "free peoples of Vietnam" and contain communism. By 1965 over 550,000 troops were sent to Southeast Asia.

In addition to the war in Vietnam, America became involved in the "secret war" in Laos. The Laotian campaign sought an edge against communist forces in the region, and in the civil war in Cambodia. The Communist Pathet Lao government of Laos, with support from the communist Vietnamese, began to eradicate any groups suspected of supporting American efforts in the region. In the civil war in Cambodia led by communist Saloth Sar (also known as Pol Pot), his Communist Khmer Rouge began to eradicate any Western influence in the country. Between 1975 and 1979 over 3 million Cambodians were killed by the Khmer Rouge in campaigns that would become known as the "Killing Fields." American involvement continued in an effort to destroy communist efforts in these countries, and between 1964 and 1975 over 58,000 Americans died. Tens of thousands were wounded, and the former Indochinese countries lost millions of people and suffered severe casualties. The United States withdrew from the Southeast Asian war effort, leaving the region under communist control. Our commitment to support the anti-communist, war-torn people brought thousands of refugees to America.

The Indochina Migration and Refugee Assistance Act of May 23, 1975, provided immediate evacuation for thousands of people fleeing the invading communist governments. The Refugee Act of 1980 again opened the door for thousands to come to America, most notably people who suffered from communist regimes. Refugee status affords certain legal rights, the right to work and to receive services from government welfare programs (Ng, 1998; Paludeine, 1998; Portes & Rumbaut, 1996; Smith-Hefner, 1998). In the first wave between 1975 and 1977, over 130,000 refugees came to America, consisting of approximately 120,000 Vietnamese, 10,000 Cambodians, and 5,000 Laotians and Hmong. These refugees were, for the most part, from upper- and middle-class backgrounds. This first group comprised people that were educated in France and Vietnam, came from large cities, and experienced more education than the groups that would follow. Chuong (1994) reports that "surveys conducted at Camp Pendleton [one of the first refugee centers] in 1975 and 1976 showed that 48% of heads of these households completed high school, while 23% completed college and 4.5% had done graduate work" (p. 6).

Between 1978 and 1979 the second wave of immigration to America brought nearly 60,000 Vietnamese, ethnic Chinese from Vietnam, Cambodians, and Hmongs to America. This second wave of immigration ranged from people with some education to people with little or none. The second wave brought enormous challenges to agencies providing support services to refugees. The third wave began in 1980, with over 95,000 Southeast Asians entering the United States. In 1981, that number dropped to 86,000, and in 1982 only 43,656 persons arrived. The third wave had the greatest impact on American society due to the large numbers of tribal people and other refugees who were "the soldiers, the peasants, the farmers, and other working groups who had no formal education, no language training, no experience with Western societies" (Walker, 1989, p. 4).

One of the largest tribal groups of refugees was the Hmong, a nomadic people who lived in the highlands of Laos, Vietnam, and Cambodia. They were specifically recruited to help the Americans fight the "secret war" in Laos and proportionately experienced more casualties than any other ethnic group during the Vietnam War era. It is estimated that they lost over 50 percent of their 400,000 population. The migratory lifestyle of the Hmong contributed to the fact that they did not have a written language until missionaries introduced this concept in the early 1950s. All of these factors contributed to the difficulty of assimilation into the American culture (Ng, 1998).

The fourth wave is associated with people who lived for long periods in refugee camps in Thailand and other relocation centers. Many children adopted a "camp culture" that is very different from that of their parents' country of origin. A favorable aspect of the camp experience was the introduction of English to the Hmong, giving them some window into American life. Many of the children from the fourth wave participated in primary education and have received information from relatives in America about their new home. Between 1987 and 1993 the number of refugees admitted from Vietnam was 173,116, from Laos 75,554 (including the Hmong), and from Cambodia 9,603 (Portes & Rumbaut, 1996). In 1996, the number of immigrants from Vietnam peaked at 39,922. However, the numbers of American-born Indochinese people are increasing due to high birth rates.

The worldview of Southeast Asians is held by people who experienced years of war, displacement, fragmented societies, refugee camps, and interruptions in their culture and traditions. Primary religions among these people are Buddhism and Animism, however

FOCUS BOX

In the book, *Passages: An Anthology of the Southeast Asian Refugee Experience*, Chai Fang a Hmong college student believes that "I must have an education. Education is the key to lead me into the future. The type of job I will have depends on the kind of education I receive. I believe the higher the education I have, the better the job I will receive to survive in this competitive world." Fang continues to address beliefs in the power of education and states, "I also believe that education is not the only thing necessary to finding a good paying job. It is a long-term process, requiring social and personal experiences, which means knowledge to improve my personal behavior and attitude." Fang recognizes that getting an education is not only about getting a job, "but to gain knowledge, to get a feeling about the environment around me and to explore the world I live in." (p. 157)

the French influence and presence of foreign missionaries introduced Catholicism and various Protestant beliefs. Culture shock, generation gaps, and the ensuing conflicts between traditional and American ways have greatly impacted these groups and complicated family and community relationships.

Pacific Islander Americans

Pacific Islanders originate from a number of Polynesian islands in the Pacific Ocean. The label *Pacific Islander* designates not one ethnic group but a collection of cultures, traditions, and ethnicity. It is common for individuals who come under this designation to have a Samoan mother and a Tongan father, yet to follow the traditions of the Hawaiian Islands in which they live (Spickford & Fong, 1999). Various countries associated with the label of Pacific Islanders are Tonga, Samoa, Guam, Tahiti, Northern Mariana Islands, and Palau. The state of Hawaii is home to the largest Pacific Islander group. The majority of these islands became colonies of the British and Dutch in the 1500s and 1600s. Guam, Samoa, and Hawaii became U.S. territories in 1899, and Hawaii became the fiftieth state in 1959. The population of Pacific Islanders grew by 41 percent between 1980 and 1990, with the largest increase among ethnic Hawaiians, followed by Samoans and Guamanians. Families contain an average of 4.1 people, compared to Asians at 3.8. The Hmong have the highest number of persons per family at 6.6, with Samoans ranking next at 4.8. Large families are associated with high fertility rates and with cultural traditions encouraging children and cohesive extended families (Palsano, 1993). Approximately 100,000 Pacific Islanders live in Hawaii, accounting for 58 percent of their number in the United States. California is home to 17 percent of the Pacific Islander population, with Washington State at 15,000 people. States with 5,000 or more are Oregon, Texas, and Utah. The remaining Pacific Islander population in the United States is distributed throughout the country.

Locus of Control and Responsibility

Previous chapters have explored the concepts of locus of control and locus of responsibility, and how these concepts drive our interpretations of our abilities and circumstances. In summary, those persons with internal locus of control and responsibility generally understand that success and failure are directly correlated with personal effort.

To suggest that Asians and Pacific islanders subscribe to one set pattern of control and responsibility would seriously generalize an extremely diverse group of people. Applications of these theoretical constructs must take into consideration the various waves of immigration for each individual ethnic group, and these waves correspond to a variety of social and political seasons in America's history. Historical conditions certainly affect internal or external approaches to personal control, and assimilation and acculturation processes have an effect on individual and group characteristics within the dominant culture.

History reveals that all Asian groups experienced prejudice and discrimination at one point during their collective immigration processes. The majority of Far East Asian groups (Chinese, Japanese, Filipino, and Korean) and Asian Indians experience pride in their racial and ethnic identity and believe that they can shape their life events if given an opportunity. They generally recognize that there are racial barriers that might interfere with their progress, but that they can attain personal efficacy within the framework of the ethnic community and eventually within the larger society. This personal efficacy develops within the context of the extended family.

The Chinese experienced a sense of community within the secluded portions of inner cities. This worldview of a strong ethnic bond provided a sense of stability within the culture and limited reactive aggression and defiance against the dominant culture. The Japanese worldview that their community must survive pushed them toward a faster pace of acculturation than any other Asian group. Racism and internment seemed to compel this population to adapt more quickly to mainstream culture to firmly establish the fact that they were proud Americans. Recent Southeast Asian immigrant and refugee groups have experienced more difficulty adapting to American ideals than did the Japanese because many are living in the margins between the dominant culture and their own ethnic past.

The Impact on the Criminal Justice System

The impact of these groups on the criminal justice system has a historical connection to attitudes and beliefs held by the dominant culture about Asians coming to America. The late 1800s were a time of numerous laws enacted to curb Asian influence in America. Examples include marriage laws outlawing intermarriage between Asians and other groups, additional state and local taxes levied against Asians, and laws limiting land purchases by Asians. These laws were enforced by local police and adjudicated by state and local courts. Federal, state, and local law enforcement helped remove Japanese Americans from their homes to internment camps in the 1940s, and, between 1964 and 1975, law enforcement was called upon to calm the civil unrest surrounding the Vietnam War.

As Southeast Asians began immigrating into American cities, police were called in to resolve cultural clashes between the immigrants and the dominant culture. Officers and public officials had little knowledge about the new cultures and less understanding of the various languages and dialects. The immigrants became victims of opportunistic and hate crimes, and they believed that the criminal justice system could do little to assist or protect them.

One of the authors was actively involved in diversity training when the newest Asian immigrants came to California. Many citizens and law enforcement officers believed that the Southeast Asian refugees who came to America were former enemies of the United States during the Vietnam War. Common were slogans such as "The war is coming here" and "These people don't belong here." This lack of awareness of history, war, immigration, and refugee programs complicated the assimilation of groups within the dominant culture.

Ethnic enclaves in American cities impact those communities and the criminal justice systems that serve them. Portes and Rumbaut (1996) noted that Southeast Asians were originally sent to four major reception centers across America. Once there they were resettled to 813 separate locations to help with the assimilation and acculturation process. By 1980, over 40 percent of those resettled to areas within which their ethnic groups were concentrated. Data indicate that Vietnamese Americans chose first to live in Orange County, California, then next in Los Angeles County, and third in San Jose, California. Chinese Americans chose first to live in New York, followed by San Francisco and Los Angeles (Portes & Rumbaut, 1996). The Hmong are among those groups that live in ethnic enclaves, and Ng (1998) notes that in Fresno, California, there was

> only one Hmong family in 1977, four families in 1978, and five families in 1979. In 1980, the largest Hmong communities in the United States were located in St. Paul, Minnesota, and Orange County, California, with estimated populations of 6,000 and 4,000, respectively. In the same year, the Hmong in Fresno numbered 2,000. But by 1981, it had risen to 7,000; by 1982, it was 12,000, and in 1989, it was about 26,000. The reasons usually cited for this increase in population are the warm climate, fertile agricultural land, Hmong politics, and the desire for a concentrated settlement in the San Joaquin Valley. (p. 102)

Secondary migration trends indicate that only a small number of selected American cities are the preferred settlement locations for the majority of Asians. Immigrant movement is directly related to economics, and as people seek jobs and opportunities, groups move to inner cities where housing is affordable and service-industry jobs are available.

> Regardless of their qualifications and experience, recent immigrants generally enter at the bottom of their respective occupational ladders. Thus, foreign manual workers are channeled toward the lowest paying and most arduous jobs; immigrant professionals, such as physicians and nurses, also must accept less desirable entry jobs within their professions and even outside of them . . . some start small, with shops catering to their own community or in riskier "middleman" ventures in the inner city. (Portes & Rumbaut, 1996, p. 45)

Historical trends in spatial mobility patterns show the newest groups moving first to inner cities and then to other urban and rural locations where they attain economic stability and assimilation into the dominant culture. The latest trends of the newest immigrant groups show that many choose to remain in concentrated ethnic enclaves. The advantages of doing so rest in the preservation of their culture, their access to ethnic community networks, and greater social control over their children (Portes & Rumbaut, 1996). The disadvantages faced by the newest immigrants living in the inner cities include exposure to and involvement with criminal activity.

Asian Gangs

As of 1996 an estimated 846,000 juveniles were involved in gangs, with approximately 5 percent of that number associated with Asian gangs (Moore & Terrett, 1998). Similar to early studies suggesting that gangs were an inner-city phenomenon, Asian gangs have their roots in the inner city. That gang activity is not limited to the inner city is demonstrated by data showing increases in such activity in suburban and rural communities.

Explanations for gang development range from theories on social disorganization and culture conflicts to individual biological factors. Though gang formation is difficult to identify and there is no evidence to support a single reason for juveniles joining gangs, gang formation does generally seem to be more related to community than to individual issues.

As Shaw and McKay studied new immigrant groups in the 1920s in the inner cities, they sought to identify reasons for a growing crime phenomenon, and theorists currently study relationships between crime and the newest immigrant groups. Southeast Asian immigrants experience similar patterns of structural changes in the family to those of early European immigrants. Children experience weak family controls, poverty, and lack of social identity within the dominant culture. This identity becomes fractured due to anti-Asian sentiment that stems from historic attitudes against Asians and prejudice as a result of the Vietnam War. Southeast Asians have moved into traditionally lower-income housing complexes with similar ethnic communities, and children experience a sense of marginality as they are drawn toward the dominant culture and away from their history and family traditions. Many of these traditions have come into direct conflict with the culture of the mainstream, and many children turn away from parental attachments to seek attachments with other youth. Conflicts within families widen the gap between parental control and youth controlling their parents. External factors increase stress on families, and the stress is pathological to relationships within the group and with society at large.

The *Sourcebook of Criminal Justice Statistics* for 1998 indicated that runaways comprised the highest offense category for Asian and Pacific Islander arrests in the sample of 9,271 agencies. Seeking a sense of identity, many juveniles leave their families and join gangs. Southeast Asian gangs and, specifically, Vietnamese gangs are highly visible in Los Angeles County and New York—areas where large ethnic enclaves reside. In addition, there are 28 Asian gangs in Atlanta. One of the most notable is the Loc Lam gang, with 26 purported gang members. Between 1992 and 1996 the gang made an estimated $250,000 to $350,000 through armed robberies, extortion, and home invasions of other Asian people. The bread and butter of the gang's subsistence was the protection money paid to them by Vietnamese business owners (Heller, 1997). Typically, victims of Vietnamese gangs are other members of their ethnic community.

Chinese criminal activity is associated with tongs and Triads, traditionally economic gangs. As discussed earlier, Triads were formed as secret societies in the late 1600s in China as a way to retaliate against oppressive governmental demands. The name Triad came from the Chinese symbol of a triangle that represents three fundamental elements of the universe: heaven, earth, and man. The tongs were a minority within the Chinese community but exercised power through violence. Discrimination and exclusion from the dominant culture encouraged the formation of secret societies to achieve economic and social goals. This transferred to Chinese communities in America. Chinese tongs typically operate within their ethnic communities in San Francisco, New York, and Los Angeles.

The Triads evolved into highly organized crime societies that are profit-motivated, engaging in gambling, prostitution, money laundering, counterfeiting, immigrant smuggling, and extortion. The most notable Chinese Triad stories involved President Bill Clinton and Stanley Ho, a known Macao gambling tycoon with connections to a Triad gang. President Clinton accepted $250,000 from Ho in 1997 at a fund-raiser. In 1996, Vice President Al Gore was photographed at a Buddhist temple in California, sitting next to Ted Sioeng, a businessman who has alleged ties to a Triad in China. Sioeng, who is no longer in America, "reportedly funneled at least $400,000 in illegal contributions to the Democratic National Committee" (Waller, 2000). Waller summarized a report from the Royal Canadian Mounted Police indicating that Triad members seek legitimacy through accepted patterns of donations to charitable organizations, universities, and political parties. Another approach used by these "secret societies" is to increase their legitimate visibility by joining service clubs and being photographed with prominent people.

Crime and victimization are underreported in Asian communities due in part to a tradition of distrust of the corrupt criminal justice systems in the citizens' countries of origin. Immigrants and refugees bring with them this resentment, and this encourages victims to let crime go unreported. The National Crime Prevention Council (1995) suggests that a majority of Southeast Asians have a deep sense of distrust toward law enforcement and the courts. One survey of Vietnamese immigrants found that

> they feel that the police are insensitive to refugees' and immigrants' cultural heritage, and they are confused and anxious about the criminal justice system, specifically the bail process. They are concerned that suspects, after being released are allowed to return to threaten victims and witnesses. They are also afraid to testify in court about a suspect. In their homeland, an encounter between suspect and witness was not required by law. (p. 15)

Some of this distrust toward police has been reinforced in America as well. Tang (2000) noted that there are a number of incidents where "much like organized crime, state forces such as the police conceal their violent activity by relying on physical coercion, partnerships with corrupt business owners, and extortion."

Established in 1988, The Committee Against Anti-Asian Violence (CAAAV) organizes community organizations to work with police to uncover possible acts of violence against Asian communities. There were 481 hate incidents reported in 1997 toward Asian Americans, a number that dropped to 429 in 1998. The National Asian Pacific American Legal Consortium (1999) reported that "the response to hate crimes continues to be an inadequate and inconsistent patchwork of local, State, and Federal civil and criminal laws; moreover, prosecutors are not adequately enforcing the hate crime laws that do exist."

The knowledge of Asian immigrant's reluctance to report criminal incidents and what appears to be inadequate prosecution of acts against Asian Americans creates another type of victimization problem. It is not uncommon for Asian crime groups to prey on their communities with assurances they will not be reported. These close-knit ethnic communities also provide the backdrop for illegal gambling and prostitution. The *Sourcebook of Criminal Justice Statistics* reports that gambling is the second most common offense occurring in Asian American communities.

Comprehensive studies of Asian and Pacific Islander involvement with the criminal justice system are hampered by broad categorizations of race and ethnicity in the reporting data. The Bureau of Justice Statistics does not differentiate between ethnic groups within the category of Asian and Pacific Islander, and many agencies do not list race or ethnicity in their crime reports or in their categorization of jail inmates (Walker, Spohn, & DeLone, 2000). Bureau of Justice Statistics data covering inmate populations list four racial categories: white non-Hispanic, black non-Hispanic, Hispanic, and other (which includes American Indians, Alaska Natives, Asians, and Pacific Islanders). Categorization of people based upon standard labels does not allow for reporting on mixed race and mixed ethnic groups. Victims, witnesses, and perpetrators may not self-identify but may be labeled by officials based upon names or appearance. When crimes are perpetrated between members of the same ethnic or racial group, there is some concern that law enforcement might not be inclined to take reports, especially from reluctant victims and witnesses. Officers experience frustrations arising from the inability to communicate with limited English speakers and the lack of cultural knowledge.

Building Relationships

Asian Americans are a fast-growing segment of the American population, and their numbers are expected to continue to rise over the next 50 years. Concentrations of ethnic enclaves are continuing to be the norm for much of America's immigrant population. Three states currently account for the majority of the 200,000 Hmong population: California is home to approximately 70,000 Hmong, Minnesota estimates 65,000, and Wisconsin over 40,000. These numbers are consistent with other Asian groups, specifically Southeast Asians, who choose to live in areas populated by their own ethnic groups. The Congressional Research Service on Refugee Admissions and Resettlement Policy (Vialet, 1999) reports that the allocation numbers for Southeast Asian immigrants dropped to 8,000 for the year 2000 compared with 40,000 in 1995, and that this is the lowest for this geographic region since the end of the Vietnam War in 1975. The immigrants include people who are from refugee camps in Thailand and Hong Kong, reeducation camp detainees and Amerasians entering under the Orderly Departure Program, and residual Resettlement Opportunity for Vietnamese Returnees and for U.S. government employees.

It is likely that new immigrants will locate in existing ethnic enclaves, and providing adequate criminal justice services for these groups is a legitimate concern for many agencies throughout the United States. The Minneapolis Police Department addressed the large Hmong population by increasing communication between this group and its officers. Sergeant Dan Wulff (2000) from the Minneapolis Police noted some important measures that were taken by Chief Robert K. Olson, and many agencies across America employ the following recommendations:

- Know the communities. It is vital to increase understanding of the culture and history of the groups in your community.
- Create a liaison program with community leaders.
- Offer training opportunities for the community to create a better understanding of the roles of law enforcement.
- Assign specific liaison officers to create a positive relationships with community leaders.

These concepts reflect community policing and represent an important step toward recognizing and validating diversity in communities. Creating a liaison between community members and law enforcement can eliminate fears and negative perceptions that many groups hold toward police. Cross-cultural training and education for criminal justice agencies can bridge racial and ethnic groups to the system and to surrounding communities. Such programs as civilian ride-along, mentoring, and school activity leagues can bring diverse communities together with law enforcement personnel. Organizations such as Drug Abuse Resistance Education (DARE), Police Activity Leagues (PAL), and Cops in Schools open dialog between community members and their children. Such dialog facilitates a partnerships in crime prevention and creates safe living environments.

The National Crime Prevention Council (1995) notes that increasing ethnic minority recruitment can eliminate many obstacles that hinder effective policing in immigrant communities. The report indicated that hiring "non-native" officers is a benefit to both the agency and the "non-native" community. The agency benefits by having officers from the non-native community who will teach their employees about cultural issues, act as interpreters, and recommend strategies to reduce cultural tension and conflict. Many ethnic communities "experienced a decrease in crime and a marked reduction in the fear of crime." Many agencies reported that the presence of non-native officers "increased non-native community access to the criminal justice system and improved trust in law enforcement and other branches of the system . . . it also increased the feeling of community safety among newly arrived groups and thus for the community as a whole."

Among the newest immigrant groups are Asians and Pacific Islanders, and they experience more confusion, mistrust, and fear about the criminal justice system than does the dominant culture. Ethnic minority officers among the ranks will help bridge the gap between the system and the immigrant community. These officers, in turn, will become "role models of good citizenship and community service" that can be effective deterrents toward crime.

Summary

Asian Americans are a fast-growing segment of the American population, and their numbers are expected to continue to rise over the next 50 years. Asian and Pacific Islander Americans include a diverse group of people who have separate worldviews incorporating distinct cultures, traditions, beliefs, and languages. These groups are not homogenous; rather they exhibit a great variety of differences that have evolved over centuries. Their histories are replete with conquest, political struggles, and struggles with nature. American immigration practices and policies toward Asian Americans reflect an "anti-foreigner stance" that is present throughout American history. However, over the last 160 years, Asian and Pacific Islanders have flourished in spite of racial ideologies that limited their access to participation in the dominant culture. Their historical struggle toward acceptance embodies the American ideal of "surviving against the odds."

Discussion Questions

1. What are some ways that the historic relationship between Asian and Pacific Islander Americans and the dominant culture affect their worldview?

2. What are key issues in building trust between this group and the criminal justice system?

3. What are some examples of racial stereotyping and its impact on the system?

4. How do the concepts of locus of control and responsibility apply to Asian and Pacific Islanders?

6

Middle Eastern Americans and the Criminal Justice System

Learning Objectives

After reading this chapter you should be able to do the following:

1. Compare and contrast world events and their effect on Middle Eastern Americans.
2. Distinguish between Arab Americans, Jewish Americans, and Middle Eastern people.
3. Define hate crime legislation and its impact on Middle Eastern Americans.

In 1978, Mehdi noted in the foreword of her book that, because of the assimilation of Arab Americans in society, many Americans are unaware of their existence. She states, "Arab Americans are 'standing up' to be counted, letting their voices be heard . . . and in the last half of the twentieth century the Arab world may be the important unknown in any equation dealing with international destinies . . . the Arab American may well help provide the balance in such an equation" (p. ix). These words have rung true in U.S.–Middle East foreign affairs from 1979 to the present; the Arab world has become an important equation in international affairs. International relations with the Middle East became complicated as follows:

1. The U.S. Embassy in Iran was taken over by followers of Ayatollah Khomeini in 1979.
2. U.S. troops were sent to Lebanon in 1983 in retaliation against attacks on Americans.
3. U.S. fighter planes attacked Libya in 1986 after leader Muammar al-Qaddafi ordered international terrorist attacks.
4. In 1986 the Iran-contra scandal involved the United States paying Iran with arms to free American hostages in Lebanon.
5. In 1991 Iraq invaded Kuwait, and the United States engaged in military efforts, called Desert Storm, in support of Kuwait and to oppose the threat to other Arab countries.
6. In 1998, in an effort to stop ballistic attacks by Iraq on their neighboring countries, the United States bombed Iraq.

These events, along with the fact that this region has the world's primary oil-producing land, impacted world politics. As Mehdi (1978) projected, the international destiny of people from the Middle East became an increasing concern to the United States.

Labels

Middle Eastern Americans have roots in a large geographic region that generally includes countries that are aligned as Arabic speaking and non–Arabic speaking (Suleiman, 1999). The following countries are representative of this population: Algeria, Armenia, Bahrain, Cyprus, Egypt, Lebanon, Libya, Iran, Iraq, Israel, Jordan, Kuwait, Turkey, Sudan, Syria, Saudi Arabia, Tunisia, United Arab Emirates, and Yemen. The non-Arab countries are Israel, Turkey, Iran, and Armenia. In fact, people from Turkey would not use the label "non-Arab country"; they would consider themselves part of the former Ottoman Empire that once claimed most of the Middle East region up to the 1800s. People from Israel, on the other hand, would refer to themselves as Jewish or non-Jewish, or Semites, or Palestinians. The term *Semites* (or *Semitic*) refers to peoples from southwestern Asia and to the Afro-Asiatic language family that includes Arabic, Hebrew, Aramaic, and Ethiopic. As of the late 1700s, the label *Semites* became somewhat synonymous with the label *Jews.* Iranian Americans would probably refer to themselves as Persian (the ancient name of the land of Iran), and people from Armenia, while living most of their existence under Turkish and Soviet oppression, would proudly declare that they are Armenian.

The labels are as varied as the distinct cultures, languages, and religion that this population brings to America. Many Americans commonly identify people from these countries into two categories: Arabs and Jews. These two categories do not define the myriad of cultures, traditions, ethnicities, languages, and religions of people from the Middle East. However, there are some general understandings about the large majority of Arabs who will likely identify themselves as Arab Americans: They speak the Arabic language, practice Islam and Christianity, and have historical roots in Middle East countries (Suleiman, 1999).

Arab Americans

Arab Americans have heritages from the 21 Arab countries in the Middle East and in North Africa, which comprises over 255 million people who call themselves Arabs (Al-Krenawai & Graham, 2000). To understand people who identify themselves as Arabs one must acknowledge the infusion of religion in their social, political, and personal lives. While the Arab countries range from military dictatorships to republics, the expression of religious beliefs is incorporated into their political ideologies. Since, the vast majority of Arabs practice Islam, the world's second-largest religion, the natural fusion of law and religion are incorporated into a legal system that is the Islamic Law.

Islam and Its Relationship to Arab Ideology

The religious beliefs of Arab Americans are as diverse as their ethnicities and culture. Joseph (1999) records that "Maronites, Catholics, Protestants, Greek Orthodox, Jews, Sunnis, Shi'a, Druze, Sufis, Alawites, Nestorians, Assyrians, Copts, Chaldeans, and Bahias" are some of the most notable religious groups among Arab Americans (p. 260). Joseph (1999) contends that the majority of Arab Americans are Christian and only in recent years has there been the growing number of Arab Americans who are Muslims. This increase in Muslims in America from Indonesia, India, Malaysia, and the Middle East has encouraged a broader understanding of Islam within the dominant culture.

Islam is Arabic for "submission to *Allah*" (which is Arabic for God), and Muslims are "ones who submit to God." Joseph (1999) further defines Islam from the Hans Wehr standard *Dictionary of Modern Arabic,* which notes "Islam comes from the same root as the word for peace (*salam*) and the most commonly used word for welcoming or parting, *salamat* and *ma' issalami* (peace on to you and go in peace) . . . peace is the free-willed reconciliation of self to God" (p. 261). Islam, a monotheistic faith, was founded by the prophet Mohammed in the seventh century A.D. and incorporates elements of two belief systems: Judaism and Christianity. It was during Ramadan, the ninth month of the Islamic calendar, that the archangel Gabriel revealed the holy book, *The Qur'an* (Koran), to Mohammed while he fasted in the Cave of Hira on the outskirts of Mecca. In 630 A.D. Mohammed claimed Mecca as the *Holy City* for Muslims, built the mosque, the holy shrine *Ka'aba*, and declared pilgrimages called *hajj* to Mecca. Over the centuries, Islam flourished and it is now estimated that there are one billion Muslims of various ethnic backgrounds throughout the world, with 6 million living in the United States. Several religious sects developed as disagreements surfaced in who shall be proclaimed the successors of Mohammed. The three most notable are the Sunni, the Shi'a, and the Druze. In general, the Sunni branch of Islam (followers called Sunnites) practice the orthodox tradition of belief, which accepts the first four successors from Mohammed as leader, whereas the Shi'a sect (followers called Shi'ites) reject the first three and accept Mohammed's son-in-law and his descendents as successors. The majority of the Shi'ites live in Iran and Iraq. The Druze sect is comprised of approximately 300,000 members who live in closed, secret, religious communities in Lebanon, Israel, and Syria and claim a different successor and his descendents to the role of leader of the faith (Haddad & Smith, 1994; Joseph, 1999).

Islam is a religion and a social order that has a divine origin and is guided by that ultimate authority (Mattar, 1999). The intertwining of religion, law, and politics provides the structure of legal systems for most Arab countries. In general, laws in America are classified based on the theory of liability: human acts are lawful or unlawful. Islamic laws are classified as human acts based on "different circumstances as mandatory, permissible, recommended, reprehensible, or forbidden" (Mattar, 1999, p. 102). Laws related to dress, gender roles, and children are based on ideas of a religious social order. For example, Islam has a patriarchal culture that views males as "the leaders and highest authority in their households, their economy, and the polity" and females as gaining "social status through marriage and rearing children (especially boys)" (Al-Krenawai & Graham, 2000). This patriarchal structure places authority with fathers who then are subordinate to their fathers, creating a legacy of respect and honor to eldest males in families. This family structure creates what some call a clan or a tribe.

The religious social order of patriarchy affects the status of women in society. For example, Saudi Arabia requires women to cover themselves from head to toe, and unmarried women are not allowed to mix with unmarried men. This is a prohibition that is designed to keep women pure before the eyes of God. In fact, Saudi Arabia's Committee to Promote Virtue and Ban Vice routinely sends out clergy with armed police officers to patrol city streets to enforce strict social codes. The Islamic legal system also has children legally in the custody of their mother until boys turn seven and girls turn nine, at that time they are under the custody of their father.

Laws related to morality and Islamic values have not changed, while other aspects of Islamic legal systems have altered to reflect the Western model of law. "Although Islamic law once had great influence on the legal systems of the Arab countries of the Middle East, many of the traditional rules of Islamic law have been replaced by rules derived from the European legal systems" (Mattar, 1999, p. 103). It is with this heritage of the fusion of religion, law, and social order that Arab immigrants came to America.

Waves of Immigration

Arab Americans have a 120-year history with America, and historians have identified two major waves of immigration associated with their coming to this country. The first wave is associated with the 1880s to World War II, and the second wave is post–World War II to the present (Haddad & Smith, 1994; Suleiman, 1999). Historical documents do show that a small number of Arabs came to America probably as slaves or indentured servants in the early 1700s, but their numbers would not reach great proportion until the early 1900s (Mehdi, 1978).

The population estimates for the first wave of Arab Americans is somewhat distorted in the early census years. Due to the fact that the Ottoman Empire had claimed a vast majority of the Middle East, people who did immigrate to America were labeled Turkish. Many of the Arabs were also lumped together with Greeks and Armenians. The Turkish Empire imposed its beliefs and culture on all newly acquired communities, which propelled many people from Syria to leave their land for opportunity in America. By 1914, approximately 106,721 poor, uneducated Christian Syrians had arrived in America. In the early twentieth century, the term Syrian American became synonymous with Arab American (Mehdi, 1978; Suleiman, 1999). This first group were village farmers and artisans who came from Mount Lebanon—with over 90 percent Christian and the other 10 percent either Muslim or Druze.

The early immigrants were known to engage in peddling of wares from door-to-door, which was a respected practice in the Middle East. While this profession was not highly respected in America, it did serve a purpose, and rural Americans welcomed immigrants. Some researchers believe it is through this peddling process of selling linens, towels, needles, thread, shoelaces, and other notions that the Syrians were able to assimilate faster in the American culture than later groups. It brought the new immigrants into direct contact with English-speaking Americans. It exposed them to the dominant culture at that time and allowed for positive interchange. In addition to the fact that the majority of these immigrants practiced Christianity, Syrian Americans would attend local churches and community events. While this contact increased their general acceptance into American life, they considered themselves in the United States but not part of the "system" (McCarus, 1994).

After World War I, many immigrants from the former Ottoman Empire came to America. Several issues blurred the actual numbers that immigrated. One is that America was not open to having former Ottoman Empire citizens, Christian or Muslims. Fear of "not getting in" drove hundreds to change their ethnic identity to that of Serbs or Turkish Armenians. Another reason for deflated census numbers is America's lack of distinction between Arabs, Turks, and Armenians. Immigration officials used the label *Arabs* for these diverse groups of people who, more than likely, would not have identified themselves as Arabs. With this in mind, the 1930 census of 130,000 Arab Americans would include a mixture of ethnic identities. After World War I, the new Republic of Turkey did not allow emigration of its citizens, inhibiting legal "Turkish" immigration between 1923 and 1941 (Bilge, 1994). The end of World War I also marked the beginning of Arab Americans' acceptance that they could not go home again. This new realization that it would be impossible to return to their former "homeland" changed the attitudes of many Arab Americans from being sojourners in America to accepting themselves as permanent settlers. The new political ideologies in their former homeland abolished their dream of returning but became the motivating factor to increase their own Americanization of their families and communities (Aswad, 1999; Seikaly, 1999; Suleiman, 1999).

As with many immigrants, searching for jobs moves people from place to place. In the 1920s the Ford Motor Company in Detroit, Michigan, revolutionized the car manufacturing industry. The assembly line process required a large labor force and Arab Americans became the predominant source. When Ford moved its company to Dearborn, outside the metropolitan area of Detroit, the Arab community followed (Hassoun, 1999; McCarus, 1994). Immigrants came for work and stayed because of the Arab American community.

The second wave of immigration begins at the end of World War II, at the close of which, another war ensued in the Middle East, placing the region called Palestine under the control of the new State of Israel. In 1948 Palestinians—Muslims and Christians—immigrated to America and settled in the Detroit metropolitan area. Seikaly (1999) noted that the new immigrants followed similar patterns of other Arab immigrant communities. The "Palestinian settlement patterns were modeled on the life they had left behind: homogenous communities grouped by family, religion, sect, and village" (p. 27). This second wave was made up of more educated and professional individuals, including students, lawyers, teachers, engineers, and doctors. The vast majority were political refugees who sought out opportunities in a democratic society.

After the Arab-Israeli War in 1967, more political refugees came to America. This was also the period in which Arab Americans began to redefine themselves within the U.S. political system. Seikaly (1999) notes that "the events of 1967 constituted a watershed in Palestinian and Arab politics . . . becoming a catalyst that ignited the political atmosphere and brought together intellectuals, student activists, and various community members" (p. 34). In the 1970s and 1980s the immigrants were distinct from earlier groups in that they "came with self-views defined as Arabs, as nationalists, and as activists of political orientations, some from within the Palestinian structures" (Seikaly, 1999, p. 35).

There are approximately 3.5 million Arab Americans, with the Metropolitan Detroit region accounting for the largest population in North America, with 250,000 people (Economist, 2000; Hassoun, 1999). The entry point for immigrants from the Arab world and the center of the Muslim community is in this region (Aswad, 1999). Population estimates also show that 25,000 to 30,000 Palestinians live in this region. The Chicago and Los Angeles metropolitan areas have the second-highest concentrations of Arab Americans.

Jewish Americans

While Israel is recognized as the "homeland" for Jews, the largest Jewish population is in the United States. Of the total 13 million Jews throughout the world, over 5.6 million live in America. Israel has the second-largest Jewish population, with 4.5 million people, which constitutes over 80 percent of its residents. France follows with over 525,000 Jews, while Canada and Russia have nearly the same number in each country—360,000 (De Lange, 2000). The five states with the largest Jewish concentration are New York with 1,652,000, California with 921,000, Florida 644,000, New Jersey 435,000, and Pennsylvania 325,000. These numbers reveal only a population of people that identify themselves as Jewish; it does not describe their diverse ethnic backgrounds. People who claim Jewish identity are from cultural groups across the world and claim religious beliefs of both Judaism and Christianity. Typically, Jewish identity is connected to the religious belief, Judaism, but this is only secondary to the connection of a history and a sense of origin shared by Jewish people (De Lange, 2000). Jews in America have a multitude of ethnic backgrounds but share a past and a sense of destiny. Their past is associated with the word *dispersion* or *Diaspora*. Sandberg (1986) acknowledges that

Jewish identity is difficult to define because there are so many different kinds of Jews ranging from religious to secular, from Jews in Israel to Jews in the Diaspora, from those who are Jews by commitment to those who have assimilated, and from those who are Jews all the time to those who are Jews occasionally. The aspects of the Jewish experience, however, that are applicable to all Jews . . . they are characterized by a sense of peoplehood focussed on Israel, responses to the meaning of the Holocaust, or merely the fact of claiming to be Jewish. (p. 105–106)

Religion

The history of the Jewish people has beginnings in the land of Israel. The beginnings of dispersion of Jewish people began when Rome conquered Israel in 70 C.E. (A.D.). Tens of thousands of people were killed, or sold into slavery and dispersed. The spirit of the Jewish people and their religion, Judaism, created both an identity and mutual experiences that united people throughout history. The Jewish religion and their "sacred books" (the Old Testament of the Christian Bible) establishes that there is only one God of all humanity. The Bible has three sections that provide the foundation for the Jewish faith. The *Torah,* meaning guidance or instruction, is considered the oldest and most sacred authoritative history of the Jewish people. Laws and regulations documented within the ancient writings from the *Torah* provide the guidelines for religious practice today. The second section, called *Neviim,* are stories from eight different prophets about God's chosen people, while the third section, called *Ketuvim,* contain Jewish poetry and other historical facts and experiences (De Lange, 2000). The "sacred books" of the Torah foretold of the dispersion of the Israelites. De Lange (2000) noted that Rabbi Eleazar expected that this Diaspora was God's will when he said, "God scattered Israel among the nations for the sole purpose that they should gain many proselytes" (p. 42). Diaspora has the root meaning "to scatter seed (the English word 'spore' comes from the same root) so it can be understood in a positive sense: just as a farmer scatters seed to bring in a richer harvest, so God scattered the people so as to win proselytes" (De Lange, 2000, p. 42). This idea of dispersion continues to be at the root of the Jewish identity.

Diaspora and Peoplehood

By the Middle Ages, two general classifications of people emerged: Ashkenazim and Sephardim, along with denominations of Orthodox, Reform, and Conservative. The Ashkenazim Jews were people from Western Europe, while the Sephardim were from Spain and Portugal. Jews traditionally lived in urban areas and generally were more educated and economically stable than other ethnic groups (Joseph, 1969). By the 1800s, Jews in Russia, Romania, and Austro-Hungary experienced a much higher standard of living than the average ethnic "countryman." In Russia, over 51 percent of the Jewish population lived in incorporated towns. The designation of "townsmen" was considered to be of a high-ranking social status. Over 95 percent of all Jews in Russia had this ranking as compared to only 7 percent of Russians. Russian peasants comprised over 86 percent of this social status, while Jews accounted for 4 percent. In Romania, Jews also had a higher educational and economic standing than ethnic Romanians. While only a small portion of the ethnic Romanian population owned and operated businesses, Jews operated over one-fifth of the large industries in Romania. In Austro-Hungary over 44 percent of the Jewish population was engaged in commerce and trade, 29 percent in industry, and 11 percent in agriculture. Similar to Russia and Romania, ethnic Austro-Hungarians were predominately engaged in agriculture (86 percent) with only 4 percent in industry and 1 percent in commerce. In all of these countries the majority of the Jewish population successfully engaged in industrial enterprises. The success of Jews became the backdrop for anti-Semitism and dispersions.

Historical accounts of the rise and fall of leaders and the forever changing boundary lines of countries impacted the Jewish people. While they would consider themselves native to a particular country, owing to their faith, they were always perceived as separate from the dominant culture; and these perceptions would propel this population across the world. For example, in 1619 Jews were pushed out of Brazil by the Portuguese and came to New Amsterdam (New York). Dispersions would continue to bring Jews to America in small numbers from 1600 to the 1700s.

The 1848 German Revolution was the major impetus for the first wave of Jewish immigration. This first wave between 1840 and 1870 brought over 50,000 Jewish people, who were educated and advanced in commerce and trade. Upon arrival, they moved to large urban areas and quickly engaged in commerce and banking. By 1870, "about 10 percent of Jewish firms were capitalized at or above $100,000; in 1890, almost 25 percent reported a minimum capital of $125,000" (Portes & Bach, 1985, p. 39).

Between 1870 and 1914, the second wave of immigration brought over 2 million Jews to America. The Russian government, in an effort to inhibit the economic success of Jews, began systematic discrimination efforts, whereby political, economic, and geographic restrictions applied to all Jewish people. To escape Russian tyranny and oppression, another dispersion brought immigrants to America, specifically New York City. In spite of anti-Semitism, quota systems, and restrictions, the Jewish entrepreneurial spirit propelled immigrants to ascend the economic ladder (Paludeine, 1998; Portes & Bach,1985). By the end of the 1930s " two-thirds of all Jewish workers were in white-collar positions . . . the 1940s Jews comprised 65.7% of New York City's lawyers and judges, 55.7% of its physicians, and 64% of its dentists" (Portes & Bach, 1984, p. 41). While the majority of Jewish immigrants became economically acculturated within the dominant culture, they continued their distinctiveness in Jewish traditions, in values, and in a "collective solidarity."

After World War I, Jewish immigrants were among the many war refugees who came to America. However, the next large wave of immigrants was after World War II. Between 1933 and 1945, Jewish people experienced the Holocaust by the German Nazi leader Adolph Hitler; over 6 million Jewish men, women, and children were exterminated. Over 3 million Jews lived in Poland prior to World War II, and at the end of the war only 50,000 people were left. Czechoslovakian Jews experienced similar devastation. Prior to the war, 360,000 Jewish people lived there, and after the war fewer than 5,000 (De Lange, 2000). De Lange (2000) notes that "even today it hardly seems credible that a nation, supposedly among the most civilized in Europe, fell prey to such appalling collective madness . . . but the European anti-Semitism, the Russian pogroms, and the Nazi policy of genocide have actually had the effect of greatly strengthening attachment to the Jewish nation, as an ideal and as a reality" (pp. 43–44).

FOCUS BOX

In *The Century,* Peter Jennings and Todd Brewster discuss the impact of the Holocaust on the Jewish people in the chapter called "The Global Nightmare." They relate that Hitler wanted the concentration camps out of sight from the German people, so the majority of the camps were located in Poland. They state that the camps "took the industrialization of killing to a new level." Now there were not only weapons factories but actual killing factories too, depositing the stench of their work into the surrounding communities, fertilizing the neighborhood flower beds, employing the local talent, and working hard to meet productivity quotas. The staff of Auschwitz, the most notorious of the Polish camps, proudly claimed to be able to "process" 12,000 inmates a day. (p. 264)

The Jewish State of Israel

The cementing of Jews across the world has resulted from the connection to the Jewish State of Israel. In 1948 the history of the state of Israel begins and continues with wars between the surrounding Arab countries and the Jewish State. The Six-Day War in 1967 established Israel as a small but mighty country. Egypt arbitrarily closed the Gulf of Aqaba to Israel, which prompted Israeli military to take action. Israel succeeded in gaining access, but with a price. Anti-Jewish terrorism flourished as a means of retaliation against Israel. From the bombing of Israeli Olympic athletes in Munich in 1972 to murders of Jewish soldiers in the disputed West Bank of Israel in 2000, anti-Jewish events have galvanized Jews throughout the world.

In support of Israel and its desire to be an independent nation, America sends over $3 billion a year in economic and military assistance (Society, 1998). American citizens support these efforts. A New York Times Poll, in 1998, found that the support is based partially on "religion, history, and contemporary politics, with 76% believing that the U.S. has a vital interest in Israel." On a different note, the survey also indicated that the first response to the question about what one thinks of when hearing the word *Israel,* 26 percent thought of war. American opinions of groups have a direct correlation to events in the world. These events affect not only Jewish Americans but all Middle Easterners.

Worldview of Middle Eastern Americans

The worldview of Middle Easterners is characterized by the position that there is not a single Middle Eastern culture. There are some similar experiences that they do share—those of exclusion and discrimination. While early immigrants assimilated more easily than later groups, being exposed to anti-Semitic and anti-Arab reactions are part of the worldview of Middle Easterners. Drawing from their individual ethnic group's collective identity sustained immigrants through changing tides of political and social unrest.

For the majority of Middle Eastern immigrants values are centered on family, religion, family honor, and pride. The extended family unit provides a sense of structure, and one's personal identity is realized within the membership of the communal organization.

There is a relationship between issues of gender, religion, and generations. The role of women in Arab cultures is intertwined with religion. The Koran identifies chastity and honor as imperative qualities for females and states that these qualities bring value and honor to the family. The one distinctive role of men involves caring economically for the welfare of the entire family. The role of women is embedded in the social order of family honor and they are responsible to uphold this honor as a "fundamental and valued element to the creation and maintenance of an Arab ethnic identity" (Ajrouch, 1999, p. 131). The values placed on gender roles also exist within the framework of the community. The value of expressing individual qualities within the sociocultural norms and values of the group provides a sense of security, belonging, and emotional well-being. The solidarity and community identity strengthens the sense of peoplehood.

A sense of family, community, and history unites Jewish Americans. The role of religion provides a moral scheme that is an essential element in the organization of their community and in the drawing together of the family. Their religious beliefs also guide their responsibilities as active members in social, political, and economic aspects of the broader community in which they live. Sandberg (1986) noted

> Jews tend to view their concerns for Jewish life in the context of their contributions to the larger community. They feel a commitment and loyalty to the U.S., the country that gave them an opportunity to deepen their roots and raise their children in safety. The concept of helping one's own people while assisting others has long been a central underpinning of the Jewish value system. (p. 2)

Middle Easterners traditionally have "helped their own people." This worldview that unites groups of people also helps them cope during stressful events. From the first Christian immigrants from Lebanon and Syria to the recent Muslim immigrants from the Balkans, the values of religion and family have helped define one's political and social identity. It is within this framework that Middle Easterners come to America and build their lives on the principles of democracy, independence, and freedom.

The Impact of Hate Crimes on Selected Groups

With the increase of public intolerance for bias-motivated crime, hate crime reporting also increases. In the closing years of the twentieth century, several heinous crimes focused attention on the devastating effects of prejudice and discrimination. Abner Louima, a Haitian American security guard, was brutally sodomized and beaten by two New York Police officers. In Jasper, Texas, James Byrd, an African American, was chained to a pick-up truck and dragged to his death by a group of young men who knew Mr. Byrd. In the state of Wyoming, Matthew Shepherd, a college student who was also gay, was driven to a rural area and tied to fence posts and beaten to death by a group of college-aged young adults. All of these events highlight the sadistic nature of crimes against people based on their race, ethnicity, religion, or sexual orientation. The Hate Crimes Statistics Act of 1990 (HCSA) established formal procedures for the U.S. Justice Department to collect data and disseminate information on hate crimes in law enforcement jurisdictions across America. Currently, there are 41 states that have special penalty enhancements for crime based on hate. In almost every state there are laws and legislation for the sole purpose of addressing bias-motivated crimes.

As defined by the Hate Crimes Statistics Act of 1990, amended in 1994 and 1996, a hate crime is, "A criminal offense against a person or property motivated in whole or in part by the offender's bias against a race, religion, disability, ethnic/national origin, or sexual orientation."

The FBI states that "Hate crimes are not separate distinct offenses, but rather traditional crimes motivated by the offender's bias." These crimes are more of a challenge to law enforcement because they are more violent, socially disruptive, random, and serial in nature than ordinary crimes, and are more difficult to solve. This is because there is a terroristic component associated with hate crimes, whereby even a relatively minor incident can breed fear and distrust across fragile intergroup lines. Research has also shown that hate crimes tend to be more violent, more traumatic to the victim, and sometimes committed by groups of perpetrators who are previously unknown to the victim. Such crimes terrorize the entire targeted community (FBI, 2001).

Hate crime laws and legislation are based on four federal statutes:

1. Title 18, United States Code (U.S.C.), Section 241 (Conspiracy Against Rights)
2. Title 18, U.S.C., Section 245 (Interference with Federally Protected Activities)
3. Title 18, U.S.C., Section 247 (Damage to Religious Property; Obstruction in Free Exercise of Religious Beliefs)
4. Title 42, U.S.C., Section 3631 (Criminal Interference with Right to Fair Housing)

In 1999, 7,876 bias-motivated crimes were reported to the Federal Bureau of Investigation (FBI). In 1998, 7,775 and in 1997, 8,049 incidents were reported; 1996, 8,759; and in 1995, 8,000 incidents. Hate crimes are still underreported, but law enforcement agencies are increasing their efforts to document and investigate these crimes (FBI, 2001; Lieberman, 2000).

Over half of all hate crimes and incidents are related to race, and religion was the second-highest motivating factor, followed by ethnic origin and then sexual orientation. In the race bias category, African Americans are the target of hate crimes more than any other group (60%), and in the religion category over 77 percent of hate crimes were

FOCUS BOX • *Hate Crime Indicators*

Hate crime indicators include, but are not limited to, the following:

- racial, ethnic, gender, and cultural differences of perpetrator and victim
- comments, written statements, or gestures
- drawings, markings, symbols, or graffiti
- involvement in organized hate groups or with their members

- previous existence of hate crimes or incidents
- victim or witness perception that the incident is a hate crime
- motive of offender
- location of incident
- lack of other motives

against Jews and Jewish institutions. Whereas African Americans have experienced the largest number of race-motivated crimes for a particular group, no other racial or ethnic group in America are more affected by world events and the onslaught of hate crimes than Middle Easterners.

In light of the recent violence in the Israeli and Palestinian West Bank territory dispute, many of the 300,000 Palestinian Americans who live in Chicago and Detroit worry about their overseas relatives, friends, and neighbors. A November 2000 *Newsweek* article interviews Palestinian American teenagers who are expressing sorrow for the young people in Israel who are being killed because of disputed land. They, too, are experiencing the burden of a failed peace process. When the spotlight is on the Middle East, they feel that it is focused on them. They reported that American coverage of the conflict appears biased, which can lead to more anti-Arab sentiment. At the Muslim Youth Center in a Chicago suburb, one 20-year-old stated that "I can speak for all of us when I say we are against that [violence]." Another 16-year-old commented that "My goal is to learn about where I came from, then educate people as to who I am. God willing, I think we could change things." Ali (2000) noted that "the sixteen-year-old's cause may be half a world away—but the hope is typically American."

Many hate crimes in America are associated with events that are "half a world away." As hostilities fluctuate in the Middle East, acts of violence against Arab Americans and other ethnic groups with Muslim religious beliefs make the victims targets of racism. A 1980 study revealed a cadre of negative stereotypes held by Americans toward Arabs. Some of the labels were "barbaric, treacherous, cunning, mistreat women, warlike, anti-Christian, and anti-Semitic." The study found that the actual label of "Arab" had more of a negative impact than such individual ethnic labels as Lebanese, Saudi, or Palestinian. Studies in the 1990s continued to find negative stereotypes about this population (Suleiman, 1999). It seems that "anti-Arab racism, like other types of racism, permeates mainstream culture and political institutions . . . and is often tolerated by mainstream society . . . it appears that Arab Americans are one of the few ethnic groups it is still 'safe to hate'" (Suleine, 1999, p. 320).

Albert Mokhiber, president of the American-Arab Anti-Discrimination Committee in Washington, D.C., reported that between August and December 1990, after Saddam Hussein attacked Kuwait, there were 41 unprovoked violent acts against Arab Americans. In San Diego, California, there was an attempted bombing of a mosque, a drive-by shooting of an Arab American–owned Dairy Queen, and hundreds of other hate crimes against this population after the media exposed the Hussein attack on television (Cohen, 1991). By the end of Operations Desert Shield and Desert Storm over 100 additional hate crimes had been committed against Arab Americans. A direct correlation between hate crimes and the media exists. The proliferation of hate crimes against Arab Americans prompted Congress to enact more laws and legislation against such acts (Saliba, 1999).

The Stereotyping of Arab Americans

The stereotypes of Arab Americans as "terrorists, oil barons who have 40 wives" escalate during conflicts in the Middle East. Such stereotyping Zogby (1998) affirms "wounds us morally and politically, and leaves us vulnerable to exclusion and defamation." Muravchik (1999) contends that stereotypes in the media continue to influence American's attitudes toward Arab Americans. When the movie industry produces films such as *The Siege,* which depicts Arab Americans as terrorists, this stereotypes this population and opens doors for hate crimes. It is difficult for many Americans to differentiate between fantasy, fiction, and fact in movies. When headlines in newspapers stress Arab violence in the Middle East and films depict violent images of Arab people who bomb, explode, kill, and wreak havoc with American citizens on behalf of their religion, the lines between real and unreal become blurred. While there are terrorists who are ethnically Arab, there are also Irish, German, and a variety of other ethnicities that engage in this violent behavior. This association of terrorism solely with Arabs produces an attitude of fear and promotes acts of discrimination against Arab Americans. Mokhiber stated "The idea that Arab-Americans have some innate knowledge of terrorism is outrageous" (Cohen, 1991). Saliba (1999) argues that one can view negative stereotypes in another light. The "racist media images of Arabs are the result of oppressive U.S. policies against people of Arab descent" (p. 310). U.S. public policies set the tone for racial stereotypes about Arab Americans, which in turn creates the environment for portraying Arabs in a negative light in films.

The negative stereotypes of Arab Americans continue to affect public policy through airport profiling, campaign funding, and political affiliations. James Zogby (1998), the founder of the Arab American Institute, refers to cases of political candidates who return campaign-support checks from Arab Americans who donated to their campaigns. He also notes that airport profiling continues to target Arab Americans unnecessarily, and identifies with the term "flying while Arab."

The relentless efforts of James Zogby to increase voter registration and turnout for Arab Americans are one method "to flex their political muscles" and to legislate against anti-Arab bias. In 1985, in Dearborn, only a small percentage of Arab Americans were registered to vote; but by 1996, over 62 percent were registered and voted. This large increase is a testament to the change in worldview about the values of the democratic process. Traditionally, Arab Americans came from countries with little involvement in politics and an attitude of acceptance of fate as it relates to social conditions. The cultural revival in the Arab American community encourages political involvement and aims to reinforce their sense of common identity (Economist, 2000). Zogby (1998) reports that

> The Arab American community has made strenuous efforts in recent years to educate Americans about who we are, to end the politics of exclusion. American sentiment has generally diminished over the last decade or so. More and more Americans, I believe, have come to realize that Arab Americans are neither terrorists nor oil sheiks, but just ordinary citizens with a paycheck, a mortgage, and their children's college tuition to worry about.

This movement toward a common identity also becomes a link to survival of traditions, values, and culture. Arab Americans are uniting against anti-Arab sentiment by creating institutions that educate mainstream Americans, renewing their beliefs with vigor by building more churches and mosques, and celebrating Arab culture with international festivals. In Dearborn, the largest mosque in the country stands as a reminder of the ethnic influence of Arab Americans on the landscape of America. The cultural revival of Arab Americans increases their collective identity, but it cannot completely insulate them from acts of hate.

Anti-Semitic Acts of Violence and Agency Responses

The FBI, law enforcement agencies, and other organizations have identified Jews and Jewish institutions as the number-one target of religion-biased crimes in the nation. California and New York experience the highest number of hate crimes against Jewish Americans. Anti-Semitic acts of hate and violence focus on places of worship. Defacing worship centers by making a Nazi swastika and other racial epithets are a common hate crime. In California, in September 2000, the West Valley Hebrew Academy was a target of this type of hate. Two suspects were apprehended by the Los Angeles Police Department for breaking windows, destroying computers and textbooks, drawing swastikas, and writing "Kill Jews" on school buildings; they caused over $100,000 in damages. The perpetrators of such crimes are generally white supremacist groups.

White supremacist groups claim the ideology that members of the white race are the chosen people of God. Their philosophy of racial superiority is supported by a religious belief that they have God's blessings to exclusively rule America. Since the Jews historically are called "God's chosen people," white supremacist groups specifically target them. These groups are highly organized, well financed, and extremely well armed. The infamous Ku Klux Klan focused their hate and violence not only against blacks but also against Jews. Neo-Nazi groups such as the White Aryan Nation, White Patriot Party, Christian Conservative Church, and the Skinheads continue to spread their hate through several means, including the use of the Internet.

Founded in 1977, the Simon Wiesenthal Center in Los Angeles has documented over 1,400 problematic sites on the Internet that focus attention on hate. In 1999, the Simon Wiesenthal Center commended Yahoo for removing 39 online hate sites. Some of the sites that Yahoo deleted were Trenchcoat Mafia Glee Club, Brotherhood of Haters, National Association of White People, Mein Kampf Nazi Spirit, Yahoo Skinhead Revolt Club, KKK for Teens, and KKK No Nigger or Gookies (Simon Wiesenthal Center, 1999).

In addition to the Simon Wiesenthal Center, the Anti-Defamation League (ADL) is a leader in national efforts against hate. Founded in 1913, ADL was committed to

> stop the defamation of the Jewish people and to secure justice and fair treatment to all citizens alike. Now one of the nation's premier civil rights/human relations agencies, ADL fights anti-Semitism and all forms of bigotry, defends democratic ideals and protects civil rights for all. It is considered a leader in the development of materials, programs and services that builds bridges of communication, understanding and respect among diverse racial, religious and ethnic groups.

ADL promotes antibias programs to decrease prejudice as it emphasizes democratic ideals and pluralistic approaches to acceptance. ADL is at the forefront in educational programs for schools, universities, corporations, communities, and law enforcement, and it is a model organization for identifying and documenting bias-motivated crimes.

The Southern Poverty Law Center in Montgomery, Alabama has dedicated its efforts to identify and track white supremacist groups in the United States. It works with law enforcement agencies and community groups to inform the public of hate and bias groups and their crimes. In addition, the National Gay and Lesbian Task Force, founded in the

1970s, focuses its efforts on eradicating discriminatory and violent acts directed at sexual orientation.

Building Relationships with the Criminal Justice System

Building relationships betrween the criminal justice system and Middle Easterners requires creating a sense of trust. This sense of trust is predominately grounded in the system identifying and apprehending perpetrators of anti-Arab and anti-Semitic hate bias violence. Many factors contribute to the increase in hate crimes. Some members of the dominant culture experience a sense of threat or fear as the socioeconomic status (SES) shifts for minority groups. As more minority groups participate in successful commercial enterprises and large concentrations of ethnic enclaves continue to develop in major metropolitan areas, racial tension increases between the dominant and the minority populations. International events spur racial and ethnic stereotypes and acts of discrimination soon follow.

The criminal justice system has emerged as the agency to enforce laws and protect our population from crimes of violence. In Massachusetts, police agencies reported to the FBI 443 hate crimes in 1999 (Meek, 2000). The ADL regional director noted that many hate crimes go unreported because many law enforcement officers do not recognize either hate crime indicators or the typology of the offenders. ADL distributed thousands of cards to officers in Massachusetts in an effort to help with the identification of hate offenders and hopefully aid in their apprehension. The Springfield Police Chief, Paula Meara, believes that the cards will aid her officers in identifying these crimes. She notes, "Unfortunately we have made arrests here in Springfield that started with name calling and hate, and that behavior escalated until it became a crime"and that each of these cards "sends a message to every officer of how important hate crimes detection and investigation are and makes them sensitive to the needs of the person who is the victim" (Meek, 2000). The ADL regional director in Atlanta comments "We don't find there's resistance [to identify hate offenders]; they're [officers] overwhelmed with other things they have to do" (Meek, 2000).

Training Criminal Justice Personnel

Training in the typology of hate offenders and hate crime indicators has increased over the last several years for criminal justice personnel. Identifying typology and hate crime motivators is an important step toward apprehension and prosecution of these offenders. The psychological impact felt by hate crime victims may be more devastating than that of other crimes. The community also experiences the impact of hate crimes. These are "message crimes" and their aim is to create fear and dread in other target members. McDevitt and Levin (1993) address the rising tide of hate crimes by identifying hate offenders, in three major categories:

1. Thrill-seeking hate offenders: generally, groups of teenagers that gain a psychological or social thrill by bashing minorities or groups that are different from themselves.

Inflicting pain gives them a sense of sadistic thrill. Their motivations range from wanting to be accepted by their peers to gaining a sense of superiority through violent acts. Attacks of vandalism, desecration, and personal injury seem to be random. The hatred of victims is relatively superficial and they can be deterred from repeating crimes if there is a strong societal response to their behavior. Example: A group of teenagers go gay bashing on Friday night after a football game.

2. Reactive hate offenders: Offenders of these crimes have a sense of entitlement regarding their rights, privileges, and way of life that does not extend to victims. It is a defensive stand against "outsiders" who seem to be threatening their way of life. They use fear and intimidation to protect or defend the perceived threat from these "outsiders." Typically, crime occurs in the offender's own neighborhood, school, or place of work. They feel justified in their response of hate because of their perceived sense of threat. Example: A new Asian immigrant group moves into a predominately Hispanic neighborhood and opens a convenience store. Other Hispanic storeowners throw paint on the new business and break the windows with the idea of "running those Asians out."

3. Mission hate offenders: Characteristics of this group include people who are disturbed and people who are experiencing some form of mental illness. They feel it is their duty to rid the world of evil and subhuman groups. Typically they feel that they have been instructed by God to further the cause of eliminating evil. Beliefs include that these "evil" groups are responsible for their misfortunes and they have suffered because of them. They perceive a conspiracy of some kind that is being perpetrated by these targeted groups. There tends to be a sense of urgency in the "mission" to act before it is too late. Example: the KKK, skinheads, and white supremacists who are on a "mission" for racial and religious purity and attack African Americans and burn a Jewish synagogue.

McDevitt and Levin (1993) noted in one study that thrill seekers were the most common offender category, with 58 percent of crimes by this group; reactive offenders followed with 42 percent, and mission offenders had the smallest percentage of hate crimes but were the most violent.

A Sense of Trust

Message crimes have impacted Middle Easterners more than any other group. Increasing criminal justice training in the identification and in hate crime motivations and in the prosecution of these crimes can help build a sense of trust. Community policing efforts have aided in building relationships between diverse communities and the criminal justice system. The California Crime and Violence Prevention Center (2000) focused their Community Oriented Policing and Problem Solving (COPPS) efforts on building safer communities by (1) improving communication between community members and between community members and law enforcement; (2) solving neighborhood problems with the help of individuals and community people; and (3) forming strong partnerships with schools, churches, businesses, corporations, law enforcement, and the community. Across the nation, efforts such as these are building bridges between diverse communities and the criminal justice system. Michael Lieberman, Washington Counsel for the Anti-

Defamation League (2000), proposes that "police officers and their agencies can accomplish much by working in partnership with citizens to implement the American vision of diverse and tolerant communities that offer freedom, safety and dignity for all."

In addition, recruitment of Middle Eastern Americans into law enforcement has a positive impact on agencies and the communities they serve. As previously discussed, when law enforcement personnel reflect the diversity within the community, law enforcement becomes a visible validation of the acceptance and inclusion of racial and ethnic groups in positions of authority. When there is an absence of diversity within government it seems to "nurture an outsider syndrome that perpetuates an us-versus-them approach to civic affairs" (Alozie & Ramirez, 1999, p. 458). The idea that society experiences reflections of individuals in the public service arena through "street-level bureaucrats" is directly related to the need to recruit minorities. The presence of minority officers increases the likelihood of police effectiveness in minority communities, and might help reduce racial and ethnic tension and discriminatory acts (Free, 1996).

Summary

Middle Eastern Americans have roots in a large geographic region that generally includes countries that are aligned as Arabic-speaking and non-Arabic speaking. There is not a single Middle Eastern American culture; however, there are some similar experiences that they do share—those of exclusion and discrimination. While early immigrants assimilated more easily than later groups, exposure to anti-Semitic and anti-Arab reactions are part of their worldview. Drawing from their individual ethnic groups' collective identity has sustained immigrants through changing tides of political and social unrest. While African Americans have experienced the largest number of race-motivated crimes for a particular group, no other racial or ethnic group in America is more affected by world events and the onslaught of hate crimes than Middle Eastern Americans.

For the majority of Middle Eastern immigrants, values are placed on family, religion, family honor, and pride. The extended family unit provides a sense of structure, and one's personal identity is realized within the context of the communal organization. There is a relationship between issues of gender, religion, and generations.

Discussion Questions

1. How do world events affect stereotyping of Middle Eastern Americans?

2. What are key issues in building trust between Middle Eastern Americans and the criminal justice system?

3. What are some examples of racial stereotyping and its impact on the system?

4. What are the differences in belief systems that impact Middle Eastern Americans?

7

The Criminal Justice System

Effective Cultural Contacts

Preparing for Effective Cultural Contact
California POST Cultural Diversity Training
Tools for Tolerance for Law Enforcement
Applications of LD 42

Summary

Discussion Questions

Learning Objectives _____

After reading this chapter you should be able to do the following:

1. Identify the impact of immigration on public and private services.
2. Discuss the differences in hiring practices of women and minority officers in various agencies.
3. Explain the impact of the media on negative images of minority groups.
4. Compare and contrast the community policing model.

The inscription over the 10th Street entrance of the U.S. Department of Justice Building in Washington, D.C. reads

JUSTICE IN THE LIFE AND CONDUCT OF THE STATE IS POSSIBLE
ONLY AS FIRST RESIDES IN THE HEARTS AND SOULS OF THE CITIZENS

Max Nordau, a German physician, writer, and Zionist, addressed the 7th World Zionists Congress in Basel, Switzerland, in 1905 and stated, "Civilization is built on a number of ultimate principles: respect for human life, the punishment of crimes against property and persons, the equality of good citizens before the law—or in a word, justice." The ideology that justice begins with individuals and is transferred to the larger society provides the framework for the criminal justice system's response to a culturally diverse society. Former President Jimmy Carter stated in a speech in New York City in 1976 that "We are, of course, a nation of immigrants, but some of us too often forget that fact. Sometimes we forget that the question isn't when we came here, but why we came here." (Eigen & Siegel, 1993). The waves of "huddled masses yearning to breathe free" do have a story to tell. The stories are associated with social and political events from around the world. Events include religious persecution, colonialization, genocides, holocausts, war refugees, and people seeking political asylum. These events tell a story of people leaving their "homeland" for a better life in a country known for its acceptance of immigrants. Changes in demographics, fear of new groups, and economic stress traditionally have made it difficult for all new groups to become part of the American landscape. Oscar Straus, U.S. Secretary of Commerce under Theodore Roosevelt, understood the stress and strain of immigrants to America. In 1907 he came to this conclusion and said, "An unprejudiced study of immigration justifies me in saying that the evils are temporary and local, while the benefits are permanent and national." His observations could be made about the many waves of immigration in American history. After major events in the world that spawn the push to America, ethnic enclaves do create vast changes in areas that will be providing public and private services.

In two short years between 1975 and 1977, over 130,000 Vietnam War refugees came to America. These refugees needed immediate financial assistance and education, as well as health services for their children. Cultural issues, language, traditions, religion, and the fact that America was socially and politically divided about involvement in the Vietnam War made assimilation difficult for this population. Overcrowded schools dealt not only with language issues, but with dietary concerns with school lunches. Southeast Asian children were not accustomed to "sloppy Joe's," "corn dogs," or milk from cows. Teachers and students found the variety of spellings for names and pronunciations difficult, so many routinely renamed children with more familiar "American" names. Stories from law enforcement officers revealed the difficulties of trying to provide services to new groups. A typical law enforcement event involved responding to a burglary-in-progress call in an apartment complex, only to arrive and find that the Hmong victims were too fearful of the police to open their doors and they, the officers, were unable to communicate due to a language barrier. Immigrant groups experienced fear, officers experienced frustration. Officers would leave the scene without much evidence and families continued in fear of police. Stereotypes by officers and new immigrants continued a wedge of mistrust and fear.

These accounts of the impact on public and private services are not new to America. In 1907, the largest number of immigrants up until that time, 1.2 million, came to America—which was probably the impetus for the statement by Straus. That record was maintained until 1990, when 1.5 million people came; then this record was broken in 1991, when over 1.8 million immigrants came to America (Paludeine, 1998). Concerns over housing, jobs, welfare assistance, and the criminal justice system have always been heightened by the impact of new groups. Straus commented that the disruptions are "temporary and local, while the benefits are permanent and national." He could not have imagined society's response in the twenty-first century to diversity and multiculturalism, but he would have anticipated that the benefits of a multicultural society are indeed permanent and beneficial.

The last half of the twentieth century was a time of reevaluating the criminal justice system's response to diversity. Changes in the ethnic, racial, gender, and sexual orientation of law enforcement and correctional officers required agencies to reexamine policing practices. In 1997, the Bureau of Justice Statistics reported that there were over 17,000 law enforcement agencies with an estimated number of 531,496 full-time officers in local police departments (Reaves & Goldberg, 2000). There has been a steady increase of minority and women in law enforcement since 1997. As indicated in Figure 7.1, racial and ethnic

Percent of full-time sworn personnel
25%
20%
15%
10%
5%
0%
1987
1990
1993
1997
Female
All minorities*
Black
Hispanic

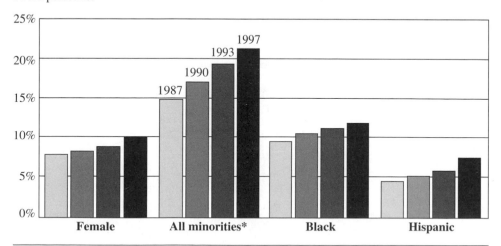

FIGURE 7.1 ***Female and Minority Local Police Officers, 1987, 1990, 1993, and 1997.***

*Includes blacks, Hispanics, Asians, Pacific Islanders, American Indians, and Alaska Natives.
Source: Brian A. Reaves and Andrew C. Goldberg, *Local Police Departments 1997*. Washington, DC: Bureau of Justice Statistics.

minorities comprised only 14.6 percent of the total full-time sworn officers in 1987 and in 1997 they were 21.5 percent.

The number of officers representing ethnic minority groups increased by 26 percent between 1993 and 1997 to over 90,000 officers, a figure that represented 21.5 percent of the total. Black officers accounted for 11.7 percent of the population, which represented an increase of 16 percent from 1993. Hispanic officers represented 7.8 percent, which accounted for a 40 percent increase since 1993. Asian Americans/Pacific Islanders and American Indians had the highest increase since 1993—53 percent—representing 2.1 percent of the total figure. In jurisdictions of 500,000 or more residents, minority officers represented one-third of sworn personnel. Women represented approximately 10 percent of all police officers, which accounted for a 26 percent increase since 1993. The highest percentage rate for women in law enforcement was in jurisdictions serving 1 million residents or more (16%). In jurisdictions with 250,000 to 999,999 residents, women officers accounted for 14 percent of sworn personnel. Overall, departments that serve larger jurisdictions accounted for the highest numbers of women and minority officer representation. White males accounted for the highest representation in smaller jurisdictions. In Table 7.1, gender and race of full-time sworn personnel in local police departments indicate a growing number of women and minorities in large police agencies.

The American Correctional Association (1998) reported that there are approximately 347,000 correctional officers. Women account for over 20 percent of all officers. Statistically, whites represent 70 percent of correctional officers, and the remaining racial/ethnic distribution is 22 percent black, 5 percent Hispanic, and 3 percent Asian/Pacific Islander and American Indian.

Internal problems related to increased numbers of women and minorities in policing typically reflected a general attitude that many officers had about diversity in the larger society. There is an old saying about workplace attitudes: "You are not going to treat the public any better than you treat each other." With this mind, the 1990s became the decade of diversity training for agencies across America. While the majority of the training focused on the responses to a diverse public, benefits of that training could be felt within the organization. Diversity training became an integral part of agencies to teach their employees to treat all individuals and groups with dignity and respect.

Preparing for Effective Cultural Contact

Preparing criminal justice personnel for effective cultural contacts with the public begins with education. Diversity education begins with understanding the social contexts that many officers experience with immigrant groups. Educating officers about ethnic and cultural diversity is significantly challenging when painted against the backdrop of an over-representation of minorities in the criminal justice system. Fears about personal safety when responding to calls in minority neighborhoods might generalize to all people from that ethnic group. People learn assumptions about groups from social settings, and these assumptions can be reinforced upon contact with minority suspects. Consequently, many police officers learn about minority people from encounters in high-crime neighborhoods (Ogawa, 1990; Wolfgang & Ferracutti, 1987). When minority populations are

TABLE 7.1 *Gender and Race of Full-Time Sworn Personnel in Local Police Departments, by Size of Population Serviced, 1997*

Population Served	Total			White			Black			Hispanic			Other*		
	Total	Male	Female	Total	Male	Female	Total	Male	Female	Total	Male	Female	Total	Male	Female
All sizes	100%	90.0%	10.0%	78.5%	72.2%	6.3%	11.7%	9.1%	2.5%	7.8%	6.8%	1.0%	2.1%	1.9%	0.2%
1,000,000 or more	100%	84.1%	15.9%	64.7%	57.1%	7.6%	17.8%	12.5%	5.4%	15.6%	12.9%	2.7%	1.9%	1.6%	0.2%
500,000–999,999	100	86.0	14.0	63.1	56.2	7.0	23.4	17.7	5.7	7.0	6.1	0.8	6.6	6.1	0.5
250,000–499,999	100	85.9	14.1	69.6	60.6	9.0	19.1	15.2	3.9	9.3	8.3	1.0	1.9	1.7	0.2
100,000–249,999	100	90.1	9.9	78.9	71.7	7.2	11.6	9.7	1.9	7.2	6.6	0.6	2.3	2.2	0.1
50,000–99,999	100	92.3	7.7	85.4	79.3	6.1	7.5	6.5	1.0	5.4	4.9	0.5	1.6	1.5	0.1
25,000–49,999	100	93.4	6.6	88.5	83.1	5.4	6.0	5.2	0.8	4.6	4.3	0.3	0.8	0.8	—
10,000–24,999	100	94.7	5.3	91.9	87.3	4.6	4.3	3.9	0.4	2.7	2.6	0.1	1.1	1.0	0.2
2,500–9,999	100	94.9	5.1	89.1	84.8	4.3	4.8	4.3	0.4	4.1	3.9	0.2	2.0	1.8	0.2
Under 2,500	100	96.9	3.1	89.3	86.8	2.5	5.3	5.0	0.2	3.2	3.1	0.1	2.3	2.0	0.2

Percent of Full-Time Sworn Employees Who Are:

Note: Detail may not add to total because of rounding.

*Includes Asians, Pacific Islanders, American Indians, and Alaska Natives.

—Less than 0.05%.

Source: Brian A. Reaves and Andrew Goldberg, *Local Police Departments 1997*. Washington, DC: Bureau of Justice Statistics.

dramatically overrepresented in crime statistics and police encounters, a causal relationship between color and deviance might be the logical result. Stereotypic labels viewed as positive or negative by officers can influence their behavior. The influence of the media in displaying violent events, the movie industry in portraying stereotypic ethnic roles, and our own history colors information we have about ethnic groups. This "colorization" can affirm existing stereotypes and influence discriminatory actions against groups. Al-Hayani (1999) explains that the problem of a lack of cultural knowledge on the part of law enforcement officers creates additional problems related to domestic violence.

In the District Court of Dearborn

Cases of domestic violence among Arabs are on the rise . . . when police officers are called to an incident of domestic violence, they address the situation by ignoring it or by overreacting. In the first scenario, the police do not take seriously the wife's complaint that her husband has been abusive, based on their experience with some Arab women who change their story later. This, according to police, happens to all groups and is not limited to Arab women. However, this attitude of the police toward what they consider Arab cultural practices makes them take such a situation lightly. From the negative information concerning the Arabs, wife beating is portrayed as an acceptable Arab behavior and custom; therefore the police ignore the complaint and fail to see the problem. (p. 74)

This lack of cultural knowledge denies Arab Americans their right to safety and protection. It affirms stereotypes by both parties; on one side, Arabs are violent, and on the other side law enforcement is for a select group, not for everyone. Lack of knowledge also contributes to fears that officers have about entering many ethnic neighborhoods.

There are varying levels of fear or apprehension that officers might experience in encountering cultural groups different than themselves. These fears might be related to personal prejudices that they have learned from the past. Children growing up in environments that attach negative labels to ethnic groups might internalize these labels and develop a belief system that supports them. Over the years, people become unaware of the root causes of their prejudice attitudes; in turn, these attitudes become buried within the personality framework.

The relationship of cultural awareness to self-awareness is dramatically evident in this context. Effective interactions between cultures are fostered by a healthy self-awareness of one's personal perspectives, as well as by mutual respect for the worldviews, morals, mores, and folkways of others. One of the underlying principles of preparing officers to interact effectively with cultural groups is the development of increased understanding of who they are and how they feel about people who are different than themselves.

To more effectively interact with groups different than oneself, knowledge about groups is helpful. Familiarity with the history of waves of immigration, knowledge about people's worldviews, and understanding of the impact of worldview on the assimilation and acculturation process all enhance positive relationships. Worldviews are not static; they are dynamic. As one immigrant group encounters the dominant culture, acculturation begins. The influences of schools, neighbors, places of worship, the workplace, and various forms of media (television, radio, the Internet) affect traditions and folkways. An example of this is marriage traditions in many Asian and Arab groups. Young girls are expected to be married in their teens in their "homeland." However, once they are enrolled in school, exposure to the dominant culture—to the value of education and prolonging marriage until they are older—changes traditions and folkways to patterns similar to the mainstream in this country.

Becoming culturally aware implies an understanding that the "recipe style" approach to cross-cultural interactions is inappropriate. Following a step-by-procedure on how to communicate with specific ethnic groups is unrealistic. For example, some "recipe style" diversity programs insist on officers learning the elements of bowing in Asian cultures, or of shaking or not shaking hands upon greeting specific cultural groups. The intentions are valid, but the design is flawed. Immigrant groups realize they are in a new country and they strive to learn the customs and norms of the new society. They do not expect the dominant culture to know the specifics of bowing or handshaking, or to participate in their cultural style. What is expected is that officers treat them with respect in spite of language and cultural barriers. Positive public contact begins with officers who display patience and use active listening skills.

Positive public contact includes the concept of effective communication. Good communicators (1) make eye contact, (2) use appropriate facial expressions when listening and talking, (3) listen to others without discounting them, (4) try to identify the main ideas of the conversation, and (5) try to connect on an emotional level. Listening techniques of attending, clarifying, restating, reflecting, and summarizing enhance the relationships between officers and the public. When officers attend to people's conversations it conveys interest and encourages further discussion. Clarifying brings vague material into focus, and might occur if officers questions further by saying, "I'm not sure what you are saying, please say it again." Sometimes it is necessary for officers to restate what they have heard to ensure that they are "on the same page" with the public. Restating also gives the opportunity for the public to agree or not agree with the message that was conveyed. The value of such reflection is that it improves the relationship between officers and community groups by focusing on the community's experience about events. Before leaving service calls it is necessary to close with a clear, concise summary of what has transpired between officers and the community. People want "to be heard"; incorporating listening techniques while serving diverse communities increases rapport and aids in building trust with the criminal justice system.

Listening effectively aids in the communication process—both verbal and nonverbal. Good verbal contacts eliminate the use of police jargon in community interactions. Using police codes, numbers, and acronyms is not informative; on the contrary, it tends to confuse and demean the public. The use of slang terms to refer to ethnic groups demonstrates a lack of professionalism and sensitivity toward those groups. For example, it is not professional to call a Hispanic "spic" or an Asian Indian a "rag head." These terms are derogatory, inhibit relations with communities groups, and detract from professional effectiveness.

In many interactions, understanding and demonstrating appropriate nonverbal behavior can bridge the gap between immigrant communities and officers. Understanding the proxemics (the study of interpersonal distance while communicating) of various groups can eliminate miscommunications and potentially lethal situations. For example, proxemics for a large majority of Arab Americans is minimal. Officers investigating a crime scene might appear abrupt and abusive if they should suggest that an Arab American witness "get back" while answering questions. On the other hand, displaying nonverbal behaviors that convey concern and respect increases the likelihood that community groups will cooperate with police.

The value of having officers who know the culture and language can also prepare departments for effective interactions. The National Crime Prevention Council (1995) notes that increasing ethnic minority recruitment can eliminate many obstacles that hinder effective policing in immigrant communities. The report indicated that hiring "non-native" officers is a benefit to both the agency and the "non-native" community. The agency benefits by having officers from the non-native community who will teach their employees about cultural issues, act as interpreters, and recommend strategies to reduce cultural tension and conflict. Many ethnic communities "experienced a decrease in crime and marked reduction in the fear of crime." Many agencies reported that non-native officers "increased non-native community access to the criminal justice system and improved trust in law enforcement and other branches of the system . . . it also increased the feeling of community safety among newly arrived groups and thus for the community as a whole." The newest immigrant groups experience more confusion, mistrust, and fear about the criminal justice system than the dominant culture. By way of building trust, hiring ethnic minority officers will help bridge the gap between the system and the immigrant community. These officers, in turn, will become "role models of good citizenship and community service" that can be effective deterrents toward crime.

Community Oriented Policing and Problem Solving (COPPS) programs concentrate their efforts on building partnerships between law enforcement and the community. The approach recognizes that the community plays a critical role in working with police to solve crime problems. This problem-solving and prevention approach to policing requires an open communication style that builds trust between individuals, neighborhoods, businesses, religious organizations, and officers. While COPPS programs are still "tough on crime," greater emphases are on "soft crime" and prevention strategies. When law enforcement is responsive to community needs, an effective crime fighting partnership develops.

In the last ten years, training programs for COPPS and diversity have increased. In departments serving 100,000 residents or more, over 60 percent have some type of community policing, and in jurisdictions that serve 25,000 people, over 80 percent of the agencies have community policing. The smallest jurisdictions, 10,000 residents, have the highest number of agencies that employ community policing as a method of increasing partnerships with the public (Reaves & Goldberg, 2000). Nearly all states have diversity training in their police academies and for in-service officers. California is one such state that has an excellent training program designed to create awareness of the nation's most diverse society. The following details how California is meeting the needs of the community.

California POST Cultural Diversity Training

California's Peace Officer Standards and Training (POST) serves 557 law enforcement agencies that employ a total of 75,600 full-time peace officers, 8,200 peace officer reserves, and 6,400 public safety dispatchers (Myyra, 1998). A governing board administers POST, and their responsibilities include the standardization of law enforcement training, as well as the creation of minimum standards of service to the citizens of California. Funding from criminal and traffic fines provides the resources for POST to set standards for hiring, officer training, leadership development, management counseling, financial assistance to support training, and statistical information for law enforcement.

An important responsibility of the commission is to set the minimum hours of training for recruits in basic police academies. Training hours in basic academies have increased over the years to a minimum of 664, with some agency-affiliated academies requiring as many as 1,000. In addition to the prehiring requirement of basic POST certification, every sworn peace officer must complete 24 hours of advanced training every 2 years.

There are over 4,000 courses certified by POST, 150 of these based on human relations training. Training mandates for POST courses are often influenced by societal issues and concerns for "safer streets," and come to bear either implicitly through political pressure or directly by legislative action. One direct influence was California Senate Bill 2680, Boatwright (California Senate, 1990). SB 2680 is a cultural and ethnic diversity awareness educational mandate for the POST system. According to the mandate, POST created a training and implementation system that allows local law enforcement agencies to structure their cultural awareness programs based upon local needs.

In response to SB 2680, POST initiated training for cultural awareness facilitators (CAF) from each local agency. Included are guidelines for community mentor committees and training guidelines for topics and curriculum to be delivered to in-service and civilian employees of law enforcement agencies. An additional component of cultural awareness training is the result of Assembly Bill 401, Epple, and includes curriculum on cultural diversity for the basic academy (California Assembly, 1993). The Learning Domain curriculum module for the basic academy, LD 42, includes the following topics, with emphasis on Section VI, Strategies for Effective Cultural Contacts:

   I. Cultural Make-Up of California
  II. Benefits of Valuing Diversity
 III. Human Rights, Prejudice, and Discrimination
  IV. Perceptions of Cultural Groups
   V. Cultural Stereotyping and Profiling
  VI. Strategies for Effective Cultural Contacts
 VII. History and Nature of Sexual Harassment
VIII. Legal Aspects of Sexual Harassment
  IX. Understanding Sexual Harassment
   X. Responding to Sexual Harassment
  XI. State Sexual Harassment Complaint Guidelines
 XII. Legal Aspects of Hate Crimes
XIII. The Impact of Hate Crimes.

(Commission on POST, 1992)

Since 1993 the minimum hours of cultural diversity training in the police academies has increased from 16 to 24 hours. In addition, many academies have voluntarily increased that number to 40.

POST also developed and implemented additional diversity programs.

1. Southeast Asian Project: designed for Southeast Asian recruit and probationary officers.
2. Teach LEADS (Law Enforcement Awareness of Disabilities): designed for core police academy, agency in-service instructors, and personnel from community-based organizations working with the disabled.
3. Building High-Performance, Inclusive Organizations: designed for agency executives and members of their management teams.
4. Law Enforcement Tools for Tolerance: designed for recruit, senior officers, and supervisors.

In addition to classroom-based courses, POST is very active in telecourse development. Telecourses are transmitted by satellite and can be down-linked at all agencies and academies. The telecourses are designed to provide the most current information along with scenario-based discussions. The advantage of telecourses is that they can be recorded for later presentation according to the training schedules of each agency.

Many telecourses were developed to enhance diversity education for law enforcement. Some of these telecourses including Hate Crimes, Law Enforcement Ethics, Cultural Awareness, Sexual Harassment, Community-Oriented Policing, Managing Contacts with Developmentally Disabled or Mentally Ill, and Law Enforcement Awareness of Disabilities were available to download at all training sites throughout California. The video scenarios in these telecourses provide opportunities for group discussion. This helps promote the development of good decision-making processes in considering issues related to diversity.

Tools for Tolerance for Law Enforcement

The most recent addition to the POST cultural diversity training is the Law Enforcement Tools for Tolerance program, developed through the Museum of Tolerance in Los Angeles. The Tools for Tolerance program is available to participants in the Cultural Diversity Train-the-Trainers course, all police academy cadets, and all law enforcement agencies. The Museum of Tolerance is a hands-on, experiential museum utilizing two principal themes: the dynamics of racism and prejudice in America, and the history of the Holocaust. The use of interactive videos, exhibits, and computers creates a unique experience for students. Museum presentations include discussions on hate crimes, valuing differences, and conflict resolution in the workplace. Facilitated small-group discussions focus on cross-cultural communication issues that might occur between officers and the communities they serve. Over the last 2 years, the Museum of Tolerance provided this program to 17,000 law enforcement officers and 4,000 law enforcement support personnel.

Applications of LD 42

Most curricula (and the cultural diversity curriculum in particular) focus on the development of cognitive processes, self-actualization of the learner, and social changes and their relevance to the student. Curriculum must be developed with special attention to the experiential level of students. Assumptions about students' abilities that instructors bring to the curriculum must be carefully evaluated when making the "conceptual leap" from purpose and process to implementation. The perceived effectiveness of the training depends upon the sociocultural processes that influence personal experience and learning within the classroom and for students (Alton-Lee & Nuthall, 1992). Consequently, the POST cultural diversity training includes ideas on cross-cultural communications, problem-solving exercises and scenarios, and ethics instruction. The diversity training considers the sociocultural processes of cadets in the basic course and in-service.

Summary

The attitudes and beliefs from the dominant culture about groups coming to and living in America have both a historical connection to and an impact on the criminal justice system. America continues to be a "home for the world." Immigrants from the Balkans, Russians from the former Soviet Union, and Chinese from Hong Kong are arriving with the dream of "having a good life in America." This dream will require both an active commitment from society and support from the criminal justice system. Members of the system can be in the forefront of preserving their rights, protecting their families and businesses, and ensuring that they too can identify themselves as Americans.

Many methods exist to increase the relationship between the immigrant populations and the criminal justice system. Community-oriented policing is one of those methods that has had a positive impact on building relationships between law enforcement and many diverse groups. The role of community policing is an important step toward recognizing and validating the diversity in communities. Creating a liaison between community members and law enforcement can eliminate fears and negative perceptions that many groups hold toward police. Cross-cultural efforts by law enforcement and other criminal justice agencies can build a bridge between the varied racial and ethnic groups in their communities. In addition, court liaisons and advocates have helped to bridge the gaps between victims, suspects, and witnesses within the court services. Further studies indicate that recruitment and retention of minority officers is rated high on public opinion polls as an effective method to reduce tension between the criminal justice system and a diversity of populations.

The proposals for effective cultural contacts are a combination of ideas from citizens, officers, and other criminal justice personnel. The goals of creating a safe environment, reducing the public's fear of crime, and building trust are contingent on increased cooperation between the public and law enforcement.

Discussion Questions _____

1. Discuss the statement that "Justice in the life and conduct of the state is possible only as first resides in the hearts and souls of the citizens."

2. What is the impact of increasing numbers of women and minorities within law enforcement agencies? and with the public?

3. What are additional effective cultural strategies to aid in communication between groups?

8

Measuring Crime

Learning Objectives

After reading this chapter you should be able to do the following:

1. Explain the differences between the various types of official reports.

2. Distinguish between the other types of reports that provide information regarding the commission of crimes.

3. Understand the advantages and disadvantages of each of the various mechanisms that are used to measure crime.

Official Reports

There are many different types of official reports compiled by private or public agencies in the form of statistical data. These provide a much needed resource for further research into the extent of crime and victimization. Those most commonly relied on are the Uniform Crime Reports, the National Incident-Based Reporting System, National Crime Victimization Surveys, and the National Assessment Program.

This chapter is adapted from Harvey Wallace, *Victimology: Legal, Psychological, and Social Perspectives* (Boston: Allyn & Bacon, 1998). Reprinted with permission of Allyn & Bacon; all rights reserved by the publisher and author.

Uniform Crime Reports

During the 1920s, the International Association of Chiefs of Police (IACP) formed the Commission on Uniform Crime Reports in order to develop a uniform system of reporting criminal statistics. The commission evaluated various crimes based upon their seriousness, frequency of occurrence, commonality across the nation, and likelihood of being reported to the police. In 1929, the commission finished its study and recommended a plan for crime reporting that became the foundation of the Uniform Crime Reports (UCR) program. Seven crimes were chosen to serve as an index for determining fluctuations in the overall rate of crime. This list of seven offenses became known as the crime index and included the following: murder, manslaughter, forcible rape, robbery, aggravated assault, burglary, larceny-theft, and motor vehicle theft. In 1979, Congress mandated that an eighth crime, arson, be added to the index. During the study phase of the project, it was recognized that differences in state criminal codes would cause the same act to be reported by various methods and in various categories. To avoid this problem, no distinction was made between felony and misdemeanor crimes and a standardized set of definitions was established to allow law enforcement agencies to submit data without regard for local statutes. In 1930, Congress enacted federal law (28 USC 534) that authorized the attorney general to gather crime information. The attorney general designated the FBI as the national clearinghouse for all data, and since that time data based upon this system have been obtained from the nation's law enforcement agencies.

The Uniform Crime Reports (UCR) program is a nationwide statistical computation involving over 1600 city, county, and state law enforcement agencies who voluntarily report data on reported crimes. During 1999, law enforcement agencies in the UCR program represented over 245 million inhabitants, or approximately 95 percent of the total population of the United States. The program is administered by the Federal Bureau of Investigation, which issues assessments on the nature and type of crime. The program's primary objective is to generate a set of reliable criminal statistics for use in law enforcement administration, operation, and management (Crime in the United States, 1994). It has also become an important social indicator of deviance in our society.

The annual crime index is composed of selected offenses used to gauge changes in the overall rate of crime reported to law enforcement agencies and is composed of those seven specific crimes discussed previously. Therefore, the index is a combination of violent and property crimes. The UCR is an annual report that includes the number of crimes reported by citizens to local police departments, as well as the number of arrests made by law enforcement agencies in a given year. This information is of somewhat limited value since the data are based upon instances of violence that are classified as criminal, and which are reported to the local law enforcement agencies. Many serious acts of violence are not reported to the police and therefore do not become part of the UCR.

A number of factors influence the reporting or nonreporting of crimes to local law enforcement. The Bureau of Justice Statistics (1992) reports that the most common reason victims give for reporting crimes to the police is to prevent further crimes from being committed against them by the same offender. For both household crimes and other theft-related crimes, the most common reason given by victims for reporting the offenses is to assist in the recovery of the property.

Violent crimes are the most likely to be reported to the police. Household crimes are the next highest reported form of crime. Personal thefts are the least likely crimes to be reported to the police.

The most common reason given for not reporting violent crimes to the police is that the crime was considered by the victim to be a private or personal matter. The second most common reason for not reporting violent crimes is that the offender was unsuccessful in the attempt to commit the crime. The most common reason for not reporting household crime or other theft-related crime is that the object was recovered.

Victims gave different reasons for not reporting crimes to the police when the offender was a stranger instead of an acquaintance. Victims of crimes committed by strangers gave the following reasons for not reporting:

- The offender was unsuccessful.
- The victim considered the police inefficient.
- The victim felt the police did not want to be bothered.
- It was not important enough to the victim to report the crime.

Victims of crimes committed by acquaintances gave the following reasons for not reporting:

- The victim considered the crime a private or personal matter.
- The victim had reported the crime to another official.

The Hate Crime Statistics Act was passed by Congress in 1990 and mandates that a database of crimes motivated by religion, ethnic, racial, or sexual orientation be collected. On January 1, 1991, the UCR program distributed guidelines for reporting hate crimes, and the first report was published in 1992. Participation in reporting hate crimes continues to grow.

With the exception of the hate crime category noted above, the UCR remained virtually unchanged for 50 years. Eventually, various law enforcement agencies began to call for an evaluation and redesign of the program. Since the UCR lists only crimes that are reported to it, and not all police agencies report crimes to the FBI and the Department of Justice, this presents a serious problem. Since the UCR relies on law enforcement agencies to voluntarily report crimes, there is the possibility of underreporting by some agencies based on political reasons (Milakovich & Weis, 1975). The UCR generally provides only tabular summaries of crime and does not provide crime analysts with more meaningful information. Additionally, the method of counting crimes causes problems. For example, only the most serious crime is reported. If a person is robbed and his car stolen, police agencies are instructed to report only the robbery. Finally, some crimes, such as white-collar crime are excluded from the UCR system. After several years of study, the FBI began to institute various modifications to the UCR program. These changes established a new, more effective crime reporting system.

The National Incident-Based Reporting System

The newly redesigned UCR Program is called the *National Incident-Based Reporting System* (NIBRS). In 1989, the FBI began accepting data, and nine states started supplying information in the new format. NIBRS collects data on each single incident and arrest within 22 crime categories. Incident, victim, property, offender, and arrestee information is gathered for each offense known to the local agency. The goal of the redesigned system is to modernize crime reporting information by collecting data presently maintained in law enforcement records. The enhanced UCR Program is a by-product of modern law enforcement records systems that have the capability to store and collate more information regarding criminal offenses.

National Crime Victimization Surveys

The National Crime Victimization Survey (NCVS) attempts to correct the problems on non-reporting inherent in the UCR by contacting a nationwide sample and interviewing citizens regarding victimization. The report was originally entitled the National Crime Survey (NCS) but was renamed to more clearly reflect its emphasis on the measurement of victimizations experienced by citizens. The NCVS was established in 1972 and collects detailed information about certain criminal offenses—both attempted and completed—that concern the general public and law enforcement. These offenses include the frequency and nature of rape, robbery, assault, household burglary, personal and household theft, and motor vehicle theft. The NCVS does not record homicide or commercial crime.

A single crime may have more than one victim. For example, a bank robbery may involve several bank tellers. Thus, a single incident may have more than one victimization. A victimization, the basic measure of the occurrence of crime, is a specific criminal act because it affects a specific victim. The number of victimizations, however, is determined by the number of victims of each specific criminal act.

NCVS is an annual survey of citizens that is conducted by the U.S. Bureau of Census in cooperation with the Bureau of Justice Statistics of the U.S. Department of Justice. Census Bureau personnel conduct interviews with all household members over the age of 12. These households stay in the sample for 3 years and are interviewed every 6 months. The total sample size of this survey is approximately 66,000 households, with 101,000 individuals.[1]

The NCVS provides data regarding the victims of crime, which includes age, sex, race, ethnicity, marital status, income, and educational level, as well as information about the offender. Questions covering the victim's experience with the justice system, details regarding any self-protective measures used by the victims, and possible substance abuse by offenders are included in the survey. There are periodic supplemental questionnaires that address specific issues such as school crime.

However, the NCVS suffers from problems that compromise its validity, such as the underreporting or overreporting crimes by respondents. Because NCVS is based on an extensive scientific sample of American households, every crime measure presented in the report is an estimate based on results of the sample. Since it is only an estimate, there will be a sampling variation or margin of error associated with each sample. Additionally, the survey is only an estimate of criminal activity and therefore cannot attest that every crime actually occurred.

Each of the methods of collecting data on violence presents a different perspective and has its own validity problems. What is certain is that violence occurs on all social and economic levels in our nation; its toll on victims is severe and long lasting. No matter which statistic or sample one uses, all agree that further research is necessary. Other researchers have gathered data regarding specific forms of violence.

The National Assessment Program

The National Institute of Justice conducts the National Assessment Program (NAP) survey approximately every 3 years to determine the needs and problems of state and local criminal justice agencies. While not technically a measurement of crime, the NAP survey identifies the day-to-day issues affecting professionals in the criminal justice system. It therefore provides a valuable insight into concerns raised by the professional whose job it is to fight crime.

The 1994 NAP survey contacted over 2,500 directors of criminal justice agencies, including police chiefs and sheriffs, prosecutors, judges, probation and parole agency directors, commissioners of corrections, state court administrators, and prison wardens, as well as other criminal justice professionals. The samples covered all 50 states and the District of Columbia. Both urban (populations greater than 250,000) and rural (populations of 50,000 to 250,000) counties were included in the survey. Respondents were asked a variety of questions dealing with workload problems, staffing, and operations and procedures.

The results of the survey indicate a great concern about the impact that violence, drugs, firearms, and troubled youth are having on society and an overburdened criminal justice system. Overall, the survey indicates that cases involving violence heightened agencies' workloads. Police chiefs and sheriffs indicated that domestic violence was primary among crimes of violence causing them increased workload problems. Prosecutors ranked child abuse and domestic violence as significantly increasing their job responsibilities (McEwen, 1995). In the opinion of police chiefs and sheriffs, among their greatest needs are programs that prevent young people from obtaining guns. In essence, it appears that law enforcement views the problem of juvenile crime in large part as a result of firearms.

Interest in community policing continues to grow. While the controversy around the effectiveness of community policing still exists, most law enforcement officials express a desire to implement all or portions of a community policing program in their jurisdiction. This approach recognizes the importance of involving the community in addressing the crime problem.

The NAP points out that we continue as a nation to become more culturally diverse. Law enforcement officials acknowledge this trend in a variety of ways. Sheriffs and police chiefs state that they are aware of the need to respond to culturally diverse populations in the wake of changing national demographics.

These findings will assist policy makers in establishing research priorities for the near future. Professionals in the field have the same concerns that researchers and citizens espouse—the need for an end to violence in our society. These official reports provide insight into the problem, but unfortunately they do not offer any concrete solutions.

Other Reports

Sources of Data on Violence

Among social surveys that have added to our knowledge of violence, *Rape in America: A Report to the Nation,* conducted by the National Victim Center, shed new light on this form of aggression. The report caused an uproar across America when it was released in April of 1992. The National Victim Center relied upon a comprehensive study entitled "The National Women's Study" to gather the information, which was based upon a national sample of 4,008 women who were interviewed regarding their experience with rape. The report indicated that rape occurred at a much higher incidence than previously accepted.

Using the 1990 U.S. Census figures, which indicate that there are approximately 96.8 million women in America, the Center estimates that one in every eight women has been raped at sometime in her life. This translates into an incredible 12.1 million women in the United States who have been raped! (See Figure 8.1.)

The information gathered from the survey in Figure 8.1 indicates that 0.07 percent of all women were raped within the preceding year. Again, using the U.S. Census figures, this translates into approximately 683,000 women who are raped each year! These figures are higher than reported in either the Uniform Crime Report or the National Crime Victimization Survey. The FBI's annual Uniform Crime Report has estimated that attempted or actual rapes reported to the police in 1990 were 102,560. The National Crime Victimization Survey reported that attempted or actual rapes for 1990 were 130,000. While the National Women's Study did not include attempted rapes, the figure is still in excess of five times that of the previously accepted number of rapes occurring each year in the United States.

One of the major problems in the area of women and sexual violence is the lack of agreement among scholars, researchers, and professionals regarding definitions and research methodology. Koss (1993) compiled various studies on rape, and her work illustrates different approaches that various researchers have used when attempting to determine the incidence of sexual violence against women in America. Depending on which article, paper, or text one reads, the estimates regarding the incidence of rape will vary. This disparity has caused problems and confusion within the professional community ever since the study of women and violence began. There are a number of reasons for the disparate figures and definitions. Following is a summary of some of the more common problems encountered when rape is studied:

FIGURE 8.1 *Survey of the Rape of Women.*

5% of the sample was unsure whether they had been raped.

39% had experienced more than one rape in their lifetime.

56% of all the women surveyed indicated they had been raped one time.

Definitional Issues: Some scholars use the term *rape,* while others use *sexual assault,* and still others define each of the foregoing terms differently. For example, one researcher may define rape as vaginal intercourse accomplished by use of force or fear, while other researchers may define rape as vaginal, oral, or rectal intercourse accomplished by force or fear. The simple addition of two terms changes the entire results of any study.

Professional Issues: The professional community approaches rape from different perspectives. For example, attorneys view rape from a legal perspective, physicians treat it as a medical problem, and psychologists approach it from a mental health point of view.

Gathering Information: Problems in the screening techniques, formation of questions, and context of questioning, as well as issues of confidentiality all impact on the validity and type of response that the researcher will receive (Koss, 1993).

Clinical studies are another source of information regarding family violence. These studies are carried out by practitioners in the field—medical professionals, psychiatrists, psychologists, and counselors—all of whom use samples gathered from actual cases of family violence. These researchers collect information from hospitals, clinics, and therapy sessions. Clinical studies normally have small sample sizes, therefore caution must be used when drawing any conclusions. However, these studies provide valuable data on the nature of abuse and assist in evaluating the different types of interventions utilized in family violence, as well as pointing out areas for further research.

Women are not the only victims of violent crime. Researchers and professionals have attempted to study violent crime from a variety of perspectives, including both offenders' and victims'. In 1989, Weiner (1989) conducted a review of the major research dealing with individual violent crime. He reviewed over forty major studies conducted by scholars between 1978 and 1987. He concludes that the farther an offender advances into the sequence of violent crime, the greater the risk that he will continue his violent behavior.

There are also other violent acts that have only recently become criminalized. Stalking became the crime of the nineties (Wallace, 1995). It is a newly emerging area of criminal law that is being studied by several experts in the field of human behavior. Zona and his associates are using the files of the Threat Management Unit of the Los Angeles Police Department in an effort to study stalkers (Zona et al., 1993). Meloy has published several articles and texts that examine the nature and extent of stalkers and violence.

Other Types of Crime Research

Although violent crime receives most of the publicity in our society, there are many other crimes suffered by citizens. Property crimes, fraud, and white-collar crimes take a tremendous toll on their victims. There are a number of reasons for the lack of attention given to nonviolent crime: the victims' movement initially focused on serious violent crime, a lack of understanding regarding the psychological and financial consequences of property or economic crimes, and a traditional underreporting of the nature and extent of this type of crime.

Sutherland's (1983) classic definition of white-collar crime offers one way of viewing this offense. He defined white-collar crime as an offense committed by a person of respectability and high social status in the course of his or her occupation. The FBI, on the other hand, defines white-collar crime as those illegal acts characterized by deceit, concealment, or violation of trust and not dependent upon the application or threat of physical force or violence. They are committed to obtain money, property, or services; or to avoid the payment or loss of money, property or services; or to secure personal or business advantage (U.S. Department of Justice, 1990). Both of these definitions deal with economic crimes, or crimes that have the gathering of assets from the victim as their objective.

Several prominent researchers have called for more information about economic crimes (Geis, Gilbert, & Stotland, 1980). Understanding the nature and extent of economic crime is necessary if we are to attempt to respond to its consequences. One of the most common forms of economic crime is fraud. A nationwide survey of fraud revealed that a sizable portion of the adult population in the United States is affected (Titus, Heinzelmann, & Boyle, 1995). Fraud was defined as the deliberate intent, targeted against individuals, to deceive for the purpose of illegal financial gain. Included in this definition were various forms of telemarketing fraud, frauds involving consumer goods and services, deceptive financial advice, and insurance scams.

The survey used a random sample of the adult population of the United States. The respondents were asked about 21 types of fraud plus a catch-all category, and were asked if they had ever been victimized or if an attempt had been made to victimize them. Fraud crosses all sociological barriers and victimization occurs in all ages, genders, races, and incomes.

More than half of those surveyed indicated that they experienced victimization, or an attempted victimization sometime in their past. Approximately one in every three respondents had been victims of potential fraud within the year preceding the survey. The attempt to defraud these victims was successful fifty percent of the time.

Economic crime is a serious form of victimization that is often overlooked by those charged with, or interested in, studying the effects of crime on individuals. The consequences of fraud will be addressed in more detail later in this text. At this stage, it is important to acknowledge that there are other forms of victimization than violence-related crimes.

Summary

It is important in the study of any discipline to know how to measure the variables affecting that discipline. Because of a number of factors that will be discussed in more detail later in this text, the measurement of crime can never be completely accurate. Official reports are those measurements of crime conducted by federal agencies. The most well-known official report is the Uniform Crime Report. This report, prepared annually by the FBI, acts as a barometer of our society. Because of several inherent shortcomings in the UCR, the National Crime Victimization Survey was developed. This survey relies on self-reporting in an attempt to determine a more accurate accounting of the nature and extent of crimes in our society.

Significantly, more and more detail is being paid to economic crimes and their effects on victims. Recent studies indicate that economic crimes, such as fraud, are widespread and occur at all socioeconomic levels within our society.

We continue to modify our measurement tools in the hopes of perfecting a valid and true method of measuring crime. Understanding the nature and extent of criminal victimization is only the beginning in a knowledge of the process of the study of multicultural issues, and it is a goal for all professionals in the field.

Discussion Questions

1. Explain the problems in using the UCR. If you were in charge of preparing it, what changes would you suggest to make it more reliable?

2. How would you improve the NCVS?

3. How does the NAP information benefit victim service professionals?

4. Compare and contrast the other types of crime research. Can you think of another method for collecting information about crime and victims?

Endnote

[1] The UCR presents a different estimate of households than the NCVS. See "Crime in the United States, 1994," *Uniform Crime Reports* (Washington, DC: Superintendent of Documents, 1994).

9

Law Enforcement

Learning Objectives

After reading this chapter you should be able to do the following:

1. Identify the purpose of staff/support functions.
2. Discuss the difference between staff and line functions.
3. Discuss how the patrol function is utilized by a modern law enforcement agency.
4. Explain the philosophy of community policing.
5. Differentiate between the organization and the function of modern-day investigations.

Administrative Services

Introduction to Administrative Services

Most law enforcement organizations follow the line structure model, which is the clearest form of organizational control. Reporting lines and responsibilities are direct. The command staff may consist of the chief of police or sheriff, deputy chiefs, commanders, and captains at the top of the structure, and, depending upon the size of the organization, a lieutenant and a sergeant, followed by police officers or deputies. Command originates at the upper management level of the department and flows in a line to the lower end.

In larger law enforcement agencies, the size of the organization dictates the addition of a staff structure. Staff responsibilities are to support the line functions, which will enable line personnel to accomplish the mission of providing citizens with law enforcement, traffic enforcement, and investigative follow-up.

The Division of Line Functions and Staff Functions

The division between line and staff functions is not always clear. For example, the function of community relations is to support the entire department; yet it interacts directly with the community in crime prevention efforts. In fact, community relations normally works best when the line officer is totally involved in the effort. Most administrators have developed programs that allow the line officer to work in conjunction with the community relations unit in giving crime prevention presentations, conducting home and business crime prevention inspections, and meeting with citizens groups to develop crime-specific prevention programs.

Reviewing the agency's mission statement is an easy way to differentiate between a line function and staff function. Although the mission statement pertains to all employees of the organization, members directly involved in attaining the mission are line personnel. For example, a typical mission statement might state: "Our commitment is to safeguard lives and property, preserve constitutional rights, actively apprehend those who violate the law and the rights of others, maintain peace and order, and promote a safe, healthy environment."

Patrol

The word "operations" encompasses the traditional line functions for which a law enforcement agency is created. An Operations Division primarily consists of patrol, traffic, and criminal investigation units. Subunits associated with these primary units can include commercial enforcement and parking control under the traffic unit; and Vice, Narcotics, and Alcohol enforcement under Criminal Investigations. Patrol may also have subunits that are identified by a variety of names, usually acronyms for some kind of special enforcement effort. For example, S.W.A.T. (special weapons and tactics) can be a special unit assigned to patrol.

The largest and most visible component of any municipal law enforcement agency is the patrol section. It consists of the men and women working in uniform 24 hours a day,

365 days a year. They handle calls for service from the public in motor vehicles, on horseback, or on foot. Patrol is the essence of the police mission (Hale, 1992). Although all aspects of the police organization have the responsibility of meeting the organizations mission, patrol usually takes the lead in this effort due to its size and visibility.

Controversy surrounds the question of what the police role is today. At the center of the debate is the fact that the duties and responsibilities of the police are generally in conflict with each other. There is no agreement among authorities concerning the meaning of the police mission. Gildstein (1977) has observed:

> The police function is incredibly complex. The total range of police responsibilities is extraordinarily broad. Many tasks are so entangled that separation appears impossible. The numerous conflicts among different aspects of the function cannot be easily reconciled. Anyone attempting to construct a workable definition of the police role will typically come away with old images shattered and with a new-found appreciation for the intricacies of police work.

The simplistic view of the patrol officer is that portrayed on television. Typically, television presents two male officers in a black and white police car. They are assigned exciting calls and usually make spectacular arrests. Major and complex crimes are solved in only one hour with four commercial breaks. The reality, however, is much different.

The basic purpose of patrol is to deter or eliminate the opportunity for a suspect or suspects to commit a crime. The role of the police is not to end any desire to commit crime; rather, it is to curtail any successful attempts to commit crimes. In addition to deterrence, a patrol unit's major functions consist of crime prevention, investigation of crimes committed, and community service.

The possibility of arrest and incarceration may influence some people into socially acceptable behavior. To a potential suspect, the possibility of arrest is usually most obvious with the presence of the uniformed patrol officer in a distinctively marked police car. Random patrolling techniques of many police organizations and officers in the field on a 24-hour basis may further curtail opportunities for criminal activity.

Another function of patrol is crime prevention. Officers are constantly on alert for situations that can lead to criminal or antisocial behavior. One example of a crime prevention activity is checking closed businesses for open doors and windows. Reporting findings and relaying potential problems to business owners can reduce chances of the occurrence of a crime of opportunity. Proper lighting in parks and other recreational areas is constantly monitored by patrol officers. Lighting and patrolling reduces the number of areas where juveniles may secretly gather to consume alcohol or use narcotics, which can lead to the commission of other crimes such as vandalism or minor thefts.

Following a crime, the investigative follow-up function is absorbed by patrol. Officers are at times successful in apprehension after commission of the crime. Also, in the course of preparing a preliminary investigative report, stolen property is occasionally recovered. This information can then be forwarded to the investigation section of the department.

Last, patrol offers services not directly connected to criminal behavior. Services that officers provide to the citizens range from opening locked cars to reporting burned-out street lights and traffic signals. Other traditional duties not related to criminal activity that are performed by uniformed patrol are searching for lost children and adults, providing traffic control, and supervising special events such as parades.

Officers assigned to patrol are paramount to the decentralization of service provided by local government. Officers can learn the "pulse" of the populace through feedback from their conversations with citizens.

The patrol division is usually the largest area of any municipal police organization. Patrol is charged with the duty of routinely monitoring the city 24 hours a day. Immediate action occurs by patrol units on any type of call for service or observed criminal behavior, even before specialized units of the department are mobilized. An example would be an occurrence of a homicide. Most law enforcement agencies have investigator(s) assigned to work homicide cases due to the complex and time-consuming investigative techniques required. Patrol will respond and begin initial investigation of a reported homicide prior to the arrival of homicide investigators. In some cases, an arrest is made and preliminary crime scene investigative work is begun by patrol by the time the investigators arrive at the scene.

Many chief executive officers of law enforcement believe that preventive patrol acts as a deterrent to criminal activity; however, little hard evidence exists to suggest this is true. A basic assumption is that criminals will not commit a crime if they observe a patrol vehicle in the vicinity. However, open drug dealing in major metropolitan areas often occurs as a marked police unit cruises by the activity.

Community Policing

As the drug problem becomes more severe, progressing from the ghetto and invading middle class schools, police and community leaders are acknowledging that law enforcement cannot win the war against drugs by itself. Crime and the fear of crime have become an ever-increasing problem within our cities. There have been numerous attempts to combat the increasing rate of criminal activity in America. William S. Sessions (1990), a former director of the Federal Bureau of Investigation, succinctly stated the problem when he said:

> In the early days of our Nation, private citizens kept the peace in their communities through respect for the law and through voluntary involvement in peace-keeping efforts. For the most part, the church, the family, and the community imposed social sanctions that were the primary controls in preventing and controlling crime.
>
> Unfortunately, as cities grew and the populations changed, this community support for law enforcement broke down. As a result, the responsibility for crime prevention shifted. Law Enforcement officers, not citizens, became society's first line of defense against crime.
>
> But as today's statistics remind us, law enforcement cannot prevent, or reduce, crime without enlisting broad-based citizen participation, cooperation, and support. Moreover, our resources and manpower are shrinking, while our responsibilities are growing and the criminal element is becoming more sophisticated. So, we must get back to the basics and use community-based efforts to control crime.

Everyone agrees with the director's statement. The problems arise when cities attempt to implement programs to carry out the purposes set forth in the statement. Scholars, police chiefs, elected officials, and community leaders have debated this issue for decades. This section offers an overview of the various approaches that have been utilized within the United States in an attempt to solve the problem of crime prevention and crime control (Goldstein, 1990; Trojanowicz, & Bucqueroux, 1990). Rather than attempt to explain how a specific activity such as a Neighborhood Watch Association functions, this section will examine the broad principles that apply to all community policing programs. Throughout, the term "community policing" is used, rather than "community relations"; the former term is used to define the program as a law enforcement activity rather than a public relations effort. A brief overview of law enforcement efforts in the past will set the stage for a meaningful discussion of community policing.

Numerous scholars and practitioners have studied the problem of crime prevention and crime control (Johnson, Misnev, & Brown, 1990). While it is difficult to name a single pioneer or early leader in the field of community policing, John Lohmann, the former dean of the School of Criminology at the University of California, Berkeley, was one of the first to publish a text in this area. His book, *The Police and Minority Groups,* is considered a classic in the field of community policing.

Community policing enters into a *partnership* with the community. The classic definition of community policing was established by the National Center on Police and Community Relations at Michigan State University:

> Police-community relations in its general sense means the variety of ways in which it may be emphasized that the police are indeed an important *part of,* and not *apart from,* the communities they serve. Properly understood, police-community relations is a concept for total orientation, not merely the preoccupation of a special unit or bureau within the department. It bears upon administrative policy, it bears upon line service through the uniformed patrol division. In short, police-community relations ideally is an emphasis on attitude, a way of viewing police responsibilities that ought to permeate the entire organization.

This definition makes it clear that community policing is an equal partnership between the community and the police. Many scholars argue that there is very little, if any, difference between community policing and problem-solving policing (Moore & Trojanowicz, 1988). However, there is a difference; it is the perspective from which the interaction between the community and the police is one involving equals.

Community policing involves the total community: the schools, churches, neighborhood associations, merchants, elected and appointed officials, and families. All of these community "citizens" work as equal partners with the police to make their individual neighborhoods safe from crime. Community policing takes the position that citizens of the community understand what their most serious problems are and what crimes are occurring in their neighborhoods. Furthermore they should have the ability and opportunity to work with the police in forming a protocol that would provide an adequate and timely response to these problems.

Community policing draws upon many different "citizen experts" and resources in responding to requests for assistance from neighborhoods. Officers work with citizens in specific, agreed-on areas of responsibility. They may also establish foot patrols to enhance face-to-face contact with citizens. Finally, departments may modify their chain of command to a more decentralized form (Pate et al., 1986).

Community policing is an attempt to work with the community in solving problems that either cause crime or contribute to the instability of the neighborhood. The following sections will explore in more depth how a police department and the community join in the attempt to accomplish this goal.

As stated above, community policing involves a partnership between the police and the community. Everyone knows what policing is or what a police department is supposed to do, but it is not so clear exactly what a "community" encompasses. Is it the entire city? Is it a neighborhood? What is a neighborhood? Are there distinct boundary lines that establish an area within a city that may be called a separate community? It is important to clarify the term *community* in the context of community policing.

It should be clear from the definition of community policing that it is a citywide program. However, most cities have distinct social-economic areas within their boundaries. What works for a newer, upper-class, suburban, residential area may not work for an older, lower-class area that is suffering physical decay. While community policing must be a total approach to a city's criminal and social problems, it must also be responsive to the individual needs of its citizens. This leads to the conclusion that community policing must be geared to react to localized problems within a city.

One scholar has defined the term *neighborhoods* as places in which people live or work near each other, where they recognize this proximity and accept is as a common trait (Hannerz, 1980). Another scholar points out that residents of cities acknowledge certain areas with "cognitive maps" that identify these areas as their neighborhood (Suttles, 1972). From these definitions, we may then draw the conclusion that a *neighborhood* can be defined as a portion of a city that has its own identity. This identity is established by a combination of factors that include: the residents' perceptions, geographic characteristics, formal city action, land-use development, and ethnic factors.

Investigative Services

An investigation of a criminal case is an effort to search for persons and/or things that will be useful in reconstructing the circumstances of an illegal act or comission and the mental state accompanying it (Weston & Wells, 1970). A criminal investigation is the process of proceeding from the known to the unknown in a logical fashion, with the ultimate objective of determining the truth.

Some believe that the only successful criminal investigation is based on techniques used by the fictitious but highly successful criminal investigator Sherlock Holmes. Sir Arthur Conan Doyle wrote of Holmes's techniques, which ranged from intuition to inspiration to imagination. Today's television viewers assume that criminal investigations are successfully concluded through the use of microscopes, computers, and intensive laboratory analyses. Others view a successful criminal investigation to be the result of routine legwork on the part of a gruff, cigarette-smoking detective.

Ironically, all of these factors can be part of the successful conclusion of a criminal investigation. Many cases have been successfully solved as a result of a detective's flash of inspiration and follow-up of a seemingly innocuous lead. A criminal case has often been solved using the combined efforts of a detective and a forensic criminalist. Using such personnel in the investigation of a criminal offense lessens the extent of reliance on eyewitness accounts and interrogations of suspects. Crime scene evidence explained by an expert witness often is more damaging to a criminal defendant than the story of an eyewitness.

Scientific Background of Investigations

Crime, like many elements within the American social structure, continues in an evolutionary process. Crime was not very sophisticated 100 years ago, with burglaries and robberies being the predominant offenses committed in America. Criminal investigations relied primarily on the use of informants for making arrests and recovering property. As crime and criminals became more complex, it was necessary for law enforcement to raise its level of sophistication.

Identification by Fingerprints

The Henry System of Fingerprint Classification is now the standard system used by law enforcement. Francis Galton (1822–1911) contributed the first comprehensive study and techniques for classifying fingerprints. Since Galton's study of fingerprints, no two sets of identical prints have been found in the system.

Sir Edward R. Henry developed a classification system that proved to be workable as early as 1901. In fingerprint classification, each print was assigned a series of symbols and numbers that would identify and individualize its total characteristics. This allowed easy and rapid access and retrieval of filed fingerprints.

There are computer systems today that are capable of comparing a latent fingerprint against a database of millions of fingerprints. States such as California have been using this system for several years. The computer operator scans the latent print, enlarges it, and then makes a tracing copy of the print. The tracing is entered into the computer, its individual characteristics to be compared against the database. The computer will respond with a single print or a number of similar prints, which are then further checked by the fingerprint technician.

DNA Evidence

Who can forget the O.J. Simpson double murder trial in which the prosecution attempted to rely on DNA evidence to convict Mr. Simpson and the defense strived to show that the DNA samples were contaminated? Mr. Simpson was found not guilty in the criminal trial, but was found to have been responsible for the deaths in a subsequent civil trial. The criminal Simpson trial raised the public consciousness of the usefulness of DNA evidence in such cases.

DNA, or deoxyribonucleic acid, is genetic material that is unique to each individual and can serve as the basis for matching suspects with a crime based upon biological evidence (blood, hair, skin, or semen) left at the scene. DNA matching began as a test for paternity and has evolved into one of the twenty-first century's most important crime fighting techniques. At least 49 states have admitted DNA evidence in trials or hearings. The genetic material is very stable and can be tested long after fingerprints or other physical evidence has disappeared.

The FBI opened its first DNA-typing laboratory in 1988, and it has become a well-known site for DNA testing in the nation. Private firms have entered this area and offer DNA testing on a fee-per-service basis. DNA testing is also being used to clear those wrongfully convicted before the use or admission of such evidence.

The use of DNA evidence will continue to expand as a tool for criminal investigations. It is another refinement of science that will allow for more accurate investigations.

The Functions of Police in Criminal Investigations

The American system of justice generally provides for the investigation of criminal activity by the police. In some areas of the country, it is also the practice for the district attorney to investigate criminal cases. Primarily, the police present investigated cases to the district attorney or local prosecutor, who will then determine whether charges will be filed. Most district attorneys are assisted by an investigative staff who perform follow-up investigations and conduct background investigations.

Police departments have the primary objective of preventing criminal activity, arresting criminals, and recovering property that has been stolen. The apprehension of criminals generally is preceded by the commission of a detected or reported crime.

The Preliminary Investigation

The multifaceted preliminary investigation is usually conducted by patrol officers, since they are the first responders. The determination of the actual existence of a crime must first be made. If there is a suspect at the scene, the preliminary investigation should include an arrest. The responding officers or investigators would also determine the crime classification. If there is no suspect at the scene, the preliminary investigation would include obtaining a description of the suspect(s) and any vehicles involved. This would enable the officer to have the dispatch center broadcast appropriate information for other field units.

The preliminary investigation also should include locating the victim and any witnesses to the crime for the purpose of obtaining accurate statements, including names, addresses, and telephone numbers. The initial responding officers would also want to protect the crime scene to preserve evidence. Also, they may begin conducting a cursory search, depending upon the severity of the crime. They may determine that there is a need for specialists to conduct the search for latent prints and trace evidence.

Officers will also determine the extent of injuries sustained by the victim as a result of the crime. They will also investigate the method used to commit the crime. Responding officers will determine the extent of property loss, and if the crime is a property crime, the value of the stolen or damaged property. Also, if deemed necessary, officers would create a sketch of the crime scene.

The Follow-Up Investigation

The preliminary investigation is reviewed and, in the event there are substantial leads in the report that could possibly solve the case, follow-up investigation occurs.

There are four purposes for the follow-up investigation: (1) to assure thoroughness of the preliminary investigation; (2) to continue investigation of any surfaced leads; (3) to explore possibilities of linking the crime with others of a similar type; and (4) in the event of an arrest, to prepare the case for prosecution (Hastings, 1982).

The review of the preliminary investigation is not intended to be a duplication of the efforts of patrol officers. Rather, the detective needs to be apprised of all existing aspects of the case prior to initiating the investigative effort.

The investigator should follow up on all case leads. The detective will make a determination as to whether the case warrants continued investigative effort or should be classified inactive, once all leads are exhausted.

One of the most important tasks for the detective is to determine if a case correlates with any other active cases being investigated by him or her or by other members of the detective section. This effort may be more difficult in larger organizations with a decentralized detective function. Career criminals may be committing similar types of crimes in various parts of the city. It is important that crime analysis sections exist in larger organizations to examine crime trends and establish crime patterns. The crime analysis unit can then publish bulletins for dispersal throughout the organization that target crime trends and assist in linkage of cases being handled in different locations.

It would be best to conduct daily briefings in smaller organizations not having a decentralized investigative effort. Each detective would present an update on active cases, pointing out any unique points. Such a briefing can provide a forum in which to compare like cases and ultimately lead to a more directed effort of investigating.

Ending a Case

The proper conclusion of a case investigation is crucial to its success. Cases investigated with due care, diligence, thoroughness, and a minimum of shortcuts lead to convictions—the ultimate goal of any criminal investigation. Concluding an investigation with the apprehension of a suspect is only a portion of the detective's responsibility. A case presented in the courts must withstand the scrutiny of the initial trial. There is also the possibility of state court appeals, as well as appeal to the Court that has final judicial review—the United States Supreme Court.

A trained investigator could begin building a strong case by first obtaining the admission of the suspect. He would then attempt to locate additional witnesses to corroborate the defendant's statement. The detective would also seek out physical evidence to substantiate the assertion that the defendant committed the crime.

Extreme care is exercised to ensure that the constitutional rights of the suspect are observed. Adherence to all rules as they apply to the Miranda rights must be followed in order not to jeopardize the case later at trial. This is particularly critical if statements were taken from the defendant. Care must also be taken if any type of lineup was used in the investigative process. If the lineup process is tainted, the witnesses to the lineup could be barred from making the identification in a court of law.

The trained investigator will also determine if there are other cases under investigation in which the defendant could be responsible. If the defendant is involved in additional cases that contain attendant witnesses and physical evidence, the chances of a conviction are enhanced—even if the original case falters.

Summary

An important, but often overlooked aspect of any law enforcement agency is the administrative services section. This section provides the support and coordination for the more visible functions of policing such as patrol. Patrol is the most visible and many believe most important function of a law enforcement agency. From the acknowledgment that police in general and patrol in particular cannot stop crime has risen the concept of community policing. This is the modern-day view of policing—a partnership between the law enforcement professionals and the citizens in the community. However, community policing cannot by itself solve the crime problem. When a crime does occur, it must be investigated and solved. In many departments, this function is handled by the investigation unit or division.

Discussion Questions _____

1. Explain the functions and purpose of staff functions within a law enforcement agency.

3. Why is the patrol function so important in a law enforcement agency?

3. Why is community policing becoming so popular in the United States?

4. Can you identify any problems with the utilization of community policing?

5. Explain the organization of a typical law enforcement investigations unit.

10

The Court System

Learning Objectives

After reading this chapter you should be able to do the following:

1. Explain the difference between the state and federal court systems.
2. Explain the roles and functions of the different parties to a criminal trial.
3. List the various types of pretrial procedures.
4. Distinguish between the different phases in a criminal trial.

This chapter has been adapted from Cliff Roberson and Harvey Wallace, *Introduction to Criminology* (Copperhouse, 1998).

The Court Structure

Introduction

It is critical that professionals in the criminal justice system understand the dynamics of the criminal court system.[1] In order to understand the role of federal and state law it is essential to have a firm grasp of the principles of how the American criminal justice system functions. There is no more confusing, frustrating, and complex environment in the legal system than the criminal court system.

The court system in the United States is based upon the principle of federalism. The first Congress established a federal court system and the individual states were permitted to continue their own judicial structure. There was general agreement among our nation's founding fathers that individual states needed to retain significant autonomy from federal control. Under this concept of federalism, the United States developed as a loose confederation of semi-independent states, with the federal court system acting in a very limited manner. In the early history of our nation, most cases were tried in state courts, and it was only later that the federal government and the federal judiciary began to exercise jurisdiction over crimes and civil matters. Jurisdiction in this context simply means the ability of the court to enforce laws and punish individuals who violate those laws.

As a result of this historical evolution, a dual system of state and federal courts exists today. Therefore, federal and state courts may have concurrent jurisdiction over specific crimes. For example, a person who robs a bank may be tried and convicted in state court for robbery and then tried and convicted in federal court for the federal offense of robbery of a federally chartered savings institution.

The State System

Historically, each of the 13 states had its own unique court structure. This independence continued after the American Revolution and resulted in widespread differences among the various states, some of which still exist today. Because each state adopted its own system of courts, the consequence was a poorly planned and confusing judicial structure. As a result, there have been several reform movements whose purpose has been to streamline and modernize this system.

Many state courts can be divided into three levels: trial courts, courts of appeals, and state supreme courts.

Trial Courts.   Criminal cases start and finish in trial courts. The trial court conducts the entire series of acts that cumlminate in either the defendant's release or sentencing. State trial courts can be further divided into courts of limited or special jurisdiction and courts of general jurisdiction.

The nature and type of case determines which court will have jurisdiction. Courts that hear and decide only certain limited legal issues are courts of limited jurisdiction. Typically, these courts hear certain types of minor civil or criminal cases. There are approximately 13,000 local courts in the United States. They are county, magistrate, justice, or municipal courts. Judges in these courts may be either appointed or elected. In many jurisdictions these are part-time positions, and the incumbent may have a job or position in addition to serving as a judge. However, simply because they handle minor civil and criminal matters does not mean these courts do not perform important duties. Many times the only contact the average citizen will have with the judicial system occurs at this level. Courts of limited jurisdiction hear and decide issues such as traffic tickets or set bail for criminal defendants.

In addition, courts of limited jurisdiction may hear certain types of specialized matters such as probate of wills and estates, divorces, child custody matters, and juvenile hearings. These may be local courts or, depending on the state, courts of general jurisdiction that are designated by statute to hear and decide specific types of cases. For example, in California, a superior court is considered a court of general jurisdiction; however, certain superior courts are designated to hear only juvenile matters, thereby becoming a court of limited jurisdiction when sitting as a juvenile court.

Courts of general jurisdiction are granted authority to hear and decide all issues that are brought before them. These are the courts that normally hear all major civil or criminal cases, and they are known by a variety of names—such as superior courts, circuit courts, district courts, or courts of common pleas. Since they are courts of general jurisdiction, they have authority to decide issues that occur anywhere within the state. Some larger jurisdictions such as Los Angeles or New York may have hundreds of courts of general jurisdiction within the city limits. Typically, these courts hear civil cases involving the same type of issues that courts of limited jurisdiction hear, although the amount of damages will be higher and may reach millions. These courts also hear the most serious forms of criminal matters, including death penalty cases.

Courts of general jurisdiction traditionally have the power to order individuals to do, or refrain from doing, certain acts. These courts may issue injunctions that prohibit performing certain acts or require individuals to do certain functions or duties. This authority is derived from the equity power that resides in courts of general jurisdiction. *Equity* is the concept that justice is administrated according to fairness as contrasted with the strict rules of law. In early English Common Law such separate courts of equity were known as Courts of Chancery. These early courts were not concerned with technical legal issues, rather they focused on rendering decisions or orders that were fair or equitable. In modern times, the power of these courts has been merged with courts of general jurisdiction, allowing them to rule on matters that require fairness as well as the strict application of the law. For example, the power to issue temporary restraining orders in spousal abuse cases comes from this authority.

Appellate jurisdiction is reserved for courts that hear appeals from both limited and general jurisdiction courts. These courts do not hold trials or hear evidence. They decide matters of law and issue formal written decisions or "opinions." There are two classes of appellate courts: (1) intermediate and (2) final.

Courts of Appeals. The intermediate appellate courts are known as courts of appeals. Approximately half the states have designated intermediate appellate courts. These courts may be divided into judicial districts that hear all appeals within their district. They will hear and decide all issues of law that are raised on appeal in both civil and criminal cases. Since these courts deal strictly with legal or equitable issues, there is no jury to decide factual disputes. These courts accept the facts as determined by the trial courts. Intermediate appellate courts have the authority to reverse the decision of the lower courts and to send the matter back with instructions to retry the case in accordance with their opinion. They also may uphold the decision of the lower court. In either situation, the party who loses the appeal at this level may file an appeal with the next higher appellate court.

Supreme Courts.   Final appellate courts are the highest state appellate courts. They may be known as supreme courts or courts of last resort. There may be five, seven, or nine justices sitting on this court, depending on the state. This court has jurisdiction to hear and decide issues dealing with all matters decided by lower courts, including ruling on state constitutional or statutory issues. The decision of the supreme court is binding on all other courts within the state. Once this court had decided an issue, the only other available appeal is to the federal court system.

The Federal Courts

While state courts had their origin in historical accident and custom, federal courts were created by the U.S. Constitution. Section 1 of Article III established the federal court system with the words providing for "one supreme Court, and . . . such inferior Courts as the Congress may from time to time ordain and establish." From this beginning, Congress has engaged in a series of acts resulting in today's federal court system. The Judiciary Act of 1789 created the U.S. Supreme Court and established district and circuit courts of appeals.

Federal District Courts are the lowest level of the federal court system. These courts have original jurisdiction over all cases involving a violation of federal statutes. These district courts handle thousands of criminal cases per year, and questions have been raised as to the quality of justice that can be delivered by the overworked judges.

Federal Circuit Courts of Appeals are the intermediate appellate level courts within the federal system. These courts are called circuit courts because the federal system is divided into 11 circuits. A twelfth Circuit Court of Appeals serves the Washington, D.C., area. These courts hear all criminal appeals from the district courts. These appeals are usually heard by panels of three of the appellate court judges rather than by all the judges of each circuit.

The United States Supreme Court is the highest court in the land. It has the capacity for judicial review of all lower-court decisions, as well as state and federal statutes. By exercising this power, the Supreme Court determines what laws and lower-court decisions conform to the mandates set forth in the U.S. Constitution. The concept of judicial review was first referred to by Alexander Hamilton in the *Federalist Papers,* in which he referred to the Supreme Court as ensuring that the will of the people will be supreme over the will of the legislature (Supreme Court). This concept was firmly and finally established in our system when the Supreme Court asserted its power of judicial review in the case of *Marbury v. Madison (1 Cranch 137).*

The Supreme Court has original jurisdiction in the following cases: cases between the United States and a state; cases between states; cases involving foreign ambassadors, ministers, and consuls; and cases between a state and a citizen of another state or country. The court hears appeals from lower courts including the various state supreme courts. If four justices of the U.S. Supreme Court vote to hear a case, the Court will issue a Writ of

Certiorari. This is an order to a lower court to send the records of the case to the Supreme Court for review. The Court meets on the first Monday of October and usually remains in session until June. The Court may review any case it deems worthy of review, but it actually hears very few of the cases filed with it. Of approximately 5,000 appeals each year, the Court hears about 200.

The Parties

The Victim

The victim of any crime is often the forgotten party in the criminal justice system. For many years, victims were perceived as simply another witness to the crime. The prevailing attitude was that the real victim was the "People of the State" in which the crime was committed. Families of murder victims could not obtain information regarding cases, and they were often ignored by overworked and understaffed criminal justice personnel. Within the last 20 years, this attitude has begun to change as we become more aware of the needs and rights of crime victims.

The Perpetrator

The perpetrator of a crime is guaranteed certain rights within our form of government. Many aspects of the criminal procedure process are controlled by the U.S. Constitution, specifically the Bill of Rights (the original ten amendments to the Constitution). These federal constitutional protections concerning individual rights are, for the most part, binding on state courts.[2]

Law Enforcement

Law enforcement's role in the court system is critical. Here, it is important to remember that its duties do not end with the apprehension of the suspect. Law enforcement must continue to work the case until it is sent to the jury by the judge. It is common in larger prosecutors' offices to have the lead detective sit with the prosecutor during the trial. That detective may know the case as well as the prosecutor and many times will provide critical advice.

The Prosecutor

We often think that the prosecutor's role is to convict the defendant. This is erroneous. The prosecutor has the duty to ensure justice, not merely to convict. Accordingly, if the prosecutor has a reasonable basis for believing that the defendant is not guilty, the prosecutor should not attempt to obtain a conviction. In such a case, if the prosecutor is the decision maker (e.g., district attorney), then the prosecutor should request that the case be dismissed. If the prosecutor is not the decision maker (e.g., an assistant district attorney), the prosecutor should present the facts to the district attorney and request either that he or she be relieved from the case or that the case be dismissed. It would be unethical for an attorney to attempt to convict an innocent person.

The Defense Attorney

The Sixth Amendment, U.S. Constitution, guarantees that the accused shall have the right to the assistance of counsel in all criminal cases. This means that no matter how petty the offense, the accused has the right to assistance of counsel; this issue has never been seriously questioned. The controversial issue is "When the accused cannot afford an attorney, when is the government required to provide the accused with counsel?"

As a general rule, the accused is entitled to the appointment of a counsel any time that the accused is subject to punishment that may include jail or prison time and the accused cannot afford to retain an attorney *(Argersinger v. Hamlin)*. (Note: If the accused can afford counsel, he or she has the right to counsel in all criminal proceedings.) Typically, the indigent accused has the right to counsel at every significant phase of the trial.

The most popular grounds for appeal in criminal courts are ineffective assistance of counsel. The appellate courts generally require not only that the defendant establish that his or her counsel made errors at trial, but also that the errors prejudiced the defendant. The courts are hesitant to engage in second-guessing trial counsel (Monday-morning quarterbacking). In addition, a defendant who is represented by a retained attorney (one hired by defendant) has a more difficult time in establishing ineffective assistance of counsel. The rationale for the latter rule is that the accused should not be rewarded for selecting a bad attorney.

No one person has a more demanding and more misunderstood role than that of the defense counsel. Too often we associate the defense counsel with the person he or she represents. However, the defense attorney's role is to be the spokesperson and representative for the accused. If the attorney can legally prevent the state from proving the accused's guilt, the attorney must do so.

The defense attorney is an officer of the court and, as such, he or she cannot present false evidence, allow perjury to be committed, or break the law in defending the accused. The defense attorney, however, is required to use any legal method to prevent the accused's conviction or, in the case of conviction, to obtain the lightest sentence possible. It is not the attorney's duty to determine what sentence is best for the accused, but it is his or her duty to obtain the lightest sentence unless requested otherwise by the defendant. An undecided issue in this regard is the defense counsel's duty either to fight the death penalty or to attempt to ensure that the death penalty is imposed when the accused is being tried for a capital offense and requests it.

The Judge

The trial judge is an officer of the court. It would be more accurate to describe him or her as the "master of the court." The trial judge's duties are varied and far more extensive than would appear on the surface. During the trial, judges rule on appropriateness of the conduct of all others involved in the court process, including spectators. Judges determine what evidence is admissible and, during jury trials, which instructions of law the juries will receive. Any motions, questions of law, objections, and, in most states, the sentence to be imposed are decided only by the judges. The senior judge in any one court or the presiding judge is responsible for the docketing (scheduling) of cases, motions, and so forth. Judges also have extensive control over probation officers, the court clerks, and indirectly, to some extent, the police.

The Jury

Even though most cases are handled with a guilty plea and only a few are tried by a jury, the jury is the focal point of the criminal justice system. The Sixth Amendment also guarantees the accused the right to trial by jury. The major issues regarding the right to a jury trial are (1) whether all offenders, including those being tried on minor offenses, have a right to jury trial; (2) the size of the jury; and (3) whether the jury verdict must be unanimous.

In felony cases, there has never been a question regarding the right to a jury trial. Prior to 1970, the general rule for state criminal trials was that in serious crimes the accused had a right to a jury trial, but not in minor offenses. In *Baldwin v. New York,* the court moved away from the serious–minor classification and established the rule that if the accused was facing a possible sentence of six months or more in jail, the accused had a right to a jury trial *(399 US 66)*. If the accused is facing a possible sentence of less than six months, then the accused has no right to a jury trial unless provided by state statute. Many states, for example, California, provide the right to a jury trial any time the accused faces a possible jail sentence.

The U.S. Supreme Court discussed this issue again in *Blanton v. North Las Vegas.* The issue in this case was whether the accused had a right to a jury trial in a case involving driving under the influence (DUI). The court ruled that if the state considered the offense a petty offense, the accused has no right to a jury trial. If the state, however, treats the crime as a serious crime then the accused has a right to a speedy trial. (Note: Nevada has a statute that classified DUI as a petty offense unless aggravating circumstances are present *[489 US 538]*.)

A related issue is whether the accused has a right to a trial by a jury consisting of at least 12 jurors. Historically, trial juries have consisted of 12 jurors; however as a result of *Williams v. Florida,* the U.S. Supreme Court has approved trial by a six-person jury. The court stated: "We conclude, in short, as we began: the fact that a jury at common law was composed of precisely 12 is a historical accident, unnecessary to effect the purposes of the jury system and wholly without significance . . ." *(399 US 78, 90).*

After the *Williams* case, many states adopted the six-person jury for misdemeanor cases. In some states, for example Florida, a six-person jury may be used in felony cases. The U.S. Supreme Court has set six as the minimum size for a jury.

A related issue is the requirement for unanimous verdicts in jury cases. The Supreme Court has ruled that in trials with six-person juries, the verdict must be unanimous. The court has approved statutes that allow less than unanimous verdicts in cases with 12-person juries. In *Apodica v. Oregon,* the court approved a state statute that allowed conviction based on the vote of 10 jury members in a 12-person jury *(406 US 404)*. The Supreme Court has never approved a less than unanimous verdict in cases with fewer than 12 jurors.

The Pretrial and Trial Process

The Decision to Prosecute

The decision to prosecute is a function of the prosecutor and is generally not reviewable. In many states and under the federal government, before the prosecutor may file felony charges with a court, he or she must obtain a grand jury indictment. In other states, the prosecutor files "an information" with the lower court.

Generally, after an arrest or on the completion of an investigation, the case is referred to the prosecutor's office. In some jurisdictions, however, the case is not referred until after the accused has made an initial appearance in court. When the case is received in the prosecutor's office, it is reviewed to determine if it merits prosecution. Because of a lack of resources, insufficient evidence, or witness problems prosecutors will not try all cases referred to their offices.

The prosecutor may also reduce the charge to a misdemeanor. Of the foregoing reasons for declining prosecution, insufficient evidence is the most common. For example, approximately one half of all drug cases in which prosecution was declined were based on insufficient evidence. The second most common reason involved witness problems, in that the witnesses were unavailable or unwilling to be involved (U.S. Bureau of Justice, 1987).

Bail

Traditionally the bail system requires the defendant to guarantee his or her appearance at trial by posting a money bond. This money would be forfeited should the defendant fail to appear in court for trial. The Eighth Amendment of the U.S. Constitution states that excessive bail shall not be required. Although the amendment does not grant the right to bail in all cases, all states and the federal government give the defendant the right to bail except in limited situations.

The U.S. Supreme Court made it clear in 1950 that the purpose of bail was "to assure the defendant's attendance in court when his presence is required" *(342 US 1)*. Accordingly, we assume that any bail higher than that necessary to ensure the accused's presence at trial is excessive and, thus, unconstitutional.

The U.S. Bail Reform Act of 1984 added the duty to consider the safety of the community when making the pretrial release decision. The act provided that bail could be refused in those cases where the accused is charged with a violent offense, has a serious criminal record and is considered a danger to the community, or is a flight risk.

Other key features of the act were its establishment of a "no-bail" presumption for certain types of cases. Many scholars thought that the "no-bail" presumption denied the accused due process since it authorized punishment before trial. The U.S. Supreme Court in upholding the constitutionality of the Bail Reform Act, stated: "The legislative history clearly shows that Congress formulated the Bail Reform Act to prevent danger to the community—a legitimate regulatory goal—not to punish dangerous individuals *(U.S. v. Salerno, 55)*.

When the U.S. Supreme Court held this act constitutional, most states enacted similar statutes. Accordingly, now in determining whether to release a defendant from custody prior to the trial, the judge must consider both (1) the likelihood the accused will be present for trial and (2) the safety of the community.

Pretrial Hearings

Felony cases are processed either by indictment or appearance before a preliminary hearing. In those states that require indictments by a grand jury, the case is normally presented

FOCUS BOX • *Pleas*

Plea of Not Guilty. A plea of not guilty denies placing the burden of proving guilt beyond a reasonable doubt on the prosecution. If the defendant stands mute and refuses to enter any plea, a plea of not guilty will be entered on the defendant's behalf by the judge. (Note: An accused has a constitutional right to be assumed innocent until proven guilty beyond a reasonable doubt.)

Guilty Plea. A guilty plea is not only an admission of guilt but also a waiver of the right to jury, the right to remain silent, the right to confront any witnesses, and the right to require the prosecution to establish guilt beyond a reasonable doubt by admissible evidence. While an accused has a right to plead guilty, the trial judge is not required to accept this plea. If the judge feels that the accused's plea is not providently entered, the judge can enter a plea of not guilty for the accused. In addition, in capital cases the accused cannot enter a plea of guilty if the state is requesting the death penalty. The rationale for this rule is that to allow the accused to plead guilty in a death penalty case would be the same as allowing the accused to commit suicide.

Nolo Contendere. This is a plea of "no contest." It is essentially a guilty plea. By entering a nolo contendere plea, the accused waives the same rights as if he or she had pled guilty. Often the nolo contendere plea is used in those cases where the accused is also liable in civil court. By pleading nolo, the accused does not admit commission of the act in question. The accused does not have a *right* to plead "nolo contendere." This form of plea is acceptable in only about one half of the states and the federal government.

Not Guilty by Reasons of Insanity. In most states, the accused may plead not guilty by reason of insanity. In states that do not allow the accused to plead insanity, the accused must plead not guilty and raise the issue of insanity as an affirmative (acceptable) defense. The normal plea in insanity cases is "not guilty and not guilty by reasons of insanity." This plea requires, first, that the government prove that the defendant committed the offense, then the issue of the accused sanity is determined. In all states and the federal government, insanity is an affirmative defense, so the burden of producing evidence as to the sanity or insanity of the accused is first upon the defense. If no evidence is entered at trial regarding the sanity of the accused, it is assumed that the accused is sane.

Statute of Limitations or Double Jeopardy. In most states, before the accused enters a plea as to his or her guilt, the defense of statute of limitations or double jeopardy must be pled. In most cases, if these defenses are not pled before the guilty or not guilty plea, these defenses are relinquished. These defenses will be discussed in more detail in Chapter 12.

to the grand jury by the prosecutor. If the grand jury returns an indictment, the indictment is then filed with the superior or district court.

In states, like California, that do not require an indictment by grand jury, an *information* is presented to a lower court (justice or municipal). The information is a charging document similar to the complaint in a misdemeanor case, and is presented to the municipal or justice court where a preliminary hearing is held. About half the states use preliminary hearings rather than grand juries. The purpose of the preliminary hearing is to determine if there is probable cause to have the defendant answer to the charge in a felony court. At the preliminary hearing, the judge can dismiss the charges, reduce the charge to a misdemeanor and try the case, or order the defendant to be bound over for trial in felony court.

After the indictment is filed or the accused is bound over by the municipal or justice court on an information, the accused is arraigned before the trial court. In some states, the arraignment may be before the lower court. At the arraignment, the accused is informed of the charge(s) against him or her, advised of the right to counsel, and a plea is entered. In addition, the judge must decide whether the accused should be released on bail or some other form of release while awaiting trial.

At the preliminary hearing, the prosecution presents its evidence, including witnesses, to the judge. The defense counsel may also present evidence favorable to the accused. At this hearing, the judge determines whether probable cause indicates that the accused has committed a felony.

The accused may plead guilty, not guilty, or nolo contendere when asked to plead. A plea of nolo contendere means that the accused does not contest the charges, and it is treated as if the accused entered a plea of guilty. If the accused enters a guilty plea, he or she admits all of the elements of the offense charged. If the accused enters a plea of not guilty, the case is set for trial. Normally both a trial date and a date for pre-trial motions are set by the judge after the judge accepts the not guilty plea. At the pre-trial motion date, the counsel are afforded an opportunity to present motions. Typical motions include: motion to suppress certain items of evidence, motion for speedy trial, and motion for dismissal of charges.

The Trial

Jury Selection

The Sixth Amendment guarantees a defendant the right to an impartial jury. In addition, the due process clause of the Fifth and Fourteenth Amendments prohibits juries that exclude members of the defendant's racial, gender, ethnic, religious, or similar groups. To ensure an impartial jury, states and the federal government require that the jury panel (potential members of the jury) be selected from a fair cross-section of the community wherein the court convenes. Most jurisdictions randomly select the jury panel from the local census, tax rolls, city directories, telephone books, drivers' license lists, and the like.

After the jury panel is selected, members are directed to appear at a certain time and place. It is from the jury panel that the actual jury is selected. The principal method used by the counsel to ensure that the jury is impartial is the "voir dire" of the jury. *Voir dire* is the questioning of the prospective jury members about matters that could influence their ability to serve. In some jurisdictions, counsel submit their questions to the judge, who then asks the questions to the individual jury members. In other jurisdictions, both counsel have the opportunity to question the prospective jurors, and can then challenge the prospective jury members. If the counsel's challenge is sustained by the judge (approved), the prospective jury member is excused.

After the voir dire is completed and the jury has been selected, they are empaneled (sworn in). The judge then gives preliminary instructions to the jury. The jurors are instructed that they are not to talk to others about the case, to read the papers, or decide on the case until all the evidence has been submitted and the jury has received their instructions from the judge.

Opening Statements

After preliminary matters have been disposed of, the jury is seated in the jury box. The prosecutor has the opportunity to make an opening statement. This statement is not evidence, but may be used to inform the jury of the direction the prosecutor will take the case. The defense counsel may make his or her opening statement immediately after the prosecution finishes, or the defense may wait until the defense presents its case.

Case in Chief

The prosecutor having the burden of proof begins the trial. Witnesses are called and evidence is presented. After the prosecution rests its case, the defense presents its case. Then, the prosecution may present evidence in rebuttal to counter the defense.

Closing Argument

After both sides have rested, the prosecution presents its closing argument. The defense then presents its closing argument. Finally, the prosecution may present an argument in rebuttal to the defense's closing argument. The reason that the prosecutor goes first and is afforded the last word is based on the concept that the side with the burden of proof has the right to open and close the case. In the arguments presented by counsel, it is unethical for counsel to indicate a personal belief on whether the accused is guilty. For example, the prosecutor may argue that the government has proved the guilt of the defendant beyond a reasonable doubt. It is unethical for the prosecutor, however, to state that he or she believes that the defendant is guilty.

After argument has been completed, the judge gives instructions to the jury. This is also called charging the jury. The instructions are used to explain the law of the case to the jurors. The subjects covered in the instructions include burden of proof, the elements of the offense, voting procedures to be used by the jury, and so forth.

The Verdict

Generally, in jury trials, the jury makes the finding of guilty or not guilty. After a guilty finding, the judge sets the sentencing. Sentencing will be discussed in Chapter 11. A jury that is unable to reach a verdict is considered a "hung jury." In such cases, the jury is excused. The prosecution either retries the case or the charges are dismissed.

Although there are no provisions for it in the statutes, juries have nullification power. The nullification process occurs when the jury brings in a verdict of not guilty despite the fact that the evidence established the guilt of the accused. When jury nullification occurs, the accused cannot be retried for that offense. The power of nullification is a common law right that juries have. It is based on the concept that the jury is not required to explain any findings of not guilty.

Before the death penalty may be imposed by a judge, the jury must find not only that the accused is guilty but also that the special circumstances that allow the imposition of the death penalty exist. Death penalty cases are generally bifurcated trials (in two parts). The first part deals with the question of guilt and the second part deals with the question of whether special circumstances are present that would allow the death sentence.

Summary

The state and federal court systems are separate and distinct. However, they are very similar in their form and functioning. Each of the seven parties in the criminal justice system has specific duties and/or obligations. It is important to understand each of these parties and their perspective. Bail serves several purposes, including protecting society and ensuring the appearance of the defendant at court hearings. The criminal trial follows a series of steps that leads to a guilty or not guilty verdict.

Discussion Questions

1. Explain the differences between the state and federal court systems.

2. Name the key players in the court system and compare their roles.

3. Compare and contrast the roles of the defense counsel and the prosecutor.

4. Why doesn't the prosecutor always have a duty to convict?

5. Explain the role and function of the jury.

6. Why does the prosecution have the burden of proof in criminal cases?

7. Explain the process of selecting jurors.

8. Would you qualify for a "death qualified jury"?

Endnotes

1. This section has been adapted from Harvey Wallace, "Role of Federal and State Law," *National Victim Assistance Academy Text* (Washington, DC: Office for Victims of Crime, 1997).

2. The Fifth Amendment's right to grand jury indictment and the Eighth Amendment's right regarding excessive bail have not been applied to the states. See *Hurtado v. California,* 110 US 516 (1884).

11

The Correctional Process

Learning Objectives

After reading this chapter you should be able to do the following:

1. Discuss how the concept of punishment has evolved over time.
2. Compare the present-day concepts of punishment to the past.
3. Contrast the different forms of sentences.
4. Identify how parole and probation differ.

Sentencing Procedures

Each rule of conduct written throughout history has required that a punishment be established for convicted violators. Usually the more serious the crime, the more severe the punishment. But which punishments should be inflicted for each particular crime has plagued society for centuries. Even today, the sentencing of a convicted offender may be the most complex part of the judicial process. Convicting the offender may be easier than deciding what should be done after the conviction. In primitive times *retaliation* was the philosophy behind punishment, and the victim inflicted any punishment he desired. As more organized societies were developed, those in the judicial process began to make an effort to fit the penalty to the crime committed. Yet vengeance or retaliation against the offender was still prevalent in the thoughts of those trying to establish appropriate punishments. The problem became what penalty the offender should be subjected to in order to satisfy society's desire for vengeance and still have the penalty fit the crime. Thus, in the early sentencing process, a thief might have a hand cut off, a perjurer might have the tongue cut out, and the male adulterer might be castrated. The punishment continued to be cruel and severe.

As time passed, imprisonment became the generally accepted way of punishing an offender, and society turned from the retaliatory approach to the *isolation philosophy of punishment*. Instead of trying to get even with the offender, society pursued imprisonment as a way of protecting itself. As long as the offender was confined, society would be free of recurrent harm. As a result, when penitentiaries were first built in the United States, they were built with the idea of confining the offenders in maximum security to isolate them from society for the prescribed length of the sentence. The offenders became known as *inmates*. These penitentiaries were fortresslike structures. There were high walls with gun towers surrounding the buildings and cell blocks. Inmates spent much time locked in their cells. They were required to wear a distinctive uniform; for a long time the uniform was made of black and white striped material. Many of the penitentiaries built in the late 1800s and early 1900s are still currently in use.

Isolation as Punishment

With punishment based on the isolation theory, the problem was how long an offender should be isolated for society's protection. Early in our history the sentencing of an offender to imprisonment was solely the responsibility of the trial judge. In most instances, there were no guidelines to assist in making the determination on how long an offender should be confined. As a result, there was a great discrepancy between judges as to the sentence imposed for the same offense. Much depended on the judge's attitude and personal philosophy. When legislators began to establish appropriate penalties for each crime, they concentrated on the felony. There is considerable difference between states on the sentences that may be imposed. In some states, legislation has been passed providing a minimum and maximum number of years that an offender must serve for the conviction of a particular crime. For example, an offender convicted of burglary may receive a sentence of not less than one year in prison and not more than ten years. In other states, the law sets forth the maximum length of imprisonment that may be imposed. The law may provide that an offender may not be sentenced for a term longer than ten years. Under this system an offender could be sentenced to a single hour in confinement, and this has happened in a few instances. As will be seen, under both systems the trial judge has great leeway in the sentence to be imposed. As legislators considered the penalties for felonies, misdemeanors were also considered. As with felonies, the length of time to be imposed was usually left to the trial judge, with the maximum set forth in the state statutes.

Other Possible Penalties

While imprisonment became one form of punishment, it is not the only penalty that may be imposed on a convicted offender. The types of sentences possible for criminal offenders are set forth in the codes of the various states. Penalty is still referred to as punishment in most codes. A penalty may be one or a combination of the following: imprisonment, fine, probation, suspended sentence, and, in some states, death. Removal from public office and the disqualification to hold public office are also listed as forms of punishment in some states.

In a few jurisdictions the terms "punishment" and "sentence" imply imprisonment. Therefore probation is not considered to be a sentence but rather a disposition of the case. However in most jurisdictions the term "sentence" is the judgment of the court after conviction. The sentence is the final disposition of the trial, whether by imprisonment, suspended sentence, probation, or fine. But punishment is sometimes more closely associated with imprisonment than are other forms of sentence. Technically, punishment means any unpleasantness that the convicted offender may suffer. Any restrictions placed upon the offender, whether by imprisonment, suspended sentence, or probation, are forms of unpleasantness, as is the financial hardship imposed by a fine.

Deterrence

As reformists in the justice system continued to study punishment, its purpose shifted from isolation theory to *deterrence*. The movement to rehabilitate the offender followed. As our study will emphasize, the isolation approach has not been entirely abandoned, as there are inmates from whom society is safe only during their confinement. Neither deterrence nor rehabilitation is applicable to some hardened criminals.

Whatever sentence is imposed, its primary purpose is for the *protection of society*. The protection may be a result of isolating the offender from society or by deterring the offender from committing future crimes, thus serving as an example to others inclined to commit crimes. The protection may also be through rehabilitation, so the offender will refrain from committing future crimes.

Probation

The suspended sentence is recognized in our system of justice today, but in most instances it is coupled with a period of probation. In many jurisdictions there cannot be a suspended sentence without probation being imposed for a prescribed period of time. In those jurisdictions that the suspended sentence is permitted without probation, the judge merely suspends imposing a sentence. The offender is free to return into society. Generally there are no restrictions placed on the offender other than good behavior during the period of the suspended sentence. If the offender breaks the law again, the judge may impose a sentence on the original charge as well as the new charge, if there is a conviction.

Probation permits the convicted offender to remain free from custody, but by being placed on probation the offender is under the supervision of some person who assists him or her in leading a law-abiding life (Byrne, 1988). The person is usually a public officer known as a *probation officer.* The primary purpose of probation is for the rehabilitation of the offender. By granting the convicted offender probation, it is assumed that there is no threat to society as a result of the offender's remaining free from custody.

Conditions of Probation

The general condition imposed on the offender, when placed on probation, is that he be a law-abiding individual during the period of probation. Many other restrictions may also be imposed at this time. For example, the judge may restrict the offender's area of travel and associates, or the offender may be prohibited from patronizing bars. Restitution for damages or injuries caused while violating the law may be required. In some instances, as a condition of probation, the offender must agree to having his or her person or home searched without a warrant at any time by either a probation officer or a law enforcement officer. When these conditions are imposed, however, it is generally held that the search may not be a harassment procedure, but is to be made only when there is probable cause to believe that the offender has violated probation. Whenever restrictions are placed on an offender, it has been stated that the restrictions should have some connection with the crime committed. For example, in one case the defendant was convicted of grand theft. Prior to the conviction, the defendant had given birth to three illegitimate children fathered by different men. As a condition of probation, the judge advised the defendant that she was not to become pregnant out of wedlock again during the probation period. She did become pregnant out of wedlock, and the judge revoked her probation and sentenced her to prison. She appealed the sentence as constituting cruel and unusual punishment. The appellate court agreed with her and reversed the case, sending it back to the judge for further consideration. The appellate court stated that the trial judge might be commended for the attempt to prevent illegitimacy, but that it should have been attempted in a different manner since the restriction on pregnancy had no connection with the crime committed. However, judges frequently require a person placed on probation to do work for charity organizations, a requirement that appears to have no connection with the crime committed. There are times when a judge may grant probation with the stipulation that a short period of time be spent in imprisonment. Some reformists have criticized the use of imprisonment for one placed on probation as placing a handicap on the rehabilitation process. Others justify the imprisonment as being a means of awakening the offender to the realization of what could happen if probation is violated.

Revocation of Probation

If during the period of probation the offender, known as a *probationer,* violates the law or fails to abide by other restrictions that may have been imposed, the probation may be revoked and the probationer sentenced to imprisonment. Whether probation is revoked is at the discretion of the trial judge. In *Gagnon v. Scarpelli*, the United States Supreme Court held that, before probation may be revoked, the probationer is entitled to a hearing stating:

> Probation revocation, like parole revocation, is not a stage of a criminal prosecution, but does result in a loss of liberty. Accordingly, we hold that a probationer, like a parolee, is entitled to a preliminary and final revocation hearing, under the conditions specified in *Morrissey v. Brewer. . . (411 US 778).*

Criticism of Probation

Generally, one would not quarrel with the primary purpose of probation, which is rehabilitating the offender. But many persons both in and out of the justice system believe that judges grant probation too often. Probation has been granted to prevent overcrowding of prisons. It has also been granted to offenders who have no incentive to mend their ways. In one case, for example, an offender was convicted of burglary and placed on three years probation. While on probation, the offender was convicted on another burglary charge and the same judge again placed the offender on probation, to run concurrently with the probationary period of the prior conviction. It is for this reason that some states have passed legislation that prohibits an offender from being placed on probation after conviction for certain crimes or for using a gun while committing crimes. In spite of the efforts to curb the use of probation, it is still extensively utilized. At any given time there are over two million probationers in the United States.

Parole

The Purpose of Parole

The release of an offender from a correctional institution prior to the expiration of an imposed sentence is known as *parole*. Parole is granted after the offender has served a portion of his or her sentence and the parole board feels that the offender can be released without being a threat to society. Parole has two purposes. It is to assist in rehabilitating the offender through release from imprisonment and in promoting a useful life in society. It is also to protect society by placing some restrictions on the offender after release from custody. The paroled offender, referred to as a *parolee,* is placed under the supervision of a *parole officer,* who assists the parolee in adjusting to society's regulations and in resisting the temptation to commit other crimes.

To accomplish the purpose of parole, those who are allowed to leave prison early are subjected to specified conditions for the duration of their terms. These conditions limit their activities substantially beyond the ordinary restrictions imposed by law on an individual citizen. Typically parolees are forbidden to use liquor or to have associations or correspondence with certain categories of undesirable persons. Typically, also, they must seek permission from their parole officers before engaging in specified activities, such as changing employment or living quarters, marrying, acquiring or operating a motor vehicle, traveling outside the community, and incurring substantial indebtedness. Additionally, parolees must regularly report to the parole officer to whom they are assigned, and sometimes they must make periodic written reports of their activities.

The Parole Board

The decision as to whether an inmate is to be released on parole is generally at the discretion of a *parole board,* usually appointed on a permanent basis to make these decisions. Whether an inmate should be released on parole is no small decision. The future conduct of an individual is impossible to predict. Will an offender who has been isolated from society for a number of years and whose daily activities have been controlled and regulated by signals, bells, and the custody staff adjust to the freedom of society?

Not all inmates released on parole are able to make the adjustment. When they do not, in most instances their paroles are revoked, and they are returned to prison to serve the remainder of their sentences. With the help of the parole officer, many parolees are able to adjust to society. But because of the number who do not adjust and who commit other crimes while on parole, the parole system has been severely criticized. Those who criticize the system overlook the fact that the great majority of offenders imprisoned will eventually be released from custody. In the long run, releasing an offender under supervision and assistance is preferable to releasing an inmate, after completing an entire sentence, with no supervision or assistance.

It is easy to understand why there are those who are critical of paroling inmates. Many parolees commit other crimes while on parole. When this happens, people wonder why such offenders were released from custody to prey upon society again. The increase of crimes committed by parolees in recent years may stem from the fact that greater use is being made of parole to relieve the overcrowded condition of prisons. Consequently, potential parolees are not always screened as well as they might be, and greater chances are taken that the parolees will conform to the regulations of society. Not all inmates are released on parole. The parole boards know that there are many inmates who will not be able to adjust to society. Hostility and hatred are so ingrained within many of them that they have no desire to conform. These inmates are not paroled and serve their entire sentences in prison. On completion of their sentences these inmates are discharged without any restrictions—other than the loss of certain civil rights by having been convicted of a felony.

Revocation of Parole

The chief restriction placed on a parolee is that of being a law-abiding person. A failure in this respect is almost certain to result in revocation of the parole. Repeated violations of less rigid restrictions may also result in revocation. Whether an inmate's parole becomes revoked is largely at the discretion of the parole board. Before parole may be revoked the parolee is entitled to a hearing, as provided by the case *of Morrissey v. Brewer.* The facts of *Morrissey* reflect that two Iowa convicts, Morrissey and Booher, had their paroles revoked without hearings. The Court held that the due process of law clause of the Fourteenth Amendment ensures that, before a person's liberty can be taken, a hearing must be granted.

Parole versus Probation

Many persons are confused concerning the difference between parole and probation. In both instances an offender is freed from custody, when he or she is not a threat to society, to participate in a supervised rehabilitation process. In the case of probation, it is often granted in lieu of any imprisonment. The probationer is under the supervision of a probation officer, who is considered to be an officer of the court. The probation officer may be a part of the trial court system or may be provided to the court by a state or county probation department. Because the probationer is under the supervision of a probation officer, any violations of the probation conditions will be reported by the probation officer to the trial court having jurisdiction over the case for possible revocation of probation.

In a few states the trial court has the authority to grant *summary probation.* After being placed under summary probation, the probationer is directly responsible to the trial judge and not to a probation officer. Summary probation is usually granted only in misdemeanor convictions and when a trial judge may have a particular interest in the matter.

Parole is granted to an offender to permit a release from custody *before serving the complete sentence.* It is usually granted to one who is serving time in a state prison, generally on a felony charge. However, a few states have provisions for the parole of an offender serving time on a misdemeanor charge in a county jail. In most instances the parole officer is a state officer responsible to the parole board.

Parole, like probation, may be refused. Although freedom from confinement is generally preferable to imprisonment, many imprisoned persons are apprehensive about being able to conform to the restrictions imposed during parole. These persons would rather serve the entire sentence and receive a final discharge than to risk having the parole revoked and being returned to prison to serve an even longer term. Both the parolee and probationer are entitled to be discharged on completion of parole or probation. The discharge means that the conditions of parole or probation have been fulfilled and the sentence completed.

The Fine

The origin of the fine as a form of punishment is lost in history. Its early use as a form of punishment served a dual purpose. Money or property was taken from the wrongdoer and paid to the victim of the crime or to relatives. The fine was also a source of revenue to the king or church, depending on the law that was broken. As other means of reimbursing the victim of a crime became available, such as civil suits, the fine was no longer used for that purpose, but fines were levied as a source of revenue for government. The fine is still employed as a form of punishment for minor crimes.

Although the United States Supreme Court did not rule out the alternate penalties, such as thirty days in jail or $30 fine, some appellate courts contend that application of such alternate penalties necessarily results in different treatment for the rich offender and the poor one. The nature of the penalty actually inflicted by the thirty days in jail or $30 fine depends on the offender's financial ability and personal choice. If the offender chooses and is able to pay the fine, imprisonment may be avoided. If he or she chooses imprisonment, the fine may be avoided. If the offender is unable to pay the fine, imprisonment cannot be avoided. Thus the indigent offender has no choice, and the alternate penalties work as a violation of the equal protection clause. However, to date, the alternate penalty procedure has not disappeared from the justice system, and fines will continue to be imposed as a form of penalty for some time to come, particularly in less serious charges.

Summary

Corrections is an important aspect of the criminal justice system. Possibly the most important part of this process is the sentencing and punishment of those convicted of crimes. The sentencing of offenders is a complex and multifaceted procedure. There are advantages and disadvantages to the different types of sentences that are used in modern America. Even with all our knowledge and technology, we still have not developed a flawless form of punishment for offenders. We must continue to examine different methods and ideals in our quest for justice.

Discussion Questions _____

1. What amendment includes the guarantee against cruel and unusual punishment?

2. Why was imprisonment not used as a form of punishment in early criminal procedures?

3. What is the primary purpose behind sentencing an offender?

4. List the different forms of punishment that may presently be imposed upon a convicted offender.

5. In what way do probation and parole differ? In what way are they alike?

12

The Second Victimization

Learning Objectives

After reading this chapter you should be able to do the following:

1. Describe the process of second victimization by the criminal justice system.
2. Discuss the traditional focus of the criminal justice system and victims.
3. Explain two theories in social psychology pertaining to victim blaming.
4. Describe and explain the types of shared responsibility.
5. List and define the assumptions of victim blaming.

The criminal justice system was created to ascertain facts, determine responsibility for criminal acts, and then to mete out punishment for these antisocial activities. In attaining these goals, the focus has been exclusively on the criminal. Although victim concerns were a part of the criminal justice process in the early years of this country, they were completely absent for well over 100 years. With the attitude of "Just the facts, ma'am," objectivity is the key and any type of emotionalism is to be avoided. With criminal responsibility determined by "the weight of the evidence," certain issues, such as victims' concerns, are seen as irrelevant and tangential. Once these first two issues of the case—facts and the weight of the evidence—are determined, the level of punishment is relatively evident, and the job of the criminal justice system is seen as finished.

The reality is that as the system goes about its "business" and completes these three tasks, the situation for victims often goes from simply being left out to being singled out as partially to blame for the crime. Today, the term for this untoward treatment is "the second victimization" (Walker, 2000). This can be intentional mistreatment, but it is often mistreatment that is incidental to the system doing its job precisely and correctly. An officer getting the facts about a burglary or a rape asks questions that are construed by the victim to imply that she did not do enough to protect or defend herself. The judge refuses in a stern, officious manner to allow a rape victim to elaborate on her response to a question. She has been shut down, her responses suffocated—again.

This chapter will look at the second victimization that is often perpetrated by the criminal justice system. Detailed examples will be given. The roots of victim blaming in our society will be extensively discussed, along with two theories in social psychology that assist in explaining this problem of the second victimization of crime victims.

Worst-Case Scenario

The following case scenario denotes the majority of the negative things that can happen to a crime victim. Although no victim would have all of these things go wrong, every instance cited has either been actually witnessed by the author or by one of his students, who have been writing papers on their own (or their family's) victimization for the past 16 years.

The scenario is as follows:

A 50-year-old African American female is at home on a Friday night at 10:00 P.M. after a long, hard week at work. She is relaxing and watching a rented movie in her living room. A 35-year-old Caucasian male breaks down her locked back door in a matter of seconds. She startles and freezes as he assaults her, beating her with his fists. He then drags her into the bedroom and rapes her repeatedly over the next hour. As he gets ready to leave, he puts his forearm across her throat and threatens to return and kill her, if she reports this crime. The force of his arm almost makes her pass out, as he runs out of the house through the front door. Dazed, crying, and bleeding, she sits on her sofa for an hour shaking. She then calls the police to report being raped.

In this worst-case scenario, the question is how is she treated from this point on by the police, the hospital, the prosecutor, and the court. From this victim's perspective, what can go wrong?

Two white, male officers with no diversity or sensitivity training arrive an hour later and slowly approach the house. Noticing the damage to the back door, they surmise that the perpetrator might still be at the scene. They enter the house in a SWAT-team fashion and nearly shoot the victim because of her agitated response to their sudden appearance.

The two officers, adrenaline running, become instantly angry with her for almost causing them to commit a fatal error. This anger sets the tone for their interrogation of her.

They ask for a description of the assailant, and as she describes him in a halting, hesitant fashion, they begin to wonder if she isn't making it up. She doesn't appear to have any external injuries, and although the bed is in disarray, there are no other signs of any type of struggling incident that she has described. They question how he got in and if the door or windows were unlocked, in what seems to her to be an accusatory fashion. They have been trained to do a bombarding, tag-team type of questioning to throw off a doubtful victim. She appears, at times, to give inconsistent, confusing answers. Due to this, they then switch their line of questioning to the "relationship" angle: "How well did you know him?" "Was this your boyfriend from a recent or previous relationship?" "Wasn't this someone you knew from work?" "Hadn't you been out earlier in the evening and met this guy?" They seem to intimate that, of course, African-American females are promiscuous.

There are no concerns expressed for her well-being or any statements about the services available. The officers fail to mention that the victim should go to the hospital for both medical and legal reasons. The interview is cold, distant, and unprofessional at best and centers on victim blaming at worst. The victim is left with more guilt and sadness and is in complete fear for her life, for she is sure he is coming back, and she is now very clear that the police do not believe her and will do nothing to protect her. In fact, the issue of protection is never raised or addressed throughout the police interview because she is not really deemed to be a victim by the officers.

After waiting in confusion and turmoil for another hour, she decides against calling family members or friends due to embarrassment and self blame—and not wanting to take the chance that their responses will be like those of the police officers. Because she is still in pain and hoping for some human kindness, she decides to drive herself to the hospital. When she arrives, she goes to the clerk at the Emergency Room counter and is told to have a seat in a packed waiting room full of men, women, and crying children with various ailments. The room is at a constant low-level roar. An hour later, she is given forms to fill out and asked for her insurance card.

An hour later, the triage nurse comes behind the front counter and announces to the clerk in a voice loud enough for all to hear that they now have a room available for the "rape victim." The clerk then turns and states the victim's name in the waiting room. She then goes back to her "room," which consists of one wall and a wrap-around curtain—offering absolutely no privacy. First, the clerk comes in to verify her financial information. Then the nurse comes in to do the intake, asking for extensive graphic details that can be heard throughout the ward. The nurse makes little eye contact and expresses no empathy for the victim, while being intent on quickly finishing her task and moving on to the next patient. She leaves abruptly and states that the doctor will be in "in a few minutes."

Two hours later, the doctor comes in and begins treating her physical symptoms, avoiding any conversation regarding how the injuries occurred. He states that her injuries are "not that bad" and intimates that she probably did not need to come in. Once he realizes what caused the injuries, he begins to focus on her relationship with the perpetrator, showing doubt for the truth of her story. She persists that it was rape, and he reluctantly does a rape exam without explaining it to her; she feels he is angry and very rough with the exam. During this interview and exam, he is called out for lengthy periods three different times. Again, this entire interaction is taking place, not behind a closed door, but behind a thin curtain.

The victim is then informed that she can go home. No counseling or social work support is offered at that time. Rape Counseling is not called, and she is given no referral numbers.

She drives herself home—back to the dark, crime scene—and spends a sleepless night shaking in her bed. Two weeks later, she gets a letter from the hospital stating that her insurance will not cover the hospital expenses, and that she must make immediate payment of a $1,300 bill, which includes the cost of the rape kit and exam.

A month later, she is called to the police station to identify the rapist in a lineup. Two individuals have characteristics like those of the rapist. She knows that she would recognize his voice, and asks that they be asked to speak. The D.A. in the room, who never identifies himself, states that they cannot do that. She is told she can leave—with no explanation about what has just happened or about what will happen in this case next.

She had expected to hear from the D.A. shortly, but hears nothing for another month. She is then called by a secretary and told when to come in. She tells her employer that she needs time off for the appointment, and he expresses amazement that the case isn't over with. He is emphatic that she can have only this one time off, unless she wants to take her vacation time.

She meets with a D.A., who is different than the one at the lineup, and is asked extensively about her behavior during the crime, including her prior relationship with the perpetrator. She is asked about her sex life in detail in a manner that is very uncomfortable to her; the intimation seems to be that she is carelessly sexually active. There is no explanation that these questions are in preparation for the defense attorney's questions. She leaves the interview feeling beaten up and blaming herself for the crime again. There is no further explanation of the criminal justice system or of what she is to expect.

Although the D.A. is aware of it at this time, she does not become aware that the perpetrator is out on bail until she reads it in the paper three days later. Again, the initial fears of further harm create flashbacks and depression.

She is called by another D.A. three weeks later and told to be at court the following Tuesday at 9:00 A.M. There is no explanation about what to expect. Her employer is extremely upset about such late notice, even though she is taking vacation time. He does not seem to believe her, expressing again that the case should have been over with "long ago." She arrives outside the courtroom at 8:45, finding that the only place to sit is across from the perpetrator and his family. Threats and innuendoes about her safety are stated loud enough for her to hear. No D.A. is to be found. Thirty minutes later, someone comes up to the perpetrator and quietly says something; quickly, he and his entourage leave, while staring her down. At 10:15 A.M., the D.A. comes flying in with several bulging cases and almost goes by her; as he sees her, he says, "didn't anyone call you? The case was delayed for two weeks or so; you can go home!"

She is unsure what "delayed" means and wonders if the case might be "dismissed." Again, no one is explaining to her that this is standard operating procedure for the defense and is partially intended to wear her down, so that she will have second thoughts about testifying. This delay *is* an issue for her for three major reasons: Her job is now at risk; she does not want to be in the waiting room with the perpetrator again; and her self-doubts and self-blame have reemerged, almost as strong as they were in the first few weeks following the crime. She still has not told family members or friends; she still has heard nothing about counseling or peer support groups. There is no "telling of her story" and no catharsis; the anxiety, guilt, and fear are all building to the point of being unmanageable. She truly feels she is "going crazy," and no one is there to tell her otherwise. She is, indeed, becoming a tenuous witness, exhibiting aspects of Post-Traumatic Stress Disorder. All of this she considers to be *her* problem.

Somehow with all of this going on, she makes it back to court, which ends up being six weeks later. She endures another scene in the waiting room and then waits patiently in the courtroom to be called to the stand. Even though the D.A. is someone she has never seen before, she welcomes her "day in court." She is expecting to tell her story to a sympathetic judge and jury. She is called to the stand, and the D.A. begins asking her questions; it is clear to her (and probably everyone else) that the D.A. knows little of the specifics of this case. Key questions about facts that indicate the lack of a relationship and the presence of threats and force are left out.

The defense attorney, who begins with a smile and a sympathetic tone, soon starts to ask pointed questions about her story. What she had said at the scene, while in shock, is not exactly the same as the report she gave later at the police station. These minor discrepancies are made to look like glaring, blatant lies by the defense attorney. Then she begins to ask pointed questions about the victim's background, and as she begins to probe about the victim's sexual life, the district attorney raises three or four objections that are sustained.

However, even though the jury is asked to disregard the questions, the damage of innuendo has been done. The victim is on trial for four hours. As she drives herself home that night, she finds herself absently driving around and getting lost twice before she finds her house. She is in shock again, without any support, while going back to the scene of the crime—still in fear that he may return at any moment.

Daily, she finds herself fluctuating between depression and anger. That evening she begins to get enraged at how she was treated; despite the fact that she may lose her job, she decides that she has to hear what the perpetrator says the next day at trial. When she gets there, she is amazed at what she sees and hears. She sees a well-dressed, clean-cut perpetrator articulating his innocence with a trace of sympathy for her pain. His girlfriend gives him an alibi for where he was at the time of the crime, while five character witnesses describe him as a harmless, responsible, good person. Throughout this process, a new D.A. interrogates all of them in a cursory fashion with the same questions. The perpetrator's previous record is not alluded to, and no other prosecuting witnesses are called. The victim leaves the courtroom confused, dazed, angry, and guilt-ridden. "Could she have made a mistake? Why didn't the D.A. ask any of her questions?" This day has been almost as painful as the day before, and that evening she decides that she will not return to court again. She then begins the process of denial and blanking the crime out of her mind. She returns to work and slowly begins to touch base again with her friends, who have noticed her absence but know nothing of the reasons for it. She simply says that she has been "very busy at work."

Two months later, she reads in the paper that the rapist is found "not guilty." In an interview on the evening news, in an ecstatic scene outside the courtroom with his friends and family, he magnanimously states that he holds no ill feelings about her false accusations. The next day she becomes physically ill, misses a week of work, and is then fired for excessive absences and poor work performance in recent months.

The Focus of the Criminal Justice System

With its roots in English Common Law, the American criminal justice system has always focused on the issue of criminal responsibility and was designed to determine punishment with a process that guaranteed certain protections to the criminal. The consistent focus for almost 200 years was on the criminal, not the victim.

The rape scenario is a product of this process and these protections. The determination of responsibility is reflected in the response level, the reaction, and the type of treatment at each step of the criminal justice system. In another circumstance, for the police coming upon the scene with a perpetrator and victim of a bar brawl, criminal responsibility (or shared responsibility) will determine who is detained, who is arrested, who is charged, and who is jailed. In this specific crime, both individuals, or neither, could be arrested or charged based upon the "preponderance of the evidence."

If one person is arrested, the prosecutor must then make decisions regarding criminal responsibility "beyond a reasonable doubt." The level and amount of responsibility will affect the original charges, the likelihood of a plea bargain, the type and time of the sentence sought, the amount of restitution ordered, and the amount of compensation allowed the victim later on. In an infamous case in Colorado, a psychiatrist who was found guilty of malpractice (an illicit relationship with a depressed patient) was ordered by the jury to pay 65 percent of the total damages. The depressed, borderline patient was deemed to be 35 percent responsible for the affair. Both were seen by the jury to be responsible for the crime, although not quite equally so.

Determining responsibility is the comfortable purview of the criminal justice system. This is why it was set up. At first, in the United States, there was some victim focus, but this was not often in writing—only in common practice. As the system evolved, especially after the 1850s, the focus on criminal responsibility and societal protection was preeminent in the law of the land. It was not until the 1970s, when the idea resurfaced that the system should also be concerned about the victim's welfare and rights (Walker, 2000). Even then, this was a difficult proposition for a system that had always focused on the criminal and since the 1950s had expanded criminal rights and protections. This shift to the victim was not made easily or quickly. In fact, the debate continues about the purpose and focus of the criminal justice system today, as seen in the discussion about the victim rights' constitutional amendment. The major arguments against this amendment focus on the original intent of the Constitution (protection of basic liberties) and its limitations (Wallace, 1988).

The major point here is that the sexual assault victim from the prior scenario was revictimized by a system that was doing its job in a very traditional sense. In order to change this reaction to the victim, the original values and norms of the criminal justice subculture need to change. The reality is that they have slowly been changing since the 1970s. However, victim blaming is still pervasive in our entire culture, not just in the criminal justice system. The next section explores the issue of victim blaming in more depth.

Victim Blaming

Why does Western society have such a long history of blaming victims for their victimization? Some of the answer comes from our Judeo-Christian roots, which state that "bad things happen only to bad people," that is, sinners. This theology has continued despite the fact that the Old Testament book of Job clearly demonstrates that plagues are visited on a righteous person. In times past, this might have been an adequate explanation, but many in our society would not intellectually accept this religious view today; however, victim blaming continues to be present. There are two major theories in social psychology that address this issue: the Theory of Cognitive Dissonance and Attribution Theory (Myers, 1996). The next section will explain both theories and then apply them to attitudes about victims.

FOCUS BOX

We all blame some types of victims. We all draw a line someplace. Where is your line? Which of the following are victims to you?: rape victim; molestation victim; burglary victim; robbery victim; auto theft victim; stolen bike victim; bar fight homicide; an abused wife who murders her husband; the molestation victim who murders father/perpetrator; Bernard Goetz; Monica?

Social Psychological Theories

The Cognitive Dissonance Theory. The Theory of Cognitive Dissonance (Figure 12.1) addresses the process by which a person's attitudes and beliefs change over time (Festinger, 1957). Although human beings view themselves as logical, our attitudes are usually more "psycho-logical"—they make more emotional sense than cognitive sense. We are often unaware of the inconsistencies in our beliefs or values, but when we *do* become aware that we are maintaining two inconsistent (dissonant) beliefs, or that we are maintaining a belief and exhibiting the opposite behavior, we become very anxious because we feel a great need to be (or to appear to be) consistent in our lives. This anxiety creates much discomfort and the immediate desire to reduce it. The easiest method to reduce this anxiety is not to change our behavior, but to change one of the inconsistent beliefs to a consistent one (Myers, 1996). When a "good" person is victimized, an ugly inconsistency raises its head, so the uncomfortable dissonance is reduced by changing our belief about the person's goodness. The world needs to be consistent and symmetrical—we feel much more comfortable with a world that "makes sense." The victim must have done something wrong, for example, not paid attention, not reacted appropriately, or said something wrong. Again, this is much easier than altering our daily behavior and checking

COGNITIVE DISSONANCE

Two opposing beliefs

OR

A belief and opposite behavior

↓

Anxiety

↓

Belief change

↓

Reduction of anxiety

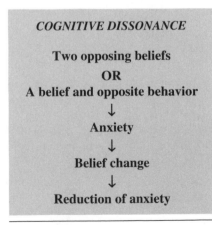

FIGURE 12.1

on the specifics of the crime, the victim's situation, the criminal's motivation, and the environment surrounding the incident. The true complicated facts about a real crime and the fact that bad things happen to good people (like us!) create psychological difficulties and inconsistencies. Therefore, one reason for victim blaming is that it is a simple, quick means of dealing with many of the inconsistencies created when a crime occurs.

Attribution Theory. The second theory, Attribution Theory (Figure 12.2), addresses causation; it discusses how we determine (attribute) the causes of events in our environment. This pertains to events in both our lives and the lives of others (Herder, 1958). We make decisions about causation very quickly to decrease our stress and anxiety. This theory states that these quick decisions are made due to two basic human needs (Herder, 1958). The first, noted above, is the need for consistency in our lives and in our environment—or at least the appearance of consistency. For humans, this is a psychological and a perceptual need. We see Christmas trees and the human face as symmetrical; we prefer balanced pictures and remember them more readily. Psychologically, we prefer that the universe be consistent and reasonable. The second need is the need for control over our environment. We have a very strong need to be the "master of our ship," and it is important for others to be in control also; if others (victims) lack control, then it reflects poorly on us and potentially puts us at risk in the future.

These two very basic needs drive us to pose two immediate questions about the causes of events:

1. Was this crime precipitated by internal or external causes?
2. Was this crime due to a general or a specific cause?

Internal causes pertain to the psyche, personality, or actions of the victim, that is, something the victim did, or failed to do, to precipitate the crime. External causes have to do with events outside of the victim in the social environment and are usually events beyond their control. General causes are situations that are present most of the time, while specific causes pertain only to this crime or situation and may only take place under certain specified conditions. Specific causes are often much easier to denote and attribute directly to the crime.

ATTRIBUTION THEORY
Internal cause
General cause
Specific cause
External cause

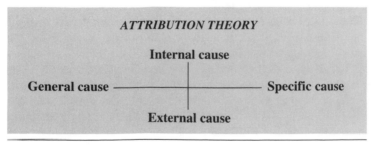

FIGURE 12.2

Think of three recent major crimes in your community. Look at the press reports. Cite examples of victim blaming. Cite examples of victim defending. How does Attribution Theory explain these examples?

In making these two decisions quickly, Attribution Theory states that we often make a fundamental error and/or exhibit a self-serving bias (Heider, 1958). The fundamental error is that in judging the events in the lives of others we always tend toward internal causation. In other words, whatever happens to others is caused by something they did. We more easily focus on them than their environment (external) because we are seldom aware of their precipitant environment or its resultant consequences. So it is a natural bias to blame others for what happens to them; this clearly pronounces that they are in control, as we would like to be ourselves. On the other hand, we apply internal causation to ourselves mainly when we succeed ("I am a self-made person."). When we fail, we tend toward external causation ("The devil made me do it."). This is called the self-serving bias. Therefore, we would usually blame others, but not ourselves, for being victimized.

Both Native American proscription to "walk in the moccasins" of others and the Judeo-Christian commandment to "love your neighbor as yourself" could be seen as attempts to overcome this fundamental bias. Both require the observer to note the other person's environment (external causes) and understand the extenuating causes of his or her victimization, instead of placing blame.

These two theories in social psychology indicate a natural human tendency to blame the victim. When the cultural norms of personal responsibility and individual independence are added to this tendency, victim blaming becomes almost automatic and pervasive. It is, therefore, understandable (but not acceptable) that our society's major institutions blame the victims of violent crime as well and actively create a "second victimization." These theories indicate that it is imperative for both individuals and institutions to be much more conscious of their own attitudes and biases in order to decrease victim blaming and to deal appropriately with victims' needs.

Types of Shared Responsibility

As previously noted, the purpose of every bureaucratic institution in the criminal justice system is to place blame for a criminal incident. Criminologists in the first half of the twentieth century focused on the criminal—his or her background, biology, and environment. Numerous criminological studies specified offender/nonoffender differences in order to clarify methods of prevention, intervention, treatment, and punishment that were appropriate for the former. As the field of victimology began in the 1940s and 1950s, Von Hentig, Mendelsohn, and Schafer began to focus on the victim's motivation; it seemed to be a logical assumption that, as there had been offender/nonoffender differences, there should also be some obvious victim/nonvictim differences (Schafer, 1968). In the various crimes that were studied, they supposedly found numerous incidents of "shared responsibility," in which the victim's psyche, biological make-up, or social inabilities caused the crime to occur (Karmen, 2001). Von Hentig wrote about the "duet frame of reference," while Mendelsohn described the "penal couple," the criminal and the victim (von Hentig, 1948).

Although most individuals in our society are the victims of a crime only a few times in their lives, the early-day victimologists believed that there were many "repeat" victims who were, in a Freudian sense, unconsiously "accident-prone." With this focus on the victim who was "accident-prone," several theoretical explanations were readily given, with minimal research support. Von Hentig used the old Lombroso argument of the "born" victim: The victim's own biological and/or genetic make-up caused him or her to be victimized (Schafer, 1968). The Freudians in psychology stated that, stemming from childhood, the victim had an unconscious "need to suffer," and the victim who was also "narcissistic" probably enjoyed the attention provided by the criminal justice system as a result of the crime. The behaviorists provided a third explanation: The victim's learned habits and attitudes caused his or her own victimization. If this "country bumpkin" visiting the big city could only be more perceptive and learn new ways of behaving, victimization would not occur. The victim could not escape responsibility for the crime: No matter what the victim did, the crime was at least partially his or her responsibility. There were biological, psychological, and sociological arguments readily available to support this victim blaming. The three arguments noted above came to the conclusion that either the victim could not change (born victim), the victim needed much therapy (Freudian), or the victim needed to be better educated (behaviorism). Whichever argument was used, the onus of responsibility and change was always on the victim. Schafer later actually elaborated three different types of shared responsibility: facilitation, precipitation, and provocation (Schafer, 1968).

With *facilitation,* the victim does something to increase the possibility of a crime, such as leaving their personal items exposed or unattended (Karmen, 2001). The unknowing, careless, negligent, foolish, naïve, or stupid (fill in with a negative adjective) victim makes the crime easier. Like a chemical catalyst that speeds up, or facilitates, the combination of other chemicals, the victim makes the auto theft or the home burglary easier by leaving the car unlocked with the keys in it or by leaving windows open and the front door of the home unlocked. (The two most common crimes to which facilitation has been applied are burglary and auto theft.) Instead of focusing on the stealth and vigilance of criminals, numerous "psychobabble" explanations noted the often unconscious motives of the victim. There has always also been much secondary gain for automobile and insurance companies in this type of victim blaming; if the victim is to blame, these two different large corporations are not responsible either to make changes in automobile security or to reimburse the victim for the loss. Unfortunately, law enforcement, when answering these types of calls, often supports such shared responsibility through its questioning, with the focus on what the victim did wrong prior to the crime—open windows, open sliding doors, unlocked cars, and so forth. With the concept of facilitation, the victim has the least amount of blame when compared to the other two types of shared responsibility.

Precipitation means that the victim is much more active and does something to initiate the criminal process; a rape victim wears seductive clothing or verbally arouses the "poor unsuspecting" rapist. The mouthy, suggestive, enticing, or scantily dressed (fill in with various hysterical adjectives) victim actually initiates the criminal incident. In the original proposals of this argument the perpetrator is deemed to be someone minding his own business who is actually entrapped by the manipulative victim. Although it may be difficult to believe today, this argument, often used against rape victims, not too long ago was also used against child molestation victims. When this author worked at Atascadero State Hospital, a common statement, with various versions, by pedophiles was that the little five-year-old had "danced seductively around the living room and aroused me"; the travesty was that some of these statements in 1976 were deemed as plausible by the staff of the hospital—and by society at that time. This "old" argument continues today as it was used as the main defense for the perpetrators in the movie *The Accused.* The Women's Movement has very appropriately spoken out against the sexism of this type of victim blaming for 30 years, but in reality this argument is doubly sexist. Its portrayal of all men as stupid, naïve, unthinking, easily manipulated, sexually preoccupied animals is demeaning and degrading also. As with facilitation, this argument seemed to be supported by some of the major theories, especially in Freudian psychology, at the time. Even the humanistic (Rogerian) perspective supported this at times by saying that women often looked for love "in all the wrong places," and needed to change this in order to prevent rape and molestation. These perspectives will be discussed below in more detail.

At other times, there is victim *provocation,* in which the wife or a drinking buddy says something or does something to make a situation, instigated by the criminal, worse. A reactive, mouthy, suspicious, defensive, or smart-ass (fill in with various active adjectives) victim responds to the criminal's initial act in such a manner that it causes the incident to escalate and, therefore, leads to the victimization. If the wife had just kept her mouth shut or not thrown the frying pan at him, he would not have hit her. If the bar-hopping murder victim had not taken such an adversarial stance, the incident would have simmered down.

With this type of victim blaming, there was actually some support from Wolfgang's early research (1958); in a study of homicide in Philadelphia, he found that 25 percent to 33 percent of the time the victim had often done something to escalate the situation (Wolfgang, 1958). These were often homicides with cocombatants using alcohol. This study and others were then generalized to spousal abuse, child abuse, and harassment— another common example of good research applied inappropriately. This had to do with homicide, only in Philadelphia, not with any of these other crimes. In this original research, the victim and offender often had a prior relationship (as in spousal abuse) related to debts, drugs, drinking, or neighborhood disputes. However, both were always men, alcohol and weapons were usually involved, and one-third of the victims had a previous record. In other words, in these early studies of victim escalation, the victims and perpetrators were extremely similar, and the roles had often been reversed in the weeks prior to the incident. Such is not the case in spousal abuse, child abuse, and harassment.

Also with victim provocation, there were readily available supportive arguments, especially from the Freudian perspective. This was a "sub-intentional death" in which the victim had a "wish to die" (mortido); therefore, the assault and murder were the victim's fault (Karmen, 2001). Even though it was equally plausible, especially in Wolfgang's "Subculture of Violence," that this provocative behavior was a way of life and the victim actually was not suicidal but saw himself as indestructible (often due to winning previous altercations), unconscious motives were much more glamorous and favored at the time. Going beyond homicide, the major problem with victim provocation is that this type of victim blaming was expanded and applied inappropriately to many other types of victims.

The result of all three types of shared responsibility was that the victim was blamed for the crime, so no changes were demanded of basic American attitudes or of the criminal justice system. The early victimologists for a period shifted the focus away from the criminal's responsibility for the crime to the victim's responsibility. In reality, this early emphasis was on victim blaming (focus on past events), not actually on responsibility (focus on future behavior). They could have taken the high road and focused on ways to help victims avoid future victimization; instead, they took the lower culturally defined road of victim blaming. However, in 1972 with the advent of the Victims' Movement, victim defending became preeminent, and since that time, victim blaming, though still prevalent, has become less acceptable in society.

The Assumptions of Victim Blaming

Even though victim blaming has had a strong theological and philosophical base in our culture, which influenced the initial authors in victimology, its influence in American jurisprudence lasted just over 100 years. Prior to 1850, victims had some control over many aspects of the criminal justice system. They often paid for the posse to apprehend the criminal and for the prosecutor to try the case when the circuit judge came to town. However, with the advent of elected district attorneys, victim rights diminished as an emphasis on public protection became preeminent. Between 1850 and 1970, victim blaming evolved into three assumptions espoused by three types of victim blamers, discussed in the next section.

The victim blaming perspective assumes that victims are different than nonvictims, just as criminology's basic assumption had always been that criminals differ from noncriminals. Various differences were discussed and researched—biological, psychological, and sociological. In other words, something is wrong with the victim. The second assumption is that the victim's difference causes the problem, that is, the crime. Stupidity, naivete, inattention, hyperactivity, poor family, need for love, or the like causes the victim to place himself or herself in a bad situation (facilitation) or to, worse yet, precipitate the bad situation. These two assumptions, accepted as truth, lead to the final conclusion that victims must change whatever is wrong with them—their thinking, their behavior, their physiology, their appearance, and so forth. Decreasing crime is in the hands of the victim—not the responsibility of the criminal (Karmen, 2001).

Noting the discussion of Attribution Theory above, the fact that these assumptions have been so readily accepted in our society makes psychological sense. The human needs for control and consistency cause us to make the quick fundamental error of external attributions for others. In reality, with a criminal incident, the human tendency (as an observer) is to blame both the criminal *and* the victim for the crime.

Types of Victim Blamers

Lack of Personal Control. Three different types of arguments have been espoused that are supported by these victim blaming assumptions. First, the American conservative tradition (law and order) supports a view of individualism that says everyone has control over his or her life and must be resourceful and self-sufficient (Karmen, 2001). Victimization is caused by persons' lifestyle—something they did, their poor judgment, or their psychological propensities. Victims must take full responsibility for altering their environment so they will not be victimized again. In business, this emphasis on total free will and self-determinism is called the "bootstrap theory." A self-sufficient person (usually a man) pulls himself up by his own bootstraps and is successful. Even though humans are social beings and any one person's success involves hard work—and luck with much social support—this myth persists and readily supports victim blaming; the victim should have been more self-sufficient and taken better care of herself or himself. In mental health, many professionals, trained to look only at individual dynamics while excluding the social environment, focus on individual motives and personal solutions; these therapeutic biases support the "great" American traditions of individualism and self-sufficiency.

Internal Causation.   The second type of victim blamers are social science academics who have developed numerous theories, especially psychological theories, that focus on internal causation. Most psychological perspectives place the onus of change on the victim and often intimate that the victim is to blame. These theories have been readily accepted by an American public that already tends toward victim blaming.

In psychology over the last 125 years, four main schools of thought have developed (Myers, 1996). Each school has a different view of victimization. The four schools are: psychoanalytic, behaviorism, humanism, and cognitive-behaviorism. The general tendency in psychology has been to purposely or inadvertently blame the victim for his or her own victimization.

The *psychoanalytic school* has almost always presented a pathological perspective. The victim of a violent crime (rape, spousal abuse, child abuse, etc.) has a negative self-concept, a father complex, an inordinate need for love, or a need for punishment; he or she is dependent, immature, perfectionistic, or self-absorbed. The bottom line is that something is wrong (a major characterlogical flaw) with the victim; that which is wrong is the problem and must be changed for the victimization to end.

Behaviorism states that all victim behavior is learned by association, reinforcement, or modeling. The person is taught by parents, peers, and others how to be a victim in life. The behavior is then reinforced and continues unless this old learning is replaced by new learning that emphasizes empowerment. Victims are required to seek out new environments and change. The responsibility for changing their victimization is squarely on their shoulders.

The point of view of *humanism* is quite different than the first two schools. Its focus is on feelings and emotions, and it is somewhat more positive about victims. All human beings, including victims, are looking for unconditional positive regard, that is, unconditional love. Everyone wants to be self-actualized to reach full potential. Victims are searching for both unconditional positive regard and self-actualization in an unproductive manner. They set themselves up to be victimized because negative attention is often much better than no attention. They simply need to "look for love" in new and better places.

Cognitive-behaviorism delves into the thinking, attitudes, and beliefs of victims. Their irrational thoughts and values get them in trouble. Victimized behavior is the result of faulty thinking patterns and evaluations of the world. Persons' beliefs about their ability to manage their world (self-efficacy) directly affect their ability to function well or poorly in their environment. Therefore, victims must change their way of thinking and their irrational beliefs in order to stop being victims.

Again, with this tendency to place blame, all of these schools of psychology usually place the burden of change on the victim, not on the criminal.

The Self-Serving Attitudes of Offenders.   The third group to utilize and expand the victim blaming argument consists of offenders themselves (Karmen, 2001). They have a natural self-investment, obviously, in victim blaming. Besides using the concept of American individualism and much of the academic "psychobabble" noted above, they utilize many self-serving arguments of their own: "She shouldn't have dressed that way," "She shouldn't have been so loose," "He acted like a country bumpkin," "They were dumb and left their lights on and door unlocked," and so forth.

Victim blaming fits well into the sociopathic reasoning of most offenders. Attribution Theory states that, with failure, the natural human tendency is to seek external causes for these failures. The criminal is just doing what comes naturally; he or she has often had many more failures than the average person, and, therefore, utilizes externalization and victim blaming more often. With this extensive practice, criminals are much better at it than most of the American public.

Summary

The purpose of this chapter has been to clearly indicate that the second victimization of victims has a long history in our culture. The subcultural norms and values of the criminal justice system supporting this revictimization were explored. Two major social psychological theories that explain the human propensity toward victim blaming were detailed. Finally, the assumptions of victim blaming and the three types of victim blamers were discussed.

Discussion Questions _____

1. Will the criminal justice system ever change its basic focus to more adequately deal with victims? What would some of the most basic legal and policy changes be?

2. Why were some of the early-day "victimologists" so focused on victim blaming?

3. What are the counterarguments to the assumptions of victim blaming?

13

A Description of Victim Services

Learning Objectives

After reading this chapter you should be able to do the following:

1. Explain the various myths related to different types of victims.
2. Outline the current services available to victims.
3. Compare and contrast the theories related to victimization, victim recovery, and victim services.
4. Explain the connection between victim issues and offender issues.
5. List and describe the victim's need for a broad array of services.

In this chapter, we will survey three major types of services for victims: rape counseling services, domestic violence programs, and victim witness programs. Realizing that there are many services for other types of victims, especially children, there will be a brief discussion toward the end of this chapter of other services and other *needed* services. Each of the three services will be outlined in the following manner: clients served, services rendered, usual staff and volunteers, and funding sources. This outline is meant to be a generic overview of these types of victim services, and in no way is this an exhaustive description of "all" types of agencies and services.

Prior to the discussion of the actual services in the three areas, the myths and dilemmas—which create the second victimization and interfere with the delivery of adequate services—will be discussed. Following the discussion of services, various theories will be delineated that explain victims' behavior and the necessity for a broader array of services. Finally, the seminal surveys that have been done in rape counseling and domestic violence and about victim/witness programs will be summarized; these surveys clearly validate both the theories and the service needs. The chapter will end by describing a general formula for the provision of victim services.

Rape Counseling Centers (Sexual Assault Units)

Rape (Sexual Assault) Myths

The fact that the reporting rate for rape is still very low (16%) and that the media continues to revictimize these women on a daily basis says that our culture still has a problem dealing with rape victims in a humane manner. Rape myths are not a thing of the past; many segments of our society still believe them. These myths, often believed by the victims themselves, continue to prevent women from seeking appropriate services. Some of the most prevalent myths are the following:

1. Women who are raped are asking for it.

    Less than 4 percent of all rape cases involve precipitative or provocative verbal or physical behavior by the victim (Amir, 1971). Also, in Anglo-Saxon law, words can never legally occasion a physical response

2. Only "bad girls" and "loose women," dressed scantily, get raped.

    Rapists choose their victims not based upon looks, but on time, place, and vulnerability (Amir, 1971). All women are at risk at any time under these conditions.

3. Women are raped when out alone at night in a back alley.

    Over 50 percent of all women are raped in their own homes, or in a place familiar to them (Amir, 1971).

4. Rape is perpetrated mainly by strangers.

    Seventy-eight percent of all rapists are known or familiar to the victim (Kilpatrick, Edmunds, & Seymour, 1992).

5. No woman can be raped against her will—she can always prevent it.

   Eighty-seven percent of all rapists carry a weapon or threaten the victim's life. Fear immobilizes the victims of most such crimes (Amir, 1971).

6. Rapes are interracial: African American against Caucasian, especially.

   Ninety-three percent of all rapes are intraracial (Amir, 1971).

7. Women enjoy being raped.

   What crimes do men "enjoy?" No victims of any crime enjoy it. Crime creates anger, grief, and depression (negative emotions) for all victims.

8. Rape is an impulsive, uncontrollable sexual act.

   Seventy-one percent of all rapes are planned (the other 29 percent probably lied about premeditation) (Amir, 1971). This is a purely power crime. About 50 percent of all rapists appear to be impotent during the crime.

9. Rape is a charge easily made, but not easily defended.

   Five of six victims do not report, so the charge must not be too easy to make; false reports are rare (2%). The statistics of 20,000 convictions annually out of 683,000 rapes mean that it is very easy to defend, often by blaming the victim (Kilpatrick, Edmunds, & Seymour, 1992).

The strength of these myths and others indicates that our society has a long way to go in changing its view of sexual assault victims and in providing better laws for their protection and the perpetrators' prosecution.

Current Services

Originally, rape counseling centers dealt only with adult rape victims but, through the years, there has been an evolution of both philosophy and funding that has led to an expansion of services. Today, these centers may provide services to adults *and* children also who are the victims of molestation and/or physical abuse. Some rape counseling centers, usually to increase their funding, have also tried to provide services to perpetrators, especially juveniles. This has not often been successful because the expertise required to assist victims is quite different from that needed to confront perpetrators.

These centers often provide a broad array of services. These would include intake at the center, the hospital, or sometimes at the crime scene. Crisis support services using volunteers are probably the most common and extensive; today, many hospital emergency rooms have sexual assault units. A key component of these is the presence of an advocate or volunteer on a 24-hour basis. Individual counseling and peer groups are the basic staples of these programs. In the early seventies, these programs were the first to use peer support groups, which research now shows is often as beneficial as standard psychotherapy. Community education in schools, police departments, churches, and social service agencies is very common; today, many programs have funding for an "outreach" advocate who exclusively makes presentations to the community. Many referrals are made

FOCUS BOX

After reading about the various types of services, what populations of victims do you think need their own specific services? Why? How would the services differ from those discussed here?

for legal, medical, psychological, educational, and employment services. From the beginning of the victims' movement, these centers have been very politically active in advocating for rape victims, with all the systems that were originally revictimizing them.

The centers were at first run by volunteers who were victims themselves. Depending on their size, they may now have two to five paid staff members, who have specialized education and training in administration, training, education, or psychotherapy. Almost all centers continue to have a large cadre of volunteers, a portion of whom have been with the centers for many, many years. Even though these centers are often better funded than other types of victims' agencies, most could not continue to offer their current level and breadth of services without these volunteers.

The primary funding for these centers comes from the Victims of Crime Act (1984 and 1989) and the Violence Against Women's Act (1994 and 1999). Most also get local funding from agencies, such as the United Way and governmental entities. In California, the funds from these two acts are disbursed through the Office for Criminal Justice Planning. In most other states, the VOCA administrator, housed in the attorney general's office, controls these funding allocations; however, these funds can be also administered by specific designees in either the judicial or the executive branch.

Rape Trauma Syndrome Theory

Before there was the official diagnosis of Post-Traumatic Stress Disorder (PTSD) (1986), the only substantial description of the rape victim's experience was the Rape Trauma Syndrome. This was first proposed as a theory to explain the emotions and behaviors of many rape victims; because of its efficacy in the field, it was quickly accepted by rape victim advocates (Walker, 2000). The tendency among rape victim advocates today is to view the grieving process following rape, not in the traditional stages, but as a series of emotions (Roberts, 1998):

1. Shock—"I'm numb."
2. Denial—"This didn't happen."
3. Anger—"Why me?"
4. Bargaining—"Let's act like this didn't happen."
5. Depression—"I feel dirty . . . worthless."
6. Acceptance—"Life can go on."
7. Assimilation—"It is part of my life."

As will be discussed in more detail below in Crisis Theory, the timing of these emotions is person-specific; the victim may cycle through all of them many times, especially when trauma cues present themselves; and through time, the intensity of these emotions usually diminishes.

The Rape Trauma Syndrome has two parts: immediate emergency reactions and delayed reorganization reactions. The immediate reactions can include: continuous crying, restlessness, irritability, agitation, anger, lack of cooperation, jumpiness, blocking, lack of concentration, boredom, inability to communicate, fear, worry about minor things, sadness and depression, loss of trust, shame, guilt, panic, self-blame, revenge, and various types of physical maladies.

The delayed reorganization reactions can include: mistrust, relationship problems, withdrawal, inability to concentrate, numerous somatic complaints and problems, irritability, dependence, phobic preoccupations, inability to sleep or eat, nightmares, regression, neediness, alcohol, drug or medication problems, obsessions, compulsions, despondence, self-loathing and shame, detachment, paranoia, sexual problems, lack of confidence, inability to make decisions, and inability to express positive or negative emotions (Burgess & Holstrom, 1974).

Today, the diagnosis of Post-Traumatic Stress Disorder subsumes this description and specifies three major types of symptoms: reexperiencing the crime, avoidance of various things related to the crime, and hyperarousal. However, prior to PTSD, the Rape Trauma Syndrome was the most extensive and complete description of the sexual assault victims' experience. Discussing this with victims individually and in peer groups often relieves their worries about their feelings of "going crazy."

Rape in America: A Report to the Nation

This section will discuss the major surveys that validate the rape trauma syndrome, as well as stressing the need for expanded services for each particular victim.

Early in 1992, the Uniform Crime Report (U.S. Department of Justice, 1992) from the FBI stated its highest figure ever for reported rapes: 100,000. A month or so later, the National Crime Victimization Survey reported 200,000 rapes for the previous year. Both figures appeared to be the most accurate ever obtained for this crime. The fact that there was a 50 percent reporting rate seemed phenomenal, since the overall rate of crime reporting had always hovered around 33 percent to 35 percent.

In April 1992, a study commissioned by the Office for Victims of Crime and done by Dr. Dean Kilpatrick of the Crime Victims Research and Treatment Center of the Medical University of South Carolina, and Christine Edmunds and Anne Seymour of the National Victim Center, reported (first in *USA Today*) that there had been 683,000 rapes in 1991 (Kilpatrick, Edmunds, & Seymour, 1992). After a period of speculation and criticism, it became clear that the report was an excellent observational/survey study of 4,008 women, done with a very good representative sample. Besides the fact that rape was 3.5 to 7.0 times higher than the FBI or the Bureau of Justice Statistics had imagined, the survey also produced other surprising facts:

1. Of all adult women in the United States, 13 percent are the victims of rape.
2. Sixty-one percent are raped before they turned 18.
3. Only one of six (16%) report the rape to the police.

4. Seventy-eight percent are raped by someone familiar to them.
5. Among all rape victims, 31 percent develop PTSD.

The extent of each of these variables had never before been imagined. With 61 percent of the rapes occurring before the age of 18, acquaintance rape education and prevention programs in high schools might be offered too late; they probably should start in junior high. Reporting rates for rape are half that of other crimes, so cultural and policy issues need to be confronted continually. "Stranger danger" is a long-held fallacy that is not true for rape; family members, neighbors, coworkers, and friends pose the greatest threat to women—at the rate of four to one. If the rate of PTSD is this high, then mental health services for rape victims need to be expanded greatly.

The other half of the study was a questionnaire given to advocates at rape counseling programs; this survey was done soon after the William Kennedy Smith rape trial in Florida, so there were questions mainly about the media and the criminal justice system. In summary, the survey stated that the programs found the criminal justice system to be more responsive to victims than ever before. The media was a different story; it was painted as lacking ethics and reporting in such a manner as to discourage rape victims from reporting the crime. The advocates stated that there needed to be more funds for public education and more laws protecting victims' confidentiality (Kilpatrick, Edmunds, & Seymour, 1992).

This report has changed both society's view and advocates' views about rape and victim intervention. It is still today the best research study done on rape. It substantiates the prevalence of Rape Trauma Syndrome and Post-Traumatic Stress Disorder. It clearly indicates the need for earlier education, more intervention, and more treatment. The fact that only one in six rape victims reports the crime would indicate a great need to question and change all agency policies. The fact that the media needs to more clearly define ethics and policies regarding rape victims would seem to be self-evident. Indirectly, this report facilitated the passage of the Violence Against Women's Act in 1994.

Domestic Violence Programs (Battered Women's Shelters)

Domestic Violence Myths

There are one million victims of domestic violence each year and about 2,000 domestic violence shelters in the United States (*National Directory of Shelters,* 1999). Seven centers were started in 1974, with the first located in Denver. The Women's Movement focused on rape and domestic violence in the initial push for victim services and rights. The women who started shelters with hot lines and peer groups soon learned that the battered women were talking about their treatment by the criminal justice and mental health systems (second victimization) as much as they were discussing the abuser and the abuse. Cultural values and myths play a large part in our society's lack of response to abused women. The fact that there are 5,000 animal shelters speaks volumes about who is valued in our society (SPCA, 1999).

Even though there have been many changes in society's view of abused women and even though the Violence Against Women's Act (VAWA) has created many positive bureaucratic policy changes, there are still numerous myths about this crime and these victims. Some of the most prevalent myths are the following:

1. The woman causes the abuse by things that she says and does.

   In most cases, she tries to "make things right" and walks on eggs. As previously stated, in Anglo-Saxon law, words can never be the precipitant of physical reactions. Her later physical response is almost always a defensive maneuver.

2. Domestic violence occurs only among minority and poor populations.

   Minority families may have more interaction with the criminal justice system, but it occurs equally among all races and socioeconomic groups.

3. Abusers are mentally ill.

   Some are, but there is no research to indicate that this is pervasive. Abusers do appear to have numerous psychosocial problems, but not to the extent that they would fit an official, diagnostic category.

4. Abuse leads to catharsis and less future abuse.

   This old Freudian analysis is true only under certain conditions. For most, the expression of aggression escalates when unabated over time.

5. Domestic violence seldom causes major injuries.

   Fifty-three percent of all domestic violence victims are treated in an emergency room multiple times. Almost 33 percent of all visits by women to emergency rooms are due to domestic violence (Mever, Seymour, & Wallace, 2000).

6. Battered women like being hit.

   Again, this is part of the old Freudian analysis that flies in the face of Freud's basic pleasure principle: Most human beings seek pleasure and avoid pain. Abused women create an environment in which there are primarily attempts to avoid the violence. What crimes do men actually enjoy being the victim of? Why would women be any different?

7. Battered women can always leave.

   Often, they do not have the financial or job viability to leave. Research shows that, by the time she leaves, she has asked for help six times informally and six times formally (Harris & Dewkney, 1994). She has tried to leave many times.

8. Domestic violence is just an "anger control" problem.

   This simplistic explanation does not explain the abuser's ability to function socially and at work. When the police arrive, he usually controls himself. He "controls" his environment very well with his anger.

9. Alcohol and drugs are the *real* causes of domestic violence.

The causal factors are very diverse and complicated. Alcohol and substance abuse occur in well over 50 percent of all domestic violence cases. (Seymour, 2000). In many cases, the violence would take place anyway, but the substance abuse often makes it much worse.

10. Violence and love are incompatible.

Both are extreme states of arousal often defined by the context. Perpetrators often confuse emotions and are unable to discriminate between them. Childhood experience may dictate no difference to them.

Current Services

Domestic violence is a stressor that is both chronic and extraordinary (note discussion below under General Stress Theory). It is often worse than other types of victimization because the basic role of the family, providing support and caregiving, is contradicted by the domestic violence. This directly violates the trust that is necessary for a family to function. Family violence is worse also because of isolation; others are unaware of the violence. Escalation almost always occurs with domestic violence over time—as with most types of violence. The fact that a woman and her children often have to leave their familiar home to terminate the abuse makes it also more stressful. Using Selye's analysis (in General Stress Theory), domestic violence often then leads to more physical and psychological problems than other types of victimization (Selye, 1956). Having a home similar to a war zone means that women and children in these homes have a much higher rate of Post-Traumatic Stress Disorder than other crime victims (except for rape victims).

Some of the first victim service programs were peer-oriented spousal abuse programs; through time, these shelters have developed a broad array of services and referral sources. These shelters provide services to women (and their children) who have been abused by a spouse or significant other. Shelters today often do not provide housing for boys over 12 years of age because they often reflect the value system and behavior of their fathers, causing the shelter atmosphere also to be abusive. Many shelters also provide services at a separate location for the battering spouse.

Shelters, from the beginning in 1974, have provided hot lines, peer support groups, and housing. At times, crisis services are available at the shelter, in the hospital, or at the crime scene. Food and shelter are central services offered for 30, 60, or 90 days; there also may be a separate facility for long-term residency. Some formal counseling may be involved, but "therapy" is provided mainly by peer support groups. Many types of education and training occur: parent effectiveness training, assertion training, house maintenance, budgeting, and so forth. For the abuser, these and courses in anger management and substance abuse are offered. An average of three referrals are made for legal, financial, medical, psychological, employment, childcare, educational, and alcohol/drug services. Advocacy in these programs is usually on a volunteer basis; it is less formal and organized than the advocacy of rape counseling centers.

Some of the earliest crisis response teams and hot lines in victim services were provided by domestic violence shelters. There are today three types of response teams: the police model, the hospital model, and the domestic violence shelter model (Roberts,

1990). In the United States, there are just a few examples of the *police model.* Domestic violence advocates are actually assigned to a patrol. They are paired with an officer and often have special training in crisis theory, mediation, and self defense. They assist the officer in defusing the volatile situation and can provide direct assistance to the victim. According to systems theory, this immediate crisis intervention should increase the victim's positive response to assistance and more readily break the cycle of violence.

The *hospital model* usually follows a set protocol with a team consisting of a doctor, a nurse, and a social worker. The purpose of this intervention is to provide the appropriate medical care and legal documentation in a professional manner. Until 10 years ago or so, this intervention went against the values of the medical subculture. It was not deemed their job to do more than provide medical care; they should not "get involved." The rationalizations were that it was a privacy issue and an added burden for which they did not have time. Many things have now changed, and the victim is not required to tell her story several times or allowed to lie about what happened. She is encouraged to tell the truth and given the appropriate assistance and referrals. However, there are still times when medical personnel balk at legal documentation, that is, acting as if they were police or lawyers.

The most prevalent response team is the *domestic violence shelter* model, which provides some direct intervention but usually relies on initial intervention through hot lines. Some of the original hot lines were pioneered by shelters in the United States. Through the years, shelters have developed several types of standard phone protocols. One is called the ABC Intervention Model (Roberts, 1990). Once the abused woman's immediate safety is assured, there are three steps to follow:

> A—Achieving Contact: Become familiar with the victim, call her by her first name; learn her children's names, and let her know your name; make it very clear that you empathize and understand her condition and concerns.

> B—Boiling Down the Problem: Have her describe exactly what is going on and what her main concerns are, what precipitated this problem and what are her needs *right now*.

> C—Coping with the Problem: What does she want and what does she need help with? Your input is important but her analysis is most important; what can she do to help herself at this moment and what does she need from you and others?

Responses to the abused woman should be calm, positive, and nonjudgmental. Open-ended questions always appear less accusatory and allow the victim more latitude to respond. Referral lists should always be handy, and a second hot line person on another phone may be needed to call the police. If possible, a follow-up call should be made to see if she carried out her plan or if she needs further assistance.

In domestic violence shelters, there is at times both individual and group therapy centering on the abuse and skill building, that is, parenting, stress management, self-maintenance, vocational rehabilitation, and so forth. Most programs do not have the funds for their own therapists, so the most common groups are peer support groups. Research indicates that these are often as productive as traditional therapy. To augment their basic services, shelters often have an extensive referral list for many support services. Most abused women who have been overprotected and isolated for years need an average of just over three referrals (Roberts, 1990). The most prevalent referrals are legal, medical, housing, child care, and employment—basic needs; the next most common referral is for Alcoholics Anonymous or Alanon. In the majority of abusive homes, there is often also a major alcohol or drug problem.

Most shelters could not exist without the commitment and hard work of many volunteers. Most programs have several employees, often including a director and a volunteer coordinator. Some programs have other employees who provide counseling, outreach, networking, and advocacy. Because of less funding, domestic violence shelters usually have fewer paid employees than other victim service programs.

Funding can come from the Victims of Crime Act and the Violence Against Women's Act, but most shelters also have various types of local in-kind and monetary funding and donations. These programs are known for their unique fundraising methods: surtaxes on marriage licenses and divorce decrees, famous people auctions, service auctions, weekend workdays with special groups, and so forth. Funding is usually not as substantial as that for other victim services.

Crisis Theory

Since domestic violence programs and shelters often deal with victims while they are in crisis soon after the abuse, it is appropriate to review crisis theory here (Roberts, 1990). In recent history, the study of death and dying has led to an in-depth analysis of the grieving process, and the discussions of crisis and grief often are similar. The original analysis of a crisis focused on stages, while Kübler-Ross's (1971) discussion of grief delineated the progressive emotions in a linear fashion. Both views have validity. In the field of victim services, there is a current bias against stage theory. They both are describing the same process in different terms. With several alterations, stage theory is still useful in understanding the victim's experience following a crime.

A crisis is defined as a hazardous event in which the individual's physical, psychological, or social safety is threatened; normal coping mechanisms soon become inadequate and the stress becomes unbearable and unmanageable. There are four stages (Roberts, 1990).

1. Fight/Flight
2. Recoil/Turmoil
3. Adjustment
4. Reconstruction

Fight/Flight is the initial response to a perceived stress. Depending on the situation, the person uses all his or her energy and resources to deal with the stress directly or to escape from the stressful situation. Recoil/Turmoil is the period of confusion, shock, and withdrawal in which the person may not be sure what happened and may be unable to interact meaningfully with his or her environment. Adjustment follows as a time when the person seems to get back to "normal" on the surface. He or she goes back to work and interacts superficially with others. Emotionally and cognitively the person may still be having difficulty adjusting to life with the loss caused by the crime, that is, domestic violence. Using the terminology in victimology today, the person in this stage is a "victim."

Reconstruction means the person incorporates victimization into his or her life view and self-concept and makes the most of personal abilities and opportunities. The victimization is not forgotten, but it is less important and put in perspective; the individual has now become a "survivor."

Regarding alterations to this theory, these stages should *never* be seen as "hard and fast." However, in the traditional view, these stages were seen as getting progressively longer, with Fight/Flight as a matter of seconds and minutes and Reconstruction as a matter of months and years. Two realities temper this traditional view of set stages. First, this is not a linear process; the person can go through the stages numerous times in a cyclical fashion; the cycle through the four stages can be cued by external events (criminal justice process, perpetrators, similar situations, victim advocates, etc.) or internal events (thoughts, feelings, dreams, etc.). Over time the cycle becomes less intense and shorter—usually. Second, it is probably the case with many types of grief that it is never completely diminished, especially for the families of homicide victims; grief reactions and crisis responses can continue for many years after the incident(s).

For victims of domestic violence, living in a perpetual crisis atmosphere, arriving at the shelter is simply one more in a long line of crises. Their survival and crisis management skills, which worked adequately for years, no longer are functional; by definition, they will need much external support and assistance to move through the crisis stages.

The General Stress Theory

Domestic violence relates to crisis theory, but because it is persistent and long-term, General Stress Theory also is applicable. For 40 years (1936–1976), Hans Selye (1956) researched and wrote about the physiological effects of stress. Most people cope with the stress in their lives in an adequate fashion—most of the time. Through basic socialization and adult experience, they learn to manage daily stress in an adaptive fashion. There are three types. *Routine stress* includes daily repetitive stressors and periodic hassles; most routine stress, by itself, seems minor, but it often has a cumulative effect. *Extraordinary stress* pertains to life transitions: job change, job loss, relocation, marriage, divorce, death of a family member, birth of a child, and the like. Whether positive or negative, life transitions are often stressful. *Catastrophic stress* refers to sudden, dangerous, overwhelming, and, usually, community events—tornadoes, hurricanes, earthquakes, mass murder, and so forth.

Selye (1956) labeled the human response to stress the general adaptation syndrome (GAS), which has three stages: crisis, expenditure of resources, and exhaustion. Each person utilizes as many physical, social, and psychological resources as possible in the face of a crisis; as the crisis becomes long-term, resources are depleted, and there is then physical and psychological exhaustion or breakdown. Selye's major focus was on the physiological aspects of stress. His perspective was that stress always takes its toll on the body. For each person, the exact toll is different; that is, it involves the breakdown of different physiological systems, leading to migranes, ulcers, strokes, heart attacks, asthma, and the like. One of his major points was that our ancestors usually had to deal with temporary stressors and then rested, but in modern society, the stress of a difficult job or a problematic relationship and/or the constant pressure to perform and succeed is persistent; the psyche and body never rest and are more prone to breakdown and illness in today's society.

In this context, many crime victims are exposed to a short-term crisis; some are exposed to persistent stress, but domestic violence, which most fits the war zone analogy, is probably the crime that presents the most persistent stress. Therefore, Selye's theory is most applicable to domestic violence victims. By definition, this theory states that the victim's resources and typical coping skills are *not* adequate for this lengthy stress. Why doesn't she leave? She needs society's assistance to leave her violent situation.

The Cycle of Violence

The most specific, recent theory that applies to domestic violence is Lenore Walker's Cycle of Violence (1979). She states that there are three stages to spousal abuse: tension build-up, explosion, and honeymoon. In *tension build-up,* the abusive husband becomes upset over little things; usually there are common patterns and common issues, centering around his childish, self-centered need for control. Over time, he becomes more and more upset over more and more minor things, until eventually everything she and the children do upsets him. The family is then constantly "walking on eggs" and catering to his needs.

Explosion is the actual abuse, which may be a shove that lasts for seconds at first and only seems to be minor; but over time, the abuse escalates until the victim needs hospitalization or is killed. As with most violence, Walker indicated that spousal abuse escalates over time.

The next day the *honeymoon* begins, with apologies, flowers, candy, and promises that "it will never happen again." At first this period may last for several weeks, and she begins to believe that he has really changed. In fact, it is these periods that reinforce to her that a positive life is possible and cause her to hesitate to leave. Walker stated, in the original analysis, that the build-up and the honeymoon would become shorter over time, and that the explosion would become more prevalent.

When this theory was first discussed at battered women's shelters, there was much support from victims for this analysis of spousal abuse. Recently, there have been confounding research results: some women state that there are three stages, while other women identify only with tension build-up and explosion—and some support only explosion as a fact of their lives (Wallace, 1998). Further research is needed to correlate both the length of marriage and the length of the abuse with the number of stages. One probable hypothesis about these recent results could be that they really represent two groups of women—one who has been married less than five years and still experience all three stages, and one group of women who have been in abusive relationships for well over five years. As Walker predicted, the explosion stage is most prevalent and perhaps constant, and the other two stages are either minimal or absent.

Nevertheless, this theory still has much explanatory power. It does describe the gradual process of abuse, some of the reasons why women hesitate to leave, and the distinct need for adequate, immediate services to break the cycle. As a type of systems theory, it supports that spousal abuse has no singular cause; that is, there is no specific individual pathology on the victim's part. Many things must go wrong for this crime to occur. Family violence happens because the family system is closed and committed to its boundaries while positively reinforcing the abuse (Van Hasselt, Morrison, Bellack, & Herson, 1988). Spousal abuse almost always escalates because the family system seldom allows intruders, and when the system is intruded on it often covers its mistakes to maintain stability.

Strategic Coping Factors

The final questions to be dealt with before we leave the consideration of theory are: What will facilitate the abused women's movement through the stages of this crisis? What can be done about the stress of domestic violence? What determines a woman's ability to deal with this cycle of violence and remove herself and her children from it?

A number of years ago, a psychologist by the name of Albee (1982) developed a theoretical formula to determine a person's level of coping. Five factors were described, as in the following diagram:

$$\text{Level of coping} = \frac{\text{Stress} + \text{Risk Factors}}{\text{Social Support} + \text{Coping Skills} + \text{Self–Esteem}}$$

Stress and risk factors decrease an individual's ability to manage stress, while the variables in the denominator increase the person's coping skills. First, the nature of the *stress* is important. Its length and intensity matter. Whether there was a warning makes a difference; surprises are more deadly. How inclusive the stress becomes is an issue. Does it threaten the person in all domains: psychological, physical, and social? The more domains involved, the less effectively the person can cope. *Risk factors* include: relationship to the perpetrator, age of the victim, previous stress, family dynamics, isolation, communication skills, availability of community resources, socioeconomic status, IQ, and any type of special status.

Social support would include family availability, friends, community resources, psychotherapy, governmental institutions, churches, and the like. This pertains to the third layer in ecological theory (Belsky) and the general societal values regarding victims and victimization (Van Hasselt et al., 1988). As these resources are helpful and positive, social support increases coping with stress.

Coping skills generally have to do with previous learning and experience. What did the woman learn from her family as normal ways of managing stress? Are they adaptive or maladaptive? What is the level of her problem-solving skills? How does she deal with negative emotions? How adequate are her social and communication skills? Does she know how to ask for help? What other types of stress has she dealt with successfully in the past? *Self-esteem* centers around her self-image. Does she see herself as a competent person? Does she see herself as controlling her own environment or not? Strong feelings of dependence probably mean a decreased ability to cope with domestic violence.

According to Albee, these are the key factors in determining what is needed to help a battered woman leave her abusive situation. Obviously, the stress and risk factors initially far outweigh the other three. External intervention is almost always needed to break the cycle of violence. She will leave when social support is provided, coping skills are increased, and self-esteem improves. These are no small tasks for domestic violence programs.

FOCUS BOX

Using Albee's coping model, apply it to a rape victim, a child molestation victim, and a domestic violence victim. Specifically, what is missing for each that is similar? How are the needed services different? What does this model say about the needs of these victims in the twenty-first century?

Surveys

There are several surveys that support Walker's, Selye's, and Albee's theories that it takes a major effort on society's part to intervene in domestic violence. To break this cycle of violence, more intervention may be needed with domestic violence than with other crimes. What does the research indicate?

As previously stated, a major survey indicated that an average of three referrals is needed for women in domestic violence shelters (Roberts, 1990). These referrals are made for legal, financial, medical, psychological, employment, child care, educational, and alcohol/drug services. This victim does not just have a few problems, but many. Most have to do with very basic needs—things that other types of victims, and most members of our society, often take for granted. Selye was correct: Basic resources have been depleted by this chronic stress.

A second, more recent survey indicates that the abused woman has asked for help many times before it finally is made available. She makes six informal requests and six formal requests prior to actually leaving the abusive situation (Harris & Dewdney, 1994). Informal requests are made to family members, neighbors, and friends. Formal requests are made to professionals and various institutions. Advice and minor interventions are insufficient. Albee was correct, at least three major areas must be addressed before her coping ability improves, and she is empowered to leave.

Victim/Witness Programs

Program Myths

Victim/witness programs were first created in 1974 through Law Enforcement Assistance Administration (LEAA) funding. As the 10 initial programs have now expanded to most jurisdictions throughout the United States, there continue to be dilemmas and problematic areas with these services. Some of the myths that perpetuate these problems are the following:

1. Increased victim services will increase victim satisfaction with the criminal justice system.

   Current surveys indicate more services have led to more dissatisfaction with the system (Karmen, 2001).

2. Increased victim services will increase victim cooperation with the criminal justice system.

   Current reporting rates of crime (33–35%) are about the same as they were in 1972.

3. Intimidation of victims is one of their major issues.

   Only 1 percent of all victims fear direct reprisal, and only 13 percent even mention it as a concern (Karmen, 2001).

4. Victim allocution is important to all victims.

   Research indicates that this varies among victims. *Those who desire it* are more satisfied when they are allowed to make a statement in court (Gregorie et al., 2000).

5. Victim/witness advocates usually reflect their D.A.'s wishes and are usually either victim advocates or witness advocates.

   Within the limits of their resources, most advocates try to do *both*. The surveys in the next section indicate the delivery of a broad array of services.

Current Services

From the first LEAA pilot programs, victim/witness services have usually been housed in district attorneys' offices. Some are in probation departments, police departments, or social service programs. In general, most are criminal justice–based, while some are community-based programs. Their clients are the victims of violent crime, who report their crime and cooperate with the police and the D.A.

Primary services include assisting the victim in filling out the Victim Impact Statement (VIS) and the compensation forms. The VIS specifies to the court how the victim was harmed physically, psychologically, socially, and fiscally. Through the compensation forms, the victim then applies for financial redress in these areas. These programs often have a small emergency fund to provide for immediate victim needs, for example, transportation, housing, and phone. They provide much information about the criminal justice system and the case status and often escort the victim through the system. They, at times, assist the victim with transportation, child care, and employer information. They also provide numerous referrals for many needed services. Victim/witness programs vary in their emphasis; some are predominantly victim programs, while others are mainly witness programs, but, as stated, most earnestly try to do both. However, these programs are sometimes more conflicted than domestic violence or rape counseling programs because they do serve two masters: the victim and the D.A. (or the system).

All victims programs, including victim/witness programs, must do a thorough initial assessment of the victims' needs. However, the information collected by the victim/witness advocate will be used in the criminal case, in the assessment of needs, in the compensation application, in the victim impact statement, and in the potential civil case; therefore, the assessment needs to be even more thorough and complete. In psychology today, there are many typologies to evaluate a victim's response to stress. An excellent discussion of assessment by Lazarus led to the development of the BASIC Profile. In 1984, Slaikeu developed this profile which encompasses all aspects of the person's life

(Andrews, 1992). It is useful in that it is both comprehensive and easy to understand. It also can be applied to the victim's experience very readily. At issue for the victim advocate is when to respond directly and when to make a referral. The sign of a "good" professional is to be well trained with a breadth of skills *and* to know the limits of those skills; reaching one's limits indicates the need to make a referral.

Each letter of the BASIC Profile stands for a different aspect of the victim's existence. The first area to be evaluated is the victim's current *behavior*. Again, with *most* victims there will be few problems indicated by this analysis using the BASIC Profile. In this first area, there are a few behaviors that need to be noted. Is the victim exhibiting extreme behaviors? On the one hand, does he or she appear to be listless, inactive, and depressed (lack of normal activity)? On the other hand, is the victim overly active, or even manic (well beyond normal activity)? The first person may have great difficulty coming to the office, while the second person will find a short meeting with the advocate agonizing. One other behavioral condition may require a referral. If the victim or the family state that the person is behaving in a manner that is unusual for them, this should be evaluated. The victim may appear normal to the victim advocate but express great distress over some aspect of his or her behavior or activity level. In this situation, a referral to a mental health professional for further evaluation would be appropriate.

The second area is *affect* or emotional responses. Victimization creates many negative responses that are normal: anger, rage, anxiety, fear, depression, guilt, and so forth. These emotions usually persist but subside in intensity over time. When this *does not* happen, and the emotions escalate in the absence of second victimization, a referral needs to be made. This may indicate complicating, unseen factors or a history of multiple trauma. As with the behavioral evaluation, if the victim or the family indicate emotional responses that are unusual for the victim, further questions need to be asked. This "unusual" emotional response may not necessarily be volatile, but it may be a very uncomfortable emotion for the victim—one with which he or she is having difficulty dealing.

As Selye noted, victims can have numerous physical, or *somatic*, responses to the stress of victimization. At times, these conditions can become chronic and require medical attention. The physical problem created by stress will vary from person to person. Victimization can disrupt any of the body's systems. Because the immune system ceases to function during a crisis, victims are more susceptible to illness after the crime than at other times in their lives. Because of society's messages that they should "get well" quickly and because of their own need to regain control over their lives, they may minimize their illness and not seek medical assistance. The victim advocate's supportive encouragement can overcome these concerns and help them obtain appropriate medical care.

Interpersonal problems at home and work and in friendships can be created by victimization. Victims lose many things through criminal acts, but the greatest psychological loss is diminished trust in others and in the world's order. The basis of any relationship is trust, and when it is absent, the relationship becomes very tenuous. For many victims, this does not affect just one relationship, but all relationships. Some research indicates that 50 percent of all rape victims have major relationship problems in the year following their victimization. Reactions toward supervisors and coworkers can create strained relationships at work. A loss of confidence can make a previously assertive person very passive and unable to fend off incidents of revictimization at the hands of friends, family members, coworkers, professionals, and the like. Depending on the situation, a referral may need to be made for individual, couples, or family therapy in order to adequately assist the victim in dealing with these interpersonal problems.

The last area to be evaluated is the person's thinking, or *cognition*. In the 1960s, an American psychologist, Albert Ellis (1962), proposed a theory of therapeutic intervention that focused on common irrational thoughts. He considered these a sign of mental illness, but for the victims of violent crime, they are common thoughts: "I am useless," "I am worthless," "I can't do anything," "I should have . . . ," "It was my fault," and so forth. An entire series of negative, self-accusatory thoughts can plague a victim's waking hours for weeks and months. If after a period of time, with the supportive input of the victim advocate (and hopefully others), there is no decrease in these cognitions, a referral would be appropriate.

The next issue is who performs these services and this assessment. The staff of victim/witness programs is usually made up of employees of the district attorney's office or the probation office. Many adjunct services are provided by the agency that houses the program. These programs also utilize both volunteers and interns in victimology, criminology, social work, and psychology from their local community colleges and universities.

Funding for these programs comes from the Victims of Crime Act (1984 and 1989) and the parent agency (probation department, district attorney, law enforcement, etc.). In-kind services and indirect funding provide these programs with many more basic resources than the other two types of programs that are community based.

Ecological Theory

Ecological theory is one of the broadest theories applied to analyzing victimization. It clearly shows the need for victim/witness programs and the diverse services they deliver. As proposed by Belsky, there are four levels (concentric circles) of analysis (Van Hasselt et al., 1988). The first level, the Ontagenic level, is the personal experience of abuse and violence; did the person experience caring and concern or neglect and abuse? Is he or she attached or detached from the environment? The Microsystem level is the family setting: Are the parent–child and parent–parent relationships caring or abusive? How is conflict resolved?

The third level is the Exosystem, which is the subculture the family lives in—neighborhood, work group, peers, ethnic group, and local institutions. Issues at this level are isolation, loss, and frustration; as these three issues intensify, the likelihood of violence increases. The fourth level is the Macrosystem; this includes various cultural values and norms of accepted behavior, especially the norm of violence as an acceptable means of resolving conflicts. Garbarino notes that the first three levels include *sufficient conditions* for crime and violence, while cultural acceptance (fourth level) is a *necessary condition*; without cultural and institutional support, attitudes, policies, and practices that revictimize crime victims do not persist (Van Hasselt et al., 1988).

This is a social reaction theory in that it looks at the "big" picture and prescribes solutions that are not simple and that deal with much more than just street crime. This theory explains victims' behavior in a complex manner, not a simplistic one. The human need discussed in attribution theory for quick, easy causes is not met by this theory. To truly understand a victim, four levels of analysis are required. Once this analysis is complete, it becomes evident that intervention and services are needed at each level. Dealing with both the first and second victimization completely requires even more intervention than is being done today by victim/witness programs. At the end of this chapter, a comprehensive continuum of services will be discussed to reflect the analysis of this theory.

Surveys

This next section will look at two surveys that support Ecological Theory and the expansion of victim/witness services. One survey was completed in 1988 and the other in 1998, so an evaluation of the progress in the delivery of victim services can be made.

The *self-evaluation* section of this survey looked at problem areas, strengths, and areas of potential change. As far as problem areas, the programs were asked to list their three biggest *problems*. The primary problem discussed by 80 percent of the programs was a lack of funding. At that time, the annual VOCA budget was about $100,000,000, with about half of it going for program administration. Seventy per cent stated that they lacked space; indeed, most had been given leftover space in district attorneys' offices. The third major problem was the attrition of volunteers; with such small staffs, volunteers were very important, but few programs had formalized volunteer training or specific coordinators to maintain continuity and stability. Other problems listed were poor relationships with the court, a lack of a police liaison, and staff turnover (Roberts, 1990).

There were five categories of *strengths* listed by a majority of the programs (Roberts, 1990). Thirty-seven per cent stated their greatest strength was the delivery of comprehensive services. Some services were cited numerous times: immediate personal assistance, 24-hour availability, compensation form assistance, collecting restitution, and crisis intervention. The second source of strength was court support and advocacy, which included court orientation, court support, and victim impact statement assistance. The third category of strength had to do with referrals and linkages (called "networking" today). Various community contacts and the capacity to link a victim up with the appropriate service were seen as a very positive strength. The most common linkages were with the police and the district attorney. Providing basic case information to victims was the fourth strength, while having a very dedicated staff and volunteers was the final strength. This last one obviously made up for the number one problem, a lack of funding.

In the area of *potential changes*, 95 percent of the programs gave a total of 390 responses (Roberts, 1990). Three general categories were evident. First, there needed to be an increase in staffing for professional services, clerical services, and for volunteer supervision. Money for better training was also a part of this change. Second, an increase of services was needed, especially in the areas of 24-hour availability, crisis services, emergency funding, transportation, and program publicity. Many cited the need to expand services that were only available on a part-time basis. The final change had to do with expanding program space and equipment: more office space, a waiting room, a playroom, cars, phones, beeper, video equipment, and so forth. Even at this time, the need for a computer was mentioned.

Although this survey is well over 10 years old, many of the same problems still exist, even with a dramatic increase in funding in recent years. Services have expanded, and staff education and retention may have also increased, but so has the demand for victim services. The next survey gives some clues about changes in victim service delivery recently.

Rural Survey (1998).   Through a grant from the Office of Victims of Crime, California State University, Fresno, did a survey of rural programs, almost all of which were sexual assault and domestic violence programs (Wallace, Edmunds, & Walker, 2000). This survey indicated that many rural victim assistance programs have the same issues that urban programs had ten years earlier.

The majority provided six major services: court accompaniment, victim assistance referrals, medical and psychological referrals, transportation, emergency financial assistance, and victim impact statement preparation. Over half of the programs had satellite offices and provided outreach to isolated victims. Most of the programs provided in-house training for their staff and volunteers but clearly noted a lack of in-depth, available training. Over half of the programs did community education but noted the need for better training of judges, police, and district attorneys on victims' issues. Computers were much more available than expected (88%), but they were being used only for word processing, not for program management, caseload statistics, or victim notification.

Major problem areas were much more basic than those in urban programs: transportation, phones, literacy, isolation, lack of privacy and confidentiality, no vocational programs, and no community professionals (Wallace, Edmunds, & Walker, 2000). The two major issues for rural programs were victim isolation and a lack of various professional services, that is, both unsophisticated clients and untrained community professionals. As with the NOVA survey 10 years earlier, a lack of funding and a lack of staff were the preeminent problems with rural programs.

Other Victim Services

This chapter has looked at three basic types of services: rape counseling centers, domestic violence programs, and victim witness programs. There are other services provided to specific types of victims, usually by various government programs. For instance, most programs for abused children are provided through the state's social service programs, especially child protective services. Abused adults and elder adults often can obtain services through adult protective services or the Older Americans Organization. Both of these are funded through several state and federal departments and programs.

There are obviously many other victim services needed. Specific victims who could especially utilize their own services would be the victims of hate and bias crime, victims of sexual harassment, and secondary victims (including those often called "survivors"). Since the early 1990s, there has been an increase in mandatory reporting of hate and bias crime; in fact, in recent years, this has been one of the few crimes that is increasing. Sexual harassment reporting has also increased since the Anita Hill/Clarence Thomas hearings in 1991. For these crimes to be dealt with adequately, specific funding and services will be needed.

The General Victim Services Formula for Recovery

After describing all of these theories, services, and surveys, what is needed in the field of victim advocacy today? This section will present a general theoretical formula that promotes victim recovery, community involvement, and potential reconciliation. Then the question becomes, "What are the necessary ingredients for this formula to become reality?" The next section looks at a proposal by Arlene Andrews to accomplish this.

The victims' movement from the beginning struggled with the issue of treatment versus retribution. In the early 1970s, the perspective was that rights needed to be taken away from the offender and given to the victim. This is not espoused as much today. Laws for offenders have been tightened and restricted, to some extent, but the two are not now seen as mutually exclusive. Offender rights can be maintained, while victim rights are expanded. In order to deal with both issues and ultimately enhance victim rights, the following formula is used as the basis for future changes:

$$Restitution + Rehabilitation \times 2 = Reconciliation + Recovery \times 2$$

This formula is a revision of one by a professor at Fuller Theological Seminary. Victim rights begin with presumptive restitution: payment by the criminal to the victim in every case in every jurisdiction every day. Treatment is needed by the victim for the physical, psychological, and social damage caused by the crime. The criminal obviously has many problems and also needs treatment—or there will be more victims in the future. Offender treatment should be both caring and confrontive, cognitive and behavioral; taking responsibility for the crime is the key issue. If restitution and rehabilitation occur, then true reconciliation and recovery may take place for both parties of the criminal act. This reconciliation is victim-specific, and the timing is not culturally determined, nor determined by the criminal's issues; it is determined by the victim's own recovery process. Recovery for the victim is extremely difficult, unless the first part of this equation becomes a fact in our culture. The reality is that, in this "big picture," victim recovery is linked to offender restitution and treatment. In her book *Victimization and Survival Services,* Arlene Andrews makes an excellent presentation of what would be entailed in a service system that did everything for the victim (Andrews, 1992). It in reality reflects her "dream model" for victim/survivor services. The reader is encouraged to review her model.

Summary

This chapter has outlined the basic myths, the current services, the applicable theories, and the surveys that apply to three types of agencies in the field of victim services. A general theoretical formula was then presented that promotes victim recovery, community involvement, and potential reconciliation. As a possible "dream model" fulfilling this formula, Andrews proposes a comprehensive system that includes four levels of service and four types of systems. It is dreaming to believe that this would all fall into place and that these four systems would work together perfectly, but with no dream, no change occurs—and the second victimization of crime victims continues in our society.

Discussion Questions

1. Why do the many myths regarding various victims continue to persist in our culture?

2. Other than the three major types of services, why have services for other types of victims been slow in developing?

3. Which aspects of Andrew's comprehensive continuum will be the most difficult to develop?

14

Diversity Issues in Victim Services

Learning Objectives

After reading this chapter you should be able to do the following:

1. Define key terms in victim services.
2. Describe the impact of crime on minority groups.
3. Compare and contrast the social psychological causes for prejudice and discrimination.
4. Explain cultural competence and its relationship to victim services.
5. Explain the guidelines for delivering diversity services.

The last two chapters have clearly shown that many victims of crime often suffer from a second victimization by the criminal justice system and other bureaucracies, and although services for these victims have expanded tremendously since 1972, there are still many individuals who receive no or inadequate services today. This problem of just and adequate service delivery is even greater for those who are not Caucasian and middle or upper class in income. For those who do not look like the "average American," or who do not fit the norm of our society in some way, there is even more secondary victimization, as well as fewer available services. When the services *are* available, they are delivered by those from the majority culture with little understanding of diverse cultures or customs; therefore, victims from these diverse cultures do not feel comfortable coming forward and asking for assistance.

This chapter will discuss the major diversity issues in the delivery of victim services. It will begin with several definitions and a description of the major minority groups that are not receiving adequate services today. There will then be a discussion of how the impact of crime on minority groups is greater and affects their entire community. This will be followed by a theoretical discussion about the causes of biased responses and treatment for these diverse groups. The majority of the chapter will then focus on how advocates can gain cultural competence and will provide a series of recommendations for the delivery of diversity services.

Definitions and Descriptions

Our normative cultural definition of a "minority group" has little to do with their numbers in our society, although their percentage of the population has much to do with their lack of power; this definition often centers on very superficial physical or cultural traits. However, the actual definition is much more complicated than these traits. A minority group has the following four characteristics (Ellis, 2000):

1. They receive unequal (biased and negative) treatment by the majority/dominant group. They have fewer social, economic, political, and educational opportunities.

2. They share physical or cultural traits that differ from those of the dominant culture. Physical traits can include skin color, hair texture, facial features, or physique. Cultural traits include customs, clothing, holidays, and the like.

3. There is predominantly in-group marriage. Out-group marriage is either forbidden or discouraged. If it does occur, there is usually a major public or private reaction against the group member. This practice is seen as a means of preserving the minority culture and of providing an emotional buffer against the unequal treatment.

4. Due to the fact that the differing physical and/or cultural traits cannot be altered or changed, membership in the minority group is involuntary.

Even though recent evidence indicates that the major physical differences between races make up less than 2 percent of our entire genetic makeup, these differences are overemphasized, and the multitude of similarities between races are often dismissed (Golden &

Lemonick, 2000). The majority group in any society always overgeneralizes the commonalities within a minority group due to a process called the "out-group homogeneity effect" (Myers, 1996). "They are all alike and different from us." Conversely, the diversity within a minority group is generally overlooked by the dominant culture. Due to the effect of mass media and a computerized culture, in America there are many more similarities than differences between the minority groups and the dominant group; that is, the cultural distinctions often begin to blend together. Therefore, the diversity within a group is often far greater than that between groups. However, for many reasons noted below, the minority cultural and physical differences are emphasized and focused on by the dominant culture, and in victim services this leads to discrimination and fewer services.

Generally, diversity distinctions have been made based upon race, gender, and age. In this chapter on diversity, there will be an additional distinction made. Diversity or minority status is applied to race which, in common usage, may also lump together ethnic and/or religious (cultural) differences; ethnic and/or religious groups are actually separate descriptions of smaller groups than racial groups. Diversity based on age would include both children and the elderly as groups often discriminated against. Diversity based upon gender places the focus on gay and lesbian individuals, who receive few victim services in our society. A final, additional group would be those who are different due to physical or physiological reasons: the disabled and those with AIDS.

As this analysis of diversity issues in victim services begins, three terms need to be defined and clarified: prejudice, discrimination, and the "isms" (racism and sexism). *Prejudice* is an automatic negative attitude toward an entire group of people, usually based upon a cultural or physical difference; this is a cognitive prejudgment caused by these general difference—not based on any facts or reality. *Discrimination* is automatic exclusionary behavior toward an entire group of people; this exclusion is usually social, political, and economic. For *racism* and *sexism* to exist in a society, there must be both the prejudicial attitudes and the discriminatory behavior—along with many institutional supports; in other words, racism and sexism only persist in societies in which the major bureaucracies support and reinforce them (Myers, 1996). These bureaucracies include the government, churches, and business establishments. The history of the United States is replete with examples of racism and sexism that continue today; this means that the provision of victim services (beginning in 1972) also continues to be prejudicial and discriminatory. The first step in changing this situation is awareness of the issue; the second step is a concerted, purposive (personal and bureaucratic) effort to make changes that will increase services for those minority groups discriminated against. This chapter focuses on ways to increase both this awareness and these services.

The Impact of Crime on Minority Groups

As a result of major cultural values of trust, respect for others, and a safe, sane, and just world, few of us expect to be the victims of a crime; therefore, when any of us is victimized, it impacts our self-concept and our worldview in a major negative fashion. For members of a minority group, the impact is even greater and more devastating. Why is this? Besides being the victims of society's major crimes, minority members of our society are also the victims of many hate and bias crimes that go unreported daily. These crimes often are much more aggressive and cause more serious injury than the average crime in America. More than any other crime, they are perpetrated by groups of offenders rather than individuals. Zimbardo and others in social psychology have clearly shown that individuals in groups tend to be much more aggressive than when they are alone. The concept used to explain this is "deindividuation"; it signifies the progressive loss of one's self-concept and moral sense while in a group or mob. There is a diffusion of responsibility—no one is responsible, no one is to blame (Myers, 1996). In a group, violence escalates much more quickly unchecked by the usual sense of moral propriety or guilt. Zajonc's experiments also indicated that groups tended to facilitate an individual's dominant response (Myers, 1996). If a person's major attitudes are prejudicial, these will be much more evident while in a group. For these reasons of deindividuation and social facilitation, minority groups experience crimes that are more violent than the dominant group. The devastating psychological effects are greater, and, therefore, the need for intervention is greater.

There are also other reasons why crimes' impact is greater for the minority members of our society. Often the reason for the crime is the physical or cultural trait that distinguishes them; it is an immutable feature that they cannot change (Ellis, 2000). All victims of crime feel a loss of control, but this person has absolutely no control over changing this feature. Dominant group victims can change their dress, lock their doors, buy alarm systems, and so forth, to at least have some semblance of control, but the minority victim can do nothing—he or she is even more helpless. Because of this distinctive, immutable feature, minority crime victims feel much more vulnerable to repeat attacks; the stress is much more persistent and pervasive than for victims from the majority culture.

Another reason for the greater impact is that 66 percent of the perpetrators of hate and bias crimes are Caucasian—from the dominant culture. Persons from a diverse group begin to believe that "all" Caucasians hate them and are "out to get them" (Ellis, 2000). Not participating in the dominant culture is *not* an option, but it then becomes perpetually frightening and stressful. As noted above in the discussion of Seyle's theory, this type of stress is much more deadly and can lead to many physiological problems. This generalized fear of the dominant culture often precludes individuals from seeking victim services, which are delivered by representatives of this feared culture (Ellis, 2000). This leads to a perpetual cycle of secondary victimization, characterized by greater impact and fewer services.

As a result of this hate crime, minority victims can attempt to isolate themselves from the majority group and the available services, or, at the other extreme, they can isolate themselves from their racial or cultural group for self-protection. This means less social support and more stress—again, a greater impact. Cognitively, a hate or bias crime creates a much greater impact for the person's worldview and self-concept, which are based partially on the immutable feature that precipitated the crime (Ellis, 2000). With no other reason (economic, power, control, insanity, etc.) for the crime than one's identity, it is much more difficult to "explain away" and resolve the cognitive dissonance.

In the final analysis, crimes against diversity members of society have both a greater personal and a broader community impact. All members of the victim's group are at risk and threatened by the crime; they have no choice but to be more cautious both because of their identity and because of the irrationality of the act. Sacred symbols and community places often are vandalized; the only places for refuge from the dominant cultural discrimination are no longer safe. The entire minority community is victimized, and members of *other* minority groups also become distinctly aware of their own vulnerability.

Theoretical Explanations of Prejudice and Discrimination

There are three levels of prejudice and discrimination that create diversity issues in the delivery of victim services. The first level is cultural and includes the general attitudes of the dominant group in society. The second level is the racism and sexism of the perpetrators of hate and bias crime. The third level, and the major concern of this chapter, has to do with the attitudes and prejudices of victim advocates, which can lead to the delivery of discriminatory victim services. The questions at hand are: Why do minority groups ask for services less often? Why does crime have a greater impact on minority members of our society? Why is there a need to focus on the delivery of specialized victim services to these groups?

If the first step in changing society is awareness, then the initial focus should be on the theories in social psychology that explain prejudice and discrimination. In the chapter on the second victimization, there was an extensive discussion of attribution theory. This theory states that as we look for the causes of a crime, we tend to blame the victim by focusing on internal causation, that is, things about the victim or things the victim did that caused the crime. This is called the fundamental attribution error of focusing exclusively on internal causes when observing others. On the other hand, the self-serving bias states that we tend to blame the environment (external causes) for bad things that happen to us. A corollary to these two human tendencies is the positivity bias, which says that we give the same self-serving break to those who are most like us; in other words, those in the dominant culture would tend to look at external causes for other members of the dominant group, while using the fundamental attribution error (internal causes) on members of minority groups (Myers, 1996). The dominant culture has a greater tendency to blame minority crime victims than other victims. So the earlier discussion of attribution theory states that, besides general societal discrimination, the process of victim blaming is also discriminatory.

Social psychology discusses three different types of causes for prejudice and discrimination. There are social causes, emotional causes, and cognitive causes (Myers,

FOCUS BOX

What are some of your stereotypes about two groups in your community that are different than you? Go discuss these with members of those two groups. What did you learn? What services do those two groups need to address regarding victimization in their communities?

1996). One social cause is social inequities. Unequal status creates set roles and expectations, as well as limited contact between groups. The minority group members fulfill set roles that are limited, and then these roles are used to prove their inferiority; in other words, the prescribed roles and behaviors become self-fulfilling prophecies. Bureaucratic support for these unequal roles justifies or sanctifies the discrimination and makes challenges to these roles an unhealthy or even deadly process.

Another social cause is called the in-group/out-group bias (Myers, 1996). This is a general bias of all group members that can be caused by group formation itself; that is, simply drawing a line down the middle of a class causes a sense of "us" versus "them." This is a tendency of all ages, sexes, and nationalities. Merely by being a member of the dominant group, advocates have a sense of belonging with "us" and a sense of being different from "them." This sense of social identity helps people feel better about themselves.

A third social cause of prejudice is the need for conformity. Conformity is the path of least resistance. It is easier to support the dominant attitudes of society than to fight them. In the South in the late 1950s and early 1960s, surveys indicated that most Protestant ministers did not support segregation but did little to change their society. That conformity, which was easier and safer for them, helped perpetuate discrimination.

The final social cause is institutional support. Segregated institutions perpetuate discrimination. Churches, even today, still tend to be segregated at 11:00 A.M. every Sunday. Until 1954, segregated schools reinforced the dominant prejudices. Media's portrayal of certain minority groups maintains these attitudes also: savage Indians, bird-brained women, macho and abusive Hispanics, African American criminals, and so forth. All of these social causes can affect the delivery of victim services. When victim advocates, with a need to conform, are members of the favored "in-group," it is difficult for them to notice and ascertain society's general social inequities and those perpetrated by the institutions for which they work. This task is not impossible, but it takes a conscious effort to overcome these biases and to become culturally competent. The aspects of this effort will be discussed below.

In the realm of the *emotional causes* of prejudice and discrimination, there are usually three issues discussed (Myers, 1996). The first is the frustration-aggression hypothesis (Berkowitz). The blocking of any goal-directed behavior causes frustration for most people, and under certain conditions, this emotional frustration can lead to aggressive behavior. The realistic group conflict theory says that the competition over scarce resources (jobs) causes the dominant group, especially poor whites, to see minority groups as blocking their financial success; this frustration then causes prejudicial attitudes and discriminatory behavior toward the source of frustration. Violent acts toward minorities do increase during economic depressions.

A second emotional cause of prejudice focuses on personality dynamics. The person who has a low self-concept or has a high need of status, or both, often has a stronger need to degrade or belittle others to feel better about himself or herself. Those who were informed that they had failed a test (lower self-esteem), then espoused more prejudicial attitudes on a later survey.

One of the oldest areas of study regarding the causes of prejudice focused on the authoritarian personality (Myers, 1996). The research on this noted a strong correlation but generally failed to show causation. The authoritarian personality was usually described as angry, insecure, morally inflexible, and submissive to authority, while having a strong need for power and a low threshold for ambiguity. It was found that this personality type tended to be very prejudicial and tended to be an "equal-opportunity bigot," that is, disliking *all* who were different. Although this was a popular area of study, the hypothesis that this personality type "caused" prejudice and discrimination was never proved. The two variables are very highly "correlated," but both could plausibly be caused by a third factor—for example, education level, parental discipline, or cognitive errors.

In this area of the emotional causes of prejudice, it could be surmised that a victim advocate, who is frustrated with his or her job and has a low self-concept (and/or a high need for status—not a common need for most advocates), might be more prone not to deliver adequate services to minority crime victims.

In order to function in our complex world while bombarded daily by new information about ourselves and our universe, we use various *cognitive* methods to simplify this information to make it more understandable (Myers, 1996). These useful methods that help us survive often become problematic when they are applied to evaluating people, especially those who are different from us. The first method is categorization: It allows us to cluster objects and people into groups in order to comprehend them better and to predict their behavior. The most powerful and common categories are sex, gender, and race. When clustering, there is a tendency to drop salient diverse traits and to oversimplify commonalities. As noted before, this is called the "out-group homogeneity effect," in which the minority group members all look alike and look different from "us" (Myers, 1996). The in-group is very aware of its own diversity, but categorization causes the loss of the out-group's diversity. Research indicates that exposure to the out-group does seem to decrease this effect. Familiarity seems to breed an awareness of differences and liking.

The second cognitive method often used to simplify our world is called the availability heuristic (Myers, 1996). This is the tendency to use what seems to be the most distinctive (available) personality or physical trait to describe a whole group. Again, it allows us to do a simple analysis of complex situations. It creates what is called an "illusory correlation" between the traits of a few individuals and the entire group: "All Italians are . . . ," "All Jews are . . . ," "All Indians are . . . ," and so forth (Myers, 1996). Any stereotype is an example of this cognitive simplification. The media perpetuates many of these stereotypes by making the common (illusory) distinctions more available in a repetitive fashion.

The most common cause of cognitive simplification was discussed earlier in this chapter: attributional biases. By attributing only internal causes for the behavior of others, we decrease our need to fully analyze their very complex situations. Minority groups *must* cause what happens to them due to diminished ability, poor social skills, or maybe even their hereditary makeup; quick, simple explanations decrease the complexities of the real world. Pettigrew (1979) said that when the fundamental attribution error is applied to an entire group, instead of just an individual, it should then be called the *ultimate attribution error* (Myers, 1996). Minorities, who have fewer educational, economic, political, and social opportunities, must have somehow caused these deficiencies themselves. On the other hand, a member of the dominant group who is having similar difficulties must have had some extenuating circumstances (external causes—self-serving bias) cause his or her condition. Again, blaming the victim is more often applied to minority victims than others.

The final cognitive simplification is the just world hypothesis: Bad things happen only to bad people. This allows us to maintain a world view that maximizes our sense of control and consistency. Injustice happens to those who deserve it. This cognitive tenet has had strong support in the dominant culture's Judeo-Christian theology (institutional support): Sinners always get what the deserve. This has led to the belief in the reverse: If they get something bad, they must have been sinners (guilty victims).

With all of these cognitive methods (categorization, availability heuristic, attributional errors, and the just world hypothesis), there is a tendency to note later information that confirms these stereotypes and to discount subsequent exceptions; this is called the confirmation bias. This tendency perpetuates prejudicial attitudes formulated by these cognitive short-cuts. With the strong human need to simplify the environment, the average victim advocate would cluster individuals into groups, reason with the use of the most distinctive (available) traits, and tend toward victim blaming (internal attribution) in day-to-day work. Awareness of these almost automatic cognitive errors is difficult under the best of circumstances, let alone in the highly volatile and emotional situation of dealing with violent crime. This seems to be an almost insurmountable situation. How can a victim advocate, overworked and underpaid, change the social causes of discrimination, calm the emotional causes of prejudice, and blunt the cognitive simplifications that diminish the delivery of adequate services to minority victims in their community? The next two sections of this chapter will attempt to answer this complex, difficult question. One section will focus on awareness and competence, and the second will delineate active and practical recommendations.

Dealing with Advocate Bias: Gaining Cultural Competence

Aronson's Solution

One of the most famous social psychologists in the United States, Aronson, in the 1960s proposed a solution to deal with racism in our society. He stated that what society needed to do was to create the opportunity for "cooperative, equal-status, interdependent" relationships (Myers, 1996). It is not enough to simply desegregate schools and neighborhoods. Individuals from diverse races and ethnic groups (add diverse sexual orientations, diverse age groups, and diverse physical abilities) have to be involved in cooperative, not competitive, activities for the common good of their communities, neighborhoods, and schools. They have to be on the same level of power and responsibility (political); this is in regards to the project at hand, but equal economic and occupational status is beneficial also. Finally, the success of the group task should require everyone's balanced synchronized effort, that is, interdependence. True integration, which diminishes prejudice and terminates discrimination, requires working together on projects that improve our neighborhood and local schools. It requires that we get to know each other and understand that we need each other's efforts to fully change our community. This fruitful familiarity creates a new "in-group" that is much more diverse and much less prone to simplistic cognitive judgments about others.

FOCUS BOX

Most victim services are delivered by Caucasians to Caucasian victims. Why is this the case? Thinking of services in your community, propose two major changes to increase the availability of victim services to diverse victims.

Aronson's proposal provides us with a "grand" solution to work from as we focus on the cultural competence of victim advocates. An advocate needs to precipitate consistent contact with groups in the community who do not usually avail themselves of victim services; an advocate needs to solicit the minority community's support of victims; all victims need to be seen as the advocate's "equal." Minority victim recovery needs to be viewed as a cooperative process in which both the victim and the advocate learn and benefit.

Personal Awareness

Dealing with advocate bias specifically begins with broadening the personal awareness of differing definitions and differing life views, or cultural schemes. Most psychological theories and most of the trauma literature is written from the dominant culture's perspective. For instance, in psychology, until about 20 years ago, there were generally two types of theories about abnormal behavior and human personality: the DEWM (dead European white male) and the DAM (dead American male) theories. Adolescent psychology traditionally was about white male adolescence. Only recently have theories had a broader cultural and gender viewpoint.

Cultural Definitions

Various cultures define a "crisis" in different ways (Myers, 1996). For some, it is a terrible event that almost signifies the end of their known world—a permanent change. For some, it is a temporary setback; for others, it is seen as a long-term, but not permanent, setback. And for others, it is seen as a great opportunity for change—maybe even a period of great anticipation and excitement. Various cultures also define "treatment" in differing manners. In the Western world, it is seen as sitting down formally and talking with a professional; it is usually viewed positively. In communal societies, outside assistance is seen as unnecessary; at times, it might even be seen as dangerous for it exposes family or clan issues to outside influences. In other cultures, the agent who actually delivers therapeutic services may differ from our Western perspective; it could be a priest, a shaman, a curandaro, an elder, and so forth. The rituals tied to treatment or therapy may be much more extensive than sitting across from a professional once a week. A victim advocate living in a diverse community needs to be very aware of these differing definitions, practitioners, and rituals.

Philosophical Schemes

Besides these practical differences, there are three basic philosophical schemes that are different in each culture: the axis of control, the axis of conflict, and the axis of life (Ellis, 2000). In the axis of control in the Western world, the emphasis is on individual internal control of one's life; in Eastern philosophy, the emphasis is on the community and family's influence on, and assistance to, the individual—external control. The Eastern view does not assume we are "the captains of our fate and the masters of our soul."

The axis of conflict denotes the varying views of a crisis as noted above. It has an evaluative component in which some cultures see conflict as "good," and others see it as "bad." There may also be cultural differences surrounding the resolution of conflict. Whether we like to admit it or not, the preference in the Western world is to resolve issues through violence, but other cultures prefer compromise, argumentation, reason, or cooperative efforts; cultural variance often denotes a preference for, alternatively, more assertive or more passive resolution efforts.

The axis of life delineates the cultural view of life and death. Again, it also has an evaluative component: Some cultures view death as a negative thing, while others see it as a continuation, simply another phase of life. The minority victim's view of his or her brother's homicide needs to be evaluated from a specific cultural perspective in order to assist him or her in recovery.

Cultural Competence

The first step in cultural competence is an awareness of the predominant schemes of the minority victim's culture. What are the other aspects of cultural competence? It is often best to clarify what is *not* included in cultural competence. Ogawa, in *Color of Justice*, discusses several things that do not indicate cultural competence. First, it *does not include* "color blindness" (Ogawa, 1999). In the 1960s, this was meant as a positive statement to emphasize racial similarities. The intent was positive, the result was negative. The result was a push for all racial and ethnic groups to blend into the dominant culture. In essence, color blindness created a "whiteout" and a progressive loss of cultural identity. The "melting pot" analogy has now been replaced by the "tossed salad" metaphor—coming together without losing our distinctiveness. Color blindness discounts the influence of the person's distinctive differences and culture, both of which are an important part of his or her makeup and victimization. It is important that the person's diverse background be recognized clearly by the victim advocate, so his or her responses can be culturally specific and appropriate. Cultural competence is *not* memorizing language and community customs; knowing cultural facts and understanding the person are two different things (Ogawa, 1999). This is a stereotypical response that assumes that all individuals in this cultural group are alike; Ogawa suggests that a victim advocate evaluate the individual victim within the context of *general* cultural schemes and customs.

In past times, cultural competence was seen as having an advocate from the victim's culture. Besides the practical problems that this poses, there is again the problem of stereotyping. The false assumption is that all members of this cultural group—advocates and victims—are similar and will understand each other better. As noted above, this "out-homogeneity effect" is a cognitive oversimplification that facilitates prejudicial attitudes.

The two individuals—victim and advocate—could be from the same minority group, but one could be first generation and the other third generation; one might be from a middle-class background, and the other could be from a lower socioeconomic group; one could adhere to the basic cultural/religious customs, while the other practices none of them. Apparent similarities could be real or very superficial. Superficial similarities imposed on actual diverse backgrounds would not create automatic cultural competence.

Ogawa (2000) states that cultural competence begins with compassion and sincerity. The basic traits needed to help any other victim are also required to help diverse victims. Without these two traits, service delivery is cold and condescending—ultimately unsuccessful. True respect for the victim's culture is also necessary. Accepting it as valid in its own right and equal in status to the customs of the dominant culture is important because this is the victim's perspective. Without this perspective, adequate assistance cannot be given.

Cultural competence includes an awareness of one's own limitations; this may simply mean an awareness that the advocate knows little about the victim's culture. This could, however, mean that the advocate must do a "prejudice appraisal" of his or her attitudes and language before this awareness is complete (Ogawa, 2000). Cultural competence means that the advocate has an openness to human differences in general; this is an attitude that praises and celebrates these differences. This attitude will come across from the initial meeting with the minority victim.

Cultural competence means client-centered learning. Paired with an awareness of one's limitations, this means that the advocate admits what he or she does not know to the minority victim, requests cultural information, and seeks out the victim's view of the crime and intervention. Once the advocate more fully understands the victim's culture, he or she then begins to utilize the cultural resources (Ellis, 2000). The advocate calls upon the family, the priest or shaman, the church or temple, and other institutions of social support and incorporates them into service delivery. In Andrews's comprehensive service system described in Chapter 13, the culturally competent advocate uses the *natural support* and *human support* systems within the victim's culture to assist in recovery.

Cultural Competence Study

Finally, a number of years ago there was a research study done by two minority psychologists (one of whom will soon be in the majority in California) on this issue of cultural competence; the study was done on psychologists, but the findings could apply also to victim advocates. After a lengthy analysis of numerous potential variables, two were found to be the most significant: professional competence and humility. Psychologists who were deemed by clients to be culturally competent were first very skilled in the practice of psychotherapy; that is, they were very well trained and delivered services in a competent and confident fashion. Second, they exhibited the trait of humility—they were open about their limitations and were willing to educate themselves by asking questions of the minority clients about their background and culture. After all the variables of advocate cultural competence are discussed, it comes down to being a highly trained professional (in legal issues, psychological issues, social work issues, etc.) in this new field of victim services and then being humbly open to new insights from victims about their many diverse cultures.

Delivering Diversity Services

General Recommendations

Brian Ogawa, in the *National Victim Assistance Academy Text* discusses "five core tenets of providing quality multicultural victim services" (Ogawa, 2000). These tenets are an excellent way to begin this section on general recommendations for the delivery of diversity services. The tenets are as follows:

1. Acknowledgment of the different and valid cultural definitions of personal well-being and recovery from traumatic events.
2. Support of the sophisticated and varied cultural pathways to "mental health" and incorporation of these into appropriate victim services and referrals.
3. Extensive cultural awareness training and competency testing to enable victim assistance staff to have the capacity to understand persons whose thinking, behavior, and expressive modes are culturally different.
4. Multiethnic and multilingual teamwork as a resource to implement and monitor effective victim services.
5. Cross-cultural perspective to benefit from the principles and methods of other cultures (Ogawa, 2000).

In the context of this discussion, the first two tenets speak to the issue of understanding the various cultural schemes of the victim. Number two also deals with the need to use the *natural support system*. Tenet number three goes beyond the issue of admitting limitations to doing something about them, that is, cross-cultural training and education.

Tenets four and five actually state that for a victim's agency to truly be culturally competent, the staff needs to reflect the community's diversity and realize that understanding other cultures has broader benefits to the agency than just providing better services; the principles and methods of other cultures can also benefit advocates and victims from the dominant culture.

Besides these five basic tenets, another general recommendation for delivering diversity services would be that victim advocates should take advantage of cross-cultural activities in their community (Ellis, 2000). They should go to local celebrations and ceremonies; they should attend church services, marriages, and funerals for representative cultures in their community. Cross-cultural education takes place through both formal workshops and community contacts and exposure. Since one of the major social causes of discriminatory services and treatment is institutional support, a final general recommendation is that victim advocates need to be very cognizant of the subtle bigotry of their own agency, their parent agency, or other agencies they commonly interact with, as portrayed in the agencies' language, policies, and procedures (Ellis, 2000). What stereotypes are infused into these three areas? What institutional traditions and behaviors are, by their nature, exclusionary—whether intended or not? Does the local media portray minority victims in a stereotypical fashion?

These tenets and recommendations would support Aronson's proposal of "cooperative, equal-status, interdependent" relationships. Victim recovery entails working with the victim and his or her cultural institutions closely, while seeing all cultures on an equal level and as a benefit to each other. It involves openness to other cultures paired with a willingness to immerse oneself in cross-cultural learning.

Practical Guidelines

From the broader bureaucratic perspective, the first practical point is that the victim's agency should reflect the diversity of the community: the board of directors, the staff, and the clients (Ogawa, 2000). True cultural competence means the agency must "walk the way it talks." Talking the game of competence is not the same as making purposive changes. Community representatives on the board may be available but never asked to participate; their participation needs to be actively solicited. Staff diversity that completely replicates the community may not be possible, but most agencies have many good ethnic candidates in their community to end the days of the "lily-white" staff. If the general recommendations about staff cultural competence and delivering diversity services are followed, diverse clients will not be reluctant to ask for services. A diverse board and staff would also increase client openness to local services.

The next practical guideline has to do with the initial contact with the victim. Know the person's proper name and find out how it is pronounced (Ogawa, 2000). A person's name is one of the two primary things he or she identifies with self-concept (the other is facial image in the mirror). Getting it right shows both respect for individuals and for their language. During this and subsequent contacts, respect, be open to their customs and, when possible, follow them. This respect will engender trust and increase their openness to services.

If the minority victim seems hesitant or nonresponsive, be open about your cultural limitations—and understanding about his or her hesitance. Acknowledge how difficult it must be for the victim to communicate with you. Make it clear that you are there both to learn from the victim and to help. Again, humility is the key ingredient. It is always important with all victims, but especially with minority victims, to address practical problems first: food, shelter, finances, safety issues, and the like (Ellis, 2000). This tangible help will be much more evident than other types of assistance and will usually be greatly appreciated, building trust from the onset.

The final practical recommendation has to do with crisis intervention. The emphasis of this entire chapter has been that all services should have a cultural focus. What is the cultural meaning of this crisis—of pain or of death? When in doubt, the advocate should ask questions and solicit cultural support, and then watch what happens, so he or she can learn from this experience. As with any victim, catharsis is often important, so have the victims tell their story. Find out if they would feel more or less comfortable with family present through this crisis. Find out from them, or their family, if there are any religious or cultural rituals that would be beneficial now or later (Ellis, 2000). The advocate should make sure the victim is comfortable with his or her being present during these activities.

Throughout these interactions with them, be aware of reducing their isolation whenever possible. Always reframe information into their cultural terms if practical; if the advocate is not able to do this, perhaps a family member or friend can. Always be aware of specific cultural communication techniques, such as eye contact and body or hand gestures.

Summary

This chapter surveyed diversity issues in victim services beginning with a description of minority groups and three specific definitions. Crime's greater impact on minority victims was discussed in detail. This was followed by a theoretical discussion of the causes of prejudice and discrimination. The majority of the chapter then focused on how victim advocates could gain cultural competence, as well as on the delivery of diversity services.

Discussion Questions _____

1. What are the reasons that minority groups in a community usually request fewer victim services?

2. What are the major barriers to gaining cultural competence in your community?

3. Which of the social psychological theories make the most sense to you? Why?

References

1 Cranch 137 (1803).
342 US 1 (1951).
399 US 66 (1970).
399 US 78, 90 (1970).
406 US 404 (1972).
489 US 538 (1989).

Abrahams, R. D. (1992). *Singing the master: The emergence of African American culture in the plantation south.* New York: Pantheon.

Affirmative Action Review. (2000). White House: Justifications for affirmative action. Retrieved from the World Wide Web July 24, 2000: http://www.whitehouse.gov/WH/EOP/OP/html/.

Ajrouch, K. (1999). Family and ethnic identity in an Arab-American community. In M. W. Suleiman (Ed.), *Arabs in America: Building a new future* (pp. 129–139). Philadelphia: Temple University Press.

Albee, G. (1982). "Preventing psychopathology and promoting human potential. *American Psychologist, 37,* 1043–1050.

Al-Hayani, F. A. (1999). Arabs and the American legal system: Cultural and political ramifications. In M. W. Suleiman (Ed.), *Arabs in America: Building a new future* (pp. 69–83). Philadelphia: Temple University Press.

Ali, L. (2000, November 27). Torn between two worlds: Arab-America teens struggle with Middle East violence. *Newsweek,* p. 57.

Al-Krenawai, A., & Graham, J. R. (2000). Culturally sensitive social work practice with Arab clients in mental health settings. *Health and Social Work, 25*(1), 9–20.

Alozie, N. O., & Ramirez, E. J. (1999). "A piece of the pie" and more competition and Hispanic employment on urban police forces. *Urban Affairs Review, 34*(3), 456–475.

Alton-Lee, A., & Nuthall, G. (1992). *Students learning in classrooms: Curricular, instructional and sociocultural processes influencing student interaction with curriculum content.* Presented at the Annual Meeting of the American Educational Research Association, San Francisco.

American Correctional Association. (1998). Correctional officers in adult systems. *Vital Statistics in Corrections.* Laurel, MD: ACA.

Amir, M. (1971). *Patterns in forcible rape.* Chicago, Illinois: University of Chicago Press.

Andrews, A. (1992). *Victimization and survivor services.* New York: Springer Publishing.

Angelo, M. (1997). *The Sikh diaspora: Tradition and change in an immigrant community.* New York: Garland.

Anti Defamation League of B'nai B'rith. (ADL). Focus on the World of Difference Institute. United Nations Plaza, New York.

Argersinger v. Hamlin, 407 US 25 (1972).

Aswad, B. C. (1999). Attitudes of Arab immigrants toward welfare. In M. W. Suleiman (Ed.), *Arabs in America: Building a new future* (pp. 177–191). Philadelphia: Temple University Press.

Bastian, L. D. (1990). Hispanic victims. Bureau of Justice Statistics, U.S. Department of Justice, NCJ 20507.

Beck, A. J. (2000). Prisoners in 1999. *Bureau of Justice Statistics Bulletin.* Washington, DC: U.S. Department of Justice, NCJ 183476.

Bennett, L. (1966). *The White problem in America.* Chicago: Johnson.

Bilge, B. (1994). Voluntary associations in the Old Turkish community of metropolitan Detroit. In Y. Y. Haddad & J. I. Smith (Eds.), *Muslim communities in North America* (pp. 381–406). Albany: State University of New York Press.

Billingsley, A. (1968). *Black families in white America.* New York: Simon & Schuster.

Bureau of Indian Affairs. (2000). Short history of the BIA. U.S. Department of the Interior. [Online]. Retrieved from the World Wide Web October 13, 2000: http://www.doi.gov/bia.

Bureau of Justice Statistics, *Criminal Victimization in the United States, 1992.* U.S. Department of Justice. Washington, DC, 100.

Burgess, A., & Holstrom, L. (1974). "Rape trauma syndrome," *American Journal of Nursing, 131,* 981–986.

Byrne, J. M. (1988). "Probation," A National Institute of Justice Crime File Study Series. Washington, DC: U.S. Department of Justice.

California Assembly. (1993). Chaptered Legislation. AB 401 (Epple).

California Crime and Violence Prevention Center. (2000). Community Oriented Policing and Problem Solving: Building Safer Communities. Sacramento, California Attorney General's Office.

California Senate. (1990). Chaptered Legislation. SB 2680 (Boatwright).

Census Bureau Facts. (2000). Asian Pacific American heritage month: May 1–31. U.S. Census Bureau's Public Information Office, Department of Commerce.

Children's Defense Fund. (1996). *The state of America's children, 1996.* Washington, DC: Children's Defense Fund.

Chuong, C. H. (1994). *Vietnamese students: Changing patterns, changing needs.* San Francisco: Many Cultures.

Cohen, C. E. (1991, February 11). As the Gulf War stirs prejudice, Albert Mokhiber fights for the rights of Arab Americans. *People Weekly, 35*(5), 87.

Commission on Peace Officer Standards and Training. (February 1992). *Guidelines for law enforcement's design of cultural awareness training programs.* Sacramento: State of California.

Conway, J., & Conway, S. (1993). *Sexual harassment no more.* Downers Grove: IL: InterVarsity Press.

Cook, R. (1998). *Sweet land of liberty?: The African American struggle for civil rights in the twentieth century.* London: Longman.

Crawford, C., Chiricos, T., & Kleck, G. (1998). Race, racial threat, and sentencing of habitual offenders. *Criminology, 36*(3), 481–511.

Curry, G. D., Ball, R. A., & Fox, R. J. (1994). *Gang crime and law enforcement recordkeeping.* National Institute of Justice.

Daniels, R. (1988). *Asian America: Chinese and Japanese in the United States since 1850.* Seattle: University of Washington.

Dave, S., Dhingra, P., Maira, S., Maxumdar, P., Shankar, L., Singh, J., & Srikanth, R. (2000). De-privileging positions: Indian Americans, South Asian Americans, and the politics of Asian American studies. *Journal of Asian American Studies, 3*(1), 67–100.

De Lange, N. (2000). *An introduction to Judaism.* Cambridge, UK: Cambridge Press.

De Vos, G. (1982). Ethnic pluralism: Conflict and accommodation. In G. De Vos & L. Romanucci-Ross (Eds.), *Ethnic identity: Cultural continuities and change* (pp. 5–42). Chicago: University of Chicago Press.

Dennis, H. C. (1971). *The American Indian 1492–1970: A chronology and fact book.* Dobbs Ferry, NY: Oceana.

Di Gregory, K. V., & Manuel, H. A. (1997). Final report of the executive committee for Indian Country law enforcement improvements. U.S. Department of Justice, Washington, DC. Retrieved from the World Wide Web October, 2000. http://www.usdoj.gov/otj/icredact.htm.

Ditton, P. M. (1999). *Jails in Indian country.* Bureau of Justice Statistics: U.S. Department of Justice. NCJ-173410.

Economist. (2000, October 14). The birth of an Arab-American lobby. *Economist, 357*(8192), 41.

Eigen, L. D., & Siegel, J. P. (1993). *Dictionary of political quotations.* London: Robert Hale/Macmillan.

Ellis, A. (1962). *Reason and emotion in psychotherapy.* Secaucus, NY: Citadel Press.

Ellis, R. (2000). Victims of hate and bias crime. In Thomas Underwood (Ed.), *Victims assistance: Exploring individual practice, organizational policy, and societal responses.* Topeka, KS: Washburn University Center on Violence and Victim Studies.

Equal Employment Opportunity Commission. Title VII of the Civil Rights Act of 1964. Retrieved from the World Wide Web July 13, 2000: http://www.eeoc.gov/laws/viihtml.

Equiano, O. (1988). *The life of Olaudah Equiano or Gustavus Vassa the African.* London: Longman.

Espiritu, Y. L. (2000). Changing lives: World War II and the postwar years. In J. Y. S. Wu & M. Song (Eds.), *Asian American studies: A reader* (pp. 141–157). Piscataway, NJ: Rutgers University Press.

Fang, Chai. (1990). Living in the USA. In K. K. Howard (Ed.), *Passages: An anthology of the Southeast Asian refugee experience* (pp. 157–58). Fresno, CA: Southeast Asian Student Services.

Federal Bureau of Investigation. (2001). Press release on hate crimes statistics. Washington, DC.

Festinger, L. (1957). *A theory of cognitive dissonance.* Stanford: Stanford University Press.

Fiztpatrick, J.P. (1987). *Puerto Rican Americans: The meaning of migration to the mainland.* Englewood Cliffs, NJ: Prentice-Hall.

Flores, B. (1990). *Chiquita's cocoon.* Granite Bay, CA: Pepper Vine Press.

Flores, J. (2000). *From bomba to hip-hop: Puerto Rican culture and Latin identity.* New York: Columbia University Press.

Foner, P. S., & Rosenberg, D. (1993). *Racism, dissent, and Asian Americans from 1850 to the present: A documentary history.* Westport, CT: Greenwood Press.

Free, M. D. (1996). *African Americans and the criminal justice system.* New York: Garland.

Fresno County Sheriff's Department. (2000). Multi Agency Gang Enforcement Consortium (MAGEC). Fresno, CA: FSD.

Garza, C. (1977). *Puerto Ricans in the U.S.: The struggle for freedom.* New York: Pathfinder Press.

Geis, S., Gilbert, G., & Stotland, R. (1980). *White collar crime: Theory and research.* Newbury Park, CA: Sage.

Glasser, I. (1999). Affirmative action and the legacy of racial injustice. In C. G. Ellison & W. A. Martin (Eds.), *Race and ethnic relations in the United States: Readings for the 21st century* (pp. 307–317). Los Angeles: Roxbury.

Golden, F., & Lemonick, M. (2000). The race is over. In W. Isaacson (Ed.), *Time, 156,* 18–23.

Goldstein, H. (1977). *Policing a free society.* Cambridge, MA: Ballinger Publishing Company, p. 21.

Goldstein, H. (1990). *Problem-oriented policing.* New York: McGraw-Hill.

Gordan, M. M. (1996). Liberal U.S. corporate pluralism. *Society, 33*(3), 221, 37–40.

Gordon, M. (1978). *Assimilation in American life: The role of race, religion, and national origin.* New York: Oxford.

Green, D. E., & Tonnesen, T. V. (Eds.). (1991). *American Indians: Social justice and public policy.* Madison: Board of Regents, University of Wisconsin.

Greenfield, L. A., & Smith, S. K. (1999). *American Indians and crime.* Washington, DC: U.S. Department of Justice: Office of Justice Programs, NCJ 173386.

Gregorie, T. et al. (2000). *Victim impact statements—A victim's right to speak—A nation's responsibility to listen.* Arlington, VA: National Center for Victims of Crime.

Grobsmith, E. (1996). American Indians in prison. In M. O. Nielsen & R. A. Silverman (Eds.), *Native Americans, crime and justice* (pp. 224–227). Boulder, CO: Westview.

Hacker, A. (1992). *Two nations: Black and white, separate, hostile, unequal.* New York: Charles Scribner's Sons.

Haddad, Y. Y., & Smith, J. I. (Eds.). (1994). *Muslim communities in North America.* Albany: State University of New York Press.

Hale, C. D. (1982). Patrol administration, presented in *Local Government Police Management,* 115.

Hannerz, U. (1980). *Exploring the city.* New York: Columbia University Press.

Harris, R., & Dewdney, P. (1994). *Barriers to information: How formal help systems fail battered women.* Westport, CT: Greenwood Press.

Haslip-Viera, G. (1996). The evolution of the Latino community in New York City: Early nineteenth century to the present. In G. Haslip-Viera & S. L. Baver (Eds.), *Latinos in New York* (pp. 3–29). South Bend, IN: University of Notre Dame.

Hassoun, R. (1999). Arab-American health and the process of coming to America: Lessons from the metropolitan Detroit area. In M. W. Suleiman (Ed.), *Arabs in America: Building a new future* (pp. 157–176). Philadelphia: Temple University Press.

Hastings, T. F. (1982). *Criminal investigation* (2nd ed.).

Heider, F. (1958). *The psychology of interpersonal relations.* New York: Wiley.

Heller, E. (1997, November 13). Grown-up war babies on trial. *Fulton County Daily Report.* American Lawyer Media, L. P.

Hernandez, J. (1996). The identity and culture of Latino college students. In G. Haslip-Viera & S. L. Baver (Eds.), *Latinos in New York* (pp. 126–146). South Bend, IN: University of Notre Dame.

Heyck, D. L. D. (1994). *Barrios and borderlands: Cultures of Latinos and Latinas in the United States.* New York: Routledge.

Humes, K., & McKinnon, J. (2000). *The Asian and Pacific Islander population in the United States: Population characteristics.* Washington, DC: U.S. Census Bureau, Current Population Reports, U.S. Government Printing Office, Series P20-529.

Jacinto, J. A., & Syquia, L. M. (1995). *Lakbay: Journey of the people of the Philippines.* San Francisco: Many Cultures Publishing.

Jackson, J. L. (2000). Race and racism in America. *National Forum, 80*(2), pp. 9–11.

Jaimes, M. A. (1999). Federal Indian indentification policy: A usurpation of Indigenous sovereignty in North America. In C. G. Ellison & W. A. Martin (Eds.), *Race and ethnic relations in the United States: Readings for the 21st century* (pp. 157–165). Los Angeles: Roxbury.

Jennings, P., & Brewster, T. (1998). *The Century.* New York: Doubleday.

Johnson, T. A., Misner, G. E., & Brown, L. P. (1990). History of police-community relations programs. In *The police and society: An environment for collaboration and confrontation.* Englewood Cliffs, NJ: Prentice-Hall.

Johnson, T., Nagel, J., & Champagne, D. (1997). *American Indian activism: Alcatraz to the longest walk.* Urbana: University of Illinois.

Joseph, S. (1969). *Jewish immigration to the United States: From 1881 to 1910.* New York: Arno Press.

Joseph, S. (1999). Against the grain of the nation—The Arab. In M. W. Suleiman (Ed.), *Arabs in America: Building a new future* (pp. 257–271). Philadelphia: Temple University Press.

Karmen, A. (2001). *Crime victims: An introduction to victimology.* Belmont, CA: Wadsworth.

Karnow, S. (1989). *In our image: Americas empire in the Philippines.* New York: Ballantine.

Kilpatrick, D., Edmunds, C., & Seymour, A. (1992). *Rape in America: A report to the nation.* Arlington, VA: National Center for Victims of Crime.

Kim, E. H. (2000). Home is where the heart is: A Korean-American perspective on the Los Angeles upheavals. In J. Y. S. Wu & M. Song (Eds.), *Asian American studies: A reader* (pp. 270–289). Piscataway, NJ: Rutgers University Press.

Kim, H. (1994). *A legal history of Asian Americans, 1790–1990.* Westport, CT: Greenwood Press.

Kim, L. I., & Kim, G. S. (1994). *Korean American immigrants and their children.* San Francisco: Many Cultures.

Kneller, G. F. (1965). *Educational anthropology: An introduction.* New York: Wiley & Sons.

Korn, J. (Ed.). (1969). *This fabulous century: 1940–1950,* Volume V. New York: Time Life Books.

Koss, M. P. (June, 1993). Detecting the scope of rape. *Journal of Interpersonal Violence, 8*(2), 200–203.

Kotkin, H., & Kishimoto, I. (1988). *The third century.* New York: Crown.

Kübler-Ross, E. (1971). *On death and dying.* New York: McMillan.

Lambert, R. D. (1981). Ethnic/racial relations in the United States in comparative perspective. *Annals of the Ameri-*

can Academy of Political and Social Science, 454, 189–205.

Lee, R. G. (1999). *Orientals: Asian Americans in popular culture.* Philadelphia: Temple University.

Leonard, K. I. (1997). *The South Asian Americans.* Westport, CT: Greenwood Press.

Levine, L. W. (1977). *Black culture and black consciousness: Afro-American folk thought from slavery to freedom.* Oxford, England: Oxford University Press.

Levine, M. L. (1996). *African Americans and civil rights: From 1619 to the present.* Phoenix: Oryx Press.

Lieberman, M. (2000). Responding to hate crimes. Washington, DC: Washington Counsel, Anti-Defamation League, Community Policing Exchange.

Linton, C. D. (1975). *The bicentennial almanac: 200 years of America.* Nashville, TN: Thomas Nelson.

Lipset, S. M. (1999). Equal chances versus equal results. In C. G. Ellison & W. A. Martin (Eds.), *Race and ethnic relations in the United States: Readings for the 21st century* (pp. 299–306). Los Angeles: Roxbury.

Littlebear, R. (1999, May). Some rare and radical ideas for keeping indigenous languages alive. Paper presented at the Fourth Annual Stabilizing Indigenous Languages Symposium, Flagstaff, AZ.

Lomax, L. E. (1962). *The Negro revolt.* New York: The New American Library.

Lucas, A. (1993). *Cambodians in America: Courageous people from a troubled country.* San Francisco: Many Cultures.

Massey, D. S., & Denton, N. A. (1993). *American apartheid: Segregation and the making of the underclass.* Cambridge, MA: Harvard University Press.

Massey, D. S., Alarcon, R., Durand, J., & Gonzalez, H. (1987). *Return to Aztlan: The social process of international migration from Western Mexico.* Berkeley: University of California Press.

Massey, D. S., Arango, J., Hugo, G., Kouaouci, A., Pellegrino, A., & Taylor, J. E. (1998). *Worlds in motion: Understanding international migration at the end of the millennium.* New York: Clarendon Press.

Mattar, M. (1999). Legal perspectives on Arabs and Muslims in U.S. courts. In M. W. Suleiman (Ed.), *Arabs in America: Building a new future* (pp. 100–112). Philadelphia: Temple University Press.

McCarus, E. (Ed.). (1994). *The development of Arab-American identity.* Ann Arbor: The University of Michigan Press.

McDevitt, J., & Levin, J. (1993). *The rising tide of bigotry and bloodshed.* New York: Plenum Press.

McEwen, T. (May, 1995). National Assessment Program: 1994 Survey Results. *Research in Brief,* National Institute of Justice, p. 2.

McGoldrick, M., Pearce, J. K., & Giordano, J. (1982). *Ethnicity and family therapy.* New York: Guilford.

Meek, J. G. (2000, December 14). *Cops get guides to hate crime.* New York: APB News Center.

Mehdi, B. T. (1978). *The Arabs in America 1492–1977: A chronology and fact book.* Dobbs Ferry, NY: Oceana Publications.

Melton, A. P. (2000). Indigenous justice systems and tribal society. American Indian Development Association. Retrieved from the World Wide Web November 10, 2000. http://www.ojp.usdoj.gov/nij/rest-just/ch1/indigenous.htm.

Meuer, T., Seymour, A., & Wallace, T. (2000). "Domestic violence," In Morna Murray, et al. (Eds.), *National victim assistance academy text.* Washington, DC: Office for Victims of Crime.

Milakovich, M. E., & Weis, K. (January, 1975). Politics and the Measure of Success in the War on Crime, *Crime and Delinquency, 21,* 1–10.

Moore, J., & Terrett, C. (1998). *Highlights of the 1996 National Youth Gang Survey.* Washington, DC: OJJDP.

Moore, M. H., & Trojanowicz, R. C. (1988). Corporate strategies for policing. *Perspectives on Policing, 9.*

Morales, A. L., & Morales, R. (1986). *Getting home alive.* Ithaca, NY: Firebrand Books.

Morell, V. (1998). Kennewick man's trials continue. *Science, 280*(5361), 190–193.

Muravchik, J. (1999). Terrorism at the multiplex. *Commentary, 207*(1), 57.

Myers, D. G. (1996). *Exploring psychology.* New York: Worth Publishers.

Myers, D. G. (1996). *Social psychology.* New York: McGraw-Hill.

Myyra, J. (1998). California Commission on Peace Officer Standards and Training, Training and Delivery Bureau, POST PowerPoint Program.

Nagel, J. (1996). *American Indian ethnic renewal.* New York: Oxford Press.

Nagel, J. (1999). American Indian ethnic renewal: Politics and the resurgence of identity. In C. G. Ellison & W. A. Martin (Eds.), *Race and ethnic relations in the United States: Readings for the 21st century* (pp. 166–175). Los Angeles: Roxbury.

National Asian Pacific American Legal Consortium. (1999). *Audit of violence against Asian Pacific Americans: The need for increased commitment to reporting and community education,* 6th Annual Report 1998. Washington, DC: National Criminal Justice Reference Service, NCJ 185028.

National Crime Prevention Council. (1995). *Lengthening the stride: Employing peace officers from newly arrived ethnic groups.* Washington, DC: National Crime Prevention Council, National Criminal Justice Reference Service.

National crime victimization survey. (1992). Washington, DC: Bureau of Justice Statistics.

National directory of shelters and services for battered women. (1999). Washington, DC: National Coalition Against Domestic Violence.

Ng, F. (1998). Towards a second generation Hmong history. In F. Ng (Ed.), *Adaptation, acculturation, and transnational ties among Asian Americans* (pp. 99–117). New York: Garland.

Nielsen, M. O., & Silverman, R. A. (Eds.). (1996). *Native Americans, crime and justice*. Boulder, CO: Westview.

Nies, J. (1996). *Native American history: A chronology of the vast achievements of a culture and their links to world events*. New York: Ballantine Books.

Office for Victims of Crime. (1998). Upon the Back of a Turtle . . . A Cross Cultural Training Curriculum for Federal Criminal Justice Personnel. Contract #96-VR-GX-0002, CCAN, OUHSC.

Office of Tribal Justice. (2000). Mission of the Office of Tribal Justice. U.S. Department of Justice, Washington, DC. Retrieved from the World Wide Web November 13, 2000. http://www.usdoj.gov/otj/otjmiss.html.

Ogawa, B. (1999). *Color of justice: Culturally sensitive treatment of minority crime victims*. Boston: Allyn & Bacon.

Ogawa, B. (2000). "Respecting diversity: Responding to underserved victims of crime." In M. Murray et al. (Eds.), *National Victim Assistance Academy Text*. Washington, DC: Office for Victims of Crime.

Ogbu, J. (1985). Variability in minority responses: Non-immigrants vs. immigrants. In G. Spindler (Ed.), *Interpretive Ethnography*. Hillsdale, NJ: Laurence Erlbaum.

Ogbu, J. (1992). Understanding cultural diversity and learning. *Educational Researcher, 21*(8), 5–14.

Olson, J. S., & Wilson, R. (1984). *Native Americans in the twentieth century*. Provo, UT: Brigham Young University Press.

Ong, P., Park, K. Y., & Tong, Y. (1999). The Korean-Black conflict and the state. In C. G. Ellison & W. A. Martin (Eds.), *Race and ethnic relations in the United States: Readings for the 21st century* (pp. 409–417). Los Angeles: Roxbury.

Ovando, C., & Collier, V. (1985). Culture. In *Bilingual and ESL classrooms: Teaching in multicultural contexts*. New York: McGraw-Hill.

Palsano, E. (1993a). *We the Americans: Asian Americans*. Washington, DC: Bureau of Census, U.S. Department of Commerce.

Palsano, E. (1993b). *We the Americans: Pacific Islanders*. Washington, DC: Bureau of Census, U.S. Department of Commerce.

Paludeine, D. S. (1998). *Land of the free: A journey to the American dream*. New York: Gramercy Books.

Parks, R. (1994). *Quiet strength*. Grand Rapids, MI: Zondervan.

Pate et al. (1986). *Reducing fear of crime in Houston and Newark: A summary report*. Washington, DC: Police Foundation.

Pate et al. (1986). *Reducing fear of crime in Houston and Newark: A summary report*. Washington, DC: Police Foundation.

Pedersen, O., & Smith, V. E. (1997, July). South toward home: Facing long odds—and painful history—blacks are at last moving back to the Old Confederacy. *Newsweek, 130*(2), 36–39.

PennState. (2000). The extent of sexual harassment. [Online]. Retrieved from the World Wide Web July 14, 2000: http://www.de.psu.edu/harass/analysis/extent.htm.

Philip, K. R. (1999). *Termination revisited: American Indians on the trail to self-determination, 1933–1953*. Lincoln: University of Nebraska.

Portes, A. (1996). *The new second generation*. New York: Russell Sage Foundation.

Portes, A., & Bach, R. L. (1985). *Latin journey: Cuban and Mexican immigrants in the United States*. Berkeley: University of California Press.

Portes, A., & Rumbaut, R. G. (1996). *Immigrant America: A portrait* (2nd ed.). Berkeley: University of California Press.

Portes, A., & Stepick, A. (1993). *City on the edge: The transformation of Miami*. Berkeley: University of California.

Reaves, B. A., & Goldberg, A. L. (2000). *Local police departments 1997*. Washington, DC: Bureau of Justice Statistics, NCJ 173429.

Report of the Attorney General. (1990). *National practices for the investigation and prosecution of white collar crime*, U.S. Department of Justice. Washington, DC: Office of the Attorney General.

Roberts, A. (1990). *Helping crime victims: Research, policy, and practice*. Newbury Park: Sage.

Roberts, D. (1981). *Raped*. Grand Rapids, MI: Zondervan Publishing House.

Robinson, C. J. (1997). *Black movements in America*. New York: Routledge.

Rotter, J. B. (1975). Some problems and misconceptions related to the construct of internal versus external control of reinforcement. *Journal of Consulting and Clinical Psychology, 43,* 36–67.

Saliba, T. (1999). Resisting invisibility: Arab Americans in academia and activism. In M. W. Suleiman (Ed.), *Arabs in America: Building a new future* (pp. 304–319). Philadelphia: Temple University Press.

Saltzburg, S. A. (1998). Non-English speaking witnesses and leading questions. *Criminal Justice*, Summer, 37–41.

Sandberg, N. C. (1986). *Jewish life in Los Angeles: A window to tomorrow*. Lanham, MD: University Press of America.

Schafer, S. (1968). *The victim and his criminal*. New York: Random House.

Seikaly, M. (1999). Attachment and identity: The Palestinian community of Detroit. In M. W. Suleiman (Ed.), *Arabs in America: Building a new future* (pp. 25–38). Philadelphia: Temple University Press.

Selye, H. (1956). *Stress of life.* New York: McGraw-Hill.

Sessions, W. (October, 1990). Focus on police and community. *FBI Law Enforcement Bulletin.*

Seymour, A. (2000). Substance abuse and victimization. In M. Murray, et al. (Eds.), *National victim assistance academy text.* Washington, DC: Office for Victims of Crime.

Siegel, L. J. (1998). *Criminology.* Belmont, CA: West.

Simon Wiesenthal Center. (2000). Press Information. Los Angeles.

Singh, J. (2000). The Gadar party: Political expression in an immigrant community. In J. Y. S. Wu & M. Song (Eds.), *Asian American studies: A reader* (pp. 35–46). Piscataway, NJ: Rutgers University Press.

Sloan, I. J. (1971). *Blacks in America 1492–1970: A chronology and fact book.* Dobbs Ferry, NY: Oceana.

Smith-Hefner, N. J. (1998). Education, gender, and generational conflict among Khmer refugees. In F. Ng (Ed.), *Adaptation, acculturation, and transnational ties among Asian Americans* (pp. 137–160). New York: Garland.

Society for the prevention of cruelty to animals annual report. (1999). Society for the Prevention of Cruelty to Animals.

Society. (1998). Israel is special in U.S. eyes (poll on American attitudes toward Israel). *Society, 35*(5), 3.

Spickford, P. R., & Fong, R. (1999). Pacific Islander Americans and multiethnicity: A vision of America's future? In C. G. Ellison & W. A. Martin (Eds.), *Race and ethnic relations in the United States: Readings for the 21st century* (pp. 486–493). Los Angeles: Roxbury.

Spilde, K. (2000). Library resource center. National Indian Gaming Association. Retrieved from the World Wide Web October 30, 2000. http://www. indiangaming.org.

Spindler, G., & Spindler, L. (1987). *Interpretive ethnography of education: At home and abroad.* Hillsdale, NJ: Lawrence Erlbaum.

Stokes, L. D., & Scott, J. F. (1996). Affirmative action and selected minority groups in law enforcement. *Journal of Criminal Justice, 24*(1), 29–38.

Sue, D. W. (1981). *Counseling the culturally different: Theory and practice.* New York: Wiley.

Sue, S., & Padilla, A. (1986). Ethnic minority issues in the United States: Challenges for the educational system. In *Beyond language: Social and cultural factors in schooling language minority students.* Los Angeles: Evaluation, Dissemination and Assessment Center, CSULA.

Suleiman, M. W. (Ed.). (1999). *Arabs in America: Building a new future.* Philadelphia: Temple University Press.

Sutherland, E. H. (1983). *White collar crime: The uncut version.* New Haven, CT: Yale University Press.

Suttles, G. D. (1972). *The social construction of communities.* Chicago: University of Chicago Press, p. 22.

Tang, E. (2000). State violence, Asian immigrants, and the underclass. *States of confinement: Policing, detention, and prisons.* Washington, DC: National Criminal Justice Reference Service, NCJ 183633.

Taylor, C. (1997). *North American Indians: A pictorial history of the Indian tribes of North America.* Bristol, UK: Parragon.

The Supreme Court of the United States. Washington, DC: U.S. Government Printing Office.

Titus, R., Heinzelmann, F., & Boyle, J. M. (August, 1995). The anatomy of fraud: Report of a nationwide survey, research in action. *National Institute of Justice Journal,* 28.

Trojanowicz, R., & Bucqueroux, B. (1990). *Community policing: A contemporary perspective.* Cincinnati, OH: Anderson Publishing Company.

U.S. Bureau of Justice (1987). *Felony Arrests.* Washington, DC: U.S. Government Printing Office.

U.S. Equal Employment Opportunity Commission. Sexual harassment charges EEOC & FEPAs combined: FY 1992-FY 1999. Retrieved from the World Wide Web July 14, 2000: http://www. eeoc.gov/stats/harass.html.

U.S. v. Salerno, 55 USLW 4663 (1987).

Uniform crime report. (1992). Washington, DC: Department of Justice.

Uniform crime report. (1994). Crime in the United States. Washington, DC: Superintendent of Documents, p. 1.

United States Bureau of the Census. Resident population estimates of the United States. [On-line]. Retrieved from the World Wide Web July 13, 2000a: http://www. census.gov/population/estimates/nation/intfile3-txt.

United States Bureau of the Census. Resident population estimates of the United States. [On-line]. Retrieved from the World Wide Web December 29, 2000b: http:// www.census.gov/population/estimates/nation/intfile3-txt.

United States Bureau of the Census. Resident population estimates of the United States. [Online]. Retrieved from the World Wide Web July 13, 2000: http://www.census. gov/population/estimates.

United States Census Brief. (2000). *From the mideast to the Pacific: A profile of the nation's Asian foreign-born population.* U.S. Department of Commerce. Census Brief 100-4.

van Hasselt, V., Morrison, R., Bellack, A., & Hersen, M. (Eds.). (1988). *Handbook of family violence.* New York: Plenum Press.

Vialet, J. (1999). *Refugee admissions and resettlement policy: Facts and issues.* Washington, DC: Congressional Research Service Report for Congress, 98-668.

Vicenti, C. N. (1995). The reemergence of tribal society and traditional justice systems. *Judicature, 79*(3).

Viola, H., & Margolis, C. (1991). *Seeds of change*. Washington, DC: Smithsonian Institution.

von Hassell, M. (1996). *Homesteading in New York City, 1978–1993: The divided heart of Loisaida*. Westport, CT: Bergin & Garvey.

von Hentig, H. (1948). *The criminal and his victim: Studies in the sociobiology of crime*. New Haven, CT: Yale University Press.

Walker, L. (1979). *The battered woman*. New York: Harper & Row.

Walker, S. (2000). "Scope of crime/historical review of victims' rights discipline," In Morna Murray, et al. (Eds.), *National Victim Assistance Academy Text*. Washington, DC: Office for Victims of Crime.

Walker, S., Spohn, C., & DeLone, M. (2000). *The color of justice. Race, ethnicity, and crime in America*. Belmont, CA: Wadsworth.

Walker, W. (1989). *Introduction to the Hmong*. San Francisco: Many Cultures.

Wall, S., & Arden, H. (1990). *Wisdomkeepers: Meetings with Native American spiritual elders*. Hillsboro, OR: Beyond Words.

Wallace, H. (1998). *Victimology: Legal, psychological, and social perspectives*. Boston: Allyn & Bacon.

Wallace, H. (Spring, 1995). Stalkers, the constitutions and victims' remedies. *ABA Criminal Justice, 10*(1), 16.

Wallace, H., Edmunds, C., & Walker, S. (2000). *Responding to rural crime victims: An overview of local, state, and national initiatives*. Washington, DC: Office for Victims of Crime.

Waller, J. M. (2000, April 17). Investigative report: Clinton donor a gangster. *News World Communications, Insight on the News*.

Weiner, N. A. (1989). Violent criminal careers and violent career criminals. In N. A.Weiner & M. E. Wolfgang (Eds.), *Violent crime, violent criminals*. Newbury Park, CA: Sage.

Weitzer, R., & Tuch, S. A. (1999). Race, class, and perceptions of discrimination by the police. *Crime & Delinquency, 45*(4), 494–507.

Weston, P. B., & Wells, K. M. (1970). *Criminal investigation: Basic perspectives*. Englewood Cliffs, NJ: Prentice-Hall.

Wilson, A. C. (1997). Power of the spoken word: Native oral traditions in American Indian history. In D. L. Fixico (Ed.), *Rethinking American Indian history* (pp. 101–116). Albuquerque: University of New Mexico.

Wolfgang, M. E. (1958). *Patterns of criminal homicide*. Philadelphia: University of Pennsylvania Press.

Wolfgang, M., & Ferracutti, F. (1987). *The subculture of violence*. London: Tavistock.

Wong, S. L. C., & Lopez, M. (1995). *California's Chinese immigrant students in the 1990s*. San Francisco: Many Cultures.

Workforce 2000. Labor Department, Bureau of National Affairs. Washington, DC.

Wu, J. Y. S., & Song, M. (Eds.). (2000). *Asian American studies: A reader*. Piscataway, NJ: Rutgers University Press.

Wulff, D. (2000). Winning strategies offered for working with different cultures. *Community Policing Exchange*. Retrieved from the World Wide Web December 12, 2000. http://www. communitypolicing.org/publicactions/exchange.htm.

Zogby, J. (1998). The politics of exclusion. *Civil Rights Journal, 3*(1), 42.

Zona, M. A., et al. (July, 1993). A comparative study of erotomonic and obsessional subjects in a forensic sample. *Journal of Forensic Science, 38*, 894.

Index